GALAXY'S BEST CHEF

BOOK 1

Ryan Duval

First paperback edition November 2023

Timeline Art by Ryan Duval
Cover Art by Grafficatz

ISBN 979-8-9892400-0-5 (paperback)
ISBN 979-8-9892400-1-2 (ebook)

MONKEY MONKEY PUBLISHING
www.monkeymonkeypub.com
firstcontact@monkeymonkeypub.com

For Kai, to prove I was kinda cool,
once upon a time.

GALAXY'S BEST CHEF

BOOK 1

CHAPTER ONE

"A space station, my ass," Clara whispers, studying the obsidian architecture around her, reminiscent of ancient cathedrals from old Earth. *Of all the materials to build such a delicate structure with, why stone? Why so dark?* She gazes at towering columns supporting vaulted ceilings as hundreds of biographers, including herself, pour into the station's docking bay. *But something's off.* Clara closes her eyes and listens to their chatter. Despite the stone surfaces, their voices remain insulated, dampened. *There's no echo...*

"It's Jupiter marble!" Clara blurts and cups her mouth.

Memories from when she wrote architect Kandara Sagran's biography, founder of the marble two centuries ago in Io's core, come rushing back. Clara groans, remembering the old architect droning on about the marble's acoustic properties only achievable with a billion years of compression and release as Io orbits Jupiter. *Thank Sol for coffee,* Clara reflects, knowing she had the undue privilege of analyzing the marble then and will never forget its texture.

She gently runs her fingers along the space station's stone column. *Soft, rough, yet impervious. Yes, this is it.* Clara imagines the entire history of System Sol rests within the marble's veins, yet her colleagues continue gossiping, ignoring the engineering marvel.

"Clueless," she mutters.

A man in white Council dress, a speck beneath massive arches, raises a hand in greeting. "The Council of Colonies welcomes you all to Parliament Station. I shall be your coordinator during your stay here. Please, follow me to Reception for processing and refreshments," the coordinator's voice effortlessly spans the docking bay's expanse.

The marble is granting his voice amplification, Clara realizes. *But how, then, is everyone else insulated?*

Ushers corral them into Reception. The coordinator takes a pedestal atop a set of stairs overlooking the crowd of biographers as receptionists perform retinal scans and assign numbers.

"Clara Ocol, Investigative Biographer, Number 736," hovers above a holotile in Clara's palm, tracking her facial features and adjusting its holographic projection so only she can read the information. She frowns. *The anticipation is going to kill me.* A familiar face crosses beyond the holotile's projection. Clara snaps her head in the woman's direction, analyzing her muscular back and short-cropped hair. *Is that Kereen?* Clara pockets her holotile and pushes through the sea of biographers to find out.

"Kereen!" Clara calls.

The woman stops in her tracks and turns around. Her eyes widen. "You've got to be kidding me!" Kereen says, smiling brightly and spreading her arms.

Clara rushes in for a hug, grinning from ear to ear. "What on Titan are you doing here!?"

"Biographies, *duh*. We gotta compete for these assignments, you know," Kereen says, releases their embrace, and runs fingers through her hair.

Clara catches the glint of a Titan Infantry ring. *Kereen still wears it?* She studies the ring's sniper division bullseye engraving, remembering their nights spent atop ridge lines, Clara with her scopes to acquire targets, estimate range, give scope corrections, and read the wind. She would then say, "Send it," and Kereen would take the shot. *"Best Sniper Team of Class 3392,"* reads the plaque on Clara's apartment wall.

A lifetime ago, she thinks. "Didn't you inherit your father's recycling center after graduation?"

"Oh, I did." Kereen's smile dwindles. "But Dad passed a few months ago and nobody writes biographies for small-time recyclers. So I wrote one myself. The Council requested I attend this interview shortly after its publication."

"I'm so sorry about David. What happened?"

Kereen sighs. "He crashed his hoverbike in Conkers Canyon. He was in the lead too, but that wasn't glorious enough, apparently. The idiot was trying to set a new course record."

"Number one, Angelo Devon, please report to Identification," the coordinator calls from his pedestal.

A man, Clara assumes is Angelo, timidly climbs the stairs to meet the coordinator, then descends an entry portal to Parliament Floor. Clara returns her attention to Kereen.

"I'm glad David went out with his boots on," she says. *But will Kereen know the reference? It's from ancient English, after all.* Clara had learned the phrase from her husband, Jonathan, who currently leads the archaeological dig of London on old Earth.

Kereen tilts her head. "He *was* wearing boots, I guess."

Lost in translation. Damn. "I mean, I'm glad he was able to follow his passion to the fullest, to the very end," Clara says.

"Still charming as ever," Kereen jabs.

"Number two, Chester Atkins, please report to Identification," the coordinator calls.

As Chester enters Parliament Floor, Angelo emerges from the exit portal. Clara expects utter disappointment upon his face. Instead, Angelo smiles with genuine glee. *Please, no! Not the first one!* She squints, watching as the next biographers enter in anxiety and exit with smiles.

"They're all happy," Clara states, deadpan, emotionless.

"Haven't lost that *Spotter* voice, I see," Kereen says, focusing on the biographers. "I think everyone's winning, interesting."

"Who do you think will get Zion Wright's biography?" Clara asks.

Kereen shrugs and motions to the coffee bar. "Come, drink."

From one biographer to the next, Clara and Kereen move with synthesized coffee in hand, bouncing conversation back and forth and gathering information. Before long, it's clear that Zion Wright's biography is still available.

After lunch, the coffee bar begins serving synthetic cocktails and wine.

Kereen grins. "This space station is more like a castle," she says, swirling a glass of red.

Finally, someone who gets it, Clara thinks.

"Number five-forty-six, Kereen Mandel, please report to Identification," the coordinator calls.

Kereen drains her wine and winks. "Wish me luck."

"Luck," Clara says, watching her friend ascend the staircase.

Kereen emerges from the exit portal nearly twenty minutes later, wearing a mischievous grin.

Clara purses her lips. "Did you get Zion's?"

"Nope," Kereen says, maintaining her grin. "I got Cillian Gundar's."

"The old chef from Venus? That's an incredible assignment!" Clara says.

Afternoon slips into the evening, and a dinner of synthesized asparagus risotto is served. Clara grimaces, thinking about the dishes her son, Aizen, makes from scratch. *The synths just can't make it right,* she reflects.

"Number seven-thirty-six, Clara Ocol, please report to Identification," the coordinator calls.

Clara stands from her seat and wades through a handful of biographers still awaiting their turn or remaining as support.

Kereen mouths, *good luck.*

Clara ascends the stairs to the coordinator's pedestal. *Be calm,* she tells herself and takes a deep Ergonos breath, one learned in her military training.

"Please, present any devices," the coordinator instructs.

She places her holotile on the coordinator's pedestal.

"Any implants we should be aware of?"

They have that information, a formality. Clara shakes her head.

"You may retrieve your holotile after the interview."

"Thank you," she says, barely above a whisper.

The coordinator extends his arm to the entry portal.

Clara descends, brushing her fingertips along its marble walls. All sound from Reception ceases, and Parliament Floor ahead remains silent.

Whoa, she attempts to say but cannot hear her voice.

"Clara Ocol, you may enter," cuts through the silence, yet no person is present.

Parliament Floor opens as she rounds a bend. *At least triple the size of Reception,* Clara gauges. Thousands of representatives from every planet, dwarf planet, moon, comet, and asteroid in System Sol, and more from every other star system, sit upon tiers of amphitheater seating, silently watching her. A wooden chair stands lonesome at Parliament Floor's center, its white oak vivid against the chamber's black surfaces. Clara wills her legs to move with confidence and grace, but she arrives several seconds later than she likes.

She does not sit.

"The chair is quite comfortable I assure you. Please, sit," says the voice.

Clara searches the many faces, studying each species' equivalent of a mouth, but cannot pinpoint who spoke.

She sits.

Like selecting *Play*, the representatives come alive, turning their gazes away and having thousands of conversations at once. All the while, Clara cannot hear a thing. She studies their silent words. *They're talking to the walls and ceiling instead of each other. Why?* Clara shifts in her chair, not nearly as comfortable as promised. When she leans to the right, another voice, deep and husky, breaks the silence.

"...She cannot possibly be the author of Kandara Sagran's biography. She's only forty-seven..."

Clara sits up straight, and the voice disappears. She leans to the left to hear a third, nasally voice.

"...Look at those pants. Titan fashion is atrocious..."

Clara narrows her eyes, analyzing the direction one representative speaks and drawing a mental line to the marble slab they face. Each appears slightly angled, no two the same. *That's right, Jupiter marble absorbs all reverberations except for one,* Clara remembers Kandara Sagran saying. The old architect had even demonstrated the phenomenon using blocks of marble on turnstiles, changing dead silence into perfect sound transmission when correctly aligned.

Clara estimates how the representative's voice might reflect off a particular slab and draws another mental line to another official.

As one speaks, the other listens.

A communication system, Clara realizes, reaching for her holotile in her pocket. *Shit, I left it with the coordinator.* She remembers how his voice also projected across Reception. *So... a completely analog communication system... producing no electrical signatures... thus, invisible to scanners...*

"...Stealth technology," she whispers.

Clara leans to the right, intercepting the voice that critiqued her age, and traces the speech to a slab left of the chamber's entry. Its reflection tracks to a group of representatives dead-center. She searches for a face to match. It takes a moment, but Clara finds a human hosting a condescending expression whose mouth follows the words she hears.

"Representative Marcey – Venus," is engraved in front of his seat.

Clara squares up to the marble slab, inhales deeply, and says, "My honorable Representative Marcey, pardon the intrusion, but I most certainly *did* write the biography on Kandara Sagran and fully understand the properties of the marble she discovered. The fact that I can use this communication system is proof enough."

The representative freezes, then looks about in a frenzy.

"Down front, Your Honor. It's me, Clara Ocol. The woman who's *only* forty-seven."

His gaze settles upon her, exuding shock and wonder. "This system is classified on levels you cannot possibly comprehend."

"I am certain that it is, Your Honor. Perhaps you might help me with something."

He hesitates. "What would you ask of me?"

"Is there a marble slab that can distribute sound to all?"

"I would never disclose such information!" The representative abruptly turns, speaking behind his hand.

The Council silences and faces Clara.

She draws a mental line, but whatever slab Representative Marcey accessed is out of view. She rises to her feet for a better perspective. *Nothing.* She steps on the seat of her chair and glimpses the top of a multifaceted slab in the back.

"What is she doing?" Clara hears another representative say.

Come on, Clara, acquire target. She places her feet on the chair's creaky arms, wobbles, balances, and slowly stands tall. The multifaceted slab reveals. Hundreds of previously hidden conversations engulf her like an avalanche. *Forty-seven meters away,* she judges and corrects her footing. Clarity cuts through the cacophony of voices. *There it is.* Clara takes another Ergonos breath, rests her hands on her hips, and lifts her chin high.

Send it.

"My esteemed representatives," she calls, "grant me your ears for a moment and I shall prove my worth."

CHAPTER TWO

Saturn fades from Titan's hazy night sky as the sun rises on Tempest City. *The eight-day-long night is finally over,* Clara thinks, relieved to be free of darkness, but she will miss Saturn's glow. *The one downside of living on Titan's tidally locked inner surface.* Tempest City's inverted dome canopy, holding Titan's crushing air pressure at bay, becomes visible, with thick clouds beyond, swirling like cream in coffee.

Clara opens her apartment door to dull sunlight trickling through the windows. She removes her shoes, sets her holotile on the coffee table, and enters the open kitchen to find a plate of cookies wrapped in rice paper on the counter. A card lays on its top with, *"For Mom,"* written on its front.

He's the best, Clara thinks, smiles, and plucks the card.

"Dear Mom. Whether you are selected or not, I am proud of you. Enjoy the cookies. Love, Aizen," reads within.

She gently sets the card aside and unwraps the rice paper layers. A waft of heaven envelops her. Her mouth salivates. Clara takes a cookie from the stack, opens her mouth, and sinks her teeth. Tastes unfold like layers of a mystery novel. The dark chunks zing with sweetness.

"My Sol!" Clara shouts, devouring two in a row. *How does Aizen do this!?* She nibbles another and moans in ecstasy.

A beeping comes from her holotile. *"Jonathan Zaid,"* hangs in its hologram. *That time already?* Clara thinks. She sets the plate of cookies on the coffee table, sits on the sofa, and waves her hand over her holotile.

A hologram of Jonathan materializes. Glass dust from London's dig powders his curly, brown hair in pastel green and collects in his forehead creases and crow's feet. A smear of darker sediment dashes across his cheek. She cannot imagine him looking any cuter until he smiles.

"Kip!" Jonathan says.

"Kip!" Clara replies, remembering the first time they *kip'ed* seventeen years ago.

They were strolling along Tempest City's reservoir boardwalk and had settled on a bench overlooking the water. They entwined their fingers and kissed. But after a moment, Jonathan pulled away, looking into her eyes, words on his lips that he did not want to say.

"What is it?" Clara asked as her anxiety rose.

"My first assignment came in," he said and paused.

"Jon, you can't stop there. I need details." Clara forced a smile but her stomach sank.

"Dr. Cho selected me for the dig of Prometheus on Luna," he said.

"Sasha Cho? The historian? That's amazing!" Clara's stomach grew even heavier. "When do you leave?"

"Tomorrow."

"For how long?"

"It's scheduled for six months, but it'll likely be longer."

"How *much* longer?"

"I don't really know."

Clara never thought people actually gulped until she felt herself do it. "What about us?"

"I can holocall everyday."

"The delays make it weird," she argued.

"But I'm certain we can make it work," he said.

Clara had met Dr. Cho during Jonathan's graduation ball and did not miss the eyes she gave him throughout the evening, making Clara feel like nothing more than a plus one. Sasha was stunning, brilliant, and, of course, *single*. And she and Jonathan would be sharing close quarters for over six months. *How can I possibly compete with that?*

"Just go," Clara muttered, letting her fingers slip through his.

Jonathan's eyes widened. He scrambled for words. "Did you know that every language, both ancient and modern, requires two or three words to tell someone you love them? You'd think at least one of these languages would create something singular. I mean. We have a word for *the fear of peanut butter sticking to the roof of your mouth*, but not this."

Clara had never seen him so rattled. "What should this word be?"

"It should be simple and light, something you can say in public without anyone realizing. Something like, *kip*."

They walked in silence alongside the reservoir. Jonathan gazed across the water, and a light breeze ruffled his curly hair. *He sure was a good one,* Clara thought, trying to figure out how to control the situation. *But Jonathan is not a target to acquire. What can I do?*

A little voice from within piped up. *Fight, you idiot!*

How? she thought.

How? He just told you how!

Clara took a deep breath, summoned her courage, and said the only thing she could muster, barely a whisper.

"Kip..."

It was so faint Clara was not sure if Jonathan heard. Six agonizing seconds dragged on. Then a word passed his lips, barely a whisper.

"...Kip."

Jonathan declined Dr. Cho's offer the following day.

Clara grins at her dust-covered husband on hologram. "How's London today?" she says.

Several seconds pass for her words to reach Earth and his response to return. *That always puts a damper on things*, Clara thinks, but she knows the quantum relays are continually improving, reducing communication delay year by year. She munches on another cookie in the meantime.

"We commenced drilling of the city's glass dome!" Jonathan finally says. "It's incredible how intense The Fall was. They say a lightning bolt on Earth is a thousand times hotter than the surface of the sun, turning the sand it strikes into glass! Now imagine that, but a billion times more intense, encasing an entire metropolis!"

"Dat amazin' 'on," Clara mumbles, mid-chew.

Jonathan squints. "Are those what I think they are?"

She nods. "Aizen may 'ookies."

♦

"Cuisine? What's that?"

"It's the art of creating delicious and beautiful food, reflecting a specific culture," Aizen says.

"Don't the synthesizers do that already?" Lucius snickers.

"Uh, no. They might understand the chemicals in food, but not the processes to combine them, and nothing about who that food represents."

"That's stupid," Lucius says. "Chemicals are chemicals. Just put them together and you get food."

Aizen scrunches his brow. "Have you ever heard of corn on the cob?"

"Cob? What language is that from?"

"Ancient English. It's the stalk that holds the kernels."

Lucius humphs. "What are kernels?"

"That's the corn!" Aizen says.

Lucius gives him a look. "Corn is a *liquid*. Don't you know that!?"

The kids on the LightTram laugh. Aizen turns red in frustration.

"Look! Aizen's about to cry!" Lucius says, making a pouty face.

"Imbeciles," Aizen mutters in ancient English.

"He's making up words!" Lucius cracks. *"In-bicycles* means awesome. Don't you know that!?"

Aizen leans his forehead against the tram's cushioned seat, trying to ignore their mocking faces. He cannot believe they will spend the upcoming class trip to Mars together. *They've already ruined the sixth grade. They'll ruin this too,* he thinks, turning away to watch Titan's farmland crops blur past his window, silos and barns scrolling slower in the distance.

"Look at me, I'm corn on the crab!" Lucius says, opening and closing his hands like claws to another round of laughter.

"Cob," Aizen whispers in protest.

The LightTram slows. *"We are now approaching Cobble Hill Station. Please, depart in an orderly fashion. Thank you for riding LightLine, the safest and most efficient way to travel."*

Aizen beelines off the tram.

"Watch out, Zion, you have competition!" Lucius calls as the door seals shut with a hiss.

The LightTram silently speeds off, its sections of white polymer enveloping in magenta light and blurring into one glowing line.

Aizen stands alone on the open-air platform, letting the gentle rustling of artificial wind replace Lucius's condescending voice. *Thank Sol for the silence,* Aizen thinks and peers up Cobble Hill. Buildings line both sides of the street, each elevating a meter or two to match the steep slope, creating a sawtooth roofline. His apartment is the highest unit of the very top building. He often wants to ask his parents why they had insisted on living there. But he knows why. Mom loves the view, and Dad loves bombing down the hill on his longboard, believing Aizen loves it too. But Aizen hates longboarding and has accumulated enough scuffs and bruises over the years to validate that. Still, Dad always insists that if Aizen tries *one more time,* he will discover its greatness. *No matter how many times I tell him otherwise.*

Aizen sighs and starts up the hill, cursing his burning thighs. He manually reduces the artificial gravity of his magsuit beneath his clothing to aid his ascent. Neighbors peek from windows. Some come into the street.

"Hi, Aizen. How was school?" says Mr. Petra.

Aizen ignores him.

"Aizen, I love your shirt, is it new?" asks Miss Jiang.

It *is* new, but he ignores her, too.

"Hey, my man, I smelled them cookies. Can I have one?" says Nigel.

At least Nigel is upfront, Aizen thinks. "Sorry. Made them for Mom."

"Oh. Well, maybe another time, then."

"Maybe." Aizen reaches his building's entry as more neighbors appear on the street. He quickly waves his holotile and enters. *It's all because of that stupid block party last year!* One he baked cookies for. *Will they ever stop hassling me for more?*

Aizen thrusts his apartment door open in frustration, kicks off his shoes, and tosses his holotile on the coffee table. It slides across the surface and bumps into another holotile, one hosting a Titan Infantry engraving on its front. He smiles wide.

"Mom!" Aizen calls with hands cupped around his mouth.

Silence.

He enters the open kitchen to find crumpled rice paper on an empty plate. *She ate them all.* A sudden thumping comes from the ceiling above him. *What on Titan?* He navigates the hallway and opens the closet door to see the attic ladder pulled down. He climbs to find Mom rummaging through Dad's old books and maps.

"Hey, Mom," he says.

She flinches, almost dropping a book. "You scared me half to death. How was school?" she says.

"Stupid, everyone thinks corn is a liquid." He sees Mom freeze and her brow scrunch. "It's *not* a liquid, Mom."

"I've never seen a solid version before," she skeptically says.

Aizen sighs. "The liquidation occurs because synthesizers interpret corn chemically, not structurally."

Mom nods, accepting his answer as fact, and returns to rummaging.

"What are you looking for?" Aizen asks.

"Your father began drilling the glass layer of London, but it's proving too thick to penetrate. He asked me to find one of his old books chronicling Earth's WorldRing tunnel system, which might provide a better solution for entry. He said it's up here."

"By the way, Mom. How'd it go? Up there?" Aizen points to where he imagines Parliament Station is still orbiting Titan.

She stops rummaging and mischievously grins.

"You actually got it!?" Aizen says. *She'll be famous for sure!* But his excitement dwindles remembering her previous assignment. "How long will you be gone for?"

She smiles brightly. "Zion Wright is here! In Tempest City!"

The Great Zion Wright has been here all this time!? Aizen ponders that. "So you'll stay?"

She again nods.

"Good." Aizen weighs his next question carefully. "Do you think I can meet Zion?"

Mom zeroes on him like a hunter. "So you can interrogate him for the trade secrets of cuisine? I'll see what I can do, but don't expect anything. Zion's the most protected person in the universe, after all."

Aizen smiles wide. "Kip!"

"Kip!" Mom replies.

◆

Clara dons a hand-me-down mining uniform, stained and worn from years of use. *The Council must have searched far and wide to find someone with the exact body proportions*, she thinks, studying the worn spots at the knees and elbows. An encrypted message meets her, specifying her hair must be tight and not to wear makeup or jewelry. She descends Cobble Hill to its LightLine station at the base.

A rush of wind brushes her bare cheeks as a LightTram slows to a stop. Its magenta light dissipates, and its hatch opens. Clara boards and grasps the overhead bar. Several miners make small talk in acronyms she does not understand and glance in her direction. Their voices quiet and become more acronym-laden as the LightTram pulls from the station.

More miners are collected at stops around the reservoir. Then they dive straight into the side of the basin, coming out on Titan's methane ice surface outside Tempest City's dome, racing through yellow tholin-rich atmosphere.

The tram slows to its final stop an hour later. *"We are now approaching*

Albert Methane Mine Station. Please, depart in an orderly fashion. Thank you for riding LightLine, the safest and most efficient way to travel."

Polymer sleeves seal around the tram doors before they open.

Clara disembarks first, strutting across the underground platform as if she belongs there, finding that if she moves with speed and purpose, she is never questioned, *usually*.

One of the miners meets her stride and smiles insidiously.

"You're new," he says.

"Transferred," Clara responds without hesitation.

"Really? Which mine? I've worked most on Titan and never seen you."

"Gregarian," she says. Having written an article highlighting Gregarian miners ages ago, Clara knows the legendary mine holds clout, and its workers are held in the highest regard. The only reason one transfers is because of serious injury.

The miner's smile drops. He looks her up and down.

Clara points to her chest. "Artificial lungs are not like the real thing."

He nods, opens the entry door, and motions her to enter first. The others get the hint and *protect her* as they descend the long, dark tunnel. Clara increases her pace, annoyed, staying ahead of the miners and light sensors, walking blindly into the darkness, recalling the schematics she memorized a week beforehand, and navigating the twists and turns by the paces.

"My Sol! How can she see!?" one of them whispers.

They come to a fork with two vault-like doors. The miner flashes his holotile on the left. Mechanical bolts screech and the meter-thick door groans open. He again motions for Clara to enter first.

She shakes her head. "This is where we go our separate ways, gentlemen." Clara waves her holotile across the right door with, *"SENIOR OPERATORS ONLY,"* engraved on its front.

Their jaws drop as she melts into blackness.

The vault closes behind her, and another door groans open in front, unveiling a sterile white room beyond. The contrast stings Clara's eyes, but she discerns people hustling in blue scrubs and long, white coats.

A woman approaches, eyes hardened by years of stress. She lifts a holotile to Clara's eye level to confirm her identity. "You're on time. That's a nice change," she says and abruptly turns, marching down a hall.

Clara takes that as her cue to follow. "Sorry, I didn't catch your name."

"Dr. Sharon, head of HR at this facility."

"What exactly *is* this facility?"

"*That*, I cannot tell you." Dr. Sharon stops at a changing room and motions for Clara to enter.

A set of scrubs and a white coat lay folded on a chair, and in a flash, Clara goes from *The Gregarian Miner* to *The Doctor*.

A knock raps at the door.

"Come in," Clara says.

Dr. Sharon enters with purpose, locks the door, and sits on an adjacent chair. "I must inform you that everything in this facility is classified. If you disclose information to anyone outside you will be tried for *treason*. Do you understand?"

Clara tilts her head. "Wouldn't that defeat the purpose of my assignment? If I cannot write my discussions with Zion, then what's the point?"

Dr. Sharon nods. "His room is deemed civilian soil. However, once you leave *that* room, everything else is classified."

"I understand."

"Can you say that into my holotile with more specificity please?" She lifts the tile to Clara's eye level.

"I understand that everything in this facility, save the room of Zion Wright, is classified, and disclosing information outside is an act of treason."

"Thank you," Dr. Sharon says, and Clara's holotile beeps. "Aside from Zion's chamber, you are cleared for the restroom, break room, kitchen, changing, and study, where you can connect to the outside for research. Everywhere else is specifically designed to disrupt signals."

"Can I not work outside, then?" Clara asks.

"Legally you can. So long as it's on a separate holotile that never enters this facility."

"Looks like I'm buying a new one," Clara quips.

Dr. Sharon frowns. "Don't screw this up. I *will* turn you in if I must."

"I'll do it all within the bounds of legality," Clara assures.

Dr. Sharon squints. "All right, let's meet Zion's physician."

◆

"In theory, he's exhibiting symptoms of gene degradation," Dr. Lee says, simultaneously worried and excited.

"What exactly does that mean?" Clara asks, her eyes locked onto him, her holotile recording.

"It's a condition where, over time, the proteins of a person's DNA slowly unravel. We believe it's an adverse side effect to the barbaric modifications made in the twenty-third century, just over a millennium ago. There has not been a single case since, until now. Somehow, those adverse effects were passed on to Zion. Unfortunately, all documentation of the modifications that might cause this was lost in The Fall."

"Does this mean Zion's DNA is different?"

Dr. Lee shakes his head. "No different than the natural variances found from one individual to another. But *that's* the problem. Without proper gene documentation, we cannot differentiate a defective modification from a normal variance. We're flying blind."

Clara thinks about that. "How far along is Zion?"

"It's early. We think. He can still use Interspeak, though his vocabulary is dwindling and substituted with gibberish. More concerning is he can no longer discern true and false and tells ludicrous stories. That's why there was such urgency to remove him from the public eye and is why we're calling on you to write his biography, before it's too late."

"There's an even more urgent matter," Dr. Sharon interjects, and Dr. Lee looks wide-eyed. "We must tell her. She's sworn to secrecy."

He sighs deeply. "Zion single-handedly saved the galaxy after The Arkathy Empire dissolved. We all know this to be true. Yet, nobody knows exactly how he united the systems left in disarray. We believe it relates to his deep understanding of food and anatomy. However, since galactic unification, the art of cuisine has declined. Consequently, alliances are growing unstable, Clara. As we speak, the Arkathy are fighting with the Cindarians again. That's also *classified*. We fear that if we cannot extract Zion's knowledge of cuisine, then our unprecedented peace may collapse."

Clara feels an anchor drop in her gut. "This is *not* what I agreed to."

"For sure," Dr. Sharon says. "But we need your help."

"What makes you think *I* can do this?" Clara sharply says.

"Because of how you write your biographies, Clara. Your little stunt in front of the Council showed them what the other thirty-four million candidates could not—an ability to understand the intricacies of your subject's accomplishments and then utilize them. Clara, it must be you."

CHAPTER THREE

Clara gently knocks on Zion's door. *No answer.* She knocks again. It opens slightly. *Still, no answer.* She pushes the door open just enough to poke her head inside.

A floor-to-ceiling hologram projects Enceladus's ocean in spring on the opposing wall. Sunlight shines through cracks in its thick, icy surface above as schools of tuna and squid swim by. Large shadows appear in the distance, swaying side to side, as ambient music plays amid the swishing of their tails.

"Rest... Relax..." the hologram whispers.

Another hologram to the right displays Zion's cardiovascular, skeletal, and nervous systems, highlighting gaps in brain tissue where the degradation disease has taken its toll.

Clara quietly steps into the room and closes the door.

Zion lies asleep in a bed to her left, extended to accommodate his height. She remembers him from years ago, giving speeches on the Council of Colonies' Capitol Building steps. He was once the epitome of health that everyone strived for but few achieved, still competing in triathlons until age 257. The Zion dissolving in bed before her is a mockery of his former self, breathing gently as if each breath may be his last. His skin is dark yet thin. Clara follows the veins from his neck to his face and around his hairless scalp. His eyes sit deep within their sockets, encompassed in violet.

She slowly sits on a stool next to his bed.

"What happened to you?" she whispers.

Zion inhales sharply and snorts, then coughs. Phlegm drools from the corner of his mouth. He raises a hand to wipe it away. "Allessandra? Where have you been?" he mumbles.

Clara sits motionless, silent, terrified.

Zion blinks hard and further wakes. "I apologize. I thought you were someone else." He places his bony hands against the mattress and hoists himself to a seated position.

Words will not come to Clara.

"I see you're quite the conversationalist," he says. "I should thank them for sending such *lively* company." A sly grin spreads on Zion's gaunt face.

Did he make a joke? Clara forces herself to say, "Hi."

"You speak!" he says, raising a hand. "Do you have a name?"

"Clara."

"Clara…?"

"...Ocol."

He nods deeply. "It's a pleasure to meet you, Clara Ocol. Now tell me, what brings you to my bedside?"

"I, uh, was chosen to write your biography." Clara feels like a bumbling fool. *This is not like me! But this is also not like him...*

"Really? *I* get a biography?"

"You, of *all* people, get one," Clara says, placing her holotile on a nightstand and dashing her finger across *Record.*

Zion eyes the holotile. "My dear, who do you think I am?"

"The Great Zion Wright, of course," she says.

He sighs. "You've been misinformed. I'm not *great.*" He rubs a hand along his corded forearm. "Just another dying old man."

"You're still the most powerful person in the galaxy," Clara says.

"Power?" he scoffs. "Power is fantasy, fiction. It does not exist."

"No. Power is what makes you great," she argues.

"My dear, allow me to show you what power *really* is." He raises an index finger to his neck and pokes. Then he grins.

Clara stares at Zion, trying to decipher his behavior, when footsteps and shouting come from the hallway outside. Four doctors, plus Dr. Lee himself, burst through Zion's door to the hologram displaying his vitals, and then they take positions around his bed, preparing defibrillators.

"What are you doing?" Zion calmly says.

The doctors freeze and turn to him, confused.

Dr. Lee checks Zion's vitals. "How do you feel?"

"Fluffy," Zion replies and motions to Clara. "My dearest Clara and I were having a *lovely* conversation when you so *rudely* interrupted. May I ask what the emergency is?"

"It's... nothing. I apologize, sir," Dr. Lee says.

"Learn some manners, *young* man! Apologize to my guest!"

Dr. Lee apologizes to Clara before leaving the room.

When the door closes, Zion bursts into wheezing laughter.

Clara cannot help laughing herself. She had imagined every possible first conversation, but nothing like this.

"Power is merely perception, Clara, nothing more," Zion says, composing himself and going into thought. "I'm in the mood for ice cream. How about you?" He again raises a finger to his neck.

After another round of emergency and apologizing, the ice cream arrives.

Clara finds it magnificent, yet Zion grimaces with each lick.

"You're disappointed," she states.

"I used to make wonderful ice cream," he says.

"Why did you stop?"

"I did not stop. The *galaxy* stopped. With synthesizers, skill is no longer required to achieve something a step above rubbish. And so, the art of cuisine is being forgotten. That's why the... the... you know, the... uh, the... zhuzubnther." Zion breathes deeply, his eyes shifting, searching.

"Why the galactic peace is destabilizing?" Clara suggests, hoping to get her first lead.

"No, it's the... you know, the... uh, zhuzub... the... the... Fuck!" Zion shouts and withdraws. "You can go now..."

♦

Clara knocks on Zion's door the following morning.

"What is it?" he calls with kingly projection.

It's the voice Clara remembers from holograms of Zion talking to dignitaries. *Not yesterday's jester.* She enters to find him facing the opposite wall, arms behind his back, standing at parade rest, the top of his bald head skimming the ceiling. The hologram no longer displays Enceladus's ocean. It's the Capitol Building on Ceres, and Zion looks about to give a magnificent speech.

"You seem better today," Clara says.

He turns, giving her an icy glare. "What makes you think you're welcome here?"

"It's me, Clara Ocol, from yesterday," she says, studying his stance.

"I know who you are. I remember telling you to leave," he sternly says.

Clara meets his penetrating stare. *He's a different person.* But she knows how to deal with *this* Zion and matches his parade rest. "No. You said that I *could* leave, placing the choice of departure in my hands. You never specified the duration of my absence or that I could not return."

He glares for a moment longer, then turns his back to her. "Let me make myself clear, then. *Leave*, and *never* return."

♦

Clara gives Zion two days and takes slow Ergonos breaths, preparing to meet his wrath. She opens the door and struts in.

"You're in the way!" Zion hollers, waving her to the side.

Dr. Lee is beside him. Both shake fists like mimes riding bicycles.

"You are the victor!" chimes the hologram.

"I won!?" Dr. Lee says, amazed.

"Not fair! You had help!" Zion points at Clara.

Again, Clara is befuddled and turns to find, *"Hoverbike Grand Prix,"* on hologram. Dr. Lee's character stands on a podium receiving a bouquet and champagne, while Zion's sits on a wrecked bike giving cut-eye.

"Thanks for letting me have another go," Dr. Lee says.

"This is *not* over, I *will* reclaim my title!" Zion declares.

Dr. Lee approaches Clara. "It's a good day," he whispers before leaving.

Zion raises fists. "Clara, wanna have a go?"

"I uh, no, not right now."

He waves the hologram away, pouting.

"Are you not furious with me?" Clara says, raising eyebrows.

"I might feel better if you played," he grumbles.

Her eyebrows drop. "I'm talking about our last session. You told me to leave and never return."

"That?" He shrugs. "I get dramatic sometimes."

"Dramatic? I thought you were going to imprison me!"

Zion's pout melts into a grin. "That would be an abuse of power."

"You said power does not exist," Clara snaps back.

"Then you should not fear something that does not exist."

Focus, Clara, she tells yourself. "I have questions for you."

"Is it about my recipes? Do you want to know the secret ingredient?"

"Do I... What? No," she says but realizes this might be an opportunity. "I mean yes, I do.*"*

"It's obviously for my signature dish."

"...What's your signature dish?"

"Really? You don't know? It's my grodote bisque soup of course!"

Clara has never heard of the words *grodote* or *bisque* before, but she knows what *soup* is. "Oh yes, my mistake, that's the one."

Zion stares hard. "The secret ingredient is… *fear.*"

"Is that a spice?" Clara says, sitting on the stool and dashing *Record.*

"You misunderstand. The secret ingredient is... *fear.*"

"Oh, you mean *Fearus?* The Arkathy flower?" Clara ventures.

"No, no, no. I mean *fear.* The *emotion,*" Zion says.

Clara narrows her eyes. "I'm sorry, what kind of joke is this?"

"No joke, my dear. You see, the grodote is a sensitive crustacean. Its body chemistry changes drastically from the emotions it feels. If the wrong emotion is felt while entering the pot, the dish is a complete ruin. However, a correct emotion can be absolutely divine. What you taste in my bisque is a chemical known as frestainician, which only releases when the creature experiences fear. It creates a euphoria calming it in times of stress. The meat is relaxed and tender. And to us humans, this tastes delicious."

"Grodotes feel euphoria? How do you even know they feel fear?"

"Because, my dear, a very long time ago, they told me." Zion raises his palms and shrugs.

"This is ridiculous!" Clara stuffs her holotile into her pocket and stands.

Zion reaches a bony hand. "Please, forgive me! I'm an old man and I like to jest. Please, my dear, can you hold my hand for a moment?"

Clara sighs deeply and reluctantly clasps his hand. *What on Titan did I get myself into?* she thinks.

"You're so warm," Zion says. "I have not felt this warmth in years. Please, stay with me. Nobody stays anymore."

Clara sits back down with a thump.

Zion innocently smiles. "Let me tell you a tale of a little crustacean who stumbles upon a much greater world..."

MERMER's TALE

Earth: 1894 – 2001

I did not know how I came into the world, but I remembered millions of us. We tossed and turned in what I later discovered were waves, the slithering shiny things were fish, and the devils from above were pelicans. They swallowed us hundreds at a time. Yet I was not afraid. I did not understand that I should be, then. But I feel incredible fear now as I reflect. All I understood was hunger. And that food was closer to the soft bottom, beneath ever torrential waves.

My legs were many, and I clumsily wiggled them, cartwheeling for what felt like an eternity until I bumped into something hard and immovable. I clamped my feet to it and crawled into the crack of a stone. There, I found my first-ever friend.

"Mermer," she said, and that was her name.

She was the same creature as me and called me, "MERmer." Quite different from Mermer, I assure you, but it may sound the same to human ears. The two of us huddled together, trying to understand our little world.

What is up? What is down? Why are we here? Do we have a purpose?

"Mermmer mer," Mermer said, and she was right.

We emerged from the crack and crawled to the bottom of our stone, where it became many smaller pieces. *Sand.* Among the sand were yellow particles that smelled correct, so we ate them and felt much better. But when venturing into the open, we quickly learned the devils from above would strike. We dodged them for years, amazed each time we returned unscathed.

But what's the point of it all?

MeerMr, another of our kind, came to us starving and asking for help. But he would not heed our warnings, racing to scavenge when it was unsafe, risking our lives as we dragged him back to safety.

On a midday venture, one Mermer and I knew to be too dangerous and turned around, MeerMr dashed forth anyway. A devil sliced through the water's surface, opening its two halves, one sharp, the other pouch-like. MeerMr had no time to react before being scooped from the water.

I had an epiphany, then. One that would forever change my life, for a creature like me should not be able to conceive one in the first place. *If one of us stands atop the stone watching the surface above as the other scavenges below, we can give a warning call should the devils come,* I explained to Mermer in our simple way.

"Mermer, meer?" she asked.

Good point. What would that emergency call be? I thought. I had another epiphany, taking all of my brainpower to formulate.

The call would be, "Mer-Mer-Mer!"

♦

Mermer gave *The Call.*

I rushed to the safety of our stone but could see no devils from above. Mermer instead told me of a creature, the same as us, but larger.

The mystery visitor remained a myth until late one evening, as Mermer finished her scavenging, a stir caught my eye. A leg at first, then another, until a massive armored head appeared. It slowly neared my dear Mermer and waved its claw. They conversed out of my hearing, and she pointed to me atop our stone.

Before I knew it, they were both returning.

This Big MerMER had been watching us with great interest, marveling at our warning system. I felt anxious, not understanding his intentions, but he knew of areas with different particles. He was so big that we knew his food source was good.

Big MerMER and I ventured into deeper waters but never out of sight of our stone, our world, with my dear Mermer atop, keeping watch. We gathered red particles and ran back to the safety of the stone, barely holding all of our loot.

They tasted different from the yellow particles collected near our stone, yet both were delicious.

I had a strange thought. I do not know why it came to me. It just did. I laid down a yellow particle, followed by a red one and then another yellow, and pinched all three together in my claw. My dear Mermer and Big MerMER looked on with interest and confusion as I inserted the particle sandwich into my mandibles.

The two flavors played wonderfully with one another, making for an ever-entertaining sensation.

♦

I did not understand why the molt was happening, only that it must. My shell felt like tight clothing that must be removed without using my claws or feet. I wiggled until I felt a sudden cracking and pulled myself from… *myself?* I noticed my dear Mermer and Big MerMER had grown larger and moved more quickly. *Had I changed as well?*

"Mer merr mer," they replied.

Amazing! I ran as fast as I could, testing my newfound speed. But then, I tripped and tumbled down the side of our stone. They never let me hear the end of it.

After the second molt, I was noticeably different from my dear Mermer, with my two arms more formidable.

"Mer mer mmerr?" she whispered, staring longingly into my eyes.

I built my courage and said, "Mermer."

She gently bumped her head against mine.

I'm the luckiest creature alive, I thought.

Big MerMER had also grown larger arms but was no longer friendly. When I asked what was wrong, he shoved me to the edge of our stone. My dear Mermer peered from a crack, frightened, just as confused as I. Then, I wondered, *What would happen to her if I fell over the edge?* That is when I realized Big MerMER wanted her for himself.

No! Despite being smaller, I pushed back with all my strength, bursting with concussive force.

Big MerMER was caught off guard, off-balance, falling backward from our stone and tumbling to the sand below. He scurried off, never to be seen again.

♦

My love and I remained on that stone for several decades, growing stronger and discovering new combinations of particles to feast upon. We slept shell to shell, and I would wrap my claws around her. *She liked that.*

Then, I noticed Mermer growing rotund and was hungrier than ever.

"Mermerm mer?" I asked.

She did not know either, but we soon found out.

It was the beginning of summer. We understood it as when the water warmed. Mermer slowly crept to the top of our stone during low tide.

So dangerous, I knew and tried to convince her not to go. But she was compelled to. And so, I kept watch as she climbed above the waterline, stretched her legs high, and shook. Hundreds of tiny creatures fell from her as torrential waves surged. It took me a moment to understand these creatures were smaller versions of myself.

This is how I came into existence, too, I thought. *But why?*

Mermer descended, exhausted, back to the size I knew. I gently bumped my head against hers and told her she was the most beautiful creature in the whole wide tide pool.

◆

I was sifting through particles, oblivious to everything else, when I heard, "Mer-Mer-Mer!" I dropped my loot and raced home, looking left, right, and above, but no devils were coming.

"Mmerr me!" I heard my love calling.

A break in the surface caught my eye, a devil opening its two halves, heading not towards me but to my dearest Mermer, instead. I sprinted to intercept, to do something, *Anything!* The devil caught Mermer's hind leg as I clutched her front claws. I gripped my legs onto the stone with a fury never before witnessed on those shores.

Still, the devil pulled Mermer from my grasp.

"MERmer!" she called as she rose to the surface.

I stared deeply into her eyes. I could feel her center, her inner light. And for the briefest moment, I was looking through *her* eyes, down upon myself, desperately reaching out. I felt the pressure around her body cease, and brightness struck. I pinched the devil with her claws, but they were much smaller than my own. I could not break its grasp.

Then a voice spoke to me more intimately than ever before.

"You have to let me go," Mermer said.

"I can't! I just can't!" I responded.

"Great things await you. I know this from the bottom of my shell. But you must let me go."

"No!" I stubbornly said.

"I'm sorry, I love you, but let me *go!*" she commanded.

I was underwater again, on our stone, in my own body.

"Mermer," I squeaked, staring at the rippling surface above, my claws still outstretched. I did not move for several hours, convinced she would soon return and gently bump my head.

♦

She's not coming, I realized after the fourth day of waiting. *I must search for her.* But only the devils would know where she might be.

I crawled to open sand, where I was most exposed, and spread my claws, taunting them. Yet, no matter how long I waited or how much I wiggled, they would not come. For my entire life, I narrowly escaped their strikes and watched them take my friends and even the love of my life. But now that I wanted to go, they refused me.

What cruel game do they play?

♦

My solitude, my atonement, lasted several years. For what crime I committed, I did not know. A slithering, shiny creature rustled the sand into a circular dune beside my stone.

"MerMer!" I scolded the shiny creature.

"Blub, blub," it said, and that was its name.

Blubblub was obsessed with cleaning his dune and rudely pushed me aside when I scavenged too closely. *Jerk.* One afternoon, I saw he had a friend, another slithering, shiny creature, and she seemed very pleased with his dune. To both my entertainment and dismay, I watched them fall in love.

Never did my heart ache so much for Mermer. *Time to move on.*

I left that stone, left everything I knew of life, racing across the sand to who knows where. I did not care. *Left, left, more left!* When I crossed areas with more sunlight and shallower waters, many devils suddenly struck. *Now they want me!?* Their fickleness was appalling. *So be it!* I stopped, and one snapped terrifyingly close. I reevaluated. *No, this is not what I thought it was!* Again, I scurried. *Left, left, left!* But they were anticipating my moves. *How do I lose them!?*

Against the direction I spent my entire life scurrying, against everything that felt natural, *I tried moving right!*

Left, left... Right! I juked.

The devils' aim faltered. They could not anticipate me. I found another stone to hide beneath. Not singular, but many together, hosting hundreds of creatures the same as I.

"Mer meree!" they cheered.

◆

Wooden piles pounded into the sand, supporting a long shadow from which minor shadows would come and go. And soon, those shadows changed, emitting a buzz that drove us mad. We eventually met the creatures of those great shadows, having soft, pink flesh, sure to perish in our harsh world. Yet, their intelligence was incredible.

And soon, their attention turned to us.

They placed hollow scoops to our left, waving their soft fingers, but we knew better and scurried right, instead. The pink creatures' frustration was magnificent to behold.

"Shit! Shit!" they said, and that was their name.

The Shitshits quickly adapted, placing scoops to either side of us the next time, but they did not fool us. We scurried in all directions. Then they tried completely surrounding us, but we remained still as their soft, pink fingers waved. One tried to pick us up.

Amateur move. We employed our claws.

The Shitshits said their names several times as we scrambled, barely squeezing between the scoops.

Another victory... But too close for comfort.

◆

A light hit the sand at dusk like it was day. We came out to investigate. *No devils, no scoops, and no soft fingers.* So, we eagerly dined.

The ground slipped from beneath our feet. The sand erupted into a thick cloud. Before we knew what happened, we were pulled from the water. We tried moving left and right and used our claws to cut what I believe was a net, but it proved too strong. The top opened, our world flipped, and we fell into several scoops, joining many more creatures of the same kind.

"Merre merr mer?" I asked, but they were just as confused.

A monstrous rumble enveloped us.

"Vroom, vroom," it said, and that was its name.

We sloshed left and right, forward and backward, holding onto each other for dear life until, at last, Vroomvroom quieted. Its massive mouth opened, and the Shitshits removed our scoops from its belly. I squeezed my way to the scoop's transparent side to survey the strange environment. The light was dim, but I could still see the ground below, hard and black. We neared a monstrous creature made with perfect corners, and its massive mouth opened, letting the Shitshits inside.

"Creak," it said, and that was its name.

Once inside, it instantly became day, and they set us atop a plateau. I waved to my friends in the adjacent scoops, but they did not see me.

Instead, a small Shitshit climbed closer, bringing its bulbous head to the transparent wall of my scoop. Glossy, white eyes shifted back and forth, soft features wiggled, its mouth became any shape it wished, and dark algae sat atop its head. *Hideous does not scratch the surface.* The Shitshit tapped the scoop, sending thunderous booms across our bodies.

I squeezed to the top, where I knew it was open, popped my head above the edge, and scolded the Shitshit good.

The tapping ceased, and the hideous creature spread its mouth wide, revealing menacing flat teeth. Its lips writhed like worms. Horrific sounds flew. Then a larger Shitshit approached, peering into the scoop, studying me, and shook its head. The smaller one closed its mouth, its features scrunched together, and water leaked from its eyes.

More of them passed through Creak's mouth and stared into our scoops, showing their teeth and rubbing their hands together.

They carried an enormous silver container through Creak's rear mouth. Then us, too. It dimmed to the night again. *So confusing.* They placed the silver container above a dancing yellow light, so beautiful in its flicker, and filled it with water that soon rippled.

The Shitshits lifted one of our scoops and held it above the bubbling water. I could hear my friends' murmurs of joy as they watched the bubbles below them. Then, the scoop tipped and they tumbled in.

I imagined the bubbles to be fun. But then, I sensed something wrong. *So very, very wrong!* Their claws wiggled as if molting. Then, they stopped moving and turned bright red.

My friends were pulled from the rippling water and placed on flat circles.

"Mer mee!" I yelled, but they did not try to escape.

Shitshits gathered around, picking up my friends, tearing their backs, claws, and legs from their bodies, sucking out their insides, and mashing them between their sickening flat teeth.

Terror washed over me, a kind I never experienced before. Another of our scoops hovered above the rippling water. I could hear their cries as they fell. Then, something coursed through my veins. All at once, horror became delight. The others were feeling it, too, almost happy to tumble to their deaths. Still, I knew this was all wrong.

I was the only one who did.

I focused away from the wonderful feeling, breathed deeply, and screamed, "Mer! Merrrrrrr!"

The Shitshits were deaf to my cries.

The last scoop, holding my closest friends and me, was carried to the bubbling water. I stared, disgusted, as Shitshits drank from cylinders, loosening their emotions, and wiggled in happy patterns to vibrating boxes.

They do not care, I realized.

I prepared to meet my end when I saw big, white eyes. *The small Shitshit!* I waved my claw. It straightened in its seat. *It sees me!* Our eyes locked. I sensed its energy, its inner light.

The Shitshit's soul? I thought.

When I reached for it, colors became impossibly vibrant, sounds cleared, and my breathing felt long and drawn. I tried raising my claws, but they had become pink hands. *I'm inside the Shitshit,* I realized. I tried telling them to stop, but this flabby mouth would not form the words I needed. Then, I found a place deep in its throat and pushed with everything I had. I do not know what I said, but it went something like, "Reeeeaaaaahhh!"

The Shitshits froze.

The final scoop tipped, and I watched my crustacean body tumble into the bubbling water. I tried standing but lost balance and fell backward, smacking the Shitshit's bulbous head against a picnic table's edge.

And then, everything went dark.

CHAPTER FOUR

"He's nuts, Jonathan!" Clara says, pacing back and forth, tears of frustration in her eyes.

"Define nuts," Jonathan replies on hologram.

"He's friends with a crab," she says flatly.

Jonathan blinks. "Hon. Is there a connection problem? Sounded like you said he's friends with a crab?"

"No, you heard me right."

"Is crab slang for something?"

"Crab as in *crab*." Clara opens and closes her hand like a claw.

"Is it a *pet* crab?"

"It's a good friend from ancient Earth, before The Fall, fifteen hundred years ago. One who taught him the secret ingredient to his grodote bisque soup."

Jonathan cocks his head. "Yeah, he's nuts."

"See what I'm dealing with!" Clara crosses her arms. "Two days ago Zion was his normal, calculative self. But *that* Zion banished me from his room. The only version that will talk to me is the crazy one."

"At least the crazy one is nice."

"Yes, he *is* nice." Clara has to give Jonathan something to make him feel helpful. "But he's fucking nuts."

Jonathan raises his hands. "Well maybe—"

"I don't need you to *fix* it. I need you to *listen*."

"I *am* listening," he says, lowering his hands and waiting.

"Well... Say *something*."

Jonathan sighs. "You're the most brilliant person I know. A brilliant biographer, soldier, mother, and wife. There is not a more perfectly qualified detective for this job. So *detect*."

He sure buttered me up there. "You think I should investigate this crab story?"

"Maybe don't listen to the words he is saying, but find their meaning."

That's my Jonathan. Clara grins. "Kip."

"Kip," Jonathan says, giving a begrudging smile. "You're a pain in the ass sometimes."

"Always, hon," she jests.

◆

Clara enters EarthRise Diner at the base of Cobble Hill to find her favorite booth open. *Yes!* A waiter nods and sends her usual brunch order to the synthesizer. Clara plops onto the cushioned bench, pulls a freshly purchased holotile from her pocket, and activates. Its hologram scans her retinas and downloads her user settings and programs.

Ready to go. But where do I begin?

"Location, location, location," she whispers, putting, *"Grodote Range,"* into the search. *Nothing.*

She tries, *"Crab,"* instead. Thousands of species appear. *How am I going to narrow this down?* She adds, *"+Speaks."*

"Crabs that spit, Crabs that squirt, Crabs that shake, Crabs that squeak," appears. She selects, *"Crabs that squeak."*

A genetically modified species on Ganymede descending from Christmas Island crabs of old Earth opens. *Information from old Earth? Rare.* Being land crabs, they migrate great distances through the forest to spawn. *That's cool.* The squeaking appeared after their introduction on Ganymede. With proper training, they make great companions. *Uh, what?*

A video of the crab opens.

Not even close, Clara thinks.

She sifts through each species, but none resemble the grodotes Zion described. Brunch comes and goes. Then, she has a late lunch. Clara soon finds herself ordering dinner. *This is getting nowhere.*

But maybe... She inputs, *"Pelican+Range+Earth."*

A link immediately pops up.

The bird still exists, Clara realizes. *But Earth's shorelines have drastically changed.* She enters *"2000AD Climate vs. Today+Animation,"* into a new search, then accesses MERGE, her favorite program, applying the information from search *A* to the format of search *B*. Before long, an animation of pelican range from 2000AD to present day develops.

But what about the humans? She thinks. *Zion described them with pink hands, which rules out much of Africa and Asia.* She inputs, *"+Caucasian."* The locations shrink to the coasts of North America and the southern tip of Africa and Australia.

A suggested link opens, *"Did you mean Brown Pelicans on Enceladus?"*

"Enceladus?" Clara whispers. *Zion never actually specified Earth.*

"Mom!"

Clara's heart leaps into her throat. She finds her son standing next to her. *How does he sneak up on me like that?* "How was school?"

"It's the weekend, Mom." Frustration crosses Aizen's face.

"Oh... Right."

"You *promised* you'd stay home this time," he says.

"I *am* home."

"This is *not* home." Aizen frowns and points around the diner.

What am I doing? she thinks. "I'm sorry, hon. I got caught up in this."

He sits down next to her, looking at the animation. "Pelicans?"

"Zion told a story about an intelligent crab who lived in coastal waters. Pelicans were his enemy," Clara explains.

Aizen releases his frown and giggles. "You mean, Mermer the Genius?"

Clara stares blankly at her son. "How on Titan do you know that?"

"It's a cartoon... Mom? You okay?"

♦

Clara thrusts open Zion's door, ready to meet whichever version of him is there. He stands in the center of the room as if waiting, his posture impeccable, his stance military. *But Zion never served,* Clara knows. *He must have learned the mannerisms for political show!*

"You have some nerve!" she growls.

"I have many nerves. My body has roughly one hundred billion of them," Zion says, emotionless. "Would you like tea?" He claps his hands sharply.

Dr. Lee enters, out of breath.

"Tea!" Zion orders and waves him off.

Dr. Lee flashes Clara a look on his way out, saying, *Not a good day.*

Clara glares at Zion. "Do you take me for an idiot!?"

"Yes," he calmly says.

Don't let him frazzle you! Clara tells herself. "That story of yours was just a cartoon you watched on hologram!"

"Just a cartoon? Have you actually seen it? It's wonderful," he says.

"So... you're fully aware that you recited a cartoon?"

"Of course."

Somehow, Clara feels like *she* is in the wrong. "I never asked you to recite a *cartoon.*"

"Oh, but you did. You asked for the secret ingredient to my grodote bisque soup. My straight forward answer was not acceptable for you, so I gave context."

"You did *not* give context. Context is *true.*"

"Do you believe the cartoon is a lie?" Zion gasps as if utterly insulted.

How on Titan did Zion make me the villain? "Yes! It's ridiculous!"

"That is no reason to call me a liar!" Zion scolds like a father.

Brilliantly done. All the blame is redirected to me. Clara takes a deep Ergonos breath. "Is this a negotiation tactic of yours?"

Zion smiles a little. "Quite effective, isn't it."

Dr. Lee enters with a pot of tea wrapped in a towel and places it on a trivet atop a small table.

"What is *that?*" Zion points at the teapot.

"It's... Tea," Dr. Lee says.

"I asked for *coffee.*"

"But you—"

"Coffee!" Zion orders and shoos Dr. Lee out of the room.

He leaves in a huff.

"He'll mutiny on you if you push him too far," Clara says.

Zion shrugs. "I'll let the good doctor win another hoverbike race."

Clara looks to the ceiling. *I must reset.* "I'm confused by you. And the other you, too. How many are there?"

"There's only one."

"But your personality changes so drastically I can never trust which version I will get."

"There are certain things you learn in life when you have lived as long as I. Sadly, intelligence is only measured against stupidity. If one excels too much, too consistently, then it's taken for granted. I've learned that keeping people guessing is the key to maintaining control. The moment they believe you an idiot is the moment you strike with brilliance. Contrast is your ally."

"So you're *purposely* acting like different people?" Clara asks.

Instead of answering, Zion shrugs.

Clara furrows her brow. "Zion, are you crazy?"

"Perhaps," he says with a mischievous grin.

◆

Aizen sits on the sofa watching MerMer the Genius with Mom like he is five years old again. Brightly colored sea creatures float about, with MerMer being the most adorable. The show pauses for a lesson.

"*F......ish. F....ish. F..ish. Fish!*" says the narrator to studio applause.

A scene in which Mermer meets a fish begins.

Mom humphs. "It's Blubblub."

"You don't know that," Aizen says.

"*...Blubblub it said, and that was its name,*" chimes the hologram.

Mom points. "See? I wonder what they call humans. Hopefully not Shitshits."

"Mom! Language!"

"It's not *that* bad of a word."

"In ancient English it is."

"Fine. So what are humans called?"

"There are no humans."

Mom scrunches her brow. "Is this a new episode?"

"It's debuting right now."

She scrunches further. "I wonder how difficult it is to get the scripts."

The show pauses for another lesson, requiring viewers to wave their hands to help Mermer confuse the pelicans. *Left! Left! Left! Right! Right! Left! Right!*"

Mom waves her hands accordingly, and Mermer finds safety.

"*You did it!*" says the narrator.

The episode ends, and Aizen watches Mom lock eyes on the credits racing by, pausing at, *"Produced by: Gabriel Perkins."*

◆

"Who is this? How did you get this number!?"

"Sorry to cold call you, Mr. Perkins. My name is Clara Ocol and I'm writing the biography for—"

"I'm not interested! Remove me from—"

"—The Great Zion Wright," she finishes, remaining calm.

Mr. Perkins pauses. "I'm listening."

"Thank you, Mr. Perkins. May I ask a few questions about Mermer the

Genius?"

He laughs a little. "Uh, sure?"

"Is the story original?"

Mr. Perkins scoffs. "Of *course* it is."

"Who's the writer?"

"Sahara Zaid," Mr. Perkins says. "It's a pen name, I think."

Clara ponders that. "Will the humans arrive with their buckets soon?"

He exhales at length. "I'm going to fire Andrew. Has it spread across the net yet?"

Clara shakes her head. "I assure you nothing has leaked."

Mr. Perkins zeroes in. "How much do you want?"

"I'm not blackmailing you."

"Then *why* are you telling me this?"

"Zion told me a story of a crab named MerMer from beginning to end."

"That's impossible. Nobody has requested the scripts."

"Are you sure?"

Mr. Perkins thinks a moment. "Andrew!"

A young man stumbles over. "Y-yes, Mr. Perkins?"

"Has anyone requested the scripts for MerMer the Genius?"

Shock washes across his face. "Well, uh, yes, actually."

Mr. Perkins turns beet red and lays into Andrew thick. Clara catches bits of his shouting. She hears, "fired," several times and then, "who?" Mr. Perkins quiets.

"Is Andrew fired?" Clara asks.

Mr. Perkins returns to his holotile. "No."

"Someone accessed the scripts, didn't they," she guesses.

"Yes."

"Was that someone Zion Wright?"

"I'm not at liberty to say."

"Are you at liberty to write it?"

"No."

"Are you at liberty to send me the access log?"

"Perhaps." Mr. Perkins turns to Andrew and nods.

Clara's holotile receives a file.

"Thank you, Mr. Perk—"

The call ends abruptly.

I might deserve that, Clara thinks and opens the file. It contains an anonymous access, several days old, accompanied by the manuscripts for every upcoming episode. *They didn't have to do that.* Nevertheless, Clara obliges herself, meticulously deconstructing the events, determining which parts Zion stole directly from the show and what he embellished.

Clara finishes early in the morning. *I've got you now.*

♦

"Clara! Wait!" Dr. Lee cries just before Clara enters Zion's room.

She turns. "What's wrong?"

He hustles to her. "Nothing's wrong. Zion instructed me to give you *this* before entering today." He hands her a card with, *"Clara,"* written in perfect calligraphy across its front.

She analyzes the lettering. *Handwritten, of course.* She rolls her eyes and opens its fold.

"Dear Clara, Did you enjoy the manuscripts? -Zion Wright-"

A pit grows in her stomach. *How on Titan does he know!? There's no way for Mr. Perkins to notify him!* Clara ponders that. *Zion must have orchestrated the entire thing, knew I would watch the cartoon, call Mr. Perkins, request the access log, and read the manuscripts.*

I cannot walk into that room, she realizes. Her vision blurs with tears of frustration that she would rather die than let be shed here. She drops the card, pivots around, and makes for the exit.

CHAPTER FIVE

Aizen wakes to a muffled sobbing coming through the wall. *Mom? Isn't she at work?* He climbs out of bed and inches down the hallway to her room. The crying is unmistakable. *It's Mom.* He knocks on her door. The sobbing stifles, and her breathing steadies.

"Come in," Mom says, feigning calm.

She's wearing a mining uniform and reading a book when Aizen opens the door. *Well, pretending.* A bookmark is between loose leaves.

He crawls onto the bed and leans his head against her shoulder. "It's going to be okay, Mom."

She wipes a tear. "Don't you have to get ready for school."

"I'm skipping today."

"You most certainly are not!"

Aizen looks into her eyes. "We need a day together, just you and me, Mom. I'm always on top of my schoolwork. One day won't hurt."

"Okay," she whispers and yawns.

"You stayed up the whole night again," Aizen says.

Mom reluctantly nods.

"Take a nap, then we'll have our day."

"Sounds like a plan," Mom says.

Aizen beelines to the kitchen. *I have just the thing to cheer her up!* He programs the synth for, *"English muffin,"* but it generates a solid brick.

Something's off. He lists the components of eggs benedict, *"Eggs, Bacon, English muffin, Hollandaise sauce,"* but they each come out as rectangles.

I must break each into its ingredients, he realizes. *But I've never gone that far before.*

He types, *"Flour,"* and receives a pile of white dust. *What the?* He dabs his finger. *Bland.* Next is sugar. *Another pile of white dust? The synth must be broken.* But the texture is different this time. He tastes. *Wow!* Next comes yeast, baking powder, and baking soda. *More piles of white dust...*

He types, *"Baking,"* into his holotile. Articles from sixty years ago appear. He refines with, *"+Muffin+English."* The search narrows to a single image of ingredients, far more than the synth indicates, and with a step-by-step process. He enters each component into the synth, and it provides him with what he needs. Until the, *"King Arthur unbleached bread flour,"* generates a loaf of bread shaped like a sword.

"Ha!" Aizen covers his mouth, hoping he did not wake Mom.

He finds his father's gardening buckets in the attic and gives them a good scrub before mixing ingredients. The dough expands and deflates. He cuts them into smaller pieces and shapes them into circles, feeling like a mad scientist. Next is something called pan-frying.

What's a pan? Aizen thinks. *What's a fry?*

He studies several pan schematics, but stainless steel, aluminum, and teflon were banned from cooking centuries ago. A black one appears with, *"Cast iron,"* in its description. He searches its composition. *It's just iron.* He accesses MERGE and applies, *"Cast iron,"* to the schematics of a pan, then sends the file to the synthesizer. It hums for several minutes before beeping. The pan appears as a black blur beyond the synthesizer's translucent door.

Okay, what now? Aizen thinks.

"Pan-fry on stovetop until golden brown," reads the recipe.

What's a stovetop?

♦

Clara wakes to the smell of burning. She leaps from bed, thrusts open her door, and chases the scent to the living room. Her eyes dart around, searching for flames and smoke. Instead, they find Aizen calmly setting the dinner table with upside-down buckets.

"What happened!? What's on fire!?" she snaps.

Aizen points to the fireplace.

A curious metal circle sits atop bamboo logs in embers, wisps of smoke drifting up the chimney. *Cooking is one of its original functions, after all,*

Clara thinks.

"You're right on time," Aizen says, placing forks and knives on either side of the buckets.

Clara takes a seat. *Jonathan's gardening pails,* she realizes. Aizen sits across from her and places his hands on his bucket.

"Remove on three, okay?" he instructs. "One… Two—"

Clara lifts her bucket early.

"Hey! Cheater!" Aizen cries.

Clara inhales deeply and laughs, recognizing the smell but never with such potency. *Such authenticity.* She expects to see a brick of eggs benedict but finds spongy circles with white orbs instead. "What's this?"

"Eggs benedict."

She cocks her head. "But it's not a rectangle."

"It's not supposed to be," Aizen says, raising his fork and knife. He seems just as confused as she. Nevertheless, he sticks his fork into the orb and uses his knife to slice it in half. Yellow liquid drools upon spongy bread, filling its nooks and crannies. He tastes and groans.

Clara follows Aizen's lead, taking an apprehensive bite. The bread feels soft yet structured. The richness of yolk coats her tongue. Flavors mix and dance, creating so many variations it becomes endlessly entertaining. She swallows, feeling its warmth run down her throat.

"Aizen, this is unbelievable! How did you do this!?"

"I synthesized the ingredients separately, then cooked the old way."

Brilliance... Clara takes another bite and brews an idea. "Would you like to cook something for Zion?"

Her son's eyes widen. His mouth drops open. He nods.

◆

Why did Aizen make cookies again? Clara wonders. But they appear charred at the edges this time. *He must have synthesized the ingredients separately and used the fireplace like he did the eggs benedict.*

When she enters the LightTram, passengers sniff the air like hounds despite the cookies being sealed within a container. *How potent are these things?* It's the same with the miners as they walk the mine's dark tunnel.

"Be careful with those," one says as they reach the two vault doors.

Doctors stop in their tracks and sniff when Clara enters Zion's holding facility. A sudden shattering of glass and heavy thumps jolts them from their olfactory trance.

"Fucking! Dammit! Jesus *fucking* Christ!" comes from down the hall.

Zion, Clara knows.

She finds Dr. Lee in his office. "What's happening?"

Dr. Lee is engrossed in a diagram of Zion's brain. "This is normal. Zion's remembering. Well, remembering that he forgot." He sniffs the air and locks eyes on the box.

"This is *normal?*" Clara tilts her head.

He shrugs. "Every three months, like clockwork."

"Shouldn't we tranquilize him or something?"

Dr. Lee lifts his eyes. "We tried that once. Resulted in four dislocated joints, three bruised ribs, and multiple dislodged vertebrae and sprains."

"Why would you do that to him!?" Cara says, appalled.

Dr. Lee shakes his head. "Zion did that to *us,* three doctors and five guards."

She scrunches her brow. "How could weak, old Zion do that?"

"Weak? He's not weak," Dr. Lee says. "He's just not ridiculously superhuman anymore. Trust me, he's still incredibly strong."

"But eight of you, and Zion was *never* military."

"I'll show you the recording sometime." His attention returns to the diagram.

Clara feels compelled to see Zion in this state firsthand and struts down the hallway.

"No! Don't go in!" Dr. Lee hollers, but it's too late.

Clara opens the door.

Zion whirls with wildness in his eyes. "What the hell are you doing here!?" He snatches a glass bottle of water and chucks it at her head.

By pure instinct, Clara catches the bottle, absorbing its momentum. *Thank Sol, for all that Ergonos training!* She shakily sets it on the table once chaperoned by two chairs. She takes a deep Ergonos breath to calm herself, narrows her eyes, and surveys her surroundings. One of Zion's chairs lies on the floor, bent out of shape, and the other protrudes from the wall like artwork.

Zion looks impressed for half a second before returning to his tantrum. "Get the fuck out!"

Clara ignores him like she would a bratty child or a wild animal, sets the box of cookies on the table, and places a card with, *"Zion,"* written in her best calligraphy atop.

Zion pauses. "Are you listening!? If you don't leave this instant—!"

Clara leaves, closing the door behind her.

"Goddamn it! Don't walk out on me!"

More objects smash.

Dr. Lee joins Clara outside Zion's door. "You okay?"

Clara looks to the ceiling. *Collect yourself.* "I'm all right."

"Stupid card! Looks like a toddler wrote it!" Zion continues shouting. "Me an *asshole!?* That bitch!"

"What did you write?" Dr. Lee asks.

"Dear Zion, You're an asshole," Clara answers.

Dr. Lee nervously chuckles.

"Stupid box! You think I'm *actually* going to look inside!? You think—!" Zion silences.

Dr. Lee whispers, "What's in the box?"

"My son made cookies, the old way."

He humphs. "I'll have to remember that." His holotile beeps. "Zion's asking for me." Dr. Lee timidly approaches the door and enters.

"Milk!" Zion orders.

Dr. Lee reappears, shrugs his shoulders, retrieves a glass of milk from the synthesizer, and re-enters.

"Leave!"

Dr. Lee again emerges and shrugs. Several silent moments pass before his holotile lets another beep. His eyes widen. "Zion wants to see *you.*"

Clara takes a moment to collect her thoughts, then enters.

Zion is sitting awkwardly in a bent chair next to his table. Once stuck in the wall, the second chair rests on the other side. The box of cookies is open. Two are already gone.

Zion points at the empty chair. "Sit!"

Clara retrieves the stool next to his bed, instead. They stare unblinking at one another until Zion evades his eyes, and all hostility melts away.

"Well played. And... thank you," Zion says, motioning to the cookies. "I must ask, how in Sol did you find Allessandra's cookies? Not even the best collectors have one."

"I did not *find* them," she says, staring at Zion, ready to bolt from the room should he flinch.

"Whatever do you mean?" His voice is strangely gentle now.

"My son, Aizen, made them," Clara says.

Zion laughs lightly, then stops. "You're serious?"

She nods.

"But many of the ingredients no longer exist," he says.

"Aizen used our synthesizer to recreate the ingredients, then pan-fried them in our fireplace." *What happened to Zion's rage?* Clara thinks.

"Of course! That's why they're like Allessandra's! She never baked them. She pan-fried!" Zion clasps his hands, going from *Zion the Monster* to *Zion the Delight*. "Do you know how to eat chocolate chip cookies, Clara?"

She gives a skeptical look. "There's only *one* way."

Zion shakes his head. "Let me show you." He pulls a cookie from the box and lowers it midway into the milk, letting it soak into the pores. He lifts. "Your turn."

Clara takes a cookie and dips.

"Wait three seconds. Now, pull it out," Zion instructs.

She does as instructed, not once breaking eye contact. "Now, what?"

"My favorite part is sucking the milk from the pores before it becomes mush." He quickly puts the cookie into his mouth and leans back, making sucking sounds.

Clara does the same. The juxtaposition of liquid, crunch, cold, and warmth is simple yet incredible. She finishes her cookie, and the previous moments, with the smashing, screaming, and chucking of the bottle, feel ages old and almost forgivable. *But only ten minutes have elapsed,* she reminds herself.

Zion closes the box, giving it a loving pat and a forlorn look. "It's best that they be savored. Cookies are a treat, not a meal."

"Zion?"

"Yes, Clara?"

"Dr. Lee said you became violent today because you remembered that you forgot."

"The good doctor said that?" Zion strokes his chin, pondering this. "I would not say I *forgot*. I misplaced a few memories is all."

"How is that any different?"

"It's like misplacing your keys. You don't forget what those keys are for, you simply forget where they are."

Do I want to tumble down this rabbit hole? Clara thinks. Nevertheless, she asks, "Which memories were misplaced?"

Zion's eyes drift to the floor. "They were of Justin..."

JUSTIN's TALE

Earth: 1994 – 2067

I did not know how I came into the world, but I remembered waking without memories as a seven-year-old boy. I could not speak, could not walk, could not eat, and could not use the bathroom. I was an infant again in every sense. Yet I dreamed of shimmering ocean shores so vividly I often wondered if the waking world was the farce.

Lying in a hospital bed, in the section reserved for those who would never wake, my eyes popped open. I was comatose for eight months, and in that time, my mind reset. *Supposedly.*

My nurse, Daniel, knew I could not comprehend a thing and made funny faces to help convey ideas. I would laugh loudly, then cry, frightened by my voice. But Daniel stayed by my side, helping me understand these strange sounds. When I grew accustomed to myself, he performed puppet shows to teach me the sounds of others, creating happy, sad, strong, and weak voices.

My god, was he masterful.

Like I was a newborn gosling, Daniel imprinted upon me. I believed him to be my father. To my disappointment, I learned he was not.

But he will forever be my dad.

My biological parents visited several weeks after I learned basic tasks such as eating, pointing, and crying when I pooped. My physician orchestrated the meeting long after I woke to lessen the psychological impact. But the anticipation must have been overwhelming for my parents. When they saw me smiling and giggling at Daniel's puppetry, they rushed to my bedside despite the doctor's order not to.

"Oh, Justin!" they shouted, grasping my arms, expecting me to hold them tight and say how much I loved and missed them.

Instead, I let out a blood-curdling scream, gnashed my father's arm, drawing blood, and kicked wildly at my mother.

♦

Daniel was finishing his best rendition of *The Magic Flute* yet, the characters at their comedic peak, and his whistling for the bells magnificent.

"Tell it again," I said and flinched at my words. *Where did that come from!?* I will never forget the shock on Daniel's face.

"Yes! Of course, Justin! Do you understand me right now?"

"I... I do!"

We both laughed until tears came.

"I love you, Dad," I said.

Daniel's smile dwindled. "Oh, Justin. I'm not your father."

"But I want you to be."

"I'm sorry. I can't. But I can be your fun uncle. Okay?"

"Okay," I said, but it was *not* okay.

Why doesn't Daniel want to be my dad?

My parents were more excited to see me when I began speaking. For a moment, I felt they might be my mom and dad after all.

But then came the questions.

"Do you remember Bernie?" Father said, handing me a stuffed tiger.

I tossed it to the floor.

"How about the Velveteen Rabbit? It's your favorite," Mother said, holding a children's book.

I shook my head.

They gave each other sad looks and sighed deeply.

I'm a disappointment, I realized.

Soon, I began to walk, then run. And one day, I discovered I was artistic, sketching underwater scenes filled with sea creatures.

"Why sea creatures, Justin?" Daniel asked, marveling at the detail.

"They're in my dreams," I said.

I never regained the memories from before the accident, only the skills. Nevertheless, there was nothing more the doctors could do for me. They discharged me from the hospital.

When my parents came to pick me up, I wailed, clutching Daniel tightly and staring into his eyes for reassurance.

"Justin, you *must* go," Daniel said, his voice shaking. He was crying.

He does want to be my dad, after all!

But then, he left the room despite my screams for him to stay, struggling wildly against these strangers I was supposed to call family.

◆

On my eleventh birthday, while visiting a local kiddie farm and after relentlessly questioning the farmer, I learned how they slaughtered and prepared livestock. I vomited chocolate cake and cheeseburger down my shirt and on the farmer's boots.

"Jesus fucking Christ, Justin!" Father cursed, apologizing profusely to the farmer. He then turned to me and whispered, "I can't take you anywhere, you little shit!"

A disgust for food consumed me. And despite my parents' and psychologist's best efforts, it would not shake. I became vegan the moment I understood the concept. But as I learned about pesticides and fertilizers, more food became taboo.

My parents believed I should make my own decisions, define how I want to live, and what faith to follow.

"Be your own man, for crying out loud!" Father would say.

To their disappointment, I followed Islam, spending hours researching obscure holidays and traditions to which fasting was relevant. I treated every day like Ramadan, over-embellishing its role and flat-out lying. After fainting in class and breaking my arm on the way down, my parents quickly ended it.

"He's a skeleton," my physician said, glaring at my parents.

In desperation, they ambushed me throughout the day, holding me to the floor and draining liquid meals via funnel and tube into my mouth.

"This is for your own good, Justin," Mother would say in tears.

Sadly, I gained weight, rationalizing the method.

The psychologists were the worst, imagining every possible reason for my desire to starve except the actual one. When I described my dreams—the loss of my greatest love and the pain of being boiled alive—they diagnosed me as schizophrenic, anorexic, and a pathological liar.

And my parents treated me as such.

The only thing I enjoyed in life was painting undersea murals. Ones that left my art teachers speechless. They spoke of my future career when they thought I could not hear, whispering, "Remember when," or, "Our beautiful disaster."

But my parents wanted my interests to lie in mathematics and current events, to go into finance or accounting just like my father had. They banished me from the school's arts excel program.

"It's a waste of time!" Father said.

"But, I love it!" I argued.

"There's no money in art! I forbid it!" He gathered my brushes, canvases, and paint tubes and burned them in the backyard fire pit.

I watched the sea creatures on canvas melt away with tears streaming down my cheeks and my body feeling ablaze as if I were in the fire myself. *There's no way out,* I thought.

There's always a way out, came a voice inside my head.

Emancipation was impossible, my so-called schizophrenia entrapping me to my parents. Nevertheless, I simply went to school on my sixteenth birthday and did not return.

◆

I worked the night shift for an illegitimate construction crew a town over while studying for my GED as best I could, sleeping restlessly alongside laborers, drifters, and ex-cons in the attic above the foreman's garage. They drank day and night, heading back to work hungover, puking, or drunk, making studying nearly impossible.

Soon, what little shuteye I grasped became plagued by nightmares. I woke screaming to rounds of laughter from the crew. Until one night, when they no longer found it funny, begging me to, "Shut up!" they offered a drink. To their dismay, the more I drank, the more I preached about falling in love, the pain of losing that love, and the horror of being boiled alive.

Again, I woke screaming, nearly blackout drunk, the crew holding me down as I lashed out, my skin feeling set on fire. They tried calming me, stroking my hair, bringing forth what looked like brown sugar wrapped in paper, liquefying it with a spoon and flame, and drawing it into a needle.

All at once, my nightmares melted away, the pain dissolved, and for the first time I could remember, *I slept.*

But even that did not last, for those nightmares trickled into my waking hours as apparitions on the job site. I desperately ignored cartoonish sea creatures swimming in the concrete we poured and birds swooping from above. And it was there, guiding a girder to its gusset plate two stories up, that I fell. I never knew whether that devil from above was real or not, but my torn meniscus and three herniated discs certainly were. Yet, I did not know what was wrong until years later. I had no healthcare.

I gritted my teeth, feeling enamel chips between my molars, and rolled from my back to my stomach. *My one goal for the day.* I saw it in the crew's eyes. They knew what future lay ahead.

The foreman booted me from the attic.

The crew guided me down the steps, handing me a nug, needle, and a phone number to call for more. The foreman gave me five twenties and hailed a cab, not once making eye contact.

"Where should I go?" I whimpered.

"Anywhere but here," he said, turning his back to me.

I stared at the nug in one hand and the cash in the other. I knew where to numb the pain.

◆

I stole when the opportunity came and worked odd jobs so long as they did not involve lifting or sitting. *So... few.* There was a period in which I resorted to less savory avenues. All so I could plunge. Each chapter of my tragedy unfolded before my eyes, but I could not stop it. I expected, eventually, that I would either face my parents' fury or die.

Death is the obvious choice!

What I did not expect was Daniel.

After spending several more years in the special needs department, Daniel began working with addicts. One of his tasks was visiting homeless shelters. It was only a matter of time before he found me curled in my own vomit beneath a table. He did not recognize me. *How could he?* But I, without a doubt, recognized him.

"Young man. Are you all right?" Daniel said. He pressed a palm against my forehead, cleaned the corners of my mouth with a tissue, checked my vitals and pupils, and knew I was high. He looked upon me with such helplessness and gently stroked my hair. "Would you like to hear a story?"

I slowly nodded.

What Daniel recited, I already knew, forever embedded into my soul. *The Magic Flute.* While the telling was less comedic and the voices less ridiculous, the whistling of the bells was just as magnificent as I remembered.

He never asked for my name or how I came to be here. Every few days, he would simply find me and recite my favorite stories.

Then, one day, he told a new story called *The Boy Who Forgot.* Never before did he speak with such passion, love, and heartache. I realized our parting twelve years ago destroyed him just as much as it did me. Meanwhile, my actual mother and father never came looking. My addiction was almost convenient for them. They were the *good parents,* and I was the *horrid son.* But here Daniel was, by my side, reciting my favorite childhood stories. And I knew why. It was so obvious.

He's my dad, and this is what dads do.

At that moment, I decided to change. To make Daniel proud. But that would take a strength I did not know I possessed.

◆

I returned home a shell of my former self, *my parent's words,* and slept restlessly on an air mattress in my old bedroom converted to an exercise room in my absence. At least I was back on Father's healthcare.

"Remember what we do for you!" he grumbled.

Knee surgery set me back months, and I was not allowed painkillers because of my history. *What fun...* I underwent several steroid injections in my spine to dull the pain just enough to begin physical therapy. Several months elapsed before I could walk, even jog. But sitting would forever equal spine pain, standing equal knee pain, turning as I walked might send me to the ground, washing dishes was excruciating, and sex? *Forget it.* Each flare-up meant months of rehabilitation, a constant reminder that I was a borderline cripple.

Nevertheless, I could make it through the day. The pain was managed. "A success story," they said. *A goddamn joke.*

And the fucking addiction lingered. Each time I got clean, I fell into old routines, returned to the same places, and went back to the plunge. It took me four years to kick it for good.

◆

I was again working towards my GED, and with all my willpower, I forced down enough food to keep my mind sharp and my muscles strong. I joined my parents for dinner, with a glare from my father and silence from my mother, but I would never actually eat in front of them. *My defiance.*

My parents viewed a GED as illegitimate and did not attend graduation. *Their defiance.*

"Mother, Father," I said during dinner. "I want to go to university."

Father chuckled and continued eating.

"Take the medicine!" Mother snapped.

"I'm serious. I want to pursue higher education."

Father lowered his fork. "You lack discipline."

"Father, I don't—"

"You're a *fucking* idiot!"

His insults no longer fazed me. "That's not a *no*."

"You don't have passion for anything useful."

"I want to overcome my fear. That's pretty useful."

"How the hell will your stupid paintings do that?"

"I don't want to study art." *More like I didn't need to.*

Hope flooded his eyes. "You want to study accounting?"

"No."

He darkened. "Then what the fuck would you do that makes any goddamn sense!?"

"I want to become a... *chef.*" Bile caught in my throat.

He dropped his fork. "I'd rather you studied art. At least you're kinda good at that."

He had never complimented me before. *Weird.* "Let's make a deal, then."

"What kind of deal?" he asked.

"If my GPA drops below 3.8, I'll switch to accounting."

"You obviously don't know what 3.8 means."

"I scored 758 on my GED."

Father glared. "Liar."

I glared right back and slid the results across the table.

He looked at it suspiciously, then to Mother.

She nodded.

"Make it 3.9 and it's a deal." He flashed a smug smile, one saying, *I've got you trapped!*

I could not wait to wipe that fucking smile off his face.

♦

My application to Anendian Institute of Culinary Arts, with my cover letter on second chances, was undoubtedly unique. I got an interview out of pure curiosity, I imagined. Dressed in the finest my local thrift store had to offer, I sat across from Dr. Sternheart, gatekeeper of Anendian Institute, hosting the country's most prestigious culinary arts program.

She reviewed my application with the most scrunched brow. "Justin. Why do you want to enter our culinary program?"

I had rehearsed my answer. "Though I am young, I've overcome much hardship. Addiction, amnesia, mental illness, and physical injury. But there is one struggle greater than the rest. I must defeat my fear of food. I believe training in the culinary arts will help me achieve this.”

Dr. Sternheart did not look impressed. “Let’s say you do well in our program, graduate top of the class, conquer your fear even. What then? What will you do *after?* Every graduate from our program has become a notable chef. Many are Michelin starred. So why would we admit someone who has little to no intention of actually becoming a chef?”

I was so focused on defeating my fear I had not considered a future. *Why am I here? The entire food system makes me sick.*

So change it, said the voice inside me.

And then, I said, “While attending your program and working as a chef, I will study agronomy to influence how agriculture is cultivated and food is processed, meanwhile maintaining the ideals of cuisine.”

She humphed. “How noble of you. But you must realize that hundreds of dishes use questionable methods. The grodote bisque soup, for example.”

I stiffened in my seat.

She caught my discomfort. “You know what a grodote is, right?”

I had dreamed of grodotes my entire life, painted hundreds of murals in which they were the centerpiece. *Do I know what a grodote is!?* I wanted to flip the desk. Instead, I willed myself down.

“I’m aware,” I grumbled.

“Then, you know to achieve the best flavoring, you must burn the feet of the crustacean before lowering it into boiling water, *alive.*”

“You *don’t* need to,” I blurted.

Dr. Sternheart sat back with a smug look. “Well, I’d love to hear how you’d reinvent Chef Dante’s award-winning grodote bisque soup. Do tell.”

I sighed. “The reason grodotes taste delicious, after burning their feet, is because a chemical is released relaxing its muscles and calming its mind in times of extreme stress. Chef Dante uses pain because he does not understand their biology. Grodotes can sense fear from one another through the chemicals they secrete. If one becomes frightened, then the others follow suit, like a chain reaction. Instead of burning the creatures, we can simply use a similar enough fragrance to induce the process.”

“And what fragrance would that be?” she asked.

“Dice an onion with a fan blowing across them.”

Dr. Sternheart frowned. “Justin, your application is quite interesting. Unfortunately, you’re not right for our program.”

♦

Father glowed. My rejection supporting his belief that I was doomed to be a leech to society.

"You can work as a *maid* for my office," he said with that grin.

I looked him dead in the eye. "Abigail's Cleaning Service brings in more annual revenue than your firm," I stated and left the dinner table.

"No, they don't." He quickly checked his phone, then mumbled, "Shit."

I entered my bedroom, slowly being reclaimed. A wooden desk I found on the roadside now sat at my window overlooking the backyard and rocky beach beyond. A used laptop adorned its surface. Cutting-edge technology, once upon a time. I refreshed my email every few minutes. *Waiting for what?* I could not say. But a message popped up entitled, *"You Were Right."*

I hovered my cursor, building my nerve, and clicked.

"Dear Justin Vagner, I diced an onion before the grodotes, just as you suggested, and delighted to say it worked! Furthermore, with the smokiness removed, I appreciated new flavors previously obscured. Many of our faculty believe this is a much better method. You have the University in quite a buzz! Even Chef Dante himself recommends your acceptance to Anendian Institute of Culinary Arts with a full scholarship. Congratulations Justin! We are very excited to have you in our program! -Sincerely, Dr. Sternheart-"

Fear, excitement, disgust, and joy surged through me. I forwarded the email to my father, heard his phone ding, tip-toed to the dining room, and watched him nearly choke on dinner.

♦

What did I get myself into? For every soup, sauce, stew, pastry, cake, steak, fish, *yadda yadda yadda*, I had to research alternative growing techniques and find healthy ranches to source meat, dairy, and eggs. But often, the recipes were given on the spot, forcing me to improvise.

"This is prime example of what *not* to do!" my professors would say, pointing at my dishes.

I swore Father would force me into accounting at any moment. But during our first-semester midterm, we were tasked with a vegan dish. *This* dish, I knew how to do and *this* dish, I aced. Factoring my core classes, ones I could do in my sleep, my GPA hit 3.9. *But holy hell, was it close!*

In the following semesters, I built upon previous experience. I developed my own growing and cooking methods, pouring over every detail and becoming more obsessed than I ever was with my painting.

How on Earth did that happen?

I approached Father one morning, my stomach in knots. "Father, I know you disapprove of my cooking, but may I use the backyard for gardening?"

"Sure, go ahead," he casually said, as if it were never an issue.

I stared in disbelief. "Uh, thank you."

I grew crops from the most natural of seeds, searched for alternatives to pesticides, and began raising chickens and pigs, using their droppings as fertilizer. *My compost was sexy as hell.* I returned from school on the weekends to seed, prune, maintain drip irrigation, and harvest ingredients for the following days. My skin tanned, my muscles defined, and I ate regularly. *All produce from my garden, of course.* As my peers adopted comical chef bellies and butts, I resembled a long-distance runner. My back and knee never felt better.

And those nightmares? *Well, they stopped.*

My parents would smile when I returned home. *So weird.* And once, while tending my garden, I overheard Father talking with our neighbor.

"How's Justin doing these days?"

"He's great!" Father said. "Graduating top of the class! I think he's going to do incredible things!"

"I'm surprised you let him pursue cooking. Isn't that a bit… You know." He let his wrist fall limp.

Father nodded begrudgingly. "Yeah, well. I want my son to follow his dreams anyway."

"Wow. I guess that makes you world's best dad."

World's best dad!? I wanted to puke.

◆

After graduation, I circulated several Manhattan kitchens, eventually landing at *Bezzanine*, a vegan restaurant led by Chef Harding, renowned for its relationship with local organic farms. *Finally, an environment pure and honest,* I thought. I busted my ass, aiding the line cooks and jumping in myself when shorthanded. Before long, I was a full-time commis. Within the year, I earned a place on the line.

"Think you can keep up, *Skinny?*" Benson, our heavyset sous chef, said.

"You bet your ass I will," I snapped back.

"Ha! Then dice these." He pointed to a crate of onions.

Tears streamed down my cheeks as my knife rattled away like a machine gun. But something smelled strange. I paused to taste the onion. A sweetness lay masked within. *Herbicide?* I thought.

"Damn, kid," Benson said, watching me dice.

"Why does this taste contaminated?" I asked.

Benson made a face. "Just do your job, *Skinny.*"

I investigated the farms we sourced from on my days off, traveling upstate and inspecting the crops firsthand. *They're not organic,* I realized. The taste paled compared to the produce I grew in my landlord's vacant Park Slope lot.

I gradually substituted Bezzanine's fraudulent produce with my own. But Chef Harding was not one to condone rogue behavior in her kitchen. I purchased a small duffle, wore running shoes, implying I had just come from the gym, and smuggled my ingredients that way. I checked the reservations nightly, focusing on food critics, notable chefs, and the occasional entrepreneur with excellent taste, and manipulated my schedule accordingly. Before long, the dishes I prepared, sides to Benson and Chef Harding's mains, were specifically praised. Many asked to pay their compliments. Chef Harding often returned to the kitchen confused.

♦

Christina Lancer, legendary chef turned columnist, particularly adored my side of roasted vegetables. She was to return on Thursday. But when I checked the prep lists Wednesday night, I found the side of roasted vegetables under Chef Harding's name. I had broccoli soup.

"Why are we serving broccoli soup? Christina hates broccoli," I said.

Benson grunted. "You pissed off the wrong woman, *Skinny.*"

Chef Harding's setting me up to fail? I thought and felt my ears grow hot. *So fucking be it!*

I returned home to my garden and plugged in my lights, illuminating my broccoli patches. Some were crawling with pests, but most were in good condition. I harvested it all, enough to make twenty bowls, not much for standard restaurants, but Bezzanine was reservation only, its meals predetermined for each guest.

I must convince Christina Lancer that broccoli isn't terrible! I thought. *My soup must be the talk of the evening!*

You'll be great, said that internal voice.

♦

"Did you try the soup?"

"Holy shit. I didn't know you could do this with broccoli."

"I know, it's incredible."

"It's so simple, but just so… MmmMm!"

Christina's guests rolled back in ecstasy with each spoonful, creating such a disturbance that Christina stopped mid-conversation. She glared at the bowl of broccoli soup at the table center.

One of her guests pointed at the bowl. "Christina, this soup is unreal."

"You should try it," said another.

Christina slowly nodded. A waiter ladled a small bowl. She leaned closer, inspecting the florets in the thick broth and taking in its scent. She spooned and sipped. Confusion, fear, and wonder washed across her face. She leaned back in her chair and waved down the waiter.

"I *must* talk with Chef Harding," Christina said.

"I apologize, but she's—"

"Now!" Christina ordered.

Chef Harding left the kitchen moments later. I peered through the door's crack, watching her approach Christina's table.

"Christina, I hope you're finding everything to your liking," she said.

"Sarah... I had no idea you could do *this,*" Christina said, motioning to the broccoli soup. "This is *phenomenal*."

Chef Harding's posture drooped. "...Thank you, Christina. It… It's a new recipe I've been experimenting with."

Christina nodded. "There was something terribly wrong with the roasted veggies this evening. But I now understand you were focused solely upon this *magnificent* soup."

Chef Harding glared at the kitchen door where I was watching from.

♦

The next day, I found a final paycheck where my prep list usually rests.

"I hope you're proud of yourself, *Skinny*," Benson said.

"You know it's all bullshit here, right?" I responded.

"It's bullshit everywhere, kid. Good luck." Benson grinned, shook my hand, and turned back to his grill.

What now? I thought.

Be the progress you want to see, said the voice within.

I had saved a little money from Bezzanine, allowing me to delve into growing in my landlord's vacant lot.

"What's that?" my landlord said, pointing to a vertical conveyor.

"It's a shelving system that rotates the next row of crops to the top every hour for direct sunlight. It allows me to grow ten times the amount of produce in the same square footage."

"Really? That's cool."

My neighbors slowly joined in, adding little corners of crops and asking for advice on how to grow naturally. Soon, young parents brought their children to look at the fruits and vegetables, the systems I built, or the bees pollinating. My produce began to sell, providing just enough income to cover daily expenditures.

I erected a greenhouse in October, but zoning did not allow for agriculture. I had been growing under the notion the garden was private. But as more greenhouses rose and more people visited, the inspectors came knocking, and my landlord had no choice but to pull the plug.

I trudged through my garden harvesting produce, potting and selling perennials, and tearing down greenhouses and conveyors, heaving their pieces into a dumpster. My back ached, and my knee throbbed.

"Justin!" my downstairs neighbor hollered from his apartment window. "Will you answer your goddamn phone! It's driving me crazy!"

It was buzzing on the floor when I opened my door, having fallen off the nightstand. *"37 missed calls,"* displayed on its screen.

"Hello?" I answered.

"My God! You picked up! Is this Justin Vagner? Previously employed at Bezzanine?"

"...The one and only."

"One moment, please." She put me on hold.

I set to speakerphone, placed four ice packs on the hardwood floor, and laid upon them bareback, feeling their bite, my only intermission from the lightning storm running down my legs.

"Hello, Justin," said a different voice. "This is Christina Lancer. Are you available tomorrow morning?"

♦

Christina and I met at Cameron's, a reservation-only café.

She gave me a sharp look. "I returned to Bezzanine looking for that broccoli soup. After sending back several horrendous servings, I realized it was not Chef Harding's creation. I interrogated that big sous chef, Benson, until he confessed it was you." She noticed I did not order. "The coffee beans are from natural farms. I thought you'd find that interesting."

How much does she know? I thought. Her expression said, *Everything*. I ordered a long black.

"They have naturally farmed oat milk if you'd like," she said.

"No thanks, I like to taste the beans."

When her latte and my long black arrived, she stared, waiting for me to act. I lifted my cup, inhaled the aroma, and sipped. I made a face.

"No good?" she asked.

"Beans are not naturally grown," I said.

"Are you certain of that?"

"Yes."

"Where are the beans from?" Her tone suggested she already knew.

"These are Sumatran. Organic, but not natural."

"How can you tell?"

I shrugged. "I can taste it."

She slid her latte to me. "What about this?"

I sipped and nodded. "Beans and oat milk are both naturally grown. Beans from Ethiopia. Oats from Kansas."

"Kansas? You cannot seriously pick that out."

"Natural farms in Kansas pair oat with buckwheat, which fruit early attracting pests normally after the oat, acting as a natural pesticide. There's a slight nuttiness in the oat as a result."

"Well, I'll be damned," she said. "I have a proposition for you."

♦

Christina funded the opening of a small restaurant of my choosing, allowing me freedom over what I cooked, how I cooked, and where I sourced produce. I built upon a recent article in *The New York Moments* magazine entitled, *"Broccoli Soup Coup, by Christina Lancer,"* and opened a venue aptly named *Soup Coup.* It was small with no seating. Just a dingy serving bar and a graffiti-covered door.

"Why *this* place?" Christina said, running a finger along the counter, grimacing at the dust.

"Soup Coup is about quality ingredients and thus, quality food. Nothing else matters. That's what I must convey," I said.

"And a shitty venue says that?"

"Well, kinda," I said. "What I truly need are several lots within New York City limits growing fresh produce. That's where we must invest."

Every day was *Soup of the Day,* made from whatever produce came in that morning from Soup Coup's lots in the Bronx, their soil now cleansed and converted into gardening spectacles. Word traveled quickly. When crops allowed for my infamous broccoli soup, lines stretched down the block.

"Need a hand, *Skinny?*" said a voice I knew.

I snapped my head up to see Benson packed in line. I wiped the sweat from my brow and grinned. "Think you can keep up, *Fatty?*"

"Oh, you little shit!" Benson cussed, rounding the serving counter and tearing an apron from the wall. He inspected the pots going strong.

Chefs from neighboring restaurants came asking how I managed such consistency in my broth or isolated flavors. What my secret ingredient was.

I would grimace and say, "That's the point of a secret ingredient," or a simple, "Fuck off!" would suffice. *They will not poach my recipes!* I thought. But there was never anything particularly ingenious to poach, only simple, clean, natural ingredients that arrived moments after harvest.

I could have easily found another venue, demand certainly suggested I do so, but this tiny, dilapidated shit-hole embodied who I was. My cussing received laughter from repeat customers and stares from first-timers. *All part of the atmosphere*. Little did they know each was to cover pain lancing down my back and legs.

But wasn't I trying to become someone better?

Looking into hundreds of eyes a day, I did not find the pair I longed for, the first pair to greet me in that hospital bed long ago. I wanted to reach out to Daniel but feared he would not remember me. I soon learned he retired to the South to be with his daughter and grandchildren.

It does not matter! I do not have the time! I convinced myself.

In Soup Coup's eighth year of operation, the neighboring restaurant chapter eleven-ed. I snatched the open lease, broke through the wall, and added a small dining room. The menu expanded to *Two Soups of the Day – one hot, one cold. No exceptions.*

I received my first Michelin star that year.

By 2066, I established five locations in New York City, one in each borough, two more in Boston, one in Philadelphia, and one in Toronto. Local agriculture shifted, inspired by my natural growing techniques, and New York City wrote natural farming of community gardens and rooftops into legislation.

I was seventy-three when I conquered the culinary world, silencing my critics, sending that middle finger to my parents, changing the agricultural climate, and overcoming my fear.

Yet, even still, it was not enough.

◆

Something's wrong, said the voice within me.

I had ignored my pain for decades, for it always existed, from starvation, my parents, my addiction, or my injuries. But, in the summer of 2067, I committed the cardinal sin of calling out of work.

"I'm sorry, Justin," the doctor said. "But you have hepatocellular carcinoma, a type of liver cancer. You most likely contracted Hepatitis C sharing needles in your youth. With your compromised immune system, it became cirrhosis, and eventually cancer. It spread to your pancreas and kidneys, too.”

The doctor's expression needed no explanation. All that work to change my destiny, to be worthy of Daniel's praise, was for nothing. I could not outrun my past.

I will always be a leech.

“How long do I have?” I said through clenched teeth.

“It's difficult to say. Maybe a year. Maybe a month.”

My parents visited me bedridden in the hospital, something I neither expected nor welcomed. They were still healthy and fit entering their centennial years, contrasting wildly with my frailty. Father wore his shit-eating grin.

“Well, I hope you had fun,” he jabbed.

I shakily waved him closer.

He stepped forth.

“Closer,” I whispered.

He leaned down.

“Go… Fuck… Yourself...” I said in a hollowed voice.

◆

Every time I hit the bottom, my dad was there to pick me up. *But where is Daniel now?* In the rare moments I could find the strength, I emailed him, asking if he remembered me. After significant silence, I was begging him to come. At any moment, I expected Daniel to enter, sit by my side, and recite *The Magic Flute*. When my door opened, my eyes shot in that direction, and my heart flitted, but it was either the nurse, Benson, Christina, or my physician.

Then, one day, a young man in pediatrician scrubs and a stethoscope hosting a rubber ducky came to visit. A look of helplessness held in his eyes, one that I recognized.

“Hi Justin, I'm Daniel Shore,” he said. “They say you've been asking for me, but I'm sorry, I do not know who you are.”

I saw the resemblance in his eyes and gritted my teeth. “I'm sorry for... confusion... but I was asking... for... your grandfather.”

Young Daniel's face washed in pain, and I realized the truth.

“When... did he pass?” I asked, my words cracking, my tears welling.

“Last year, I'm afraid. It was a heart attack while hiking.” Young Daniel gave a questioning look. “How did you know my grandfather?”

He was my dad! I wanted to shout. Instead, I said, “Did he ever... tell you stories?"

Daniel's questioning look deepened. "They are some of my fondest memories. I recite them for the children I work with now."

"Did he tell you... *The Boy Who Forgot?*"

He suspiciously nodded.

"Daniel… I'm… *The Boy.*"

Young Daniel exhaled deeply and leaned over me, giving the most loving of hugs. I realized I was somehow important in this young man's life, a conduit through which he could say goodbye to his grandfather. And the conduit was working both ways. I found one final remnant of strength and clutched young Daniel tightly, tears streaming down my cheeks.

♦

"Any day now," doctors and nurses said, not once glancing in my direction, as if I could not hear their words or see their looks.

I'm already dead to them, I realized. So imagine my surprise when I woke to a young geneticist radiating with excitement.

"Justin," she said, placing a hand on my arm. "My name is doctor Wong Kwai Lan. My team and I have been experimenting with organ cloning and believe we can help you. We obtained cells from your liver, kidneys, and pancreas several months ago and regrew them in our facility. All three organs have successfully matured without a trace of cancer. We only need your authorization to perform the surgery."

I blinked, dumbfounded. "Why wasn't... I told?" I whispered.

Dr. Wong nodded. "It's nearly impossible to regrow cancer-ridden organs without them becoming cancerous as well. It was written off as a potential treatment. However, with recent tests confirming the new organs are clean, we've determined a triple transplant could save you. But it must happen now. Are you willing to undergo the procedure?"

"Yes," I squeaked.

♦

I woke from the anesthesia, but instead of being greeted by a nurse with a cookie, I found Dr. Wong looking stern, with dark circles around her eyes.

"Justin, I'm so sorry," she said. "We don't know why, but your body is rejecting the organs, even when they were grown from your exact DNA. This has never happened before…" she drifted off.

I knew only moments remained. *But it cannot end this way! My past cannot defeat me!* I tried sitting but could not find the strength, then speaking but no words came forth. All I could do was stare into Dr. Wong's eyes. So that's what I did, boring my gaze until I sensed the doctor's inner light, her soul.

I've done this before, I realized and reached into her light.

I was suddenly looking upon my body through a different set of eyes. It lay twig-like. Its skin was yellow with jaundice and its chest shuddered with each breath.

Then it shut down, bit by bit, function by function, like the lights of an apartment building switching off.

CHAPTER SIX

Clara stares at Zion sitting in his mangled chair, sucking milk from another of Aizen's cookies. Again, the story takes place before The Fall, and again, it's on the edge of crazy. But how Zion told it seemed honest. *Well, honesty from a lunatic,* Clara thinks.

Zion finishes his cookie and notices her staring. "Clara, my dear, is something the matter?" he says, handing her the last cookie.

Clara apprehensively dunks it and sucks the milk. It actually helps. "You weren't in the story," she says.

Zion looks surprised. "Why would I be?"

"Your misplaced memories were of Justin, which means you knew him."

"You don't have to know someone to have memories of them," Zion says matter-of-factly.

"I don't follow."

"Justin's life was tragic, brilliant, misguided, yet courageous. There is a lot to learn."

"But I'm trying to learn about *you*."

"Are you not?" he asks.

Fine, I'll play, Clara thinks. "So what did Justin teach you, then?"

Zion smiles slightly. "Most people, even today, believe their destiny cannot be changed, are convinced life is too complicated, they have too many responsibilities, or the opportunity has passed. But I guarantee ten years from now those same people will look upon today and think, *if only I started then*. If they still do not act, then another ten years will pass and again they will say, *why didn't I start then?* Justin's life is an incredible example of turning a situation around at its darkest moment, and yet even *he* could not find the courage or moment to engage the only person he loved. Truth is, there's never a perfect moment to begin something new or to pursue something frightening. The key is simply *doing*. Aizen understands this. I suppose that's the fearlessness of youth." Zion gives the empty box of cookies a curious look. "May I help your son?"

"How so?" Clara asks.

"This year's Human versus Machine is fast approaching, and will host its first ever cooking competition. But the human competitors will never beat the synthesizers. Aizen, however, thinks as the old chefs did. If he truly discovered stove-top cooking the old way, completely on his own, then he'll give them a run for their credits."

Clara gives him a look. "How would you help him?"

"I can enter Aizen as Titan's champion."

"I'm sure they've already selected—" *Zion can do whatever he wants,* she realizes. "*Only* if Aizen feels ready."

Zion studies the empty box again. "Oh, he's ready. The question is, are the judges?"

♦

"Ladies and gentlemen! We at Tempest City Productions are pleased to host this year's Human versus Machine!"

Audience members jump to their feet, whistling and cheering as a camera makes its pass.

"Previous years exhibited incredible feats of athleticism and genius, nail-biting martial arts and chess tournaments, ultra-triathlons, spelling bees, and even a mathletes. And how could we forget last year's near upset when Ezekiel Arbor almost defeated Swimbot 3200 in a seventy kilometer under-ice swim from Athens to Troy! We all remember when Swimbot's batteries nearly succumbed to the frigid temperatures, its backup heaters kicking in at the last moment. Never before have the machines come so close to defeat!"

Cheers and boos erupt.

Host Charlamain raises a hand to hush them. "Yes, yes. In all two hundred and thirty-six years of competition, the machines have never lost. However, this year we bring a competition like nothing before. One combining finesse and artistry. Welcome to Human versus Machine's first ever cooking competition!"

The audience's roar vibrates in Aizen's chest even when backstage. He glances at chefs to either side of him, each a master programmer trained at the best universities and wearing chef uniforms straight out of historical documents. Aizen feels goofy in his, tailored last minute to fit his small stature. *The kids from school will never let me hear the end of it,* Aizen thinks and can almost hear Lucius saying, *Hey, mushroom head! Not mushroom in there for brains!*

"Let's meet this years human competitors!"

Applause rises as each chef walks on stage and bows beneath a spotlight. But when it comes to Aizen, the audience pauses. He timidly walks to center stage, taking his bow in silence. Then comes their roar.

"Wow! The people's champion has already been chosen! Everyone put your hands together for Aizen Ocol! Human versus Machine's first ever youth competitor!"

The chefs take positions behind cooking stations hosting customized synthesizers, except for Aizen's, which has proper cooking equipment.

The Machine competitors come on stage—Chefbot 7000, Bourdain 2018, Sir Mince-Alot the III.0, and the favored-to-win, Kramer 3400. They wear chef hats stretched over their square frames and wheel to their stations.

Host Charlamain asks each machine what separates them from the rest.

"Perfection."

"Perfection."

"Perfection."

"Perfection and taste."

"And taste, now there's a surprise." Host Charlamain chuckles and turns to the human chefs. "And what separates you?"

"Finesse, only achievable through experience."

"Nuances that cannot be understood by a computer."

"Grandma's secret code."

"My superior programming skills."

"And what do you feel separates you from the rest, other than age?" host Charlamain says to Aizen, and the audience giggles.

Aizen feels their eyes upon him, shifts uncomfortably, and leans to the microphone. "I cook the old way."

The chefs snap their heads towards Aizen, confusion writ upon their faces. But then, their expressions melt, convinced he is joking.

"Now *that* would be a treat!" host Charlamain says, dismissing the statement. "Let's meet our judges! May I introduce notable food critic all the way from Ceres, Emilia Herst!"

Emilia stands and takes a bow.

"Next is the newest judgment protocol system with a database of over fifteen trillion recipes, MasterJudge 3000!"

MasterJudge appears on hologram as an old man in a suit taking a bow.

"And I am pleased to announce that Kramer Industries' very own quality control inspector has joined our panel. Please, meet Oscar Delicourt!" Host Charlamain pauses. "But we have another surprise judge. He was a professional chef from nearly three hundred years ago. May I present the one, the only, Chef Cillian Gundar!"

A man well into his centennial years hobbles on stage, waving to audience members who leap from their seats.

"Whoa! Please, calm!" host Charlamain insists.

The audience settles.

"The goal of this year's competition is quality. Each competitor will have *one* hour to complete an appetizer, main, and dessert, and given the freedom to choose what dishes to prepare. However, there's a secret ingredient that must be incorporated into all three courses." Host Charlamain pauses. "Do you want to know what the secret is?"

"Yes!" the audience shouts in unison.

"The secret ingredient is..." Drum-roll. "Pineapple!"

A spotlight hits center stage as a portion of the floor opens, and a platform lifts, overflowing with the fruit.

"Let the competition begin!"

Aizen stares at the pineapples in shock. He should not be surprised, having been told the secret ingredient in advance to brainstorm like the others, but the variation in color and size of the fruit rising from center stage is startling. *Something hidden lies within the secret ingredient itself,* he thinks and walks from behind his station to the platform.

The audience stirs, and host Charlamain approaches.

"Chef Ocol, what are you doing?" he says, tilting his mic.

"Investigating," Aizen says, lifting a pineapple and catching a scent. *It smells ready.*

"Investigating what?" host Charlamain says with a chuckle.

"Why each of these are different." Aizen suddenly notices Chef Cillian Gundar staring at him, grinning. *That's weird,* Aizen thinks and carries three pineapples back to his station. With a thwack, he chops their tops, and the audience flinches. He brings his holotile close, running through structural profiles to determine which synthesizer had created them. Instead, the holotile searches Earth, zeroing in on a region once called Brazil.

A real pineapple! Aizen realizes, almost dropping it. *Each is worth a fortune!* He cuts a small piece and slowly places it into his mouth. Bliss squeezes from its cells. *The pineapple itself must be the focus.* Aizen searches for produce from old Brazil and compiles a small library of ingredients.

The Appetizer.

Aizen is determined to introduce the pineapple alone to exemplify how its juices can caramelize. He synthesizes brown sugar, granulated cane sugar, and stalks of sugarcane and digs his knife around the pineapple core, using a corkscrew to pull it from the flesh.

"Will you look at that! Aizen is performing heart surgery!"

Aizen jolts at the audience's laughter. *Keep moving,* he tells himself and chops the sugarcane into smaller pieces, scrapes its skin, allowing sweet sugar to ooze, and stuffs them into the hollowed pineapple.

His vintage stovetop ignites with a woof and a plume of flame.

The neighboring chef leans over. "You *can't* be serious!"

Aizen winks, placing a pot on the flame and dumping an unhealthy amount of avocado oil and brown sugar. The mixture comes to a boil. Sugar combines, caramelizes, and foams. Aizen surgically dips the pineapple with tongs and then races to set his vintage oven to 204°C. It ignites. The conveyor feeds kindling first, adding large pieces of bamboo as the flames take. After the pineapple marinates in the sugar pot for ten minutes, Aizen relocates it to the brick oven and sets a timer for subsequent dunks.

The Main.

In his research, Aizen learned that meats generate more or less correctly, for they were the first products synthesized to reduce stress upon colony ecosystems. *The ancient chefs must have ensured their accuracy,* Aizen had guessed. He types *"Pork"* into his synth. A list of cuts appears. He selects *"Pork Belly, Raw."* The cut materializes in less than a minute, and Aizen places it in his vintage pressure cooker alongside potatoes, onions, capsicum, and chilies.

An idea strikes him. He synthesizes coconut milk, pours it into a saucepan, and adds chilies, cardamom, anise, and cloves. The aroma spreads like wildfire, and both judges and competitors stop to inhale.

The audience catches a whiff and gasps.

"My goodness, Aizen! You should be a professional perfumer!" says Host Charlamain.

The audience silently watches Aizen furiously work as his competitors calmly type into their synthesizers, produce bricks, and adjust algorithms.

Aizen chops the second pineapple into thin rings and tosses them onto a cast iron pan. After a moment, he turns them, revealing charred sides and getting an, "Oooo," from the audience. He drizzles the spiced coconut milk atop.

His timer rings. *Ten minutes already?* He dashes to the oven to retrieve the roasting pineapple. *Golden brown.* He dunks it into the sugar pot and returns it to further roast.

The Dessert.

Aizen chops the third pineapple into rings as well and sets another cast iron pan on the stovetop, adding butter, and brown and granulated sugar.

This is going to be one sweet meal! Aizen thinks and laughs.

"Having fun there?" the neighboring chef says. "You're making us look bad, you know, but I'm excited to see someone cooking the old way!"

"Thanks," Aizen responds. "And for the record, I have no idea what I'm doing."

Almost on cue, frothing sugar spills onto the burner, sending another woof. The chef reels with a hearty laugh.

Aizen combines flour, baking powder, baking soda, brown sugar, and eggs. He places the pineapple rings onto the second pan, pours in the cake mix, and sets it into the brick oven next to his roasting pineapple.

Again, his timer rings, and Aizen dunks the roasting pineapple, *dark amber.* Then, his pressure cooker dings.

He opens it to inspect the pork belly, and his fork pokes clean through. He finds four shallow bowls, situates a grilled pineapple ring at their centers, gently placing tender pork belly slices and setting another pineapple ring atop like a sandwich.

The machines hum to life, having finished their calculations, catching the attention of chefs, judges, and the audience.

"There they go!" says host Charlamain.

Aizen's timer goes off a third time. He gives the roasting pineapple its final dunk, *dark honey.* He sees the cake has risen in its pan, moves it from the oven to his cutting block, and flips. It lands face down with a solid thump. Everyone turns. He wiggles the pan, feeling it loosen from the seasoned surface, and lifts it to reveal a golden cake with translucent pineapple rings.

A round of applause grows from both the audience and chefs.

"One minute remaining!" host Charlamain calls.

The chefs set their plates of synthesized bricks garnished to beautify onto their serving carts. The machines spit dishes already plated and garnished geometrically.

Aizen retrieves his roasting pineapple. *Completely black.* He lays it on his block, on its side, gently resting the blade of his knife on its skin. The weight of the blade alone is enough to slice clean through.

"Ten, nine, eight…," the audience chants.

Aizen rolls the thin caramelized slices into tubes and delicately lays them onto his plates.

"Six, five, four…"

He ditches his knife and places his plates onto the cart.

"Three…two…"

Aizen steps back, raising his hands as if under arrest.

"One! Time is up!"

♦

Cillian Gundar stares at Aizen's dishes as the other judges banter. The old chef's eyes shift to Aizen standing beside the chefs and synthesizers at center stage.

"This has been a contest for the ages!" host Charlamain calls to the crowd. "And now the moment you've all been waiting for is here! But first, let's give all our contestants a round of applause!"

Their excitement rises and falls like an ocean swell.

Each set of dishes wheels before the judges, receiving nods of approval until reaching Cillian Gundar, who shakes his head.

"They're all the same," the old chef says. "The same techniques, the same tastes, the same dishes. Where has the creativity gone?"

"Oh, there's no pleasing a palate of Chef Gundar's magnitude!" host Charlamain chides.

The old chef again stares at Aizen's dishes yet to be tasted.

"Let's take a look at the leader-board!" Host Charlamain waves to the hologram. "With only two contestants remaining can the Kramer 3400 hold onto its lead?"

Sir Mince-Alot the III.0's dishes wheel to the judges.

MasterJudge 3000 analyses the appetizer, main, and dessert at the base of its holographic projection. The AI on display says, "Analysis complete. Sir

Mince-Alot the III.0 has tapped into an obscure sector of my archives. I am very pleased."

Cillian makes a face. "I hold to my previous comments. However, Sir Mince-Alot *does* have a more accurate configuration of how the flavors should combine."

The scores come in.

"We have a new leader!" Host Charlamain cries, then turns to Aizen. "One contestant remains! Can the young Aizen Ocol pull off the impossible!?"

Both cheers and boos come as Aizen's dishes wheel to the judges. Aizen's stomach is in knots, and beads of sweat form on his forehead.

"They look beautiful," Emilia says.

"Nice to see they're not bricks," another judge quips.

Cillian Gundar narrows his eyes and leans over each dish, tilting the plates to get a better view. He inhales their scent. "Where did you learn to cook like this?"

They all turn to Aizen.

"It...it just felt right," Aizen squeaks.

The judges start with his appetizer, the caramelized pineapple tubes with sugarcane core.

"Holy #&%^!" Oscar Delicourt shouts as real-time censorship beeps.

They dig into Aizen's main course and then the dessert.

"My Sol!" another judge shouts.

Their ravenousness sends the crowd into laughter. But Cillian remains still, staring at Aizen, his eyes not wavering, his face like stone. Aizen looks away but still feels the old chef's eyes on him.

The audience suddenly gasps.

Aizen snaps his head back to see MasterJudge 3000's hologram flickering wildly, its AI figure shouting, "Impossible!... Impossible!... Wait!... Incredible!... Incredible!... No!... Impossible!... Wait!..." Its hologram becomes a solid blue.

CHAPTER SEVEN

This is a mistake, Jonathan thinks, descending another cylindrical shaft carved into London's glass dome by archaeological teams nearly a century ago. He stares at a thin cable clipped to his envisuit's harness. *It'll hold,* he tells himself, trying to quell his anxiety. He knows what the weight limit is. There is no chance of failure. But his predecessors must have thought the same before meeting their ends. Even with carbon blast gear over his envisuit, Jonathan feels immense heat radiating from the shaft's glass walls, becoming a darker shade of green as he drops. He activates his helmet lamp, lowers the last few meters, and anchors his boots to its slick, glass floor.

"Reached bottom," Jonathan calls through his com, and Zach stops the winch. "Beginning bore."

He inserts the first length of bit into his Miskito drill. Its motor winds, sending dust-like shards of glass whipping into a green cloud. He relies purely on his sensors to navigate. *"One meter,"* his helmet visor indicates. He adds length to the bit. *"Two meters."* He adds more. *"Three meters."*

There's no hissing associated with penetration. *But there should be,* Jonathan knows. *A millennia of bacteria breaking down organic matter and releasing gasses into the air should have built immense pressure beneath the dome. So, why nothing?* He feels it in his gut. *There's still more depth to go.* He sighs with a mixture of frustration and relief. As much as he wants to penetrate the dome, decompression can be violent, as discovered with old

Barcelona, the first of old Earth's cities reached, its entire archaeological team lost in the blast. *Do I want to take that chance?*

Jonathan studies his blast gear, accumulating green dust like snow. *It's no guarantee of safety.* He thinks about the historical documents surviving The Fall. Ones depicting archaeologists enduring pit traps, giant rolling boulders, and supernatural creatures. *The dangers of archaeology have not changed much since,* he reflects. He adds a fourth length of bit to his drill and presses on. It suddenly creaks.

"Jonathan! It's about to fracture!" Zach calls into his earpiece.

Jonathan holds his breath, maintains RPMs, and slowly retracts the bits from the glass.

"Clear!" he calls as his Miskito drill winds down. "I drilled another four meters, but there may be hundreds more." He snakes a sensor down the hole.

"Incredible," Zach says.

"Incredible and inconvenient," Jonathan responds. "Zach pull me up."

The cable grows taut and lifts Jonathan from the shaft. His headlamp plunges into the dark glass walls, highlighting blurry silhouettes of London's skyscrapers frozen mid-collapse. *So close, yet so far,* he thinks. The only city more impossible to reach is Paris. *A lost cause,* Jonathan knows. *Everyone knows.*

Blinding sunlight washes over him when he reaches the shaft's opening. He turns off his headlamp and removes his helmet, making out Zach's figure operating the winch as his eyes adjust. Angela and Vincent are enthralled in their holotiles analyzing information pouring in from the sensor he placed. Zach swings the crane from the shaft, setting Jonathan onto the dust-covered glass dome. His boots detect the slickness and bite into its surface.

Jonathan unclips the cable, removes his blast armor, unzips the top of his envisuit, and stretches his limbs like Da Vinci's Vitruvian Man, letting the breeze run across his bare arms and back. "It was hotter than hell in there today," he says. "Can we determine a thickness?"

Angela looks up. "Too thick, as usual." A sudden beep comes, and she snaps back to her holotile. "Oh, we *do* have a thickness. One hundred and forty-five meters remain."

"Practically Paris," Jonathan says, and his team nods. "I think it's time we seriously consider the old WorldRing tunnels."

Zach rolls his eyes. "And you think *drilling* is difficult?"

"I'm not saying it'll be easy, but at least we know there was a hub in London and that its tunnels lead out in several directions."

"They've most likely crumbled by erosion or collapsed during The Fall," Zach argues.

"We don't know that for sure."

"Finding them is *impossible*," Zach emphasizes.

"Until someone actually tries," Jonathan urges.

"Whatever."

The four lock belt coilers to the winch and rappel down the side of the glass dome to London's jungle below. After a short hike, they reach base camp alongside several other drill teams trickling in from their sites.

"We heard you got a reading!" Captain of Team Four says, approaching Jonathan, his crew eagerly looking on.

"Only a hundred and forty-five meters left," Jonathan sarcastically says.

Team Four's excitement dwindles.

"Practically Paris," says their captain. "Well, at least you know. How long are we going to keep this up?"

"Funny you should say that." Jonathan heads to the camp's center. "I need everyone to gather around, please!" he calls. Several more crews cluster. "We've been drilling the old locations for almost a month and are no closer to reaching London than the expeditions before us. It's time to change our approach."

"Change? To what?" one says.

"If we can locate the WorldRing tunnels, we might find a way into London from below," Jonathan says.

"But *how* do we find them?" the one says.

Jonathan remains silent. Even the old books and maps Clara scanned for him are nothing more than recreations sketched from memory by survivors of The Fall, their accuracy dubious at best.

I need an exact reference point, he thinks. *Practically Paris.*

♦

Clara sits at the edge of her seat, watching Human versus Machine conclude on hologram while Zion calmly sips his tea. Her hands tremble. Her heart pounds. She can only imagine how Aizen must feel.

"You saw how he went straight for the pineapples," Zion says smugly. "He understands the importance of agriculture."

Clara scrunches her brow and turns to him. "Is this how you brought the galaxy together? By understanding their agriculture?"

Zion perks up. "Well, that would certainly help."

"Is that what you were trying to tell me with Justin's story?"

"Aren't you perceptive today," Zion snides.

Clara senses Zion is slipping to a less desirable version. "I've lost you, haven't I," she pointedly says.

"Please, give Aizen my congratulations. Good day, Clara," he says.

Mr. Politician, Clara knows. She gathers her holotile and exits the room, but as the door shuts, she hears Zion whisper, "...Zhubzar gundari shoonter."

Clara stops in her tracks. *What the hell was that!?* She places an ear against the door.

"Clara?" Dr. Lee says from down the hallway.

She raises an index finger to her lips, silencing him, and listens to Zion whisper to himself. *There's a rhythm to it.*

Dr. Lee approaches and whispers, "Zion often loses his speech."

"No, this is *not* speech loss," she says. "This is a language."

Dr. Lee tilts his head. "I need to show you something." He wanders back down the hall, but Clara does not budge. Dr. Lee pauses. "Trust me, you'll want to see this."

Clara reluctantly follows to Dr. Lee's office, where he opens a hologram depicting a brain firing violently, then two others looking calm.

"Which one is Zion?" Clara asks.

"They *all* are." Dr. Lee points to the calmest. "This is Zion most of the time." He points to the second hologram, slightly more active. "But when he threw his tantrum, it changed to this."

"Why?"

"To be honest, we don't know."

Clara spies the third violent diagram. "What's with the crazy one?"

"This is Zion's brain right now. I happens whenever he speaks that gibberish." Dr. Lee hesitates. "Remember when I told you he disabled eight of us when we tried to tranquilize him?"

"Uh, how could I forget?" She crosses her arms. "You owe me a viewing by the way."

He nods. "In the few seconds it took him to dismantle us, his brain was erratic as well. I believe his gibberish and violence come from the same source."

"Zion has no military training. Even if he is incredibly strong, eight of you should have been more than enough to restrain him," Clara argues.

"But!" Dr. Lee raises his voice. "What if it's *not* Zion?"

"Who could he be, then?"

"Not the right question."

Clara sighs. "Can we stop with the riddles?"

Dr. Lee frowns. "All human brain activity, even at its most stressed or stimulated fires in more or less the same way. However, *this* wildness is not possible for humans to produce. We don't know *what* he is, let alone *who*."

Clara peers into the diagram, feeling like something is off, orchestrated. *Medical sabotage is one of Zion's favorite games, after all.*

♦

"Clara, right on time. I'm pleased to see you today," Zion says, sipping his tea. An unused pot of coffee rests next to a teapot.

Clara grins. "Messing with the good doctor, I see."

"Always, of course."

She cannot pinpoint which version of Zion this is. He shares the mannerisms of *Mr. Politician* but emits warmth like the *Jokester. This is new,* she realizes.

"How are you changing your brain patterns?" Clara says.

Zion nearly chokes on his tea. "Took you long enough to figure it out. I place my holotile next to my brain implant, which runs on a private frequency one tick away, causing interference."

Clara humphs. "Dr. Lee thinks you're not human."

Zion chuckles. "His deer in the headlights look is the best part."

What's a headlight? Clara thinks. *What's a deer?* She places her holotile on the table, about to dash *Record,* when Zion raises a hand.

"Clara, you've been asking many questions, for my biography I know, but I realized this morning that I know little about *you.* I have questions, if you do not mind me asking."

Clara strangely likes the reversal. "I guarantee my life is boring."

"Oh, quite the contrary," he says. "You've done great things and at such a young age. Considering Aizen's cooking, it appears your entire family is gifted. I am now interested in the partner in your life. You have not mentioned them in the least."

Clara smiles. "Well, Jonathan, *my husband,* is a few years younger than I. We met in university. He's a fellow history geek and is somehow getting cuter with age, which is quite annoying."

"So he's an investigative biographer too?"

"My Sol, no. *Two* writers under one roof? Could you imagine? We would implode." That gets a smile from Zion. "He's an archaeologist."

"Oh, that's wonderful!" Zion says. "Je bust heek English."

"You speak ancient English?" Clara asks but should not be surprised. She remembers watching his negotiations on hologram as a child, marveling at xeno-species talking in impossible tongues and Zion's holotile translating on the fly. After a moment, Zion would turn it off and start responding with slow, inhuman sounds, picking up his pace until he comfortably spoke their language.

Zion grins. "You must speak it, too."

"Only the cuss words, I'm afraid," Clara says.

He gives a sharp laugh. "Is Jonathan on assignment?"

"He's currently leading London's dig, but he's having trouble penetrating its glass dome. It's just so thick."

"They're *still* trying to drill through the dome? Interesting. To think, not a single archaeologist has thought to use the WorldRing tunnels," he says.

Clara zeroes in on Zion. *How could he have guessed that!? What game is he playing!?* "That's *exactly* what Jonathan is trying to do," she responds.

"Really? Sounds like he's encountering a problem."

"Most of the tunnels have collapsed. It's practically Paris."

"Not at all," Zion says lightly. "The sea-lines were designed to flex with ocean currents requiring additional reinforcement at the cliff-side entry. These points of entry most likely survived."

How does Zion know so much? "But how can Jonathan find the opening with the raised sea levels of today? He needs a precise position."

Zion rests his chin on his fist, thinking. "Would an image suffice?"

"No images exist from before The Fall," Clara says.

Zion stands abruptly and struts to a closet. Before Clara can process, an easel, canvas, and several paint tubes, brushes, and trowels appear. Zion slathers blues and whites onto his palette board.

"The granite at the tunnel opening has a sort of hook, like a nose," Zion explains, quickly laying down blues for what looks like an ocean.

"Zion," Clara quietly says. "How do you know what the old shoreline looks like?"

The ferocity in Zion's painting dwindles. He lowers the brush and turns from the canvas, terror in his eyes. "It's difficult to explain..."

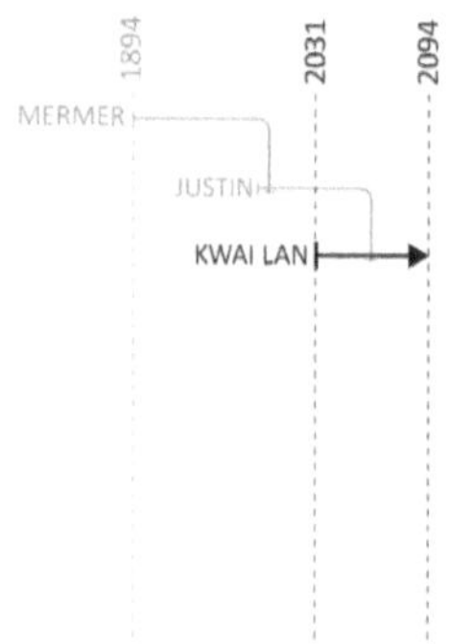

KWAI LAN's TALE
Earth: 2031 – 2094

I did not know how I came into the world. Much of my life was a blur. I remembered the first half like an old movie. One riddled with outdated jokes, continental accents, and cliche cinematography. And no matter how amazing that life may have once been, I simply could not relate. I was at the mercy of medicine during this time. First, as a patient, then as a geneticist.

◆

The First Half

I was barely five years old when my kidneys started to fail. My parents were both recessive carriers of Polycystic kidney disease, yet they did not know they possessed the trait until my symptoms began. Another year passed before my diagnosis, but by then it was too late. The damage was done. I needed new kidneys.

Mother arrived at the hospital every morning with the best dimsum I had ever known, the recipes perfected by my grandmother, before her, my great-grandfather, and before him, my great-great-grandfather. I could smell her arrival, and the doctors and nurses turned their heads as she walked to my room, soaking in the dimsum's aroma. Or my mother, for she was stunning. She wore a deep shade of red lipstick that never faded, projecting her smile to the darkest corners of my world, melting all my worries away.

Together, we dined on all the greats—shrimp dumplings, barbecue pork buns, chicken feet, sticky rice in banana leaf, and my favorite. Pan-seared turnip cake called *lo bak go.*

Mother taught at the University of Toronto during the day while I stared at the ceiling, bored. The hospital lunch remained untouched, and dinner was reluctantly picked at. Mother would return late, rescuing my stomach with ha fan noodles and quietly singing lullabies. I stared as her lips formed syllables, hypnotized by their deep hue.

But the more often Mother visited, the more distant Father became, coming only once every few weeks with an adorable stuffy. I knew exactly which one I would snuggle, Henry the Hippo, but I was protesting Father's absence and refused to touch them. As my impending surgery neared, he disappeared altogether.

"Is it because I'm sick?" I whispered to Mom.

"No, Pumpkin. *Absolutely* not."

"I'll get better. *I promise.* Tell Daddy, I'll get better."

"Your father leaving has nothing to do with you. It's *my* fault. *I* drove him away," she insisted.

Lying to protect me, I knew.

◆

"I don't know how much longer we can wait," I heard the doctor whisper to Mother one morning. "She's dwindling to skin and bone."

I imagined myself melting into the hospital bed like cheese and the sound of the dialysis machine as a second heartbeat.

The doctor entered my room and sat beside me. "Kwai Lan, how do you feel today?"

"I'm okay," I said. *Why is he talking to me alone?*

"You've been so strong. We're *very* proud of you." He paused. "We found a kidney, but it's only a thirty-six percent match with your DNA. There's a chance that the transplant might not take, but another opportunity like this may never come. We believe we should perform the surgery. Is that okay with you?"

I thought it over. The idea of someone else inside me was weird. "What happened to the donor?"

"He was very old when he passed away, but very healthy."

"Did he have kids?"

"Oh yes, and grandchildren too. They would all love for his kidney to save a young girl such as yourself."

I breathed deeply. "Okay..."

I remembered the apron wrapped around my waist and the coolness of iodine spread on the small of my back. But then, just before the anesthesia, the surgeon grew furious and called off the procedure.

My doctor looked at me with helplessness in his eyes. "I don't know what to say, Kwai Lan. The kidney did not survive travel. I'm afraid you must wait a little longer."

Another kidney will never come, I knew.

"Take mine!" Mother shouted from the hallway, talking with the other doctors. "I'm at least a fifty percent match!"

"But factoring in your own latent Polycystic Kidney Disease, there's only an eight percent chance it will take," they said.

"So there *is* a chance!" Mother argued.

The doctors sighed. "Technically, there's a chance."

♦

Mother went into surgery first, and I watched her bed roll in next to mine. She opened her eyes a crack, still groggy from the anesthesia. "You got this, Pumpkin..." she whispered.

I counted backward from ten with a mask over my mouth but only reached six before I was asleep.

♦

"This is incredible. The kidney should not have taken," I heard the doctor say as I regained consciousness.

"But it did," Mother responded from the bed beside mine.

He scrunched his brow. "Typically, people with latent Polycystic cannot be donors. The kidneys are simply *too* weak."

"Maybe Mom's kidneys are stronger," I said, knowing her immense willpower had made it possible. *And that strength now resides in me!*

In the following months, I painstakingly peeled from that hospital bed and worked through the physical therapy, determined to live up to my new kidney's expectations.

"Ready to go home, Pumpkin?" Mother said, her smile proud.

♦

Mother sang lullabies to me every night, even when I outgrew them. But I listened without complaint all the same. I knew it was her way of coping with a daughter once facing certain death and my father's abandonment. That and her flawless smile. *Her armor against the world.*

The only time she was not racked with worry, not putting up a flawless front, not wearing her red lipstick armor, was when she cooked. And she cooked all the time. It did not matter what time of day it was. When she was not working, she was cooking. *I was learning.*

"We're late!" Mother called up the stairs. "Get your butt in gear!"

I looked at the time. *So what?* I thought.

"Kwai Lan!" she called again.

I looked at my dress shirt and slacks, then at my poster of Acid Flux in torn jeans and chains, holding guitars and drumsticks like weapons. *I'm a sellout,* I thought and slowly made my way downstairs.

Mother was waiting at the door, dressed to impress, red lipstick armor freshly applied, and holding a container of her masterful lo bak go. She looked me up and down.

"Not bad, let's go," she said, opening the door.

"Do we have to go *every* year?" I said, once in the car.

Mom pressed the ignition. "It's Chinese New Year, of course we do."

We pulled into our local community center a short time later. Mother entered first, proudly holding her container of lo bak go. The faces of my elderly neighbors lit up as she walked by, their eyes following the container.

"They're not excited to see *you*, Mom. They want the *food*," I said. "They never bring anything. Why do you bother?"

"Oh, to be fifteen years old again," she said and sighed. "For many of our neighbors, especially those raised in Hong Kong, this is one of their few remaining links to home. That alone is reason enough."

"Whatevs," I said, rolling my eyes. But, I knew of the hardships surrounding China's reincorporation of Hong Kong and how its local traditions, culture, and language were being systematically erased. Mother constantly discussed it while cooking, herself having escaped Hong Kong's lockdown with my father and pregnant with me.

She handed me the container of turnip cake and pointed at the buffet table. "Make sure everyone gets one. Except Mr. Dai. He's allergic. And Ms. Chuang even if she guilt-trips you. She's on a diet. And watch out for Mr. Lao stealing an extra. He somehow manages it every year."

I looked at the container in my hands. "What?"

"Be useful, serve," she said.

"Um, what will you do, then?"

Her posture straightened, and she checked her reflection in a wall-hung mirror beyond circular tables, ensuring her lipstick was perfect.

"Kevin is single," Mom said, turned abruptly, and strutted to a table hosting a handsome man with shocking silver hair.

He looked my mother's way. Sudden recognition showed. "Kat?" He sprang to his feet and gave her a warm embrace.

♦

"This is incredible," Kevin said, joining our weekend dimsum ritual. *With me doing the cooking and them flirting like teenagers!*

"Bombs away!" Kevin called, tossing uncooked dumplings at Mother, resulting in flour being tossed back into his face.

I was endlessly annoyed and gave him all the over and under-cooked pieces. He complimented them all the same. *Why won't he just go away!?* I thought, then caught Mom smiling without her red lipstick armor. *Shit...*

"Kwai Lan," Mom said, sitting me beside her and Kevin one day. "We have some important news to share with you."

Oh no! No, no, no! I thought.

"Kevin and I are getting married," she said.

I sighed deeply, studying Mother's smile. "Okay," I mumbled.

"And..." Mother took a breath. "I'm pregnant."

Tucker was born just before my seventeenth birthday. *Overshadowing it, of course.* He was annoyingly perfect, born with soft hair sticking straight up, and would laugh and smile on cue.

"Oh, isn't he a sweetheart," Mrs. Ho, our next-door neighbor, would say.

Whenever I snubbed him, he gave a smug look, saying, *I know you think I'm adorable, too.*

He stumbled to me one day, giving my leg a clumsy embrace, and looked up, flashing a flawless smile. *Mother's smile.* That's when he said his first word, but it was neither *Mama* nor *Dada.*

It was "Gai wan."

Close enough, I thought, unable to restrain a smile. *Cheeky little bugger knows how to get to me.*

♦

Where are they!? It was nearly a half-hour since class finished. *What a day for them to forget to pick me up!* I stared at the torrential downpour outside the school's entry doors. Several calls and texts went unanswered. Tendrils of anxiety reached my stomach.

I walked home in the rain, clothes clinging to my body and shoes squishing, to find the driveway empty. But the living room lights were on. Mrs. Ho peeked through the curtains.

What's she doing here?

She slowly opened the door and met me on the stoop. "Kwai Lan, there's been an accident."

Kevin's sister was at the hospital when I arrived, horror on her face. "A semi-truck lost traction in the rain," she said robotically. "Kevin died on impact." She paused. "Tucker and your mom are still hanging on."

I watched Tucker through a window, resting in his tiny, intensive care bed, with screws drilled into his pristine skull securing a neck immobilizer.

"Despite being strapped into his car seat, his neck was broken," the doctor said. "But he's a fighter. We've never seen anything like it."

The doctors were hopeful of recovery until rampant infection from a ruptured appendix was discovered. Tucker passed away as I slept in the waiting room.

Mother was still fighting wildly in her subconscious despite having a crushed liver, pancreas, and kidney.

"She should have died in the ambulance," they told me.

I gently stroked Mother's hair, avoiding the stitches where she hit the windshield. And then, her lullabies flowed past my lips, broken and off-key, but they were the sweetest songs in the world.

◆

"We have a liver and pancreas right now!" I shouted at the doctor. "Can't you do *that* surgery while we wait for the kidney?"

The doctor shook his head. "I'm sorry, Kwai Lan. Your mother cannot survive back to back surgeries. Even the one is ambitious. It must be all three organs at once, or not at all."

"Then, we put the liver and pancreas on ice!" I snapped.

The doctor's face dropped. "They cannot wait. Other patients with much higher chances of success need them."

I held my side, where my mother's kidney was. "Take mine!"

"You know we can't do that. I don't know what else to tell you, Kwai Lan." He lowered his head and left the room.

That familiar beep of the dialysis machine accompanied the silence. I turned to Mother, looking peaceful on the outside. *Engaged in epic battle within,* I knew.

"It's all my fault," I whispered.

Mother stirred. Her eyes cracked open, despite the induced coma, looking right at me. "Be strong, Pumpkin," she whispered as all her breath slipped away.

◆

School. Home. Sleep. Cry. Maybe eat. *School. Home. Sleep. Cry.* Maybe eat. *Therapy, therapy, therapy. Birthday at neighbor's house. Their family. Their friends. Is it to brag? Alone. Kevin's sister, sometimes. Mrs. Ho, too often. Food, bad. Cookbook, dusty. Mom's stuff, basement. School. Home. Sleep. Cry.* Maybe eat. *School. Home. Sleep. Cry.* Maybe eat.

"Scientists Successfully Regrow Nose for Burn Victim!" flashed across the school bus's seat-back display.

I shook my head, snapping out of my daze. *What?*

A doctor on screen pointed to before and after images of a burn victim's face. *"We grew the nose directly on the victim's own forehead, encouraging new skin cells to develop around artificial cartilage. We then cut around the new nose's perimeter and flipped it from the patient's forehead to where their nose had once been, without severing major blood vessels."*

"You can't be serious!" I shouted, and the other students on the bus turned in my direction.

I raced from the bus stop home, past Mrs. Ho cooking dinner in the kitchen, and up to my room. I researched every article I could relating to cloning and regeneration. *This could be it!*

◆

Read. Read. Sleep. *Read.* Sleep. *Read.* Sleep. Sleep—

"Kwai Lan!"

I lifted my head from a medical journal, the page sticking to my cheek, and drool on my lip. Mrs. Parsons, our school librarian, stood over me.

"Have you eaten today?" she said.

"Of course," I snapped and returned to reading the journal.

Mrs. Parsons crossed her arms. "You have not left this spot since nine o'clock this morning."

I checked the time. *Seven in the evening.* My stomach growled. But again, I focused on the journal.

Mrs. Parsons sighed, returned to her counter, and pulled out her holotablet. Twenty minutes later, she plopped delivery on my table.

"What's that?" I said, annoyed.

"It's called *food.* You should try it some time."

I rolled my eyes. "From where?"

"Soup Coup. It's their broccoli soup today, lucky duck."

Soup Coup? They're supposedly revolutionary, I thought, but I hated broccoli. I thanked Mrs. Parsons and offered to repay her. She refused. I ignored the soup until Mrs. Parsons coughed to get my attention. I rolled my eyes again, opened the bag, pulled out the piping hot container, and removed its lid. I spooned a bit, blowing across its surface to cool, and slurped it in. Richness spread across my tongue, creamy yet not too much, seasoned to perfection.

"Damn," I whispered. *I guess I like broccoli, after all.*

I felt a presence over my shoulder and whipped my head around to find Mrs. Parsons staring at the medical journal I was reading.

"You know, U of T has a great genetics program," she said.

◆

I sat with the Dean of Medicine and my professors just before graduation to discuss my research proposal, culminating my seven years at the University of Toronto.

"Kwai Lan, how is Regenerative Cloning any different than regular cloning?" the dean asked. "The ban on harvesting embryotic stem cells will likely never lift."

I tilted my head. "Regenerative Cloning does *not* require the transfer of nuclei from embryotic cells, yet grows an organ with identical DNA to the original."

"How is that possible?"

"The blueprints in human DNA, like all mammals, become dormant after formation of limbs and organs in the womb. Which is why we can heal, but not regenerate whole body parts like flatworms, starfish, and lizards can. My thesis is to find those genes allowing for regeneration in flatworms and transfer them into our human DNA."

"The chances of you finding these procteins are slim to none," the dean argued.

"True," I said. "But because the transfer of embryotic nuclei is not required, Regenerative Cloning is *legal.*"

They discussed my proposal behind closed doors, returning an hour later. "Congratulations, Dr. Wong Kwai Lan, we grant you permission to pursue Regenerative Cloning."

◆

"You actually found them? Where were they?" Cassandra, my one lab tech, said.

"Locked between genes 3992344 and 3992750," I responded.

"But that's just genetic junk."

"It's not junk. These genes are viral in origin and horizontally transferred into the first mammal-like creatures, maybe even the first synapsids, when they diverged from reptiles in the carboniferous period." I pulled the section of DNA up on the screen. "Gene 3992566 is one of the genes responsible for the protective lining of the amniotic sac, making placental pregnancy possible. Without it, our immune system would destroy the fetus." I pulled up another section. "The group I've isolated here clearly shows that the genes responsible for regeneration were abruptly changed in mammals during this time period, too."

"So the mutations were of viral origin?"

I shook my head. "These mutations likely originated from another complex organism, horizontally transferred into a virus, then transferred into synapsids. The virus is just the carrier."

"What does this mean for humans?" Cassandra asked.

"If we program RNA to retrieve these active proteins from a flatworm, then we can insert them directly into human cells."

"And it would take effect immediately? People can regenerate?"

"Not quite," I said. "But if we inject the borrowed genes into human stem cells, we can theoretically regenerate any organ or limb within incubators, inserting reference cells at the right moments of development."

♦

"We have our first patient," I said to Cassandra, grinning.

She gave me a confused look. "Regenerative Cloning is far from FDA approval."

I handed her my holotablet, the patient's case file in its projection.

She cocked her head. "An orangutan!? You can't be serious!?"

"Abbey lost her arm as a baby in Indonesia's Lumber War, becoming the poster child for animal rights activists," I said. "Having her as our first case would catapult us into the spotlight."

Cassandra mulled it over. "I guess an organutan's DNA is almost identical to a humans."

"Ninety-seven percent identical," I said.

♦

Cartilage and bone grew first – an ulna, radius, carpals, and phalanges, attached to an artificial elbow for support, the size of a needle. We fed reference cells into the mix, ligaments, muscle tissue, and skin from Abbey herself for our altered stem cells to reference.

"It twitched!" Cassandra pointed to the arm nearly five months into growth, a foot in length now, with orange hair beginning to sprout.

"It's time to send it signals," I said.

We identified the nerves at the elbow, connecting them to a computer that sent electrical pulses to contract each finger, making a fist and then working with more complex gestures as the muscles slowly developed.

Weight training began at the ten-month mark. The hand held a two-kilo kettlebell for a few seconds before slipping out. But two kilos quickly became ten, fifty, then the weight of a grown female orangutan.

"Abbey's here," Cassandra said.

We met Abbey in a playroom alongside her caretaker.

"Abbey, it's wonderful to meet you," I said as the caretaker signed.

Abbey signed back, her eyes darting about, nervous.

"She says she's scared," the caretaker translated.

"Does she understand what we are trying to do?" I asked.

"She watches Animal Rescue on hologram. I told her it will be like the surgeries on the show, that you will rescue her arm."

♦

We visited Abbey three months after the attachment surgery.

"Abbey, how does the new arm feel?" I asked.

Abbey replied with both hands.

Both hands! I snapped my head to the caretaker, my heart racing.

The caretaker smiled. "Verbatim Abbey says, *Funny, like lost tooth, and have new one.*"

"The nerves are reuniting with unprecedented vigor!" Cassandra said, watching signals shoot from Abbey's brain to the arm on hologram.

A year later, Abbey was swinging from branch to branch as if her arm was never lost.

♦

"We are back with Dr. Wong Kwai Lan, the brainchild of Spare Parts!" Dr. Kingston of Science Today said. "Kwai Lan, is it true that in your six years of operation, with over three million replacements grown, you've never had a single limb or organ rejection?"

I tilted my head. "There's always complications during surgery. But yes, we've never had a rejection of a regenerated organ or limb."

"How is this possible?"

"Our regenerations are literally your own body, inherently possessing perfect ABO compatibility, a one hundred percent HLA tissue match, zero anti-body reaction, and perfect serum acceptance. The only uncertainty is the surgery itself."

Dr. Kingston thought about that. "But considering those same factors, why can't a recently severed limb be reattached like one of your regenerations?"

"Trauma plays a significant role in a surgery's success," I responded. "Severed limbs experience significant damage to the nerves, making them nearly impossible to reattach. Donated organs fair better because they function passively, but they still experience reduced functionality. The replacements grown at Spare Parts, however, have never experienced trauma. And, instead of rushing them from one traumatic event, on ice, to a second traumatic event of surgery, we can time the maturation of our replacements with the scheduled surgery and carefully transport them in portable incubators. If needed, they can wait in the hospital until the perfect moment. Urgency is often the largest contributor to failure. We have removed that factor."

"But there's still one hurdle you have yet to cross," Dr. Kingston said. "Regrowing organs for cancer patients."

◆

Cassandra rushed to me as I entered Spare Parts's front door, opening a case file on her holotablet.

I hung my coat. "What's up?"

"This is it, Kwai Lan. The one you've been searching for."

"Describe."

"Justin Vagner, seventy-three years old, triple transplant."

"Car accident?"

"No, but Justin has been through hell and back. He suffered retrograde amnesia as a child, became a drug addict as a teenager, was anorexic and schizophrenic, and suffered a serious back injury. He somehow overcame all of that to become a Michelin starred chef."

I humphed. "What restaurant?"

"Soup Coup."

I paused. "No shit."

"Yeah, I know. Unfortunately, Justin contracted hepatitis C which became liver cancer, spreading to his pancreas and kidneys."

The same three organs... Mother's smile flashed through my mind. I breathed deeply. "Regenerating clean organs from potentially cancerous cells is nearly impossible. It's why we don't take cancer patients."

"Sooner or later, we'll have to cross that bridge." Cassandra's holotablet buzzed. "They need me in incubation. Please, think about it."

I did think about it, *dreamed about it,* and found myself ordering Soup

Coup every day that week. I dug through Mother's belongings in the basement, her last words echoing in my head as tears ran down my cheeks. I opened a box marked *"Toiletries."* At the very bottom was a familiar brass tin. I slowly opened it.

"Oh..." I plucked one of the cylinders, removed its top, and twisted its shaft. A deep shade of red emerged like a phoenix from the ashes. A chill ran down my spine, followed by warmth as if Mother had embraced me.

"Be strong, Pumpkin." Her words were so clear.

Slowly, unsteadily, I applied her red lipstick armor.

◆

I waded through Spare Parts's Incubation hall, resembling a nursery. Families gathered around incubators, peering through the glass as if beautiful newborn babies peacefully slept within. Instead, a pair of lungs inflated and deflated, or a heart pumped with fervor.

I continued to the Limb Wing, met by a lone arm, with lean muscle shoulder down, curling a dumbbell next to a pair of torso-less legs running swiftly on a treadmill.

A triple amputee stared in disbelief. "Are those really mine?"

I gently touched her arm-less shoulder. "You'll be running again before you know it," I said.

"How much longer until the surgery?" she asked.

I studied the legs running in their harness and the arm curling, imagining the rest of her attached to them, her muscular torso flexing just as mechanically. *She might become an even stronger runner now.*

"Another month," I said. "But intense physical therapy will be required before you can race again."

She wiped her tears. "I just want to hold my little girl."

"And you will." I gave my leave and continued to a cordoned-off section of incubators, where Cassandra was extracting samples from Justin's organs.

"Do you know how much cost we've eaten?" Cassandra said. "Everyday, I'm finding more cancer spots."

"The fact that any of Justin's organs have matured this far cancer-free is a miracle," I said. "What are we down to?"

"Of the original twenty copies, we have two livers, three pancreases, and two pairs of kidneys."

"Shall we, then?" I said.

We began with Pancreas 17, analyzing each of its two hundred samples. On slide 147, I saw a deformed clump.

"Shit," I whispered.

Cassandra turned. "Really?"

"Yeah, it's there."

She removed the organ from its incubator, placed it in a bio-hazard bag, and then set the bag into the bin. Pancreas 12 was the same. *Such a shame.* But when I finished Pancreas 3, I felt giddy. Cassandra finished her slides just after me and turned with a grin. *It was clean.* Both Livers 6 and 11 proved absent of cancerous cells, too.

The kidneys gave us trouble. *Of course they would,* I thought and rolled my eyes. Kidneys L5, L7, and R19 all had cancerous spots.

"R2 is our moment of truth," I said.

Cassandra and I finished our slides and faced each other.

"Clean?" she whispered.

I nodded. "Yours?"

"Yes," she squeaked.

My stomach fluttered. A wave of euphoria hit. "Swap slides!" I said.

We went through them again. And then again.

"Kwai Lan, it's three in the morning," Cassandra eventually said, resting her head on the table. "We should send our findings to Oncology for confirmation."

"Okay," I said.

I returned in the early afternoon the next day. My research teams stood deathly silent at their stations, watching me approach Oncology. Cassandra was already there, staring at the results. I felt a rock in my stomach until she looked my way with a brilliant smile.

◆

"Take the WorldRing, I'm telling you," Cassandra said, having used the transit system herself just a week earlier to assess Justin's condition. "It's the fastest way to New York City."

"But it's a prototype line," I argued. "It may shut down for some unforeseen technical issue. It's too risky."

"But Justin needs the organs *now,*" Cassandra said. "Everything else is too slow. And the WorldRing has offered us free use of their system."

◆

I stored Justin's organs safely in portable incubators and secured them to a private RingShuttle's floor.

"Dr. Wong," a shuttle attendant said, "We thank you for trusting in our WorldRing line to New York City. Please, buckle your harness and feel free to ask any questions."

"You say the entire trip will be a half-hour long," I said. "Will we be subject to tremendous g-forces? The organs are extremely fragile."

"Not to worry, Dr. Wong. Acceleration should feel no different than a plane during takeoff. However, instead of thirty seconds of acceleration, we continue for ten minutes, reaching a cruising speed of Mach two. When we near New York City we will gently transition to a ten minute deceleration. All without turbulence. There is no safer way to travel."

I barely noticed the acceleration phase and stared at trees and farmhouses blurring by my window. We dipped below the surface of Lake Ontario, and I tried picking out the hulls of cargo ships. Then we rose from the water to penetrate the Appalachian Mountains. A gentle deceleration began in upstate New York. The city quickly neared. The line dipped beneath the earth and settled into a WorldRing hub below Grand Central Station. *Just under thirty minutes. Incredible.*

The ambulance from Grand Central to the hospital swerved side to side, with its siren wailing.

"Slow down!" I shouted at the driver. "The organs are delicate!"

We arrived twenty minutes later, and I meticulously checked the organs. *No damage, thank god.* I then thought about the smooth ride aboard the WorldRing. *I'm sold.* I handed off the incubators to assistant surgeons and signed a release form transferring responsibility to the hospital.

"Dr. Wong, Justin will wake soon," a nurse said, leading me to his room.

I peered through the window at a skeletal man, yellow with jaundice. "He looks about to pass away at any moment," I said.

"Trust me, Justin's a fighter, despite how he looks. He's ready for the procedure," the nurse said.

I entered his room, hit by a sweet stink in the air, and sat beside his bed. His yellow eyes opened into slits and wandered the room before finding me.

"Justin," I said, touching his twig-like arm. "I'm Dr. Wong Kwai Lan. My team and I have been experimenting with organ cloning and believe we can help you..."

◆

"I don't understand, Kwai Lan," Justin's doctor said. "The surgery was flawless. And you say the organs were grown from Justin's *exact* DNA?"

"As with *all* my patients," I responded, my mind racing. "There's no way his body rejected them. Was there infection?"

"We checked again. There's nothing that would inhibit the surgery."

"Was it an act of God, then!?" I snapped. *Was I flying too close to the sun? Did I push too far?* I thought. *No, it should have worked!*

The doctor paused. "I don't know..."

"How much time does Justin have?" I asked.

He sighed. "Maybe an hour."

"I'll deliver the news, the organs were *my* responsibility," I said.

The doctor nodded.

I entered Justin's room and sat on the stool next to his bed.

He stirred. His eyes slowly opened.

"Justin, I'm so sorry," I said. "We don't know why, but your body is rejecting the organs."

His eyes filled with pain and then rage. His facial muscles twitched and rippled. He gripped the bed frame and tried to sit, but he was so weak. His lips curled back like a wolf bearing its teeth, but after several moments, Justin settled. He stared deep into my eyes instead.

A sudden vertigo gripped me. I nearly fell to the floor. Alarms rang. Nurses ran into the room to Justin's side. One grabbed my arm, helping me to my feet. My head pounded. It felt crowded. *Felt different.*

I stumbled out of Justin's room, down the hall to the elevators, through the ground floor lobby, and out of the hospital. I waved my hand wildly to hail a cab. *Home, I must go home...*

◆

The Second Half

A gnawing in my stomach grew so intense I wanted nothing more than death. I was starving, but I could not eat, and my body dwindled to skin and bone.

I lurched awake, grasping my belly. "What the fuck?" I whispered, checking myself to see that I was okay.

I melted a brown sugary cube into honey with a spoon and flame and drew it into a needle. The pinch in my veins was nothing compared to the lightning shooting down my back and legs. *Just make it all stop!* I kept thinking. Then a rush of pure heaven pushed the pain away.

My god, this feels good, I thought.

It does, said a bitter voice in my dream.

I lurched awake again, clutching my arm at the elbow, expecting to find collapsed veins. But again, there was nothing.

Soft sand beneath my many feet. I scurried from one rock to the next, looking up to see my greatest love being taken by a devil from above. I could not stop it. I could do nothing.

Empty, so empty. Greatest love... gone, said an innocent whisper.

I woke in tears, confused.

Burning! Skin melted away. Arms and legs tore from my body. I watched them disappear into giant mouths. Sounds of "Mmmm," and "Oh my!" accompanied hundreds of screams from my brothers and sisters.

I leaped from bed, patting down my body. I wiped my eyes. *Another dream,* I thought, confused, scared. *I need Mom.*

I wandered downstairs to the kitchen. My stomach growled.

I opened the cupboard. There it was, my mother's cookbook covered in dust. I thumbed through the pages, smiling sadly at the alterations scribbled in the margins. *The family's secret ingredients.* I thought about Mom's political ranting, her passion, her fire.

I cooked all night long, finding I was more skilled than I remembered being. I studied the secret ingredients. *Something's missing,* I realized. When I made further alterations, a new clarity in flavor came forth.

◆

The more often I cooked, the less intense those nightmares became, until one night, I dreamed of Mother cooking her masterful lo bak go, humming quietly. She stopped and turned to me.

"It's about time you came," she said, her voice so real, so present.

"I'm sorry, mom," I said.

She made a face. "Sorry for what?"

"I couldn't save Justin, I've let you down."

"Pumpkin, I don't give a damn about Justin."

"But he required the same organs as you, which means I could not have saved you either."

She grinned. "I never needed saving. But you know what does?"

"What?" I asked.

Mother pointed at the lo bak go.

I calmly woke, went to the kitchen, and started making Mother's lo bak go. That's when I saw what I never expected, reflecting in the microwave glass. *A smile.*

◆

I returned to Spare Parts in a bizarrely good mood and brought my containers of dimsum to the company canteen. Heads turned, sniffing the air. Cassandra appeared as if waiting around the corner.

"Is that the Wong family dimsum?" she said with her eyes locked on the containers.

"I've made improvements," I said, opening their lids.

Cassandra snatched a pair of chopsticks and plucked a chicken foot, steam rising from its glaze. She inspected it with the same scrutiny she did her work, then inserted a toe into her mouth. A kaleidoscope of expressions crossed her face, then she spat the stripped bones into a napkin.

"Holy hell! What did you do!?"

◆

Five days a week at work became four, then three, then two, then one.

I invited Cassandra out for coffee.

"Kwai Lan," Cassandra said and sat down next to me, latte in hand. "Sara's organs are nearing maturation, this is huge, we need you at work."

I grinned. "You're doing great on your own. Sara's organs are clear of cancer. Congratulations."

"Thanks, but what's up with you? You've been absent for practically the whole year."

"It's just… Spare Parts doesn't do it for me anymore," I said. "I have no desire to work. I think I want to cook dimsum, instead."

Cassandra sipped her latte. "For as long as we've been friends, you've *loved* your work. I know you love cooking too, but how has this suddenly become more important? Is it Justin's case? What happened?"

"I've been having strange dreams..." As I described them, I filled the gaps, telling a story I did not know I knew. I realized I was reciting someone else's life. *Justin's life.* But I was not afraid of it anymore.

Cassandra lowered her latte. "Kwai Lan, those are incredible dreams, but they do not rationalize a career change."

"Why not?"

"Because you cannot change the world through cooking. Not like you can at Spare Parts. You of *all* people know this."

No, food can change the world! I thought. "What about the French Revolution?" I said. "That started with famine."

"Well—"

"The Indochina War?"

"That's because of World War II," Cassandra argued.

"China's One Child Policy?" I raised an eyebrow.

Cassandra pressed her lips tight. "Are you planning to feed all the starving nations? Save Africa and India with *dimsum?*"

"That's not what I mean."

Cassandra gave me a strange look. "What do you mean, then?"

I thought about Mother and blurted, "Our culture is being erased as we speak. The only people who still use traditional characters or speak Canto are those who grew up abroad, like us. Mandarin is the only language in Hong Kong now. All we have left is our cuisine. If we let that get manipulated, then what? Dimsum is the last opportunity we have to save our heritage."

Cassandra thought it over. "The world cannot accept *real* dimsum. You will fail."

"I've been told that before and beaten the odds," I said.

I've also beaten the odds, said the bitter voice from my dream.

Me too, said the innocent one.

♦

"It's small, but in a good location," Cassandra said, studying the dusty street-facing dining hall. "What's the name?"

"Kat's Dimsum," I said.

She humphed. "Of course."

Cassandra dragged several researchers to Kat's Dimsum's grand opening.

"This is incredible," a researcher said, trying my shrimp with roe. "I didn't know you could do this, Dr. Wong."

"Please, call me Kwai Lan," I said. "And thank my mother. She was the real chef in the family."

"Is anyone else coming?" Cassandra said, glancing at the empty tables and Harold, my lone waiter, scrolling through his holotablet on a bench.

A young Asian-Canadian couple passed through the door.

"Guess so," I said.

Harold lurched to his feet. "Welcome to Kat's Dimsum. Please, have a seat," he greeted, distributing menus and order sheets.

"What's up with the characters?" the boyfriend said, looking at the menu.

"They're traditional Chinese," Harold said.

"Um, why not use simplified characters?"

"Kat's Dimsum strives to preserve the authentic cuisine and culture of Hong Kong."

The girlfriend suppressed a snicker.

"I think we're good," the boyfriend said, closing the menu.

They quickly left.

♦

I was about to send Harold home early after another idle morning when an elderly group stumbled in. Harold seated them at a circular table with a rotating glass tray at its center.

A man from the group pointed at the glass tray. "I haven't seen one of these in decades," he said in old Hong Kong Cantonese.

I snapped my head from my holotablet. I watched their faces light up when they saw the menu's characters and become ecstatic, realizing what dishes they described.

"Lo bak go!? They actually have it! Get extra!" one said.

"And chicken feet! Get the feet!"

The poor guy, checking boxes on the order sheet, desperately fought off his friends.

"You checked the wrong box!" a third shouted, plucking the sheet from his hand.

"It's correct! Look!" he said, reaching to reclaim the sheet.

When it reached my hands, it was torn in two places, with every box checked. They ordered three times what they could eat, and I culled it for sanity's sake. I took a moment to watch the shrimp dumplings go out from the serving window.

The group sniffed the air, wonder melting across their faces. Harold placed two baskets on the table, one atop the other, then separated them. Once animated, the group now stared motionless.

"Tony, you try first, this was your favorite as a kid," one said.

Tony peeled a dumpling from the parchment paper with serving chopsticks, dipped it into chili sauce, and placed it into his bowl. He then lifted the dumpling with his personal chopsticks and inspected it thoroughly.

"Just eat it already!" one of them said.

Tony slowly inserted the dumpling into his mouth and lowered his head to the table, thumping his fist against its surface. He lifted his head, fighting back tears.

"Is it as good as you remember?"

He finished chewing and swallowed. "I… I can't believe I'm saying this. I think it's better."

♦

My holotablet beeped early morning. *A call from Harold?* I checked the time. There was still an hour before opening.

"What's up?" I answered.

"You won't believe it!" Harold said, turning his tablet.

A line of elderly men and women stretching down the block appeared, chatting in Cantonese.

"Are you opening or not!" one of them said.

Harold spun the holotablet back around. "You gotta come here now!"

"Keep the door locked! I'll be there in fifteen!" I said.

The crowd nearly bulldozed us over when I unlocked the door.

That week, I hired more waitstaff, several cooks, and hosts to contain the mob at the door. But no matter how much produce I ordered the night before, I had to send couriers to the market during peak hours to keep up with the sudden demand.

"Kwai Lan, the man at table two is asking to sample one of each type of dimsum," Harold said.

I studied the man staring at the menu, meticulously reading each item. *He must be a food critic,* I thought. I prepared his dumplings using Mother's masterful wrapping techniques I rarely used because of time. The dumplings in those baskets were gorgeous, and my newly hired cooks, experts in their own right, looked upon them with awe.

When they were delivered to table two, the man straightened in shock and frantically looked about the restaurant. His gaze returned to the dumplings. He plucked one. His hand shook.

Maybe not a food critic, I thought.

He took a small bite, then dropped the dumpling and chopsticks.

Harold ran over to check on the man, conversed, and then he came to the kitchen. "He's asking to meet the chef."

I slowly approached as the man scanned the dining room. His gaze settled upon me, and the blood drained from his face. His deep-set eyes shifted down, looking at my red lips.

"Kat?" he whispered.

I shook my head.

His face further drained, and he gulped. "Pumpkin?"

Shivers went down my spine.

"It's been a long time," I said.

He offered the seat across from him. I remained standing.

"You look just like your mother," he said.

"What do you want?" I snapped.

"I wanted to know who made the dumplings."

"*I* did." My eyes bore into his.

"So, the Wong legacy lives on," he said.

"It does, despite you," I spat, venom on my tongue.

"I'm sorry, for everything."

I cocked my head. "You're *sorry?* That's it? You think apologizing absolves you of any wrongdoing? Am I supposed to throw my arms around you and shout *Daddy!?*"

The guests at adjacent tables gave concerned looks.

"No, no, of course not," he said, his face reddening.

"You ran away when I was about to die!" I shouted, pulled out a chair, sat with a thud, and aggressively ate the dumplings I had made. My father was silent. "I'm waiting for you to defend yourself! Come up with a stupid excuse! At least a stuffed animal!"

"Kat never told you," he said with discovery in his voice.

My eyes met his. "Never told me *what!?*"

"I'm not your father."

"That is the dumbest thing I have ever heard!"

He sighed. "Your mother and I were both tested for polycystic kidney disease during your diagnosis. She was a carrier, which meant I must also be a carrier for the disease to be dominant in you. But I tested negative."

I so badly wanted to believe he was lying, but remnants of my past began making sense. The whispered arguments outside my hospital room, and how everyone said I clearly took after my mother.

He lowered his eyes. "I tried being there for you, I truly did. But the pain it caused me every time I saw your mother. I could only see her betrayal. I started drinking and lost my job at the university. I tried seeing you after the surgery, but your mother forbade it, saying I threw away my chance."

I stared down at the table, stunned. *Mom? Why?* I didn't know what to say except, "You seem okay now."

My father smiled weakly. "I'll be sober six years this May."

"Are you working at the university again?"

"I manage a bookstore."

"Oh."

"No, no. It's great work. I'm learning more now than I did in a university environment. I learned all about Spare Parts."

"I gave that up," I said.

"Kat would be proud of you for doing so. I'm proud of you, for what it's worth."

"Not much," I said bitterly. "Why are you proud of me for leaving a multi-billion dollar startup to cook dimsum?"

"Pumpkin," he said and motioned to the other guests. "We all know what this restaurant symbolizes."

♦

My father insisted on coming every day, and I made it a point to personally prepare his orders, employing Mother's beautiful wrapping techniques to twist the knife in his heart or giving him all the broken, overcooked, and undercooked pieces to vent my anger. Once, I made barbecue pork buns but purposely omitted the filling. His laughter traveled to the kitchen with that one.

He came in again.

We made brief eye contact before I escaped to the kitchen. My anger boiled when his order sheet reached my hands, but the boxes were empty. Instead, he wrote, *"Table 7, Jennifer Long in disguise—"*

I snapped my head up. A woman dressed in a torn jacket with matted hair sat at table seven, yet her hands were oddly manicured. *My staff is ignoring her,* I realized. I stared at Harold until he looked in my direction. I waved him to the kitchen.

"What is it?" he said.

"Table seven."

"We'll remove her."

"No, that's Jennifer Long."

"The food critic? No way."

I gave cut-eye.

Harold straightened. "Yes, of course. What do you want me to do?"

"Treat her like any other customer, not too nice or she'll know what's up. Take her order. *Wait.* Give her tea and walk away for a moment, *then* take her order."

Harold nodded and left the kitchen.

I read the rest of the note. *"—Don't use Kat's wrapping, but make sure they are delicious. I'm leaving so you can work without distraction. Good luck, Pumpkin. -Stephen-"*

Why does he have to be nice? I thought, angry with myself for being less angry with him.

You must focus, said the bitter voice.

♦

Jennifer Long returned the following day in full makeup and elegantly dressed but found herself waiting in line with everyone else. She was eventually seated at table four, close to the entry, so she felt a chill when the door opened. Jennifer frowned, quickly checked boxes, and raised her sheet for Harold to retrieve. After a minute of being ignored, she lowered and scrunched her brow. Harold set a teapot on her table. She lifted her sheet again, but Harold moved on to another table. He finally returned to take her order sheet. Confusion spread across Jennifer's face, but she was grinning.

She ordered the same dishes, and I made them identical.

When the basket of shrimp pork with roe arrived, Jennifer inspected the pieces and then nibbled. Her eyes closed, her posture slouched. After swallowing, she waved to get Harold's attention. She pointed to herself and smiled. "I'm Jennifer Long. May I speak with the chef?"

"Yes, of course." Harold hurried to the kitchen. "Jennifer Long wants to meet you," he said to me.

"Wish me luck." I strutted from the kitchen.

Jennifer gave a quizzical look and gestured her hand, offering a seat. "Literally the exact same treatment both times I dined here. How wonderful to have such consistent and unbiased service," she sarcastically said.

I grinned and sat. "At Kat's Dimsum, everyone deserves to experience the best Hong Kong has to offer."

"What gave me away the first time?"

I pointed to her manicured nails.

Jennifer studied them for a moment. "Do you know why I'm here?"

"I confess that I don't," I said. "I thought you never critiqued dimsum."

"I need my dimsum fix, just like any other CBC," she said. "My brother raved about this place."

"So you're not here to judge?"

"Well..." She tilted her head. "Chef Wong, do you know *why* I gave up my cooking career to become a critic?"

"I do not."

"I was trying to achieve what you're doing now, though a bit more extreme. I tried to bring dimsum to Paris."

"That's... brave."

"Insane, actually. And that's what everyone told me. After struggling for two decades and draining my life savings, I now agree." She looked into my eyes. "But *you* can fail a thousand times and not dent your savings."

I winced. I hated talking about money. It was never my goal with Spare Parts. Nevertheless, Jennifer was right.

She read my discomfort. "I'm not asking for a handout. I know I wasn't good enough, especially after trying *this*." She waved to the baskets. "I couldn't compete with French cuisine. But maybe *you* can."

"But why Paris?" I asked.

"It's a major pillar of cuisine. And now that dimsum is officially banned in Hong Kong, we cannot rely on our own people to keep up the tradition. If you truly want to preserve our culture, then you *must* cement dimsum into the culinary landscape, you *must* win Paris."

◆

My Ringshuttle from Toronto slowed into London's station.

Our attendant stood from his seat. "London welcomes you to the newest station on the WorldRing international network. Passengers destined for Paris please remain seated, those visiting London, you may now remove your restraints."

Passengers from Toronto and New York City timidly unbuckled their harnesses and stood from their seats.

"You can't be serious," a passenger said. "It's only been an hour since we left New York."

The attendant smiled. "I assure you, we are in London. We reached a cruising speed of Mach three while crossing the Atlantic Ocean. However, with no reference point in the ocean's vastness, it's difficult to judge speed, and therefore time."

A set of fresh faces took the seats of those who departed in London. The attendant quickly checked harnesses and properly stored loose luggage.

"Thank you for traveling the WorldRing. May you enjoy this short trip from London to Paris. I will be with you the entire way. Please, feel free to ask questions, I know this is new for you all," he said before sealing the door with a decompression hiss.

Acceleration gently pressed me into my seat. London's yellow tunnel rings blurred by, becoming one constant hue. Yellow steel became gray concrete as we entered the ground and appeared transparent when we emerged from a granite cliff-side, just below a thrust of rock resembling a person's nose. The new passengers grew anxious as we plunged beneath chopping waves.

"Not to worry," the attendant said. "We submerge the Ring-lines below the surface to avoid complications with weather and tides."

A shadow in the distance quickly proved monstrous, its propellers churning the water above.

"What you see above is the hull of a super-container ship," he explained.

Heads twisted to glimpse the ship now out of sight behind us.

"We have now reached top speed. Please, prepare for deceleration."

Our chairs swiveled 180 degrees, and a three-minute deceleration commenced. We inclined at the French shoreline, broke above the water's surface, and lifted above the cliff.

"The divots in the earth and concrete rubble at the cliff edge are impact craters and broken bunkers from WWII, now reclaimed by grassland."

Countryside, castles, and small towns raced by. Then the towers of La Defense appeared in the distance.

"And there's Paris," the attendant said with a prideful look. "Vertical farm AeroTowers have filled the gaps between old commercial skyscrapers of La Defense. You can see several more AeroTower clusters in each of Paris's traditionally low-rise districts. All food required to sustain Paris now comes exclusively from within city limits, becoming the first metropolis to achieve self-sufficiency."

"Oh wow, like Havana," one passenger said.

"Yes, but on a much larger scale, supporting a much larger population."

But can they grow the produce I need? I thought.

♦

"Chinese broccoli doesn't exist here," Francis, my newly hired produce courier, said in rough French, his accent sounding East African, maybe. "Just use European broccoli like the other takeout places."

"*Takeout?* Is that what you think I'm doing?" I responded in rusty French-Canadian.

For reasons I could not fathom, this amused him. "Chinese food is all the same. *Fast* and *cheap*."

"I'll be the judge of that," I said coolly. "Are there *any* farms in Paris open to growing niche crops?"

He shrugged. "Maybe the roof gardens, but you can't afford them. Just use European broccoli. It's certified organic."

My anger boiled. "Let's say I *can* afford them. Who must I talk with?"

A smug look crossed Francis's face. "It's too expensive for *Chinese*. I'll give you the number for Ponte de Flandre's AeroTower. They can supply you with certified organic European broccoli."

He likes to say certified organic a lot! I thought, ready to explode.

That's because he's lying. None of this is organic, the bitter voice said.

I've seen the certification, I thought back.

Certification means little.

How do you know?

I can taste it. Which means you can too.

Francis gave a confused look. "Are you okay?"

Shit! Was I speaking aloud?

No. Check the green onions, the bitter voice said.

The onions appeared organic enough, but I felt oiliness when holding them. I sniffed, then took a nibble. There was a sweetness, almost like candy. I snapped my head to Francis. "You sneaky shit! This is covered in herbicide!"

"No! It's certified organic!" he said, producing his holotablet. "Look at the certification!"

"This is Glyco-Phospherus 72! Ring a bell!?" *How did I know the exact product?* "Get this shit out of my face! If you ever pull this again, I'll report you to OFRAC!"

His eyes narrowed, and his jaw clenched. "There must have been a mix-up." His voice became malice. "I'll bring the correct produce tonight."

"And find me some fucking Chinese broccoli!" I shouted.

Francis fumed, piled his crates onto his auto-truck, and sped off.

You could have done that with a bit more tact, the bitter voice said.

Francis will do exactly as I say now, I thought back, confident.

Oh, I doubt that.

◆

Francis did not return that evening as promised. Then Gabriel, my meat courier, missed his delivery. My calls went unanswered.

"What's going on?" Harold asked.

"I think we've been blacklisted," I said.

"By the purveyors? Can they do that?"

"Apparently so."

"What are we going to do? We open *tomorrow*."

I had invited every critic from Paris. There was no way to change the opening now. *But I have only half the ingredients.*

"I need to think," I said.

Harold got the hint, leaving me alone in the kitchen.

"What the hell do I do?" I whispered.

Cull the menu, said the bitter voice.

No shit! But what do I cull!? I snapped back.

You got us into this mess! You figure it out! the bitter voice spat and left.

Asshole, I thought.

He's not that bad, said the innocent voice.

I don't suppose you have any ideas, I thought.

You can make turnip cake, right?

Not without dried shrimp.

Please, don't use shrimp, it said.

I have to. Otherwise, it won't be authentic.

Why does it always have to be authentic?

To preserve Hong Kong's dimsum culture. We've gone over this.

But you can't do that with nothing at all, it said.

The voice is right, I realized. *Damn.*

♦

Jennifer Long cocked her head and made eye contact with me. I neared her table and saw her baskets were barely nibbled at.

"What's going on?" she said, pointing to the dumplings.

"Supply issues, I had to improvise," I whispered.

"This is not at *all* what I expected."

"Is it bad?" I asked.

She thought. "It's delicious in its own way, but not *authentic*."

"Once I fix the supply issues, I'll cook authentically."

Jennifer shook her head. "You opened with *this* style of dimsum. *This* is what will be written about. *This* is what people will read about. *This* will become your standard."

The next day, Harold set his holotablet on the table.

I looked up to see *"La Revue Culinaire,"* in its hologram. "Well, let's have it," I said, leaning back in my chair.

Harold flicked to the page. *"You Dimsum, You Lose Some, by Jennifer Long,"* translated to English on hologram. Harold nodded with every critique and grinned at the few positive remarks. Then he paused.

"What?" I said.

"—I would love to say Kat's Dimsum embodies the essence of what dimsum should be, brings a slice of home to those of us who cannot return, but I am obligated by the truth. Kat's Dimsum is not authentic." Harold stared at the hologram. "Jennifer doesn't know what she's talking about."

"No, she called it how it is," I said.

I thought I could live with that until I saw the disappointment in the eyes of Paris's local Chinese community, excited to finally have a taste of home. They smiled all the same, saying, "It's delicious." But little by little, they stopped coming.

♦

A vacuum-sealed head of broccoli with a note was at Kat's front door when I arrived one morning. I wanted nothing more than to throw it straight into the bin. Instead, I opened the note.

"It's certified organic. -Francis-"

We met after hours at the restaurant, just as my night cleaner arrived. He gave Francis a knowing glance before passing through the kitchen door.

"You two know each other?" I said, pointing at the kitchen.

"It's a small circle," Francis grumbled.

"Which kind of circle is *that*?"

He glared. "The barely escaped with our lives, kind!"

The Ethiopian Revolution, I realized. "That's been over for a year now."

His eyes narrowed. "It's just a ceasefire. Those don't last."

"So you'll never return home, then?"

He scoffed. "Did you try the broccoli or not!?"

"I did. It's certified organic, just as you promised," I said.

"Will you accept it?"

"No."

"Your loss." He made for the door.

"Francis!" I snapped. "Everything has been taken from my culture, just as it's being taken from yours! I understand what your people are going through!"

He turned, radiating malice. "You do not understand! You never lived through it!"

"No shit, Francis! But my parents escaped Hong Kong with nothing but the clothes on their backs, me in my mother's belly, and that damn cookbook!" I pointed furiously at the table it sat upon. "So I can very well empathize with your plight! Now, can you put yourself in my shoes for *one* second!? Imagine if, on top of everything else, they took *injera* from you too!"

His eyes widened like a frightened horse.

Hot tears rolled down my cheeks, and my hands trembled. "I *will* save my culture! With or without your help!"

Francis grunted, pulled out his holotablet, and flicked contact information my way. "There's your stupid Chinese broccoli."

♦

I held my breath as Francis unloaded his crates, afraid to break our fragile alliance. "How are the crops growing?" I asked.

"Sign here," he grumbled.

I replaced white onion with green onion and dried pork with dried shrimp, returning to the authenticity I promised.

"You fixed them… good," said a few regulars.

But I still needed Chinese broccoli. And from what Francis said about the rooftop gardens, that would be a significant expense.

I called his contact.

"Selami yihi Roberito newi, inideti liredahi ichilalehu?" a man answered, speaking Amharic or Oromo. I could not guess.

"Allo?" I responded in French. "Parles—"

"How did you get this number?" he interrupted, switching to French.

"Francis gave it to me."

"I don't know a Francis. You have the wrong number. Goodbye."

"W…wait!" I said.

I heard a woman in the background speaking the same mystery language.

"Oooh," the man said, then returned to our call. "Sorry, sorry, I *do* know a Francis. I'm Roberto. How can I help you?"

"Francis said you can grow specialty produce," I said.

Roberto brightened. "Yes! We own our roof and can give you a good price! Much cheaper than the AeroTowers!"

Cheaper than AeroTowers!? My anger with Francis ballooned.

◆

"You actually came!" Roberto greeted me through the lobby intercom of an old stone building. "Come up the stairs to the very top. Then knock two short, one long, three short, on the door and I'll let you in."

The stairwell held the scents of a hundred tenants come and gone, each floor unique. After several minutes of climbing, my thighs burning, I reached a rusty door at the top. I knocked the pattern. A deadbolt screeched, and the door slid open. Blinding sunlight hit me, but I discerned a short man's silhouette waving me forth. I stepped onto the roof.

The man gave me a curious look. "You're not French?"

"I'd think my name would give that away."

"I see, I see." He gave another curious look. "My wife says I should know these things." He abruptly extended a hand to shake. "I'm Roberto."

"It's a pleasure to meet you," I said, grasping his hand.

He shook furiously and a bit too long. "It's nice to meet you too, Miss Wong. Come, come, I'll show you around."

He led me through several patchwork gardens, multi-tiered hydroponics, and vertical conveyors built from mismatched metal. He casually pulled a winch, rotating a conveyor's next tier of crops to the top level. Despite his equipment appearing homemade, the produce grew brilliantly. We entered a greenhouse hosting young citrus trees floating in shallow pools, their roots entwined in foam acting as pontoons.

"Aquaponics!" Roberto declared, pointing at the trees. "AeroTowers think they're the only ones who can do it. But no, no, Aquaponics were invented by the Aztecs thousands of years ago. And look here!" He raced to tiers of cabbage with simple hoses at the soil. He squeezed, and water droplets appeared. "It's just like the ones from ancient China! That's your people! They invented this!"

What am I getting myself into? I thought.

This is delightful, said the innocent voice.

Aquaponics is not easy. Incredible, said the bitter voice.

But this garden is unlicensed, I thought back.

In the next greenhouse section stood a tall woman and young girl operating on seeds like surgeons, peeling back shells, slicing one in half, and combining it with another.

"Hon, this is Miss Wong," Roberto told the tall woman.

She ignored him, holding her breath and working her tweezers. A moment later, she looked up. "Hi, there," she said to me, then turned to Roberto. "You caught me in the middle of it."

"Sorry. I should know these things," he said.

"It's okay." She kissed his cheek, then turned to me and extended her hand. "It's an absolute pleasure to meet you, Dr. Wong. I'm a big fan of your work in genetics. Please, call me Sylvia."

With a sudden shift, Roberto made for the gardens outside, his attention captivated elsewhere. I shook Sylvia's hand, feeling like I finally met the brains of the operation.

"Sorry about Roberto," Sylvia said. "He's a wonderful man, but like a child sometimes."

"It's perfectly fine. I enjoyed the tour."

"He's very proud of his Aquaponics."

"I assumed that was your doing," I said.

"Oh no, Roberto's a bit aloof, but brilliant with his hands. He has that magic touch."

"That sounds annoying."

Sylvia grinned. "Very."

The little girl finished with her seeds and tugged her mother's hand.

"Yes," Sylvia said, kneeling to her daughter.

"I'm all done. Can I go play?" the girl whispered in perfect French.

"Make sure you put the seeds in the freezer," Sylvia said.

Memories of my mother flooded me. My stomach twisted.

The girl ran to the freezer, placed the seeds, and galloped to the gardens. Roberto looked up just as she jumped into his arms.

"How old is she?" I asked.

"She'll be six next month."

"It's amazing to see her splicing."

Sylvia gave a look. "You have no idea. My husband is a genius with his hands, can build anything, grow anything. I graduated valedictorian from Addis Ababa's Agriculture Institute of Technology. Now believe me when I say our daughter makes us look like idiots in comparison."

"Incredible. What school is she enrolled in?"

Sylvia frowned. "Dr. Wong. There is no school for Cecilia to attend. We work to scrape enough money to hire tutors. My brother, Francis, most of all, working for the AeroTowers under the table. Cecilia will make us all proud one day. She's going to seed Mars."

◆

Roberto and Sylvia silently watched as I nibbled the first harvest of Chinese broccoli.

My God, this is almost naturally grown, said the bitter voice.

"Only twelve credits a kilo?" I asked. "How much are the AeroTowers?"

"Fifteen," Sylvia answered.

"I'll match fifteen. No point in underselling yourself."

Roberto smiled, but Sylvia shook her head. "Our profits must remain minimal. We don't want to become a target of OFRAC. Take it at twelve or not at all," she said.

I nodded. "Twelve, it is."

◆

My Chinese broccoli dishes went to their tables later that week, the addition of green brilliant among a palette of brown, orange, and white.

"Finally!" someone shouted, and the other tables chuckled.

My morning regulars were finishing as a more tourist crowd trickled in. Among them was a small family dressed in their finest. It took me a moment to realize it was Roberto, Sylvia, and Cecilia. Roberto wore a blazer and bow tie that made his smile even goofier. He vigorously waved to me as Sylvia rolled her eyes. She wore a yellow dress that accentuated her height, and Cecilia wore a smaller version matching her mother, but bright blue.

I left the kitchen to meet them. "I'm glad you came," I said, showing them to a table.

"We had to see what you were cooking? Khasam said your food is saving Hong Kong," Roberto said.

"Who's Khasam?" I asked.

Sylvia frowned. "Khasam is Francis's real name."

As if waiting to be called, Francis entered wearing a light-blue blazer matching his niece's dress. He silently approached the table and sat.

"Nice to see you too, Francis," I said.

A spectrum of emotion crossed his face. He looked to Cecilia, which seemed to sway him. "It's nice to see you," he mumbled, opened the menu, and gave a disgusted look. "You eat feet?"

"Yes, chicken feet, they're delicious. Shall I prepare some?"

"Yeah, the feet!" Cecilia said, bouncing in her seat.

"Uh, no. *No* feet," Francis said.

Cecilia pouted until Harold set a teapot on the circular glass tray and spun it around.

"What do you suggest we order?" Sylvia asked.

I pointed to the menu's images. "Definitely the shrimp dumplings, barbecue pork buns, sticky rice in banana leaf, and pan-seared turnip cake. And you can always order more if that's not enough," I said.

"That sounds great!" Roberto said.

I added chicken feet to their order purely to see the look on Francis's face. When they arrived, he froze, grew red, and snapped his head toward me. Cecilia saw the feet and bounced in her chair.

I approached, restraining a grin. "Is everything okay?"

"I said *no* feet!" Francis grumbled. "We're not paying for this!"

Sylvia flinched, and I heard a thud from beneath the table. Francis grunted and his eyes went wide. But then, he glanced at Cecilia and reeled back his anger. He reached for a dumpling with his hand.

I pulled the basket from the table. "You will *not* eat with your hands in my restaurant."

His eyes bore into mine. "Can I have a fork?" he growled.

I smiled sweetly. "Over my dead body."

His face dropped, and Cecilia giggled. Francis again looked to his niece, weighing his level of anger. He slowly picked up his chopsticks, stabbed through a dumpling, and inserted it into his mouth.

"It's good," he reluctantly admitted.

"Uh-huh, real good," Cecilia said, easily using her chopsticks.

Only then did Francis smile, shedding his hard exterior.

"Uncle Francis?" Cecilia said.

"Yes, dear," Francis tenderly responded.

"Try the feet with me."

His smile vanished.

♦

A banging came from the front door as I closed down for the night.

What the hell? I locked the safe and peeked through the serving window to see Sylvia in her yellow dress, her arms stained red, and her palms smearing the door's glass. Cecilia was beside her, lost to hysterics.

I raced to let them in.

"Lock the door!" Sylvia shouted. "Turn off the lights!"

"What happened!?" I asked.

Sylvia brushed by me to the kitchen.

I quickly locked the door, shut off the lights, and joined them in the kitchen. I rinsed a towel under warm water and washed the blood from Sylvia's arms, searching for the cut, but she was not injured. *It's not hers.*

"What happened? Where's Roberto?" I asked.

Sylvia's face melted in pain. "They... killed him."

"Who's *they?*" I asked, but Sylvia was as manic as Cecilia. I shook her shoulders. "Who's *they!?*"

Sylvia whimpered, "OFRAC was waiting for us. Roberto went up first."

"Why would he go?"

"They come every month demanding money to ignore our garden. But there was yelling. Something heavy dropped to the street."

Thrown off the roof, I realized.

"He had a pulse. I tried to resuscitate, but his head was... open."

"Sylvia, we need to call—" I stopped, realizing OFRAC was a subdivision of the police.

Sylvia shook her head. "I'm sorry we came here. I didn't know where else to go."

"It's okay," I said, hugging Sylvia and Cecilia tightly, my mind racing.

The storefront glass suddenly shattered, and heavy footsteps entered the dining room. My heart leapt into my throat. Sylvia and Cecilia silenced as if they had practiced it a hundred times. I frantically motioned to the exit door to the back alley, but when we neared, the handle wiggled. I heard picking.

Come on, work the problem! I thought.

The deep fryer next to the kitchen door, said the bitter voice.

I tiptoed to its controls and switched it on high. Before long, I could smell burning oil.

Fill the mop bucket with—

I get the idea! I found a ladder, leaned it against the kitchen door, and set a water-filled bucket on the top step above the fryer. I then tied a rope around the wiggling door handle with the opposing end secured. I heard the lock click. The door lurched, but the rope caught.

An officer in black armor peered through the crack. "They're in the back!" he called, pulled a knife, and sawed at the rope.

The fryer's oil ignited in flame.

Sylvia and Cecilia sat frozen against the wall. I flipped a stainless steel prep table to its side and slid it against them.

"Crouch down!" I said.

Sylvia curled around Cecilia as I wrapped the blood-soaked towel over us, peeking my head above our table barrier.

The rope severed, and the exit door whipped open. Officers spilled in, fanning around us with rifles aimed. Their commander raised a hand, looking about to speak, when the dining room team came through the kitchen door, tipping the ladder and dumping the bucket of water into the deep fryer.

Deafening pops were followed by an eruption. I ducked as flaming oil covered the towel over us. I shrieked and threw the fireball off to see officers rolling on the floor engulfed.

"My eyes!" one cried. Desperately wiping the burning oil.

More officers rushed in, patting down comrades to find their own palms ablaze. I saw a black rectangle amid a wall of fire, like the entrance to hell. *Our salvation.*

"Move!" I shouted and pointed to the open exit door.

Sylvia stood, cradling Cecilia, and made for the door. Gunshots rang. Spurts of blood puffed from Sylvia's legs and torso like pink smoke. She dropped to a knee and turned, using her body to shield Cecilia from a second volley. Then, she slumped to the floor, motionless.

I ran to Cecilia, still wailing in her mother's arms, when something struck my leg and stomach. I dropped to the floor next to them. An officer approached with his shoulders on fire and eyes full of fury. He trained his pistol on my head.

A gunshot rang, but it was the officer who tipped to the floor.

A figure rushed through the open exit door wearing a desert-tan bulletproof vest and utility belt with holstered pistols. The butt of a rifle was pressed firmly to their shoulder. *Francis!* I realized. He strafed through the kitchen, shooting slugs, putting burning officers out of their misery.

"Get Cecilia out of here!" Francis hollered and crouched as a second squad entered from the dining room. He switched to fully automatic, sending two bursts through the kitchen door before flicking out the rifle's empty magazine.

"Fucking go!" he yelled, thrusting in a full magazine.

I tried climbing to my feet, but the pain in my stomach was paralyzing.

Let me deal with it! said the bitter voice.

The pain reduced like volume suddenly lowered. I inched towards Cecilia. She was no longer wailing but staring at her mother's body.

"Cecilia, you need to run," I calmly said, but she continued staring. "Cecilia!" I said louder with no response.

"Here they come!" Francis called as a heavy, metallic tumbling came into the kitchen. "Fuck! Cover her ears!"

I pressed Cecilia's head into my chest, covering her eyes and ears, just as the burst came, like the heart of a thunderclap. My ears pushed inward, and wetness filled my drums, sending a wild ringing through my head. Even with my eyes closed, my pupils felt fried. I pried open my lids to see Francis struggling to a knee. He opened fire as officers flooded through the kitchen door. Bullets impacted walls, thudded into Francis's bulletproof vest, and squished into his exposed limbs. His arm blew off at the elbow, but he did not seem to notice, drawing a pistol with the other. He nailed two officers in the head before I saw the back of his own skull burst open.

A single officer remained, bleeding from his leg with a quickness that screamed, *Artery.* He limped to Francis, shooting several more slugs. Then, he dropped to a knee, shaking his head, trying to stay conscious. We made eye contact, and he swung his pistol my way. I covered Cecilia as best I could as bullets drove into my back, hitting my vitals.

Hitting Mother's kidney.

The officer's eyes became vacant. He dropped his pistol, crumbled to the floor, and convulsed in a pool of red. Aside from the flame's flicker and roar, all was silent. I slowly raised my head to find Cecilia unharmed.

"You have to run… through the door," I whispered.

Cecilia stared blankly.

She's not going to run, said the bitter voice.

How do we get Cecilia out of this? I thought.

We make the jump, said the innocent one.

The jump? I don't understand.

I know, Kwai Lan. I'll take it from here.

I looked deeply into Cecilia's eyes. "Be strong, Pumpkin."

CHAPTER EIGHT

"Does the name Wong Kwai Lan mean anything to you?" Clara says, standing in Dr. Lee's doorway clutching Zion's paintings.

Dr. Lee swivels his chair, wearing an intrigued expression. "It does, actually. She's a legendary geneticist from before The Fall, rumored to have developed limb and organ regeneration. Something we've yet to rediscover. Why do you ask?"

Clara sets the paintings on the floor against the door frame. "Zion told me a story about her childhood and research in genetics. Then about her late career as a chef."

Dr. Lee humphs. "Kwai Lan devoted her life to her research. The chef thing sounds like one of Zion's confusions. As to her childhood?" He shrugs. "Another missing piece of history."

Clara reflects upon Zion's stories and how one influences the next. "What do you know about multiple personality disorder?"

Dr. Lee gives her a look. "That it's impossible."

"Why?"

"Personality is the result of synapses in the brain dictated by our DNA. And although injury, experience, or disease can have an effect on personality, there is still only one. What you're experiencing with Zion are misfiring synapses caused by his degradation disease."

"But, the last time we spoke you said his brain looks different depending on his mood. And that you had no idea why.”

“True, but I’ve been monitoring him during your sessions. When he tells those stories, his brain is normal.”

Clara eyes the live feed of Zion in his room, hovering above Dr. Lee’s desk. “What about reincarnation?”

“Clara, you’re tumbling down a rabbit hole. You must focus on discovering what tactics Zion used to bring the galaxy together.”

Clara glares. *“Don’t* tell me how to do my job. It requires a full investigation into all aspects of Zion, lunacy and all. Rest assured, when I have the entire picture of who he is, it *will* include how he stabilized the galaxy.”

“We don’t have the time. The Council wants answers *now.* You need to give them something, otherwise they’ll pull the plug on this.”

“I can navigate my way around the Council.”

Dr. Lee hesitates. “I’ve been getting incredible data during your sessions. You’ve stimulated his mind in ways we cannot. His degradation has actually paused. I would hate for this to end.”

And there’s his true motive, Clara thinks.

Dr. Lee’s holotile beeps. He sighs. “Zion wants tea, again.”

Clara catches Dr. Lee’s arm on his way to the break room. “Just put coffee in the teapot.”

A grin crosses his face.

Clara watches the holo-feed of Zion pacing back and forth. Moments later, Dr. Lee enters his room, holding a teapot wrapped in a towel and placing it on the table. Zion points accusingly at the teapot.

“What is that! I ordered coffee!” he says.

Dr. Lee lifts the teapot, and coffee pours from its spout.

Zion’s brain diagram goes berserk. Clara jolts back but finds it normal again. *Was it my imagination?* Her gaze returns to the live feed. Zion stands with arms crossed as Dr. Lee sets the coffee-filled teapot on the table.

“Get out of there,” Clara whispers.

Seconds after Dr. Lee exits, Zion snatches the teapot and chucks it, shattering the porcelain and splashing coffee across the wall. The brain diagram again goes haywire for a fraction of a second.

Dr. Lee returns triumphantly. But when their eyes meet, his smile drops. “What is it?”

Clara points at the diagram. “Zion’s brain did the thing. Twice.”

Dr. Lee replays the moments of wildness. Sweat appears on his brow.

"But you said it was interference between Zion's brain implant and his holotile?"

"Zion *lied*," Clara says. "Dr. Lee, I need to see that recording of him attacking you and the guards."

He opens a folder entitled *"Zion's Greatest Hits,"* but it's empty. "What the hell?" he mutters, restoring the folder to no avail. "I swear it was here yesterday."

Scrubbed thoroughly. Professionally, Clara knows.

♦

"So, what is cuisine again?" Lucius asks, following Aizen like a lost puppy past rows of old books.

Is he trying to make a fool of me again? "You forgot already? *Idiot*," Aizen quips, and kids at a table giggle.

"Quiet," says a librarian.

Aizen imagined having them laugh at Lucius would be satisfying for a change, but Lucius looks sad now. "They're expressions of one's culture," Aizen says.

Hurt still holds in Lucius's eyes. "What if you don't know where you come from?"

Aizen ponders his own heritage. *Dad was adopted at age five, a lost child of Mars. His lineage is a guess at best. Mom is an Ocol, but they're all over the place.* "If it makes you feel better, Lucius, I don't know where I come from either. I've always considered myself Titan."

"Does that mean Titan has its own cuisine?"

Everything's pulled from a catalog of a million digitally interpreted dishes. Nothing specific to Titan, Aizen realizes. "I don't think it does, actually."

"Shouldn't it though?"

"Yes, it absolutely should," he admits.

♦

Aizen returns home to find Mom scanning paintings into her holotile. One depicts waiters delivering baskets to tables, another has cooks pinching bags of dough, and a third is of an Earth-like cliff meeting ocean. All portray a woman with red lips.

Mom looks up with a smile. "Kip!"

"Kip!" Aizen responds. "What are you doing?"

"Zion made this for Jonathan." She points to the cliff painting. "Then he continued with the others."

For Dad? "Um, why?"

"I mentioned Jonathan was having trouble reaching London and Zion suggested using the WorldRing tunnels."

"Dad's already trying that."

"But he can't find their exact location. Zion painted this to show where the line from London to Paris enters the English cliffside."

"That could be anywhere along the coast," Aizen says.

Mom shrugs. "It's better than nothing."

"How would Zion even know that?"

She pauses. "He knows a lot about things no one should. It's partially why I'm sending this. If this helps find a WorldRing line, then Zion might know more about old Earth."

"Might he know where we come from, then?" Aizen asks.

"That's a good question. I've always considered us Titans."

"But we're all of different origins. Lucius says Titan doesn't even have its own cuisine."

"You're talking to Lucius? Isn't he your nemesis?" Mom gives a look.

"He's not much of a nemesis anymore."

She humphs. "Good for you."

"Do you think Zion knows what Titan cuisine is?"

"I would not be surprised if he did."

"...May I speak with him?" Aizen timidly asks.

Mom's look sharpens. "I do *not* want you in the same room with that man. He's not well."

"A holocall, then? *Please.*" Aizen senses turmoil in the scrunching of Mom's brow.

"Maybe," she says. "Don't you have to get ready for the interview?"

"Oh, yeah," Aizen says, sensing Mom's evasion.

◆

TWN anchor Celina Cobalt sits on a cushioned red chair, flipping through a notepad, searching for a factoid, perhaps. Aizen feels it's an act for the audience seated beyond a dozen cameras and blinding lights. A stage manager commences a countdown with his fingers. *"Five. Four. Three. Two..."* He gives a thumbs-up.

Holograms flash *"APPLAUSE."* The audience obeys.

Celine raises her hand, hushing them. "We are back with Aizen Ocol, the first *ever* human champion on Human versus Machine. Aizen, thank you for taking the time to speak with us. We are baffled by your triumph over the synths. How did you accomplish such a feat?"

Aizen stares at the blinding lights and then turns to Celine. She smiles friendly enough, but he senses urgency for a response. "I used cuisine."

"Yes, it's a cooking competition after all. It's all cuisine."

Aizen shakes his head. "Cuisine is a celebration of who we are, where we come from, what we believe in, and what connects us. I was speaking with a friend recently who made a good point about Titan cuisine."

"Oh, what point is that?" Celine excitedly says.

"We don't have one."

She appears confused. "How did this help you beat the machines?"

"The pineapples that rose from center stage were grown in old Brazil."

"Grown? Really?"

"Really," Aizen says. "When I discovered this, I searched for what other crops likely existed in that region during the twenty-second century. Once I had a small library, I imagined which tastes might compliment one another."

"But how do you know those dishes once existed?"

Aizen shrugs. "I kinda made them up. The reason I compare them to cuisine is because I pulled from that region to establish a theme. While my competitors had nearly identical creations, my dishes were unlike anything the judges ever tasted."

Celine thinks about that. "You say Titan has no cuisine, but there must be something."

"Maybe before our fields were monetized to grow synthesizer mix."

"That was a hundred years at most. The recipes must exist somewhere."

Aizen nods. "You would think so. But I've scoured the net and haven't found a single one. I can't shake the feeling that they've been erased. But I believe that with enough trial and error we can recreate the cuisines developed before The Fall!"

Awkward silence envelops the audience.

"Aizen," Celine cautiously says. "That information is lost forever."

His frustration grows. "No, it lives within *us*."

◆

Jonathan sits shotgun as their hover-skiff zips along the English coastline, dipping in and out of cliffside bends. Zach maintains a distance of fifteen meters as radar and X-ray map its topography and geology. Angela and Vincent furiously categorize portions of the rock into possible matches with Zion's painting from the back seats.

Jonathan again raises the scan Clara sent him on holotile and catches

Zach's sideways glance. They're all on edge, especially Zach, who has no faith in his direction and with a painting as their lead. Jonathan dares not tell them Zion is the artist. Instead, he said it was a relic from before The Fall recently scanned for the digital archives. *Still insane.* Except that the brushstrokes and hues appear almost identical to what Jonathan sees outside his window. They round another bend, and he notices a thrust of granite resembling a nose.

"Focus on that formation there," he says, pointing.

Angela and Vincent send X-rays to map the rock beneath the water and vegetation.

Angela turns to him. "It's a 98.47% match."

Zach sets the hover-skiff to hang a meter above the water.

"Angela, bring the radar gun," Jonathan says.

"You really think there's something this time?" she asks.

"Yes, I do."

Zach scoffs. "This is a waste of time. Just like the other thirty-four close matches. The other teams are making their way through London's dome while we play hide-and-seek."

"We're archaeologists, Zach. Hide-and-seek is our job," Jonathan responds. "The others are making the same mistakes as our predecessors."

"This is practically Paris," Zach says with disdain.

Jonathan gives a cold stare. "Yes, *practically*. Which means there *is* a chance. I believe *this* is the way."

Zach clenches his jaw. "Find another operator. I'm done after today."

"You can't leave now!" Jonathan says.

"Oh, watch me."

"Are you sure you want to do this?"

"I am, unless there's some *miracle*." Zach rolls his eyes.

"Fine!" Jonathan pulls on a baggy envisuit and hits the vacuum button, sucking it tightly to his body, and dons a helmet set to *gills*. "Angela, you coming!?"

She glances at Zach and slips on an envisuit.

"Suck up," Zach mumbles.

Jonathan points right at Zach. "Coward!"

Angela and Jonathan dive feet-first into the water and swim to their diving scooters. Jonathan kicks his scooter into high gear, pulling him into the water's depths.

"Jonathan," Angela calls on a private channel. "Don't listen to Zach. He won't really leave. He's just frustrated like the rest of us and doesn't know how to express it."

"I appreciate you defending him, but I think he's serious," Jonathan says and makes out the granite nose formation in the murky water.

"You shouldn't have called him a coward. He's sensitive."

"He shouldn't give it, if he can't take it." Jonathan points at the tip of the nose formation. "The WorldRing tunnel should be just below."

They flip on helmet lamps as the water grows dark and find a solid wall covered in seaweed where the tunnel entry should be.

"Shit, Zach may be right, after all," Jonathan whispers.

"Wait," Angela says, aims her radar gun, and sends a ping.

A schematic materializes across Jonathan's visor, confirming the cliffside to be solid granite formed millions of years ago. Then a cylindrical portion appears filled with newer granite like a bricked-up window.

"It's here! But blocked for several meters!" Angela says.

Zach calls in, his previous skepticism vanishing in a heartbeat. "I can remote drill a hole and place explosive! It should clear a path large enough to squeeze through!"

"Told you he was still with us," Angela says.

Angela and Jonathan return to the hover-skiff but remain in envisuits, ready to dive again.

Zach dons VR goggles and gloves as a scooter, outfitted with their Miskito drill, does the work below. With his legs splayed and holding a virtual drill at his hips, Zach sways back and forth like a rock ballad guitarist. He snakes explosives, removes his goggles, and turns to Jonathan. "It's set. Wanna do the honors?"

Jonathan shakes his head. "I'm squeezing as much work out of you as I can on your *last* day."

Zach frowns and pushes the button.

Stone and sediment blast from the drilled hole, clouding the water below. Once it settles, Jonathan and Angela dive. Visibility is zero. They rely purely on visors for guidance.

Angela finds the blasted hole and sends a ping.

"It's clear through!" she says.

Jonathan assesses the hole's varying widths. "I won't fit."

Angela fist-pumps. "The glory is mine!"

"Linking my display to yours. Be careful in there," he says.

"I will." Angela sets her scooter to its slowest speed, inching along, her lamp illuminating the jagged passage. "Damn, this is tight!" She emerges from the other end to an endless black hole and blows bubbles, following as they rise. They coalesce against a fuzzy curved surface, then stretch into one long linear bubble and slowly drift away. "It's soft, like algae." She pries at the fuzziness, uncovering smoothness beneath. "It's concrete!"

She gives another radar ping, and a perfectly cylindrical tunnel fifteen meters in diameter, continuing for several kilometers, materializes on visor.

"There's your miracle, Zach," Jonathan says.

At seven kilometers, the scan blurs.

"What happened?"

"That's where the tunnel rises above sea-level," Angela says. "We'll have to ping again once we reach that point. There's quite a bit of debris along the way. It's dense, like calcium, weird."

"We must prepare a proper expedition in the morning," Jonathan says.

♦

Jonathan, Angela, and Vincent wake with giddiness and vigorously eat their rations as Zach silently sits, giving longing glances to his former crew. Last-minute items are secured to their MULE sub, and they suit up. The moment Jonathan seals his helmet, Angela calls in.

"You're not seriously going to leave Zach behind!" she says.

"Yesterday was his last day. He said so himself."

"Don't be an *asshole*, Jon!"

Jonathan sighs deeply, grabs the last envisuit hanging on the wall, and approaches Zach. "You have *two minutes* before I change my mind." Jonathan has never seen a suit go on so quickly.

The four drop into the water, then lower the MULE. Zach commands their hover-skiff to land above the cliff.

"You ready?" Jonathan says and sees thumbs go up.

He sets his scooter to full, leading the way through the blasted hole they spent yesterday widening for the MULE. They enter the pitch-black tunnel and spread equally around its circumference, each of their headlamps illuminating a quarter of the surface as they descend.

"It's not in pristine condition like we expected," Vincent says, analyzing miniature impact craters. "These look like bullet holes."

Jonathan ponders this. "That may explain why the entry was blocked up. It would have made the perfect invasion point during The Fall."

"Could be the opposite," Zach says. "To keep London's population from escaping."

"Doesn't explain the calcium deposits," Angela says. "The first one is just ahead."

It fades into view, appearing like a bleached coral reef at first. But then, Jonathan recognizes a human aspect.

"Fucking hell..." he whispers.

Skulls, femurs, and rib cages. Tens of thousands of skeletal remains envelop them. Their scooters stir loose limbs, giving the illusion they are reaching out to grab them. Armored vehicles lay among the remains, so deteriorated they resemble cheesecloth.

"This is incredible," Vincent whispers.

Mid-afternoon, a long linear bubble appears at the top of the tunnel and lowers to midway its height.

Sea level, Jonathan knows.

"This is where the radar scattered," Angela says.

"What are the conditions above water?" Jonathan asks.

Zach remotely sends his scooter to the surface and extends a probe arm.

"Air temperature is quite cool," Vincent says.

"Of course, we're underground," Jonathan responds.

Vincent shakes his head. "The heat built-up within London's dome is estimated at five-hundred thirty-four degrees centigrade. If this tunnel is indeed connected to the city, then it should be similar."

Jonathan checks the reading. *"35 degrees."*

They establish Basecamp several kilometers beyond the tunnel's shoreline. Its inflatable dome, airlock, and cooling and atmosphere systems slowly rise into place. Compact cubes unfold into mattresses, a portable kitchen, and a waste incinerator. Then, they lay their many drones, designed to map the tunnels, across the floor for final calibration.

"What time is it?" Angela asks, her hands covered in drone grease. "I'm exhausted."

"Nearly five in the morning," Jonathan says. *The darkness is playing tricks with our circadian rhythms.* "We need to rest."

They try, but with the symphony of insects and animals they had grown accustomed to in London's jungle replaced with utter silence, the slightest movement or sniffle feels like an alarm.

Then, Zach begins to snore.

CHAPTER NINE

A recording greets Clara first thing in the morning. *From Jonathan? Why not call?* That familiar uneasiness in her stomach unfurls. *A recording means Jonathan is either inside London and communication is limited, or this is his last will and testament.* Thankfully, he predicted her frantic thoughts and entitled the recording, *"I'm Not Dead."*

Clara breathes a sigh of relief and opens the message. Jonathan materializes, looking tired and greasy. She recognizes the metallic material of Basecamp in the background.

"Kip!" Jonathan says and waits.

Clara gets the hint and plays along. "Kip."

"Geez, I thought you were going to leave me hanging," he says as if the recording is an actual call. "You look lovely today."

Clara inspects her sweatpants and runs her fingers through her disheveled hair. "Thanks, hon. You always know what to say."

"Why, thank you for noticing. I've been working out," Jonathan says, like Clara had returned the compliment.

Oops. The magic fades, and Jonathan, on recording, knows it too.

"Clara… We found the WorldRing tunnel. Zion was right," Jonathan says, appearing both excited and troubled. "We've explored sixty-five kilometers of tunnel, but there are dozens of branches to investigate. It's slow going, but the discoveries are incredible."

A second hologram of the tunnel entry below water appears projecting what looks like a coral reef.

"Skeletons," Clara mutters under her breath. A chill runs down her spine.

Jonathan takes a more serious tone. "I'm not certain how long it will take for us to reach London. I'll send another message in a few days with progress. I miss you. Kip!"

"Kip," she whispers as the recording dissolves. *Be careful...*

Clara showers, dresses, and makes her way to EarthRise Diner. She finds her booth and orders her usual eggs benedict but grimaces when it arrives. *Aizen's spoiled me.* She forces it down anyway and begins searching, *"Zion+Military, +Martial Arts, +Boxing, +Judo, +Jujitsu, +Ergonos, +Fighting."*

Nothing.

She inputs, *"Zion+Attacks,"* and several headlines appear.

Finally, she thinks.

"Zion Attacks Glurkin Trade Policies Calling Them Non-Conducive to Galactic Stability, Read More Here."

She flicks to the next headline.

"Zion Thwarts Attack Upon Archedian Duchess by Sniffing Out Kathazen Cyanide in Her Soup, Becomes First Non-Archedian to Receive Knighthood, Read More Here."

Clara rolls her eyes and flicks to the next.

"Zion Drafts Plan of Attack to Solve Zardonian Hunger, Receives Fourteenth Galactic Peace Prize, Read More Here."

She is about to give up when an alternate suggestion appears.

"Did You Mean Brown Pelicans on Enceladus?"

"No! I did not mean pelic—" People are staring, and Clara collects herself. *It's the second time this suggestion has come up,* she realizes. She inputs, *"Zion+Pelicans+Enceladus."*

One item appears.

"Zion Christens Opening of Pelican Wildlife Sanctuary on Enceladus, Read More Here, (Clearance Omega)."

Why is this Omega? she wonders.

The link leads to, *"Access Denied."*

When Clara refreshes, the headline disappears. *Real-time scrubbing,* she realizes, staring into the hologram. *Someone's hacked into my holotile.*

♦

"Mom, can you sign the permission form for my school trip to Mars?"

Clara sets her luggage on the bed and pulls out a new holotile. "Send it my way."

Aizen flicks it over, then says, "I thought you were staying home."

"I know. But I need to go to Enceladus for a few days." She signs the permission form and sends it back.

"Enceladus? What for?"

"To follow a lead."

"Is this related to Zion's biography?"

"Kinda, yeah."

"I wish you told me. I would have made you something for the trip," Aizen says, giving sad eyebrows.

"Don't even *think* about swindling me," Clara says. "I already asked Zion to discuss Titan cuisine with you."

"You did!?" Aizen smiles wide, and his eyebrows spring back up.

"He'll be contacting you tomorrow afternoon." She stows the last of her things. "Happy now?"

He nods. "Can I see you off?"

Mom grins. "Of course."

They descend Cobble Hill to the LightStation at its base, ignoring neighbors praising Aizen's performance on Human versus Machine. By the time they enter the tram, Aizen looks beyond annoyed.

"Fame sucks, doesn't it," Clara says as they take seats.

He raises his eyes. "You have no idea. Lucius and his goonies follow me around asking an endless string of questions. Even my teachers give me admiring looks."

"I can see how that's weird." Clara notices a girl about Aizen's age approaching with a holotile in hand and a cookbook on hologram. "Aizen, someone's coming to talk with you. Want me to send her away?"

"It's okay, Mom," Aizen says, stands from his seat, and politely greets the girl.

She smiles brightly. "I wasn't sure it was *actually* you, you look different without the chef hat."

Aizen blushes but does not miss a beat. "Oh, that? It felt like a giant sock on my head."

She laughs and shows him the cookbook she is reading. Aizen seems genuinely interested. He even signs it.

"It's a pleasure meeting you," he says and goes to shake hands.

She hugs him instead, takes a holopic, and dashes back to a group of girls, giggling.

Stunned, Aizen slowly sits.

"Fame's not all that bad," Clara says.

"She was nice," Aizen says, glancing in the girl's direction.

She bashfully smiles back.

"Was the book interesting?" Clara asks.

"I've read it before. It's all right."

Clara glances at the girl. "She's cute. What's her name?"

Aizen scrunches his brow.

"You didn't get her name?"

He shakes his head.

Clara sighs. "Maybe you should go ask for her name." *Aizen's just as clueless as his father,* she thinks.

♦

A siren cuts through Jonathan's dream. He rolls to his side, using a pillow to cover his head. But when his brain registers the emergency, he leaps to his feet.

"Seventy-four, seventy-five degrees!" Vincent hollers. "This is a heat draft! We have less than three minutes!"

They pull envisuits over pajamas, push vacuum buttons, and don helmets set for smoke filtration, gas reconfiguration, and temperature control.

Zach furiously sets Basecamp to blast mode. The dome becomes aerodynamic toward the incoming draft, and they crouch as the ceiling lowers. Zach anchors its cleats into the concrete tunnel floor and turns to Jonathan, worry in his eyes.

"We're going to be okay, Zach. But I need you at your best," Jonathan says. "If temperature rises above shell tolerances, what do we do?"

"Set the air recyclers into overdrive," Zach answers.

Jonathan knows that will burn out the air-handling unit, marking the expedition's end. But it is better than death. "And if that is not enough?"

"Purge water supply into shell inter-layer."

"And if *that* is not enough?"

"Hope and pray," Zach says.

"No! Get inside the MULE!" Jonathan sees the look on Zach's face. *The MULE is back at the waterline.* Jonathan's thoughts go to Clara and Aizen. There is so much he wants to tell them, so many things he wishes he had done differently. *I must put my thoughts on hold!* "Let's go!"

They pile into the airlock and purge oxygen. Basecamp's metallic skin ripples like a flag in a gale-force wind as the heat draft intensifies. They brace their hands against the sides to stay upright.

"Heat is 564 degrees!" Vincent calls.

Jonathan turns to Zach.

"Air recycler in overdrive! No effect!" Zach says, working furiously on his visor. "Routing water supply!"

Basecamp's skin calms as water fills the inter-layer, then puffs like a balloon as water becomes steam. It bursts.

"Heat is still rising!" Vincent calls.

The silver skin melts to dark brown and ignites.

"What do we do, Zach!?" Jonathan says.

Zach raises his head. "Hold tight!"

Basecamp lurches, tumbling them to the floor like a rug pulled from under their feet. Jonathan struggles to regain his footing and peers through the airlock window. He realizes they are caught in the heat draft and cruising down the tunnel like a bullet through a barrel. *Zach unscrewed the anchors? Why?* Jonathan realizes the seawater at the tunnel entrance is still cool. "Prepare for contact with the water! The moment we do, open the doors and dive!"

Steam engulfs them.

"One more kilometer!" Angela says.

"Heat has peaked at 982 degrees centigrade!" Vincent calls.

Far above Basecamp's limit, Jonathan knows. His suit presses around his body. *Zach must have over-pressurized the airlock to ensure the door blasts open instead of holding closed.* "Lay on the floor! Feet towards the door!"

They lie waiting, like sardines in a can, watching the airlock door bubble and warp with the heat.

"At the water!" Angela confirms.

"Set helmets to *gills* and hold your breath until beneath the surface! Zach, the door!" Jonathan says.

They shoot from the airlock, skipping across the water like stones across a pond, side by side. Each contact with the water feels like a baseball bat against Jonathan's butt and feet. The others pull ahead of him. *I'm the heaviest,* he realizes. Their formation becomes a diagram of weight. Zach is the next heaviest. Vincent and Angela skip out of view.

Jonathan's foot is caught by the water's surface, tumbling him end over end like a pinwheel. Pain lances through his shoulders and hips until he settles below the surface. The helmet's gills hum as they suck in seawater and separate oxygen. Jonathan takes a deep breath. *I must check on the others!* But when he raises a hand to access his visor display, fire shoots through his shoulder. "Fuck!" He tries the other arm, but it is the same. "Voice activation!"

"Voice command system initialized, ready to assist," spreads on visor.

"Medical report."

"Severe contusions to gluteus maximus, rectum and genitals. Fractured metatarsals in both feet. Both shoulders dislocated. Adrenaline high, heart rate elevated, cholesterol level good, vitamin C intake optimal, vitamin D intake..."

"End medical. Team status."

"Angela Mendez, unconscious, breathing, heart rate returning to normal. Vincent Hong, conscious, conducting medical report. Zachariah Cordon, cardiac arrest, suit administering CPR..."

Shit! Jonathan thinks. "Reset shoulders!" he orders but forgets to administer local painkillers first. He shrieks as the suit pulls, his left shoulder crunching back into place, followed by his right. "Administer painkillers!"

The needles prick, and the pain dulls.

"Locate dive scooters," he says after several deep breaths. His visor displays them at the shoreline, still operational. "Bring them to each of our positions."

It takes a good ten minutes for them to reach Jonathan. His scooter slows as the others race ahead. He grasps the handles as best he can and prepares for the pain.

"Bring me to Zach!"

Vincent is already there when Jonathan arrives.

"The suit got his heart going again, but he's in critical condition," Vincent says, pointing to Zach's limbs kinking ninety degrees midway through his forearms and shins. "He's bleeding bad. There's only so much the suit can do. We must get him to help."

He must have pinwheeled against the tunnel wall, Jonathan guesses. "I'll stay behind with Angela."

Vincent straps Zach to his scooter. "I'll return after dropping him off at headquarters."

"Understood. Good luck," Jonathan says. "Suit, take me to Angela," he commands and grits his teeth.

Where sea level meets the tunnel ceiling, dark streaks continue along the concrete underwater for several meters. Jonathan finds Angela motionless. Polymer plates protecting her hands, knees, and feet are nearly worn through. Jonathan envisions her pressing them against the ceiling to slow herself. Her helmet is sanded down to the gills. Dread fills him.

"Status on Angela's air," he commands.

"CO2 is escalating. She requires oxygen immediately."

"Can I umbilical my helmet to hers?"

"Umbilical is possible if intake has not been compromised."

"Where's the intake?"

"Just below the gills."

It's sanded right up to the umbilical, Jonathan realizes. He pulls the cord from Angela's helmet and one from his and locks them together.

"How's the seal?"

"Thirty-two percent of oxygen will be lost in the transfer."

"Can we boost output from my gills to compensate?"

"Yes, but you cannot do so indefinitely."

"How much time will we have?"

"Approximately two hours forty-seven minutes."

"How long to exit the tunnel?"

"At full-speed, approximately two hours and forty-three minutes."

"Do it!" he says. His helmet vibrates as its gills go into overdrive, and a countdown appears on visor. He tandems the two scooters, strapping Angela around himself, and lashes his hands tight to the handles. He then prepares for the most excruciating pain of his life.

♦

Aizen sits at his desk with his stomach in knots, staring at his holotile, waiting for Zion's call. He checks the time, *"14:57,"* and has done so every few seconds for the past ten minutes, convinced that if his attention strays for just a moment, Zion will call, Aizen will miss it, and he will never have this opportunity again.

At 14:59, Aizen's holotile beeps.

Zion's face materializes on hologram, looking thin and frail. *Mom said he was not well. But what happened?* Aizen thinks. Nevertheless, he recognizes strength in Zion's posture and grace in his mannerisms.

After a moment of silence, Zion grins. "Aizen Ocol, it's a pleasure to meet you."

A pleasure to meet me? Aizen realizes that he is staring. "It's an honor to meet you, Your Excellency."

Zion makes a face. "Please, call me Zion. Nobody's called me *Excellency* since... well, since I left office."

"Yes, Mr. Zion, leader, sir," Aizen says, feeling foolish. Mom warned that Zion is a master of directing conversation, but she never mentioned how intimidating he is. Not with aggression but omniscience.

"I suppose *Mr. Zion, leader, sir* will have to do," Zion says, leaning back in his chair and sipping from a teacup. "I saw your performance on Human versus Machine. You did well."

"Thank you, Zion," Aizen says.

"You were immediately drawn to the pineapples at center stage. You could sense something different about them, couldn't you."

Aizen nods. "They were so imperfect that they felt perfect." *What on Titan did I say?*

Zion's eyes widen. "Well said, well said indeed! This is fundamental to quality food. Nature has spent millions of years perfecting its ecology for an entire ecosystem that includes humans. We were never meant to invent agriculture. Archaeologists have even found our hunter-gatherer ancestors were far healthier than most humans today. Nevertheless, we domesticated these wild species because of a sudden dip in Earth temperature around 20,000BC. Since then, we slowly altered them to become what we perceive as perfectly human. But therein lies a conundrum, the more we genetically modify, the more we tailor food to be human, the less nutrient rich and delicious they are. Truth is, people evolved to both enjoy and be nourished by food's natural state. One can say synthesizers create perfect human food. But is what they create wonderful?"

Aizen soaks it all in. "They're perfectly boring."

Zion laughs. "Are you familiar with the term *Wabi Sabi?*"

Aizen shakes his head.

"It's from ancient Japanese meaning *to find beauty within imperfection.*"

"That sounds wonderful. I didn't know a term like that existed." Aizen feels like he is finally loosening up.

"Unfortunately, most ancient terms were lost with the creation of Interspeak after The Fall." Zion pauses.

Aizen seizes the opportunity to steer the conversation. "Cuisine has also been lost. Something happened where it's become simply a fuel source instead of cultural heritage. I've been wondering about Titan cuisine and which Earth cultures it comes from."

Zion thinks about this longer than Aizen expects. "The first to settle Titan were from France, Ethiopia, and the United States. Have you heard of these ancient countries?"

"Not Ethiopia," Aizen says.

"Really? That country is very important, especially for you."

"For me? Why is that?"

"You descend from its people."

"How do you know that?"

"Your last name, *Ocol,* is of Ethiopian heritage. The country once resided in East Africa and, because of its near equatorial location, constructed Earth's first space elevator, becoming a dominant economic center when humanity expanded into System Sol."

Aizen processes. *Nobody in the galaxy can possibly know this.* He dashes *Record* on his holotile. "Is there a specific cuisine from Ethiopia?"

"Oh yes, a very good one, too. It's called injera and involves one of the most important grains to ever exist, *teff.* Descendants of this grain are still used today as the base protein in synthesizer mix. Traditionally, it was used to create a fermented flatbread, on top of which varying mixes of vegetables, meats, and spices local to Ethiopia were placed. It even became the national cuisine of Mars when they declared independence."

"Ethiopians settled Mars, too?" Aizen asks.

"Ethiopian culture and cuisine was quite prolific because of a very important person who harnessed the unique properties of teff. Her name was Sha Tolera, the foremost agricultural engineer during The Great Expansion..."

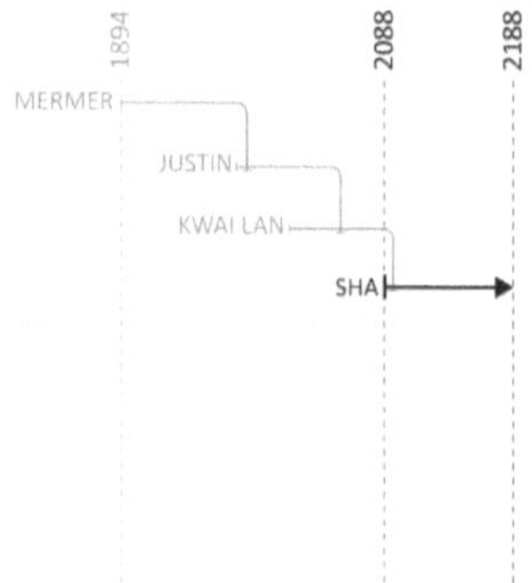

SHA's TALE

Earth / Mars: 2088 – 2188

I did not know how I came into the system, but ever since I was a little girl, my destiny was to turn Mars into a garden of Eden. But first, I had to survive the streets of Paris. Luckily, I had the help of three imaginary friends. But before we unpack *that* nugget of information, I would like to tell you about my name.

My real name is Sha Tolera. I have had others along the way, but this one was given to me at birth and used at my death. *Bookends of my life, I guess.* My parents gave me this name because it sounded nice in both Hindi and Oromo, though the name itself had no origin.

Or so I thought.

♦

Ethiopian Highlands

"Please, I must know. How did they meet?" I asked, desperate to learn anything regarding my parents.

My Aunt Nobi grinned. "Your father, Abed Petal, immigrated to Ethiopia in 2074 to teach at Addis Ababa's Agriculture Institute of Technology. There, he met an incredible student, your mother, Masani Tolera."

"She was his student?" I asked.

"They were certainly an unexpected pair," Nobi said. "Masani was tall and severe, commanding the rooms she walked into, and your father was short and goofy, often overlooked. Masani would debate everything Abed would teach causing him to become so frustrated he often asked her to leave his class. But would you know it, their debates turned into discussions outside of the institute, which became ideas, and then developed into legitimate projects. All their time was spent together, laughing, arguing, and innovating. Thinking back, it was no surprise when Masani asked for Abed's hand in marriage after graduation."

"Incredible," I said, remembering how opposite they were.

"That was a beautiful moment in a difficult time," Aunt Nobi said with a sweet smile.

"Difficult how?" I ventured.

Nobi's smile dwindled. "Foreign metacorporations flooded our lands soon after, hungry for our tantalite deposits. Their quota obsessed CEO's pushed local farmers into hard labor, and turned our villages into company camps. And what choice did we have?"

"I'm guessing none," I said.

"That's what the world thought, too," Nobi said. "But just when Ethiopia appeared doomed, our government enacted brilliance, passing the Equal Education Bill, one ensuring every citizen received a university education. In women, they particularly invested. Our country went into massive debt, but the resulting education boom was a thing of beauty. Millions of Ethiopian women flooded universities both locally and abroad." She paused. "Your mother was among them and, despite being your father's student, she was actually his elder. After Masani's graduation, they moved to the farm to help your uncles Sonam and Khasam and myself stay afloat as the metacorporations encroached upon our fields."

"How did you survive?" I asked, looking across the lush teff fields.

"Something unexpected happened," Nobi said. "Small Ethiopian-owned mining ventures emerged, re-mining deposits considered exhausted by the metacorporations, tapping into generations of knowledge, and finding tantalite in unforeseen locations. They muscled into the economy, reclaimed those company camps, and plastered the horrific living conditions across the news. The metacorporations were hit with a disparity tax. Then, the Ethiopian government instated its Industrial Buyback Program, forcing foreign corporations who fell below a set profit margin to sell shares to local Ethiopian ventures. But we should have known not to kick the beehive, for when the metacorporations grew desperate, they banded together to declare Corporate Law upon our country."

"The Ethiopian Revolution," I whispered.

Nobi's eyes blazed. "But they once again misjudged us! Believed we were still poor and uneducated! They were not prepared for Ethiopia's mighty roar!" She raised her fists to the sky.

I soaked it all in, but a question lingered. "How'd I get to Paris?"

Aunt Nobi's eyes settled on me. "What a year for you to be born, deep in the belly of a cargo ship in the Red Sea, fleeing the bloodshed. On that ship, you were named Sha. But once landing on Italy's heel, you became Cecilia. Your mother became Sylvia. Your father became Roberto. And your uncle Khasam became Francis. For five years, you trekked across Europe until settling in Paris, just in time for its Agricultural Renaissance."

♦

Paris, France

Mother, Father, Uncle Francis, and I stood on an empty rooftop, imagining how to fabricate equipment, what crops we should grow, and if we could generate enough income to survive.

"How'd you find this place?" Uncle Francis asked.

"I followed my instincts," Father said, grinning.

"It's above a hospice, no other farmer will touch it," Mother responded. "The landlord is desperate."

"Just imagine the passing of souls will enrich our soil," Father said.

Even at five years old, I cringed.

"There's no denying the price," Uncle Francis grumbled. "But how do we break into Paris's produce market?"

"We focus on niche crops, ones the AeroTowers consider unprofitable," Mother said.

Uncle Francis ground his jaw. "We won't find another opportunity like this. We should take it."

We fabricated equipment from scraps, developed topsoil from compost, and established a personal seed bank. We lived in a section of greenhouse hosting three beds, a small kitchenette, and a washroom. It was tiny and partially open to the elements. But where most children had a living room to play in, I had a garden of Eden. I remembered running among flowering crops, helping father tend seedlings, mother splice seeds, and grumpy Uncle Francis catalog produce for delivery. But we had to be careful, for we were asylum seekers, *sort of.*

"It will cost us our life savings," I overheard Uncle Francis say. "But OFRAC will allow us to live and grow here so long as we don't raise a red flag by making too much profit and give them a monthly cut at the same time. It'll be tight, but we can make it." Uncle Francis paused. "Sadly, Cecilia cannot attend school without being discovered. If that happens, we'll be deported into a war zone."

"But she *needs* an education," Mother defiantly said.

"I have an idea," Father said. "A few professors I worked with in Addis Ababa now work here in Paris. Maybe they can help."

Professors would visit our rooftop a few evenings a week, marveling at the produce growing strong despite our shabby equipment. They taught me English, French, math, and history as often as possible, initially simplifying their lessons but soon giving me their full university courses.

"She's brilliant. I've never seen anything like this," Aurelien Giraud, my mathematics professor, told my parents. "Are you certain she's never had schooling before?"

"No. Nothing," Mother said in choppy French.

"I believe Cecilia might have a real chance of being selected for the Eden mission to Mars scheduled for 2109. They will have a particular need for young agricultural engineers. She will be the perfect age by then."

"You can't be serious," Mother scoffed.

I bounced excitedly at the thought and talked nonstop for the next month about Mars's gravity, atmosphere, soil, and ice caps, imagining using all those resources to create a garden just as beautiful as our rooftop.

"Cecelia, is this something you truly want?" Mother asked me.

I nodded with vigor.

"Do you understand what this means?"

"Yep!" I said.

"I still think its ridiculous," Uncle Francis said.

Father shook his head. "She needs a dream to pursue. Even if Mars doesn't work out, the skills she'll learn will be invaluable. It's a good idea."

Aurelien introduced me to his partner, Professor Alejandra Korda, an astronautical engineer and physicist. She sat next to me, opening a hologram of planets orbiting a sun, with calculations appearing next to each.

"What do you think about System Sol's planets?" she said.

I smiled. "Mars is my favorite!"

"Mine, too, but Mars is *very* far away."

"Thirteen months, four days away," I said.

"That's a good assumption, but the distances change depending on its proximity to Earth. For example if we left Earth today..." Professor Korda put the date into the equation next to Mars and let the holotile do the calculations. "...It will take thirteen months, four d—" She snapped her head to me. "How did you know!?"

I shrugged and pointed at the equation.

"Cecelia, these equations require quantum computation," my professor said, looking lost. "How did you do that?"

"It's easy," I said and pointed at Venus. "Nine months, fourteen days."

Professor Korda ran the equation on her holotile. She covered her mouth and whispered, "Oh my god."

◆

A lady came to our rooftop interested in the seeds we were splicing. Mother was so excited to talk with her, spending hours bantering back and forth, their laughter echoing from the greenhouse. Uncle Francis would often shake his head and leave. Father would try to join their conversations but was unable to keep up. One thing I knew for certain. *This lady is smart.*

"Where are we going?" I asked as Mother slipped a new blue dress over my head.

"Remember that nice lady? We're going to her restaurant for dinner."

"But you said not to go to new places."

"I know Cecilia, but Kwai Lan is a friend. We'll be okay."

I remember the chicken feet, how they looked gross but tasted delicious, and how hilarious it was to watch Uncle Francis try them.

The next thing I knew, I was running faster than I thought possible, tears streaming down my cheeks and my throat raw. I stopped in a sunny park with people smiling and laughing. It was morning. *Where had all the time gone?* I regained control of my legs. Pain registered in my feet. I had been wearing sandals at the restaurant. Now, I was barefoot, and my soles were bleeding. My once beautiful blue dress had singed at its frills and was speckled with dark and crusty... *blood?* I was not sure. My nose was aflame, smoke the only scent I could discern.

I searched for Mother and Father and Uncle Francis. Several strangers approached, giving pitiful looks, and I ran, just as Mother taught me to, crying out as pebbles embedded into my raw feet. I found a secluded spot beneath a bowing tree and sat on the cool grass.

"We need to get her someplace safe," said a friendly voice, so close.

I lifted my head. No one was there.

"But where do we take her," said another voice, feminine yet strong.

"Shut up you two!" said a third, grumpy voice. "I think she can hear us."

I caught a thin silhouette barely distinguishable from the surrounding air. It turned its shoulders.

"Can you hear us?" it bitterly said, reminding me of Uncle Francis.

The moment I thought this, the figure became more visible, and its features defined, becoming my uncle. But this impostor was not him. *I am no fool.* But to answer fake Francis, I nodded.

"God dammit!" he said, further resembling my uncle.

"Watch your language! She just said she can hear us," said the feminine, strong voice.

Her outline became visible, too, taking the form of my mother. She looked almost real. Almost solid. I desperately wanted to hold her hand and reached out, but it passed right through.

"Pumpkin? Can you *see* us?" she said in disbelief.

Something happened to my mother and uncle. I knew it in my soul. "Is Papa gone, too?" I said, sobbing.

The friendly voice spoke. "I'm afraid he is, I'm so sorry."

"Don't tell her that, you idiot!" said fake Francis.

The friendly voice took the form of my father.

And these were my three imaginary friends. I did not know where they came from, but they stayed by my side ever since with a decided interest in my well-being. But they annoyed me to no end like it was their job. *Like right now.* I gave fake Francis a glare. I called him *Jerkface*, which was quite fitting, let me tell you.

"Come on, you didn't have to say that," Jerkface said.

"You get what you deserve!" I responded. I liked to imagine him wearing funny clothing. That day, I chose a bright pink suit with a green bow tie and snakeskin boots.

Jerkface looked at himself. "You can't be serious."

"Now you really look like a jerk!" fake father said and laughed.

I called him *Papa* because he truly reminded me of my father. I imagined him wearing a secret agent tuxedo.

Then, there was my third imaginary friend taking the form of my mother, but she often looked like the lady from the restaurant. I don't know how, but she could control her image. She called me, "Pumpkin." *I'm not a fruit. I don't get it.* But it made her happy to say it. *Whatever.* I called her *Susan* because I always liked the name.

With Susan's help, I found Professor Giraud's address.

He lived in a strange housing development just outside Paris. The homes were skinny and vertical, three stories tall, with front doors and ground floor windows facing the street.

I was too shy to knock and peered through the window, instead. A familiar woman in a form-fitting dress sat swirling a glass of wine on a sofa. *Professor Korda!* I realized. Aurelien entered the room, setting a board of cheese and meat on the coffee table, then he leaned into Professor Korda, gently kissing her. Their bodies melted together, and they rolled back into the cushions. As Alejandra set her glass on a side table, her eyes met mine.

"Oh my god! Cecilia!?" She pushed Aurelien off and made for the door.

♦

"Where are your parents?" Alejandra again asked, scrubbing filth from my back with a warm cloth.

"Gone," I whispered.

"Where did they go?"

I shrugged.

She sighed and lifted my hair to wash my neck. "Is that gum?" She looked closer. "That's gum. What have you been eating?"

"Street food."

She gave a concerned look. "What do you mean by *street* food?"

"The people who sell in the park gave me some."

"That's smart of you," Alejandra said. "How did you find Aurelien's address? How did you get here?"

"I used a computer at the library to find his address and a bus. The driver said I didn't have to pay."

"You never cease to amaze, Cecilia," she said, looking sadly at my hair. "We're going to have to cut this. I'm sorry."

"It's okay," I quietly said, wrapping my arms around my knees and curling into a ball. I sobbed as strands fell to the floor until a lump of hair-tangled gum landed with a thud, and I laughed for half a second.

Alejandra found a pair of Aurelien's shorts, a binder clip to cinch the waist, a white T-shirt that fit me like a dress, and a flowery tie for a belt.

"Isn't that better?" she said, handing me a mirror.

The white T-shirt and flowery tie reminded me of a dress my mother once wore. I began to cry.

"Cecilia. What's the last thing you remember of your parents?" Aurelien asked when I calmed down.

I sniffed. "We were having dinner at a Chinese restaurant," I squeaked.

They looked at each other, dread upon their faces.

"Aurelien, you think it's… what we heard on the news?" Alejandra said.

He slowly nodded and knelt to me. "Cecilia, you will have to stay with us from now on. Do you understand?"

My lip quivered. "Yes."

♦

"Where did Professor Korda go?" I asked. "Will she come back?"

"Yes, she will *absolutely* come back," Aurelien said.

"Promise?"

"I promise."

And she did. We sat at the dining table, and Professor Korda placed her holotile in front of me.

"Cecilia. You're probably wondering where I've been these past two weeks," she said.

I nodded.

"I used to teach at Ghana University several years ago and went back to find something that will help you live with us." She raised an image of a little girl on holotile. "This girl's name was Maria Dhaka. Her family went missing."

"Like mine?" I whispered.

"Yes. But Maria has been missing, too... For a year now." She sighed deeply. "Her father was originally from Ghana and her mother from Ecuador." Professor Korda's voice started shaking. "D...don't you look just like her?"

I looked past my professors to see the ghostly apparitions of Papa, Jerkface, and Susan calmly listening.

"You *do* look just like her," Susan whispered.

I looked at the image again. "Yeah," I said.

"This is Maria's birth certificate." She opened it. "We added Korda to the last name."

"Like yours?" I asked.

"Yes. Cecilia, we have to change your name."

I looked down. "Cecilia is not my name..."

My professor cocked her head. "What's your name, then?"

"Sha Tolera."

"Why was it changed?"

"Mommy said it was not a safe name," I said.

"I see. I'm sorry to say that Cecilia is no longer a safe name either. Please, repeat after me. My name is Maria Dhaka-Korda."

"My name is Maria Dhaka-Korda," I whispered.

◆

"Can anyone tell me which planet in System Sol is closest to Earth?" Professor Couture said to his Advanced Placement Astrodynamics class. Typically a university course, enough lycée students tested advanced, and now a group of sixteen-year-old brats had a class of their own.

"Mars!" Dillon shouted.

"Wrong!" Professor Couture snapped with his blunt, Usonian accent. "If you're going to be an arrogant ass, be correct!"

Dillon's face dropped. "You can't talk to us like that."

The Professor glared. "I'm an astronaut! I've been to Luna, Venus, Mars, Phobos, Deimos and Ceres, and was the first person to ever set foot on Mercury. I am not your babysitter! If you cannot handle me and this course, then leave. That goes for *all* of you!"

Dillon stared, stunned. His face flushed red, but he stayed in his seat.

"Glad to see you're not a bunch of wimps." Couture waved his hand, and a hologram of System Sol materialized on the back wall. To the left was the sun, with planets Mercury through Neptune appearing sequentially at their astronautical units. "I ask again, what is the closest planet to Earth?"

"Venus!" Dillon said, sure of himself.

"Wrong!" Couture said, amused. "It's not too late to leave."

Dillon was getting all in a huff.

"Mercury," I said flatly.

The students laughed.

"Correct!" Couture said.

Their laughter ceased like someone dashing *Mute*.

"Can anyone tell me why?" He searched our faces, resting on mine.

I sighed. "This diagram depicts the distance of planets from the *sun*, not from each other. You must consider each planet's varying distances as they orbit and that any space vessel, no matter how fast, must travel elliptically around the sun. When you do this, Mercury, on average, is the closest planet to Earth."

"Correct." The diagram became a top view of their orbits. "Can anyone tell me what the closest planet to Mars is?" The room was silent. Couture's eyes again found me.

"Mercury," I said.

"Correct! What about Jupiter?"

"Mercury?" Heloise said.

"Yes! Saturn?"

"Mercury!" Dillon said with full confidence.

"Wrong!" Couture said, and Dillon's face dropped. "A joke. It's indeed Mercury. What does this mean, Dillon?"

"Mercury is the closest planet to every other planet in System Sol?"

"Welcome to the class," Couture said with a sarcasm Dillon could only dream of. "Why is this important?"

Hyun raised his hand. "Being almost geo-locked and so close to the sun, Mercury has limitless solar energy."

"What else?"

"They can develop powerful laser propulsion technology?"

"Yes, but what else?"

"It's the most logistically strategic position in the system," I said.

"Right!" Orbital trajectories appeared on hologram. "A launch from Earth to Mars, averages eleven months. However, a launch from Mercury to Mars, with comparable technology, averages seven, granting the future Hermians the inherent ability to outpace any ship in transit. Meanwhile, they will also enjoy the highest frequency of launch windows. Such an advantage, coupled with near limitless energy, means whoever is brave enough to settle Mercury will control all of System Sol."

"But it doesn't have water!" Dillon blurted.

Couture's eyes twinkled. "It has ice in its north pole crater, I've seen it myself. But it's not enough to sustain a large population and food production. One could say Mercury does not have a true water source. However, what nearby planet, besides Earth, has a massive amount of water just waiting to be harvested?"

"Ceres," I said, realizing the lesson's true purpose.

"What does Ceres also have?" he asked.

"The asteroid belt. A near limitless supply of rare earth metals," I said. "Whoever colonizes Ceres will have control of nuclear power."

"Yes." Professor Couture let that sink in. "*Two* centers of unprecedented power. *One* source of water... What could *possibly* go wrong?"

◆

"Money only goes so far," a mercenary in handcuffs said on hologram during an exclusive interview. "I have never in my life met such strength, such ingenuity. The rebels defeated us years before we knew it." He glanced at guards flanking him wearing yellow, green, and red striped armbands. "I only hope I can be forgiven. But you must understand, this is the only way I can support my family."

"So *your* family is worth more than millions of Ethiopian lives?" the interviewer prodded.

"Well, yes. What kind of father would not die for his family? *Kill* for his family?"

"What about the metacorporations paying you?"

"CEO generals... They dangle carrots that can never be reached," the mercenary said. "If they knew what was good for them, they'd get out now. Like I said, money only goes so far."

Three months later, holograms of Ethiopian rebels and soldiers dancing alongside government officials and civilians, crowding the center of Addis Ababa, plastered the news.

Newly elected President Kidsta came into view, approaching a podium, standing proudly, overlooking a sea of survivors in Addis Ababa's crumbled center, and cried, "The Ethiopian Revolution is at an end!"

The crowd exploded into cheers.

She held her hand high to hush them. "But now we must rebuild. The Ethiopian People's Republic calls upon all of it's citizens, calls on those who fled years ago to return. We must work together like we never have before. We must forgive past discretion, become united as *one* people. For we have an opportunity never thought possible. With the help of the United States, France, Japan, and United Korea we have devised a plan to change Ethiopia forever. To change *humanity* forever. Earth's first Space Elevator will anchor into the Ethiopian highlands!"

♦

Seemingly overnight, engineering factions were established.

Nucleheads developed in-depth plans for rare earth mining operations in the Asteroid Belt, eyeing Ceres as their base of operation, while *Lightweights* designed solar harvesting systems for Mercury.

And the metacorporations that once pillaged Ethiopia were begging for forgiveness, desperate to be included in the new space race. They poured money into the research and development of Mercury and Ceres and, by proxy, Ethiopia itself.

And Mars, with its third gravity, difficult atmosphere, unpredictable weather, and lack of exploitable resources, was abandoned. Most of its funding was pulled. Nevertheless, some people still believed. *People like me!* To us, Mars was the only other place in System Sol that could generate the galaxy's single most valuable resource. *Topsoil.*

We are *Dirtdevils.*

♦

"Maria," Alejandra said during dinner.

I was researching agricultural engineering institutes and lost to the world, but I recognized uncharacteristic tension, snapping me back. "What?"

"Remember that business trip we took to Addis Ababa?"

"The conference," I stated.

"We were not truthful with you. We met with President Kidsta."

"Um, okay?"

"She's offered Aurelien and me positions on the space elevator's design team."

Wow! I thought, but I sensed more. "And?"

"We must move to Addis Ababa. We hope you will join us, but you're an adult now and must make your own decision. However, if you're serious about Mars, Ethiopia is the place to be."

Addis Ababa's Agriculture Institute of Technology was still a pile of rubble, yet they began accepting students well before reconstruction. *But this is not something they need to play coy with.*

"What are you *really* trying to say?" I asked.

Alejandra pursed her lips. "We found relatives of yours that survived the revolution. They would love to meet you."

"You did what!?" I stood, knocking my chair to the floor. "We worked so hard to cover my identity! How can you throw that away!?"

Aurelien raised his hands. "Your identity is safe. Your uncle Sonam and Aunt Nobi believe you're Maria Dhaka-Korda, a student interested in an internship on their teff farm. I told them about your thesis on Off-World Grain Development."

♦

Ethiopian Highlands

Uncle Sonam and Aunt Nobi's fields stretched far into the horizon, undulating with variations in highland topography. I watched a family of rams descend from the cliffs to graze on juvenile grains.

"You're okay with them eating the teff?" I asked, using what little Oromo I remembered from childhood.

Uncle Sonam nodded. "We encourage it in fact. They are essential to grassland ecology. Without them we cannot maintain proper soil nutrients. But we make sure the rams only graze the teff halfway through maturation, so they can regrow for harvest. With the rotation of crops we maintain this relationship throughout the year."

"Is that what the drones are for?"

"The rams *will* stay clear of them, but their primary function is locating and eliminating pests, especially during locust season. However, if a pest is endangered, the drones relocate them instead."

"Won't they just return?" I asked.

Sonam shrugged just like Mother once did. "The drones never stop. It's the best relationship to establish. No chemicals, minimal impact on species. Come, you must see the grain mills."

We boarded his small hover-skiff and zoomed just above a lush teff sea, wind rippling the grasses like waves. Grain mills stood ominous in the distance, with massive turbine blades slowly turning like monuments from ancient history. We stopped at one's base, and my uncle waved his holotile to unlock its door. Exposed gears above rapidly spun, engaging smaller ones until spinning a grinding stone as proficiently as any industrial mill could.

My uncle grasped a handful of teff flour from a barrel to show me its smoothness. "This is the most cost-effective way to grind, even with the advancements of the last two centuries. I cannot understand how most of the world still uses electricity to power hydraulic mills when they could simply remove electricity and hydraulics altogether."

Jerkface appeared by the barrel and gave me a look. "Please."

Despite my inclination to deny him, I needed to know, too. I took a pinch of flour and licked.

"Unbelievable," Jerkface said. "This is completely natural, no pesticide or herbicide. No modification. Nothing. I wish I grew up in this era... Minus the genocide," he added and faded away.

Dusk was upon us. We returned to my uncle's modest yet strangely advanced hut to find Aunt Nobi heating a circular stone for injera. I loved watching her pour the batter onto the stone in a spiral motion, from outside to inside. She covered the injera with a conical lid until the scent of toasting came. She pulled the lid, tugged the edges free with bare fingers, slipped a thin disc beneath to peel, and tossed it into a basket.

She waved me over to try.

I spiraled as directed but was terrified to peel the injera from the stone, convinced my fingers would singe. The injera burned. Nobi began yelling. Then the ghostly apparitions of both Jerkface and Susan were yelling, too. All three synchronized facepalmed as the smoke detector rang.

Dillon entered with my cousin Koran.

"Hey Maria! What's burning?" he said in English with his crooked grin.

I swore Dillon was following me. First to Professor Couture's class, then to AA-Tech, and guess who showed up on the first day of the internship to learn drone construction with my cousin.

"Dillon!" Nobi said with excitement, having just lifted the lid from another injera.

Dillon reached over and effortlessly peeled it from the stone.

"See, that's how it's done," Jerkface said.

He's even charming my imaginary friends!? It's a good thing he's stupid! But the more time I spent with Dillon, the more I understood his aloofness was a sort of brilliance.

◆

It took me two months, but I finally pulled the injera from the stone at the right moment and tossed it into the basket with a slight spin to keep the bread from bunching.

"There you go, Sha," Aunt Nobi whispered, gently squeezing my arm.

Sha? I turned to my aunt. "How do you know?"

She grinned. "You may have my stump of a husband fooled, but I've been staring at that Tolera nose for over thirty years. Your uncle Sonam has it, your uncle Khasam had it, your mother Masani had it, your cousin Koran has it, and will you look at that, *you* have it, too."

"Please, no one can know. It would cause a lot of trouble for my adoptive family," I whispered.

Aunt Nobi nodded. "Your secret is safe with me, *Maria.*"

On the last day of our internship, just before Dillon and I returned to Addis Ababa, my aunt woke me from my bunk at dawn.

I wiped sleep from my eyes and was about to speak, but she motioned me to remain quiet. I followed her through the kitchen, out the front door, and to the warehouse, where drones lay upon worktables in various stages of completion. A small door in the back opened to a laboratory. Thick dust covered stainless steel tables, and early sunlight percolated through its clerestory. Nobi flipped a switch, and a wall of canisters upon shallow shelves, organized to obsession, lit.

My mother's work, I knew, and plucked a canister.

"Khan Dan Teff—Low light, low temp for winter greenhouses," read the label.

I inspected several more before noticing Aunt Nobi at the far end.

She calmly pointed at a canister. "Your mother spent years splicing different varieties of teff to exploit their unique properties. But she was on a quest to create a super seed able to grow in any environment. She called it— *Spectrum Habitat Adaptability.*"

SHA, I realized. *All this time, I'm just an acronym?* My frustration climbed, but my curiosity rose faster. My hand reached for the canister. No description was on its side.

"What am I supposed to do with this?" I asked

"Masani was certain the work should continue even if she were not able to do it herself. I thought you might be interested in picking up where she left off."

♦

Addis Ababa, Ethiopia

The SHA seeds germinated on my dormitory window sill within a morning and grew ten centimeters a day. In a week, the teff matured, self-pollinated, and produced seed. Sadly, the seed's nutritional value was negligible, and they were sterile. *When Aunt Nobi said it was incomplete, she wasn't kidding,* I thought. But if a few crops survived in a harsh environment, they might sow the next season, then the next, and the next. Until a grass perfectly adapted to that environment emerges. *But how many generations would it take? A hundred? A thousand?* I wondered. *First things first, I must discover why the seeds are sterile.*

A knock rapped upon my door. My holotile displayed, *"Dillon."*

"It's open," I said.

He entered, dressed like a sloppy lord-ling in a three-piece suit with his shirt partially untucked, his vest unbuttoned, and his hair unkempt. "It'll be visible tonight! Wanna come!?"

"It's like finding a needle in a hay stack," I said. "And even if you find it, it'll look like a tiny speck."

"That's not the point, Maria. Tonight's the first time we can see the elevator's tether descending with the naked eye. It's history in the making."

"He's right," Susan said, appearing next to me.

"You still won't find it," I said.

Dillon grinned. "Maybe you can help. You know more about it than the rest of us, having family on the inside."

I sighed. "Fine, I'll come, but you owe me."

"Drinks on me, then." He hurried off to gather more classmates.

Susan gave me a grin. "You should dress up. Dillon looks handsome."

"He looks like an idiot," I snapped.

Susan surveyed my jeans and T-shirt. "We can make this work. Those red heels, a shade of red lipstick, and that short blazer of yours."

I shook my head.

"Don't say I didn't try," Susan said, fading away.

Dillon, Heloise, Hyun, and I rose to the top of Eleon Tower, recently constructed in Addis Ababa's financial district, reaching six hundred meters in height and granting views above the highlands.

"How'd you get tickets?" I asked Dillon.

"...Dad." If anything brought Dillon back to reality, it was mention of his affluent father. "I haven't talked to him since leaving the family business."

Granger Laser, I knew.

"He likes reminding me of what I'm missing with gifts like these," Dillon continued.

"Does he know you're planning to take the Mars trials?"

"He sent a Dirt Devil vacuum to my apartment last week."

I grinned. "At least he has a sense of humor."

The elevator doors parted, revealing men and women dressed as if attending a gala. A lounge band with slick-backed hair played, "Fly me to the moon..." over the chatter.

I looked at my jeans and T-shirt and realized how out of place I was.

"Alicia! But of course you're here!" Dillon said to a gorgeous brunette, his voice suddenly changing.

That's not Dillon, I thought, hating how he must put on a facade to fit into that world. Alicia embraced him, kissing his cheek.

Susan appeared next to me dressed just as lavishly, donning red lipstick. "And now you've lost Dillon."

I do not like Dillon! I thought back.

"Whatever you say." Susan waded into the crowd and reached for a glass of champagne from a waiter's platter, her ghostly hand passing through. She pretended to sip anyway.

Dillon returned with a crooked grin and kiss prints on his cheeks. "Our reservation is on the terrace."

"I think she fancies you," I said.

Dillon gave me a confused expression.

"Alicia. Likes. You," I said bluntly.

"What makes you say that?"

I pointed to my cheek. "It's the impression that I get."

Dillon pulled a handkerchief and wiped the prints, realizing how close they were to his lips. "You really think she's into me?"

"Like a hermit crab to its shell," I blurted and wanted to die.

"Wow, Maria, you sure know how to paint a picture." Dillon led us to our table and ordered rounds of drinks and hors d'oeuvres as the sun dipped below the horizon.

"It's happening so fast," Heloise said. "I wonder how they're lowering the tether without destabilizing the construction station's geostationary orbit."

They turned to me.

I rolled my eyes. "All right."

They smiled wide and leaned closer.

"The construction station is actually two massive spools of nano-fiber oriented back-to-back, continually being replenished by 3d printers on Luna turning silica in its regolith into glass fibers and launching them into Earth's orbit. As one tether lowers from the construction station's spool into the Ethiopian highlands, another stretches far into space acting as a counterweight, keeping the entire elevator stabilized during construction. Once anchored to the ground, hundreds more strands from Earth will run up its length, braiding into a more substantial tether. Lastly, non-recyclable waste will be compressed and sent to the counterweight's end to keep the entire elevator taut with centripetal force."

"But that's so dangerous," Hyun said. "Centripetal force being its only means of structural stability does not allow for redundancy. If the tether breaks, the entire thing comes down."

"It will *never* come down," Dillon said.

I humphed. "The titanic was considered unsinkable."

"That's just one example."

"New Orleans's levees, the Twin Towers, the—" I listed off.

"Okay, okay, I get it," Dillon said. "So what happens if the tether fails?

"Millions of people die," I said.

"Come on."

"Think about it," I said. "A fifty-seven thousand kilometer long tether, five meters wide, crashing down along Earth's equator, wrapping the planet multiple times, crushing towns and cities, setting forests and cropland ablaze, creating tsunamis, the list goes on. It's why the elevator schematics are the world's most highly guarded secret and the anchor site hosts more military than a small country. It's the perfect target for anyone against expansion."

They stared, processing it all until our holotiles buzzed or pinged in unison. The city lights below ceased, and people gathered on the terraces of neighboring towers to gaze into the night sky.

I found Polaris, then constellations Ursa Minor, Major, and Orion, my favorite. As the sun set, the Milky Way's entire arm became visible, and hundreds of faint satellites traversed the sky in prograde orbits. But one swayed back and forth.

"What is it?" Heloise whispered to me.

"That's the anchor."

"Wow, Eagle-eye Maria," Dillon said, a little too close.

I could smell alcohol on his breath and gently pushed him to arm's length. Hurt flashed in his eyes. He left our table in a huff.

Susan appeared in his seat. "Would a little romance be so terrible?"

You never dated, I thought back.

"In retrospect, I wish I had."

I returned my gaze to the stars. *The Mars trials are coming. I cannot be distracted.*

♦

Gobi Desert, East Turkestan

"Wasn't the written exam... supposed to be... the most difficult part!?" Dillon said, breathing heavily, plopping onto the snow-covered sand at the halfway mark of today's marathon in the desert, bound in layers to keep from frostbite.

"You must keep moving, Dillon, and don't you dare sweat," I said. "Sweating kills us."

"Where's Heloise?" Hyun said.

She came wavering from the mist moments later. "Team 137 dropped out," she said. "I stopped to make sure they were okay and called the evacuation crew."

"Come on, Dillon. Only two more days," I said, pulling him to his feet.

"Two more marathon's you mean," he grumbled.

Our pockets buzzed. I pulled my holotile and opened its projection. *"182 of 586 teams remain."*

"We're dropping like flies," Dillon said.

"The hardest part is almost over," I said. "They say the trials get easier."

"Because Antarctica sounds like a breeze." Dillon smirked.

"Let's go," Hyun said, trotting ahead with a funny hiccup in his step.

♦

"D-didn't they s-say the G-Gobi Trek w-was the hardest p-part of the t-trials?" Hyun said, his teeth chattering as he fumbled to relight his torch in the blizzard's complete white-out. A monstrous gust of wind almost knocked him over. He shifted his legs to brace.

"Breathe Hyun," Heloise said into his earpiece. "Yes, you're the last one, but racing to relight the torch will only cause mistakes. Precision is key."

"E-easy for you t-to say, y-you're a w-welder," Hyun argued.

"And after today, you will be one, too."

We watched Hyun's progress from Basecamp's hologram, heat blankets around our shoulders, feet in hot water, teeth still chattering like machine guns from our times in the blizzard. At the bottom corner of the hologram was a pass-fail tally. Only twenty-four teams remained.

"G-got it!" Hyun said as the bright light of his torch flickered on hologram.

"And sealed!" Heloise confirmed to a round of shivering cheers.

Hyun entered Basecamp several minutes later, tore off his envisuit, embraced his heat blanket, then us.

"Great job, Hyun!" Heloise said.

Hyun looked at the hologram. "O-only twenty-f-four teams?"

"Not to worry, Hyun. I hear the trials get easier after this," I said to nervous chuckles.

◆

Atlantis Base, Mariana Trench

"Maria, do you copy?" Dillon called into my earpiece, feeding me instructions as I worked on our version of an airlock in the crushing black abyss. Our fates were tied in this trial.

"What is it?" I responded, my heart racing.

"You look cute. That is all." He was grinning his stupid grin from beyond Atlantis Base's thick glass.

"You're an idiot!" I responded, my frustration climbing.

"Roger that."

I spied the candidate on my left, *Heloise? I could not tell*. One by one, the others cranked their last bolts tight and entered their airlocks. *Am I behind?*

"Never-mind them. They're rushing," Dillon said like an imaginary friend listening to my thoughts.

After several hours, I was the last and cranked the final bolt tight.

"Replacement complete," I called.

"You are cleared for entry," Dillon responded.

I manually rotated the door's locking mechanism open, entered the airlock, and cranked the door tight behind me. *Moment of truth.* After several uncomfortable seconds, the lighting turned green. I let out a monumental sigh of relief and removed my helmet once the water drained. The inner door cranked open, and a wash of cheers nearly knocked me flat.

"You were phenomenal! We passed!" Dillon said, shaking my shoulders.

It wasn't until I emerged that I realized we were one of only two teams in the green.

♦

Kennedy Space Center, Florida

"Welcome to Magnetic Artificial Gravity Suit training!" said a man I knew all too well, a man I respected and kinda feared. Professor Couture made eye contact with me and grinned. When he found Dillon, he frowned. "Magsuits will be the difference between space exploration and space colonization! Are what our crews currently use on Mars, Ceres, Mercury, and Luna to maintain muscle mass and bone density! Hundreds of micro-electromagnets are woven into the magsuit's titanium weave and will pull evenly across your body towards a steel floor, providing Earth-like gravity. However, they cannot add Earth equivalent to your organs and blood, which may cause unexpected physiological effects."

"Like shitting your pants," Dillon whispered.

"Yes Dillon!" Couture called, staring daggers at him. "With your history of adolescent bed-wetting *you* will be shitting your pants!"

Dillon's jaw dropped, and his face reddened.

How did Professor Couture even hear that? I thought.

"You're miked," Papa said, pointing at a dot on my collar.

"You may have noticed many new faces in the room!" Couture said and gave a menacing look over the trainees. "Most of you are getting a free pass because of the money-hungry corporations you work for looking to exploit the natural resources of Mercury or Ceres! I hope when you are up there, approaching those gorgeous planets, you learn to respect the resources from which you are about to leech! Understand that they *can* run dry! Just like they have on Earth! Don't make me regret giving you this training!"

The new faces adopted horrid expressions.

"For those heading to Mars, who *actually* underwent the grueling trials, I respect you! Nevertheless, this will be the first long-term space mission for you all!" He grinned mischievously. "Training will commence *right now!"*

A door to a gymnasium swung open behind Professor Couture, and we followed him single-file through. When I stepped upon the steel-laced flooring, my magsuit's electromagnets activated, spreading pressure across my shoulders and arms and traveling down my hips and legs. The suit's wrist hologram rose, showing simulated gravity at, *"+10%."*

Our muscles screamed as we trotted around the gymnasium.

"Feel the burn!" Couture said and increased the pace.

"Who is this guy?" a soft man with red hair said, sweat pouring down his face.

"It's Captain Couture," I responded between huffs. "The only person to set foot on every planet and moon between Sol and Ceres."

The soft man raised his eyebrows. "*That* Couture? I thought he retired!"

"Samuel! As long as there is life in me, I shall live it!" Couture shouted from the front and went into a full sprint.

It was only a ten-minute run, something I normally did in my sleep, but with magsuits, it felt like hours.

Samuel dropped to his knees, gasping.

How will this guy keep up? I thought.

Dillon helped him to his feet. "Wish you stayed home now?" he said.

"You know each other?" I asked, sensing their familiarity.

"Sammy works for my dad. He's not much of an athlete, but he's the best laser physicist in the world, probably."

"So you're heading to Mercury." I said.

Samuel gulped air. "I'm directing... a crew to construct... the initial... solar arrays."

I humphed. "And so it begins."

Samuel's heavy gasps ceased like it was an act. He gave me a penetrating stare, his pale eyes chilling me to my core.

"Don't trust that one," Papa suddenly said.

Agreed, I thought back.

Samuel broke eye contact, turned to Dillon, and put his innocent charm back on. "What does she mean?"

"Tell you later." Dillon pointed to the front.

Professor Couture stood tall, showing no hint of fatigue. "There will be times when you will not have a magsuit! When energy rationing will be necessary! When you are in environments devoid of iron! Or planning a return to Earth. Regular over-training will compensate for bone degradation and muscle atrophy during such times!" He raised his hologram with, *"+10%G,"* in its display and flicked his finger, bumping it to, *"+11%G."*

"You can't be serious?" Samuel whined, playing the victim.

"I do not tolerate smart-asses! Line up!" Couture commanded.

Within a month, we walked around at *+25%G* and trained at *+150%*. My muscles became stone. My joints were like steel hinges. Even Samuel trimmed up, yet he found every excuse to downplay it.

"I am not a beautiful actor but the director of a play," he would say.

His crew of scientists and astronauts smiled endearingly at his antics, would stop everything just to hear what he might say, and bring him coffee or dinner as he obsessed over calculations in the evenings.

"He's the future!" one of the astronauts heading to Mercury said. "He's going to change the universe as we know it!"

They worship him, I realized. But I could not shake the unease of his stare.

The launch windows soon came. Samuel's Lightweight crew left for Mercury first. A few months later, the Nucleheads left for Ceres. And finally, at year's end, we Dirtdevils went to Mars.

♦

Camp Harmony, Mars

"There's a potential aquifer eighteen clicks north, but it's impossible to judge if water is still present," Dillon called in. "We'll have to drill."

"It'll have to wait," Chiayu said through com. "Night's coming in fast, and you're on dinner duty." She furrowed her brow and faced me. *"Ken* thinks he found another one." Chiayu twitched her nub of a thumb, a casualty of the Great Freeze of 97', when both reactors went offline, forcing the crew to divert battery power from heating to air-recyclers. She had lost three toes, a thumb, and an ear to frostbite and did not grow replacements, bearing her injuries as a badge of honor, as all of the older crew did.

"Welcome to Camp Harmony, *Ken and Barbie,"* they said upon our arrival, looking at our pristineness with disdain.

"Ken's got shit for brains, but look at that baby smooth skin," they'd say to Dillon or Hyun.

"Barbie thinks she can do equations, go back to your little garden, darling," they'd say to me or Heloise.

After the first month, I chopped my hair short and uneven. When Dillon burned his arm, he wore sleeveless magsuits to show off the bandage. And Hyun exaggerated his hiccup stride, showing off an old track injury.

But Heloise was the first of us inducted into their pirate ranks. A minor quake occurred as she welded in the field, and she burned straight through her envisuit's glove. Thinking quickly, she continued welding the titanium weave of her magsuit beneath, sealing the hole but sacrificing a pinky and ring finger.

Harmony's doctor took one look at the hand and shouted through the public com, "A Martian is born!"

The old crew howled to the ceiling like wolves.

Heloise now looks down on us, too.

Just before sunset, Dillon returned in Rover 2 and found me in Avenue H, tending to my sickly buckwheat.

"Hey, what's with you?" he said, sensing my frustration. He just came from the locker room and smelled like Satan's breath.

"It's this fucking perchlorate saturated sand. Nothing takes," I said.

He pointed at a bed of lentils growing strong.

"Soil's from Earth," I snapped.

He pointed at the quinoa, looking happy.

"Using our feces for nutrients."

Dillon grimaced. "Well, it works, doesn't it?"

I glared. "Our own shit is neither sustainable nor healthy."

"Seems to be a steady supply of it at least."

"Maybe from you."

"Ha!" He pointed at the compost box. "Isn't this working?"

"We only have a few cubic meters. We need hundreds of thousands to grow enough food to support Harmony."

"What about hydroponics?"

I glared. "Find an aquifer first, then we'll talk."

"I'll find one soon enough," he said with his crooked grin.

"They laugh at you when you're out there," I snapped. "They've been here for twenty-three years and didn't find one. So how will *you*?"

"Thanks for the vote of confidence, Maria!" He left in a huff.

Jerkface appeared with a look on his face.

What the hell do you want!? I yelled in thought.

He pointed to where Dillon exited. "He's your ally. Don't burn him."

Why does everyone like Dillon!?

Papa appeared next to Jerkface, shaking his head. "Dillon has been getting the worst of it from the crew. He needs a friend."

I thought long about that. *I guess I can be a friend.*

Susan appeared. "We should give him a taste of home."

I'm saving that for a special occasion, I thought back.

"Right *now* seems special to me," she said bluntly.

I found Dillon alone in the kitchen, holding dehydrated pea soup and sobbing quietly. *The rest on dinner duty bailed,* I realized.

"Pea soup is nothing to cry about," I said.

Dillon stiffened and turned my way. "Who said I was crying?" He forced a smile, but it dwindled. "They ditched me."

"I know." I walked to the cold storage's hatch. "Come, I want to show you something."

Motion-sensored lights illuminated a frigid corridor overflowing with supplies. I stopped at a sealed case, knelt, and input my code. Its lid sighed and opened, revealing several burlap bags within.

"What's that?" Dillon said.

"Guess."

He pulled a bag from the case, stroking its burlap like an old leather-bound book, then squeezed. "No! It can't be! How did you get this?"

"Sonam and Nobi sent it last shipment. It's their Instant-Fermentation Teff Flour, specifically designed for injera."

"Must have cost a fortune," he said.

"Ethiopian discount."

He gave a knowing look. "They must really like you." Then, he spied a round disc beyond the case. "Is that an injera stone?"

I grinned and rolled it from behind the case. "Dill, let's teach these pirates a thing or two about cooking."

When we returned to the kitchen, Dillon unplugged the industrial burner and lugged it into the dining hall.

"Make way!" he hollered, setting it on a table.

As Dillon heated the injera stone, I poured teff flour into a mixing bowl and added water. The flour immediately reacted, and the scent of rapid fermentation struck my nose. I filled a watering can with the batter and joined Dillon in the dining hall to see a group of curious crewmates forming a semicircle around him.

"You're nuts *Ken*, you know that?" one said.

"Yep," Dillon responded, spreading oil across the stone and flicking water droplets that crackled.

I handed Dillon the batter-filled can. He carefully tilted, and a slow stream of batter poured onto the stone. He spiraled outside to inside, just as

Aunt Nobi taught us.

"I think we need a thinner mix," he whispered. "It won't settle in this gravity."

"The heat should help it," I said.

The batter soon spread flat.

"You better get those sides ready," Dillon said.

"On it." I returned to the kitchen.

"We should do collard greens," Susan said, appearing at rehydration.

"It's called *gomen*," Jerkface corrected, appearing next to her.

"And the lentils, and split peas," she continued.

"Miser whet, aterkek aletcha," Jerkface again corrected.

Susan shot him a look. "You're so arrogant."

"We don't have the ingredients to make proper sides," Jerkface said.

Improvising is a way of life at Camp Harmony. Why should this be any different? I thought, dumping veggies into pots to rehydrate.

"No! You can't!" Jerkface shouted.

I queued up The Regolith Assassins' new album, maxing out the volume.

"Hell yeah!" Dillon shouted from the dining hall.

Jerkface waved his hands wildly in protest.

I cupped a palm around my ear and mouthed, *I can't hear you.*

Once rehydrated and mixed with spices, I brought my improvised sides to the dining hall as Harmony's crew poured in.

One grew excited. "I didn't know we had injera on the menu! The last time I had this, I was a kid!"

"You Ethiopian?" I asked.

"Not with a name like, *Jared.* I'm talking about Brooklyn back in the day, before the fire of 2081."

"How do you eat this?" his friend said.

"Tear a piece of injera and scoop a filling. *Duh*," Jared said, rounding the table, placing injera on plates and scooping sides. "You're gonna need all the help you can get with this," he said, turning to Dillon. "It's Dillon, right?"

"Yeah." Dillon peeled another injera in one relaxed pull and tossed it like a disc into a basket.

Jared nodded. "Now that's skill."

♦

My first vacation day in three years finally came, and I was determined to sow the new and improved SHA seed I engineered to produce fertile seeds for future seasons. *Well, in theory, it should work.* I strode past greenhouse avenues barrel-vaulted in Martian concrete, protecting the crops from direct radiation but robbing them of sunlight, forcing us to rely upon LEDs. *Such inefficiency.* I reached Avenue H, Grain Development.

Deb gave a look as I entered. "Isn't it your day off? Please, tell me you have something else to do."

"I do," I said.

The LEDs cut, leaving us in darkness.

"One, two, three, four…" I heard Deb counting.

On five, the LEDs shot back on.

Deb sighed with relief. "Looks like Dave and Hyun started repairing the reactors."

"Let's hope it's quick," I added. *Poor Hyun,* I thought, imagining all the insults Dave must be giving him.

That's when I saw it. My buckwheat had buckled under its own weight in the night. *Another month of work down the drain.* At this point, I should not have been surprised. We, the Eden team, were supposed to whip Agriculture into shape. Instead, we were failing on all fronts. Dillon with aquifer hunting, Hyun with soil composition, Heloise with infrastructure, and myself with grains and produce.

I sighed and set my canister of SHA seeds on a potting bench, tossed the dead buckwheat into the compost, retrieved several seedling trays, and took a healthy portion of Hyun's soil. I mixed the soil one to one with Martian sand and planted twenty seeds. *They should be poking up in a few hours,* I hoped.

My holotile beeped, *"Dillon."*

"What's up?" I said as his face appeared on hologram.

"It's your day off, right?"

"…What are you scheming?"

"I'm about to drill that aquifer. Wanna come?"

"I have plans."

"Bullshit, you're in the greenhouse right now. I really need your support with this."

Papa would say I should be a good friend. I sighed. "What lock are you departing from?"

"Northwest. Meet you in ten!"

Carlos gave his usual looks as we suited up. "Two of you won't find this aquifer any easier than one. Waste of oxygen."

"Do you know how difficult managing multiple drones while drilling is?" Dillon said. "Looks like *you're* the newb."

Dillon, why? I thought.

Carlos gave a steely glare. "The only substance resistant to the battery acid corrosion that caused the Great Freeze's reactor shorts, is *enamel*."

"What of it?" Dillon asked.

Carlos smiled wide, revealing his metallic replacement teeth. "*I*... fixed the leak."

"That doesn't mean any—" Dillon began to argue.

"Shut! Up! Dillon!" I yelled.

"I'd listen to *Barbie* if I were you," Carlos said, reluctantly handing us our helmets.

After passing through the airlock and loading Rover 2 with drones, drills, and omni-bits, Dillon turned to me. "Why'd you cut me off back there?"

"You were digging your own grave."

"Was I? I wish they'd get over this hazing. It's been three years now." He kicked the rover into high gear, which wasn't very fast, and followed the path he had previously taken. The tracks had swept away in the wind, but our visors superimposed a blue line to follow.

"I thought about cutting off a finger or toe. Something that doesn't matter much," Dillon blurted.

"Dill!? What the fuck!?"

"You cut your hair," he argued.

"Hair. Grows. Back!"

He shrugged. "I can grow replacement fingers if I must. I'm pretty sure that's why Heloise did it."

"Heloise is an accomplished pianist, you've seen her *play*. Even with replacements, there's no way she'd do that just to fit in."

He looked unconvinced. "There were others working machinery and welding during the quake. They were fine. Heloise happened to be alone with no cameras, and that weld was a little too perfect."

That weld was indeed too perfect. I thought about how happy Heloise had become, finally accepted by the crew. "You know what'll shut these pirates up? Finding that aquifer."

Dillon chuckled. "If you can't *join* them, *beat* them."

"Dill. Promise me you won't start chopping body parts," I said.

He gave a look. "I'll be good."

"*5h24m, to destination,*" appeared on visor with a path leading around Yang's Canyon.

"You've got to be kidding me," I said.

"It's actually longer with the patches of loose sand," Dillon said.

After an hour, I saw a pinching in the canyon's cliffs and pointed. "We should build a bridge right there."

"Ha! With what funding?" Dillon responded.

We eventually rounded the canyon and climbed the crater's rugged crown to find its interior flat instead of dipping back down.

"Holy shit, Dill!"

"See what I'm talking about!?" he responded. "I'm not *completely* crazy you know."

"How can I help?" I asked.

He pointed at the drones. "Activate and place them around their case. They'll know what to do once calibrated to the wind." Dillon lugged his massive drill to a marker. "This is the first of several locations I want to drill today."

I circled the drones around their case, synced my visor, and selected *On*. They calculated wind patterns, then blinked yellow.

"We have a warning. Wind turbulence is high," I said.

"They've been saying that for weeks. They'll be fine."

I studied the crater's ridge, dust rising like smoke from a chimney. "What did Chiayu say?"

"That it's normal this time of year. We have satellites monitoring wind patterns. No need to worry," Dillon said.

The drones took off in unison, tilting to compensate for the wind. I switched my visor display to aerial. As the drones spread, their camera angles generated a topographical map. A slight bulge the size of several city blocks was at the center of the crater. Iron deposits were scattered below the first drill site. *Dillon will have to thread the needle around them all.*

Dillon fed the first omni-bit length into his drill, backed to a safe distance, and connected through visor.

"Beginning bore," he said, slowly waving hands to remotely navigate the drill's omni-bit. He looked high on drugs.

When he lifted his leg to disengage the clutch, I laughed.

"This is serious, Maria," he said, inserting the next bit length.

An itch formed on my ankle. I wiggled, trying to rub against the lining of my suit. After ten minutes, *agony.* "How much longer will this take?"

"Shhh," he whispered and again raised his leg, disengaging the clutch. "Six hours."

"And *what* am I supposed to do!?"

"Take the rover for a spin. The other drill locations need to be spiked." He fed another bit length into his drill.

I rolled my eyes, hopped on the rover, and connected my visor. Several markers appeared. The closest was fifteen minutes away. I sped off, spitting dust in my wake, and spied the drones overhead, circling the next location like vultures. *"X,"* appeared on visor, and I slowed to its spot. Dillon was tiny in the distance, resembling a lone Tai Chi master in a vast red sea.

I accessed the drones' radar and X-ray and started understanding Dillon's logic. I initially felt the scattered iron deposits were hindrances to navigate, but I now understood the areas between them were solid metal. I hammered a sensor spike into the ground and moved to the next.

As I reached the fourth location, a sudden gust of wind pushed against the rover, almost tipping it. The drones above flashed red on visor. One fell from the sky.

"What's going on over there!" Dillon called in.

"We lost a drone!" I said as it impacted the ground, sending a plume of dust to the wind.

"Oh… no..." Dillon whispered.

"DUST STORM APPROACHING!" flashed on visor.

"All personnel, report to Harmony!" Chiayu called across all channels. "A storm's coming fast from the south, t-minus four hours thirty-two minutes until lockdown. Drop everything, now!"

"Coming to your position, Dill!" I said, spinning the rover and bee-lining his direction. My visor estimated, *"32m,"* to reach him, then, *"5h24m,"* back to Harmony. *We won't make it,* I realized.

"No! Head straight back!" Dillon responded with conviction. "From your position, you'll return just in time!"

"Dillon's right!" Chiayu said, jumping into our channel. "Otherwise, you'll both be stranded for who knows how long."

"You want me to leave him!?" I shouted, appalled.

"Maria, this is a direct order! You will—"

I blocked Chiayu's connection. I raced past the drill sites I had spiked, imagining Dillon hunkered down, whimpering as dust covered him and his air supply dwindled. "Dillon, I'm heading your way!"

"No! Don't you dare!" he said.

"Heading your direction whether you like it or not! I have a plan!" I lied about the plan.

"But!" Dillon began, then sighed. "Roger that."

Carlos called into our channel. "Maria! Return this inst—"

I blocked everyone save Dillon and thought to my imaginary friends, *I need your help.*

My right hand raised to my visor possessed, searching alternative routes back to Harmony. *It's Susan.* Then I heard, "No, stay off the loose sand." *Papa's helping too.* Jerkface came into my view, pointing to a peak in the distance. "Dillon needs to move two klicks south."

"Dill, go to position 143,279,98!"

"But that's atop a crest!" he protested.

"Just trust me, and get there fast!"

Dillon's beacon started bounding southward. His white speck appeared against the red sky like a kangaroo in the outback. He scrambled up the peak and grabbed the rover's roll cage when I arrived, hoisting himself into the passenger seat and strapping its harness.

"What's the plan?" he gasped.

Yeah, what is the plan? I thought, then studied our previous tracks winding down the crater and around Yang's Canyon. *"5h24m."* Another route suddenly appeared on visor, taking us straight down the crater's side to that pinch in the canyon walls. *"1h36m."* An image of a man in stars and stripes riding a motorcycle appeared in my mind.

"Dill? Have you ever heard of Evel Knievel?"

"No." He searched the name. "Oh! You've got to be joking!"

My foot went rogue, punching the accelerator, launching us down the near vertical slope. My hand popped the rover to neutral, letting gravity take over. Patches of rock came quickly. It was all I could do to swerve. Then, it was hard-packed sand right to the canyon edge.

"We're not going to make it!" Dillon hollered as we hit an upturn in topography.

We were airborne, sailing above the canyon floor, but a sudden gust of headwind slowed us. Our rear axle crunched against the canyon's opposite edge, sending the rover's butt skyward, tumbling us end over end, the roll cage justifying its existence. By the time we stopped, breakfast coated my visor. *But we made it!*

Chiayu found a way onto our channel. "Maria, Dillon! We have a beacon malfunction! What's your position!?"

Dillon took a deep breath. "No malfunction... We jumped the canyon. We're at 128,24,58. Rover 2 is destroyed, but we can make it on foot."

Chiayu paused. "We're sending Rover 3 to meet you halfway!"

After an hour of trudging, Carlos appeared from the red-out in Rover 3, waving his arms.

"*Shhh...* That was one *hell* of a stunt... *shhh...* pulled back there! I can't wait to see... *shhh...* helmet footage!" Carlos said, with what I swore was respect in his voice. "But don't you ever... *shhh...* that again!"

The storm intensified as we returned from Harmony, visibility dropping to zero. Carlos grew nervous, muttering to himself with his com off. But I could make out his profanities by reading his lips.

Camp Harmony suddenly appeared, and Carlos slammed the brake. We nearly ran into the northwest hatch.

We raced through the airlock and out of our suits, and met the rest of the crew in the Command Center, transfixed on its central hologram. A few glanced in our direction and nodded respectfully.

I nudged Dillon and whispered, "I think we did it."

He pointed at central hologram. "Hyun and Dave are still outside."

Rover 5 was getting battered by the storm, their blue line veering off course.

"No... *shhh...* time... *shhh...* backup... *shhh...*" came through com.

"Don't do it, Dave!" Chiayu shouted.

A look of dread spread across the older crew.

Rover 5 suddenly turned, leaving Hyun's beacon in the sand.

"Main reactor is still offline. Fuck!" Chiayu shouted and turned to Carlos. "Is the backup reactor properly grounded?" she asked, slowly reaching for a glass-enclosed lever.

"It *should* be," Carlos said but grew pale.

I realized that Dave meant to wait out the storm inside the reactor. *But if that airlock door opens, static electricity generated by the storm will fry the reactor's circuits,* I knew.

All eyes trained upon the lights above.

"It's *grounded*," Carlos muttered to himself.

Power cut, leaving us in darkness.

"One, two, three, four... *five...*" Carlos counted. "Goddammit!"

All was silent but the howling of wind and scraping of sand.

"We cannot survive both a dust storm *and* a power outage," Chiayu said quietly. "It's been an honor serving with you all." She pulled the lever and a line of strobe lights dropped from the ceiling, leading to escape pods.

"Emergency evacuation initiated. T-minus five-minutes."

We stood motionless, processing the moment.

"Move your asses! They will not wait for us!" Chiayu cut through.

I need the SHA seed! I knew it in my soul and gave Dillon a look.

"Oh, no you don't!" He reached for me.

I ducked, spun, and strode out of the Command Center, dashing through the Junction and down agriculture avenues, their doors closing off sections as the station went into lock down. Avenue H was still open, but just before entering, I was tackled to the floor. The door to Grain Development sealed. I cracked my tackler in the face several times before I was released.

I stared through the door's window at my beautiful seedlings growing lush in the poisonous Martian soil. The canister of SHA seeds, embodying my hopes and dreams, sat on the table beside them, just out of reach.

"Fuck this shit!" I screamed.

Susan, Papa, and Jerkface all appeared. "You have to let it go!"

"Fuck you! Fuck all of you!"

"This is not the end of the world!" Papa said.

"Yes, this is! Why can't you see that!" A rage I did not understand rose. My fists pounded against the door.

"Get a hold of yourself!" Susan said.

"Shut your mouth! You've never lost your life's work! You gave it away to cook food! You *coward!*" I yelled.

I did not know my imaginary friends could slap me until Susan took control of my hand and struck my cheek hard.

"You think my life's work was genetics!? Dimsum was everything! And I gave that up, for *you!*" She raised a ghostly finger to my forehead.

"Don't do it," Papa said. "She's not ready."

"Are we ever!?" Susan snapped and unlocked a memory.

◆

I woke from a nightmare I knew was real, adrenaline pumping through my veins, a fiery hell-space and gunshots consuming my thoughts.

"Hey, look who's awake," Dillon said.

I jolted, nearly striking him, and began to shake. His eyes held tremendous worry. The left socket was purple where I had punched him.

"You gave us quite a fright," he said. "You've been screaming out for three days straight."

Us? I sat up, trying to get my bearings. *We're in an escape capsule.* There was barely room for Dillon, myself, and *Chiayu.*

"You're getting a psych evaluation once we reach Mercury!" Chiayu yelled.

I looked to Dillon for clarification.

"You were screaming at fictitious people when Chiayu found us in agriculture. She thinks you have schizophrenia."

"What do *you* think?" I asked Dillon.

"Not schizophrenia," he said. His tone conveyed an understanding.

Chiayu glared at Dillon. "She's nuts, and you know it!"

We slowly stabilized outside Deimos's orbit, staring at the dust storm consuming all of Mars below. Six months later, Hermian drone retrieval vessels docked with our capsules, ready to take us to Mercury.

"My Sol, look at this thing?" Dillon said, drifting from one compartment to the next. "They have steam stalls, an exercise room, canteen, and even individual sleeping closets."

Chiayu opened a panel to the recycling systems and stared at its components. "This is light years ahead of us."

When I wandered into the canteen, I saw a shiny machine bolted to the counter, with containment orbs around its spouts. *An espresso machine.*

"We have *coffee!*" I called.

◆

Icarus, Mercury

"Welcome to Icarus, System Sol's first extra-terrestrial city!" the Hermians greeted, and we smiled. "Now, let's get you to work!"

Our smiles dropped.

They pulled up our records. "This is perfect, we have plenty of young talent, but none have experienced true adversity," they said. "Carlos Rivera… you survived the Great Freeze, correct?"

Carlos smiled insidiously, showing off his metal teeth. "I was the one who fixed the reactors."

They stared at him like he was a god.

A month quickly turned into several. A year quickly became two.

◆

"So, what did you tell the guy?" I asked Carlos as he recounted his latest run-in with the new electrical tech. He and Jared had just finished their shifts, and I was about to begin mine. Carlos swigged his end-of-shift ale as I sipped my morning coffee.

"To pull the wires manually," he said.

Jared facepalmed. "Please, tell me New Guy didn't listen."

Carlos chuckled. "Let's say he's learned a lesson."

"Teacher of the year," I said and finished my coffee. "Send my regards to that poor kid."

I left the boys for the underground greenhouses in the lowest section of Icarus, a hundred and seventy levels below the surface. Several agricultural techs hustled about distributing another soil shipment from Earth into newly dug greenhouse sections. *Oh, to have such funding,* I thought. *But such dependency on Earth soil is troubling.*

"Professor Korda," Shelly, a young tech, said.

"What's up?"

"How'd you grow on Mars without soil shipments?"

"We didn't."

"But you were developing soil integration with Martian sand, right?"

"That was Hyun's department. I was working with grains."

"And nothing took?"

The SHA seedlings came to mind. "No, nothing took," I lied.

"When will you return to Mars?"

"We're not going back."

"Why not?"

"Yeah, why not?" Susan suddenly said in my mind.

Weren't you the one who said to let it go? I thought back.

"Now you want to talk!" Susan shouted. "It's been *two* years!"

Forget I asked, I thought.

"Professor Korda? I didn't mean to bring up bad memories," Shelly said, snapping me back to reality.

"Oh, no bad memories," I said. "We just don't go back to Camp Harmony because nobody will fund a second expedition."

Shelly looked unconvinced. "But Professor Korda, don't you think Mercury being solely dependent on Earth soil is a problem? We passed five thousand inhabitants last month and look to double that within the year. I think The Director will listen."

The Director, Sammy... Can I bring myself to trust him? He was like a little emperor on Mercury, yet I saw so much more ambition in his eyes. We were already indebted to him for our rescue. Asking him to fund a return trip to Mars would put us further into his pocket.

"But the girl's right. It's the *only* way to retrieve the seed," Susan said.

"I know!" I yelled aloud.

Shelly stepped back.

"Sorry, it's not you," I said, trying to recover, but everyone knew of my episode on Mars.

"Oh, okay," Shelly said, quickly finding another tech to talk with.

"Smooth," said Jerkface's condescending voice.

No, no, no! Just go away! I thought back. *No one can know about you!*

"Dillon can help," said a third voice, Papa's voice. "He's still close with The Director. Both of you negotiating a return trip would be far more effective than you alone."

I did not want to go down this avenue, beg a man who I knew would do anything in his power to take advantage of the situation for help. But I could see no other way.

♦

"You could not grow in Martian soil before, so why is now different?" The Director asked with a pleasant grin. But he was chomping at the bit. I could feel it.

"That's not entirely true," I said. "We had seed growing in fifty-fifty Martian sand. A kind of teff developed to adapt to marginal environments. But, we left it behind during the evacuation."

The Director thought long, the wheels turning behind those pale eyes. "Let's say we retrieve this seed. Can we continue its development here, on Mercury?"

I shook my head. "We need wind, light, water, day and night cycles to allow the microbes to break down the grasses into topsoil. Mercury cannot grant these on a large enough scale. Mars is the only planet in System Sol that can truly terraform."

The Director frowned. "Terraforming Mars. The Dirtdevil's creed. It's a fantastic idea, but will take a thousand years to achieve. No, I will not fund an expedition to terraform Mars."

"But—" I began to say.

"But!" The Director's voice rose. "I *am* interested in this seed, and will fund a small retrieval mission. However, you must realize the sensitivity of the matter. Camp Harmony is Earth's property, and this seed is, too."

I again shook my head. "Actually, this seed was developed on my family's teff farm. It's mine by right."

Dillon shot me a confused look.

"We'll still be trespassing on Earth property," The Director said.

"Sammy, why not invite astronauts from Earth?" Dillon said. "That way it's a joint venture."

The Director gave a sly grin. "You surprise me Dillon. Yes, I will approve a return to Camp Harmony, to assess its condition, as a goodwill mission with Earth's astronauts. Meanwhile, *you* must retrieve that seed." He pointed right at me.

What deal with the devil did I make?

The Director sent us the official dossier several days later. The crew consisted of Dillon, Carlos, Jared, Shelly, and myself from Mercury, and Chiayu and Couture from Earth.

I pointed at Couture's name. "Hey Dill, it's your *best* friend."

He glanced at my holotile and scoffed. "Should have known." He looked closer. "They're coming to Mercury first?"

"It'll take less time to come to Mercury then launch to Mars, as it would to launch directly from Earth. It's more efficient this way."

"Mercury's the closest planet to every other planet," Dillon said. "I really hate that guy."

◆

"Maria, it's an absolute pleasure to work with you," Captain Couture said, then turned to Dillon. "Dillon, you're like a barnacle. You know what a barnacle is, right?"

"Do you want to see the arrays or not!?" Dillon snapped. "I can easily turn this rover around!"

I gently grasped Dillon's forearm, our signal to calm.

The rover hummed alongside monorail tracks stretching into Mercury's horizon, with the sun just below the surface, keeping its searing rays from cooking us yet illuminating rocky terrain like an overcast day on Earth. We stopped at a convergence point in the tracks, donned helmets, and emerged from the rover's rear airlock.

"The solar arrays run along tracks keeping pace with the slow rotation of the planet, allowing them to continually stay in sunlight." Dillon pointed at an array coming towards us, compacted, resembling an oil drum on wheels. "Once every seventy-two hours, an array detaches from the train, returning to the dark side for maintenance and upgrades as the rest continue on. It will eventually rejoin the train at the head."

He stopped the array before us and selected *Unfold*. It twisted and turned, unraveling hundreds of metallic petals like a rosebud blooming.

"How much area does this cover?" Couture asked.

"About a football—sorry, *soccer* field."

Couture humphed. "Incredible."

"Thank you," Dillon said.

Couture gave a surprised look. "*You* designed this?"

"I helped develop the tracking system and maintenance cycle."

Couture had nothing to say except, "Have you become a Lightweight?"

Dillon gave Captain Couture a dark look. "I was born into a Lightweight family, but I gave that up to be a Dirtdevil."

"And how quickly you've returned."

"At least I do something other than just step on planets." Dillon stomped his foot. "Look at me! I'm Captain Couture! Look at this amazing step I took! Write me into the history books!"

"Whatever makes you feel special, Dillon," Couture said, turning his attention to the rocky landscape. "I'm sorry my love, I've left you in the hands of an imbecile."

"Children, we're on the same side," I said. "And in case you need reminding, Captain, Dillon is the reason you have this opportunity."

Couture crossed his arms. "You're planning to stay on Mars, aren't you?" Our silence validated his statement. He sighed. "I respect your determination to try again, but Earth will not allow it."

♦

Chiayu joined me on LightLine's underground platform in her envisuit, ready for launch. The Nautilus stood before us in simplistic glory, its fuselage a blunt cylinder twenty-five meters tall, looking like a paper towel roll on end, ready to be pushed from Mercury's gravity by energy collected on the planet's light side and reconfigured into a propulsion beam.

"Maria," she said.

"Chiayu," I returned. "It's good to be going back."

She narrowed her eyes. "I'll be watching your every move in transit. If I suspect anything is off, I *will* ground you."

So much for easing tension. "I'll prove you wrong, then."

"My goal is *safety*, and right now, I consider you unsafe. I *hope* you prove me wrong," she said.

"Oh, she's all right, boss," Carlos said, arriving with Jared, Dillon, and Shelly.

Captain Couture entered last. "So, this is the Nautilus."

Jared looked upon its white, polymer hull. "Are we the test subjects?"

"Yes and no," came The Director's voice. He emerged from the ship's entry hatch midway up the Nautilus's fuselage. "We've begun using LightLine to trade with Luna, Ceres, and Earth's space elevator. However, we have yet to land upon a planet with significant atmosphere. In this respect, Mars will be a first."

I saw confusion cross Couture's face. He made eye contact with me. *He sees the change in Sammy, too,* I realized.

"Oh Sammy, quit with the show!" Dillon said, still oblivious.

The Director gave a tour of the ship's exercise facility, living quarters, and engine room. The Bridge was like a private theater with seats facing a large holowall, yet it hosted no controls. *Completely automated,* I knew.

The Director smiled gently. "I look forward to the status of Camp Harmony, and if it can breathe life once again," he said, but all I could see in his eyes was, *Find that seed!*

Technicians strapped us into seats, secured helmets, and sealed the hatch.

"Please, enjoy your transit to Mars, once cruising speed is reached you will be free to move about the cabin. Thank you for riding LightLine, the most safe and efficient way to travel," chimed the Nautilus.

I prepared for incredible G-forces, performing pre-launch breaths. But the acceleration was gentle. Rings of structure blurred past our window as we escaped the underground. Icarus shone as a pinpoint of light at the planet's north pole crater below, with its monorails spooling around the planet, their solar arrays open like daisy chains on the light side.

The Nautilus's hologram indicated we were traveling almost three times faster than any ship ever had, our transit time to Mars only two and a half months instead of seven. *Another record set by the Hermians.*

◆

Camp Harmony, Mars

"Scans indicate Camp Harmony's northwest airlock is the most probable point of entry," Chiayu called from the Nautilus.

"Uh, it's almost completely buried," Jared responded.

"Maybe we can scoop the sand from the door." Carlos set his case on the sand, dropped to his knees, and pulled at the dust drift with gloved hands. It tumbled back into the divots.

"Try the northeast lock," Chiayu said.

"Negative," Couture said. "The drift is even deeper there. But I'm certain we can devise a better digging strategy." He theorized several hand positions, each with pros and cons, and calculated how much weight was pressing against the door.

Dillon glanced at me from behind his visor, his eyes saying, *You've got to be kidding me.* He slinked away.

"If we hold our wrists like this," Couture continued, "We can most efficiently scoop sand from the door." He had Jared, Carlos, and Shelly holding their wrists awkwardly. "Maria, come join," he said and looked around. "Where's Dillon?"

The airlock door shuddered, and Couture lurched back. Dust pressing against the door poured into the opening airlock, coalescing around a pair of envisuit legs. *Dillon's envisuit legs.*

"Let's go," Dillon said and disappeared into the airlock's depths.

One by one, we followed, activating our headlamps.

"How did you—" Couture began.

Dillon pointed at a ladder at the airlock's mid-point. "Drone deployment hatch opens to the roof."

"What about the sand covering the exterior door's track?" Couture said. "It will compromise the seal."

"That's why we have redundant mid-lock doors," Dillon casually said.

Jared opened the mid-lock door and then plugged his envisuit's finger into the lock's inner doorjamb. "There's no air pressure inside."

"Can we open the door?" Carlos asked.

"Yeah, we're good to go."

Carlos set his case on the floor and attached cords to the door's sill and head. "You might want to back away." A disc appeared on hologram. Carlos placed a hand in its projection and turned. Voltage increased. Sparks flew. He detached the case and tugged the door's edge, sand pouring from inside.

"The corridor beyond is nearly filled," Jared said.

"What do you think happened?" I asked.

"Rear bulkheads must have malfunctioned," Carlos said.

Dillon unfolded a rover drone from his pack, tossed it between the sand and ceiling, and remotely guided it deeper into the camp through his visor. It reached the Junction, where department corridors converged like streets meeting at a central plaza. Dillon spun the camera, taking the status of each department. One corridor was packed solid with dust.

"Agriculture took the hit," Dillon said, giving me an uneasy glance.

"Can we get inside?" Couture asked.

Dillon pointed at the sand. "It's only this deep for a few meters. With your *efficient* hand techniques, I'm sure we can clear it in no time."

Jared, Carlos, and I snickered. Couture grew red-faced. Shelly rolled her eyes, pushed by us, and started pulling at the sand.

◆

Little by little, we liberated departments from entombment. Then we started on agriculture, taking chisels to the packed dust, breaking it apart like brittle concrete, revealing compressed leaves and grasses within.

"It looks fossilized," Dillon said.

The overhead LEDs suddenly lit.

The reactor's back online! "Hell yeah, Carlos!" I cried on the public channel, hearing the others cheering.

"Only took a month!" Carlos responded. "For future reference, we're completely submerging the reactors. Twice this shit's happened!"

"There's not going to be a future," Couture interjected.

"Whatever you say, *Dad,*" Jared said, and we chuckled.

"Carlos, did you find Dave's body?" Chiayu asked.

"Uh, no. That's kinda weird," Carlos responded. "Actually, it looks like multiple people camped here."

♦

"Maria, Avenue H's door is missing. That's your old stomping ground, right?" Jared called in during his dig shift.

Dillon and I quickly donned envisuits and raced to meet Jared.

He pointed at the rim of the hatch. "The door, it's gone. Looks like scorch marks."

We cleared more sand, and Jared plugged his suit's finger into the jamb. "It lost pressure a few days after we evacuated," he determined.

I waded through knee-deep sand, searching for clues as to why Avenue H, of all avenues, was open. I found my workstation and its thrashed equipment. Everything was accounted for except the canister of SHA seed. *But I left it right here!* I frantically pawed the sand to no avail. I felt it in my gut. *It's gone.* I checked the rear hatch of Avenue H.

"Rear hatch is sealed," I reported, masking my panic, and returned to the corridor. "Decompression didn't come from Avenue H."

"Maria, we found the inner hatch clear across the corridor," Dillon responded, pointing at the charred, warped hatch. "It was blown."

We reconvened on the Nautilus.

"It appears purposeful," Chiayu said.

"You think someone broke into Harmony during the storm?"

"I do. But what could be so valuable in Avenue H?"

All eyes shifted to me.

"Maria, is there something you'd like to tell us?" Chiayu said. "After all, that's *your* spot, and it was *you* who initiated this expedition."

Dillon jumped in. "We're just here to check the camp's status."

"Dillon! Shut up!" Couture gave him an icy stare.

Chiayu glared. "Maria, I will not ask again. Tell us what you know, or you will be grounded for the rest of the mission."

"I... developed seed that can survive in Martian sand, but left it here during the evacuation. Our true objective is its retrieval," I confessed.

"I see. And where did you leave this seed?" Chiayu followed up.

"At my station, in Avenue H."

"Well, did you find it?" Couture said.

I shook my head. "It's gone."

"Who else, aside from Dillon, knew about this seed?"

"Heloise knew, but she never seemed interested," I said.

"Hyun thought it was the greatest thing," Dillon interjected. A look of understanding crossed his face. "Oh."

"And Dave's body was not found in the reactor," Carlos added.

Chiayu seethed. "Dave and Hyun *must* have orchestrated the reactor shutdown so they could infiltrate Harmony, steal the seed, and erase all traces."

◆

We reached Avenue Y a week later.

"Both its interior and exterior hatches were blasted from their seats," I reported to the Nautilus.

"Roger that. This must be where Hyun and Dave entered."

Jared welded the outer hatch shut, Carlos flipped the switch, and the air recyclers roared back to life. After a full day of pressurization, we unclasped our helmets and inhaled the greasy scent of Camp Harmony once again.

◆

"Found something," Shelly called from the dunes.

I was in the Command Center with Captain Couture and opened her video on hologram. "We're watching your feed. What is it?"

"Not sure yet."

A black object appeared, jutting from the sand like driftwood washed ashore.

"No way, it's a hand!" Shelly said and scooped the sand away, revealing more of the arm. "I didn't know Camp Harmony issued black envisuits."

"We didn't," I said.

Shelly hauled the body in Rover 1 straight into the infirmary. Couture delicately removed the suit, revealing the preserved body of an athletic young man. His face was clean-shaven and holding a peaceful expression.

"This suit's amazing," Jared said, inspecting its surface. "Watch when I apply current." He attached clamps, and the black material became the white of the dissection table beneath. He then placed a red screwdriver below. It became visible on the suit's surface.

"A chameleon cloak," Couture said, and we turned to him. "A rumor."

"So like, invisibility?"

Couture nodded. "It employs reflectivity to transmit whatever lies behind to the front from any angle." He turned to the peaceful young man. "We need to determine where he's from."

"How do we do that?" Dillon said.

Couture donned a set of scrubs, mask, face shield, and gloves, reminding us that he's the leading physician in off-world health.

"Making incision," he said, slicing down the young man's chest, peeling back his skin, and then removing muscle. He took a whining circular saw to the ribs, removed flesh and bone like a puzzle piece, scanned the exposed heart with his holotile, and compared it to samples from colonists on other planets and moons.

"Magsuits maintain Earth equivalent muscle mass and bone density, but do little for internal organs, especially regarding the weight of blood and size of heart. Our friend here has been living in one third gravity for many years." Couture scrunched his brow. "But his heart doesn't make sense. Despite being atrophied, it's too robust for even Earth."

"What does that mean?" Chiayu asked.

"This young man's heart has been genetically modified. It looks like that of a horse," Professor Couture said. "Only one place in the system allows such experimentation."

"Mercury..." Chiayu muttered. "That explains how they were so responsive with the rescue pods during Harmony's evacuation."

I thought about that. "But something went wrong. If they had retrieved the seed, then The Director would have never agreed to this mission."

Jared went to work hacking the suit's computer. Several hours later, he channeled its last recording to central hologram.

"It's only several days worth. Seems he was regularly uploading," Jared said and rewound the recording, x50 speed, beginning in darkness, but as time regressed, the black became rust, then the Martian red we knew. The hue lifted into a flurry of sand, and a faint circle of light shown above. *The obscured sun.* The video soon righted itself and spun around.

The young man's on his feet, disoriented, I knew.

"Whoa, what's that?" Dillon said.

Jared paused the recording. "What's what?"

Dillon pointed at an area swirling with dust. He selected *Trace* and stretched his arm into the hologram, outlining a portion of what looked like nothing at first glance. Then I saw it, just like I did my imaginary friends for the first time, barely distinguishable from the air. *A second figure.*

"My Sol," Chiayu whispered.

A third person wearing a Martian-issued white envisuit soon revealed, lying in the sand. They lurched to their feet as flashes returned to the cloaked figures' pistols. The Martian raised a hand, holding a canister to the storm. A darker cloud coalesced and entered.

"Stop." Chiayu turned to me. "What was released from the canister?"

It took every ounce of strength to whisper, "The seed."

"Are you certain?"

There's no mistaking it. I nodded.

"Continue," Chiayu said.

The Martian turned as the cloaked figures ran in reverse. But the Martian strode with practiced steps, accounting for the loose sand and with an unmistakable hiccup in their stride. The recording ended.

All was silent. I saw tears in Dillon's eyes.

"Hyun was trying to save the seed," I whispered.

♦

On the last day of our mission, Dillon convinced us to visit his aquifer, quoting the price of the drill left behind to sway Chiayu and Couture.

Carlos jump-started three rovers.

"It's just over here," Dillon said as we crested the crater's ridge.

I caught Chiayu's expression when she recognized the flatness.

"I always thought this was just a crater," she said.

"Yeah, I know," Dillon said, launching a drone to locate the drill buried in the sand. "That's odd."

"What's odd?" Chiayu responded.

"There's a darker patch of sand around the drill site." He lowered the drone to the location ahead of us. The surface rippled in the drone's draft.

"It's water!" Couture gasped.

When Dillon raised the drone, the ripples ceased too quickly to be liquid. But I had seen this movement on Uncle Sonam and Aunt Nobi's farm.

"No! It's grass!" I cried, strode forth, knelt, and gently stroked the grass's red blades with gloved fingers. *Only five centimeters tall but mature.*

"But, how?" Couture asked. "The radiation, cold, toxicity, atmosphere."

I turned to him. "Hyun released thousands of seeds into the storm. If even one is slightly more resistant to the cold, radiation, or perchlorates, it can kick-start the adaptation process."

I collected samples as the others freed Dillon's drill, and then we began the five-hour trip back to Camp Harmony.

"Their roots must extend deep into the sand, through cracks in the iron deposits, reaching water beneath," Dillon said.

"Are you saying Dillon's aquifer is an *actual* aquifer?" Chiayu said.

"It *must* be. Where else would they be getting water from?" Dillon's excitement was contagious. "I believe wherever we find teff, we find an aquifer, too!"

"Have you mapped out the other craters?" Couture said.

"I have a list of potentials from before the evacuation and can start searching in the morning."

"I'd like to join you, Dillon. If you'll allow it," Couture said with unexpected respect in his tone.

Dillon turned sharply in surprise. "I… Of course."

"But the ground is frozen solid. How can their roots penetrate it?" Jared said.

I thought about that. "The perchlorates in the sand lower the freezing point of water to where a few hours a day in summer, liquid droplets exist," I said. "SHA seed is extremely fast growing and a few hours a day is enough for germination and growth. But the teff appears to be further concentrating the perchlorates within their cells, lowering their internal freezing point, like antifreeze. It found a way to seep its roots through the permafrost."

"Are the seeds edible?" Chiayu asked.

I shook my head. "They'll be highly toxic."

"Then they're useless."

"I disagree," I said. "Teff roots can interweave like a fabric, allowing the sand it resides upon to become resistant to duststorms."

"Like sod," Shelly added. "But without the microbes to break the dead grasses down."

"What's required for the microbes to work?" Chiayu asked.

"An Earth-like atmosphere around the teff," Shelly said.

Chiayu's turmoil was visible on her face beyond her visor. *It's against protocol, against mission directive,* I imagined her thinking. But the prospect of sowing the surface was serenading her Dirtdevil soul. I could sense it.

"Put together a list of materials and I'll see what I can find!" she said.

"Aren't we supposed to leave tomorrow?" Shelly asked.

"Harmony's food store was nearly full when we evacuated," Chiayu said. "With just us, we can survive for a few years if need be."

♦

"Fifty-seven aquifers!" Captain Couture said in disbelief, having just returned after three weeks in a rover with Dillon and smelling horrid. "Each was marked by grass, just as Dillon suspected!"

"Maria, you wouldn't believe the variety," Dillon continued. "A ravine had grass with tall, fat blades to reach sunlight above the edge. And another location on the dunes were spreading like kudzu vines."

Couture slapped a hand on Dillon's shoulder. "Let's get drilling!"

Dillon and Couture hit liquid water at the third marker of Dillon's Aquifer. Its outpouring spilled across the surface, soaking the land and returning to the aquifer from which it came. New teff quickly connected the sparse patches into one continuous prairie.

"Maria, four inflatable emergency habitats are up and ready. How many do you think you'll need?" Carlos said.

"For experimentation, I'd say ten."

Carlos nodded. "Consider it done."

We soon had ten inflatable habitats growing teff.

"Each has a different atmospheric composition, starting with Mars actual," I explained, motioning at a patch growing outside. "All the way up to Earth equivalent." I pointed at the far inflatable habitat packed full of grass. "The teff flourished once we added sufficient oxygen, allowing them to properly metabolize Mars's carbon dioxide-rich air. Once the teff is metabolizing there's a runaway conversion of carbon dioxide into oxygen. But Mars's low air-pressure won't permit microbial growth. It wasn't until we increased pressure to 25mbr that decomposition began. However, the perchlorates pulled from the sand returns to the soil maintaining a high toxicity. So in habitat five, we started removing the dead grasses before they decomposed, serving to dilute the perchlorates in the sand to non toxic levels. Only then did we allow the teff to decompose on site, which will eventually create topsoil suitable for agriculture."

♦

Dillon called us to habitat ten hosting Earth equivalent air. We packed among its lush vegetation around a heatcube, maintaining a steady fifteen degrees. We removed helmets and gloves and breathed the topsoil scent in deep.

"That brings me back," Jared said. "It's kinda chilly in here."

"Oh, right." Dillon pulled a canteen from his pack, popped its top, and poured red, steaming liquid into cups.

"Mulled wine!?" Shelly said, inhaling the spice.

Dillon raised his cup high. "To new beginnings."

"Here here!" Carlos said and drank.

Chiayu looked into her cup, then to the lush teff, and sipped.

She's with us, I knew.

Couture cleared his throat. "Dillon, there will be no new beginning."

Dillon squared up to him. "How can you stand on the brink of greatness, the beginning of a new era in colonization, and say, *nope?* What are you so afraid of? Earth? What will they do? Slap us on the wrist? They would not dare, not when we've legitimately sowed the land with Maria's seed. They have *no* claim, and we have *every.* Mercury? We have all the evidence we need to keep them in check. So what has you tied up?"

"The mission is to assess Harmony's condition. Earth's investors—"

"Mars no longer answers to Earth's investors!" Dillon snapped.

Couture sighed. "You speak like Mars is its own country."

"Why shouldn't it be?" Dillon asked.

We laughed nervously, but Dillon did not budge.

"Do you remember what you said during magsuit training?" Dillon continued. "That most of us were from money hungry corporations looking to exploit the natural resources of your beloved planets. How can you now represent those companies? Meanwhile, here we are, turning Mars into a garden of Eden. We're not exploiting a resource, but creating one. How can *this* be wrong?"

My excitement rose, the lunacy of what Dillon suggested becoming less.

Couture humphed. "So, in this independent Mars, are *you* the president? Earth would never take you seriously."

Dillon grinned. "No. The President of Mars must be someone respected system-wide, someone with an established legacy, someone who wants to preserve the beauty of this planet, someone who knows every influential person in politics, and is absolutely fearless."

"Wow, Dillon, good luck finding such a person," Couture chided.

"I've already found one," Dillon said.

Couture rolled his eyes. "And who is this *amazing* person?"

Dillon raised his cup. "You..."

Couture's sneer melted. He stared, unfocused, lost in another realm. After a long while, he peered into his cup and swirled. "Goddamn you, Dillon," he said and sipped.

And so, with a population of seven, Mars declared independence from Earth. Within a decade, Mercury and Ceres did the same.

♦

The Martian Republic

Dillon returned from his morning shift in the fields to find Susan and me mid-conversation. "Hey, Susan," he said, leaving his boots by the door and hanging his coat on the hanger.

"Hey, Dill," Susan responded with a grin.

I rolled my eyes. "Susan says, *hi.* How do you always know who I'm talking to?"

"You have a tone for each," Dillon said. "Notice I'm never around when you talk with Jeff." Dillon hated my name for Jerkface, calling him *JF* instead, which eventually became *Jeff.*

"Da, da, da!" came a little voice from the playpen.

Dillon turned and smiled brightly. "How's my little girl!?"

With her infant-sized magsuit, complete with a cranium hood, Masani resembled a miniature scuba diver. Dillon lifted her from the pen and gave her a puckered kiss on the cheek. He then scrunched his nose, turned her around, and sniffed her butt.

"My Sol! She must get this from you!" he said to me, grimacing.

"Thanks for volunteering." I pointed at a box by the door. "Liners arrived while you were out."

Dillon disappeared into the next room with Masani and a fresh liner.

Susan gave a smug look, one she started giving me after Dillon and I became a *thing.* But we were not the only ones to succumb to primal instincts. Jared and Shelly were the first, followed by Couture and Chiayu. In fact, Dillon and I were the last of the original seven. And it did not end there. Everyone who immigrated to Mars became obsessed with procreation. Our reputation quickly reached the other colonies, and they affectionately re-dubbed us *DIRTYdevils.* Surprisingly, no psychologist or biologist could explain the phenomenon. Susan simply called it, *Martian Fever.*

"Where were we?" I said.

"The Director's proposal," Susan responded.

"Right. We need to figure how to power a LightLine station on Mars without relying on Mercury for that power. There's no way we're becoming dependent upon that man," I said.

"What about Ambassador Riker's proposal, then?"

"A propulsion system designed by Mercury, powered by reactors from Ceres is risky. Tensions between the two are already high after Ceres cut their ice-water shipments."

Dillon returned wearing a frown as Masani smiled in his arms. "Your daughter is becoming more difficult by the day."

"You okay?" I asked.

"I'm just glad we're not in micro-gravity like Ceres or Luna, could you imagine?"

Masani looked at the empty chair Susan was in and pointed.

"Oh, can she see me?" Susan said.

I shook my head. "My attention is this way, she wants to know why."

"But one day she might start sensing us."

"We'll just have to wait and see," I said, glancing at Masani, hoping she did not inherit my lunacy.

Dillon checked the time. "Sorry Susan, but we have to go."

"Already? Well, best of luck. And don't go easy on Sammy," Susan said, pointing at Dillon.

"I'll make sure he doesn't," I said.

Susan faded away.

"Make sure I don't what?" Dillon asked.

Masani opened her arms in my direction. Dillon handed her off to me.

"Make sure I don't what?" he repeated.

"That you don't go easy on Sammy."

"Oh, you don't have to worry about that," he said.

I most certainly do! I thought.

We left our tiny brick farmhouse in the fields atop of Dillon's Aquifer, now domed, pressurized, and hosting an Earth-like atmosphere, and dropped Masani off with Jared and Shelly's teenage son next door.

At the dome's airlock, we donned envisuits and took a rover straight down the crater's side to our old Knievel jumping point at Yang's Canyon, now dubbed *Maria's Way.* And where I once wished for a bridge to exist, a bridge now stood. Translucent farming domes atop several more aquifers appeared in the distance. We docked directly inside Camp Harmony's airlock, *a new feature,* and changed into Council dress. Hundreds of people now crowded its halls. The old greenhouse avenues were converted into a hospital, university, rec-center, and pub. A newly constructed government wing sat proudly where Avenue Y once was, appearing like fresh growth on an ancient tree.

Jared, Carlos, Shelly, Chiayu, and President Couture were at their designated seats around a circular table when we entered Senate Chamber. The ambassadors of Earth, Luna, Ceres, and Mercury entered moments later and found their names hovering above chairs. The Director stood silently across from President Couture. His hair had gone entirely gray and was pulled into a bun, and he wore a thick black cloth textured to subtly catch the light. The pleasantries he once used were no longer present.

The Director in full, for all to see, I thought.

"Good afternoon, ambassadors and senators, you may be seated," President Couture said, taking his seat. The rest followed, except The Director, who took an extra moment. President Couture did not let it fluster him. "We have gathered here today to discuss the culturing and distribution of Martian topsoil and to review the Mars Orbital Transit proposals from the United Hermian Tribes, the Ceran Republic, and Earth Federation. Senator Dhaka-Korda, you have the floor."

"Thank you, Mr. President," I said as a grassy field appeared on hologram at the table's center. "Teff has become key to the Sequential Terraforming of Mars. Sequential in that we are not focusing on the planet entirely but creating habitable pockets atop known aquifers, irrigating and sowing the land within, and introducing oxygen and atmospheric pressure conducive to decomposition. When enough topsoil has been generated, we raise the pocket's atmospheric temperature, pressure, and composition to Earth equivalent and begin proper farming. As Sequential Terraforming provides us with topsoil and food for short-term habitation, we allow our high metabolizing grasses to spread across the Martian surface creating sod to reduce dust storms, meanwhile gradually converting the global atmosphere from carbon dioxide to oxygen. We hope to begin true terraforming in the lowest regions of Mars in three centuries." The hologram zoomed out, showing thousands of markers across the planet's surface. "Senator Granger, you have the floor."

Dillon stood. "Currently, one hundred thirty-seven farms are generating topsoil, but another twenty-one thousand potential aquifers have been identified. In the next decade, we expect to generate roughly eleven billion cubic meters of topsoil a year. This soil is what brings you all here today."

President Couture raised a hand. "Thank you, Senator Dhaka-Korda and Granger. Senator Rivera, you have the floor."

Carlos stood as Camp Harmony's power infrastructure appeared on hologram. "The old nuclear reactors have been replaced by cold fusion reactors of Ceran design, completely separated and individually grounded to ensure another shutdown is impossible..."

The floor opened to questions from the ambassadors, and they did their best to uncover the faults in our logic. When they could not, they quieted.

President Couture turned to the ambassadors. "Let us continue on to today's main agenda. The Mars Orbital Transit System proposals. Ambassador Song, the floor is yours."

"Thank you, Mr. President." Ambassador Song stood. A diagram of Mars and a station in geosynchronous orbit materialized on hologram. "We believe developing a space elevator is essential to opening Mars to System Sol." He went through the mechanics of oscillating the elevator to dodge Phobos. "Ultimately, we believe it better to accelerate Phobos into deep orbit to avoid a conflict with the elevator."

The Director cleared his throat. "Ambassador Song, you must realize the engineering gymnastics you are proposing. Phobos is already on the verge of collapse. Tempting it further by applying dynamic forces is preposterous. Even if you pull that off, it will take three decades to relocate the moon, and another decade to construct the elevator. We cannot wait forty years."

"Then, we oscillate the space elevator to dodge Phobos," Ambassador Song said.

The Director shook his head. "Such oscillation can only be achieved once the elevator's tether is anchored to the ground and centripetal force is applied to the entire system. How do you propose the tether will dodge Phobos while lowering to the surface during construction? Will you politely ask the moon to wait? A space elevator is simply too risky and cost inefficient for Mars."

The Director's right, I knew, recalling my adoptive parents working on Earth's space elevator and the nights I spent running calculations with them.

Ambassador Song slumped into his chair.

"Thank you, Ambassador Song," President Couture said. "Director Williams, you have the floor."

The Director stood. A real-time video of a ship in Mars orbit and another depicting its cargo hold appeared. "These are components for a LightLine propulsion system we can gift to you *today.* We estimate a LightLine station to be operational in one Martian month. Any questions?"

Ambassador Song darkened. "Have you even considered Mars's

atmosphere? Any ship entering and exiting Mars will be subject to *air friction*, which will burn your LightLine polymer to ash."

The Director grinned. "LightLine polymer hulls are designed to absorb light waves from our propulsion beam, which will super-heat any local atmosphere, thus creating a vacuum tunnel to travel through. Atmosphere and air friction are no longer issues. Welcome to the twenty-second century."

"Enough," President Couture said. "We understand the superiority of LightLine. But we cannot overlook that it requires over ten petawatts of energy to operate. Our reactors cannot generate such power."

The Director nodded. "Which is why constructing a microwave receptor on the surface of Mars to receive energy beamed from Mercury is essential. The energy boost will also accelerate the development of your cities."

President Couture shook his head. "Doing so makes us completely reliant upon Mercury's solar fields. We cannot allow such a dependency."

The Director clenched his jaw. "Like how Mercury is dependent on Ceres for water? On Earth for food? And now Mars for soil?"

President Couture locked eyes with The Director. "*That* is the price you pay for too quickly exploiting Mercury's resources and exponentially growing your population without considering the ramifications. Mercury, Ceres and Luna have all overextended themselves in search of riches. A mistake Mars will *never* make."

"Then, you're living in the past," The Director grumbled.

"No. We are completely self-sustaining. *That* is the future," President Couture said, staring down The Director.

"We're willing to give you LightLine as a gift," The Director said.

"No, you are not," Couture said. "LightLine is a means of transporting topsoil from our planet to yours. Allowing its construction on Mars is a gift from *us* to *you*."

The Director gave an icy glare. I could almost see his lip curl, his teeth about to tear out President Couture's throat. But The Director composed himself and sat. "If not from Mercury, then I assume you'll build a new reactor."

"Which is where Ceran engineers come into play." President Couture motioned to Ambassador Riker. "You have the floor."

The ambassador stood, giving The Director an uneasy glance. "Our reactors are capable of generating twenty petawatts of energy, more than sufficient to power a local LightLine connection between Mars and Phobos. Because of Phobos's minuscule gravity, several propulsion types can be accommodated allowing the moon to serve as a universal space station. Such reactors can be prefabricated on Ceres and delivered to both Mars and Phobos in twenty-two months.”

◆

In the Martian autumn of 2188, our population reached one million.

“We did the impossible, Dill,” I said, watching thousands of people on hologram celebrating in streets, plazas, and fields across the Martian world. “We maintained self-sufficiency through it all.”

“We certainly proved everyone wrong,” he said, fumbling with his pack.

The hologram switched to a view from Phobos staring upon Mars’s surface. Thousands of domed aquifers, producing topsoil and food, specked the red desert with green life. Thin strands of vaulted farmland spanned between them, creating a continuously traversable landscape. Views from within the domes and vaults took over, showing people trekking the terrain and living and working in the covered fields. It had become a Martian right of passage. But with our busy schedules, Dillon and I never had the time to claim ours until now.

I caught Dillon sneaking a holotile into his pack.

“The whole point is to disconnect from technology,” I snapped.

“It’s just in case of an emergency.”

“Watching the newest episode of Ceres Brigade is *not* an emergency.”

“Fine.” He set the tile on the table.

I rolled my eyes. “Come on. We need to make Torus Town by nightfall.”

Dillon donned his pack.

“Goodbye house,” we said.

“Goodbye Sha Tolera and Dillon Granger, safe travels,” the house responded before going to sleep for our seven-month absence.

“Sha Tolera...” Dillon said. “I still have trouble saying it.”

“Well, get used to it. This is who I am,” I bitterly responded. It was strange with Dillon. He had an easier time accepting my imaginary friends.

He sighed. “It’s only been a month since you revealed your true identity, and what happened to your family.” He gave a sheepish look. “I’m sorry, I wasn’t thinking about how you felt keeping it a secret for so long.”

“I’ve dealt with it,” I said. “What’s truly getting to me is the media. It’s why I want to disconnect for our right of passage.”

“Shall we get going, then?” Dillon said and grinned.

I grinned back. “We shall.”

Sorghum, wheat, barley, corn, millet, buckwheat, and teff lined the main street, running down the center of Dillon's Aquifer. A fold of sheep, munching on young grains in the distance, wore expandable magsuits over their growing wool, looking like balloon animals. The roof of a house peeked above the crops.

"Look at that, Jared and Shelly are putting on an addition," Dillon said.

One of the carpentry crew on the roof cupped their hands around their mouth and called, "Good luck!" It was their grandson.

We waved. It continued like this, and when we reached the end of Dillon's Aquifer, my arms were as tired as my legs.

We trekked a vaulted strip of cropland into rugged terrain, quickly becoming an aqueduct. Slivers of water ran to either side of a cobblestone road with pumpkin, squash, and cucumber dangling over the edge. We then met a thrust of land and the aqueduct became a canal, the crops now climbing steep slopes. We met two sources of water. One was pumped from Dillon's Aquifer and traversing home, the other was from Torus Town.

Dillon scooped the water from Dillon's Aquifer and tasted it. "Yep, salty." He tried Torus Town's. "Also salty. Jeff, can you tell the difference?"

"Can you?" I asked Jerkface.

He appeared next to Dillon, looking younger than both of us. *He could be our son, even grandson,* I realized. I knelt and scooped the water.

"Torus Town is cleaner," Jerkface said. "Less trace sulfates."

"Torus is cleaner, less sulfates," I relayed to Dillon.

He submerged salinity tabs into each source. "Damn, Jeff. Spot on."

We entered Torus Town's bubble at its highest elevation, granting magnificent views of fields and township below. A church bell rang nine times as we reached a Traveler's Campground.

♦

We had an early start the following morning, heading toward Aang, an estimated nine days of travel. On the fourth day, a farmer recognized us, me in particular, but did not ask for a holopic, *thankfully.* There was something off in his manner.

"Is everything okay?" I asked.

"Yes, yes, everything is quite all right," he said. "Well, my daughter is studying on Ganymede, and I'm sure you know."

"We do not. What happened?"

"The Hermians blockaded Ganymedan space yesterday."

The fourth of Mercury's water colonies to declare independence, I knew. "Why would they suddenly blockade now?"

"Ganymede applied to the Ceran Alliance," he said.

Now that makes more sense, I thought.

"First Ceres cuts off water exports to Mercury, then they take Mercury's water colonies." The farmer gave a nervous look. "Is this retaliation?"

"The Hermians are just trying to make a point," I said, but my stomach sank remembering The Director's pale eyes.

"I suppose you're right," the farmer said. "Good luck with the rest of your passage. Make sure to take advantage of the stops along the way, they might be crowded, but they have drinkable water, and charging stations."

♦

Aang appeared in the vast dune sea five days later, its many domes merging like an insect's compound eye. We entered through lush grasslands, soaking water from an aquifer much larger than Dillon's and releasing rich moisture into the air. Towers rose to support convergence points in the compound dome enclosing intimate urban fabric below, reminiscent of Paris.

"On y va!?" Dillon said, his French sounding foreign to me now.

We checked into Just Inn at sunset.

I scrubbed Martian dust from my wrinkles and looked into the mirror. *Old... But I should look older,* I knew. Mars's gravity had pulled significantly less on my skin than Earth's would have, yet my muscles and bones remained strong thanks to the magsuits. Dillon and I were turning centennial this year, but I did not feel older than forty.

Nevertheless, Dillon had knee replacement surgery and regrew a liver and spleen. I lost an eye. My body rejected the first seven replacements before one finally took. And we both required constant skin replacement therapy, like everyone from the early days. Finally, in 2167, pigmentation was applied to the domes, saving younger generations from cancer.

But it did not save Masani.

At age four, the melanoma began, requiring Masani to undergo skin grafts throughout her childhood. Then, she was diagnosed with leukemia at twelve. She fought wildly for three years and won. But just when we thought she would return to everyday life, the lymphoma came. *But my Sol, did she fight.* By age twenty-one, Masani was finally cancer-free. She followed in Dillon's footsteps, taking to drone construction and geology like it were second nature. After graduating from UHarmony, she joined Ceres's deep-space survey program, taking her to Ganymede, Europa, and Enceladus. But on Titan, she met a young organic chemist. They had a son we always meant to see in person, but duty had always called.

GALAXY'S BEST CHEF | 181

Then, at age thirty-eight, a fatal heart attack occurred while Masani was training for her first trip to Earth. The doctors determined she suffered significant heart damage from her chemotherapy as a child.

We had only prolonged the inevitable, I realized.

Dillon emerged from the shower and caught my expression in the mirror. He wrapped a towel around his waist and another around my shoulders, then hugged me gently from behind.

"I miss her, too," he whispered.

◆

A banging on the door woke me.

"Dillon! Sha! Are you in there!?" A familiar voice called.

Dillon rolled to his side and placed a pillow over his head.

"Please, this is urgent!" the voice said.

I peeled from bed, donned a T-shirt and shorts, and approached the door. *"Senators Holden and Sady,"* shone on hologram.

"Dill, get dressed! It's Shelly and Jared!" I said.

I heard him shuffle, then say, "What?"

I opened the door to find them in Council dress, their assistants crowding the Inn's hallway beyond.

"Would it kill you to check your holotile?" Jared said. "We searched every inn, hotel, and hostel in Aang to find you."

Dillon approached, working an arm through a sleeve. "What's the emergency?"

"It's Mercury," Shelly said.

"We know, they blockaded Ganymede."

She shook her head. "The Hermians *invaded* Ganymede and Europa."

"Invaded? With what military?"

"We don't know," Jared said. "But they somehow marched an entire fleet across System Sol undetected."

"They didn't use LightLine," Dillon said. "We would have seen their signatures."

"Or they've figured a way to hide it," I said.

Dillon turned to Jared and Shelly. "How can we help?"

"President Liu called an emergency session at Pouhallah Station to discuss the matter directly with the Hermian ambassadors."

◆

Pouhallah Station, Phobos

A LightLine beam guided our LightShuttle into one of Pouhallah

Station's hundreds of docks alongside lavish pleasure cruisers and private yachts, drab mining rigs, and proud emissary vessels resembling tropical fish, eels, and sea anemones, granting Phobos the appearance of a coral reef.

Weightlessness fluttered my stomach as I stepped through the airlock, my magsuit switching from shuttle power to station power.

"Ugh. Gets me every time," I said.

Dillon did not acknowledge. "Couture warned us as kids and we've worked so hard to ensure Mercury and Ceres stayed civil. We should have averted this," he said, looking pained. "I wish Couture was still with us."

I gently grasped his arm. "He believed in us. When the time comes we'll know what to do."

The adjacent lock opened. A young couple emerged from a flamboyantly colored yacht with, *"Obradovic,"* engraved on its side. They possessed an air of royalty in the upturning of their noses and manner of dress. The young woman held an infant in her arms who surveyed the terminal with intelligent eyes. They rested upon me, and he smiled, but his mother quickly turned him away. A train of attendants and luggage followed the family to the suite they booked. The infant whirled its head around, making eye contact with me again.

We entered the United Solar Nations Congressional Hall, consisting of a single circular tier of seating. President Liu stood at its central speaking podium below. We caught her eye, and she quickly rushed over.

"I'm sorry to cut your journey short. I know you've wanted to claim your right for so long. But you knew The Director best of all," she said.

"We understand," I responded.

Dillon and I took positions at our designated seats as ambassadors from Earth, Venus, Luna, Ceres, Titan, Enceladus, Europa, and newly independent Ganymede entered. We waited for the Hermian ambassadors.

A gong rang, signaling the USN was in session.

President Liu waved to her assistant and whispered into his ear. He nodded and left. "Has anyone seen the Hermian ambassadors today?" she informally asked.

"They were dining at The Phoenix less than an hour ago," Ambassador Riker answered.

The Phoenix? Even for Hermians that's extravagant, I thought.

"Let's not be distracted, then. You may be seated," the president said. "We are here today to discuss the Hermian occupation of Ganymede and Europa. Ambassador Kelly, you have the floor." President Liu stepped back from the podium.

The lone ambassador of Ganymede approached. "Thank you, Madam President. At 04:27TIA, Jovian satellites became unresponsive. At 07:52TIA, we received a distress call from Ganymede's north-pole observatory via tight-beam. The message reads, *Unidentified objects entering Ganymede's atmosphere. Stop. Formation of objects suggests man-made. Stop. Aurora break detected. Stop. Second wave of objects is entering atmosphere. Stop. Objects approaching our position.* At 14:22TIA, we received another distress signal from Europa, but its message was scrambled. We believe these objects entering Ganymede's atmosphere to be Hermian vessels. The Aurora breaks, as described, only occur when LightLine beams contact oxygen molecules in an atmosphere."

Ambassador Chen of Luna raised her hand. "Ambassador Kelly, using LightLine does not automatically incriminate Mercury. We all use the technology in some capacity. We cannot assu—"

President Liu's assistant returned flanked by soldiers. The president lurched to her feet. The assistant whispered into her ear.

"Lock the doors!" the president shouted.

The soldiers triggered the emergency lockdown. Titanium shutters fell like guillotines at the doors.

"The Hermian ambassadors have been found dead in their quarters," she announced and turned to her assistant. "Are we secure?"

"Yes, Madam President." He produced an envelope. "I found this with the ambassadors, addressed to you. It's safe to open."

President Liu tore its seal and read aloud, "Dear President Liu and members of the United Solar Nations, trusted colleagues and friends. Our world's have come to an impasse, one The Director cannot ignore. The injustices done to our people, this moratorium of water, food, and soil, has left us no choice but to assume control. The Director wishes you not to resist, but understands it is human nature to do so. I write this letter not as a declaration of our intentions, but as a warning to you, my friends. Leave Phobos while you still can. May Sol have mercy on us all."

"You feel that vibration?" Papa said and appeared kneeling.

I did. "We need to evacuate now! I feel vibrations!"

The ambassadors stared at me, confused.

"I feel it, too!" Dillon lied.

The president gave me a trusting look and opened Phobos's emergency channel. "All personnel, this is President Chiayu Liu. This is not a drill!

Phobos's structural integrity has been compromised. Please, proceed to the nearest escape pod or docked vessel and depart immediately, we will rendezvous in Deimos orbit. I repeat this is not a drill!"

A hologram opened in the center of USN's chamber, displaying Phobos's internal heat rising, but it was not from the reactors, as I assumed.

"Structural failure imminent. Evacuation sequence initiated," said the hologram and oors opened around the chamber's perimeter to escape pods.

The floor violently swayed before we could reach them. Power cut, and our magsuits ceased their pull.

I lost my grip on the table's edge and tumbled end over end in the microgravity to the chamber's center. I caught glimpses of Dillon still holding tight. He pointed at me, then at the escape pod on the opposite wall. He placed his feet between his hands like a swimmer diving into the backstroke, then delicately somersaulted back, planted his feet against the wall, and pressed. He drifted across the chamber, appearing closer with each of my somersaults. I caught his hand and we spun like two suns orbiting a common center, nearing the opposite wall. We pulled tight, our revolutions speeding up, dodging the grasps of flailing ambassadors. My hand found a pod's handle. *Designed for one but has room for two,* I knew. We crammed in, sealed the hatch, and hit the switch. Compressed gas launched us through a tube.

We rose from Phobos alongside thousands of pods, yachts, and pleasure cruisers leaving Pouhallah Station's docks. A hairline crack formed on Phobos's surface, slowly widening until the moon clove in two. The inside sparkled like a geode's crystals as thousands of power mains ruptured. The smaller half of the moon dipped to Mars, crumbling in its gravity, shattering hundreds of escape pods and vessels in its path. The larger half rose to a deeper orbit, slowly disintegrating, leaving a dust cloud in its wake, each particle between a grain of sand and a house in size.

The cloud is coming closer, I realized. "Dill," I whispered.

"I know," he whispered back, staring into my eyes. "Since the moment we first met, you've been the light of my life. I love you, Sha."

I pulled him close, gently kissing his trembling lips. But then, with a heavy thrust, he pushed me into the pod's chair.

"What are you doing!?"

"Saving you!" He reached for the bladder to seal me within.

"Don't you dare!" I kicked and punched. "We go together!"

"Susan, Papa, Jeff, hold her down!" Dillon shouted.

My arms and legs stiffened.

"Sha. *You* must live on. *They* must live on," Dillon said.

I knew he was right. "Okay," I whispered, and my arms were released.

"Here it comes. Get in the bladder," he said.

I donned an oxygen mask and pulled a transparent film across myself like a blanket. It flashed at the seam, and air sucked out, shrink-wrapping me within. Dillon lay atop, facing me, with his back to the window. *My shield.*

"This is it, hold on tight," he said.

I peered beyond him to see the dust cloud shredding through hundreds of escape pods and ships. Larger rocks punched through a pleasure cruiser's delicate hull, spilling wiggly objects into space. *People,* I realized.

Grains of sand picked against our pod's hull, escalating like an approaching storm. Then the glass cracked.

"Right in the back of the leg!" Dillon yelped.

More granules pierced the hull, through Dillon's flesh, and into mine. But for every shriek I let out, Dillon gave ten. His face became every expression of pain until droplets of blood formed in his tear ducts, and he relaxed. All became still, silent.

We only grazed the edge of the cloud, I realized. Air hissed through hundreds of pinholes, slowly pulling Dillon away from me, his body and face speckled red.

"Wake up, Dill," I whispered.

"Pumpkin," Susan said, appearing beside me. "Dillon's gone."

No! I must go with him! I thought.

Papa appeared with his hand on my shoulder. "I thought the same at one time, but we owe it to our loved ones to live on."

"A ship is coming," Jerkface said and pointed at Mars below.

A brightly colored dot against the planet's surface grew in size, little puffs of gas nudging it closer. It was a private yacht with a bright blue head fading to yellow, its once fabulous tail now riddled with holes. The name *"Obradovic"* was barely legible on its side. *How had they survived?* The crew within scrambled to put out fires and patch the hull as a young couple with an infant in the mother's arms stared at my pod from the yacht's observation deck. *The royal couple from earlier.*

The father turned away, shaking his head. Then, the mother turned away, too. But a pair of intelligent eyes met mine. *The infant.* He gave me a toothless smile and pointed.

"It's enough," Papa said.

CHAPTER TEN

Salt, real ocean salt, gently mists Clara's face. She closes her eyes, letting it exfoliate her skin, knowing the frigid cold of Enceladus will soon be upon her, and that its pelican sanctuary must shut down for the evening. The sun slowly dips, and the moon's population, people and animals alike, march to salvation beneath the ice.

A young guide approaches Clara with, *"Cheryl,"* on her name tag. "Ma'am. We muzt dezcend," Cheryl says with an Enceladan dialect.

Clara nods and follows the guide, joining a steady stream of tourists, biologists, and students to the elevator. She sighs, anticipating another of Enceladus's eleven-hour nights. One in which Clara will wake several times wondering why she is here. Nobody could recall a visit from Zion. Yet, she had seen it on her holotile as clear as day.

Cheryl glances at Clara, looking about to ask a question. But then, the elevator begins its descent. All attention turns to its transparent walls and the thick layers of ice beyond, growing a darker shade of blue until blackout. The icy layers become liquid. City lights from below dimly illuminate schools of fish pursued by modified tuna. Then, they scatter off.

"Oh, you're in for a treat," Cheryl says and points.

Swaying silhouettes come from the depths, the city lights outlining their sharp fins, tails, and gaping mouths of triangular teeth.

"Great white zharkz of old Earth were zolitary creaturez," Cheryl says.

"But they became pack hunterz on Enceladuz. We call them the White Wolvez." With a twitch, the wolves organize into pairs and dart after the tuna. "And there they go."

The ocean floor fades into view with hydro-thermal vents spewing clouds of nutrients.

"The building blockz of aquaculture," Cheryl informs. "But they alzo heat New Troy." She points at an underwater city made of hundreds of structural orbs resembling a phosphorescent cluster of frog eggs. Beyond appears to be a skyscraper on its side, contouring to the ocean floor. "That iz old Troy," Cheryl says. "It onze rezided on the zurface, with itz length penetrating through the ice, like a nail hammered into wood. It waz zent to the bottom of the ocean during The Fall. New Troy waz built below the ice, to enzure zuch an accident cannot happen again." The shaft tilts towards New Troy. "The elevator zhaft'z accordion zegmentz continually adjuzt to abzorb a fluctuating length az the icy cruzt above zwayz independently of the rocky floor below."

"Thank you for the lesson," Clara says when the elevator stops.

Cheryl scrunches her brow. "You're not here for the wildlife, are you?"

"How'd you know?"

"You haven't been looking at the animalz, not in the way mozt touriztz do. You zeem more interezted in our ztaff."

That's perceptive, Clara thinks. "I'm searching for truth to a story. But it seems to be only a rumor in the end."

Cheryl grins. "What'z the rumor?"

"That Zion Wright christened the pelican sanctuary's opening."

Her grin dwindles. "Um, do you have a moment?"

"Cheryl, all I have are moments."

They stop at a bar called *The Aquarius*. Despite its glamorous location at the city's edge, Clara knows a local watering hole when she sees one. Schools of fish swim by the curved, structural glass, peering in at the humans on display. Biologists at tables raise glasses when Cheryl enters. On hologram is, *"Happy Hour – The White Wolf."*

Clara and Cheryl sit at the bar corner.

"The uzual for me," Cheryl says to the bartender.

He nods and eyes Clara.

Clara points at the drink special. "The White Wolf."

His face brightens. "Yez, Ma'am!"

Cheryl grins. "Remember, the White Wolvez are pack hunterz."

The bartender sets shot glasses of varying heights on the bar, the shortest representing a shark's pectoral fins and the tallest representing dorsal and tail fins.

"Lookz like we're drinking for a group tonight." Cheryl takes pectoral fin glasses and pushes one to Clara, lifting the other to her nose.

Clara follows suit, detecting gin and low tide, and knocks it back. When the fire dissipates, she says, "Now's our moment..."

Cheryl purses her lips. "There'z a reazon you're not getting information about Zion'z vizit. Nobody here iz old enough to remember. But my grandfather uzed to work with pelican babez long ago. He told many ztoriez about the zanctuary'z infancy, but one in particular ztuck out. It waz an incident involving Zion. But he told it like a ghozt ztory. I never thought there waz any truth until you mentioned it. Let me zee if he can join uz."

Twenty minutes later, an elderly man with a resting smile enters. His eyes focus on Cheryl, then move to Clara.

"You muzt be Mz. Ocol. My granddaughter zayz that I might aid you with your rezearch." He extends a hand to shake and looks at the shot glasses. "My goodnezz."

Clara shakes his hand. "It's an honor to meet you, Mr. Nadir."

"No, no. The honor iz all mine. But I azzume you're not here to write my biography. Zo, how can I be of zervice?" He takes the stool next to Clara and reaches for a shot glass.

"I'm here about an incident occurring ninety-seven years ago during the pelican sanctuary's christening. One involving Zion Wright," she says.

Mr. Nadir's resting smile dwindles. "Oh, that iz nothing but a ztory I uzed to tell the children."

"I would love to hear it still."

"I cannot quite recall," he nervously says. "I'm wazting your time."

"Mr. Nadir, I protect my sources fiercely, this is off the record."

He thinks long, then knocks back his shot. "The true verzion, then?"

"Yes, please."

He nods. "I waz twenty-zeven yearz old when Enceladuz'z pelican program began. Tranzferring zpecimenz from Earth waz not difficult, but training them to move below ground for the cold zpellz waz. Many were lozt, but thoze that zurvived raized their babez to go underground az we had taught them. Within a decade, we opened the zantuary to the public, which coincided with Zion'z campaign through Zyztem Zol. He waz running againzt Zlurgezta Jguta of Glieze, a fierze battle of ecological prowezz. Zo, it made zenze for Zion to chrizten the zanctuary. I never met hiz Excellency, I confezz, but I did *zee* him. After giving hiz zpeech, Zion and hiz zecret zervice ztrolled the boardwalk above my work zector. He azked to be alone and waz watching me acclimate pelican babez to the cold zurface. Their motherz were often agitated by thiz. A few znapped at me, and one flew off. I expected her to zwoop down upon me but heard zhoutz from above, inztead. The pelican went ztraight for Zion."

"The look on hiz face iz zomething I'll never forget. For a man who pacified the bloodthirzty Trogdanz, who make our White Wolvez zeem cute, I waz zhocked to zee zuch fear in hiz eyez. He curled upon the boardwalk plankz az hiz zecret zervice came to zhoo the bird. But before they could, zomething... I don't know how to explain it. Juzt that Zion became different. Hiz crying cut, he lurched to hiz feet, and he znatched the pelican'z bill."

Mr. Nadir reaches for another shot glass. "Zion killed the bird. But what zcared me waz the brutality of it. He zwung the pelican like zhe were an ax, uzing her bill az the handle. Her wingz and legz broke. And I watched in horror az he twizted her head round and round. The zecret zervice there to protect Zion were inztead trying to zave the bird from *him*."

Clara shakes her head. "No wonder it was covered up. Did Zion pay you for your silence?"

"He did not need to," Mr. Nadir says, breathing deeply. "Zion turned on hiz own zecret zervice, mazterfully parrying their movez, redirecting their momentum, and manipulating their jointz. I have practized Ergonoz for over eighty yearz, Clara. I'm zeventeenth Dawn. Yet, I have never zeen a more terrifyingly beautiful dizplay of the art."

♦

Clara boards her LightShuttle home, pops hangover pills, and furiously drafts Mr. Nadir's account, still fresh in her mind. *If Zion's a master of Ergonos, then he must have enlisted!* She scours his early culinary career, xeno-cultural cooking theories, and brilliant negotiations during the Arkathy Blockade, all without raising a finger in violence. She cannot find a gap in his timeline. In separate holograms, she opens MerMer, Justin, and Kwai Lan's tales. *What if?* She places one tale atop another at the moment each protagonist meets. Her holotile analyzes for chronological inconsistencies, finding none. Clara highlights the technological advancements. When holotiles replaced phones, ringways replaced airlines, human regeneration replaced organ donation, and natural farming replaced industrial.

This is lost history, she realizes. *This is all true.*

A sudden beep comes from her holotile, causing Clara to jolt. A message from Aizen with an attached recording appears. *What the?* She jumps straight into the recording.

Zion materializes mid-conversation. *"...On top of which were varying mixes of vegetables, meats, and spices local to Ethiopia. It even became the national cuisine of Mars when they declared independence."*

"Ethiopians were the first to settle Mars, too?" says another voice.

That's Aizen! Clara recognizes.

♦

Mom's going to kill me, Aizen thinks, standing in line to board a LightShuttle to Mars. He rationalized leaving a week ahead of his class trip to avoid the press and planned to meet up with his classmates in old Aang. *Still, Mom's going to kill me.* He packed two pairs of clothing, extra socks and underwear, his holotile and ID card, and his cast-iron pan. *Poor choice in retrospect,* he thinks. Aizen's name is mumbled a few times. He tries hiding his face in his jacket's collar.

"You're Aizen," a man finally says.

Aizen turns to find a middle-aged couple. "Hi..."

"My wife thinks I'm crazy, but do you know what I did after watching your interview?" the man says. "I quit my job to start a bakery."

That's brave, Aizen thinks. "What's its name?"

His wife gives him a look. "Yeah, what *is* its name?"

"I haven't figured that part yet. I quit my job though."

"Why are you heading to Mars?" Aizen asks.

"It's the only place in System Sol that still grows actual crops other than Earth. I figured if I'm to start cooking the old way, I better go there. That's why you're going, too. Right?"

No, but it's a great excuse, Aizen thinks. "Yeah, it is."

A woman inches her way closer. "You're starting a bakery? Me, too."

Another couple perks up. "We're opening a ramen shop."

"What type of food are you going for?" the man asks Aizen.

"Injera," he says and sees confusion. "It's a traditional Ethiopian dish that became Mars's national cuisine."

"I didn't know there were national cuisines!" the man says.

"We are now boarding LightShuttle 4726 to Harmony Spaceport, Mars. Please, proceed in an orderly fashion with your holotiles at the ready," echoes through the terminal.

Aizen descends the portal, enters the LightShuttle, and finds his seat.

First class? He looks at the attendant.

The attendant winks and says, "On the house."

Aizen catches up on the shows he missed because of his schedule. His agent calls several times in a frenzy. Mom, on the other hand, does not call once. Although delaying his punishment, Aizen feels insignificant. *Always second to Mom's work.*

◆

He wakes the second day to see a thin debris ring of what used to be Phobos circling a green, blue, and red Mars out his window. A deceleration beam catches the LightShuttle, navigating it deftly around moon debris and into an earth-like atmosphere. They touch down just outside the archaeological ruins of old Camp Harmony.

"We have arrived at Harmony Spaceport, the local M-time is 21:47. Please, gather your belongings and disembark in an orderly fashion. Thank you for riding LightLine, the most safe and efficient way to travel."

Aizen books a small yurt outside Camp Harmony. *My first area of investigation.* He rides a hover bus, racing just above lush fields of grass in the night, with student archaeologists adorning badges of the History Recovery Guild. Aizen's excitement rises. *This must be how Dad feels when embarking on a dig!* The last time he spoke with his father was after the accident in the WorldRing tunnel. He was groggy from the meds and could not speak for long. *Just glad he's okay,* Aizen thinks. Small, white yurts appear before a glass dome containing the original Martian atmosphere around Camp Harmony. The hover bus stops, and they disembark. A host asks for holotiles to confirm reservations.

When she scans Aizen's, her eyes light up. "Yah are—"

"Yep, I am," Aizen quickly responds.

She shows him to his yurt. "It's not much, but yah 'ave ah bedroll, sittin' mats, ah net connection, and incinerator toilet. Dis is like *real* campin'. Please, contact me should yah 'ave any needs."

Real camping? Aizen often camped and fished with his father in Caldon Reserve, south of Tempest City's basin, only packing a sheet of poly, bedrolls, protein packs, and a heatcube. There was no toilet or shelter, and they ate the fish they caught. Aizen's favorite part was how his father always tried to teach him how to bait a hook or start a fire. Ultimately, Aizen caught and gutted the fish and started the fires to roast them. But then, Dad's time off would end, and he would leave for another dig.

Second to Dad's work, too, Aizen thinks.

CHAPTER ELEVEN

Zach lies buried at the edge of London's dome alongside hundreds of archaeologists before him. "Sooner or later, it happens to every crew," they told Jonathan when he first arrived in London. He had refused to believe it, made certain to follow every safety protocol, and even invented a few. *But I couldn't break the cycle,* Jonathan thinks, feeling his chest tightening.

"Cutting it close," Angela says. "The quarry said the headstone would arrive today, right?"

"Yeah," Jonathan says, thinking about how Zach's widowed wife and three daughters will arrive tomorrow.

Vincent sighs. "I don't think we'll find anyone quite like Zach again."

Jonathan nods. "He was pure talent, and such an asshole."

Angela smiles sadly. "Our asshole, though."

A speck in the sky slowly descends, setting the headstone on its marker. Rockets unstrap themselves and return to whichever quarry they came from.

"Here Lies Zachariah Cordon, Beloved Husband, Father of Three, First Class Archaeologist," hovers in the headstone's hologram.

Jonathan waves a hand to open Zach's biography. The quality is far below one of Clara's pieces, but it captures Zach's role in discovering the WorldRing entry and saving their lives.

♦

Zach's eldest daughter, Hazel, arrives the following morning.

Alone? Jonathan wonders. *Where are the others?*

Hazel locks eyes with him. "Where is it?" she says bluntly.

Jonathan leads along a line of headstones that gradually become newer until reaching one in pristine condition.

She stares for a few seconds, pivots, and struts back to camp.

Jonathan hurries to catch her. "Hazel, you okay?"

"You wouldn't understand! You're all the same!" she snaps and disappears into her lean-to.

Angela approaches Jonathan. "What did you say?"

"Nothing really. Is it strange that only Hazel came?"

"Perhaps the rest will come when it's not so fresh."

♦

Two days later, while studying old maps of London, focusing on its WorldRing station and tunnels, Jonathan hears a knock on his office door.

"It's open," he says.

The door creaks and Hazel steps in.

"Well, I'll be. Please, have a seat." Jonathan motions to a wooden chair across his desk, but there is barely room for all his books and sketches, let alone two people.

She squeezes into the seat and inspects the strangely organized chaos. "Just like Dad's study back home. Fewer maps and manuals though."

Jonathan closes his holotile. "I saw the flowers you left. That was nice."

She shrugs. "He deserves something, I guess."

"Hazel, were you not close with your father?"

Her eyes meet his. "We were *very* close, when he was *actually* home. But the schedule, one year on and off, was torture."

Jonathan thinks about his last week with Aizen before leaving for Earth. They camped in Caldon Reserve, and he taught his son how to fish. *Well, Aizen may have taught me a thing or two,* Jonathan reflects. A sudden sorrow grips him, remembering how sad Aizen was when he left.

"I'm so sorry, Hazel," Jonathan says. "We tried our best to save your father."

Hazel sighs. "It's not your fault."

But I'm responsible, Jonathan wants to say.

Hazel eyes a stack of antique maps set high on a bookcase. "Paris, 2097," she says. "A reprint I assume. You think we'll ever reach it?"

"Not in our lifetimes," Jonathan says and sees that only a corner of the map is visible. *How'd she guess?* "You know your maps."

"Dad and I used to collect them."

"You just finished university, correct? What did you study?"

She points at the stack of maps. "Cartography."

"Any specialization?"

"Infrastructure."

"Are you not yet assigned?"

"I *was* about to accept one mapping uncharted labyrinth tunnels dug by the native Sorgan civilization in System Centauri, but I had to decline."

"Why? That's a great assignment," Jonathan says, but she remains silent. "Oh, sorry." Again, his chest tightens.

"Stop it," Hazel says. "Dad always spoke highly of you."

Angela and Vincent stroll through the door. "Jon, how's the shou— Oh, didn't know you were busy."

"It's all right. I'll be going," Hazel says.

"Actually, Hazel," Jonathan says. "We're about to review the WorldRing tunnel extents we mapped before the accident. Would you care to join us?"

She thinks a moment and gently nods.

"The library has more room," Angela says.

Hundreds of old text recreations on bookcases surround several tables in the library. Angela places her holotile on a table with the WorldRing tunnel extents in its projection.

"You made it quite far," Hazel says.

Angela makes a *not really* face. "There are dozens of branching tunnels. We can't figure which way to go." She layers color coding onto the tunnels. "Red represents collapsed tunnel. Blue is where our drones reached before the blast. Our relays fried, so we don't know their current locations or conditions."

"How do we regain connection?" Jonathan asks.

"We must reset the relays, which may be impossible with tunnel temperature so high," Vincent says.

"Practically Paris," Jonathan says, and they nod.

"What about their *Find Me* function?" says a quiet voice, Hazel.

Angela tilts her head. "Say more."

"If we know their serial numbers we can ask the manufacturer to ping their locations and check their temperatures."

"But they're deep underground. It's why we don't have a connection," Angela says.

Hazel shakes her head. "The *Find Me* function is quantum. It does not require line-of-sight or frequency."

"How do you know that?" Jonathan asks.

"I read the manual with Dad before he left for London." She opens her holotile and flips through the manual, stopping at a small paragraph. "The manufacturer is obligated by law to track their products if stolen or lost. The information we receive will be minimal, but at least it's something."

"That's a good start," Jonathan says. "Hazel, would you like to contact them?"

She stares into the diagram. "Where did it happen?"

Angela activates the crew indicators, adjusting to the moment after the heat blast. Zach's name appears in red, Angela's in orange, Jonathan's in yellow, and Vincent's in green.

"The waterline?" Hazel says.

"It was your father's idea. The heat was beyond our basecamp's rating, so he removed the anchors and sent us back to the water. He saved us all."

Hazel slowly nods. "I'll think about it."

♦

Walls, comprised of rusty concrete, are completely devoid of windows. *Depressing,* Aizen thinks, wondering how Sha and Dillon must have felt living in such conditions. The tour group reaches The Junction, connecting Camp Harmony's many departments. Their headlamps peer down corridors, revealing crisscrossing cracks in vaulted ceilings.

"If you please follow me, we will now enter the Command Center, where all communication was conducted," their guide says, and the group follows.

An incoming call blinks in the lower right of Aizen's visor, *"Jonathan Zaid."* *Oh, shit,* he thinks, scrambling to remember his backstory. It stops. He breathes a sigh of relief until his father calls again. *He never calls twice.*

Aizen answers, audio-only. "Hey, Dad."

"Hey, buddy," his father responds. "No video? Did I catch you at a bad time? It's mid-afternoon for you."

On Titan, it is, Aizen thinks. "My holotile is having camera trouble."

"Sounds like you're having audio trouble, too. There's an echo, like you're inside an envisuit," Dad says.

"Funny how that is."

His father pauses. "You're responding too quickly. Where are you?"
Aizen hesitates.

"Aizen Jakob Zaid Ocol! Tell me what is going on this instant!"
The middle names, dammit. "I'm, on Mars," Aizen confesses.

Dad adopts a terrifyingly calm tone. "Why are you on Mars?"

"I came early to avoid the press," Aizen says. "I'll be meeting up with my class in old Aang."

His father considers this. "Your mother never said anything to me."

Aizen activates the video, and his father appears, looking exhausted. But his arms are no longer in slings, and of the bruising that had crawled up his neck, only a faint green remains.

Dad narrows his brow. "You're in an envisuit? Why?"

"I'm exploring old Camp Harmony."

His father blinks, and all his calm anger washes away. "Since when were you interested in archaeology!?"

Phew, Aizen thinks. "I had a holocall with Zion. When I asked about my heritage, he said Mom and I are from Ethiopia. Then, he told a strange story about the first people to settle Mars."

"Fascinating. You think Camp Harmony might help validate his story?" his father says, strangely accepting.

"There are several moments I hope to find truth in. But I need to search Avenue H. You studied here for a semester, right? Do you remember anything called that?"

"I'm not familiar with the name. But if you describe the room, I might be able to help."

"It has several vaulting tunnels branching off a central corridor."

"Sounds like the medical wing."

"Zion *did* say they became a hospital later on."

"Can you flip the camera?" his dad asks, and Aizen flips. "You're in the Command Center, head back to The Junction."

The tour group is entranced by an animation depicting settlers, scientists, and engineers working seamlessly, smiling and laughing like one happy family. *If only they knew.* Aizen slinks behind a tourist whose suit bulges in the middle like a vase and slowly backs out of the Command Center.

At The Junction, a hologram indicates, *"Medical Wing."*

"What about this section interests you?" Dad asks.

"The woman in Zion's story worked at Avenue H. How far is that?"

Dad grins. *"You're* the archaeologist now. Use your English."

"Come on! Please?"

"Nope, remember what I taught you."

"Dad. Is. Jerk," Aizen says in choppy English.

"My son isth immachair," his father responds so fast Aizen only makes out the first two words.

Aizen frowns. "A. B. C…" he recites in ancient English, passing vaulted avenues, each hosting an exhibition of experiments once conducted. "…G. H." He stops and realizes the exhibit is about nutrition. "Hey, they actually got this correct."

When Aizen enters, his visor superimposes engineers tending seedlings and picking fruit. *"Agriculture is the support system of society. Every synthesizer today relies upon the vitamins and proteins only nature provides. Camp Harmony's settlers worked diligently to en—"*

Aizen mutes and removes the graphics. Then he walks the rows of empty tables. Halfway down, he stops.

"What is it?" Dad says, breaking the silence.

"She worked at this station, but it's not the original. There's nothing here for me."

"That's usually how archaeology goes," Dad says.

Aizen studies his father's video square. "You look better. How's the crew?"

"You remember Zach, right?" Dad's voice drops.

Aizen met the guy just before Dad left for London. "I do."

"He… didn't make it." Dad's eyes become glossy.

Aizen wishes he could hug his father. "Dad, it's gonna be okay."

♦

Clara takes several Ergonos breaths as she approaches two hulking men in black suits outside her apartment building's entry. *Please, don't be here for me,* she thinks.

"Clara Ocol, please come with us," one says, pulling a badge that says, *"Chief Security Officer."*

"Can I shower first?" Clara probes.

"I'm afraid not." The Chief waves and a hovercar appears from thin air.

Clara formulates how to escape but then listens to their breathing. *Together, they're beyond my ability,* she realizes. The car door lifts vertically, revealing a man and woman in white Council dress facing one another.

The woman smiles with impossibly white teeth. "Ah, Clara Ocol, it's a pleasure to meet you."

"Is true," says the man.

"Please, join us. This won't take long, we promise."

Clara gives the Chief a sideways glance and enters. The door quickly shuts and the hovercar lurches forth.

"We must ask for your holotile," the woman says, opening a box.

Holotile, singular. Clara places the one she uses for interviews into the box. But when she had reached into her pocket, she grazed her finger against her second holotile, activating it, then navigated blind, disconnecting from the nets and dashing *Record.*

"Fantastic, now we can talk freely," the woman says. "Please, address me as Representative Vesta and my colleague as Representative Fordham. We were present during your interview at Parliament Station."

"Weren't all the representatives present?" Clara asks.

Fordham chuckles. "My goodness no. Only from a few select sectors."

Clara thinks about the timing of their visit. "Does this have to do with Enceladus?"

Fordham again chuckles. "We were very surprised you went there and with whom you spoke to."

"I promised him safety," Clara says.

"And Mr. Nadir will certainly have it. *If* he keeps his mouth shut," Vesta says. "But you, Clara, are another matter. We did not expect you to point your nose that direction."

"I'm an investigative biographer, pointing my nose is my job."

Vesta gives a sharp look. "You were instructed to find Zion's secrets to maintaining galactic stability. This side-project of yours, Zion's senile stories, are a waste of time. We need concrete facts, and we need them *now.*"

"You've hacked my holotile?"

"Don't be naïve, Clara."

Clara breathes deeply. "Representatives, I understand what you have asked of me, but in order to follow through, I must comprehend Zion's complete person, insanity and all. And as I'm sure you know, my traveling to Enceladus had nothing to do with Zion's stories."

Fordham humphs. "We know you've been discussing them with your family. That Jonathan has found a WorldRing tunnel as a result, and Aizen is investigating Camp Harmony as we speak."

Aizen's on Mars already!? Clara almost cries out, struggling to remain calm. *That cannot be!* Then again, she had skipped over Aizen's message. Another thought creeps into her mind. *They're tracking all of us.*

"Clara, we *strongly* suggest you focus on the task at hand," Vesta says as the car slows. "And here we are, ending exactly where we began."

The vertical door opens to reveal the Chief and his Deputy standing exactly where they left them.

"May I have my holotile back?" Clara asks Representative Vesta. "My interviews with Zion are on it."

She reluctantly opens the box. "It would be wise to cooperate," she says, flashing her impossible smile.

The door shuts, and the car speeds down the street, disappearing from view before the first bend.

"Now that wasn't so bad," the Chief says with unexpected candor, extending his hand. "Take care of yourself, Clara."

Clara apprehensively shakes it, feeling stiffness in her palm.

The Chief and Deputy abruptly turn and enter a second vehicle.

She opens her palm to find a small card with, *"Clara,"* written in calligraphy. She lifts its fold.

"Install program 4729GX# on your holotiles. -Zion-"

◆

"Three drones are still operational," Hazel says, pointing at their locations on hologram. "But two have stopped."

"A dead-end, cave-in, or equivalent," Angela responds.

"But this one is still going strong." Hazel zooms out, and the English shoreline becomes recognizable. A series of green dots appear. "Six days ago, it traveled beneath the English Channel, arriving in old Netherlands." She connects the dots.

Jonathan studies the trail leading to Europe. "This is getting us *farther* away from London."

"The WorldRing lines alone are an unbelievable discovery," Vincent says. "We may have to put London on hold."

Jonathan's chest tightens. His frustration climbs. "Zach wanted nothing more than to get to London! So that's what we're going to do!" He looks at Hazel but cannot read her.

"But Jon—" Angela begins to say.

All at once, Jonathan's frustration becomes anger. "I need to think!" He brushes by his crew and descends the hallway to his office. His chest burns, and his jaw clenches. He barely reaches his office, slamming the door closed before crumbling into heaving sobs.

◆

Jonathan wakes on the floor, curled. Beneath his head is a soft pillow. Across his body is a warm blanket. Sleeping in his desk chair is Angela. When he rises, she stirs.

"Hey you," she says.

"Can you keep this a secret?" Jonathan asks.

She raises eyebrows. "Everyone heard you through the wall."

"Oh." *They've seen me weak, broken.* Yet, Angela is smiling something strange. "What?"

"It's nice to see you human, for once," she says.

"I'm unfit to lead."

"You had a good cry is all. We've been worried about you for awhile. Do you want to see a psychiatrist?"

"My Sol, no," Jonathan says but ponders it. "Well, maybe. I don't know. What time is it?"

"Six-ish."

"Breakfast?" Jonathan says.

Angela gives a look but nods.

When they enter the canteen, several crews give shifty glances.

"Ignore them," Angela says and steps in line.

Vincent and Hazel join.

Jonathan makes eye contact with Hazel. "I—"

"Don't," she says. "I get it, you're sorry. Can we just pick up where you left off. That's what Dad would have wanted."

"Is this what *you* want?"

"Well, I'm still here, aren't I?" she says.

♦

Hazel bursts into the library. "You have to see this!" She sets her holotile on the table with the drone's pathway on hologram. "The drone shot southwest, covering hundreds of kilometers in just a few hours!"

"That's impossible," Angela says.

"I know." Hazel locates the newest dot and zooms. "Look at the way it's moving."

Angela studies. "It's tracing a perimeter, first protocol when in a city."

Vincent clears his throat. "If it's impossible for the drone to move so far in a few hours, it may be malfunctioning. It could be wandering a field in old Russia for all we know."

"Practically Paris!" Angela says in frustration.

Blood drains from Hazel's face, and her jaw goes slack. She lifts her finger, connecting the drone's dots, then continues the line, estimating where it might move next. The drone's next dot perfectly matches Hazel's prediction, then comes a second, third, and fourth match.

Jonathan recognizes the outline of a sprawling city, a river splitting down its middle, and an island at the center.

"Oh my Sol," he quietly says. "The drone is in Paris..."

◆

"Is Mr. Nadir well?" Zion says after a long stare-down.

Clara maintains eye contact. "I don't know what you're referring to."

"Because you didn't travel to Enceladus and talk with the good man?" Zion takes a sip of his tea. "Have you installed the program?"

"I have."

"Activate it if you're concerned."

Clara does, but nothing happens. "What does it do?"

"It's a clever bit of code that analyzes our previous conversations to construct a fictitious one."

"Won't it simply predict our actual conversation?" Clara asks.

"It knows not to use its best calculation."

"What about Dr. Lee's recording?"

"The program is already installed in his office and will synchronize with your holotile."

"So you think we're safe?"

"I *know* we are." Zion sips again. "What were you searching for on Enceladus?"

"Don't you already know?"

"I do."

"Then why ask?"

"For the art of conversation?"

"Is that what we're doing? Creating art?"

"Clara, we're always creating art, whether we realize it or not."

"Like the art of Ergonos."

"Ergonos?" Zion cocks his head. "I've never practiced it."

"I don't believe you."

Zion shrugs. "It's the truth."

Clara ponders another way to prod. "Why are you terrified of pelicans? You've dealt with far more menacing creatures."

"Unknown to most, a deep phobia of birds vexes me. Should my competitors discover this, they'd certainly use it against me."

"You *don't* fear birds. The Thoravians are birds and you spent years with them," Clara says.

Zion frowns. "Thoravians adapted for life upon a gas giant planet. Flight is their existence. Representative Sasta was a most wonderful host with elegant wings and the equivalent of feathers. But a bird she was not."

Clara zeroes in. "You are Mermer, and you fear pelicans, *specifically.*"

"Clara, I'm not Mermer."

"How else can you know so many things from before The Fall? You're also Justin, Kwai Lan, and Sha."

A grin spreads on Zion's face. "How did you hear about Sha?"

"Aizen recorded your story. He's smart, you know."

"Oh, I know, more than you realize."

"Did you tell him Sha's tale to coax him into going to Mars on his own?"

"He was asking about Titan cuisine—"

"And you steered him in the direction you wanted."

Zion humphs. "I find Aizen quite difficult to steer. He's very strong-willed, like his mother."

He's steering me right now! Clara refocuses. "If you don't know Ergonos, then what happened with the pelican?"

"Clara, I don't remember. One moment it was coming towards me. The next, it was dead on the boardwalk. My secret service dealt with the creature while I was curled on the planks. Even that was too detrimental with the election, so we covered it."

No, it cannot be like this. "This is *not* an isolated incident. You attacked Dr. Lee and the guards in the same manner."

"What an imagination Dr. Lee has. Have you talked with the guards?"

"I have."

"What did they say?"

"That you got in a punch or two, but were quickly subdued."

"So, you are basing your theory solely from Dr. Lee's account?"

"No. The guards' stories were identical." Clara pulls up the recordings.

Zion listens, calmly sipping. "What does this prove?"

"That they're lying."

He gives a perplexed look. "That's ludicrous."

"I've been interviewing people for over two decades. One absolute I've learned is that the truth is messy. Of seven interviews, I should have received seven differing versions of what happened."

"So, their truth is too consistent to be truthful? Fascinating," Zion says with genuine wonder.

A gentle knock raps on the door, and Dr. Lee pokes his head in.

"Refill?" he says, pointing at the teapot.

Zion peers into the pot. "Why, yes, perfect timing."

It's not perfect timing, Clara thinks, hoping Dr. Lee remembers exactly what they coordinated earlier that morning.

As Dr. Lee leaves to refill the teapot, Clara further digs into Zion, but he maintains his denial. *Perhaps Zion does not know that he knows.*

Dr. Lee returns with the teapot wrapped in a towel, steam gently rising from its spout. *Is the tea actually hot?* Clara wonders, but Dr. Lee gives her a reassuring glance. *How did he fake the heat?*

Zion sets his empty teacup on the table's surface.

As Dr. Lee tips the pot and tea pours from its spout, he stumbles, causing the tea to shift from the cup onto Zion's lap. Clara leans forward, studying Zion's facial expressions and mannerisms for any sign of Ergonos.

Zion's eyes widen, and he inhales sharply. Then, he exhales through his teeth in a controlled manner and calms.

A perfect Ima Herdum Ergonos breath! Yes! I knew it! Clara nearly jumps from her seat with excitement. *Will Zion leap out of the way or grab the pot!?*

Zion locks eyes with hers, instead, letting the tea drench his lap.

"I see why they chose you, Clara. That was masterful," he says, turning to a terrified Dr. Lee. "And a brilliant stumble. Now fetch me a change of clothing and some *hot* tea. Clara and I have a lot to discuss..."

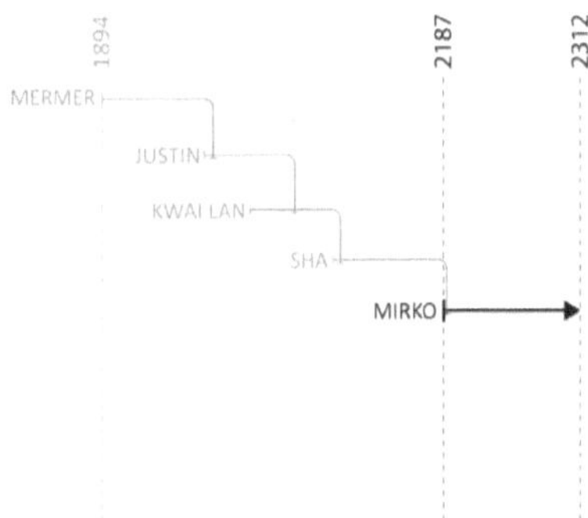

MIRKO's TALE

System Sol: 2187 – 2312

I did not know how I came into the system, for I was not privileged with such time to ponder. War and sushi were all I knew.

My first memory was of my parents vaporizing before my eyes. Yet, I did not cry as I should have. I was just an infant boy. A man, I believed was my father, rushed me to a capsule and launched me into space with a year's supply of rations and an auto-nurse to raise me. And from there, with a toothless smile, I watched the ship's oxygen tanks rupture in a brilliant blue display.

Adrift, I learned to roll in zero-g and push off the capsule's sides, guided by figments of my imagination. I often pressed my nose against the cool glass, staring at never-changing stars. *My comfort, my stability.* Until one day, my capsule was swallowed by a metal monster. The hatch opened, and a crew in military dress pulled me from my crib.

I was delivered to the Ceran Military Academy, as was protocol for all orphans of The Hermian War.

From the moment I arrived, I excelled, and Ceran Command deemed me a *super-genius.* But I am not a super-genius, not even a regular genius, for I could never solve the elevated IQ puzzles. Yet, I was discussing the philosophy of war at age two and reading at a collegiate level by age three. Meanwhile, my genius peers, possessing double my IQ, were still pooping their pants and crying at every discomfort. *Such babies!* I remember thinking. But I could not explain the things I could do or know, only that I felt echoes of a thousand mistakes made and learned from.

♦

Saltwater and fishiness, the scents of Ceres Market, greeted me when I snuck from class. I loved watching schools of fish swimming in their enormous ice-cube aquariums, each species separated by temperature curtains, and the suppliers and buyers bartering and grading fish. Soldiers returning from their tours would flock to the market chefs for the dishes they dearly missed.

Chef Misano-san was my favorite. He never cracked a smile but possessed a hidden sense of humor embedded in his seriousness. I remember his fondness for knives, spending the earliest part of each morning meticulously sharpening their blades. Only when adequate for the day ahead would he rest them upon his cutting board, close his eyes, and breathe deeply, awaiting the first trickles of market calamity. He did not speak to me for the longest time, but he was certainly aware of my gaze.

I had just turned seven, but there were no celebrations for us orphan cadets. And I felt so alone. Misano-san must have sensed it, for he waved me to the other side of his station that day. He placed a stepstool at the table, raising me to the correct height, and wrapped an apron around my waist. Then, he presented an old, worn knife and a slab of tuna. He pointed two fingers from his eyes to his slab, leaned at an angle, slowly ran his blade through the flesh, and layered one slice upon another on a dish. He turned to me and waved his hand in a manner, saying, *now you.*

When I picked up the knife, the balance and the dimples worn into its hilt felt like home. I held it differently than Misano-san did. Nevertheless, he nodded. I leaned into the same angle and slowly sliced the tuna.

"Sugoi," Misano-san whispered.

"Indeed," said another voice.

Commander Lam, I realized.

"So, this is where you've been running off to, Mirko," he added.

"Sorry, sir," I said.

"Skipping class to participate in Ceres's most celebrated tradition is nothing to be sorry about."

"Yes, sir," I said, but I knew this was the end. I was part of the genius class, intended for more extraordinary things. I stepped off the stool, untied my apron, and glanced at Misano-san.

He extended the worn knife hilt first my way.

I stared at it with wanting, then looked to Commander Lam.

"Go on, take it. You've earned it," the commander said, voicing Misano-san's thoughts.

I sharpened that blade every night and smuggled my fish rations to our sleeping quarters to practice my cuts. "Weirdo," I heard from my peers. But they did not understand. I earned this.

♦

On our tenth birthday, Commander Lam and Sergeant Kee took us to watch the bleeding of tuna, a method called *Ikejime*. A chunk of ice was pulled from an aquarium top, revealing tuna swimming furiously below. Two anglers approached the opening, one of them I knew.

"This is Misano-san, renowned fisherman and chef from old Japan, known as Sector 25 today," Commander Lam said. "And this is his assistant, Sato-san. They will teach you the most important lesson in life. The necessity to kill to survive."

Sergeant Kee gave us a hideous grin.

Wearing rubber boots, waders, gloves, and belts of hooks and knives, Misano-san and Sato-san approached the churning water with a baited line and tossed it in. An electrical wire was attached to the hook line. *To stun the fish,* I understood. A tuna immediately took it, thrashing as it was muscled from the water. Sato-san held the tuna between her legs as Misano-san knelt at the head, placing a punching dagger on its crown.

"Don't!" several children cried, tears running down their cheeks.

Misano-san pushed in with a crunch and pulled out a cylinder of flesh, skull, and brain. Sato-san handed him a sharpened rod to thread down the spinal cord. The tuna's tail thrashed, and its mouth opened as if screaming, but no sound came forth. I looked on with interest as my peers wailed. Even Sergeant Kee grew pale. Misano-san opened the gills in a few quick slices, inserted a large hook into its slits, wrapped a cord around the tuna's tail, and raised it over a drum to collect the blood.

The cries escalated.

"Sergeant Kee, take the *weaklings* home!" Commander Lam ordered.

"Stop your crying this instant!" Sergeant Kee barked, gathered those who could not dry their tears, and marched them back to the barracks.

Their bunks and belongings were gone when the rest of us returned.

♦

The Hermian War remained a figment of our imaginations. Was nothing more than simulations, games, and fun times with friends... until that siren rang. Our professors marched us to the emergency elevators, joining thousands of students from the regular classes, lowering us deep into the ice.

I felt vibrations in my chest, yet my peers and instructors were oblivious. Only when the lights flickered did concern cross their faces. The cab shuddered, and they braced their hands against the walls. *No, we'll break our limbs that way,* I somehow knew. I turned off my magsuit and lifted my legs, floating in the air.

My professors saw what I was doing and ordered the rest to follow suit.

Rumbles came far away at first, like thunder rolling in. *What's thunder?* Deafening cracks were soon atop us. The elevator cab walls racked, concrete floor tiles shattered, and the lighting blew. We continued our descent in darkness, the blasts from the surface becoming less intense. The doors opened when we reached the bottom, revealing students screaming upon the floor, bones protruding through uniforms, their limbs bent into question mark shapes. The floor was slick with blood.

They braced against the elevator walls and floor, I realized.

Commander Lam met us. "The Hermians targeted academies all across Ceres."

"They went for the children? How could they?" Sergeant Kee said.

Despite the attacks, Ceran Command refused to pull the Armada from Jovian space, for that planetary system was too crucial to our allies. But after a fourth academy strike, losing over twenty thousand children, the Ceran Armada abandoned Jupiter's moons to secure Ceres's orbit.

◆

At sixteen, we began combat training. The prospect of super-geniuses on the battlefield, especially me with my natural way, had Ceran Command drooling. But combat felt genuinely unfamiliar. Jujitsu, muay thai, boxing, wrestling, gunkai... *But you name it, I sucked at it.* My peers, on the other hand, were learning at incredible speeds, shown techniques only once, and performing them flawlessly.

They nicknamed me *Target Practice.*

"Mirko, you can't get out of this! Submit already!" Cadence said during jujitsu class. She had me in a rare naked choke, and I was passing out. "You do this every time! Just give up!"

Give up!? Like hell! I made gurgling sounds meant to be defiant remarks. Then, I passed out. I woke to Cadence at my feet, lifting my legs to return blood to my head. She extended a hand to help me up.

"I can teach you the proper escape after class," she whispered.

"They won't let you," I said and spied Sergeant Kee, glaring at me. He'd been advocating for my discharge at every opportunity.

"Target Practice! Back on the mat!" he barked, pointing at Giorgione, our jujitsu valedictorian.

I sighed and prepared to pass out again.

♦

"Welcome to kali silat!" Commander Lam said as variable blades and simsuits were distributed.

"Why are they adding another program now?" Kota, our kickboxing phenom, whispered.

"Quiet!" Sergeant Kee barked.

"The heat components of your V-blades have been removed for training!" Commander Lam continued. "But the real thing can cut any material save diamond!"

Sergeant Kee handed me a V-blade. "Get ready, kid."

It felt too light in my hand. I found a weight calibration parameter, placed its balance forward, and extended its blade several centimeters. It now felt like an extension of my body, and I smiled like an idiot.

"What are you smiling at!" barked Sergeant Kee.

"These are called simsuits, designed to seize where struck, simulating injury!" Commander Lam said, demonstrating the proper way to wear them.

While we fiddled with our blades and zipped our simsuits, lost in our own worlds, the sergeants ambushed us, slicing at our vitals. I watched my peers crumble to the floor, their simsuits paralyzing their legs, arms, and necks. Sergeant Kee spun from a seized-up Giorgione, locked eyes with me, gave a hideous smile, and lunged.

He's going for my hamstring, I thought as Sergeant Kee dipped low. How I knew this, I could not guess, but I quickly lifted my knee, bridging the gap between us and plunging it into the sergeant's incoming face. His nose popped, and his head snapped back, but I had only awoken the beast. *Now he'll go for my groin,* I thought, again mystified by such clairvoyance. I tipped my blade's point to Sergeant Kee's extended wrist.

His eyes widened in disbelief, but it was too late. My blade touched his wrist, and his simsuit seized, forcing him to drop his knife.

I continued slicing up his forearm, theoretically carving tendons in the elbow, ripping through his bicep, and plunging into his armpit. Finally, I twisted the blade, running it across his jugular.

The simsuit constricted milliseconds later, from wrist to shoulder to neck, curling Sergeant Kee's arm and hurtling his fist at his face. His eyes grew even wider before he cracked himself in the socket and thumped to the floor.

Commander Lam released the simsuits, and my peers rose to their feet, staring at me in disbelief.

Sergeant Kee regained consciousness seconds later. "What the fuck happened!?" he barked, staring daggers through a swelling eye.

"Stand down, Sergeant," Commander Lam said. "The boy filleted you like a fish. Then, you punched yourself in the face. You're lucky you lost your blade beforehand, otherwise you would've stabbed yourself in the brain." The commander turned to me. "There's hope for you yet, cadet."

My peers were terrified, and the sergeants gave me wary glances the following week until they remembered how I spent my nights practicing my cuts and attributed my freakishness to that. But in that moment, I had understood the mechanics of the human body more intimately than ever before. Had tapped into a strange well of knowledge.

♦

Giorgione pressed a forearm across my face, pinning me to the mat as he isolated my arm. But, I was entranced by the musculature of his neck, his Adam's apple, and the gap between them. I could sense a pulsing. *His artery? What happens if I poke it?* If I extended my arm, he would checkmate me. *I'll have to be quick.* I made a fist, raising my index knuckle like squeezing a trigger, and thrust it forward, descending it into his neck. He grunted, swiveled around my outstretched arm, and pulled it straight. I grabbed my own fist in defiance, refusing to tap.

"Dammit, Mirko! Just give—" Giorgione's grip suddenly loosened, and he fell back, convulsing.

Medics rushed him to the infirmary.

He rejoined jujitsu class several days later, tapping one opponent after another as if nothing had happened.

"Target Practice!" Sergeant Kee barked at me, then pointed at Giorgione.

I saw fear in Giorgione's eyes as I approached. He inadvertently reached to his throat but played it off like a knot was in his neck. He turned to Sergeant Kee. "Can I have a *real* challenge?"

Just then, Cadence tapped her opponent. Sergeant Kee pointed at Cadence, and Giorgione quickly headed that way.

Was what I did that bad?

Kota's strikes were fluid, her balance impeccable, and her movement hypnotizing. And I was stiff, predictable, and had a broken nose again. When I circled away from her jabs, she would nail my thigh with her indestructible shin.

"Check that shit, Target Practice!" Sergeant Kee barked.

I ate a punch every time I tried. *But what if I could hurt the shin itself?* I thought upon the bones and ligaments of her lower leg and the tarsals in her foot. *That's where the weakness lies.*

"Nice movement," Kota said.

"What?" I became more aware of myself.

She jabbed, but my body weight was different this time. I wanted to move forward instead of circling out. I tilted my head, slipping the jab, and closed the gap, nearly kissing Kota. She was standing straight up, and my foot was behind her heel. Her eyes said, *shit.* I nudged her chest with my forearm, tripping her to the mat.

"Target Practice got you good!" Cadence said.

Kota scrambled to her feet, her eyes furious, and stormed, lashing faster and harder. *She'd been going easy on me before,* I realized. She again nailed my leg with that shin. *But the tarsals.*

"Look at him move! He's like water!" I heard Giorgione say.

Yes, be like water, I thought and loosened up more, moving in, out, and around, then striking back. My jab grazed Kota's cheek.

"Damn!" Cadence said as more gathered. "When did he learn that?"

I noticed Kota was falling into a pattern. *The kick will come now,* I predicted and evaded. *Water, water,* I mantra-ed, knowing exactly what she would throw. *Jab, jab, cross.* Then, her hips twisted for the kick.

What now? I thought.

Be a rock, said a voice inside my head.

What the fuck!?

Rock! it shouted.

My feet planted on the mat. My center of gravity lowered and the tip of my elbow was pointed at the top of Kota's incoming foot. Her tarsals flexed around the point of my ulna and snapped. She returned to her stance, looking to continue on, until her brain caught up with her foot and her face turned pale.

"Why'd you stop?" Cadence said. "You okay, Kota?"

"I'm... fine." Kota removed her gloves and limped to the infirmary.

"I can't *wait* for graduation!" Kota said, standing tall, her foot mended.

"You realize graduation is a one-against-seven brawl against the drill sergeants, right?" I said, lying on my meditation mat.

"That's why I can't wait," she said with fire in her eyes.

"All combat styles are allowed," Cadence said, glancing my way. "Even kali salat, if you can wrestle a blade from a sergeant."

"So, even Target Practice has a chance?" Giorgione chided.

"You *actually* think he'll reach two minutes?" Kota said.

"I'm *right* here," I grumbled. "And what makes you think *you'll* last?"

"Look at me," Kota said, gesturing to her muscular core. "I'm going be the first to ever reach three minutes."

"I'm just aiming for two," Cadence said.

I won't last more than a few seconds, I knew and rolled to my side.

Giorgione nudged me. "Hey little buddy, you're gonna be fine. Try actually meditating in today's session. Works wonders for me."

"I can't turn off my brain," I said. "It feels like I have several brains, actually." I thought about how every time I tried the breathing exercises, all I could feel was a cacophony of thoughts racing back and forth.

"Just try," Giorgione insisted.

Our instructor entered and we assumed lotus positions.

"*Breathe* in… two… three… four… five… six… seven… eight… *and* out… two… three… four… five… six… seven… eight…" she began.

For reasons I did not know, I was becoming lulled. I found myself surrounded by endless white space and wearing fishing attire. *That's neat,* I thought, but I did not remember our instructor saying anything about this. The chatter of merchants rose, and a fish market faded into view. I walked among stations, studying fish on ice, octopus and squid, seaweed and kelp, and several types of roe. I stumbled upon a station selling crab. I leaned closer to inspect the crustaceans and found one staring back at me.

Weird, I thought.

"I'm not weird," the crab said.

I flinched and opened my eyes. The fish market slipped away, and the meditation room returned. But when I looked down, the crab was on the mat before me. I must have made a noise, for my peers were staring at me.

The crustacean waved its claw. "It's okay, Mirko. They cannot hear or see me. I've been wanting to meet you for a long time."

"Eeeeaaahhh!" I shouted and ran from class to an eruption of laughter.

Every time I dozed off, that stupid crab was waiting. *There's no choice but to face it*. During our next meditation class, I walked the fish market in my mind and sat on a bench alongside an aquarium. The little crab appeared on the water side of the cube, raised its claw, cut a circle, and stepped through.

"Hi," I said.

"Shhh," our instructor scolded.

"You must *think* to me," the crab responded.

Okay... What's going on? What is this? I thought.

"This is a relationship."

I don't understand.

"I don't expect you too, not yet. But we've been with you ever since you were adrift."

I thought that was a dream.

"It was not."

Why are you in my head? What do you want?

"We want to help."

We?

"I don't have time to explain, but rest assured, we are here for you."

This is stupid, I thought. *I'm leaving.*

"Thank you for talking with me," the crab said. "And good luck with graduation tomorrow. If you need help, return to this part of your mind."

◆

Commander Lam entered the Combat Arena, leading a train of sergeants who took positions opposite us. Each face was blank, machine-like.

Commander Lam took the center. "Today is the day you've worked so hard for! The day that will determine which of you will lead Ceres to victory! It has been an honor watching you grow into the strong men and women before me now! I am proud to have raised each one of you!"

Seven sergeants came forth, simsuits on and training blades at their hips.

"Kota Xavier!" Commander Lam called and stepped back.

Kota unbuttoned her gray cadet uniform jacket, revealing her simsuit, strode to the arena's center, and bowed to each sergeant. She then slid into her favored Muay Thai stance.

"Begin!" Commander Lam called.

Kota came forth, stalking the sergeant directly in front of her. *Jab, jab, slip, duck, cross.* Then, came her shin. The first sergeant dropped to the mat holding her thigh, her femur fractured, no doubt. The next sergeant came anticipating Kota's kick, raising their shin to check. But Kota adjusted mid-kick, swiveling her leg like a question mark and going high, instead, cracking the sergeant in the jaw.

I checked the timer. *Two sergeants down in the first minute!*

A third and fourth sergeant came together, one lashing, forcing Kota on the defensive. When Kota found the opening and unleashed her shin, the second sergeant swept her back leg, dropping her to the mat. Kota switched to jujitsu, snagging the heel of the closest sergeant with the crux of her elbow and twisting, sending an audible pop from his ankle. But then, a fist came, digging into Kota's nose, splattering blood down the front of her simsuit. Her tooth tumbled across the mat, settling before us.

The hologram flashed as the two-minute mark was reached, but Kota would not let up. *She's really trying for three minutes!* I realized.

Kota found her way back to her feet and became a fury of elbows and knees as the sergeants closed in. But she could not slip all the strikes and winced each time her ribs were struck.

"*02:51,*" displayed on hologram when they finally submitted her.

Medics led Kota to an empty chair among the sergeants. They fed her arms through a crisp white officer's jacket and pinned graduation stripes upon her chest. Ceran Command bowed before her.

Fresh sergeants took the place of the injured.

"Giorgione Sepertella!" Commander Lam called.

Giorgione strutted into the arena, removed his jacket, and bowed confidently.

"Begin!"

Giorgione ducked low for a sergeant's leg, and when they sprawled, he rolled back, pulling the sergeant down atop him. The moment the sergeant outstretched an arm to brace their fall, Giorgione coiled around it, pulling to ninety degrees and rotating back, farther and farther, until the sergeant's upper arm snapped. Another sergeant went for Giorgione's legs, trying to isolate his ankle. But Giorgione masterfully torqued over like an engine until the sergeant's head and arm somehow became wedged in Giorgione's elbow. He squeezed like a python until he was cracked across the jaw by another sergeant. Giorgione rolled back in a daze. Several more strikes came before the medics called the match.

"*01:58,*" hung on hologram.

My heart sank for Giorgione, but I could not show it.

Giorgione slowly crawled to us, pulled his gray cadet jacket back on, and shakily stood at attention, a look of shock and pain upon his face.

"Cadence Shi!" Commander Lam called.

Cadence breathed deeply and strode into the arena, hands by her side.

The Earth stance of ninjutsu? I thought, confused.

"Begin!"

Cadence stood motionless, relaxed, almost bored, as the timer ticked away. The sergeants glanced at one another. At the thirty-second mark, one rushed. Only when his shoulder met Cadence's waist did she spring into action, snatching the sergeant's blade from its sheath, running it along his back, and seizing his simsuit. Cadence rolled off, flicking the knife, striking a second sergeant in the solar plexus, seizing them, too. She leaped to the side, evading another sergeant's grasp, proving as slippery as an eel. With a combined effort, the sergeants cornered her. But before sending a knockout blow, Cadence tapped. The confused sergeants turned to the hologram.

"02:01."

She passed, and without a scratch on her, I realized.

Cadence calmly walked to the opposing side of the arena, donned her white jacket and graduation stripes, and sat next to bloodied Kota.

Commander Lam gave her a respectful nod. Then, his eyes met mine. "Mirko Obradovic!"

The sergeants were still breathing heavily from chasing down Cadence, and I knew their favored styles. Still, when I removed my cadet jacket and stepped forth, my legs wobbled with anxiety. *Calm,* I thought. I was about to bow when Commander Lam raised a hand.

The exhausted sergeants marched to the sideline, and seven fresh opponents entered. Sergeant Kee was among them, directly behind me.

Set up to fail? Typical! said a bitter voice inside of me.

Commander Lam's eyes bore into mine, saying, *Show me what you got!*

I remembered what that stupid crab said. I closed my eyes and breathed deeply. Soon, I was in my mental fish market. The little creature was waiting.

I need help, but I don't know what you can do, I thought to it.

Three more figures appeared. A thin man, a woman with red lips, and another with severe features.

"We can help so long as you remain in this meditative state," said the crab. "Do not open your eyes."

But I can't see, I thought.

"You won't need to." The crustacean melted into my leg. "Reach out Mirko, stretch your arms and legs, feel their breathing, their sweat, their heartbeats, their souls."

But I can't.

"Then, I will see for you," the severe woman said.

"I will guide you to their weak points," the woman with red lips said.

"And I will show them pain," the thin man grumbled.

When they melted into me, my senses exponentially grew. I could detect minuscule sounds, heat, and even anxiety. Each felt specific. Each familiar. I stretched my hands to either side and widened my stance. Silhouettes began to form. *The sergeants?*

"Yes, Mirko," said the severe woman.

I could sense them all, but it was so much more, like a 360-degree field of heartbeats. Some were slow and steady. Others fast. One was full of adrenaline, *Sergeant Kee.*

"Begin!" Commander Lam called.

I felt my body swaying back and forth, navigating around sergeants who appeared in slow motion and gently poking their necks with my knuckles.

Then, I heard screaming.

"Mirko! Stop!" Commander Lam was shouting.

Stop? But only a few seconds have passed, I thought. I opened my eyes to see medics rushing to sergeants laying motionless on the mat, splayed around me like I was the center of an explosion. My peers shook their heads in disbelief, eyes wide and mouths agape.

Commander Lam knelt to a sergeant, pressing fingers against their neck. He placed the sergeant's arms across their chest, kissed their forehead, and rose to his feet, furious.

"He was a good soldier! He deserved better!"

I studied the sergeant on the floor, arms crossed and eyes vacant. *Sergeant Kee was dead.*

◆

"They're sending you to the front line?" Commander Kota Xavier said as the rest of my peers kept their distance. "But your graduation was incredible, despite the accident. You should be leading the Armada."

"They'll never let me near the controls of an Orion class ship, let alone a whole armada," I said. "I'm too dangerous, too unpredictable, apparently."

"But sending you to the Jovian System. On the *ground*." She shook her head. "That's a death sentence."

"Isn't this *all* a death sentence!?" I snapped and boarded my transport ship, taking one last look at the geniuses I spent my childhood with.

They stared at me like I was a monster.

♦

Four years of battle. My platoon had repeatedly dropped smack into the mayhem, each time emerging unscathed while the Hermian Tribal Infantry smashed the rest of our battalion. When I would not die, Command accused me of hiding while our comrades were decimated. I was almost dishonorably discharged until they analyzed the footage.

"We thought you went AWOL," First Officer Kota Xavier said on recording. "Then, we found you dance-fighting in the middle of the battlefield, right in the faces of their equalizers. You're insane, you know that? The Hermians pulled several troop ships from Earth orbit and are heading your way. They're coming hard. Be careful."

♦

Eight years of battle. I now led all of Ceran Infantry on the ice of Ganymede. Decoration upon decoration was pinned to my chest, but it did not matter. Ceran Command and my soldiers still feared me.

Forever the monster, the weapon, I thought.

My only semblance of friendship was with the enemy. For when I was discovered on the battlefield, Hermian Infantry, especially their monstrous genetically modified equalizers, would raise gatling guns to the sky, open all frequencies, and shout, "Mirrrko the y'Untouchable! The Destrrroyer! The Ghost! The Harrrbingerrr y'of Death! We y'are honorrred to face you!"

♦

Twelve years of battle. We liberated Ganymede's capital of Sundow, only to lose it the following day, vaporized from unknown parts of space.

"We're searching far and wide for this weapon, Lieutenant," Vice Admiral Kota Xavier said on another recording. "We believe it's the same one used to destroy Phobos, starting this war. But, every time we take an asteroid or station rumored to host the technology, the Hermians incinerate it," she said. "They're sending another fleet to Jovian space. You have them spooked. Keep up the good work."

♦

Sixteen years of battle.

"Your movement and redirection of momentum. It's like a ballet of destruction. How do you do this?" Ceran Command would ask, growing frustrated when I could not answer. Nevertheless, they reverse-engineered my movements, studied my breathing techniques, and charted pressure points they'd seen me use, developing the fundamentals of Ceran self-defense. *Ergonos.*

Thousands of us now danced through Hermian ranks, slicing hamstrings and severing spines with our V-blades, sending the rest into a panic. Yet despite our best efforts, *despite me,* the war waged on.

♦

Twenty years of battle.

"Five tours is enough," Ceran Command said despite the Jovian System still being occupied by the Hermians.

"You think!?" I snapped, staring down the admirals and generals, then I removed my jacket, hosting twice the medals they had. *Did I make a difference in the end?* I thought, handing it over.

"I'm sure we'll see you soon," General Lam said, expecting me to grow bored of civilian life and re-enlist like the others had.

"Fuck you," I said, turned my back to him, and boarded the transport home to Ceres.

♦

I walked Ceres's fish markets once again. But several aquariums had frozen solid, and the chef stations had dwindled to just a few. I neared the stations, desperately searching. *Not him, not him, not him...* Then I found a man standing at an angle, slicing tuna with such care, such precision. He did not glance in my direction when I neared, going straight into slicing and plating tuna sashimi. *How did he know what I wanted?*

"Arigato," I said but did not take the dish.

He stood up straight with a grimace, saying, *Not good enough for you?*

"Have you ever wanted to do anything else?" I asked.

He waved a hand, gesturing for me to come around. As I tied an apron, he placed a slab of tuna before me, *lower quality, of course,* and then a blade.

"No need," I said, unsheathing my old knife, shorter now, thirty years of sharpening its blade and practicing my cuts taking its toll.

Misano-san's eyes narrowed. Recognition showed, but he did not voice it. Instead, he sliced his tuna with inhuman speed and precision. He then turned to me and pointed at my slab. I leaned into my angle and sliced just as quickly, but my cuts were inconsistent in size. Misano-san gently pressed my right shoulder lower, changing my angle.

No! I thought. *My posture's been incorrect this whole time!?*

Young cadets approached the counter.

Misano-san nodded and said, "Tomorrow."

Day after day, he further corrected my form and introduced variances in technique depending on what portion of tuna was cut. After three months, he placed grade-A tuna in front of me.

Customers approached, usually signaling the end of my session.

"Tuna sashimi, onegaishimasu," said a young girl in cadet uniform.

Misano-san entered the back office.

"Hi," said the cadet, staring at me. "Tuna sashimi, onegaishimasu."

"Uh, yes, com—" I began.

Misano-san grunted from the office.

Right, I thought. Misano-san never spoke to his customers, only nodding and going to work, creating the illusion they were about to experience something rare and beautiful. *Something unspeakable.* I nodded slowly, leaned into my angle, and curled my fingers atop the tuna to hold it in place. I pulled my knife across the flesh in one smooth motion, severing a small rectangle from the slab. I repeated the motion until six were free, placing them atop shredded radish on a charcoal dish and adding a spot of wasabi. No soy sauce.

The cadet gave a content look. "Arigato."

I nodded and made eye contact with the next customer.

"Tuna and salmon nigiri, onegaishimasu," he said.

I've never cut salmon nor placed anything atop rice before, I thought.

But you've watched Misano-san do it countless times, said the thin man's voice within me.

The wave of customers finally passed. Each smiled as they dined on my sushi. *I did it! I've made it!* I thought. But then, Misano-san stormed from his office, pointing at the first cadet I served and giving me a horrid look.

"Get out of my sight!" he barked, tearing off my apron.

Heat flushed up my neck. *What could I have possibly done wrong!?* I studied the cadet who was happily eating her sashimi, lifting the pieces with chopsticks, inserting them into her mouth, and biting down... *Oh shit! I never needed to bite Misano-san's sashimi,* I realized. Every piece was perfectly sized to each customer like he had measured the mouths of the entire Ceran population.

◆

When I returned the next morning, Misano-san treated me like any other customer, serving me perfect sashimi. The second morning was nigiri. The third was maki. There was zero recognition in his eyes.

I retreated to my quarters and thanked Sol for soundproofing, for here I was, *Mirko the Destroyer—Scourge of Hermian Tribal Infantry,* crying over sushi. I stayed in bed the next day, breathing my meditative breaths. *I need help,* I thought and waited for the crab.

Instead, the thin man appeared.

"You're pathetic," he said.

What?

"Look at me, *poor little* Mirko," he mocked. "For the first time in my life I'm not perfect at something. Are you going to see Misano-san or not!?"

He doesn't want me, I thought back.

"Oh, grow a goddamn spine!"

But?

"But what!?"

It's just sushi.

"Just!?" He threw his arms up in disgust. "It's not *just* sushi! It's art! Nothing less than perfection is acceptable!"

Misano-san is being unreasonable, I argued.

"Like hell he is! You tarnished his reputation! I would have thrown you out of my kitchen, too!"

I pondered that. *You had a kitchen?*

"I'm a chef! A damn good one! And if you ever hope to become one yourself, then you must never break!"

I never said I wanted to become a chef.

He gave me a look. "I see you smiling when you practice your cuts and sharpen that blade. But, just because Misano-san sees something in you does not mean this will be easy."

What should I do, then?

"Stop being *pathetic* and go back to Misano-san!"

What if he won't accept me?

"Go back the next day! And then, the next! Until the only way to rid himself of you is to teach you!" The thin man turned and marched off.

Asshole, I thought.

"Coward!" he responded, fading away.

♦

I returned every morning so Misano-san could not deny my existence. Nevertheless, he did. Until, after several months, I found him waiting at a dining table in rubber boots and waders. He stood when I arrived and strutted towards the aquariums. After several paces, he turned with an expression saying, *Are you coming!?*

I nearly tripped, catching up to him.

Misano-san moved as if he were still thirty years old. His pace was military, and I matched cadence. We passed market vendors to the tuna prep area. Hundreds of tuna, pulled from aquarium cubes that morning, lay on their sides, Ikejime holes in their heads and covered in ice. Beyond them, butchers sliced around their collars, broke through their spines, and removed their fins.

"Who's correctly breaking down the tuna?" Misano-san suddenly said.

I studied each of the butchers.

The first furiously worked a traditional saw, shedding bits of flesh to the floor like sawdust to remove the head. He used a smaller knife to scrape thick scale, then a sword to cut spines from the vertebrae. *Why not use a single blade?* I thought.

Another used a heated wire to melt through flesh and bone, but the meat was singed at the edges. *Such a waste.*

Then, I found a woman using a simple, rounded blade. She pushed it around a tuna's collar, then pulled it back, using its sharpened heel. A short chop of the spine severed the head and fins in one clean piece. With the same blade, she scraped scale from the skin, then pushed forward along the spine, rotated the fish, and pulled back along its side, quartering a chunk of flesh. Her movements were relaxed, patient, and precise, yet she broke down the tuna faster than the rest.

"Her, with the round blade," I said.

Misano-san nodded. "Sato-san will teach you the way."

♦

"Why do you use a rounded blade?" I asked Sato-san, marveling at the folded imperfections of being hand-forged.

"I would have loved to own the traditional knife sets," she said. "But I could never afford them. Instead, I modeled my blade after a Taiwanese fillet knife I remember my father using."

"Don't you feel guilty abandoning the old ways? Aren't you tired of being hassled by the other butchers?" I asked.

She did not hesitate. "The Usonians introduced salmon to Japan in the 1900's. It was initially considered garbage fish, but slowly found its way into grocery stores and eventually seeped into sushi. Those who critique me for balking with tradition, yet serve salmon on their menus, are hypocrites."

I pointed at the knife. "You actually made this yourself?"

"Come with me," she said, leading to an abandoned section of the market with twisted metal from ships that returned home in rare form. She pointed at the metal. "Ceran Siclecell Titanium armor is simultaneously stiff yet flexible, designed to absorb shock waves. Once forged into shape it will always return."

"How is this important to butchery?"

She grinned. "It's the perfect material for a fillet knife, once forged into shape, it will never dull."

◆

After my first year, I began understanding Misano-san and Sato-san's teachings. After another, it was second nature. I woke every morning excited, smiling stupidly.

After the morning rush one day, Misano-san gave me a strange expression. "It's been three years today since you asked me that question. Let me ask it back to you. Would you ever want to do anything else?"

"I can spend a lifetime doing this," I answered, feeling the truth of it.

"And I have," Misano-san said, grinning.

◆

"I should've known to find you here. How are you, Lieutenant?" A familiar voice said.

I lifted my eyes to see a crisp uniform with decorations on its breast and a tag reading, *"Admiral Kota Xavier."* I pointed my blade at the menu choices.

"Tuna sashimi, onegaishimasu," Kota said.

I sliced and plated her sashimi.

"Arigato," she said, found a table, and waited until my shift ended.

I closed up shop, approached Kota, and sat across from her.

"You have some balls, Lieutenant," she said.

"Behind that table I answer to only one person."

"The old man."

"Misano-san, one of the last master chef's of his kind," I snapped.

"I did not mean to offend."

I narrowed my eyes. "The last time we spoke in person was when I departed for Jovian space. You looked at me like I was a monster then. So what brings you here now?"

"A part of me is glad to see you happy. But make no mistake, I'm still wary of you. I would not have come unless it was important." Kota took a long Ergonos breath. "The Hermian's have taken Enceladus."

"In the Saturnian System?" I said, confused. "Our presence is far too strong there. Why would they make such a move?"

"We don't know," Kota admitted. "But they've moved a massive fleet into Enceladan orbit. They're up to something."

"You think it's the weapon?" I ventured.

Kota shrugged. "They've commandeered one of the research stations called Troy."

"What for?"

Again, Kota shrugged. "Both Athens and Troy stations extend several kilometers through the ice, to its liquid ocean below. Whatever they're doing, they're working hard to conceal it."

I thought about that. "What does this have to do with me?"

"Everything, I'm afraid," she said.

♦

Enceladus shone a dim white on hologram, its fractured icy surface speckled with pin lights at its research station, Troy.

"Your objective is to land upon Enceladus's surface undetected in the night, infiltrate Troy to liberate the scientists, and capture the Hermian's elusive weapons-system! All without their fleet in orbit knowing!" Kota briefed my regiment. "But as you know, Hermian instrumentation is extremely sensitive! All electrical and heat signatures will be detectable from thousands of kilometers away! Which means you must insert without the use of heaters, lidar, holotiles, and communication!"

Completely dark. I finally understood why I must lead this mission. We donned envisuits and climbed inside powerless insulation balls colored white to match the ice. Within each was oxygen tanks, food, water, and fecal containment, as that could also be detected.

We shot from our fleet, hiding in Titan's shadow, and coasted silently through Saturnian space to Enceladus. Gloves with reflective palms attached to our insulation balls' exteriors were used to capture the sun's rays and signal upcoming maneuvers in Morse code. Particles from Saturn's E-ring soon bounced against our hulls, reducing our velocity as we entered Enceladus's tenuous atmosphere.

I raised my glove, flashing thrice. We released oxygen from our tanks in thirty-second spurts, decelerating us to non-suicidal speeds. The atmosphere warmed us with friction, but we did not burn, for our insulation balls absorbed the heat to maintain an exterior temperature equal to the surrounding atmosphere.

The surface quickly came. I pulled a ripcord, inflating a doublebladdered airbag around my ball, and sensed my regiment pulling theirs, too. But a few failed to deploy. Their pulses skyrocketed before they smeared on the surface. The rest of us bounced like masterless basketballs across a court. Once settled, and my double bladder deflated and detached, I kicked a breakaway panel and slipped achy legs through insulated sleeves, ending at heavy boots. I rocked back and forth, righting myself. My soldiers were spinning aimlessly, disoriented in the pitch-black night, growing more panicky by the second. Like a penguin, I waddled to the nearest, grasped her glove, and tapped my name into her palm with Morse code.

She tapped back, *"Private Mathers."*

"You are first," I tapped.

I pulled a cable from a winch within my ball and handed her the end loop. She assumed the caboose position of a string of soldiers I would round up like a sheepdog. One by one, I greeted them. They clipped to my cable and shuffled back, bumping into those already linked. Like a game of centipede, we navigated the ice, careful not to turn too sharply, often bypassing soldiers if it meant colliding with our tail. But, inevitably, someone slipped, toppling us like dominoes.

After seven hours, I reached the last.

"You 194," I tapped, then, *"You last."*

"Understood," he responded.

I pulled the cable taut and tapped my palm, *"Private Collins, Sergeant Seranin, Sergeant Yu, Private Tan, Private Smith, and Major Garcia did not make landing. We will take a moment of silence before we move."*

Several shed tears in isolation but pulled themselves together. *As they always do,* I thought.

"We must reach Troy's sister research facility, Athens, before sunrise," I tapped. *"Follow carefully, hold the line, and be ready for my commands. We must navigate several crevasses in darkness. Let's go!"*

In unison, they thumped the line.

◆

We woke in a shallow depression a klick away from Athens. Early morning sunlight unveiled the obstacle course we had navigated in the night. My regiment lay coiled like a snake still attached along my cable. I unhooked and thumped their insulation balls one by one as a wake-up call. I then stretched my senses to the bottom-most point of Athens, to its reactor and submarine port, three kilometers below the ice, the only way to access the moon's subterranean ocean. Several hundred souls were huddled around the reactor for warmth.

My regiment quickly formed a semi-circle around me.

"Survivors in Sector Twelve. Team One with me!" I signed and released my insulation ball's clamps, cracking it open like an egg, exposing my inactive envisuit to the elements, sending an immediate chill through me.

Fifteen others emerged with old assault rifles devoid of electronic components and connected to oxygen tanks for round combustion.

"Let's go!" I signed and took off towards Athens's airlock, eyes closed. My platoon filed in behind me, rifle butts against shoulders, barrels down. *"Nobody guarding entry!"* I signed over my head.

We turned back-to-back at the airlock door covering a 270-degree range as Private Mathers stepped upon a pump to generate a minuscule current to hack into Athens's system.

"Lock is depressurized, opening," she signed.

The door shuddered open and we poured in, sealing it behind us. Private Mathers checked the inner lock door, confirming the upper portion of Athens station was depressurized. We found glow sticks on the floor leading down its staircase when we entered. *Placed by the inhabitants,* I assumed. At level minus two fifty-four, the floor grating no longer sparkled with frost and unmarked boxes were piled high in adjacent research labs. We reached the station's lowest airlock, deep within the ice.

"It's pressurized," Private Mathers signed.

"When was it last used?" I asked.

"Yesterday, twice."

Out once, in once, I knew. *"And before that?"*

"Twenty-seven days ago."

"They'll know we're here the moment we start decompression," I signed. *"Let's say hello."*

Private Mathers decompressed and negotiated the outer door open. I entered and pressed a palm against the lock's inner hatch, sensing eighteen souls on the other side, rifles trained my way.

"This is Lieutenant Obradovic, Task Force 473 of Ceran Infantry," I knocked in Morse. *"We've come to liberate you."* No response. I knocked again, adding, *"We know that six hundred and thirty-seven souls are here."*

One lowered their rifle and knocked back, *"Lieutenant Obradovic? They say you can sense things no other person can. Prove yourself."*

"Eighteen of you are pointing rifles at the door," I replied.

"How many fingers am I holding up?"

"Two fingers, one thumb, behind your back," I answered.

The rifleman then raised his middle finger to the door.

◆

"Do you know anything about the Hermian forces occupying Troy?" I asked, relieved to finally speak.

William shook his head. "We do not," he said in a thick Enceladan accent. "We were EMP'd, frying communicationz and zending our reactorz into cool-down. Luckily, we retained itz rezidual heat in the lower levelz."

"Do the Hermians know you survived?"

"They muzt know. Their inztrumentation iz too zophisticated not to. But containing uz iz more advantageouz, they need only wait for uz to freeze."

"I see. Might you know how to enter Troy undetected?" I asked.

"Zokka might. Zhe waz ztationed there for zixteen yearz."

"May we setup Basecamp in Athens?"

"Your body heat iz welcome, but we cannot zpare any food."

"We brought our own rations."

William thought it over. "You may zet camp next to the airlock."

◆

Later that day, a microbiologist strolled into Basecamp.

"I was told I could find Mirko Obradovic here," she said.

Private Mathers pointed in my direction.

She studied me. "*You're* the mighty warrior? You look like a nerd."

My soldiers stiffened in shock.

"That's because I *am* a nerd," I responded. "Who do I have the pleasure of speaking with?"

"Dr. Sokka Shen. William said you needed my assistance." She glanced at the soldiers staring daggers at her.

"Let's walk," I said.

We strolled the edge of Athens's central atrium, winding down several levels of Enceladan encampment with each person carrying glow sticks, resembling a cavern of fireflies from above.

"Can you really see through walls?" she abruptly asked.

I grinned. "When I need to."

Her eyes narrowed. "You're full of shit."

I let out a snorting laugh. "You don't have an Enceladan accent."

"Nice perception skills, *Mirko the Wise,*" she said. "I'm Earth born."

I stopped in my tracks. "I assumed you might be from Ceres."

"Because of my name? Or because you're an idiot?"

"Because I'm an idiot, I suppose."

"Correct," Dr. Shen said. "I'm from the Siberian region of old Russia."

"How'd you end up out here?"

"I was obsessed with microbiology as a child and came to Enceladus after university to help introduce the necessary organisms to convert the ocean's water chemistry to accommodate aquaculture. It was working, too, before the Hermians came. The tuna strangely took to the deep waters."

"How can that be?"

"A side effect of their genetic modification to extreme cold is a heightened ability to withstand water pressure. They began hunting the cephalopods at lower depths."

"I wonder how they taste," I said.

"Like *tuna* maybe." Her tone said, *Duh.*

I shook my head. "Tuna take on the flavor of what they hunt. On Earth, you can tell from what region they lived in by tasting the prey they fed upon in their flesh."

"How do you know that?" she said, giving me a funny look.

"After retiring from Ceran Infantry, I apprenticed with a sushi chef named Misano-san." I pulled my worn knife from its sheath. Sokka laughed when I spoke of Misano-san's seriousness and how crushed I was by his critiques. *I cannot believe I shared that.* Before long, we were several levels lower, surrounded by scientists.

"Mirko, it's getting late. But let's talk again soon," Sokka said, placing a hand upon mine and gently squeezing, sending lighting bolts through me.

"Uh, yes." I felt high as I climbed back up the atrium to Basecamp.

Private Mathers approached with urgency. "Sir, what have you learned from Dr. Shen? Do we have an entry strategy for Troy?"

Oh, right... I turned around and marched back down to find Sokka.

♦

We crammed into Athens's submarine lock at the bottommost point of the station, opening to the liquid ocean below. We again were sealed within our insulation balls and strung along my cable. Private Mathers pointed at several dozen oxygen tanks welded to my lead insulation ball.

"The output of O2 is designed to propel us through the water. But use it sparingly," she signed.

I nodded and turned to my regiment. *"This is just like our night crossing,"* I signed. *"Relax as best you can as I lead you to Troy and prepare for insertion in approximately eleven hours. Unlike Athens, Troy has an open airlock that uses air pressure to hold water at bay. Once we secure the airlock we will EMP the colony, knocking out their systems. After the pulse dissipates we activate our heat vision and V-blades. Any questions?"*

"Are there creatures in the water? We've heard stories," one signed.

"Tuna and squid. I'm more concerned about the jaggedness of the ice's underside. Remain as still as possible. Is that understood?"

They thumped the line.

I twisted the airlock valve filling the chamber with water. I closed my eyes, opened my senses, and dipped into the ocean current, swiftly dragging the rest of my regiment along. I felt a tingling on my right, *North.* I faced south instead, letting the current guide us for several hours. Creatures swarming hydrothermal vents became intense to my senses. A curious group of cephalopods approached, each the length of my arm from body to tentacle. They clung to my frame and inspected our insulation balls.

I extended a finger to meet one's tentacle. *The Creation of Adam,* I thought. *But who's playing God?*

What be you? the squid seemed to ask.

Um. We're human, I thought back.

No, you giant eggs.

We're inside the giant eggs, I thought.

It abruptly released my finger and jetted away, and I felt the feverish rush of hundreds of heaters closing in with *food, food, food, food,* on their minds.

The tuna, I realized.

We encountered more schools of fish, each having a unique demeanor, and were greeted by another school of tuna just before reaching Troy's open airlock. But their fever felt different. More like, *run, run, run, run.*

"Mirko? What are those?" the stupid crab said, appearing beside me.

Tuna, I thought back.

"No, what are, *those?"* It pointed its claw deeper into the abyss.

What do you— I felt massive objects swaying back and forth, slowly, purposefully, organized in pairs, and communicating. They guided the tuna like a pack of wolves herding prey.

Left, Left. Right. Keep straight, the wolves said with childlike voices.

One turned our direction. *What this? Look. I find.*

A pair peeled away from the group, coming closer.

Big eggs? Food? one said.

Taste! Taste! They bolted towards us.

I cranked the oxygen tanks open, blasting us ahead and feeling my regiment's pulses skyrocket. We were at Troy's insertion point and about to break the water's surface when I felt a monstrous tug.

Outside bad. Taste bad, the wolves said.

Another violent jerk racked the line.

Inside good!

I burst from my insulation ball into the lock and grabbed the line to drag the next soldier from the water. Mighty yanks pulled us back, but as more of us joined the tug of war, we slowly overpowered our opponents. When the last ball was dragged from the water, we backed away, aiming rifles at its surface. All was still. I could no longer hear the childlike voices.

"What the fuck! You said there was nothing to fear!" my soldiers signed.

"I don't know what those things are!" I responded.

"Things? You mean they weren't the Hermians!"

"They were hunting the tuna! We must focus on the miss—"

Lights flooded the airlock. Doors burst open. Hermians in heavy impact armor rushed along catwalks above and pointed their rifles down upon our skulls. But Private Mathers had pulled the EMP from her gear and twisted its switch, sending an electromagnetic pulse milliseconds before the Hermians pulled their triggers. *A medal is in order for her!* The circuits of their rifles, heavy impact armor, and magsuits fried, sending the Hermian soldiers stumbling about. The lighting cut. I felt hundreds of heart rates within Troy spike as the Hermian Tribal Infantry, the most advanced in human history, was cast into the Stone Age.

◆

Commander Turk had not uttered a word. Her vitals did not waver. And I had exhausted every humane interrogation tactic.

"Let's talk," Kota signed from surveillance, knowing I could sense her through the wall.

"I'll be a moment. Do you need anything?" I asked Commander Turk.

The commander gave a funny look. Her stomach growled.

Kota met me in the hall. "They're impossible."

"Well..." I thought about Commander Turk's stomach. "Permission to raid the canteen?"

"I don't see how that will help, but permission granted," Kota said.

I turned and headed that way.

"You can't just leave without being dismissed, Lieutenant!"

"Reprimand me," I said and kept walking.

Slabs of tuna lay across kitchen prep tables for dinner. *For us soldiers who fought the grueling battle of Troy?* I thought. After Private Mathers fired the EMP and we overwhelmed the confused Hermians, working our way up level by level to the top, Kota's fleet had come to life in orbit, ambushing the Hermian fleet. But I was not privy to this information and was stunned when sections of Kota's Hopper Camp—a command center, barracks, canteen, and detention center—landed a klick outside of Troy, and Kota herself came knocking on our front door.

I cut a portion of tuna from the slab, wrapped it in paper, found rice just made, grabbed seaweed, a wasabi tube, ginger, and a cutting board, and returned to Hopper Camp's detention center.

Commander Turk was kneeling by her cot when I entered her cell.

"...May he shepherrrd y'us y'into the light," she whispered.

I set the cutting board on the interrogation table and unwrapped the tuna. "Have you had sushi before?" I asked. "Most don't realize that sushi is an umbrella term for several styles. For example, sashimi is the fish by itself," I pulled my knife from its sheath and curled fingers atop the tuna. "You must slice in single strokes. Like so." I sliced and plated the pieces, then set the dish at the table's center with two pairs of chopsticks. I lifted a pair, placed a spot of wasabi on a piece of sashimi, and inserted it into my mouth.

Commander Turk picked up the second pair and clumsily tried one, a second, then a third. When she finished, I set pickled ginger on the dish.

"Ginger to cleanse the palate," I explained.

Commander Turk's eyes flicked to my knife resting on the cutting board.

"Next, I'll make nigiri."

Commander Turk ferociously ate the nigiri.

"Now, I'll make maki." I set my knife on the cutting board and carefully rolled the maki. "The key is to maintain a consistent roll."

Commander Turk snatched my knife and slashed at my throat. But I sensed it coming and lifted a hand, knocking her wrist upwards. The knife whiffed above my head. She regained her balance and thrust straight at my heart. I slapped her wrist downward this time, the blade chopping the maki roll I just finished.

"Not bad," I said. "But you want to cut the pieces smaller so they can be enjoyed in a single bite."

Commander Turk studied the roll she inadvertently cut.

"If you hold like this." I adjusted her hand. "And pull back in one stroke, your cuts will be cleaner."

She released the knife and backed away. "Who y'are you?"

"Lieutenant Mirko Obradovic."

"The Harrrbingerrr y'of Death," she whispered, her eyes wide.

I shook my head. "Sushi chef, one day, hopefully. But I had to come out of retirement because of you."

"Chef? But you're y'a monsterrr! You rrrape women and drrrink the blood y'of babies!"

"I can also shape-shift into a bat," I said deadpan and her eyes went even wider. "For the love of Sol! I don't do any of that! I don't want to partake in any of this! But you threaten the existence of everything I hold dear, so here I am!" I sighed. "Commander Turk, I just want to go home and work on my sushi. The only way I get to do that is if I find this secret weapon of yours. If you help me, I promise to go away forever."

The commander locked eyes with mine. "y'It doesn't worrrk like you think y'it does. Therrre y'is nothing to be found."

"Then, how does it work?"

She shook her head. "Forrr the sake y'of my brrrotherrrs y'and sisterrrs, I will say y'only this. y'Evacuate, *now*."

◆

I was preparing for bed in Hopper Camp's officer quarters when brilliant light blasted through my window, nearly frying my retinas. I covered my eyes, dropped to the floor, and opened my other senses. I felt Troy's foundation softening like a candle and water pooling at its base. Then, the entire station dropped through the ice into the ocean abyss below. Hundreds of Hermians, Enceladans, and Cerans trapped within screamed as water pressure crushed the station like a boa constrictor. I could not watch anymore and let my senses go. The light finally dissipated.

With blurry eyes, I raced to Hopper Camp's Command Center. "What the fuck is going on!?"

Kota turned to me. "It matches the description of the weapon we've been searching for. It struck Troy. I've called for the evacuation of Ceran and Hermian fleets in orbit."

I thought upon the warning Commander Turk had given. I peered into the hologram to see thousands of escape pods fleeing from Kota's battle cruisers embracing Hermian fleet ships with their drawbridges still penetrating Hermian hulls from the insurgency. I then thought about Sokka.

"What about Athens?" I asked.

Kota turned to a coms tech. "Send word to Athens resistance, they must evacuate now!"

Several minutes later, another light beam struck, its brightness sending us again to the floor, covering our eyes. I sensed it landing several hundred klicks north of our location.

"They struck Athens," I said. *Did William and Sokka get out in time?*

A third beam hit both Hermian and Ceran fleets in orbit. We watched their oxygen tanks rupture alongside nuclear core detonations on hologram. Shrapnel flung in all directions, striking support ships and causing them to shatter like a chain reaction. Kota's flagship commander appeared on hologram with flashing alarms and billowing smoke in the background.

"Admiral Xavier! The entire fleet is coming down! Our projected crash zone is right on top of Hopper Camp! You *must* evacuate!"

Kota snapped her head to me. "Lieutenant Obradovic! Take my capsule and get as far away as possible. You have to survive!" She tossed her holotile to me, then called for Hopper Camp's evacuation.

I stood frozen. "But Kota—"

"That is a direct order, Lieutenant! Don't make me drag you there!"

I stood straight and saluted, then sprinted down hallways, passing hundreds of soldiers donning envisuits. Detention cells opened, and Hermian prisoners raced to open others. I waved Kota's holotile across her door, entered her fitting closet, pulled on an envisuit and helmet, and pencil-dove above her bed as covers and mattress pulled away to reveal a cylindrical capsule below. I landed hard inside and gritted my teeth as compression bags immobilized me. The glass hatch was sealed shut, and the capsule shot off at crushing speed before I could prepare. My vision narrowed as the pod's display screamed, *"10.3g... 10.4g."*

Finally, after several kilometers, my capsule stopped on the ice, just in time for me to see a firestorm crossing Enceladus's black sky. It was Kota's flagship in several pieces, flanked by hundreds of shredded battle cruisers and support ships. I held my breath. Impact tremors hit, causing my vision to blur and my teeth to chatter. A horizontal avalanche followed, tumbling my capsule, compacting ice around its hull, and entombing me three meters deep.

Then all cataclysm ceased.

I opened a channel to Hopper Camp. "This is Lieutenant Obradovic of Task Force 473, calling Admiral Xavier! Do you copy!?" *Silence.* "Admiral Xavier! Kota! Do you copy!?" *Still silence.* I searched for any active frequency, finding one. "This is Lieutenant Obradovic! Does anyone copy!?"

A crackling voice came, *"Shhh... copy... shhh... is Sokka... shhh... Athens Resist... shhh..."*

The ice above me crunched, and sunlight appeared through its cracks. Gloved hands pulled chunks from my capsule's hatch. A face appeared from behind a visor. *Sokka.*

"You okay in there?" she said through com.

"You sure took your time," I grumbled, having drunk recycled fluids for eight days straight.

"We had to help the important people first." Her deadpan delivery caught me off guard. "A joke, Mirko." She continued chopping the ice around the hatch until she cleared enough to open. She hooked a carabiner to my envisuit's harness and winched me up.

"Have you found others?" I said.

"We have several parties searching for pods. We've picked up sixteen from your regiment, thirty-seven from Kota's fleet, and four Hermians."

"That's it?"

Sokka pointed beyond me.

I turned around. The once flat ice had shattered in the fleet's impact. Jagged edges glimmered as far as the eye could see. One slip, a brush against a shard, could slice an envisuit. *Dr. Shen risked life and limb to retrieve me,* I realized. "What's your status?"

"We packed inflatable habitats, fuel cells, and several months of dehydrated food stuffs during our evacuation. We're okay for now. But we'll have to scavenge fleet wreckage if we want to survive long enough for Titan to pick us up."

"You've made contact?"

"No. We haven't gotten through to anyone. Satellites must have been hit."

After several hours of striding, inflatable habitats appeared in the distance, looking like sausage links. Construction crews meticulously shaped chunks of ice into massive bricks. I turned to Sokka.

"Once we encase a habitat in ice, we'll deflate them, heat from within, and let refreeze to create an airtight seal," she explained. "We'll repeat the process as much as is required to house incoming survivors. But there's a limit to what our air-recycler can handle."

♦

I raised my fist, signaling what remained of my regiment to halt. A dozen Hermian soldiers surrounded a wrecked ship ahead, *the Saint Samuel.* Among them were two equalizers wielding dual gatling railguns and an auto-self-destruct mechanism should ammo deplete or their heartbeats stop. Even I knew to get out of the way if they came charging in their thick armor-plating painted Hermian red and screaming proverbs on every frequency. *They're safeguarding whatever lies in that ship.*

"*We must steer clear,*" I signed.

The next day, we found the thrashed remains of the Ceran fleet alongside several mangled pieces of Hopper Camp, much of it still ablaze. We searched the wreckage, finding charred and dismembered crew, but not Kota's body. I sensed scavengers conversing in Ceran sign language when we reached the flagship's remains.

I flashed my glove against the faint sun in Morse, "*This is Lieutenant Obradovic of Ceres Infantry. Identify yourself.*"

One looked in my direction and returned flashes. "*This is Corporal Shu of Ceres Fleet. Glad to see you survived.*"

Corporal Shu looked defeated when we reached him.

"*We've been wandering for months, surviving off what little food was in our pods, trying to find others,*" he signed. "*We finally set up camp here.*"

"*You're welcome to join us,*" I signed. "*We've erected habitats and have foodstuffs from Athens before it dropped through the ice. We're searching for air-recyclers to accommodate our growing population.*"

Corporal Shu thought about that. "*There should be one at the flagship's bridge for the eventuality of separation.*"

We found the recycler in several pieces in the ship's mechanical room.

"*Can it be repaired?*" I signed.

"*Not without the proper tools,*" Corporal Shu responded.

"*What about the ship's aft section?*"

"*Perhaps. But it's been claimed.*"

"*By the Hermians?*"

"*No, Cerans,*" the corporal signed.

"*They should be friendly.*" I sensed Corporal Shu's hesitation. "*What happened?*"

"*We weren't far when the fighting began,*" he signed. "*The Cerans, now occupying the aft section, drove out another group of Cerans who originally camped there.*"

How had it come to this already? I thought. "*We need that recycler. Can you show us the way?*"

We made camp a klick from the aft section, preparing to sleep within our envisuits when flashes lit the sky.

"*You can sense what's happening out there, right?*" Corporal Shu asked.

I closed my eyes, focusing on a group of souls approaching the ship. *"There are two distinct camps. A-team is in pike formation, shooting, but not to kill. It appears they're trying to pull B-team away from the ship wreckage. But B-team is vigilant,"* I signed.

"Do we help A-Team or B-team?" Corporal Shu signed.

"We take neither side, Corporal."

The shooting stopped. A-Team scattered across the ice to a depression where they had set up a temporary camp.

"A-team is retreating. No casualties, no injuries." I opened my eyes.

"Sir, what do you suggest we do?"

"We make contact in the morning, unarmed," I responded.

"That's suicide," signed the corporal. *"They'll open fire on us."*

"No, Corporal, we have not become savages just yet."

Tremors woke us in the dead of night, and the sky flickered like the fabled lightning storms of Earth. A-Team fired flamboyantly, appearing like a more significant force. *Sloppy.* Again, B-team did not break formation. The firestorm soon died down. I was about to open my eyes when I sensed a third group masking their approach within the terrain. *Two squads of four, each with a monstrous soldier at their centers.* My stomach sank.

"Hermians are coming in fast from the west!" I signed.

My regiment jumped to their feet.

One of the monstrous soldiers broke into a sprint.

"They've sent an equalizer!" I signed. *"Private Mathers, can you amplify the output of our stuns?"*

She nodded. *"We can daisy-chain our rifles to make the range and penetrate their armor. But we'll only have one shot."*

"Do it," I ordered. *"And congratulations on your promotion, Major Mathers, I leave you in charge."*

"Yes, sir!" Major Mathers signed.

Corporal Shu cocked his head. *"Sir, are you leaving us?"*

"I must convince our Ceran comrades to put aside their differences and focus on our true enemy."

"But they'll see you coming. They'll shoot you."

"They won't." I shut down my envisuit's life support systems, leaving only the air hissing on analog, becoming truly invisible to scanners. Then, I closed my eyes and slipped into darkness. I sensed the equalizer come into range of B-team, and open its rain of destruction, rumbling the ice beneath my feet. Incendiary rounds melted through the ship's armor like a hot knife

through cheese as B-team hunkered down. A-Team stopped in their tracks on the ice and faced the commotion. *Run, you idiots!* But they did not, and it all made sense, then. *They're neither Infantry nor Navy,* I realized.

The equalizer detected A-team and swung that way.

Where's that stun!? I stretched my senses to Major Mathers. She was still furiously working to daisy-chain the rifles.

I bound for the wreckage, now free of the equalizer's rain, to meet B-team poking heads above the debris. I arrived in full stride and leaped clear over them and their barrier, landing delicately inside the ship. I spun as they lifted rifles, opening my hands to show I was unarmed.

"Two Hermian squads just west of us," I furiously signed. *"An equalizer is firing upon the Cerans who were flanking you."*

Their leader slowly lowered her rifle and signed, *"Let them deal with it."*

"Unacceptable," I signed back. *"Our comrades out there are not trained for combat. You know this."*

"We do," she signed.

"Then, you know they're either engineering or medical personnel, both essential to our survival."

"Who are you?" she signed, again aiming her rifle.

"Lieutenant Obradovic of Task Force 473."

She pulled the rifle's butt tight against her shoulder, then thought better of it and lowered.

I nodded. *"My regiment is due east. We have a plan to take out the equalizer, but I need you to distract it so I can get our comrades out there to safety."*

"Won't the equalizer detect you?" she signed.

"No." I bolted back onto the ice.

The equalizer opened fire on A-Team, but a moment later, B-team sent a volley, their shots bouncing off the Hermian's ridiculous armor. The monstrous soldier lifted both gatling guns, sending spurts into the would-be sky, and resettled upon the ship wreckage.

I reached the first hobbling Ceran of A-team and hoisted him over my shoulder without slowing my pace. I passed another on the ice, severed at the waist. *Alive but gone.* A third was wrapping her arm with an amputator. It flashed, her arm fell to the ice, and her suit instantly sealed. I grasped her intact arm and pulled her along. The rest of A-team limped to shelter in a shallow valley. I dove over its edge with the two injured Cerans in my arms, tumbling down to meet them.

One pointed a stun pistol centimeters from my visor. *Just what I need.* I jammed my titanium-tipped finger behind its trigger before it was pulled, yanked down on the barrel while lifting the hilt, dislocating the Ceran's wrist, and confiscated the pistol.

"Stay put. Two squads of Hermians are coming from the west. We're taking care of the equalizer," I signed to the bewildered Cerans and slipped back into the darkness.

The equalizer pitched forward, fixated on B-team, driving its massive legs into the ice, dropping one of its gatling guns depleted of ammo, with the other still spraying, all the while signing, *"The Father, the Son, and the Holy Spirit,"* across their chest.

A sudden wavelength rippled across the ice, concussing against the equalizer in full tilt. *The stun!* I realized. *And one hell of a shot!* The Hermian became jelly, crumbling to the ice belly down. Its gatling gun ceased rotation. *Did it run out of ammo?* I waited for its cataclysmic self-destruct. Instead, I felt a second equalizer charging from the west with guns raised.

But it's out of range of the ship, I thought.

"No, Mirko," said the severe woman's voice within me.

I studied the equalizer's posture and the angle at which it held its guns. *The equalizer lying unconscious is the target,* I realized. *They intend to set off its self-destruct, taking us all out.* I checked my new pistol's charge. Enough to stun once at full power. But given the equalizer's armor, it must be at point-blank range. I knew only one way to get that close, having witnessed their destruction for years vaporize everything but a half-meter zone just in front of them, caused by the limitations of their armor. *A safe corridor if you're stupid enough to stand there.*

I retrieved my V-blade, extended its edge just enough to cut through the equalizer's armor plating without compromising the envisuit's seal beneath, and strode into the equalizer's kill zone. The monstrous soldier picked up my blade's signature and jerked its gatling guns my way. But I was already in full stride, too quick to focus on. The ice behind me vaporized, the shards nipping at my heels. When one of their guns paused to auto-reload, I pivoted, coming straight at the Hermian, right up the safe corridor. It lurched in surprise, digging its heels into the ice and plowing a mound of snow.

I set my magsuit to, *"2.0g,"* and hurdled over the mound, planting my feet on the equalizer's breastplate, my magsuit recognizing it as, *"Floor."*

The Hermian thrashed as I carved into its armor, ditching its gatling guns and grabbing my legs. Despite the two-G, the ungodly soldier was pulling me off. I increased to six-G and sucked back to the armor. Pops sang down my back, and pain shot through my knees. *Almost there!* I finished the carve, dropped the V-blade, and pried the armor with my suit's magnetism. Still, the Hermian was lifting me off. A millimeter crack appeared. I placed the tip of the stun pistol and let my shot fly.

The vise grip around my ankles relaxed, and the monstrous Hermian tipped forward. I fumbled to disengage my magsuit but was too slow.

Pinned beneath a sleeping giant.

My regiment came racing to roll the equalizer off of me.

"My Sol, sir!" Major Mathers signed. *"That's a first!"*

I did not respond, focusing upon the rest of the Hermian squads, slowly walking our way, hands up in surrender, held at gunpoint by my regiment. I powered up coms to meet a cacophony of cheers. Then, came a murmur from the Hermian's captain kneeling before me.

"Mirrrko, The Destrrroyerrr. y'It was y'an honorrr to face you."

♦

"Recon Four, calling Athen's Basecamp," Corporal Shu called in as his squad swept around the hole Troy had fallen through.

"We read you, Corporal. What's up?" Sokka responded.

"We found another deserted camp around Troy's abyss."

Dr. Shen turned to me. "That makes the fourth."

"They were using radioactive isotopes to keep warm," Corporal Shu said. "You think they succumbed to radiation sickness?"

"It doesn't explain the inhabitants' disappearance," I responded.

Corporal Shu approached several frozen-over holes. "What about the holes, sir? You think they were trying to dive to Troy's wreckage?"

Dr. Shen studied the holes on hologram. "I think they were fishing."

"How do you know?" Corporal Shu asked.

"I used to ice-fish on Lake Baikal." She turned to me. "Something's not right though."

I nodded. "Sit tight, Corporal. We'll be there in a few hours."

When we arrived, Corporal Shu's squad was searching a storehouse made of a compartment once part of Hopper Camp.

"Sir, what do you make of this?" he said, pointing to dehydrated foodstuffs, Ceran symbols on their packaging. "They had enough food to last several months."

"Sokka, are you sure they were fishing?" I asked.

She approached the frozen holes. "The way the central hole is chopped suggests so. But the ice should be several kilometers thick, not ten centimeters." She neared another hole, frozen over. "The holes at the perimeter are melted from below instead of cut. You can see the isotopes beneath."

"Why would they keep the area shallow?"

"It would make it easier to re-chop the central hole." Sokka studied the camp. "Have you found anything that could be used as line and reel?"

"They had a winch with nano-cable," Corporal Shu said.

"I'd say they were ice-fishing," Dr. Shen concluded.

◆

Sokka and I found Corporal Shu's squad kneeling around the central fishing hole, staring into its depths, the following morning.

The corporal turned to me. "Sir, there's a fish. We chopped open the hole expecting it to flee, but it stayed. Weird."

Weird, indeed, I thought. I strode closer, but my legs suddenly gave out. I fell flat on my face.

"Mirko, the Graceful," Sokka said.

What the hell!? I thought.

The little crab appeared in front of me. "It's a trap!"

I felt monstrous creatures rushing from the watery depths, heading straight for Corporal Shu's squad. *It's the wolves!* I realized. The ice fractured where the isotopes were placed. Corporal Shu's squad was flung into the air and plunged into the frigid water. One was immediately dragged into the depths, where I sensed their limbs being torn from their body. Another soldier was pulled under, and then a third.

Good! So good! the wolves said.

Corporal Shu was struggling to get atop the ice.

Give me back my legs! I thought to the crab, and they were released. I lunged, sliding across the ice on my stomach, reaching for Corporal Shu's hand, but he was ripped from my grasp.

One more! the wolves said, watching me but not with their eyes.

I reeled from the edge. *Go away!*

No! We wait for you, one who speaks.

◆

What's going on out there? I thought, staring at the stars overhead, trying to imagine what kept Ceres, Mercury, Earth, or Titan from making contact. *Why the seventeen years of silence?*

Supplies dwindled. Bodies atrophied. Hope eroded.

Great equalizers came to us anemic, their gums bleeding, teeth falling from their heads, and their bodies shriveled and bruised. But we could not help them, for our own supply of vitamin C had nearly depleted.

Childlike whispers came to me every minute of every day, beckoning me back to the water. The wolves knew where our camp was and would congregate below the ice, discussing how good we tasted.

♦

I again woke screaming at the sensation of Corporal Shu being chewed.

Sokka was by my side, stroking my sweat-soaked hair. "Mirko. These visions are not real. Please, stay strong. Promise me you'll stay strong."

I promised I would but did not know how much more I could take.

"I'm zorry to interrupt," William said at the entrance of our room. "But we have to dizcuz the vitamin zituation."

Sokka kissed my forehead. "Stay, rest, try to sleep."

I shook my head and slowly rose. "I'm okay."

We followed William to our makeshift infirmary.

"Mirko, Zokka, William," Dr. Zeal said. "Our vitamin C zupply iz at an end."

"Can we not get vitamin C from our food?" Sokka asked.

"We went through our greenz and citruzez yearz ago."

"We can search more wreckage, there *has* to be more," I said.

"Mirko, it'z all gone," William said.

"Can we modify our GLO gene to allow our bodies to produce it themself?" Sokka asked.

"No," Dr. Zeal said. "Modification of that gene would cauze the unraveling of DNA."

"Then, we're screwed," Sokka muttered.

Something nagged in the back of my mind. I thought about the fishing holes at the deserted camps. *Why did they bother fishing when they had food? Oh,* I suddenly realized. "Tuna are one of the few vertebrate fish that produce their own vitamin C," I quietly said.

Horror washed across Dr. Zeal and William.

"So, we must face the wolves," Sokka said.

♦

We returned to the deserted camp with a full platoon to find Corporal Shu's icy grave still kept thin by the radioactive isotopes in the water. A volunteer, clad in equalizer armor and tethered back to the winch, inched towards the frozen hole, ice pick in hand.

"They're watching us," I whispered to Sokka. "I can sense them."

She gently squeezed my hand.

The volunteer chipped through the ice and knelt, peering into the depths. "There's nothing down there," he said.

They're all down there, I knew. But they did not rush to the surface.

We set a pulley above the hole, draped a baited hook over its wheel, and lowered it into the abyss. The day passed without a nibble. But then, we woke to shouts from the night watch.

"Flag is raised!" they hollered.

Sokka neared the cable, staying off the shallow ice, and felt the vibrations on the line. "We're hot!"

We slowly cranked the winch, reeling whatever was on the line from the depths. The wolves below dispersed, and, for a moment, their voices did not haunt me. Then, I felt the fury of a tuna. It took three hours to crank to the surface, and it barely fit through the hole we chopped. Its eyes were almost gone and its coloration was completely white. The changes in anatomy left the biologists gasping.

"What now?" they asked once it was pulled atop the ice.

"Sokka, straddle the tuna," I instructed and unsheathed my knife, placed its tip at the tuna's crown, and crunched through its skull. "The rod!" I hollered and threaded it down the tuna's spine. I slit its gills and strung it above a drum to collect the blood.

We baited the hook and lowered it back into the abyss.

♦

"Eighteen tuna!?" William cried in disbelief when we returned. "What about the wolvez!?"

"They kept their distance, just observing. I don't know why," I said.

"How are we going to break all thiz down?" William said.

I grinned. "We have plenty of Siclecell titanium lying around."

We forged fillet knives from twisted armor, and I taught them how to break down the fish. With several butchers working around the clock, I returned to the ice, monitoring the wolves below and notifying anglers when they neared. But I could not always be there.

Major Mather's squad was on the ice when I was at camp. As their angler baited the hook, the wolves rushed to the surface, breaking the ice and sending them into the water, just as before. But their equalizer armor proved too thick, and they slugged at the wolves' snouts with metal fists. When Major Mather's squad returned, they presented a tooth, triangular in shape, the size of a hand.

"What are we dealing with?" I asked.

Biologists shook their heads in disbelief. "It'z a great white zhark, but triple the zize of thoze found on Earth."

"Sharks? But they communicate with one another, work as a pack. It's why we call them the wolves."

"The *white* wolves," Sokka added. "The rapid adaptation modifications have done their work and then some."

My anger rose. "Why have you *never* mentioned great white sharks were introduced to Enceladus!?"

Their smiles dwindled. "We introduced hundredz of zpecies before the Hermian occupation, but never great whitez, nor any zhark for that matter. We're juzt az zurprized az you, Mirko."

♦

"Lieutenant y'Obrrradovic," Commander Turk said, letting the R's roll across her tongue. "You must know how much y'it pains me to come to you like this."

"I do. But you're not surrendering in the conventional sense. We are no longer bound to this war."

Her eyes widened. "You've made contact?"

I shook my head. "No. But we've been stranded here for forty-six years. According to interplanetary law, thirty years without setting foot on our respective home worlds means we are no longer citizens of them. Therefore, we're no longer obligated to fight one another."

The Hermian commander thought about that. "The Dirrrectorrr wishes his disciples to rrrise y'above the petty life y'of morrrtals, to claim y'our rrright y'as gods," she said, staring upwards.

"How's that working out for you?"

Commander Turk winced. "The Dirrrectorrr has y'a plan. You will see soon y'enough."

"Does this plan involve your people dying?"

"Y'it would be y'an honorrr."

"Yet, you're asking to be rescued."

"To die glorrriously y'in the heat y'of battle y'is differrrent than letting y'ourselves dwindle."

"How can we trust you if you long to die in battle?"

The Hermian thought. "Hundrrreds y'of my rrregiment have died y'of scurrrvy, the cold, y'or by the white wolves. Surrrviving this moon y'is the battle now."

I thought about the white wolves. "Why did you introduce great white sharks to Enceladus?"

Commander Turk shrugged. "That was y'above my rrrank. y'Only the geneticists knew. They y'are y'at the bottom y'of the y'ocean now."

I wanted nothing more than to reject Commander Turk's surrender, but I knew they were hoarding something. I thought upon the wreckage of the Saint Samuel and the equalizers still protecting it day and night. "What's in the Saint Samuel?"

Commander Turk shot me a look but then breathed deeply. "y'Our y'equalizerrr y'units."

And with them, a surplus of energy cells, each enough to power our magsuits for an entire year, I knew. "If you're willing to share your power cells with us, then we will help you."

Commander Turk thought it over and nodded.

With watchful eyes, we welcomed the Hermians into camp.

"There are so few of them," Sokka said, leaning against me.

"I know," I said, studying their gaunt faces.

The equalizers were hit the hardest. Their once massive musculature had eroded, leaving loose skin draping over skeletal frames like towel racks. Then, I saw former Ceran Fleet personnel light up as a tall woman entered, her head held with dignity. Our eyes met. *Kota!*

William stepped forth. "Fellow Enceladanz, we welcome you into our home. The grievancez of the pazt will be forgotten, for a new beginning we now have."

Commander Turk shook William's hand. "May this be y'an y'alliance to rrrememberrr."

♦

We donned loose magsuits, appearing like children in parent's clothing. When they cinched tight, our ribs and joints became horrifically visible. The hologram displayed, *"+0%."*

"You ready?" William said and watched us nod. He flicked the hologram to, *"+1%."*

Weight spread across our shoulders, vertebrae popped, and pain lanced through knees and hips. Howls echoed, followed by laughter. We adopted hunched postures. *Old age, all at once,* I thought. Nevertheless, Kota strolled effortlessly with, *"+3%,"* hovering in her wrist hologram. *Damn her!* I thought but could not help smiling at her unyielding competitiveness. I eyed scars crawling up her neck.

"What happened? How'd you end up with the Hermians?" I asked.

She sighed. "Commander Turk pulled me unconscious from the burning wreckage of Hopper Camp and nursed me back to health."

"And held you prisoner," I said.

She shook her head. "We worked together to survive."

Did she have a hand in planning their raids? I wondered. "I see."

She grinned nervously. "Do you still have that stupid knife?"

When I pulled it from its sheath, worn to a nub, she cackled.

♦

"With our high protein diet, we zhould be near Earth equivalent gravity by now," said Dr. Zeal. "But we've peaked."

"What do you mean, peaked?" William said.

"A number of uz are regrezzing."

Now that Dr. Zeal mentioned it, I pulled gravity back from *+12%* to *+11%* a few days ago but told myself it was only a momentary reprieve.

A loss of motor function followed our inability to gain muscle. Then, headaches and respiratory failure came.

I found Kota sitting in the corner crying one morning.

"You okay?" I asked.

She looked up with unfocused eyes. *Blind, like several others,* I realized.

And then, the light of my own world slowly dimmed. But I could still sense living creatures, warmth, and even magnetism. *I can still fish.* I spent nearly every waking hour on the ice giving directions to a team that blindly stumbled around the holes. I feared an attack from the white wolves, but even they knew something was wrong.

Rotten meat, no eat, they began saying after catching one of us.

♦

While breaking down a recent tuna catch, I smelled something chemical. I sniffed its exposed vertebrae. *What the?* I cut a bit of meat along the spine and inserted it into my mouth. It was subtle, almost non-existent.

"Alcohol," the thin man said, becoming visible in my darkness.

It couldn't have gone bad. We caught it yesterday, I thought.

"It's not fermentation," he said.

The woman with red lips appeared. "Mirko, your symptoms point to methanol poisoning."

But from where would methanol come from?

The severe woman joined them. "The hydrocarbons emitted by the thermal vents at the ocean floor are being absorbed by the shellfish and tube worms that feed on them. In turn, they're eaten by more predatory fish, who are then eaten by the tuna. The hydrocarbons must be concentrating as they move up from one tier of the food chain to the next, causing the apex predators of this moon to become toxic."

Which is the Tuna, I thought. *But why did it take so long for our symptoms to show?*

"Your bodies must be storing the toxins within your fat cells," said the woman with red lips. "As you've burned fat with the increased weight of the magsuits, the toxins are being released at once."

"Then they must stop eating the tuna," the thin man said.

The woman shook her head. "They're the only source of vitamin B and C, essential proteins, and countless more natural fats and oils."

"What do they do then?" he said.

Nothing changes, I thought to them.

"That's suicide."

But eating the tuna gives us more time. I let my senses go, and their apparitions melted away, leaving me blind once again.

♦

"It's my 127th birthday today," I whispered to Sokka, lying in her cot, deep in a coma. *One she'll likely never return from.* I imagined her telling me to quit my sulking. "I know. I must get back to work." The fuel cells needed juice, the air recyclers must be in working order, and we must be fed. *I am the father of two thousand deathly ill children.*

"Mirko, this might be the end," the little crab said.

I refuse to believe that, I thought back. *There's still time.*

The woman with red lips appeared. "That time is gone. You cannot come back from—"

"Shut the fuck up!" I shouted aloud.

Two individuals ran to the doorway, more vibrant to my senses, their hearts pounding strong. They stared at me like I was a wild animal.

"What? Can't I get a little angry now and then?" I grumbled.

The individuals looked at one another.

Wait... "Can you see?" I asked.

They ran off.

♦

I was breaking down tuna when I again sensed the two individuals standing alongside others who took comfort in the sound of my chops and slices. *Their vitals are so strong.*

"Welcome back, who are you?" I said.

They again looked at one another and took off.

♦

The third time, I was traversing the ice to our fishing hole with a handful of anglers strung along my cable. I stopped and turned. The two individuals were not far, their arms moving, signing to one another. *They can really see.* The signs were familiar but not Ceran. I could not place them until one used the Hermian signal to turn a statement into a question.

"How can he know the way?" one signed and looked at me.

"He's certainly blind. I don't know how he does it," signed the other.

"Wait here," I tapped to my anglers, then disconnected from the cable. The two individuals froze as I approached. I raised a hand in greeting and signed with rusty Hermian, *"What camp are you from?"*

They remained still as if that made them invisible.

Chameleon cloaks, I knew. *"I saw your sign language."*

"That's impossible," one signed to the other.

"Not impossible," I responded. *"What camp are you from?"*

They hesitated. *"Are you the leader here?"*

"No. What camp are you from? I will not ask again."

"We're not from one of your camps. We're stationed in orbit."

My heart leaped. *"Are you here to rescue us!?"* I furiously signed.

♦

The warmth of propulsion engines seeped through my envisuit as a small drop ship nestled into a depression in the ice outside of our encampment.

"Feels like an Earth ship," Kota said through com, walking beside me, listening for my direction should an obstacle cross our path.

"But you said they werrre Herrrmians," Commander Turk said.

"They use Hermian sign language, but they seem different. I don't know who they are," I said.

The drop ship's engines cooled. Its docking bay door lowered. An impossibly large soldier emerged first. *An equalizer, shit...* But, he was unarmed and held no hostility in his posture. His soul felt pure and innocent. *He's in love,* I realized. More followed, tall, elegant, their vitals fresh and healthy. *Teenagers.* They lined either side of the ramp, standing at attention as a young woman descended down the middle. Her vitals were as vibrant and strong, yet she contrasted greatly, her stature stout. *The runt of the litter?* I thought. She stopped several paces before us. I could feel her eyes surveying our ill-fitting envisuits.

"y'Enceladans," she spoke on our agreed frequency and placed her fist upon her shoulder. "y'I y'am Captain Sharrrpe y'of the Rrreforrrmed Peoples' Alliance y'of Sol. We have come to y'aid you."

Her words were Hermian English, but barely. We hesitated, slowly piecing together what she said.

William broke our silence. "I am William Ztern, leader of Athenz Colony. We welcome you to Enceladuz."

Captain Sharpe cocked her head. "y'I y'ap-ol-og-ize," she said slowly, enunciating her words. "We... thought... you... spoke... y'Eng-lish..."

"We y'are speaking y'English," Commander Turk said, thickening her own Hermian accent.

Captain Sharpe paused. "¿Hablas Español?"

"Mirko," William said to me.

I stepped forth and signed, *"We are speaking English, but it seems time and isolation has made us incomprehensible to you."*

As we neared our encampment, I acted as a translator and could not help but notice Captain Sharpe marveling at how I navigated blind. We passed through the airlock into a waft of putrid air. Captain Sharpe's young crew grimaced at those on their deathbeds, unable to control bodily functions and bathe. A sudden embarrassment took hold of me.

"How have so many of you survived?" Captain Sharpe signed.

"We catch tuna below the ice to keep fed, and provide vitamin C."

She paused. *"Do you not know what plagues you?"*

"We believe the tuna is bad. But we have no way of confirming."

"Yet, you still eat them."

"No choice," I signed.

"We can investigate whatever this is, but I cannot guarantee we can find a cure," she responded.

"We understand. Once we return to Ceres, we can grow new organs."

"You're Cerans?" she signed.

"Most of us are Ceran or Hermian, stranded in the Battle of Enceladus, in 2221. Both fleets crashed upon the surface and the research stations were sent to the bottom of the ocean. We've had no contact since."

Captain Sharpe perked up. *"Is one of these stations called Troy?"*

◆

Captain Sharpe's crew stayed for several weeks, giving medical exams and treating the sick as best they could. In exchange, I aided them in preparing a dive to explore the ruins of Troy, with which they were obsessed.

I must discover why.

Captain Sharpe's first officer, Taam, the equalizer, approached. *"Captain Sharpe wishes to speak with you privately,"* he signed.

Must be about Troy again, I thought and studied the gentle giant of a man. He led me to a section of habitat where they had inflated several tents. The equalizer stopped at the largest and motioned for me to enter. A lack of scent struck me as I split its self-healing fabric entry.

"Mirrrko, thank you forrr meeting with me," Captain Sharpe said but did not look up from her desk. Her holotile was open, but I could not sense what was on its display.

I was acclimating to their dialect, imagining they were from another era. It felt foolish, but I imitated old Hermian, excessively rolling my R's. "Thank you for helping us. We would not have survived much longer."

She snapped her head up. "Finally, you speak y'english."

"It's not that we've lost our ability to speak, it's that you speak a century's old dialect," I said and felt her pulse jump.

She set her holotile aside and turned squarely to me. "Mirrrko, you werrre y'once y'a grrreat soldierrr, corrrect?"

"I was a lieutenant, in a war, before your time."

She shook her head. "y'I rrrememberrr y'it well."

"That's impossible. I would put you at sixteen years old."

Her pulse lifted again. "That's y'exactly rrright. But y'I was five when The Fall y'ocurrred. The surrrvivorrrs y'of Merrrcurrry put y'us childrrren y'into stasis y'in the Kuiperrr Belt. When we woke, sixty-five yearrrs laterrr, we found System Sol y'in shambles."

"What's The Fall? What happened? We know nothing," I said.

"We don't know much y'eitherrr. y'Only that we must rrrestitch the surrrvivorrrs forrr y'our species to surrrvive y'as y'a whole."

"How many colonies have you reached? Who survived?" I asked.

"Pluto y'and Trrriton perrrished. Titan barrrely surrrvived. Theirrr knowledge y'of what happened y'is little. y'Enceladus makes the fourrrth colony, but we did not y'expect surrrvivorrrs herrre."

"I wouldn't call us survivors. I'm sure you've confirmed we have methanol poisoning." Her silence validated my suspicion. "We must get off this moon. Might you transport us to Titan?"

"The G-forrrces rrrequirrred forrr lift-off would kill you."

"Then, put us into stasis for the trip," I said.

"We y'are not going back to Titan. We must push y'on to the colonies not yet connected."

My frustration swelled. "Are you really connecting us? If you did not expect survivors on Enceladus, then why have you come?"

"You wouldn't y'underrrstand."

"What is there to understand!" I snapped. "Why are you obsessed with Troy!"

Captain Sharpe darkened. "Calm yourrrself Mirrrko. We will detain you y'if we must."

"You couldn't detain me if you tried!" I spat.

"Delusional," she said as if recognizing a symptom. "Yourrr fellow y'Enceladans say you have voices y'in yourrr head."

"Those voices have kept us alive!"

"So y'it's trrrue." She moved to the side of her desk and reached below its surface. "Mirrrko y'Obrrradovic, The Harrrbingerrr y'of Death, y'is not y'of sane mind."

"You're reaching for a gun," I said.

"y'I'm y'imprrressed with yourrr y'awarrreness." She raised the object to her mouth. "But this y'is not y'a gun," she said, her voice now muffled.

My body suddenly became rubber.

"Asphyxiation!" the woman with red lips from within said.

I rushed Captain Sharpe but stumbled to the floor.

Her pulse became wild. "You killed my fatherrr's brrrotherrrs and sisterrrs! You took the light frrrom the perrrson y'I loved most! y'And now you will pay forrr yourrr crrrimes!"

I placed my hands on the floor and raised to a knee. "Crimes!? It was Mercury who started this war!" I desperately reached for my knife, but my hand wobbled. I could not grasp it.

"Cerrres cut y'our waterrr supply! *That* was the beginning!" Captain Sharpe knelt and pulled my knife from its sheath. "y'I wonderrr how many lives this blade has taken!?" She placed its flank against the edge of the table.

I heard a ping and metallic pieces dropping to the floor.

"No!" I wiped my hands across the floor, searching for the pieces.

Captain Sharpe cocked her head. "Don't worry Mirrrko. Yourrr brrrain will soon starrrve to death. Yourrr pain will soon be overrr."

I huffed, trying to extract oxygen from the saturated air. *What do I do!?*

The little crab appeared. "Do what we've always done, Mirko."

But I cannot see! Yet, I could sense adrenaline pulsing through Captain

Sharpe's veins and her heart pumping strong. I focused on her inner light, burning so bright. *I don't need to see,* I realized, and reached forth.

Sight returned, but I saw through a different set of eyes. And what I saw would forever haunt me. There my shriveled body was, convulsing on the floor, gasping for air, next to the shattered pieces of my knife.

CHAPTER TWELVE

"It's going to be okay," Clara says, rubbing Zion's back as he sobs.

"It feels like yesterday," he says. His eyes widen. "It *was* yesterday."

"No, it's 3406. You're on Titan now."

"It was *yesterday!*" he shouts and begins to shake.

Clara's holotile beeps. *Zion's brain pattern is shifting. Time to go.* She slowly stands and makes for the door.

"You're going to leave me? Typical!"

Clara stops in the doorway. "Do you want me to stay?"

"No. You should go. Before *it* returns."

"Before *what* returns?" Clara questions, sensing Zion's struggle to maintain composure.

"It!" he shouts and abruptly stands.

Clara quickly steps out and closes the door, pulling the handle as if Zion will tear it open. Instead, she hears him say, "Kandoother zungo de joontner."

◆

Cliff-Nesters swoop up and down like old fighter jets, threading the needle between the structural members of a bridge Aizen stands upon, chasing the wasps that nest in Yang's Canyon's rock walls. Aizen leans against the railing, watching a Nester hunt, when his eyes lock onto the bridge's footing at the canyon's edge. *It can't be,* he thinks.

A holoplaque on the railing opens, *"Ekon's Bridge. Constructed Kanya 12th, 2870, Dedicated to Lauren Ekon for her contributions to Martian literature."*

The original bridge deteriorated long ago, Aizen realizes. He climbs the steep grass slope of a crater's backside. In the distance, beyond the restricted zone, surfers prepare to bomb down the crater's near vertical drop on grassboards. One with wild hair places his board's tail at the edge and wavers back and forth, building his courage. *If only Dad were here,* Aizen thinks as the surfer tips forward and cascades down the slope, carving side to side, biting his board's edge into thick grass blades that would slice his body from head to toe should he tumble. But he does not fall and plows to a stop at the bottom. Cheers come faintly in the wind, their excitement palpable.

"Wow," Aizen whispers.

He reaches the crest to see grasses stretching the entirety of the crater's interior. Concrete footings of an ancient dome peak above the vegetation, their iron components rusted and returned to the soil long ago. The grasses become taller as he wanders into the depths until towering overhead. He imagines them as the maize, wheat, and sorghum from Zion's story. A small clearing drops a few centimeters, and a holoplaque describes the foundation of a granary. The pathway beyond feels like an ancient road, but the grasses grow dense, and he cannot press through. *Something's on the other side of this.* He climbs over the top instead.

"Please, return to the designated tourist area," his holotile chimes.

Aizen dismisses the warning and continues trudging before taking a spontaneous left. His step dips into the ground. *Another foundation?* Sudden dizziness grips him. He sits on the foundation's edge to regain himself, but his eyes betray him. Tears release.

"Why yah cryin'?" says a sweet voice.

Aizen lurches to his feet, searching through blurry eyes. Only when she moves does Aizen see her. Red mud cakes her face and clothing, and grasses stick out of her hair.

"Yah shouldn't be 'ere," she says. "Dey never let tourists come dis fah."

"Why not?" Aizen responds.

"Dey afraid of us."

Afraid? But she appears so innocent. "What's there to fear?"

"My broders want what yah 'ave."

"I don't have much. What's your name?"

"Emma. What yah's?"

"Aizen," he cautiously says, but she does not react. "Aizen Ocol," he repeats. *No recognition. Thank Sol.*

"Nice tah meetcha, Aizen," she says. "But yah should go before my oldah broder's find yah."

"Thanks for the warning." He turns for a moment, soaking in his surroundings. "Which way should I—"

She's gone.

Martian winds stir the grasses. All else is silent. Aizen kneels, scooping soil and clipping grass samples, keeping an open ear for footsteps. He sits upon the edge of the foundation, imagining what the structure was once like. All he can think of is Dillon and Sha bickering about who will change Masani's diaper. A chill settles in the air. *Time to go.* He returns the way he came, following parted grasses yet to spring into place until they again grow dense. It feels more difficult to press in this direction, the blades of grass pointing toward him rather than away.

"Damn," he says and backs off.

"It designed tah keep yah from escapin', boy," says a voice.

Aizen whirls to meet a menacing smile, rising to well over two meters tall, with grasses in his hair and clothing granting him the appearance of a sunflower.

"I don't have anything," Aizen says, suppressing his anxiety.

"I'm sure yah 'ave someding of value," comes another more intelligent voice, appearing from the grasses, too. "De bag," he orders.

Aizen relinquishes it and backs away, bumping into solidness behind him. *A third sunflower.*

"Yah ain't goin' nowhere." The third grabs Aizen's collar.

Aizen's heat cube is tossed as if useless, and his clothing, bedroll, and thermal blanket are dismissed like a joke. They pocket his holotile. When they find his cast iron pan, they pause.

"I never knew de rich tah cook," one says.

"I'm not rich," Aizen responds.

"Boy, look at yah clodin', yah rich."

"I'm Titan middle class."

"Yah 'ad enough cred tah come all de way from Titan? Like I say, boy, yah rich."

"It's only twelve thousand credits," Aizen argues.

Darkness emanates from the sunflowers. "Spoiled li'l shit!"

Aizen struggles against the sunflower holding his collar.

"Now 'ere we go." One pulls Aizen's ID from the bag. "Spoiled li'l shit's passport. It'll fetch ah good price."

"I need that!" Aizen yells.

"Like 'ell yah do, yah can get anoder... Aizen Ocol?" the sunflower reads. "Why does dat soun' familiar?"

"Is dat de kid who beat de machines?" says another.

"Someone dat famous would never come all de way out 'ere." The flower ponders that. "Yah not dee Aizen Ocol, are yah?"

"No," Aizen says a little too quickly.

"Yah ah bad liar," the intelligent one says. "Yah will fetch ah good ransom, I imagine."

Aizen glances at the sunflower holding his collar and notes that he is missing a thumb. *It won't take much to break!* Aizen karate chops the sunflower's wrist. It's sloppy but enough to knock his collar free. Then, without thinking, Aizen kicks between the sunflower's legs.

"Li'l fuck!" the sunflower cries, doubling over.

Aizen dashes into the grass, hearing the sunflowers' swift footsteps gaining. But Aizen is striding better as he goes. His steps grow in length. He shifts side to side like a speed skater, maintaining a slight lead.

"Catch 'im already!" a sunflower calls.

Voices come from ahead, a cheering alongside blaring music, sounding like a party. Aizen explodes into a clearing at the crater's rim, with surfers chanting *Go! Go! Go!* as one teeters on the edge. A camera hovers above, recording it all.

Aizen grabs a board from a rack.

"'Ey!" its owner shouts but reels back when the sunflower brothers burst from the grass in pursuit.

The edge nears, looking like the end of the world. Aizen's mind races with all of Dad's longboarding lessons. He does not hesitate, does not timidly drop in. Aizen dives over the edge, head first.

◆

Jonathan zips through the WorldRing tunnels on his hoverboard, setting relays at forks and bends to maintain communication with HQ. *If only Aizen were here to see this!* he thinks and banks into another bend. According to their estimates, they should be below the English Channel. *This is far enough for today,* Jonathan knows. His legs are like jelly, fueled by adrenaline. He uses what little energy he has left to set up a micro-tent to prepare dinner for when Vincent, Angela, and Hazel arrive with the full habitat and equipment typically used for archaeological digs on Mercury. They are triple the cost and quadruple the weight but can withstand temperatures above a thousand degrees.

Dinner is ready when the rest arrive, and they quickly set up Basecamp around Jonathan's micro-tent kitchen.

"Hazel, how much longer 'til we reach the English Channel?" Jonathan asks, handing her a bowl of rehydrated protein. Her hair lies flat, and she emits a musk they will never speak of.

"Give me a second," she says, breathes deep, and regains composure.

She's made of tough stuff, Jonathan thinks.

"We should have reached the channel yesterday," she says.

"What does this mean?"

"Maybe a draft caused the drone to cover ground more quickly than anticipated. I don't know for certain."

◆

Jonathan suits up early the next morning as his crew breaks down Basecamp. For several hours, he winds through the tunnel on his hoverboard. He prepares to bank for the next bend, but his proximity alarm does not sound. He sends a radar ping. The tunnel ahead materializes, a straight two hundred kilometers in length.

"Angela, what do you think?" he calls in.

"This appears to be below the English Channel," she responds. "Can you cover it today?"

"I'll have to drop most of my gear here for you to pick up. Wish me luck." Jonathan moves more swiftly with the lighter load but does not dare reach max speed, fearing slight imperfections in the tunnel's surface may snag his board. What proves most challenging is keeping perfectly straight. With clenching toes, Jonathan constantly corrects, unable to find that exact zero-degree angle. The stability muscles in his shins scream. After a few hours, the bottoms of his feet are cramping. He stops, swigs from his suit's electrolyte-filled reservoir, and stretches his calves and toes as best he can. But the moment he steps back on his board, the cramping returns.

"Angela, you copy?" Jonathan calls.

"Did you make it already?"

"I'm about halfway, but my legs are done. I'll have to sleep here in my envisuit tonight."

◆

The next day, Jonathan reaches the end of the tunnel, a granite wall.

Sealed off like the sea-side entry, he realizes.

"It's a dead end," he calls in.

"But the drone's path goes clear through," Hazel says.

"Link to my visual if you don't believe me," Jonathan says, listening to them bicker in the background.

Hazel suddenly laughs. "Um, look up."

Jonathan does, his headlamp illuminating the ceiling of the tunnel. "What am I searching for?"

"Is there a gap?"

"Uh, just a maintenance hatch."

"You sure it's a hatch? This tunnel once functioned at near vacuum. Any break in its seal would be disastrous. Can you get closer?"

Jonathan eyes his hoverboard. "Maybe."

He accesses its settings, maxing out *Lift*. He balances as best he can, rising several meters above the floor, and looks up. His headlamp illuminates triangular sections of the square when he shifts side to side.

"It's a hole," he says and sends a ping. A shaft materializes on visor. "It's perfectly square, weird."

♦

Representative Sckoonez stands ominously beside Clara's booth as other Earthrise Diner patrons stare, speechless. The squareness of the representative's shoulders contrasts greatly with its thin, wispy legs. *Cindarians use body heat to keep upright like a balloon,* Clara remembers from her xeno-biology course in school.

"Sss… Claraaa Ocolll," the representative says with an ashen voice, like water pouring on a campfire. "Mayyy I ssspeak… withhh youuu…? Sss…"

"Y-yes," she says, offering the seat across from her.

"Ssshalll weee... walllk inssstead? Sss…" It says, moving along the floor with gecko-grippy feet to keep grounded, sounding like velcro.

Clara quickly saves her work and hurries after the representative.

"Claraaa… dooo youuu know whyyy... I ammm herrre…?" It asks.

"Is it regarding Zion's biography?"

"Cccertainly isss…" It looks up to her with serious eyes.

Despite appearing like a silly balloon, Clara cannot help but be impressed by the representative's aura.

"Myyy peopllle... arrre sssuffering, Claraaa… The Arkathyyyy… havvve commmanderrred our emberrr minesss," the representative says, becoming upset. "Ourr emberrrr minesss... arrre wherrre ourrr chhhildren... arrre borrrn... Ourrr futurrre... isss being takennn frommm usss... Alll ssso the Arkathyyy... cannn feeed... theirrr citiesss..."

Clara's stomach drops. "That's horrible."

"Yesss... Buuut Zzzion... manyyy yearsss aaago... wasss aaable... tooo ssstop themmm... Thoughhh weee dooon't... knowww hhhow... Cannn youuu... hhhelp usss?"

"I'm trying my best to pull that information from him as we speak, but I'm not sure that I can."

"Whhhy...? Sss..."

"I'm not at liberty to say."

The representative stops. "Claraaa... I ammm nnnot onnne tooo beeeg... buuut I ammm beeegging youuu nowww... Pleassse tryyy harrrderrr... Weee willl foreverrrr... beee innn yourrr deeebt... Sss..."

Clara nods. "I'll try harder, but I cannot make promises."

The representative gives Clara a hesitant glance. "I sssenssse... I ammm nnnot theee firssst... tooo approooach youuu... Sss..."

She remains silent.

"Dooo beee carrreful... The Arkathyyy arrre... maaaking a plaaay... fooor Suprrreme Minisssster..." It says. "Maaany representativesss arrre... in theirrr pooocket... Sss..."

"How do you know that?"

"I'mmm nnnot at... llliberrrty to sssay..."

CHAPTER THIRTEEN

Six days of crawling through passageways barely wide enough for Jonathan's shoulders to slip through and sleeping within his envisuit, putting its waste-to-water recyclers to the test is taking its toll. Besides the vertical hoist from the WorldRing tunnel, it's been a perfectly horizontal shot to Paris.

"Let's take a break," Jonathan says and rolls to his back, relieving the pressure on his lumbar. He brushes a gloved hand along the tunnel's stone, marveling at its perfection. *Neither dug nor drilled.* Corners meet at perfect right angles. *What made you?* He swigs from rehydration and rolls back to his stomach. "Shall we?"

"Can I take the lead?" Angela asks.

"Sure," Jonathan says, relieved.

They shuffle on, face down, only looking up to maintain a proper distance from the person in front. Even still, lancing pain runs through Jonathan's neck each time he does. He grits his teeth and looks again to find Angela has suddenly picked up her pace.

"There's something ahead!" she calls and drops from view. Her helmet pops back into the square opening. "It's a chamber!"

Jonathan shuffles forth and pokes his head through the opening, then extends his palms to the stone floor and pulls himself free. Hazel is just behind him, followed by Vincent. Their gear, piled atop Jonathan's hoverboard, set to follow, comes last. They work out the kinks in their joints, wincing with the aches.

Hazel kneels on the stone floor. "The chamber's construction is only a few centuries old. It was made after The Fall."

Angela gives it a long look. "Agreed."

Jonathan runs his hand along the chamber walls. *Again, precision cut.* "Whoever made the passageway had their hand in this, too."

One chamber leads to the next, each climbing several centimeters in height like cascading terraces. Thousands come and go. They pass through crystalline metamorphic rock formed before the Permian era, transitioning to Triassic and Jurassic clay. After three more days, the Jurassic clay gives way to Cretaceous chalk.

Then, the moment Jonathan's inner child has been waiting for comes. A thin white layer of compressed stone slashes diagonally through the chambers like a scar.

"The Cretaceous-Tertiary extinction event," he whispers. "The end of the dinosaurs."

Yellow limestone overtakes them, and the chambers end at a low passageway.

"Whoa," Angela says, looking closely at the passageway's rock. "This structure is much older." She pings. "Beyond is full of calcium."

"Like before?" Vincent asks.

Angela nods and cautiously enters. "Holy shit!"

Jonathan follows, nearly rolling his ankle on bones lining the floor. The passage walls are constructed of femurs with skulls placed at datum lines, crucibles, and doorway-like frames.

"I thought the catacombs were a rumor," Hazel says. "There must be millions of them."

"This will be a treat for our friends in HQ." Jonathan opens his pack, handing scanners to each of them. They disperse through the catacomb.

"Jonathan? Can you come to my position for a moment?" Vincent says several minutes later, a little too calm.

Jonathan senses the panic behind the calm. "Coming."

The next turn is washed in orange light. *Did Vincent change his lamp's color?* Jonathan then sees Vincent's shadow projecting against the wall. *Another light source.* A skull is missing from the bone wall. In its place is an illuminated stone pulsing as if breathing.

Vincent stares, hypnotized. "It's incandescent."

"Is it hollow?" Jonathan asks.

"It's solid. Is there stone on Earth that emits light?"

"Only under ultraviolet." Jonathan hovers a gloved hand over the stone. "No heat."

"What are you two staring at?" Angela says, then sees it, too.

Hazel is the last to arrive and gasps.

More glowing stones illuminate the corridor ahead, positioned at twists and turns. They round another bend to meet a different light source, bright and warm. *Sunlight?* Jonathan steps forth, ascending an ancient staircase. He passes beneath stone archways to an open doorway with cobblestone streets lined by low buildings.

"This is it… This is Paris," Jonathan says, stepping through the doorway. "May the world of archaeology be forever changed."

♦

With her head cocked, Clara listens to Zion explain the secret ingredient to his grodote bisque soup. "Zion, you've told me this before."

"I most certainly have not. The secret ingredient is—"

"Fear," Clara says flatly.

"Fe—" Zion gives Clara a skeptical look. "That's an *incredible* guess."

"No. You've told me this story."

He scoffs. "Impossible."

Clara sighs. "Mermer was a grodote who accidentally transferred his consciousness into a young boy just before being boiled alive."

Zion's face becomes pale.

"Should I come back another time?" she asks.

"No! I'm fine!"

Clara catches something in Zion's tone. "Is this Justin speaking right now? Or perhaps Mirko?"

Zion stares hard. "How do you know these names?"

"You've told me their stories as well."

His face twitches. "Have I told others?"

Clara opens the drafted tales on holotile, describing how one leads to another.

Zion appears frustrated yet impressed. Then, he leans back in his chair. "Clara, it's incredible how you've broken them down like this. You really take your assignment, and me, seriously." He rubs his hands nervously. "For the longest time I thought the doctors were making it up, my lapses in memory. But I must have told you these stories. No one else could have.

How many times have I repeated myself?"

"Just this once with Mermer. But Dr. Lee mentioned that you tell strange stories before we began. Perhaps you've told him."

"God, I hope not," he says.

♦

Clara finds Dr. Lee waiting outside Zion's door the following day.

"Come with me," he says, his voice cold.

Clara follows to his office, where he points at the scan of Zion's brain.

"His deterioration had stabilized when your interviews began. I hoped to keep him from further descent, possibly stage a recovery. But he's entering a new phase of degradation where the synapses in his brain are rapidly uncoupling. I didn't notice until he stopped asking for coffee when I brought tea." Dr. Lee gives a desperate look. "There's not much time left, Clara."

The live feed shows Zion kneeling at his bedside with his hands pressed in prayer. But when she enters his room, he's sitting in his chair. She sets her holotile on the table and dashes *Record*.

"I didn't know you were religious," she says.

"What makes you say that?" Zion gives a funny look.

"I saw you on hologram kneeling in prayer."

He grins strangely. "I don't know what you were watching, but it certainly wasn't me."

Not that he knows of, Clara thinks. "I've met with Representatives Vesta and Fordham. They're concerned about what'll happen to the galaxy should you pass away."

"A useless lot those two are," Zion says. "They're under Arkathy hypnosis."

Is that what Representative Sckoonez meant? Clara thinks. "Zion, I must be truthful with you. I was chosen not only to write your biography but to discover the methods you used to establish galactic unity."

He laughs slightly. "I'm surprised you're telling me this. Are you not afraid of the ramifications?"

"I'm using the program."

"What program?"

He's forgetting so quickly, Clara thinks. "Zion, I need to know how you brought the systems together."

"Clara, I could transcribe every meeting and teach you every cuisine, but it would not matter."

"Why not?"

"Because what we're encountering today is no different from the events proceeding The Fall." He pauses. "I don't expect you to believe me."

"Your painting led Jonathan to the WorldRing entry. I believe you."

"Painting?"

Shit! "Please, tell me why it's not so different."

Zion shrugs. "History tends to repeat itself, though at larger scales each time. There was incredible prosperity before The Fall, unlike anything humanity ever experienced. But the resulting war nearly wiped us from existence. Now, considering how great of a galactic peace we've experienced these past centuries, one can only imagine the consequent chaos."

"We should stop history from repeating, then," Clara argues.

"We cannot stop the ebb and flow of life. But perhaps we can control it. We must break this peace before tensions reach a tipping point."

"You're not seriously suggesting we encourage the galaxy to collapse."

Zion grins. "Anything that builds pressure must be allowed to release. Therefore, smaller skirmishes *should* occur. Our galactic unification will be imperfect, but the best systems of governance are often messy."

Clara ponders that. "So you must know the Arkathy and Cindarians are fighting again."

"I do. I'm surprised that *you* know this."

"Representative Sckoonez came to me searching for an answer to their situation."

Zion frowns. "Take what Sckoonez says with a grain of salt. It tends to withhold crucial information."

"But the Arkathy are mining Cindarian embers to power their cities."

"Yes. But the Cindarians also mine those embers to birth children."

Clara scrunches her brow. "I would think the children win."

"Any rational person would. Until you consider Cindarians theoretically live forever and their population is well beyond the limits of their home system. And the ember mines they're currently fighting over actually belong to the Voldars. But the Voldars only understand that selling their embers generates income. I imagine it'll be a rude awakening for both the Arkathy and Cindarians should the Voldars finally say, *no*."

"We should support the Voldars," Clara says.

"That would result in the extinction of both the Arkathy and Cindarians."

"Then, how do we choose?"

"We don't. By letting their tiny war play out, all three species live on."

"In agony," Clara says.

"Life is never perfect."

Clara scoffs. "But what happens if their civilizations crumble?"

"That Clara, is when they begin anew, discover who they truly are, and how amazing they could be if they worked together. With Cindarian immortality, Arkathy technology, and Voldar resources, they could be the first beings to reach new galaxies. Yet they cannot see it."

"Can we not just explain this to them?"

Zion shakes his head. "They must come back from the brink of extinction. Must experience the consequences of their actions firsthand. Just like humanity did."

"Are you saying we've only come so far because of The Fall?"

"Yes."

"There's no logic to that."

Zion humphs. "Humanity's most horrific moments are often rooted in *Logic*."

"How did you come to this conclusion?"

Zion becomes vacant, stonelike, lost within the depths of his mind. When he returns, he stares with intensity.

"Clara, I have witnessed unspeakable things done in the name of peace, and lived through the aftermath," Zion says in a different voice. "I know what questionable acts I have myself committed. I am not proud. But had I not done what needed to be done, then humanity would have perished long ago..."

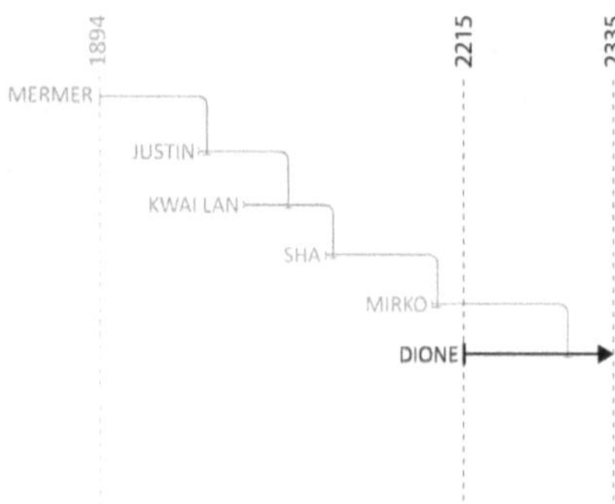

DIONE's TALE
System Sol: 2215 – 2335

I did not know how I came into the system, and I did not care. All that mattered was where we went next. And we were always going. From one ghost colony to another, searching for those who survived and remnants of history to preserve. The atrocities I have witnessed, a reminder that perhaps humanity *should* have been extinct, were only balanced by traces of hope. But they grew fewer by the moment, and my faith hung by a thread.

I was Hermian, raised to believe my culture was the most righteous in System Sol and that we were responsible for humanity's ascension to godliness. *But what does this mean after The Fall?* Since I was a little girl, I loved the concept of the Hermian mission until it was enacted to its fullest. Then, it became my responsibility to stitch humanity back together.

But there was a time long ago when such weight did not bear upon my soul. When I had a family.

◆

My mother was Abigail Kesler, admiral of the Hermian Armada, her duty lying far in the Jovian System. I do not remember much of her during that time. Nothing beyond a pair of eyes staring at me in my crib, a peaceful expression rimmed by hardness, stress, responsibility, and dread. My father told me countless stories of her conquests on Ganymede and Europa but never spoke of his own achievements despite being decorated. He was

Tomas Sharpe, commander of the Hermian Tribal Infantry. His DNA was enhanced by simian and equine to heighten muscle tissue, endurance, heart strength, and lung capacity. As were all of us to a degree.

I loved watching soldiers and officers walking Icarus's halls, guessing which DNA mixes they were enhanced with by their musculature and gait. The first time I saw an equalizer, I nearly laughed out loud. Monstrous shoulders, forearms, and thighs awkwardly filled out his uniform, making his head look tiny.

"Gorilla," I whispered.

The equalizer stopped dead in his tracks, whirled in my direction, and flexed his shoulders and forearms. "Ooo! Ooo!" he called just like a gorilla, thumping his chest with his palms.

I ran off, giggling in terror as his monstrous laugh echoed down the hall.

◆

When I was five, I began the modifications. But instead of receiving the Infantry or Equalizer package, I was given Navigation.

"Dione, this will only pinch a little," my doctor said.

I studied the syringe's shaft. "What is it today?" I whispered, trying to mask my anxiety.

"DNA from the brains of mother elephants who once roamed Earth's savannas. They'll help with memory recall and navigation."

"Does Mommy have them?"

"She sure does, and did you know she can navigate the entire Jovian system without a nav-computer?"

I believed him, having already noticed changes in myself from the previous injections. DNA from frogs to strengthen my cell walls during cryo-freeze, stem cells from eagles and owls to enhance my eyes, and bat proteins for precision hearing. I could now hold ice in my hand without so much as a chill, eat ice cream as fast as I could without a headache, recognize friends and family from kilometers away, and pick out whispers amid a crowd.

"Am I gonna fly ships?" I asked my doctor.

"We certainly hope so. Wouldn't that be great?"

"I guess," I halfheartedly said. The lighting changed, and I knew Daddy had come to pick me up.

"Hey Poops, was it bad today?" Daddy said with his downward smile.

Come to think of it... "I didn't feel a thing!"

"Nor should you," my doctor said, placing cool liquid on my arm that closed the small puncture on contact.

I hopped off the table. "Can I have ice cream?"

Daddy looked as if something important had dawned on him. "You know what? I think you've earned it today!" He turned to the doctor. "Thank you, comrade."

"Always an honor, Commander. Young Dione must return for the rest of her DNA package on the twelfth of next month," the doctor said, pressed a fist against his heart, and stood up straight. "For The Director."

We matched salute. "May he shepherd us into the light."

I held Daddy's hand as we entered the surface lifts. Diffuse sunlight showered us when the doors opened. Within Mercury's north pole crater, and with no tilt in the planet's axis, the sun appeared perpetually about to rise, gently illuminating Icarus's domed orchards, granting just enough ultraviolet radiation for its citrus trees to flourish.

I tugged Daddy's uniform cuff and pointed at the Cold Market, where the ice cream vendors awaited my patronage, *no doubt.* But he was fixating on a thin magenta line outside the dome, decelerating a shuttle from the Hermian Armada orbiting above.

"Your mother's home," he said and smiled sweetly. "I bet you cannot wait to meet her."

I heard so many stories of her greatness that I was unsure of my worthiness. "I guess," I quietly said.

"Come on you sourpuss! Let's get some ice cream!"

The chill of the Cold Market no longer fazed me, but Daddy shuddered. We approached Miss Ri's station. I stared, mesmerized, as she pushed cream across her stone table with a spatula in each hand, breaking ice crystals to keep its texture smooth. She must have had the same injections as I, for she periodically touched the frigid stone with bare hands, not once flinching. She noticed me staring.

"You again? My goodness you have a sweet tooth," she said.

"Afternoon, Miss Ri," Daddy said. "Three packs of insta-cream, please."

"Three?" she said. "Has Admiral Kesler returned?"

"She has. We're going to make ice cream tonight."

Miss Ri ceased kneading and rushed to the freezer, pulling three unmarked packs. "I was saving these for when we win the war, but if I can help welcome our admiral home, please take them."

"Thank you kindly," Daddy said. "What makes these so special?"

"Oh, you'll know when you try them," Miss Ri said, winking at me.

We moved on to other stations, where Daddy bought two bags of limes and something called wine. I listened to the bottle with my modified ears.

"It doesn't whine," I said.

Daddy barked his laughter.

He's so happy to see Mother, I realized. Daddy had met with psychologists almost every day, and I often heard him cry through the wall late into the night. Walking through the market now, I finally saw him happy, complete. *Mother must be the missing piece.*

"I'm ready to meet Mom," I said and smiled.

"Me too, Poops." He led me to the meats section. "Should we have real fish tonight?"

I nodded.

"Which one should we get?"

I studied the meat cubes printed in the underground factories and the natural fish hanging on the wall beyond, shrink-wrapped. I never truly thought about how they became food until then. A pit formed in my stomach. I pointed at the cube.

"But that's printed," Daddy said.

I gave him *the eyes.*

"Oh, all right." He waved to get the butcher's attention, leaned close, and whispered. "Do you have real halibut?"

The butcher nodded. "It'll cost you though. It's from before the war."

"It's a special occasion. Can you cut it to look like a printed cube for the little one?" Daddy said and smiled my way.

I pretended not to hear him as clear as day.

We returned to our apartment several hundred meters below the surface, spread groceries on the prep table, and put the ice cream in the freezer.

"Wanna be my sous-chef?" Daddy asked.

I made a face. "A shoe shelf?"

He barked his laugh. "Sous-chef, silly. The chef's sidekick." He placed a step stool, raising me to the tabletop. "I need you to prepare the lime bath. You think you can do that?"

I nodded.

Daddy placed the juicer with a ribbed knob and a large bowl in front of me and went to work, halving the limes and sending them my way to twist upon the knob. When its reservoir filled, I poured the pulpy liquid into the bowl. Citric acid seeped into my cuticles, causing my fingers to burn. But I was the sous chef and refused to complain. I washed my hands as Daddy cut the halibut into smaller cubes, tossed them into the lime bath, and added minced cilantro. It was ready to cook in citric acid for the afternoon.

I was playing *Marauders versus Farmers* in my room when I heard the front door open. Daddy hustled from the kitchen, and I heard murmuring from who could only be my mother. Before long, footsteps neared my door.

"It's unlocked," I whispered, knowing she could hear me.

The door gently opened. I looked up to meet the mighty warrior, but my gaze overshot her. I had assumed Mother would be exceptionally tall like the other captains, guided by their DNA concoctions. Instead, she was short and stout. She read my confusion and raised a hand to the height a captain should stand. I could not help but grin.

"May I come in?" she said.

I nodded.

Mother's steps were soft and graceful. She sat on the floor next to me.

"Wanna play Marauders versus Farmers?" I asked.

She looked at the figures on hologram. "I would love to."

"You can be the farmers," I said.

Her eyes darted from one figure to the next. She gathered the civilian characters and tools and redistributed them with lightning efficiency. "Ready," she said, her voice cold.

I brought two marauders outfitted in armor and swords from a grassy hill to meet a farmer in a wheat field. "Hello little farmer," I said. "I'm a nice traveler looking for some water. Can I borrow some?"

Mother gave a stern look. "I stab the first marauder in the jugular with the farmer's pitchfork then bury a forester blade into the second's eye socket."

My two marauders lay on the ground dead.

"Wait! You can't!" I yelled.

Mother ignored my protest. "I use the farmer's intruder whistle alerting the townsfolk. They set the crops ablaze with flintlocks."

A ring of fire lit around the hill, the flames quickly igniting grasses higher in elevation. My marauder troop at the hilltop had nowhere to run, screaming as they burned alive.

"Farmers win!" chimed my holotile.

"You cheated!" I shouted. "They just wanted water!"

"They were heavily armed and obviously lied about their identity," Mother calmly said. "They could not be trusted."

"But! That's not fair!" Tears cascaded down my cheeks.

Mother's expression melted to horror.

Daddy ran through the door, apron around his waist. "What's the matter!?"

"She cheated!" I pointed accusingly.

Mother appeared utterly confused. "I was just playing the game."

We ate ceviche with a side of elote and grilled plantains in silence.

Mother looked at Daddy every so often. "The ceviche is fine. You're getting better, Tom," she finally said.

"Dione helped make it, believe it or not," Daddy responded.

Mother looked at me, and I slumped into my chair, pushing a cube of halibut around my bowl.

"Well done, Dione, it's delicious," she said.

I pouted.

"What do you say, Dione?" Daddy said.

"...Thanks," I whispered but gave mad eyebrows.

After dinner, Daddy pulled the packs of insta-cream from the freezer. I kept my pout as best I could and broke my pack's internal compartment, starting the chemical cooling process, and massaged the bag to keep large crystals from forming. Mother handled hers just as deftly as I, while Daddy fumbled with mittens to keep his fingers from frostbite.

"Black sesame from Mars, before Phobos's destruction," Daddy said.

It was incredible, just as Miss Ri promised.

Bedtime soon came. I gave Mother another scowl, went to my room, climbed into bed, and pulled a pillow over my head. But I could still hear them whispering.

"She's a spoiled brat, Tom!" Mother whispered. "We cannot afford to treat her like a little girl!"

"But, Abby, she *is* a little girl."

"When I was her age I was—"

"Mastering war games, I know," Daddy said.

"And you were southern hemisphere wrestling champ by age six!"

"That was a different time, before we won the Jovian System."

"She's weak, Tom! And you know it!" Mother hissed.

♦

"My next deployment just came in," Mother said at dinner a week later.

"But... you just got home." Daddy's happiness deflated. "In the Jovian system again?"

Mother shook her head. "It's here, on Mercury."

Daddy beamed a smile. "Don't scare me like that!"

"Where on Mercury will you be?" I quietly said.

Mother barely glanced my way. "Godfire Station as General of the Hermian Army." She thought about that. "Technically, it's a demotion."

"But it's home. That's what you earned," Daddy said.

Even so, she was gone most days, returning after Daddy and I ate dinner, and I was in bed. I heard their whispering as I played Marauders versus Farmers in my room, breaking down Mother's tactics. She did not try to lie or deceive. *Her decisiveness won,* I realized.

One evening, Mother returned early, joining us for dinner.

"Admiral Kesler," I said.

She turned to me. "It's general now. But you can call me Mom."

"Mom..." It felt weird to say. "I want to play Marauders versus Farmers."

"Your father is a better *playmate* than I."

"But I want an *opponent,*" I emphasized.

Her eyes focused. "Very well, but I will *not* go easy on you."

"Abby, come on," Daddy said with an exasperated look.

"Fine, I'll go eighty percent, but don't you start crying again."

We sat on my bedroom floor with my holotile displaying farmers in the fields and marauders on the grassy hill.

"Who do you want to play this time?" she asked.

"Marauders."

"Again? The farmers have the advantage," she said.

"I know."

We set our pieces and rolled for initiative. I was first. I brought a single, unarmed marauder from the hill to a farmer. "Hi there, I'm very thirsty and was hoping to buy some water."

My mother thought. "You may purchase water in town."

"But I'm so thirsty. Can I buy one of *your* water-skins?"

My mother thought again. "Yes, for two baht."

The farmer bent over to retrieve the water skin, and I saw the opening.

"I pull the farmer's knife from his belt and slit his throat," I said.

Mother craned her neck. "The farmer shouts an alert. The others light the crops. Game over."

But the farmers were not alerted, and no crops were set ablaze. Mother further craned her neck.

"He can't shout. I slit his throat," I said and saw Mother's eyes wildly dilate.

Mother began sparing moments every evening to play, explaining the pros and cons of each strategy. And I soaked it all in.

"Mom," I said after a grueling match. "I'm not a spoiled brat."

"You heard that?"

I nodded. "Daddy's afraid I'll get hurt, and without me, he'll be lonely."

"Daddy needs to grow a pair of—" Mother stopped to reassess. "I've missed him, I suppose."

From the moment Mother returned, I noticed that my parent's body language was off. "Do you love Daddy?" I asked.

Mother's lips pressed tight. "I love his genetics. And he had a great career on Ganymede, before his defeat. It's why I chose him as your father. Our DNA is complimentary."

"Daddy never talks about Ganymede. What happened?"

"Your father once had twelve siblings. Did you know that?"

I nodded. "Where are they now?"

She sighed. "They were on Ganymede holding the capital city of Sundow when Ceres unleashed its secret weapon."

"Was it a type of nuke?"

Mother shook her head. "It was a super-soldier unlike any other. We still don't know what modifications he's undergone. But from survivor accounts, we know he does not require his eyes to see. He moves beautifully, like performing ballet. And we have a name, Mirko."

"Mirko..." I repeated, archiving the name forever. "What happened to Daddy's siblings?"

Mother gave a look. "Mirko *killed* them, Dione. And would have killed your father too if he had not fled like a coward."

"Daddy's not a coward!"

"You're right. I'm sorry. It was because of his *retreat* that we learned of Mirko's presence, prompting us to use Godfire Station. But Mirko somehow escaped." She paused. "Listen to me, Dione. When it's your turn to lead this war, if you ever come across Mirko, or any soldier like him, do not hesitate. You must *kill* him, quickly and without mercy, even if you must sacrifice your life in the process. Mirko cannot be allowed to exist. Do not think, just do, okay?"

"Like the game?" I asked.

"Yes, like the game."

♦

Daddy and I were making ice cream when a knock came on the front door. Mother answered. Her breath skipped, and her posture straightened. She placed her fist against her shoulder.

"Your Excellency, to what do we owe the pleasure?" she said.

Daddy almost dropped his ice cream pack.

"Must I have a reason to visit my most trusted general?" came a voice I often heard on hologram. *The Director.*

"Please, come in," Mother said and gave me an urgent look.

I set my pack on the table and hurried to the door as The Director entered. His gray hair was pulled into a bun, and he wore black from head to toe, the fabric deeply textured, capturing the light as he moved.

Daddy tore off his mittens and apron and gave a salute.

"Commander Sharpe, at ease," The Director said and turned his pale eyes upon me. "You must be Dione." He knelt to my height. "I hear you've become quite the Marauders versus Farmers player. What's your secret?"

"Don't hesitate. Just act," I responded.

The Director grinned. "You'll make a fine captain one day." He stood abruptly. "General Kesler, Commander Sharpe, I must speak with you privately."

They entered the study.

"It's time you know the true objective of this war and your parts to play." I heard The Director say through the wall. "Operation Eraser is omega level classified. Is that understood?"

"Yes, Your Excellency," Mother said. "Allow me to set an audio sphere."

All became silent.

I finished massaging the ice cream packs and set them in the freezer. Then, I played several rounds of Marauders versus Farmers.

"I hope you understand why this must be done," The Director's voice suddenly returned. He emerged from the study and gave me a grin. "Dione, I would be honored to play Marauders versus Farmers with you one day."

"Yes, Your Excellency," I said, placing my fist against my shoulder.

He responded in kind and let himself out.

I heard heavy breathing from the study. I entered to find my parents embraced. Daddy was sobbing with his big ups and downs as Mother sat statuesque, a single tear rolling down her cheek.

"What's wrong?" I asked.

Daddy tried to collect himself. "It...It's nothing to worry about, Poops."

With awkward silence, we ate ice cream. Then, Daddy went to bed.

"Dione," Mother said. "You will begin flight school tomorrow."

"But, I just turned six."

"Your scores show that you're ready."

"I don't want to fly ships," I pouted.

"I'm afraid you have no choice. The Director wills it."

"The Director is *stupid*," I said.

Mother's hand lashed like a coiled snake. Pain rippled across my cheek. "*Never* talk about The Director like that!" she hissed, looking around the room as if we were being watched.

I stared back, stunned. "Okay," I squeaked.

♦

"Where are the other cadets?" I asked Miss Melendez, my professor of Astrodynamics.

"Dione. You are meant for an extraordinary mission. We must choose your peers carefully," she soothingly said. "More will join soon enough."

"What's the mission?"

She tightened her lips. "You will be told when the time is appropriate. For now, let's calculate the trajectory from Pluto to Neptune."

"...Okay," I said.

Instead of learning war tactics and intercept patterns, invasion, and boarding procedures, like the other cadets, Hermian Command had me memorizing orbital trajectories, constellation maps, and repair and maintenance manuals for a strange ship called *Regeneration*.

"It's a special ship that you will one day captain," Miss Melendez said, but again, she would not tell me why.

Soon, I was in orbit above Mercury, undergoing zero-g training in the sphere years ahead of the curriculum. There was always an emergency procedure or puzzle to solve, trajectories to plot, and reaching a new high score in Marauders versus Farmers. And despite not knowing what it was for, I loved every minute of it.

♦

Taam was the first kid to join me. His frame immediately gave him away, *an equalizer.* Yet he knew the trajectories by heart as well. *He has the navigation package, too,* I realized. When I heard his barking laughter, just like Daddy's, I knew we would become best friends.

Acara joined next.

"What game are you?" she asked.

"What do you mean?" Taam said.

"I'm high score on *Piglet's Fortification*," she said.

"The construction game?" I asked.

She nodded. "What are you?"

"I'm *King of the Anthill*," Taam said and looked at me.

"Marauders versus Farmers," I said.

Both Taam and Acara snickered.

"What's so funny?"

"Um. That's a little kid's game," Taam said.

"So are yours!"

"But ours are tactical."

"Marauders versus Farmers is tactical, too!" I defiantly said.

"If you're in the Stone Age!" Taam barked his laugh.

Daddy and Mother were overjoyed to see me when I returned home on the weekends. They hugged me non-stop and made black sesame ice cream despite the expense. Although it felt like we became the happy family I dreamed of, something nagged. *What are they hiding?*

◆

I was back in orbit and had just finished the day's zero-G training session in the sphere. I studied Mercury's northern hemisphere spinning below us. Citrus trees beneath Icarus's dome shined brilliantly against Mercury's surface, and magenta LightLines stretched to the Hermian Armada in low orbit. Every few days, a microwave beam would emit from Godfire Station, sending energy to one of our water colonies or fleets in Martian, Jovian, and Saturnian space. I had memorized the schedule and could anticipate when each beam would come, imagining Mother orchestrating their release.

Something suddenly caught my eye. All thirty-seven million solar arrays on Mercury's light side were unfolding. *But the next beam is tomorrow.*

"Tag! You're it!" Taam said, slapping my shoulder, rotating out of my retaliation swipe, and drifting across the zero-G sphere to join the other children.

My attention returned to the unfurling arrays below, absorbing immense power. The tip of Godfire Station glowed. My swirling hair straightened out stiff, and a blinding beam erupted. I covered my eyes as Taam and the others shouted. After several seconds, the beam stopped, and my hair became limp again.

"Wow!" Taam said and looked at the surface.

I anticipated the arrays would close now that the beam was sent, as was protocol. But their petals remained open, and Godfire Station's tip again brightened.

"Cover your eyes!" I shouted.

Again and again, the beams erupted. Between blinding flashes, I saw Taam crying, curled into a ball, floating.

I glided to him. "What's wrong?"

"I can't see," he said between sobs.

"Children! Get out of there this instant! That's an order!" It was Miss Melendez with panic in her voice.

I helped Taam to the sphere's hatch, guiding his hand to the wall.

"What's wrong with him!?" Miss Melendez snapped.

"His eyes."

She knelt, cupping palms around his jaw, holding his head still. "We have replacements," she dismissed. "Children, there's ice cream in the canteen."

Some of my comrades stifled their cries. "What kind?"

"Any kind you want," Miss Melendez said, and the children brightened, but I was not fooled.

When we passed the bridge, I glimpsed the moons and planets of System Sol displayed on holograms with their cities and colonies flashing red. Officers stared wide-eyed, shaking their heads and covering their mouths.

We paused.

"Children!" Miss Melendez snapped. "Do you want ice cream or not!"

I focused my bat-like hearing on the conversations on the bridge as we continued to the canteen.

"General Kesler's lost it! We must stop her!" one of them said.

"It cannot be stopped! That's the whole point of Godfire Station!"

"But we can destroy the solar fields!"

"You can't be serious! That would doom us all!"

"Just enough of them to reduce the beams to non-lethal levels! Hail Admiral Rues! His fleet's in orbital position!"

Miss Melendez served us large bowls of our favorite ice cream in the canteen. I could not stomach anything but felt compelled anyway, as if it were calling to me. My comrades inhaled their bowls, smiling and laughing, forgetting what they had just witnessed. Even Taam, in his blindness, happily fumbled with his bowl.

I spooned my ice cream.

Utensils magnetically snapped to the table, and my friends began snoring. *Why are they sleeping? Where's Miss Melendez?* I looked around. *When did she leave?* I felt unbelievably tired and stumbled to the canteen door. *Locked?* I fought my heavy eyelids for as long as possible before slumping to the floor and falling asleep.

♦

I woke in a cryo-tube alongside twenty-seven other children, shivering violently. *We're aboard Regeneration,* I realized. A hologram opened with Daddy smiling in its projection, but his eyes were sad.

"Hi, Poops," he said.

"What happen—" I tried asking, but with chattering teeth, I bit my tongue.

"I know you have many questions, but you must remain calm," Daddy continued. "You've been in hibernation for sixty-five years."

What!? I frantically searched the hologram, finding *"2286AD, Kuiper Belt,"* in the corner.

Daddy began shedding tears. "Dione, you are about to embark upon your first mission. You must extract Niotrodium from Makemake's core…"

♦

After mining the Niotrodium, we slipped back into hibernation, waking again for Iridium extraction of several comets. *But for what purpose?*

We cried, whined, and argued with the recordings, then with each other, not understanding what these missions were for, why we were put into hibernation, and why we were alone.

"Maybe there's no one else at all," Acara said at dinner one night.

With that in mind, we quickly took matters into our own hands. All my trajectories, Taam's geology, Decan's medicine, Acara's fabrication, Kaden's drilling, Sara's linguistics, and Lilly's tracking, were recalled.

By the time we were eleven years old biologically, we were seventy-eight to System Sol. But we did not comprehend this until Pluto.

♦

Again, my cryo-tube opened, and I started the shiver exercises to warm. After an hour, I could lift my arms and curl my fingers into fists. The scheduled recording opened. *Daddy.* I smiled despite chattering teeth.

"Hi, Poops," Daddy said with eyes of sadness. "You must be eleven now."

"Y...y...yes," I chattered.

He looked away. "You'll soon reach Pluto. On its surface is a water colony we established just before The Fall. Your objective is to make contact with its inhabitants and assess their condition. Full mission brief can be accessed via your holotile. I love you, Poops." The recording ended.

Tears pooled in my eyes, blurring my vision, until Regeneration's gravitational spin began. We emerged from our cryo-tubes and headed to steam rooms to rinse off the foul cryogel. Then, we met in the canteen, groggy and grumpy. Protein porridge, with a splash of sugar and cinnamon, came from the printers.

"Good morning, Captain," Taam said, breaking the silence. His golden replacement eyes settled on me. He slid a cupcake with a candle shaped like an *11* in my direction. "Happy birthday, I mean."

"Happy birthday," everyone groaned.

I almost forgot about the birthday celebrations the first month after the thaw. As captain, mine was on the first day when nobody was in the mood. I leaned forward and blew out the candle.

"Thank you," I said, breaking a piece of the cupcake for each of us to nibble on. "Have you reviewed your briefings?"

"They mentioned The Fall again. What are they talking about?" Acara asked.

"We'll find out when we make contact with Pluto's colonists."

"If they're still alive," Decan said.

"They are!" Taam said. "Hermians never go down without a fight!"

The rest nodded, but not enthusiastically. We were meeting other Hermians, *meeting adults*. The thought of them establishing parental control was unbearable.

"We should expect the worst," I said. "Decan, if there are survivors, your skills will be needed. You too, Sara."

Both our doctor and linguist sat up straight and pressed fists against shoulders. "Yes, Captain!"

We landed on Pluto's blood-red tholin-rich ice, activated our boots to grip, and slowly approached the colony's opaque huts. We could not detect electrical signals. Sunlight was too dim for unmodified eyes, but our owl pupils saw silhouettes on the ice.

"Something's wrong! Go silent!" I commanded and switched off all frequencies. I knelt to the first body, studying the red ice crawling from the surface to wrap around the frozen torso. *"Decan, what do you make of this?"* I asked, using Hermian sign language.

Decan stroked the red ice. *"Blood. These are cuts,"* he signed.

"Heat blades?" I asked.

"No, they would seal the wound. This looks more primitive."

Airlock doors had been torn from their seats, and food stores were empty. Sara waved to get our attention and led us behind a hut to two bodies. One wore a different envisuit.

"*Kaden, is this military?*" I signed.

Kaden studied. "*The exo-skeleton looks like a mining unit.*"

"*What's that?*" Sara pointed at a slab of metal on the ice.

I recognized it from Marauders versus Farmers. "*A machete,*" I signed.

"*A what?*"

"*It's a tool for cutting.*"

Acara synced her envisuit to an airlock's jamb. "*Power was cut and airlocks were blown forty-two years ago,*" she signed.

"*But these Hermians were once great soldiers with a full armory. How could they be sabotaged like this?*" Taam signed.

"*Back to the ship, now!*" I ordered.

We changed into relaxed uniforms and sat down to dinner.

"Whoever attacked didn't use weapons," I said.

"You think they used EMPs?" Decan asked.

"No, all circuitry is functional," Acara said.

"They didn't take the harvesting equipment," Taam said. "What were they after?"

"Food and medicine," Decan said. "They couldn't spare weight for anything else."

"But it's all standard issue," Taam argued.

"Standard issue becomes valuable if the source is cut," I responded.

"Food, yes, but the infirmary didn't look raided to me," Kaden said.

"The penicillin is missing," Decan said.

"They can print that."

"Assuming their printers are functional," I said.

"They're designed for twenty years, but can last longer if well maintained," Acara said. "The protein supply would deplete first."

"But how were the colonists overpowered by tools?" Taam asked.

I pondered that. "Whoever came won the trust of the local population by coming unarmed, then struck with a coordinated attack, blasting the airlock doors and slashing envisuits with homemade machetes when least expected. It's what I would have done in Marauders versus Farmers."

"That's what your game is for!?" Both Taam and Acara shouted.

I shrugged. "That's how I won."

"But, that's not fair," Kaden said.

"Fairness is irrelevant," I said. *Mother's words,* I realized.

"Now I *need* to know why I was chosen," Lilly, who rarely spoke, said. "Mine's *Kitty the Cat Burglar.*"

Decan turned to her. "Was it *you* who stole my socks!?"

She fought a smile and slowly pulled the balled pair from her pocket.

Decan snatched them. "Why would you do that?"

"I like the smell," she squeaked.

♦

We reached Neptune fifteen years later in hibernation, biologically thirteen now, and emerged from our cryo-tubes profoundly changed. With his equalizer genes, Taam's shoulders had grown monstrous, his height had doubled, and the muscles of his forearms and legs had swelled. He gave me a shocked look when I stepped from my tube.

I must be different, too! I thought and looked down to find dried blood coating my legs. *Oh, shit.* Our briefings said it would occur either this thaw or the next. But knowing and experiencing was proving quite different.

"Ladies!" I commanded. "Steam clean! Boys, prepare breakfast!"

We split into groups, the boys hurrying down one corridor and the girls down another. Taam looked back with concern. *But he knew this would happen.* I approached my sisters and realized my eyes were level with their chests. *Why are they standing a full meter taller than me?* Their bodies were elegant hourglasses, augmented by the DNA injections reacting to puberty, creating optimum height and reach, and molding facial features that demanded respect. *They were striking.*

I caught my reflection in a corridor window and nearly jumped back. *No! Please, no!* I studied my body. I was not taller, was not an hourglass shape, and did not have a chiseled jawline or structured nose. At that moment, I understood how similar I was to my mother. Doomed to be short and stout. And I'm sure the doctors promised she would be tall and elegant, too. But the Keslers were stubborn. It was how Mother rose to the very top of the Hermian ranks. Stubborn as stubborn could get. *Down to the DNA, apparently.* I breathed deeply, lifted my chin, and strutted into the steam room to face the supermodels.

We entered the canteen to find the boys inhaling protein mixes like ravenous dogs, their musculature showing through their crisp uniforms and stubble growing on their chins. Their deep voices sent shivers through me, but when our eyes met, they did not hold. The only eyes that did were Taam's, emitting concern. My uniform sleeves extended several inches beyond my fingertips. I had rolled the cuffs and sucked my stomach for the zip to reach the top. But when I sat next to Taam, the zipper split.

"Captain Sharpe?" Taam quietly said.

"Not a word!" I snapped and felt their eyes on me. I stood, grabbed my tray, and left for my captain's quarters.

Footsteps neared my door. By the cadence, I knew it was Taam.

"I don't want to see you!" I grumbled.

"But, Captain Sharpe. It's a matter of great importance."

"Go away!"

"Dione. Please."

I gave the door an icy glare but opened it a crack. Taam was grinning with hands behind his back. I peered down the corridor to see we were alone and fully opened the door. "What's so important?"

He brought his massive hands to his front, holding a cupcake with a candle shaped like a *13,* looking miniature in his paw.

"Happy birthday."

♦

Triton appeared dull blue, tinted by Neptune's reflecting light.

"Our mission is simple!" I said as our dropship descended to the icy surface. "We make contact with Triton's water colony and learn the status of System Sol. Is that understood!"

"Yes, Captain!"

"Coms off, we're running silent from the beginning this time!"

As we neared the water colony, we saw that their airlock doors were blown, just like on Pluto.

"Search the rooms, touch nothing," I signed.

We reconvened an hour later.

"There are no bodies," Taam signed. *"But we found personal items on shelves, maps and blueprints set across tables, and fresh magsuits and uniforms folded on beds. It feels like they were preparing for another day of work. What does this mean?"*

"That these people did not leave," I signed and felt a pit in my stomach.

Decan came bounding over. *"The canteen has power!"*

We followed him to the kitchen. He pointed to the burner and flipped a switch. The coil glowed red.

"Captain, the freezer looks full of meat," Acara signed.

We walked the freezer's rows, staring at the slabs hanging from hooks, frozen solid. Decan scanned them.

"It's real meat," he signed.

"But the water colonies cannot raise livestock," I said. One of the slabs caught my eye, having a little square tattoo. *"That's a stem-code. It might tell us where it originated from."*

Decan scanned the stem-code. *"It's from Icarus. But that doesn't make sense. They'd never send real meat."* Decan cocked his head, then violently heaved in his helmet.

Lilly raced to his side.

"What's wrong, Decan!" I signed.

He regained himself and sent the analysis to the rest of us.

"Corporal Stephan Kean, Ice Mining Division, Hermian Tribal Infantry," showed brightly on visor. *It's people!?* Nausea struck, and my knees weakened. I wobbled to the floor, fighting the urge to puke, when immense paws pulled me back to my feet. It was Taam.

Something registered out of the corner of my eye. I turned to find a strange figure standing in the doorway with a helmet looking comically large compared to their toothpick limbs, like a scarecrow.

I raised my hand in greeting and waited for a response.

The scarecrow reached for the freezer door, instead.

Taam bolted to intercept as the door slammed shut and leaned into it. *The door will certainly crumble before his inertia,* I thought. Instead, it flexed like rubber, absorbing Taam's kinetic energy and sending him hurtling backward.

"Who the hell was that!?" Kaden signed.

Diagrams at the edge of my visor vanished, our headlamps went dark, and the gentle hiss of air ceased. I tapped my visor. *Nothing.* My pupils opened, making out my crew.

"We've been EMPd. Suit power is out," I signed.

Acara pressed a hand against the door, then signed, *"Siclecell Titanium. We're not getting through without a V-blade."*

"We left them in the dropship," Taam signed.

I peered at the hanging meat. *"Those without Cuvier Whale DNA would suffocate within minutes. But we can last for hours. Take one last breath. Our captors should return once they believe we have suffocated."*

Fifteen minutes elapsed. Any unmodified human would have surely succumbed, yet the door remained closed. After an hour, the cold seeped into my fingers and toes, signaling the descent into hibernation.

"They must know of our heightened oxygen absorption," Decan signed.

"Will we suffocate or freeze first?" I signed.

"Most likely freeze. Why?"

I waved to get everyone's attention. *"Our captors are not taking any chances and are waiting for us to slip into hibernation."*

"What do we do, then?" Acara asked.

"How long can each of you hold your breaths for?" I asked.

"Three hours twenty minutes... Three-fifteen... Two-fifty... Two-forty-five... Three-ten... Three-five," they signed.

"Two-ten," Taam signed.

I studied Taam. *"Are you sure? Your lung capacity is several times larger than ours. Two-ten is almost up. Do you feel oxygen-deprived?"*

Taam scrunched his brow. *"No."*

"How did you determine two-ten?"

"They had me sprinting in vacuum as a child," he signed.

"If you use minimal movement, you can significantly extend that time."

"How does this help us? We'll freeze first," Decan signed.

"We must huddle around Taam using our body heat to keep him thawed," I explained.

Taam grinned. *"And then, I give them hell when they come."*

I nodded. *"But you must capture them alive."*

Taam crouched to the floor, and we wrapped around him. The freeze crept in, and I desperately wanted to sleep. I forced my eyes open a final time to see Taam looking back, centimeters away.

We'll be okay, he mouthed.

♦

A paw wiped the hair from my forehead, and I slowly opened my eyes.

"Look who's back," Taam said with a grin.

"How long was I out for?" I moaned.

"Two months," Decan said. "You went into deep hibernation."

"Why only me?" I asked.

"Your mass is significantly less. You nearly froze solid."

My crew lit up when they saw me awake and speaking.

"I'm glad we all made it," I said.

"A few of us were still conscious when it went down!" Acara said, placing a hand on Taam's thick forearm. "You should have seen Taam! He caught the guy who trapped us, then carried us as one frozen lump to our dropship, all in one breath!"

"Five hours and thirty-four minutes!" Taam said proudly. "I had no idea I could do that!"

I focused on Acara's hand, gently squeezing Taam's arm and him allowing it.

"What about our captor?" I commanded.

Acara recoiled her hand and stood at attention.

"He refuses to speak or eat," Decan said. "We have him on IV, but he will not survive long."

"What are we feeding him?"

"The same protein mix we eat."

"It's probably disgusting to anyone who isn't Hermian."

Decan scoffed. "He eats *people* and thinks *our* mix is disgusting?"

"Fair point. What do his vitals say?"

"He's slightly malnourished. It seems he has vitamin supplements."

"Injuries?"

"Several old broken knuckles and toes, nothing significant otherwise. His injuries align with a career in mining."

"So he's one of our water colonists."

Decan shook his head. "Outside of general DNA scrubbing he's unmodified. I believe he was a commercial miner."

"That means he's Ceran." An idea brewed. I stepped from my cryo-tube, my legs wobbly. Taam reached to help, but I waved him off. "I wish to speak with this Ceran alone in the canteen in two hours."

"Yes, Captain!" they said and saluted.

I took a long steam, and when I returned to my quarters, I found gifts from my crew. A new uniform lay upon the end of my bed, different from what I remembered. A note was placed on top.

"A uniform fit for our Captain. - Acara-"

I tensed, reading it like an insult at first. *But Acara only means the best,* I knew. New lines ran along the sides of the uniform where additional material was added. Its seams were perfect, the sleeves were hemmed from the shoulder side to keep the cuffs pristine, and the pants were contoured to my short, muscular legs. The zip reached the top, and I breathed deeply.

"Damn, she's good," I whispered. But then, I thought about her hand on Taam's arm and frowned. *Taam... Where's his gift?*

Upon my nightstand was a book, *"Poetry From Beyond, by Taam Kapoor."* I cautiously opened to the first passage.

"Mars is red... Neptune is blue—"

"You've got to be kidding me!" I blurted.

"—We're in this together... All here for you."

I found artificial cream, sugar, and cocoa in the ship's reserves and entered a private room. The scarecrow sat shaking in a straight jacket with an IV feeding nourishment. *"143 years old,"* his blood analysis told us. *A time capsule of information. If we can only get him to talk.*

I whisked cream with sugar and cocoa in a small bag and placed it in a larger sack with ice cubes and salt to lower the temperature. I then shook, kneaded, and spun every which way, frost forming on my fingers. The scarecrow grew both confused and intrigued. When I stopped, his eyes darted to mine, then to the sack. I pulled the smaller bag from within and opened its seal. The cream had crystallized. I tasted. Its sweetness was not quite enough, and the cream was too thick, but the essence of chocolate ice cream was there.

I heard a whine. The Ceran craned his neck to view the contents. I scooped a bit. His eyes grew wide. He opened his mouth, and I fed him like a baby. He moaned. Comically so. *Embarrassingly so.* I felt myself blush. His head listed side to side.

He slowly regained himself and lifted his head.

"Do... you... want... more?" I said.

He processed my words and nodded slightly.

"I... am... Captain... Dione... Sharpe... What... is... your... name?"

Again, he processed, then groaned, "Mmmischa."

We emerged from the canteen smiling to find my crew anxiously waiting. I had removed Mischa's straight jacket, and Taam swelled into a defensive posture.

"Calm," I signed at my side, then said, "Everyone, I'd like you to meet Mischa Kozelsky, Captain of the Ceran mining freighter, Taka."

Mischa's eyes shifted nervously. He dared not look at Taam. "Mmmeeted you, nnnice," he mumbled.

Sara closed her eyes and nodded as Mischa spoke his gibberish, putting her parakeet genes to work. She soon responded with Mischa's drawn-out slurs, growls, grunts, and whines.

"His crew was in the Kuiper Belt mining comets for heavy water and Iridium when all communication in System Sol cut," she translated. "They eventually landed on Triton, helping the water colonists survive."

"You really understand this?" I asked.

"Yes, Captain! It's a mix of Japanese, English and Russian, with many words substituted for guttural sounds!"

"Meh kata no same I mmm vod son," Mischa said.

Sara laughed. "He's wondering why we look the same."

Mischa's eyes locked onto mine. *Except for you,* they said.

We allowed Mischa free movement in the canteen and made a point to include him in meals. He stared at the protein mix in disgust and at us for not noticing its horrid taste. He tried again and gagged.

"Ffffuckin shit," he muttered one evening.

Decan grew furious. "But eating *people* is okay!?"

Mischa looked up in shock.

"He had no choice," Sara said. "The water colony was attacked by pirates. Mischa was in the field and returned to find the colony slaughtered and his ship stolen. He consumed the dead to survive."

"Bullshit!" Decan spat.

"Mischa told the truth," I said. "His vitals did not waver."

Decan glared at Mischa. "You're a fucking monster!" He flicked his bowl of protein mix into Mischa's face.

"Decan! You are relieved!" I ordered and stood, though I was a third shorter than him.

His menacing gaze met me. "You're *defending* him?"

"He's innocent in this!"

"Innocent!? You disgust me!" he cried.

My eyes shot to Taam. He was suddenly behind Decan, his massive arms wrapping around and lifting him off the floor.

Decan flailed his feet. "Let me go you stupid oaf!"

Taam squeezed. Decan's mouth opened wide, and his legs calmed. Taam set him down and unwrapped his arms.

Without a word, Decan left the canteen.

♦

Kaden called my holotile. "Captain! I found Mischa in the steam room beaten to a bloody pulp!"

"Shit. I'll be right there. Tell no one," I said, hustling through the halls to the steam room.

Kaden was at the doorway. "It's bad, someone really worked him. You think it was Decan?"

"I don't know," I said, studying Mischa crumpled on the floor, soaking wet, his arm broken, and his front teeth missing. "We need to bring him to the infirmary. We can talk with Decan directly."

A grin twisted on Decan's face as he inspected Mischa's crushed nose, missing teeth, and broken ribs and arm.

"Decan," I started.

"I had *nothing* to do with this, Captain," Decan said. "Check the recordings, I've stayed clear away from him since the canteen. Just as you requested." He saw the look on my face. "Not to worry. I'll fix him up."

Kaden came to me later that day. "Everyone has an alibi and there's nothing on security.*"

"Did someone tamper with the feed?"

"It seems untouched." A look crossed Kaden's face. "How did Mischa get out of the canteen without anyone noticing in the first place?"

A few days after Mischa's release from the infirmary, we again found him beaten within an inch of his life. This time in suit fitting.

◆

"Captain! He's outside!" Kaden called from Regeneration's aft airlock.

Sara and I raced to meet him.

"Kaden, suit up! Get that airlock open!" I ordered.

"He's overridden the controls!" Kaden said. "How the hell did he do that!? How did he get here without us knowing!?"

"He's been a captain for over a hundred years!" I said. "He knows the inner workings of ships better than we ever will!" I peered through the window. Mischa was wearing his old, ratty envisuit several meters out, facing the dull glow of Triton below. "Sara, talk to him."

She spoke in his slurred mix of languages, but Mischa did not move. I checked his vitals. His breathing was steady, and his pulse low. I'd never seen him so relaxed.

"Mischa," I said quietly on com.

He raised his hand to hip height and emitted a minuscule puff of gas from his palm thruster, spinning him to face the ship. *A perfect single-axis rotation, better than I could dream of performing.* He puffed closer to the window. I saw that he was grinning beyond his visor's reflection. Our eyes locked as his hands pressed the glass surface, absorbing his gentle forward momentum.

Goodbye, he mouthed and pushed away, little puffs of gas propelling him towards the dull glow of Triton below. His scarecrow silhouette became a pinpoint. And then, he was gone.

◆

We woke from hibernation in the Saturnian system and gathered in the canteen for breakfast.

"Where's Decan?" Taam said.

"He had an accident during hibernation," I said. "He's in the infirmary with two broken arms and legs."

Taam gave me a look. "Accident, or *accident,*" he said.

"I don't know, actually."

"Are we going to find out who did it?"

"I don't think we will," I said.

Taam nodded in silent agreement.

Decan joined us for breakfast a week later, his arms and legs mended, and gave each of us a long stare but said nothing. He sat at the table's far end, peering into his porridge.

"Listen up!" I said as we finished. "We're nearing Saturn for our deceleration assist. Its rings will be fully facing the sun this time of year. I want you dressed and on the observation deck in ten minutes!"

Their faces brightened. "Yes, Captain!"

We stared in silent awe as Regeneration drifted safely above Saturn's rings, our minuscule gravity rippling ice particles like a raft on still water.

"Look at the gravitational wake chains!" Acara said, pointing at ice particles looking like strings of pearls before breaking apart.

"It's beautiful," Taam whispered.

A fuzzy, yellow ball emerged from Saturn's shadow.

"There's Titan," I said.

Regeneration released compressed gas to slow our approach. Titan's gravity pulled Regeneration into orbit, looping us around its dark side.

"If there's a break in the clouds, if an atmosphere bubble is visible, then there's a good chance its population survived," I said. "Get ready to push into geosynchronous orbit. Kala City should be rounding the horizon in three, two, one..."

No clear pocket was evident in Titan's haze.

My stomach sank. "Any power signals?"

"Nothing, Captain."

Smaller settlements rounded the horizon. Still no bubbles.

"Wait." Taam pointed at a tiny clearing in the southern hemisphere.

"What town is that?" I asked.

"There was never anything there before," Taam said.

"Lock into geosynchronous orbit above that spot!" I ordered.

Regeneration rose, stabilizing above the mysterious atmosphere bubble. *It's atop a basin,* I realized. A brown surface shone within, its center becoming green.

"That's dirt!" Taam blurted. "Maybe agriculture!"

"Landing team, let's go!" I called to a round of cheers.

Ten of us marched from the Observation Deck to Regeneration's aft airlock, suited up, packed into our drop-ship, and dropped into the thick yellow atmosphere.

"Initiating deceleration!" I said. "Hold tight! This is our first descent into atmo! It'll be bumpy!"

Our heat shield hissed like an awful snake as flames licked the window, dying down as we slowed. Then, retrorockets thrust, lurching us forward, but our restraints caught us. Titan's rough, icy surface finally revealed itself as we skimmed toward the mystery settlement. A shallow inverted dome appeared, spanning the entire basin. We landed just outside its southern edge, where we determined an airlock might be.

Taam pressed his hand against the dropship's door, checking its systems. "You ready?" he said, and we nodded.

Titan's thick pressure flooded the airlock. We emerged, staggering to the dome's entry hatch.

"What's pushing against us?" Acara asked.

I stopped and raised my glove sensor to analyze. "This is wind," I said.

"So that's what wind feels like," Taam said.

Acara linked her envisuit to the bubble's airlock terminal. "The lock is offline." The more she negotiated, the more frustrated she became.

"What is it?" I said.

"It's not even connected to a power source, whoever constructed this had no intention of leaving."

An act of desperation, I thought. "Is there another way to open it?"

"Manually, but there's nearly nine tons of force being applied to the door."

"What do you suggest?"

Acara welded a hook to the door and tethered it to our dropship. It took several minutes for the ship to build enough force to crack the door open, just enough for Titan's air to rush inside and equalize.

"Acara, patch the airlock into our dropship's power cells for our return," I ordered.

"Yes, Captain!" Acara responded and landed the dropship.

We entered and sealed the outer hatch. Taam grasped the inner lock door's wheel. "Pressure is one and a half times stronger here than inside.

We'll pop like a cork."

Like a cork, indeed. We tumbled across the ground, curled in brace positions, until we settled.

"Everyone okay?" I asked, receiving a round of thumbs up and giggles. Readings spread across my visor. Atmospheric composition and temperature were Earth equivalent. Saturn showed enormous above, and I extended my glove to analyze. UV was high, mostly emitting from the planet itself.

"We'll get a tan for sure," I said, unclasping my helmet.

"Captain, wait!"

I let it roll back and took in the air. Decaying soil hit my olfactory sense, and I laughed. A strange rustling met my ears. *Wind has a sound,* I realized. My crew stared at me befuddled, then furiously unlatched their helmets.

As we moved to the basin's edge, the ground became dark and moist.

"Topsoil!?" Taam scooped his paw into the dirt. "How in Sol do they have topsoil!? There is no silica on Titan!"

The basin's steep wall hosted wisps of green, mixing with reds and yellows at the basin floor. Soon, we traversed a lush prairie. Square depressions, filled with water, hosted a green sponge-like substance.

"Algae, oxygen producer," Taam said.

A gray swirling was below.

"Fish!" Kaden hollered.

"At-ten-hut!" I called, and my crew snapped into position. "It's clear someone, if not the Titans themselves, are alive and well. We need to understand where they are and how they survived. Lieutenant Kapoor."

"Yes, Captain!" Taam responded.

"What is the lay of the land?"

"We're in the lower portion of a two-tiered basin with a layer of topsoil atop the methane ice surface. The algae ponds appear to be fed by underground springs, its water running into the fields via irrigation canals. Cleansing the water of toxins is tricky, so I imagine they want to keep irrigation separate from drinking water. Their settlement should be in the higher tier of the basin to the north."

"Private Faulkner, accompany Lieutenant Kapoor to the northern tier. Observation only. However, if you make contact, establish communication and convey that we are here to help."

"Yes, Captain!" Sara said and nodded at Taam.

I grouped the rest of us into pairs and assigned directions. "We'll be running dark. Use manual timers, and reconvene here in two hours."

"Yes, Captain!"

Decan and I headed southwest to the highest peak for an overall basin view. He glanced at me warily.

"You may speak freely, Decan," I said, once out of earshot of the others.

"You ordered me beaten during hibernation, didn't you?" he snipped.

"It was *you* who ordered Mischa beaten, was it not?" I retorted.

He thought. "No. It was not."

"And I did not order such an attack on you."

"But you didn't search for who did," he argued.

"That's because you deserved it."

"But I'm not a cannibal! I'm Hermian, your own kind!" he grumbled.

I stopped midway up the basin wall. "The Hermians are gone, don't you understand that? Pluto and Triton were our last hopes of establishing a water supply before The Fall."

"But we have Ganymede and Europa."

"Why have we not heard anything, then? Why the complete silence?" I said. "Decan, we may be going extinct."

"That's why we must protect our kind," he said.

"I mean *humanity* may be going extinct. Hermian, Ceran, Martian, Terran. These distinctions died long ago."

"But The Director would never stand for cannibalism."

"The Director is *dead.* And for all we know, Hermian survivors may be resorting to cannibalism as we speak. Would you forgive them if it ensures the survival of the Hermian race?"

Decan remained silent.

"We've been collecting resources in the Kuiper Belt and making contact with old colonies, Hermian and Ceran alike. Soon we'll reach Mars, Ceres, and Earth. We're few, with no weaponry. We're not military. I believe our true objective is to save what's left of the human race."

We reached the top of the basin wall and archived irrigation canals running north-south in two parallel lines and feeding depressions of vegetation into our elephant brains. I saw the others reach their vantage points in the distance, and Taam and Sara dip into a reed-like forest at the northern tier.

"Decan, we need you at your best," I said. "Need you for the weak and the dying, including heathens and former enemies. But, you must decide for yourself how you want to contribute to this new future we're creating."

Our timers buzzed, signaling our return. We descended in silence and met at the rendezvous point. Teams scouting farther north reported leafy green shrubs, vines on trellises, and tall stalks.

"Where's Taam and Sara?" Kaden asked.

"They went into the northern tier to investigate. We should expect them to be a little late," I said.

A little late turned into two hours late.

"We should go look for them," Kaden said.

"No need." I pointed. A speck appeared at the ridge, sprinting down its side. From the silhouette alone, I could tell it was an equalizer.

"That's Taam, all right," Kaden said.

"Wow. Look at him go. He must be doing sixty kilometers."

"Well, he knows he's late."

We chuckled.

"Where's Sara?" Lilly said, sniffing the air. "I smell blood."

My eagle eyes focused on Taam's speck, making out his shoulders dipping side to side. *He's charging hard.* Something hung limp in his arms. *Another person.*

"Sara's injured!" I shouted and turned to Decan.

He held my gaze for a second, then tore off his med pack, opened its contents, and threw a small box into the grass that auto-unfolded into a gurney.

"How bad is she bleeding!?" Decan called.

A red river flowed down her arm. "It's a lot!"

Taam's facial features became recognizable, and his mouth opened wide. Several seconds later, we heard his monstrous voice shout, "Run!"

Strange thumps resonated in the ground. I retracted my telescopic vision and panned up to the northern tier. Little sticks appeared, wiggling back and forth, heads shone, bouncing up and down, then torsos came. Long secondary faces appeared, followed by sets of thin quadrupedal legs.

"What the hell are those!?" shouted Kaden.

Centaurs? I thought. *No.* "The Titans are on horseback!"

Several dozen cascaded down the wall in pursuit of Taam, their beasts long and spindly, their strides delicate and slow, yet they covered incredible ground.

Decan, who was furiously setting up his equipment, was now furiously breaking it down. We sprinted towards the southern wall as fast as we could, making for the airlock Acara had made operational, *hopefully.* Taam caught up to us, slowing to match our speed.

"Don't stop! Don't look back! Just go! Get to the southern wall! Get the high ground!" he cried.

We all listened. *How could you not with those howler monkey vocal cords of his?* I peered over my shoulder, nevertheless. The Titans were gaining, several standing upon the backs of their steeds with javelins ready. I assumed they could reach us even from over a hundred meters out. I felt my short legs tire. I drifted back. My crew remained focused on the southern wall. *But none of us will make it in time,* I knew. Grasses crunched beneath my feet, reminding me of that first Marauders versus Farmers game against my mother.

I snatched a flare from my belt and twisted its top. A bright blue flame screamed, and smoke billowed. I turned sharply east into a depressed wheat field and lowered the flame, setting the crops ablaze.

"Nay! Wheat o thee shall saveth!" a rider cried, pointing at the others who broke off pursuit of my crew, half rushing to an irrigation canal, half convening upon me.

I continued dragging my flare and pivoted to the more valuable crops. A whoosh came through the air, and I caught a glint. *Thank Sol, for those eyes and ears!* I ducked just in time, the tip of a spear intended for my heart brushing my cheek instead. My steps began to squish as water filled the wheat field, squelching the fire. I scaled an elevated pathway separating wheat from sorghum, rising six meters tall in the adjacent depression. I turned and held my flare dangerously close to the sugar crop. The cavalry approached, ready to strike, carefully watching the flare in my hand.

I spied my crew in the distance, scrambling up the basin's wall and turning around when reaching its peak. The largest of them waved hands wildly and looked about to charge back down, but the rest converged, holding them back. *Holding Taam back,* I knew. And it took all of them.

"Dione!" he cried, his voice echoing across the basin like God himself.

The spindly horses reared, nearly throwing their masters. I wasted no time, twisting the cap of my flare, snuffing it out, and darted into the thick sorghum, where the Titans could not pursue on horseback.

◆

With howls, the hounds found my envisuit glove or boot, left behind to confuse them. It was proving only a mild distraction. They were right on my tail. I had not slept in six days nor eaten in two, and I finished my water reservoir early that morning. My knees were weak. I had to sit.

I was in a cornfield now and saw an ear in the low light of dusk. I plucked it from the stalk and tore its husk. It was young, the kernels small. I retrieved a memory of my father making elote. *Yes, young.* I sank my teeth anyway, feeling kernels pop and juices flow. *Oh, such flavor!* I was lost in ecstasy when a hand pressed upon my shoulder. I slowly turned to meet a pair of eyes with pupils as wide as mine.

"Lilly?" I whispered.

"Hey, Captain," she said and sat beside me on the ground. She wore a jet black, formfitting fabric caked in mud and pulled a canteen from her belt. "Thirsty?"

I stared at the canteen with lust and chugged its contents. The condensed electrolytes flooded my bloodstream. All exhaustion melted away.

"Good stuff, isn't it?" Lilly said, laying on her back, hands comfortably wrapped behind her head.

Her relaxation sent my anxiety skyrocketing. "How'd you find me? How'd you get past the hounds?"

"Inferior olfactory senses, easily tricked." She pointed to the night sky. "Do you hear them?"

Their rustling and howling were more distant, I realized. "How?"

"You had the right idea about ditching your suit. Except that you're now radiating. But I took care of that." She gently tapped her nose. "Grizzly Bear. A hundred times more sensitive than any *hound.* I know exactly where they are." She breathed deeply. "And they just found your underwear."

Howls came in the distance, followed by hooves thumping that way.

"My underwear?" I asked.

"I raided your hamper before coming."

"Lilly. That's disgusting."

"You're welcome, Captain." She stood. "Wanna get outta here?"

I nodded.

A wicked smile spread across her face. "Then we're going to have to do something about your scent." She pulled a massive pair of underwear and two pairs of socks from a pack.

"Are those Taam's?"

"It's funny. With all the advancements these past four centuries, smell is the one sense that has never been cracked. Chemicals yes, but not scent specifically. So, we gotta mask your scent with stronger scent, and Taam is by far the stinkiest."

I caught a whiff and gagged.

"Arms," Lilly ordered, and I reluctantly outstretched them.

She slipped a sock up each of my arms and legs. Then, came the underwear, my head through one leg hole, my arm through another. The stench was overwhelming, and I dry heaved. Lilly stuck plugs up my nose.

"Baby," she said. "How do you think I feel? I know his entire body chemistry." She sniffed the underwear. "Your boyfriend's a healthy one."

"What?"

Lilly darted into the corn stalks.

I almost tripped on Taam's floppy socks to catch up.

"Taam's not my boyfriend," I whispered.

"Coulda fooled me. It's a pheromone bonanza with you two."

"But, I thought he and Acara..."

"Oh, Acara wishes, but she's got nothing on you, Captain."

Despite the hounds hot on my tail and the dirty underwear around my neck, a massive weight lifted from my shoulders.

"Lilly, I like you. But *never* touch my underwear again."

♦

Sara's eyes wandered the infirmary, delirious.

"Her fever is over forty degrees," Decan said with a hard stare. "Even with her modifications, it's killing her."

"Do we know what this is?" I asked.

Decan gave a *kinda* look. "It's acting like bacteria."

"Bacteria? But they were eradicated long ago."

"It appears this particular strain found a way to survive."

"Does this mean we'll get sick, too?"

"Taam seems fine. But he wasn't run through by a javelin either."

I studied Sara's wound, a two-centimeter hole through her right shoulder, festering up her veins. "How do we fight this?"

Decan raised a hand to his chin. "Old Earth would use penicillin."

"Penicillin," I whispered and thought about Pluto and Triton, how that was the only medicine taken. "We can print that, right?"

"Technically yes, but the strain will be from a century ago. The bacteria might have grown resistant since."

"We have to try," I said.

We breathed a sigh of relief as Sara's fever reduced, all but Decan.

"The infection has only stalled," he said. "We must ask the Titans for help. Either they have penicillin of a newer strain, or bacterial immunity."

"That might be complicated," Taam said. "I'm pretty sure I killed one or two of them when they ambushed us."

I sighed. "Sara dies if we don't ask for help." I turned to Lilly. "We'll need your help getting close to them undetected."

She nodded. "I have just the thing, Captain."

♦

Lilly, Taam, and I landed during Titan's fifth day of darkness, wearing the same black fabric Lilly wore to retrieve me.

"In the water," Lilly ordered.

"What?" Taam said.

"Just trust me on this."

As we waded into an irrigation pond, the skintight fabric swelled, becoming a centimeter thick. We emerged several kilos heavier.

"Now, roll in the dirt," Lilly said, tumbling to the ground, kicking and wiggling like a dog. Soil clumped to her waterlogged fabric.

"Can't we just wear chameleon cloaks?" Taam asked.

"The hounds will smell us," I said.

"Yep," Lilly said. "This is good stuff."

I knelt, grabbed a handful of soil, and rubbed it on my arms, but was shoved to the ground. A mess of muddy hair was pressing against my face.

"Lilly, what are you doing?" I said.

"Your smell with my smell, my smell with your smell," she chanted and pointed at Taam. "Get in here, stinky!"

The three of us rolled, mud flying, faces rubbing against one another and giggling up a storm. After a moment, I realized it was just Taam and me. We looked up to find Lilly standing with her arms crossed.

"You done *fooling* around?" she said.

"But you said to—" Taam started.

"Taam! Get off me!" I ordered.

We reached the basin's northern tier. I imagined having Lilly's nose, sniffing the air. *Fresh cut vegetation*, I discerned, then I caught smoke. "They're northwest of us."

Lilly grinned. "I think you get me." She became serious.

"What is it?" Taam asked.

Lilly turned to Taam. "The ones you supposedly killed. I caught their scents just now. They're alive."

We continued along a trail until Lilly waved us off and called for sign language only. Two Titans were making their rounds, their hounds by their sides, sniffing loudly.

"This way," Lilly signed, disappearing into the reed forest.

"Taam, what is this?" I signed.

"Bamboo," Taam signed and ran his paw across a stalk.

A clearing opened with several Titans around a campfire wearing little clothing despite the chill. They were tall and thin but not sickly. Their musculature appeared stretched. They were teenagers, *like us*. They spoke quietly to one another, holding cups and sipping steaming liquid.

Lilly sniffed the air wildly. *"It's tea!"* she signed, then pointed at two titans across the campfire. One wore a bandage around her torso, and another had their right leg and arm in splints. *"That's them."*

I faced Taam. *"You attacked girls!?"*

"They're the ones who javelin-ed Sara!" he signed in his defense.

I turned back to Lilly, but she was gone. *"Where'd she go?"*

After several minutes of searching, Taam pointed at the campfire. Next to the injured Titans sat Lilly, entranced by a real fire. She lifted a javelin from a pile at her feet and gently stoked the flames. The injured Titans glanced in her direction but returned to their conversation. When their brains registered the stranger among them, they lurched from their seats.

"Who is't the hell art thee?!" they yelled, grasping for their javelins to find them missing.

Lilly gently tapped the pile at her feet.

What is she doing!? I thought, turned to Taam, and signed. *"Stay out of sight! You'll scare the shit out of them!"* I stepped from the bamboo.

Lilly smiled. "Hi, Captain, meet the gang." She turned to the *gang*. "Gang, meet our captain."

The Titans spread away from me like oil on water, pointing frantically.

"Yond's the one! The flibbertigibbet yond burn'd our crops!"

One of them rushed me, but Taam's massive paw, nearly the width of the Titan's chest, emerged from the bamboo blocking his path. The Titan scrambled back.

Taam slowly retracted his paw into the forest.

This is bad! The Titans need their security! I pointed at the pile at Lilly's feet. "Lilly, return their javelins."

"Eh, Captain?" She looked at me like I lost my mind.

I marched over, retrieved a javelin, and approached the Titan who had rushed me and presented it, butt to the ground, tip to the sky. I released my grip and let it teeter. The Titan snatched and raised it to attack position, but I crossed my arms and stared him down. His eyes flicked to the bamboo where Taam was hiding. He handed the javelin to his companion.

"Yond one's mineth," he said, pointing at the one in Lilly's hand.

"Lilly, give the man his stick," I said.

She frowned, admiring its ornate shaft, beautifully carved and oiled, a hilt wrapped in leather, and a head made of bone. She tossed it gently over the fire into the Titan's hand and reluctantly distributed the rest.

I sat on a bamboo bench and patted the empty spot next to me. The Titan sat, gripping his ornate javelin.

I raised a hand to my chest. "Dione." I then pointed at Lilly.

"Lilly," she said.

The Titan raised a hand to his chest. "Steve." He jutted his chin to the bamboo as if to point.

"Taam!" came his booming voice, and the Titans flinched. Taam emerged from the bamboo.

"Hwaaaaa," the Titans gasped, looking him up and down with wide eyes.

"How many m're of thou art h're?" Steve said.

I shrugged my shoulders. "I'm afraid I don't understand you."

He frowned. "Bringeth Martha h're!" he ordered.

A Titan dashed into the darkness. I shielded my eyes from the campfire to see a woman with shriveled skin emerge from a small hut and approach the campfire, squinting terribly.

"What is all the ado about? I wast sleeping!" she groaned.

"We has't visiteth'rs from outside," Steve said.

She snapped her head to me and came in close, her nose almost touching mine.

"It's a pleasure to meet you, Martha. I'm Captain Dione Sharpe."

Her cloudy eyes went wide. "Ah!" She placed hands on her cheeks. "Ahahahahaha!" she cackled and abruptly stopped. "Di-O-ne." She held each syllable. "I have not heard this dialect in a hundred years. Welcome to Tempest," Martha said in near-perfect Hermian.

♦

We erected a small medical habitat within Tempest next to Martha's hut and carefully transferred Sara from the dropship.

Martha gently pressed her lips against Sara's forehead. "Forty-seven degrees," she whispered. "How long has she been like this?"

"Three weeks," Decan said. "Do you have the medicine?"

Martha shook her head. "That was gone long before any of these kids were born. But you may study us. We are all survivors of this plague."

Decan took her blood. "You're a hundred and eighty-seven years old?"

"Am I? What a surprise," she said, grinning.

"Martha is ev'rything to us," Steve said as he gave blood.

"Why do the young Titans speak so strangely?" I asked.

Martha gave Decan and me a smug look. "Those light beams destroyed our cities and towns, and with them, our technology, history, and education. Everything, but my late husband's books in this basin's remote research station. He was a doctor in Shakespearean literature as well as a pedologist. This basin was an experiment to develop Titan soil using plastic pellets as aggregate instead of silica. Hence, why it was not targeted by those light beams. It became Titan's only point of refuge for those who escaped the destroyed cities. The young Titans today speak this way because that literature is the only education they know."

Decan made eye contact with me, his mind racing, as was mine.

The light beams...

◆

"The inoculation was a success," Decan said. "Unfortunately, Sara's cells were severely damaged. She cannot survive another hibernation."

"What are you saying?" I asked.

"She must remain on Titan."

My face dropped. "Have you told her?"

Decan shook his head.

I entered Sara's room to deliver the news.

"Hi, Captain," she groggily said but grinned.

"Hi, Sara," I said. "How are you feeling?"

"I'm awake. So, I'd say *better.*"

I took a deep breath. "Decan says you're going to be fine. But—"

"I'm not coming with you, am I," she said.

"How'd you know?"

"Steve told me."

I thought about that. "How'd Steve know?"

"These Titans are smarter than you think."

"I don't want to leave you."

"Don't worry about me. I'm finding things quite fascinating here." She glanced out her habitat window at Steve husking corn in the morning light, shirtless. As if he knew Sara was watching, he flexed his stomach.

I grinned. "Sara, I don't know how we'll get along without you."

She smiled. "Just remember, no matter what language is spoken we're all essentially the same. Actions always speak louder than words anyhow."

"What will you do here?" I asked.

"The Titans need a teacher. I imagine those courses crammed into our brains, the ones we cannot forget, will be useful."

"I never knew you wanted to teach."

"It's a void I can immediately fill." Sara paused. "Actually, I've always dreamed of creating a universal language. One that borrows from all of humanity's past, focusing on commonality, so it can be learned by anyone. I'll have time on Titan to finally start. When you wake in Ceres orbit it'll be a decade for me, its development will be far along by then."

"That's a *phenomenal* idea," I said, myself excited. "I'll leave a tight-beam transmitter and power cells so you can reach us with progress."

"Consider it done, Captain."

I emerged from her habitat to find Kaden waiting.

"Sara needs to rest," I said.

"Actually, I came to talk with you." He grew nervous. "I've been exploring west of Tempest's dome with one of the elders who used to be an organic chemist. There's a massive hydrocarbon reservoir I can help them tap into. With our knowledge combined, we can develop a significant plastics industry. There's incredible potential here."

"You're not staying," I said firmly.

"I understand how you feel, Captain. But my contributions are mostly finished. Makemake, Pluto, Triton, all the comets we mined. From here on things are political. And, we cannot leave Sara alone."

"She'll be okay," I said.

"Dione, I'm staying," he stated.

"No! You can't!" I responded.

"Please, Captain. I've done everything you've asked without question. I deserve this," Kaden said.

"Fine!" I stormed off.

♦

We gathered for goodbyes the next day. Kaden stood next to Sara, tending to her every need, dare I say doting. But Sara kept glancing at bare-chested Steve.

"Young love, so complicated, so pure. So *obvious*," Martha whispered.

"I hope Kaden won't get hurt," I responded.

"I was referring to *you*," Martha said.

My heart leaped into my throat. "I don't know what you mean."

She gave a knowing look. "That big, handsome, clueless oaf has you in quite a twist. Doesn't he?"

I ignored the comment. "If all goes well on Ceres, we'll send them your way with trade goods."

Martha held her knowing look, waiting.

"And yes… the clueless oaf has me in a twist," I mumbled.

Martha grinned. "Good luck."

We donned envisuits, entered Tempest's perimeter airlock, staggered to our dropship, and rose to Regeneration waiting in orbit. But before we slipped into hibernation for our trip to Ceres, we took a short three-day detour to another of Saturn's moons, Enceladus.

◆

"What do you mean, Troy is missing?" I said, studying Enceladus's white surface below and the dark spot that was once a research facility.

"Athens is gone, too. But we're still picking up their reactor signatures," Acara said. "They must have fallen through the ice."

"Let's hope not," I said. "Our objective is to retrieve Project Infinity from Troy's research facility."

"What *is* Project Infinity?" Taam said. "They failed to give details."

"I don't know," I said. "But it's our highest priority mission so far."

A portion of Enceladus crept into the sunlight, highlighting black specks scattered across the white surface.

"Oh wow!" Taam said. "Two entire fleets are wrecked on the surface."

"Captain, we're getting a minuscule signature west of the wreckage," Acara said.

"Can you pinpoint its location?" I asked.

She zoomed onto a pile of ice. "It's rectilinear, it seems built."

Lilly approached. "Let me check it out."

I nodded. "But no contact with the survivors. Who knows what state of mind they're in."

Lilly returned in the dropship the following day. "Do not open the lock! I found hundreds of them, but they're horrifically sick!"

I looked at Decan.

"Quarantine kit is in the third compartment to your left. Change into the sensor suit so we can monitor you for the next ten days," he said.

The days came and went. Lilly was fine.

"I need to have a look myself," Decan said to me.

I knew the danger. *But those inhabitants might know what happened to Troy.* "Okay, but under no circumstance do you make contact."

"Yes, Captain. But I'll need to see how they are living."

"Lilly, can you get inside without detection?" I asked.

Lilly nodded. "They're completely sensory deprived and their airlock is easy to hack."

♦

Decan and Lilly spent a week on the surface.

"It's not an illness in the viral or bacterial sense. Something else is happening," Decan called in with a concerned look. "And one of the inhabitants is affected *differently*."

"Explain," I said.

"He's blind like the others, I'm certain of it. But he moves effortlessly, and works day and night fishing and preparing tuna. He's single-handedly keeping them alive." Decan turned to Lilly.

"With cloaks, we should be invisible even if he can see," she said. "But the way he turns to face us. It's like he can see without eyes."

Where have I heard this before? Memories from childhood flooded me, ones of Daddy sobbing in his room at night and Mother explaining what happened to his siblings. *Don't hesitate. Kill him!* Her words were so clear. I breathed heavily. Sweat beaded on my forehead.

"Captain?" Lilly said.

Decan narrowed his brow, studying me.

"Follow this man!" I ordered. "Go everywhere he goes! Report everything he does!"

♦

Lilly called in the next day. "He's made contact. We were tailing him to their fishing holes when he suddenly approached and signed in Hermian."

"Sign language requires sight," I said.

Decan raised palms. "He even knew what we were signing through our chameleon cloaks."

"Is he Hermian?"

Lilly shook her head. "He signs with an accent."

"We need blood samples!" I blurted, and Decan gave me a look. "To understand how he can see. He must be uniquely modified. Snakes can sense heat. It must be snakes!"

"Captain. This is *not* part of the mission," Decan said.

"The mission has changed! This is *top* priority!" I yelled.

♦

Our dropship's landing gear gripped the surface, and its airlock ramp lowered, revealing four skeletal figures waiting on the ice. I searched them over, trying to identify the super-soldier. I fixated on the tallest with broad shoulders, but the hips held curvature. *She is not him.* I studied her companions. Their envisuits hung like deflated balloons. *Mirko, the Harbinger of Death, is not among them.* I switched channels.

"Enceladans," I said and saluted. "I am Captain Sharpe of the Reformed People's Alliance of Sol. We have come to aid you." I feared saying *The United Hermian Tribes* would cause panic.

They looked at one another, confused.

One broke the silence. "Ic pro William Stern, lâttêowa râd Athens. We wilcumian êow æthebban Enceladus."

I looked at Taam. He shrugged.

"I ap-ol-og-ize," I said, enunciating my syllables. "We… thought… you… spoke… Eng-lish…"

"We stêpan word–cwide English," said another, slightly more clear but still incomprehensible.

God, I wished Sara were here, I thought. "¿Hablas Español?"

The smallest of them stepped forth and signed in Hermian.

No, this is all wrong! I thought. *How can this little man be the one!?* But he moved with such grace, effortlessly guiding us through their colony and slicing tuna with incredible skill. His hands moved with a mind of their own, reminding me of Miss Ri maneuvering ice cream with her spatulas.

"It's incredible how he found Vitamin C in the tuna!" Decan said.

"He saved them all, Ceran, Enceladan, and Hermian alike!" Taam marveled.

But I could not accept Mirko's heroism. Every word he signed. Every smile he gave. Every joke he made underscored my father's sorrow. *Don't hesitate. Kill him!* Mother's words resonated in my soul. But I still held doubt. This man appeared more like a bookworm than a super-soldier. *But that's how he snuck behind enemy lines! Don't let him fool you!*

◆

I spent weeks carefully watching Mirko help my crew locate Troy until I could not take it anymore. I could not believe he would be willing to aid us without an ulterior motive. I pulled up his file on my holotile, reviewing the accounts from survivors of his attacks. I requested to speak with Mirko alone.

When he entered my habitat, he began speaking in our exact dialect.

How is this possible!? Only Sara can learn a language so quickly! From his blood, we knew Mirko was not modified. His DNA was even dirty, like he was from the twentieth century, before genetic scrubbing.

For reasons I do not understand, this next moment was fuzzy despite me having perfect memory recall. I vaguely remember Mirko asking me to bring the Enceladan population to Titan. But he did not understand that the g-forces from lift-off alone would kill them.

Then, he began questioning our missions. Questioning Troy.

He's too dangerous! I must act now! I dashed my finger in my holotile, reversing the air-recycler, building carbon monoxide in my room instead of scrubbing it.

Mirko shook his head, seemingly aware of what I had done. He lunged forth but stumbled to the floor. Somehow, he summoned the strength to crawl, reaching for his knife. *Now that's the Mirko I heard about!* I could not help but marvel at his grit.

I quickly pulled his knife from his sheath before he could and snapped it in half, causing him to cry out. Then, I took one last breath from my oxygen mask and watched Mirko Obradovic, *the Harbinger of Death,* die.

My head spun, and my limbs quivered, asphyxiation finally affecting me. I heard Taam race through my door as the alarm rang.

♦

I woke to find Decan deep in thought on his holotile and Taam curled on the floor beside me, snoring.

"Taam," I groaned.

He stirred awake and smiled. "Welcome back, Captain.

"What happened?" I asked, feigning ignorance.

"Someone sabotaged your air-recycler."

"Mirko?" I asked.

Decan turned with confusion. "Looks that way, but it doesn't align. Mirko certainly had his issues, but he never displayed ill intent." He sighed. "I don't know how we're going to dive without him."

"Dive?"

Decan frowned. "To Troy... the whole reason we came to Enceladus, *remember?* Troy lies at the bottom of the ocean just as we feared. The only way to reach it is by using their old equalizer suits."

"Acara is repairing them as we speak," Taam added.

"Mirko was explaining how to navigate the water column through the ice and said we'd have to negotiate with the inhabitants below," Decan said. "Whatever *that* means."

"I'm sorry Decan, Taam," I said.

Decan glared. "It's too late for apologies. We're *screwed*. And I can't imagine how we'll tell the Enceladans that their Messiah is dead."

"We don't," I said.

Both Taam and Decan's faces dropped.

"You *can't* be serious," Taam said, his eyes worried.

"We must complete our mission as originally planned and leave for Ceres before we lose the launch window."

"What about all these people?" Decan asked.

"They're terminal. We cannot help them," I said.

"I can't believe I'm hearing this!" Decan stormed off.

I turned to Taam, my stomach in knots. "You understand, right?"

His mouth was tight. "I don't agree. But I understand."

"Retrieving Project Infinity is our *only* priority," I said.

"But we don't know the way," Taam said, sullen.

I felt a pull in my stomach. I looked in its direction. "It's that way."

◆

"Where's Decan?" Acara asked.

"He's not coming," Taam said.

"But he was learning the route from Mirko. How do we get there now?"

"I know the way," I said.

"But—" Acara began to say.

I glared, and she silenced.

The refurbished equalizer armor was nearly rusted through, their once bright red hues were brown, their joints were crusty and grinding, and their smell was atrocious. Pressure rings clamped around our joints, designed to shift the armor with our movement, making several tons of metal feel light as a feather. We dropped into a fishing hole tethered to winches and descended a deep water column. Icy walls shifted in layers from bright white to cobalt blue. Then, complete darkness. I felt both Taam and Acara's heartbeats. *That's strange.* Then, I discerned something looking up with curiosity.

They be in shells, said a child's voice.

"Keep the line clear," I ordered.

Acara unmuted. "We didn't say anything."

I checked their mics. *Both had been muted.*

The water column ended.

We activated our floodlights, but they disappeared into the open ocean.

The one who speaks has come, repeated like echoes around me.

When I blinked, bright lights appeared like hundreds of outlines swaying side to side. I held my eyes closed. *What the hell is this?*

This is our home, a swaying light said, coming closer, taking the shape of a creature I had learned about at the academy.

I unmuted my com. "Taam, Acara, promise me you won't panic."

"Um, okay?" Taam responded.

"Hundreds of sharks have surrounded us," I said as the creatures slowly came within our floodlight's range.

Acara inhaled deeply. "My Sol..."

"Sharks my ass!" Taam said. "These are fucking dinosaurs!"

Why in water? one said as if directly in my mind.

We're here for the wreckage, I thought, but it was not *me* thinking it.

Wreck-edge? Not know.

I resisted the urge to answer, but I knew the words. *Long ago, a great stone fell from above,* flooded my thoughts.

Our home now, the shark responded.

That is where we must go, I thought against my will.

Why? It asked.

We left something behind.

Why?

We did not know it would fall.

Why?

We were attacked.

Why?

There was a war.

Why?

I don't know... It was my own thought.

The shark paused. *You get, then leave.*

"So... I think we just got permission," I said on com.

"What the hell are you talking about!" Taam yelled.

Six sharks escorted us to the ocean floor. Troy's outline appeared as a skyscraper draped upon the rough topography like cloth to a body. Then, our escort darted off with effortless lashes of their tails.

I studied the wreckage. "Acara. What portion of Troy is this?"

"You see that protrusion there?" she said and pointed. "That's the suspension strut Troy once hung from."

"Hung?" Taam asked.

"Yes. The thickness of Enceladus's ice fluctuates throughout the year, which means the only stable foundation is at the surface with the station hanging into the ice." She pointed farther down. "The bottom-most point is where the reactor and research facility are."

Juvenile sharks swam in and out of gaping holes in Troy's hull, so many it seemed the former inhabitants had simply morphed into aquatic form.

"Jesus," Taam said, studying skeletons with limbs torn from torsos.

I motioned to an airlock hatch. "Can we enter here?"

Acara connected and gasped. "There's still power! It's pressurized!"

We passed through the airlock to a dimly lit corridor.

"How's everything still running?" I asked, studying the dim lighting.

"The bottom-most section seems to function as an emergency shelter able to withstand the water pressure," Acara said. "Our equalizer armor is too bulky to maneuver its hallways."

"Leave them behind, but remain in envisuits," I responded.

We crawled out of the armor and began sweeping the rooms.

"Captain, I found a group of scientists in Lab 4B," Taam called in.

I raced over, expecting to find scientists talking with Taam. Instead, they were huddled on the floor, their bodies shriveled like raisins.

"They were shot," Taam said, pointing at their wounds.

More groups were discovered, riddled with bullets or having gashes in their wrists. Then, we found hundreds curled on the reactor room's floor.

"Warning, radiation leak detected," our envisuits said.

"Are we safe?" I asked.

Acara rushed to the reactor's hologram. "Our envisuits should protect us for a limited time," she said. "Captain?" She selected a red icon.

A firm locking sound followed.

"Radiation levels decreasing," our suits said.

"The reactor door was opened on purpose," Acara said, looking at the curled bodies. "These people died of radiation exposure."

"Do we know when?" I asked.

Acara checked the access log. "Sixty-seven years ago..." she cocked her head. "There's a recording addressed to the United Hermian Tribes."

I nodded, and Acara opened.

Gaunt scientists appeared on hologram. *"We, the researchers of Project Infinity, have become prisoners of our own making. Several attempts to reach the surface, to bring our discoveries to The Director, were made. But the very creatures we created turned against us. We have survived as long as we can on what food-stores remain. But after so many years, it's painfully clear we are alone in the universe. However, if we are wrong and you are watching this, please forgive our weakness. All we can offer you is our research stored within this terminal. With Project Infinity, The Director will bring peace to System Sol. May he shepherd us into the light..."*

◆

"Captain, may we speak?" Decan asked, entering my quarters.

"You missed quite the dive," I said. "Take a look at this."

He timidly approached, his eyes shifting to the oxygen mask beneath my desk, then to the hologram. "Sharks?"

"This is Project Infinity," I said.

He gave me a wary eye. "Why is shark DNA so important?"

"I'm hoping you can interpret its genetic code to answer that."

"The animals we've been modified with, I can. But sharks are out of my knowledge."

"You'll have plenty of time to research the matter when we reach Ceres." I closed it down. "What did you want to discuss?"

"That's just it." He took a deep breath. "I'm *not* coming."

"You most *certainly* are," I responded, my eyes boring into his.

Decan stood vigilant. "On Titan, you said I should decide how I want to contribute to the future. I've decided to stay and help these people."

"Decan, there's nothing you can do for them. They're *terminal.*"

Decan's hands shook, his face reddened. "I know it was *you* who reversed the air-recycler in your chamber, not Mirko!" he blurted. "I never thought *you* would be the one to commit murder! And after all the grief you gave me with Mischa!"

"Decan. How can you accuse me of such a thing?" I said, remaining calm, not giving a tell.

He gave a cold look. "If you let me stay, with the equipment and personnel I require, then I'll keep your secret. *That's* the deal!"

How Decan figured it out, I could not guess, but I could not afford the rest of my crew even thinking it. And so, Decan and Lilly stayed behind as the rest of us slipped into hibernation.

◆

Ceres appeared dusty from a distance, but as we neared, each speck proved to be a fragment of pulverized ship in orbit.

"Descending to or ascending from the surface is impossible," Acara said.

But perhaps more impossible was when our ship slowed into geosynchronous orbit, we received a call from the surface, via tight-beam, addressed to me. A man in Ceran uniform appeared on hologram, older than I, but young, nonetheless.

He raised his hands and slowly signed in Hermian, *"Captain Sharpe, we've been waiting for your arrival with much anticipation. My name is Commander Meeks. We're in need of your help."*

"Commander Meeks, we have indeed come to help," I responded. *"But how did you know of our arrival?"*

Commander Meeks studied my hand movements and nodded. *"We restarted our tight-beam three years ago, sending signals to every colony in desperation. All was silent, until one of your crew on Titan, Sara Faulkner, responded. She told us of your journey through System Sol and the exact date and location of your arrival to Ceres."*

"...And taught you Hermian sign language I see," I responded.

"She said there's a doctor among you. We're desperate to find a solution to our muscle atrophy and bone degradation," Commander Meeks signed.

I became aware of his gauntness. *"Unfortunately, our doctor stayed behind on Enceladus. The survivors there have been living exclusively on the Tuna below the ice for over eighty years, but the hydrocarbons from the moon's hydrothermal vents has caused severe methanol poisoning."*

Commander Meeks thought about that. *"We might be able to help. We're running at minimum power. But if we clear our skies and begin mining the asteroids again, our aquariums can grow to supply the Enceladans with fresh food while providing us power for our magsuits."*

"Were your cities not destroyed?" I asked.

"Our grandparents told us the light beams struck all the colonies save Ceres. Once the ships in transit across System Sol learned of this, they came rushing into Ceran orbit. But we could not support them and forbid landing. When their supplies dwindled, they raided one other. A reactor detonation caused a chain reaction destroying all ships in orbit. Their debris showered the surface collapsing our greenhouses and ports, but the deeper chambers survived. But with our skies filled with so much debris we cannot reach the asteroids to resupply. We've diverted all power to our most base life support systems. We're almost completely depleted now."

"What about your Spare Parts facility? Is it still functional?" I signed, excited by the prospect of helping the Enceladans, surprising myself.

Taam smiled at me with renewed faith.

Commander Meeks sighed. *"It was taken apart long ago, its power cells used for life support."*

"Can you rebuild it?"

"There are no engineers alive from then. The knowledge is lost."

"What about Earth?" I signed.

"Only silence."

"Mars then?"

"A graveyard," Commander Meeks signed.

"No. The Martians' creed is self-sufficiency. They must be okay."

"But their Spare Parts facilities burned with their cities."

I thought about that. *"Step one is liberating you of this debris."*

♦

Acara led a team piecing together old Hermian vessels in orbit from schematics memorized as a child, drifting from one hunk of ship to another. After two standard years, six hundred and twenty-eight Hermian transport, mining, and military ships were haphazardly rebuilt, but they would never be space-worthy again.

"Together they'll function as a space station," I signed.

"More like a junkyard," Command Meeks responded. *"How can we be certain it won't be struck? It's like a grenade ready to explode."*

"We must rebuild the other ships before that happens. How's your team coming along reverse engineering Ceran ship schematics on the surface?"

"Slow. We're learning how to build these things from scratch. We don't even know if the ship debris in orbit is from the same models."

♦

Little by little, Commander Meeks's crew sent schematics to help Acara's team rebuild Ceran ships. Orders were barked using Sara's new universal language. We mostly heard, "No!" from the Ceran engineers on the surface, followed by, "Idiotos." It came as no surprise when the first edition of Interspeak proved to be a cesspool of cussing.

"What will the first intelligent species we contact with think of us?" I messaged Sara.

Her response returned a half-hour later. "I know, I know. This was never my intention. Even the Titans are learning the curses so quickly. I can't tell you how often I've wanted to wash my son's mouth with soap."

"Sara, we *must* fix this. Taam accidentally called me a twat yesterday. I nearly broke his jaw," I sent back.

She smiled devilishly in her next message. "There might not be many curse words for men, but we can certainly even the playing field."

The first time I called Commander Meeks a *flaccid cock,* he paused.

Then, roaring laughter came through com.

In our fourth year in Ceran orbit, we finished the reconstruction of the first Ceran mining barge, christening it *Impotence*.

"We need to find the right shit for propulsion," Commander Meeks said. "Something like—"

"Niotrodium," I said.

"Yes, how did you know?"

Our early missions in the Kuiper belt were starting to make sense. *The Director must have anticipated this scenario,* I thought. *But what about Project Infinity? The Sharks? What's their purpose?*

♦

After seven years in Ceran orbit, we joined the crew of Impotence, returning from its maiden voyage to the belt with its uranium-rich payload, and touched down on the Ceran surface.

"Welcome to Ceres!" Commander Meeks's crew greeted us.

We raced the payload to underground processing plants for refinement and formation into rods. The first reactor came back to life. Aquariums thawed, eggs hatched, and tuna, mackerel, salmon, and hundreds of other species matured within a year.

I walked among massive aquarium cubes, running my hand along their icy walls. *I belong here,* I thought. My legs led to an abandoned section with food stations, dusty and dark, knives hanging upon their walls rusted to near disintegration. One station felt familiar. I entered its small office in the back. A desk, once oak, appeared almost black. Upon its surface lay a yellowed envelope with, *"Mirko,"* written on its face. My heart raced, and my hand trembled. I reached forth. The envelope crackled in my grasp, and its seal effortlessly released. A letter was written in Ceran, but I could read it.

"Mirko, I trust you will someday return, and although I will be gone, our legacy must live on. Remember the lessons I taught you, for they will serve you well in both life and this business. But above all else, make sure your cuts are clean and your portions are appropriately sized. And never speak to your customers. Keep the mystery alive, Chef Obradovic. -Misano Okino-"

Mirko, a chef? I wondered what kind of person he might have been if not for the war.

A memory suddenly pulled from my archives of a little boy meticulously running a blade across a whetstone. *His first kill?* I thought. The boy pulled a container from his pouch with a small cut of mackerel. He leaned to the side, drew his blade across its flesh, and sliced a piece clean.

Another memory took its place. *The boy's older now,* I realized. Again, he was sharpening his knife and cutting fish, this time tuna.

The boy became a young man amid battle. I could feel an equalizer's gatling gun beneath his feet and see the rubble the young man knelt behind eroding away. Yet, he seemed unconcerned, bringing forth his blade, sharpening its edge, and peacefully slicing his rations.

Decades seemed to pass, the knife slowly wearing away until I recognized it, worn to a nub.

Then, he was a boy again, looking up at an old man. *Misano-san,* I understood. He extended the knife to the boy, hilt first. Its blade was longer, yet its handle hosted dimples from previous lifetimes of use. The boy held it with such care, such love.

It's an heirloom from the only family this little boy ever knew, I realized. *And I destroyed it right in front of him.*

Who's the monster now? whispered a voice.

I spun around, trying to find where it came from, but I was alone.

♦

Our first shipment of fish, vegetables, a small reactor, and a tight-beam transmitter reached Enceladus.

Decan immediately called. "I never thought I'd hear from you again. And you're giving us supplies?"

"We're also researching ways to rid the tuna of hydrocarbons," I said.

Decan gave a look. "But you'll miss your window to Mars."

"They don't need our help."

"How do you know?"

"It's a feeling," I said.

He narrowed his eyes. "You were set on abandoning Enceladus for the window to Ceres, but now you're helping us instead of continuing to Mars based on a *feeling?* What's changed?"

I made sure I was alone. "Something happened between Mirko and I when I killed him," I whispered.

Decan's eyes went wide. "You confess—"

"I do. But Decan, right now, I need you as a psychologist," I said.

"...Okay?"

"I somehow absorbed Mirko's memories." I told Decan of my visions in the fish markets.

"Perhaps your mind manufactured these memories to deal with your guilt," he said. "But I don't know for sure. I'm not a psychologist."

"Thank you, Decan," I said. *It's more than guilt,* I knew.

Lilly came into view and whispered into Decan's ear.

"They need me," he said coolly and ended the call.

I sighed deeply and thought about the Enceladan mission, the refugees I left behind, Troy at the bottom of the ocean, and Mirko… *What was it all for?* I pondered Project Infinity again and opened the shark's genetic code. I had made surprising progress on my own, and was at a section of proteins related to the shark's immune system. As I scrolled down, my finger flicked back up. I shook my head and scrolled down again. But my stupid finger flicked back up. "Oh, come on!"

"You all right?" Commander Meeks said, standing in my doorway.

"I'm fine."

"The Imbecile is returning if you want to welcome the crew home."

"I'll be there in a moment," I said.

He nodded and left.

I was about to close my holotile when I paused.

Interesting. This is almost human, said a woman's voice inside my head.

My finger went rogue, highlighting several lines of code. I shook my head and stared at my finger. Then, I slowly closed the hologram, pretending nothing strange had just occurred.

♦

"Captain Sharpe!" Commander Meeks said, finding me strolling through the revitalizing fish market.

"What is it, Commander?" I said.

"Mars just called us! It seems that despite their network of domes being destroyed, they survived above and below the surface!"

I felt pride flushing through me. "*Above* the surface? But how?"

"Apparently, chunks of Phobos falling from orbit added tremendous amounts of hydrogen and oxygen to the atmosphere allowing the lowest altitudes to host near breathable air!" He paused, shaking his head in disbelief. "They dug into ancient lava tubes, spilling heat into the atmosphere, warming it just enough to farm on the surface!"

"They'll still have to wear face masks," I said. "But that's incredible!"

Commander Meeks gave a look. "What I'm about to tell you, does not make sense. While every other colony in System Sol has plummeted to near extinction, Martian population has septupled."

"Martian Fever," I whispered.

"What?" he asked.

"It's a Martian phenomenon," I said.

"How do you know these things?"

"Someday I'll tell you, Commander," I said.

He grinned. "Will you be joining us to Earth?"

Most of my crew had left for Enceladus, Titan, or would stay on Ceres. Only Taam and I remained to complete our quest.

"We leave Earth and Mars to you, Commander," I said. "Our launch window to Mercury is fast approaching."

♦

Taam and I woke from hibernation to a massive sun blazing through Regeneration's tinted windows. We met in the canteen for a breakfast of bland porridge.

After a few spoonfuls, Taam dropped his spoon into his bowl. "I just can't eat this shit anymore."

I remembered the look on Mischa's face when we tried feeding him this. "We have fish in storage," I said.

"But nothing to cook with," Taam said flatly.

"We don't need *heat* to cook."

He gave a funny look. "I don't follow."

"We have limes."

"...Still don't follow."

I found tools similar to utensils and laid them on a canteen table. "You're going to be my sous-chef."

"A shoe shelf?" he responded, giving a confused look.

I burst with laughter and accessed the memory of my father and me cooking ceviche. Instead, I found thousands of other memories, unlabeled and scattered, a disastrous mess of recipes, techniques, and cuisines. *What is all this?* I sifted through them, looking for Daddy's ceviche but finding so much sushi. *Are these Mirko's?* Then, I found vegan dishes, steamed meat and vegetable buns, and large flatbreads with lentil mixes. I had only scratched the surface when a paw grasped my shoulder. I blinked hard, coming back.

"You were just staring into space there," Taam said.

"For how long?"

"Like two minutes, you weren't responding at all."

I spied the utensils and ingredients on the table and knew it was all wrong. "Taam, I apologize for what's about to happen."

Ceviche, sashimi, nigiri, maki, gazpacho, crushed cucumber, spicy tofu salad... Everything we could make cold, we did. I wrung Taam dry, barking orders and scolding mistakes. Treating him like a true sous-chef. *Poor Taam.* At first, he protested, but eventually, he kept his head low and chopped, stirred, and minced wordlessly. I did not know where my dictator-like behavior came from.

But look at what we created, said a bitter voice inside of me.

"Let's eat!" I declared.

Taam glared at me, took a maki piece, sniffed, and made a *not-bad* face. The entire roll vanished. The nigiri disappeared next. And then, the ceviche was gone.

"Taam!" I shouted, but there was no stopping him. I raced to pick at the dishes before my vacuum cleaner of a first officer finished them all.

"My Sol! How did you do this!?" he said, smiling brightly.

◆

"Hi Poops," Daddy said with Mother by his side. "I wish we could tell you why The Fall happened. Why twenty-seven children woke in the Kuiper belt to cryptic recordings entrusting you with complex missions. But to ensure you found a path forward untainted by old prejudices, it had to be this way." He looked at Mother to continue.

"You must be a mature woman now," she said, "experienced so many situations I cannot begin to comprehend. You may even be a mother. But no matter what, I hope you have become someone you are proud of. Someone who can see the *truth...*" Mother gave a look I saw once before when she slapped me as a child. I noticed her pupils rapidly dilating.

Old Morse! I realized and followed along. *Blink* −.. . ... − .−. − − − − −.− − *Blink* .. − *Blink* −.. . ... − .−. − − − − −.− − *Blink* .... .. − − *Blink.*

"Destroy it. Destroy him," Mother was saying.

Daddy was in tears, oblivious to Mother's message. "Poops, I wish I could greet you on Mercury, but we died long before you woke in the Kuiper belt. I'm so sorry for having put you through this. Only one task remains. Deliver Project Infinity to the survivors on Mercury."

◆

With only Taam and me, Regeneration's bridge felt frozen in time. I imagined the crew at their stations analyzing the information pouring in. Mercury, where it all began, was shining through the window. Icarus's north pole dome was deflated and dark, and the rails wrapping the planet were splintered. We slowed into orbit, rounding its light side to see thousands of circular dunes covering the surface like brushstrokes upon a canvas.

"A coordinated asteroid attack?" I whispered.

"No," Taam said, staring in awe. "They look detonated from just above the surface."

"Nuclear," I said. "How can there possibly be survivors?"

"Only one way to find out," he said.

The first thirty-seven of Icarus's sub-levels were incinerated. Beyond its mid-lock, we found the entire Hermian population in envisuits, holding each other tightly, perfectly preserved. I held my breath as I passed my old residence. I neither paused nor glanced at the door.

"I didn't look at mine either," Taam said quietly through com.

We passed the lowest lock to the mechanisms of the city. Water and air-recycling systems and fuel cells were depleted. The meat factories, with their long conveyors and cellular printers, were dusty. And the underground greenhouses were crop-less.

"That's it," Taam said as we reached the feces-to-fertilizer recycling vats at Icarus's bottom-most point.

I felt that pull in my gut. "There's more." I pointed at the recycling vat.

"Nope. No way," Taam said.

"Please?"

"No!" He crossed his arms, standing his ground.

"I'll make you *ice cream...*"

His eyes lit up, then he glanced at the vat and frowned. Then, his eyes lit again. "I hate you," he eventually said and submerged into the sludge. After forty-three meters, he hit denser material. "The particles have separated over time." He dug his gloved paw into the thicker silt, hitting steel. "Reached bottom. What am I looking for?"

"Not sure, but you're close, I think," I said.

"Why am I doing this again?"

"Ice cream."

"...Fine," he grumbled.

"Clear a larger radius. You're so close," I said. *Have I lost my mind?*

"Got something," Taam suddenly said. "Looks like a lever. To purge the sludge maybe?"

Not maybe. Definitely. "Pull it," I said.

Taam tugged the handle. A loud clang came. Molasses-like water slowly drained, revealing Taam in his nicotine-stained envisuit. A second clang rang, and the handle rose to chest height. A hologram displaying a grassy hill, figures in armor at its top, with others working fields below, opened.

"Marauders versus Farmers!?" I shouted and came running.

◆

I won a hundred and thirty-four times, yet nothing happened after each victory.

"It's been four hours, Dione. I don't think there's a point to it," Taam said.

"Taam, who would put a game at the bottom of shit recycler without a purpose? And of all games, it's *mine*." I was easily winning, but it felt like I was missing something. I pondered the point of the game. *Infiltration? Sabotage? Negotiation?* That's what I believed as a child. It wasn't until Enceladus that I felt the game was hokey. *But what if?*

I started another match and brought the entire Marauder troop from the hill to meet the farmers in the fields. I removed their armor and swords and tossed them on the ground.

"How can we help?" I said.

The farmers looked relieved. *"We could use two farmhands here. Kurdam's farm is looking for aid, too."*

"Which direction is that?" I said.

The farmer pointed.

I ordered four marauders to help Kurdam's farm and continued distributing the rest to several more farms encircling the grassy hill.

The crops began changing from wheat to sorghum. Then, they became lush orchards and vineyards. Villages grew into towns. Stone buildings replaced straw huts. I could no longer differentiate the marauders from the farmers. *They're just people,* I realized. Residents from all the towns began construction atop the grassy hill. *A shrine? No, it's an observatory now.* The observatory became a launch platform, then a space elevator, a LightLine system, and finally, a massive ship I did not recognize. The entire population gathered, waving goodbye as half boarded the strange ship and launched from the grassy hill.

"Congratulations!" spread across the hologram.

Another clang rang, and the floor below me twisted open like a camera iris.

"The bottom of the tank is an airlock!" I said.

The hallway beyond was sterile white, and the iris sealed tight above us once we entered.

"Atmosphere is good. Temperature too," Taam said and slowly removed his nicotine-stained envisuit, grimacing all the while.

I breathed deeply, expecting the smell of bleach or citrus, but I caught lavender, the scent of choice to cover cryo-gel. "Someone's coming out of hibernation."

A white hallway stretched several kilometers long. I ran as fast as I could, met by Taam's jogging.

"I see something ahead!" he said.

The hallway opened to a massive room with ringed tiers above, each hosting hundreds of people in cryo-tubes. Their faces were smooth, and their hair was red. *All identical.* The tiers above were the same, except younger. Their frames were enormous.

"Equalizers," Taam muttered and turned to me. "They're *all* equalizers."

A black cryo-tube stood lonesome at the bottom tier's center, hosting a small window revealing a raisin-shriveled creature beyond. It was a man I recognized, a man I knew. When I peered through the window, he slowly opened his pale eyes.

"Please, step away," The Director's voice said, but the man within did not speak. "Step away now. We must tend to him."

Several identical equalizers in lab coats and scrubs approached The Director's tube. I could see Decan's skills as they checked his vitals. *They're engineered beyond an equalizer.* The cryo-tube cracked, spilling foul gel across the floor. The clones reached in, grasping The Director's joints to support him. He was thin, sickly. They pulled tubes from his mouth with a heaving of oxygen-rich liquid.

The Director slowly lifted his head and whispered, "Dione, my how you've grown."

◆

"What is this place?" Taam asked.

"I don't know," I said, but I sensed it had a greater purpose.

One of the monstrous clones approached us. "Muscle stimulation is complete, The Director will see you now."

The Director was dressed in his trademark textured black cloth and seated at an elegant dining room table, flanked by his clones. He spread his hands wide. "Dione... Taam... My brightest stars, welcome home. Please, sit. Tell me of your perilous journey. I wish to hear everything from the beginning."

The Director nodded with each element we mined in the Kuiper Belt and winced when I spoke of Pluto and Triton's fate. Then, came Titan.

"They call their settlement Tempest? Fascinating," The Director said. "It's incredible the lengths they went to, to survive."

"If you think that's amazing, then you should hear about Enceladus!" Taam said.

The Director's eyes sharpened. "Tell me."

"They survived by eating the tuna beneath the ice! And their leader, you won't believe it! He was—"

"—the one who told us what happened to Troy," I cut Taam off before he uttered Mirko's name. "It was sent to the bottom of the ocean."

Taam gave me a confused look but did not protest.

"And what about Project Infinity?" The Director said.

The clones trained upon me, analyzing everything I said, every facial twitch I gave. *Truth testing,* I knew. My mother came to mind, her eyes dilating, "*Destroy it. Destroy him.*" I steadied my pulse. "Troy's research facility was destroyed. Project Infinity was no where to be found."

The clones searched every inch of my stone-like demeanor for clues until Taam shifted in his chair. The clones focused on him, instead.

Stay still, Taam! I wanted to shout.

Without a word, four of the ten clones left the room.

The Director frowned. "Please, continue."

When we told of Ceres's reconstruction, The Director's frown deepened, and when we spoke of skipping Mars, he stopped us.

"You didn't even go?" he said.

"The Martians have done exceptionally well on their own," I calmly said. "Their population has actually septupled when the rest of humanity was nearly wiped out. They're completely self-sustaining."

The Director darkened. "That's *directly* against orders."

"Our mission was to restitch System Sol, was it not?" I said. "By helping rebuild the shattered ships in Ceran orbit and clear their skies, we re-established trade between the colonies, including Mars. You weren't in the field. I had to make the call."

The Director gritted his teeth. "Very well. You still achieved your arrival time to Mercury. But this means you did not reach Earth either."

"Ceres went to Earth in our stead," I said.

"You let *Cerans* go alone?" he said, disgusted.

"We're *allies* now," I said and felt confused. *Wasn't helping all of humanity our goal? Wasn't that the point of Marauders versus Farmers in the end? Does The Director not understand his own directives?*

A clone entered with urgency and whispered into The Director's ear.

He clenched his jaw. "Where's the rest of your crew?"

They're searching our ship, I realized. "They stayed behind to help rebuild the colonies. Only Taam and I returned."

"Where did you hide Project Infinity?" he pointedly asked.

"We never retrie—"

"Where!?" he barked, his eyes furious, knowing.

♦

A clone unlocked my room door. "The Director wishes to speak with you." She made a gesture implying, *this way.*

I cannot take an equalizer, I knew and followed her up the many tiers of cryo-tubes. The Director was at the top tier with tubes hosting embryos.

He turned to me. "Dione, we've put you through so much, kept you in the dark, leaving you to question our objective." He took a deep breath. "We had to implement protocols should Earth and its allies do the unthinkable. Your parents were integral to its execution."

A name from childhood came to me. "Operation Eraser," I whispered.

The Director tilted his head. "Earth's dependence on fossil fuels could not be shed, thus their ships continued to rely on volatiles. They were like a cancer. And Ceres's hoarding of water illustrated their greed. Then, they did the unthinkable. They launched a full-scale nuclear attack upon Mercury. We were left with no choice but to enact Operation Eraser, and wipe the slate clean."

I recalled the barrage of microwave beams emitting from Godfire Station. *We nearly destroyed the human race as retaliation?*

"You're lying. Mother would have *never* done that," I said.

The Director humphed. "Are you familiar with Memory Immersion? We developed it to investigate how our platoons were being wiped out on Ganymede by experiencing the final memory of those who were killed." He turned square to me. "Do you want to know what your mother did?"

My jaw clenched. *I need to know.* I nodded.

"I must warn you, Dione. You will think everything your mother thought, feel everything that she felt."

"I understand," I said.

The Director pointed at a chair rising from the floor. Once I sat, he presented a syringe. "This will... hurt."

♦

"They should have never disobeyed!" General Kesler shouted, studying the bodies of her crew slumped across Godfire Station's control panels, the blood oozing from their backs, and the pistol smoking in her hand.

Central hologram flashed with nuclear warheads passing Venus's orbit and from where they originated, *"Earth."* General Kesler raced to its controls. *Earth somehow evaded our detection systems!* By chance, her scouts had spotted them with their eagle eyes from the cockpits of their corsairs. But, the warheads were slowly sailing beyond her scout's visual range, disappearing into the blackness of space. *There's no stopping them.*

"If Earth and its allies mean to destroy us! Do they not deserve the same fate! Initiate Operation Eraser!" General Kesler ordered.

Earth materialized on hologram displaying the populations of its cities. She selected Earth's most populous metropolis and pressed *Fire.* Solar arrays on the light side of Mercury unfolded their petals, absorbing energy at full capacity. Within minutes, power peaked, channeled into microwave emitters, and sent a ten-second beam toward Earth.

"In twenty-seven minutes, the population of Tokyo will feel the air warm and tingle, and the smell of fresh ozone will hint at a thunderstorm," General Kesler whispered, imagining how it would unfold. "As they stare upwards, their bodies will engulf in flame, automobiles and buildings will shed their surfaces, and structural steel will become molten. Static electricity will lift clouds of dust above the city and, as heat further increases, will coalesce into glass, entombing them within. Those who survive the heat and molten steel rain will face starvation and suffocation." She stared at Tokyo on hologram, tears welling in her eyes.

No! Don't you dare weep for them! They started this! General Kesler stood straight, pulled back her tears, selected Mexico City, and pressed *Fire.*

"Now Beijing! Jakarta! New York City! Paris! London!" she hollered.

The holograms surrounding her screamed with incoming calls, and thumps and shouts rang outside the command room's blast doors. Tokyo flashed red on hologram as the first beam reached its mark.

"Fuck..." General Kesler whispered as the reality of its annihilation set in. *I must finish the mission!* She fired next upon the cities of Luna, Mars, and the Jovian and Saturnian moon colonies. Then, she opened Ceres on hologram, breathed deeply, and pressed *Fire.* But, the solar arrays did not collect energy, did not transfer to the emitters, and did not send light beams to the icy dwarf planet.

Someone cut power! But how!?

As if to answer, Admiral Rues's fleet, firing upon Mercury's solar arrays from orbit, opened on hologram.

My own people are destroying them!? she realized.

Command room power dwindled, leaving General Kesler in darkness. A torch pierced the heavy blast door, crashing it to the floor. Gunshots burst. Bullets penetrated the general's back and exited her chest. But she did not flinch, her modified nerves dulling the pain.

The shots ceased, and a set of footsteps approached.

"General Kesler," said a familiar voice.

"Commander Sharpe," she whispered. "I'm ready."

"But, I'm not," he whispered back.

General Kesler gave a sideways glance. "Tom, you must do your part in this," she said as the iron taste of blood seeped into her mouth. "Please, do this. If not for The Director, then for me. I cannot bear this on my conscience any longer."

Commander Sharpe slowly lifted his pistol to the base of the general's skull, his arm trembling. "As...as granted by Article 746 of the Hermian Tribal Infantry, I am both judge and jury. I find General Abigail Kesler... guilty of mass genocide. Her sentence is death. Immediately."

"Dione is strong, Tom. She'll set things right," the general said.

"I love you," Commander Sharpe whispered, closed his eyes, desperately fighting tears, and pulled the trigger.

◆

"Fuck!" I shouted, coming out of the memory, dropping to the floor, and vomiting my breakfast.

"Sedative and water!" The Director ordered his clones.

Mom, Dad, no... I thought, trying to make sense of it. *How could they?*

They had no choice, said a voice from inside. *But your mother has given one to you.*

I had experienced this shock with Mirko's memories before. I breathed slowly, calming my body and mind, and stood as the clones came running. *Collect your thoughts. Look at your surroundings. I'm in a massive incubation facility. Why?* I pointed at the embryos in the cryo-tubes. "What does *this* have to do with Operation Eraser?"

The Director cocked his head. "You recovered on your own. Nobody's ever done so without significant counseling."

"I've had worse." I again pointed at the tubes. "How is this related?"

"I cannot imagine what you've been through." The Director shooed the clones away. "Should Ceres or Earth survive Operation Eraser we must ensure they never again corrupt System Sol. But we need resources, Niotrodium and Iridium, for example. Most importantly, we need Project

Infinity. Once we have it, we can bring Hermian greatness to all peoples. Rebuild System Sol. Share water, soil, and food equally, and develop the most cutting-edge clean energy systems. But to achieve this, I need a new kind of soldier completely loyal to the Hermian cause, an army that understands exactly what I am doing." He motioned to the embryos. "An army of *me.*"

I shook my head. "Even with identical DNA, they'll have a choice."

"That's where Project Infinity comes in."

What can shark DNA do? I thought. *I don't understand.*

But I do, said the woman's voice from within. A vision of the shark genome and its highlighted immune system came to me. *The pores in the cellular lining of the human brain are too tight for antibodies to pass through, protecting the brain from its own immune system. However, the antibodies of great white sharks are nearly identical to a human's but are small enough to wiggle through the lining. If correctly applied, shark antibodies can allow us to treat mental illness and alter synapses like never before.*

Alter synapses? Do you mean, memories? I thought back.

Yes. Memory, thought, and personality, the voice said.

I snapped my head to The Director. "You want to copy your consciousness into your clones! You want to create a literal army of you!"

The Director's mouth went slack. "Dione, I am impressed. I thought I was the only person in System Sol who understood this. But there's more. We've learned to stop the aging process and can treat every physical ailment. All except for matters of the mind. But with shark antibodies, Alzheimer's, Parkinson's, cancers of the brain, among thousands of other conditions, can be cured. We can finally achieve bio-immortality and reach unknown corners of space." He motioned to the cryo-tubes. "These embryos, this Ark, is not meant for retaking System Sol. It will be the first of many colony ships to reach Proxima Centauri and begin a fresh civilization. Two and a half centuries of time distance ensures that if System Sol plunges into another war, humanity cannot go extinct." The Director raised his arms like a conductor. "Dione, will you help finish what your parents started? Will you help humanity reach the stars?" He lowered his arms. "This is your last chance. Project Infinity. Give it to me."

I met his stare and gritted my teeth. "We *never* found it."

The Director frowned and snapped his fingers.

Paws grasped my upper arms, lifting me clear off the floor. I was carried down the tiers to the very bottom. At the center was an equalizer on their knees, stripped naked, forearms kinking, and bones protruding from the back of their hands. The concrete floor was shattered and spattered red. The equalizer's head lifted as I neared, and golden eyes locked onto mine.

"Taam!" I shouted and struggled against the clones until they released me. I rushed to him and frantically clutched his head against my chest, systematically checking his injuries. *Self-inflicted,* I realized.

"I'm sorry," Taam moaned. "Dione, I'm sorry. I tried to fight it."

"It's okay. You're okay now." I said, feverishly kissing his forehead, temples, nose, and lips. He winced but pressed back with hunger. The clones pulled me away, Taam's blood running down my chin.

"Dione!" shouted The Director. "I'm done asking nicely! Give me Project Infinity, *now!"*

"I've told you all that I know," I said.

The Director frowned. "Taam held strong for three hours, he is truly loyal, but he eventually confessed where you've hidden it." He looked into my eyes. "Aperire mihi!"

My arms and legs froze. *What is this!?*

"Give it to me now!" he barked.

My abdominals flexed. Bile crawled up my throat, working the holotile in my gut up my esophagus. My hand reached into my mouth, retrieved the holotile, and extended it to The Director.

Taam, I'm sorry, I thought. *Mom, Dad, I'm sorry... And Mirko, I was wrong about you. You are just as much a pawn as I... I'm so sorry...*

I forgive you, said Mirko's voice. A ghostly soldier appeared between The Director and me. His posture held strength despite his small stature, and his eyes emitted such understanding. *You were right about me, Dione. I killed your father's siblings and would have killed him, too, given the chance. I am everything you were told. I am Mirko, the Harbinger of Death. And now, so are you.* He placed his hand atop mine, and I suddenly had control.

With all my strength, I crushed the holotile in my palm.

"No!" The Director shrieked.

I let the pieces fall to the floor and found my tongue. "I know what my destiny is. I was never meant to *help* you. I was meant to *destroy* you."

"Aperire mihi!" The Director spat.

His words no longer affected me. I calmly walked forth.

"Aperire mihi! Aperire mihi!" He turned to his clones. "Kill her!"

The clones lunged, the first reaching her paw to crush my little neck. But she appeared to move in slow motion, and I could not help but notice she was overextending. I raised my hand to the base of her thick wrist, found the correct points, and curled it down with almost no effort. I then pressed my heel onto her toes. Two hundred kilos of pure muscle hurtled to the floor, face-planting into the concrete with her body curling like a scorpion's tail. A snap rang from her neck, and her body tumbled limp.

I breathed deeply and closed my eyes as the remaining clones came.

When I opened them, ten equalizers lay on the floor. Taam stared at me in disbelief. My hands were now around The Director's neck. His shoulders and hips were dislocated. *I did that? Yes.* Such confusion held in his pale eyes.

Memories from a previous life superimposed what The Director once looked like. His hair went from gray to red, and his wrinkles smoothed. His eyes soon held dark circles as he furiously established Mercury's first solar arrays. In his thirties now, Dr. Williams was in research and development, his face fresh and plump. Then, an overweight young man wearing a magsuit and huffing and puffing as he ran an obstacle course was staring back at me.

"Sammy," a voice said through me. "Look at what you've become."

Recognition showed in The Director's eyes. "No... It cannot be... I killed you..." he gargled.

My rage surged, and my grip tightened around his neck. "This is for Dillon! For Sokka! For Mom and Dad! For everyone!"

♦

The bones in Taam's hands and arms had mended. Scars on his knuckles and face healed white. His replacement teeth were even more bright.

"It's a good idea, strangely," he said.

Commander Meeks nodded. "It's remarkable The Director developed such technology, despite his intentions."

We stared at the Ark's ringed tiers with thousands of vacant cryo-tubes.

"What will become of the clones?" I asked Commander Meeks.

"Most will help reconstruct the solar arrays upon Mercury and rebuild System Sol's colonies. The younger clones will be raised in foster families. We believe integrating them into all walks of life is the best way to override The Director's ambitious nature. It's either this or exterminating them."

"And we've finally had enough of genocide, right?" I said.

"That's where the Arks come in. It'll take two hundred and eighty-seven years to reach System Centauri, ensuring whatever happens in System Sol will never reach System Centauri, and vice versa," Commander Meeks said.

"We must collect embryos from all across System Sol," I said. "Who we send to System Centauri should represent humanity as a whole."

"I'll spread the word. Babies for everyone," Commander Meeks said and pointed at a cryo-tube containing a tiny embryo. "Boy or girl?"

Taam brightened. "We're leaving that to chance."

"I like that," Commander Meeks said and took his leave.

I wrapped my arm around Taam's massive forearm and leaned my head against his shoulder. "What do you think about, Anda?"

"After my grandfather?" Taam said in surprise. "That's wonderful."

"We have to specify Anda's future occupation for the new colony. You think construction? Physics? Maybe medicine?"

Taam thought a moment. "Centauri should develop a heart and soul of its own. Perhaps something artistic."

"Like a chef?" I suggested.

"Yeah! That would be perfect!" Taam gently placed a paw on the cryo-tube's glass. "What do you think, Anda? You want to be a chef?"

CHAPTER FOURTEEN

"Clara, I hope this message finds you well," Jonathan says on a recording. "I wanted to tell you first, before we announce to System Sol. The WorldRing tunnel did not lead us to London, but to Paris, instead."

"Paris!?" Clara shouts, almost spilling her glass of red on the sofa.

"I know," Jonathan says, having predicted her reaction. "But something's not right. The streets are so clean that we're leaving dirty footprints behind. And when we return to areas already explored the prints are gone. The city may have had an automated maintenance system long ago, but I cannot imagine it still functioning today. Temperature is tolerable. The air is breathable."

"My Sol," Clara whispers as recordings of Paris appear in a second hologram. The city should be in complete shambles, with buildings blackened and crumbled and streets littered with skeletal remains, yet the limestone structures look as if no cataclysmic event occurred. The only sign of The Fall is the wavy glass dome looming overhead, refracting sunlight like rippling water.

"It's beautiful," Jonathan says. "The architecture. The care that went into building this city. It's unlike anything I've ever seen." He runs a hand through his greasy hair. "Clara, can you see what else Zion knows. He led me here for a reason. I'm certain of it."

Clara cannot agree more.

"I miss you, hon. Now more than ever. Kip," Jonathan says as the recording ends.

"Kip," Clara whispers.

♦

"Aye's de one, I'm tellin' yah," a man says from an adjacent table, his hair wild and his chest bare. "Nah really, I saw de li'l dude on 'ologram."

Aizen hides behind his menu. Several days ago, he changed into traditional Martian clothing, bought a new holotile, and found a man who could make a fake ID. *I cannot be Aizen Ocol. Too dangerous,* he thinks, studying his new ID with Lucius Gonzalez's name next to Aizen's photo.

"'Ey, li'l dude," says the man, standing beside him now.

Aizen reluctantly looks up.

"Aw, it is yah! Dis is crazy!"

It's pointless. All of System Sol knows my face, Aizen thinks. "Hi, nice to meet you. Do you want an autograph?"

"Autograph? 'Ells nah." The man gives a funny look. "Yah famous, li'l dude, but not *dat* famous. I been droppin' in fer sixty years and don't ever sign nah autographs. Dat's corporate shit."

Aizen thinks about how people always want his name on something. *It is stupid, is corporate,* he agrees.

"I just wanna know 'ow yah done it, li'l dude. I never seen anyone tap de zone like dat."

Tap the zone? Aizen lowers his menu. "What do you mean?"

"Yah don' know? Check dis!" The man plops into an adjacent seat and opens a video on his holotile entitled, *"Little Surfer Destroys Maria's Drop."*

The video begins in bird's-eye view of the drop zone with a surfer perched at the edge, then pans over to reveal treacherous patches of rock jutting from grasses down the long, steep slope. Martian hip-hop fades in with its intricate rhythms and love affair with horns. As the surfer looks about to drop in, a small figure sprints into view, grass board in hand.

That's me, Aizen realizes and notes the sunflower brothers are conveniently out of frame. He watches himself leap over the edge like a base jumper. The camera view switches to below, showing Aizen's silhouette against the green sky. Before meeting the grassy slope, he places the board below his feet and wraps his hands behind his back, crouching.

"Dat's slice man. It's like yah longboardin'."

Aizen watches himself grasp the board's leading edge, kicking out the tail to maneuver rocks and getting airborne at one point. His control is incredible, his balance is perfect. *I look just like Dad,* Aizen thinks. When he reaches the bottom, he carves by the camera, hops off the board, and sprints off to an eruption of cheers.

"Nah one, I mean nah one *dives* in like dat man. 'Ow'd yah do it?"

Aizen reflects upon the ride but cannot remember a thing. "I don't know."

"Come on, li'l dude, 'ow can yah not know?"

"I closed my eyes."

"All right, keep yah secrets," he says with a smile. "I'm 'Armond Kitzsto."

Harmond Kitzsto? Aizen recognizes the name from Dad's videos. "Lucius Gonzales," Aizen says and realizes his fake identity will become famous, too. *Damn.*

"Watcha gonna 'ave?" Harmond asks, pointing at the menu.

"Injera," Aizen says.

Harmond shakes his head. "Not 'ere, man. Gonna get dat syndesizer shit. If yah want tah 'ave real injera come wid us to Shakoperan."

"What's that?"

Harmond leans close and whispers, "It's ah local 'oliday celebratin' first contact after De Fall, li'l dude."

"Is it a secret?"

"Kinda. Dey don't let dose widout bloodlines in."

"Do you have a bloodline?"

"Yah see Scone dere?" Harmond tilts his head back to his table. "Tall one wid de sharp nose. Aye's Zondan, a tribe from de soud pole. Dey don't believe in magsuits. Is why aye's so tall. Aye's gonna get us in. I'm sure aye'll 'elp yah, too."

A pull to join them grips Aizen. "I would love to come, but I need to get to Aang."

Harmond laughs. "Shakoperan is *in* Aang, li'l dude. Might as well travel togeder."

◆

Rugged mountain trails rise above and below breathable altitude, forcing Aizen and his new companions to repeatedly don oxygen masks. Scone knows which ridges to follow and in what valleys to make camp. They sleep beneath the stars, bundled in every layer they have, the cold lulling them every night. Aizen helps chop through frozen ponds to catch the trout beneath and start fires with flint and steel. He closes his eyes, feeling the Martian breeze prickling his cheeks and the campfire clouding his nose. *Real camping,* Aizen thinks. *Dad would love this.*

They reach Toldan outpost.

"Aye Lucius, can yah give me ah 'and?" Scone says, towering over Aizen, even when crouched, reminding him of the sunflower brothers. Scone pulls a hunk of metal from his pack in the shape of a scalene triangle, its longest side looking razor sharp. "Eva use ah knife before?" Scone asks, handing the blade to Aizen and laying two trout on a large stone. "Before we cook de fish, yah must gut dem. Yah understand my meanin'?"

Aizen grins and pulls the first trout closer, slices from the belly to the base of the head, slits beneath the jaw, and pulls the guts from the gill to vent from the flesh with forefinger and thumb. He then runs a finger along the inside of the spine, removing the kidney.

Scone blinks hard. "All right, den! Now we slice de flesh along deir sides and rub salt and mala into de cuts."

"Mala?" Aizen asks.

"Dey ah dried peppercorn seed dat's spicy, but in ah numbin' way. It enhances de flavor." Scone crushes mala peppercorns with the flat of his blade and slides the pile Aizen's way to rub into the cuts. Then, he pulls a large cast iron pan from his pack, its surface glistening from years of use. He spreads veggies around the edge, placing the first seasoned fish at the center and burying it in bright red chilies. The pan goes directly into the flame with another turned-over on top. "It called ah glacier oven."

Scone lifts the overturned pan, releasing a spicy aroma, causing Aizen to cough. When he pulls it from the fire, the fish's skin crackles and wriggles with heat. Scone serves the group.

Tender meat slips off the spines, burning with both spice and temperature. Aizen's eyes water, and his nose drips. Mala numbs his tongue. His companions swig beer.

Aizen stares into his cup. "I've never drunk before."

"Part of de experience," Scone says.

Aizen sips and feels its carbonation prickle.

They sweat from hairlines and suck air through their teeth but cannot stop eating. Then, the fish is gone. Silence encompasses them. Numbness lingers upon tongues and lips.

"Shall we 'ave de oder?" Scone says, more a statement than a question, and places the second trout on the pan.

◆

The dishes are different for each meal the rest of the way to Aang, and Aizen makes sure to help, marveling at Scone's recipes, nonsensical until tasted. Chilly and mint are common ingredients. And his nose constantly runs.

"Dey ah designed tah combat de buildup of Martian dust in de sinuses," Scone explains.

On the eleventh day, they summit a peak to see a city with golden towers surrounding a center of crumbling stone.

"Welcome to Kamala, li'l dude," Harmond says.

"But you said this was Aang."

"De ruins at de center is old Aang. Dat's where Shakoperan will be. But we gotta be careful."

"Why's that?"

"Mars is divided, li'l dude. De tribes who terraformed dis planet, were taken advantage of when dey reopened trade. 'Undreds of companies rushed tah Mars tryin' tah capitalize on its soil, an' now dey ah tryin' tah monetize its agriculture." Harmond retrieves coins from his pocket, each shiny around their edges but rusty in the center. "It written in de currency. De outside is gold, silver, an' oder alloys from off-world. But at de center of every denomination, is Martian iron. Economy at de edge. Soul at de center. And dey at odds wid one anoder."

They join hundreds of tribes navigating the ring city of Kamala towards old Aang, each in fine ceremonial garb with their heads held high. They pass Kamalans in power suits conducting walking meetings, dodging the tribes-people who refuse to change course. *A silent, slow march. A show of defiance,* Aizen realizes. The tribes-people tower over the Kamalans, having forsaken the use of magsuits. Tension is palpable. Aizen can see it in the glances, receiving mixed looks, some saying *traitor,* others saying *welcome.*

A tall woman makes eye contact with Scone and says, "DNA testin'."

Scone stops in his tracks. "Anyone not willin' tah risk arrest, leave now. If yah want tah continue, come wid me."

A few say their goodbyes and join the backward flow of people. Harmond stays despite looking out of place. Aizen takes this as a sign that everything will be fine.

Scone leads to an alley and pulls skin-colored tabs from his pocket. "Apply dese tah yah dumbs, dey're laced wid de DNA strains de detectors ah lookin' for."

Aizen watches Harmond apply his tabs, their coloration shifting to match his leathery thumb. Aizen presses tabs to his olive thumbs.

"Once in de testin' zone dere is nah turnin' back," Scone warns.

A part of Aizen wants to run, but the pull to experience the cuisine beyond is stronger. They funnel into border check lines, two at a time, ushering into testing. Thumbs are pricked, with either a beep and passing through the gate or a buzz and security escorting them away.

Scone goes first, his height alone confirming his heritage. The scanner beeps, and he is through. Harmond and Aizen are next in the queue. Harmond extends his thumb to the detector.

The guards stare at his blonde hair.

"Ahms," their captain says.

Harmond's face drops as the technician raises a detector to his shoulder, instead. His eyes meet Aizen's just before he sprints for the gates.

"Get 'im," the captain says.

Two guards with taser rods quickly catch up to Harmond.

"Fuckin' Pigs! Yah can't gate-keep culture! Yah can't... Grgghhhrhlll!" Harmond says as volts run through his body.

"Yah next," the captain says to Aizen with a grin.

Aizen stands frozen, watching the guards cuffing Harmond while Scone calmly walks away without acknowledging his friend's arrest. The technician presses the DNA detector against Aizen's shoulder. He feels the prick and waits for the buzz. *How am I going to explain this to Mom and Dad?*

A beep comes, instead.

The captain's grin dwindles. "Try de oder ahm."

Another beep.

"It looks good, sir," the technician says.

The captain skeptically eyes Aizen. "Move along, den."

CHAPTER FIFTEEN

Why did Vincent survey the same plaza twice? The error is no cause for worry until Jonathan looks closer. The first survey recorded several stone benches lining the plaza's perimeter, but the second survey has them clustered at the center.

"They moved," Jonathan says and turns to his crew, wondering if they were playing a joke on him. *But moving them would take serious equipment.*

Twenty minutes later, when they reach the plaza to investigate, the benches are situated around the perimeter, matching the first survey, with no scuffs or scrapes on the cobblestone.

"I don't understand," Vincent says. "I'm certain they were at the center."

That night, Jonathan wakes to tremors coming through the ground and rolls to Hazel.

"Hey. You awake?" he whispers.

No response.

"Hey." He nudges her shoulder. "You awake?"

"Now, I am," she grumbles.

"Great. You feel that vibration?"

Her eyes fly open and she sits up, pressing a hand on the ground. "It feels like construction."

The vibration stops. Jonathan stands, tiptoes to the airlock, and dons his envisuit, careful not to wake Angela and Vincent. "Let's go check it out," he whispers.

When they pass a museum of stone construction surrounding a glass pyramid, they again feel the vibration. Hazel places her holotile on the cobblestone with a compass-like needle wavering on hologram. *"112.3 meters below grade."*

"The sewers," Hazel says, pointing at a circular disk textured like a tortoiseshell.

Jonathan pulls a driver from his pack and locks onto the first pristine bolt. *They should be fused with the cover from centuries of corrosion,* he knows, but his driver effortlessly unscrews the bolt. He removes the rest and pulls at its lip. "We need a pry bar."

Hazel points at an iron lamppost.

"Absolutely not!" Jonathan says.

They search the museum plaza for debris, anything that might work, but everything is impeccably clean. Jonathan turns a blind eye as Hazel cuts down the lamppost.

"I found this piece of debris in the back of the museum," she mocks.

"You found it, *you* do the honors," Jonathan grumbles.

She stuffs the end into the cover's lip, pushing and pressing, eventually bumping it above the edge and sliding it from the hole. A cast-iron ladder drops down a cobblestone shaft, continuing the palette of Paris into the sewers. They descend. At the bottom, they find vaulted stone ceilings spanning dry canals with sidewalks on either side. They traverse the canals, recording it all.

"I see something," Jonathan says, running ahead to a square hole cut into the floor. "It's just like our passage from the WorldRing tunnel to the catacombs."

Hazel touches the cut stone. "It's wet. Condensation?"

"No, the rest of the rock would be weeping, too. This is freshly cut," Jonathan says. "We'll have to come back tomorrow with the winch."

♦

When they return the next day with Vincent and Angela, their excitement electric, the opening is gone, as if it never existed.

"They can be closed," Jonathan says, looking concerned.

They track more vibrations in the following days, each time finding freshly cut shafts that seal before they can investigate.

Jonathan tracks yet another far north, but it is getting late. *I'll have to return tomorrow with the others.* He marches back to camp, passing streets now memorized, his legs on autopilot, scrolling through information on visor. He passes Vincent's plaza with his head down. A pair of legs come into his peripheral.

"Hey, Vincent, didn't know you were out," Jonathan says.

"Vincent's at Basecamp, Jon," Angela responds through com.

Jonathan lifts his head. "But he's—"

An incredibly tall creature stands before him, legs not of black envisuit poly but like leather. The musculature of its calves and thighs is magnificent. The torso swells deep with breath but expands side-to-side instead of outward. Its shoulders are broad and heavily built. Its arms stretch long, ending with chisel-like fingers. Its featureless face looks at him, but there are no eyes.

"Why are you here?" the creature says in a deep register.

♦

"Paris?" Zion says, confused.

"The painting you made for Jonathan led him to Paris," Clara says.

"Painting?" Zion's expression says he should know this.

"You told me about Kwai Lan and Sha Tolera. Told me about Paris. Then, you made Jonathan a painting to help him locate a WorldRing tunnel."

"WorldRing!" Zion says triumphantly. "Yes, I know!"

Clara breathes a sigh of relief. "Zion, the painting worked. Jonathan found a way into Paris."

Zion scrunches his brow. "Paris?"

She gives him a sweet smile and stands. "Thank you, Zion."

He smiles back. "Anytime, Allessandra."

"Clara," she corrects.

"Yes. That's what I said." Zion lies back in his bed and whispers, "That's what I said."

Clara meets Dr. Lee in his office. "It's bad."

"I know," Dr. Lee says. "I've never seen him like this. I fear we may never discover how he united the galaxy."

"But we've learned so much, we now know what caused The Fall."

"If it's true," he says.

"You still don't believe his stories?"

"Clara, it's just so fantastical."

She thinks. "Do you know who Allessandra is? He's mentioned her a few times now."

Dr. Lee shakes his head. "I have no idea."

♦

The next day, Zion is out of bed, sitting in his chair, and sipping tea when Clara enters.

It's a good day, she hopes. "Zion. Please, tell me about Allessandra."

"Allessandra?"

"The woman you mistook me for during our last session."

"I have never mistaken you for anyone."

Clara sighs. "Who is she?"

"It's not important."

"Why not?"

"She was nobody."

"Why do you say that?"

"People live and people die. After living as long as I, you understand it's best to let them go."

"Have you let her go, then?" Clara asks.

"Don't you want to know about Paris?" Zion says, evading the question with bait that she cannot resist.

Another time, Clara notes. "You remember Paris now?"

"I never forgot," Zion says.

Clara takes the seat across from him and sets her holotile to record. "I would love to hear about Paris."

He breathes deeply. "I do not know how I came into the world. Much of my life was a blur. I remembered the first half like an old mov—"

"Kwai Lan," Clara says deadpan.

Zion's eyes shift side to side. "Oh, I've told you this." He then brightens. "Of course! My mistake... I do not know how I came into the system, but ever since I was a little girl, my destiny was to turn Mars—"

"Sha," Clara says.

Zion rubs his bald head. "Those were the only two stories of Paris."

"But Zion, there has to be more. There has to be a reason why Paris is in pristine condition."

His head snaps to her. "What do you mean?"

"Jonathan is in Paris right now. The city is perfectly preserved, as if The Fall never happened."

"Jonathan is in Paris? Right now?"

"Yes, I've been trying to tell you this for two weeks."

"That's *impossible*. Paris is *impossible*," he says, growing nervous.

Clara opens Zion's painting of the WorldRing at the cliffside on holotile.

"*You* painted *this* to help Jonathan find the tunnel leading to Paris."

He studies the painting, looking about to protest, but his mouth purses. "This is indeed my work. You said Paris is in pristine condition?"

"Yes." She plays Jonathan's message, accompanied by recordings of the shafts, chambers, catacombs, and city streets.

Zion gasps and covers his mouth. "He needs to leave now!"

"Why?"

"It's dangerous! They will protect their home, violently if they must!"

"Who are *they?*"

"...Unless, I sent him there on purpose," Zion mutters, giving the scanned painting a deeper look. "But why would I do that?"

"Who are *they!?*" Clara asks more sternly.

Zion frowns. "They were humanity's first test in the interstellar arena..."

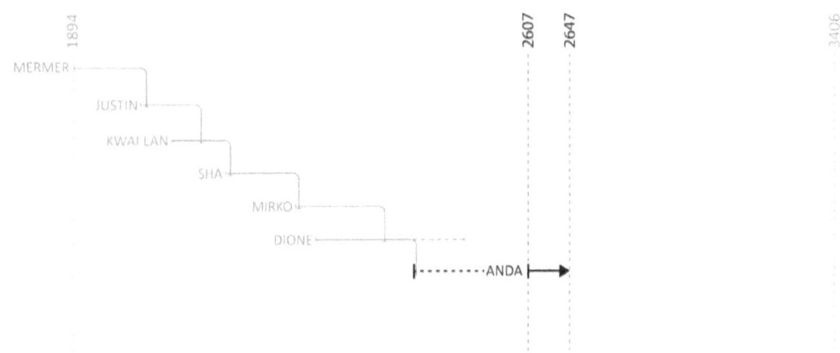

ANDA's TALE

System Centauri: 2607 – 2647

I did not know how I came into the galaxy, but from the moment I opened my eyes, they gazed upon a smiling cabbage. And I loved it so, rubbing my face into its soft fabric and chewing its cotton leaves. More than once, it had to be cleaned of my saliva. We all had plush stuffies of a sort, some shaped like construction equipment, others like medical and engineering tools, and a few like starships and drones. But mine was a cabbage because I was supposed to be a chef one day. At least, that's what my DNA parents decided nearly three centuries before my birth.

♦

T-minus twenty years.

Three thousand of us were simultaneously born on Archangel 1, the first of many Arks nearing a potentially habitable planet named Sorgan, orbiting an unremarkable red dwarf called Proxima, the smallest of System Centauri's three suns.

We were pulled from incubation tubes, wailing, terrified by the light's brightness and the air's chill. But then came soft humming and a slow rocking. I was one of five boys matched with five girls, as was standard for all three hundred clutches. I felt I knew everything about my clutch's caretaker before ever setting eyes upon her. She was safety, warmth, kindness, and love. Her name was Lanna. My brothers and sisters loved

Lanna just as much as I, no doubt, but my connection was special, for I could finish her sentences even as an infant.

"Rock-a-bye baby, on the hull-top—" Lanna would begin.

When solar winds blow, the cradle will rock, I finished in thought but could not voice it then. Nevertheless, I was the first of three thousand infants to speak, and it was not *Mama.*

One day, as Lanna lifted me from my crib, I said, "Good morning!"

She stared at me with bulging eyes. "Um, good morning?"

"I'm hungry!"

The other caretakers would not believe Lanna, for I became shy when she tried to get me to speak. Then, one day, while I was in caretaker Tray's arms, I felt my bowels stir.

"I'm gonna poop!"

Tray gasped. "Well, that's convenient."

♦

T-minus fifteen years.

We gathered in the canteen to celebrate our fifth birthdays. My clutch-mates stared, mesmerized by the sticks on fire atop spongy bread. Snigdha, my sister, reached towards the flickering light.

"Oh, Snigdha, be careful," Lanna said, guiding her hand away. "The flame can burn you."

"What is it?" Ford, my brother, asked, pointing at the spongy brick.

"This is cake." Lanna saw our blank faces. "It's a treat to commemorate your fifth birthdays and the beginning of your training."

"What do we do with it?" Snigdha quietly said.

"Blow out the candles," I answered.

"Candles?" Felipe, another of my brothers, said.

I pointed at the sticks on fire.

"Why, yes, Anda. That's correct. Good job," Lanna said. "Who taught you this?"

"Nobody," I said.

Lanna gave me a perplexed expression.

Soon after eating the cake, we were ushered to our first class.

"All right, children, now watch as I press three times," Professor Nadoo said during our *Intro to Communications* class. He pushed the lever of his telegraph, sending three distinct beeps.

"*S,*" appeared on hologram, but we were lost to giggles.

"If we give three longer taps we get an *O,*" he continued.

More beeps and giggles later, *"O,"* appeared next to the, *"S."*

"Now if we make another *S,* we complete the universal signal for *help.* The most important word to learn."

"Why not spell, *help*?" I asked, finding it strange.

"Good observation, Anda. But we use *S-O-S* because it's the easiest to tap in Morse code."

I tapped my telegraph.

"Help," appeared on my hologram.

"My goodness! Well done, Anda!" the professor said. "Lanna must have taught you already."

I shook my head.

He gave me a confused look. "Perhaps we should stay with SOS for now. Okay children, let's give it a try."

A calamity of beeps, bops, and blips flooded the room. Gibberish appeared on their holograms.

"Well, that's certainly a good try," Professor Nadoo said and saw that my hologram was blank. "Anda, give it a go."

I tapped quickly.

"Why?" appeared on my hologram.

"Very good Anda, but we must first learn the basics."

I tapped again.

"This is too easy," appeared.

"No, Anda, this is very difficult. Even adults must train diligently."

I huffed, scrunched my brow, and furiously tapped.

"That's because you're stupid!" displayed for all to see, and my clutchmates exploded with laughter.

That earned me my first of many detentions.

♦

T-minus ten years.

"Today is your first day of specialized training," Lanna said. "I know it's scary, but you'll still have your core classes together, and we will always live as a clutch. *That* will never change."

Ford raised his hand. "But what if I don't want to be a drone engineer."

"Yeah, I don't want to be a botanist," said Corian.

"I'm scared of blood," Felipe said.

"I don't want to do construction," Samantha said.

"I *hate* math," Snigdha scoffed.

Lanna sighed. "I know this is hard to understand. But your professions are based upon your donor's DNA and backgrounds."

Snigdha heatedly pointed at me. "Anda's donors were soldiers! Why is he a nutritionist?"

"It's what his donors wanted, and his mother's DNA aligned." She turned to me, realizing I had been silent. "Do you want to be a nutritionist?"

"Yep," I said without pause.

Lanna looked pleased. "See. Anda understands."

Snigdha crossed her arms. "Mommy's favorite!"

I raised an eyebrow. The insult was weak. A word lingered in my mind. One that would make for a phenomenal comeback. "Don't be a *bitch*, Snigdah!" I retorted.

My siblings cocked their heads, confused.

"Anda!" Lanna scolded with horror on her face. "You shouldn't say things like that! Do you know what that word means!?"

"A female dog," I said. *Why don't my siblings know?*

Snigdha smiled. "I like dogs. I'm a *birch*."

Lanna shook her head. "Snigdha, we're not using—"

"It's with a *T*, not an *R*," I corrected.

"Anda, no!" Lanna protested.

My siblings gave her a look, wondering why this word held such power.

"Like... *bitch?*" Corian said and giggled.

Lanna raised her hands. "Children! Please, you can't use this word!"

"Bitch! Bitch! Bitch!" they chanted.

The forbidden word quickly spread to the other clutches, and Tray came to see Lanna. They entered a separate room and spoke an old tongue from System Sol, keeping us in the dark, having exclusively taught us Interspeak.

"I hate when they do that, it's not fair," Snigdha said.

I listened through the door. The words felt familiar.

"Condotimane, secoge le domonadara," Lanna said.

"Woreds harke learn sihes *bitch*," Tray responded.

The more I listened, the more I understood, until it clicked.

"We purposely removed these words from Interspeak," Tray said. "How could you be so careless?"

"You think *I* taught them this!?" Lanna snapped.

"The other children say they learned it from *your* clutch. You must have slipped."

"No. Anda just said it one day. He even knew what it meant and how to use it as an insult."

Tray's voice paused. "Can I talk with him?"

I knocked gently on the door.

Lanna opened. "Oh, Anda, we were just wanting to see you," she said, switching to Interspeak.

♦

T-minus five years.

"Anda, you don't need to mix it, just pour it into the printer," Professor Florence said.

I rolled my eyes. "This is *not* cooking!"

My professor frowned. "I've been working printers for twenty years. I've been a nutritionist longer than you've been *alive.*"

"Yet you don't know your ass from your elbow!" I said, frustrated by this buffoon. Five years of chemical breakdowns, proteins, and vitamins essential to the human body, all without consideration for texture or taste.

My professor's face remained blank, registering my curse but not reacting. Otherwise, it would spread like wildfire through the clutches.

"Anda, please escort yourself from this classroom," he calmly said.

"You're an ignorant cunt!" I said and stormed out. *It's all bullshit! I* thought. *All a lie! Where's the love, the joy, the creation!?*

I entered my clutch's quarters and slammed the door. My siblings were still in class. *Good.* I dragged my safe box from beneath my bunk and rummaged for the burner and steel plate I *borrowed* from the chemistry department. I pulled several bags of *borrowed* dry goods and combined flours, adding enough water for a smooth mix.

"I heard you got kicked out again," Snigdha said from the doorway.

I snapped my head up. *She must have snuck from class.* "Come check this out."

She shut the door and knelt next to me, studying the mix. "Is that for the printer?"

"It's designed to firm up when placed upon heat."

"Why would you want that?"

"Remember that time I poured the batter into the printer's vent."

She nodded. "You had detention for a week."

I grinned. "Professor Florence had me clean out the printer's internal components by hand. That's when I noticed the mix contacting the heat sink had firmed into a brittle sheet. I had an urge to try it. So I did. The texture was incredible." I lit my burner, heated the steel plate, and spread a spoonful of oil.

Snigdha gave a funny look.

"It prevents the mix from adhering to the steel," I said, placing a small dollop of the mix onto the plate. It slowly spread, bubbling through and firming around the edges. I slipped a thin sheet of metal beneath and flipped. When the other side solidified, I peeled it from the plate.

"It's similar to the cake we had on our fifth birthday, but flat," I said, breaking a piece for Snigdha to try.

Her eyes lit up. "It's the cake!"

♦

"We gotta go!" Snigdha said, keeping watch of the hallway as I stuffed freeze-dried veggies and lentils, anything I could, into my pack.

"I need to find teff," I responded.

"But that's meant for the printers."

"Says Professor *Shithead*."

"You're so weird, Anda," she said.

I found burlap sacks, slit one open, and peered inside. It was full of seed. *But what kind?* I placed one on my tongue. *This is it!* I poured as much as I could into my pack.

"Anda! Now!" Snigdha growled.

"Coming!"

We closed the food store's hatch just as someone rounded the corner and shuffled home. As we neared our quarters, I sensed people ahead and grasped Snigdha's wrist, pulling her down a side passage.

"Anda, home's that way," she said.

"Mom and Tray are coming," I said.

Lanna's laugh reverberated down the main corridor. We lowered into a ladder-way connecting to the deck below. I lifted the knife I had made from scrap metal, polished to a shine, just above the floor for Snigdha and me to see via its reflection. Instead of passing by, Lanna and Tray came into our side passage.

"Lanna, not here," Tray whispered.

"Yes, *here.*" Lanna pushed Tray against the wall and pressed her lips against his.

"What are they doing?" Snigdha whispered.

"I think it's to show affection," I said.

Hands suddenly planted on my cheeks, turning my head. Snigdha's warm lips were against mine.

"Mm! Mm!" I protested and dropped my knife, sending clangs down the ladder rungs.

"My Sol!" Lanna laughed, and she and Tray ran like kids in trouble.

I pried Snigdha off and peeked my head above the floor to find our passage empty.

"What's wrong?" Snigdha said. "Don't you like me?"

"Yeah, but you're my sister."

"Aren't Tray and Mom siblings?"

"They were raised by different sets of biological parents."

"We have different biological parents, too."

"True." I thought about that. "But it's just not meant for us."

"Oh," she said, looking down.

We returned home to find our clutch waiting.

"What took you so long?" Corian asked.

"We were almost caught by Mom and Tray. Where's Samantha?"

"She couldn't get out of training, but she delivered the containers earlier today. What's it all for?"

I set up five burners and placed Samantha's metal containers above them, filling the deeper with water and the shallower with oil. The water boiled. I added lentils. Ford watched over them as I assigned tasks to the rest.

"Corian, did you get the grinder?" I asked.

"Yeah, but I don't understand. Teff should be planted."

"Trust me on this," I said. *Trust yourself,* I thought.

We soaked chilies and ground them to a paste. Potatoes were cut into cubes. I placed a large steel bowl on a burner and filled it with oil. Then, I combined ground teff with water and salt, pressed it thin, and dipped the dough into the oil. My siblings watched with wonder as it sizzled and popped. The dough puffed from the bottom and self-capsized, frying the other side. With pliers, I pulled it from the oil. Snigdha was there with a towel to pat down the excess oil. I placed bits of chili paste, lentils, potatoes, and other spices and tasted them.

"Less chili paste, and add salt to the lentils," I said.

"Salt?" Ford cocked his head.

"Sodium preservative," I corrected.

"Why preservative?"

"It brings out the flavor."

He held the block above the pot. "How much?"

"Just until it tastes alive."

He thought about that, scraped the block, and tasted it. He lifted his head with a smile. "It's alive!"

I tried it again. "Now this is more like it!"

Each of my siblings took a bite. Confusion and wonder spread across their faces, then spicy coughs erupted. I turned to Snigdha, who was sucking air through her teeth.

"What do you think?" I said.

She gave a sad look and mumbled, "It's delicious, as always."

Something's wrong, I thought, but I could not figure out what. Snigdha sent me more sad glances as I cooked until Ford started a conversation.

We just sat down for dinner when the fire alarm rang.

Footsteps scrambled down the hallway, and our door was kicked in. Professors Florence and Nadoo bounded into the room wearing envisuits and holding expandaplast canisters to snuff out the blaze. The unmistakable whining of inflatable walls to contain fumes came from the corridor.

"Is everyone okay!?" Professor Florence shouted.

I found my voice. "We're just cooking."

"You're... what?" he said.

"Cooking. You know. *Making food,*" I responded.

The professors inspected the burners and containers giving off steam and checked their visors.

"There's a slight increase in heat, but it's safe," Professor Florence said. He unclasped his helmet and went into a coughing fit.

Professor Nadoo stepped to the burners and studied what we made. He released his helmet and inhaled but did not cough. "Chantili cuisine is part of your nutrition curriculum?"

I shook my head.

Nadoo pointed. "May I taste?"

I nodded.

He tore bread, scooped toppings, and placed it into his mouth. "A touch more spice. That's how my grandmother made it. Where did you learn this?"

"I invented it," I said, saddened to learn it was not original after all.

◆

T-minus one year.

We slept soundly in our cryo-tubes, suspended in frigid gel, protecting us from the deadly g-forces of nuclear blast deceleration as we passed System Centauri's heliopause, officially entering Centauri space. When we reached cruising speed, we woke groggy, shivering, and sputtering oxygen-rich liquid from our lungs. Then, we ate printed porridge.

"This is horrendous," Ford said.

"I have just the thing." I pulled a small bag from my pocket.

"Is that dirt?" Snigdha whispered.

I grinned, opened its seal, and sprinkled a pinch into our bowls. "Brown sugar and cinnamon."

"Wow!" Felipe said after tasting. "It makes such a difference."

After breakfast, we assembled in Archangel 1's observation deck.

Professor Nadoo pointed at a red spot of light in the darkness. "Ladies and Gentlemen, this is Proxima Centauri, our sun." He then highlighted a speck, almost invisible. "And this is Sorgan, a planet one point four times the size of Earth and hosting all the resources we need. This is our new home." He turned to us. "In the next few months we will be running arrival simulations."

♦

Felipe and I returned to our quarters dead-tired after another day of building virtual food printers and bioreactors to grow probiotics for gut health and blood for transfusions. The rest of our clutch was already there, lying exhausted on the floor. We joined them on the cool steel.

Ford rolled to his side and said, "I'm hungry."

They turned their heads my way.

"No rest for the weary," I said and peeled myself from the floor.

Then, before we knew it, we were celebrating our twentieth birthdays in orbit above Sorgan, gazing down upon its rocky surface bathed in our red dwarf's crimson rays.

♦

Touchdown.

"The drones will go first," Professor Nadoo instructed, "Piloted from Archangel 1's Command Center, destined for life in one of Sorgan's horizon belt craters, theoretically warm enough to host liquid water. Finding these reservoirs is our single most important endeavor."

We turned to Ford. This was his moment to shine.

"Wish me luck," he said and stepped forth with the other drone specialists, one from each clutch.

♦

A month later, Ford wandered into our quarters.

"Ford!" Snigdha shouted and raced to hug him. "You look terrible."

"What's wrong?" Felipe said.

"The drones keep disappearing," Ford said. "I just lost my fifth. They gave me a few days off to rest."

I pulled the lid from a deep pot filled with vegetable curry, its steam engulfing our quarters.

Ford wildly sniffed the air. "Now *that's* what I've been missing!" He raced over with his bowl.

"Ford, might the sun's radiation be interfering with the drone's guidance system?" Samantha asked.

He shook his head. "The systems are fine. It's just... the drones suddenly fall hundreds of meters until signal loss."

♦

A week later, Ford again burst into our quarters. "It called home!"

"What called home?"

"One of the drones I lost suddenly regained connection. It's five hundred forty-seven meters beneath the surface and reporting a temperature of forty-three degrees. The planet's more geologically active than we thought," Ford said, smiling. "There might be an entire underground system of lava tubes or caves. It explains why we can't find water even though it was detected centuries ago. System Sol wants me to put together an investigation team!"

"A team? Of who?" Samantha said.

"You! Our clutch! We're going to be the first ones to set foot on Sorgan!"

♦

Without an atmosphere, sunlight did not refract as it did in Archangel 1's Earth-like air. The contrast of crimson light and pitch-black shadow on the surface was stunning.

"Depth perception will be useless. Lamps off," Ford instructed. "Prepare to cross Draconis Crater's shadow-line."

"But we'll be blind," Felipe said.

"I've mapped the terrain with the drones. It's all on your visors."

I crossed the shadow line last, nervous of the sensory limbo, but found I could easily negotiate the rocky terrain. I sensed a divot just ahead, one not accounted for in the map. "Ford, watch your step."

"Anda, I got th—" Ford tripped, landing hard in the one point two-G.

I extended my hand, but Ford did not reach for it. *He can't see me,* I realized. "Ford, reach three o'clock high."

He fumbled for my hand, and I pulled him to his feet.

We continued for hours, slowly negotiating treacherously loose rock down the side of the crater.

"Why are... our thighs... burning like this?" Ford said, huffing. "We've trained... our entire lives... at Sorgan gravity."

I thought about that. "The confines of Archangel 1 prepared us for sprints instead of marathons," I said, feeling fine.

"Archangel 2... will have to... change the program… when they wake," Snigdha said.

"It's not so bad," I responded.

"Oh, shut up!" she snapped.

We finally reached the crater's bottom, where we set up Basecamp for the coming weeks. Then, I prepared protein blocks diluted in water for dinner. My clutch-mates looked on with disappointment until I pulled a canteen from my pack, slowly opened its lid, and sprinkled a spicy mix.

"Anda, honestly, what would we do without you?" Felipe said.

"Live a shitty, flavorless existence," I responded, sending them into giggles.

"Lanna says you've spoiled us," Snigdha said.

"Have you seen the *caretakers* try my creations? They inhale it like cocaine." I saw their blank faces. "Like drugs." Still blank. "Never mind."

Ford joined us after his debriefing. "Mom says they're missing several spices from their food stores and wanted me to ask if—" He glanced into the pot to see the porridge peppered red, then grinned. "I didn't see a thing."

♦

We adjusted Ford's maps daily to account for unexpected terrain until we finally reached the location his drone had called from.

"I don't understand," Ford said and sent his reading to the rest of us.

A perfectly square shaft descending 547 meters into the planet's crust materialized on our visors.

"I think this means we descend," I said and felt their anxiety spiking around me. *That's weird.*

"Any volunteers?" Ford asked.

Everyone was silent.

"I'll go with you," I said.

"With *me?* Right," Ford responded.

"I'll go, too!" Snigdha blurted, fidgeting about.

Ford, Snigdha, and I set up a winch above the shaft, and Ford clipped a tether to his envisuit. He inched towards the edge, peering into its depth. "Ready to descend," he said but did not budge. "Okay. Ready to descend." His legs began to shake. "Okay. Ready to *descend.*"

I placed a hand on his shoulder. "Let me take the first plunge," I said, sensing his relief.

For three hours, I dropped, ending at a horizontal tunnel where Ford's drone sat in pristine condition. Ford came next. Then, Snigdha touched down as Ford was downloading the drone's data.

"I never want to do that again!" Snigdha hollered, detaching from the tether like it was cursed.

"Check this out." Ford sent us a schematic the drone constructed. "There's a series of shafts, corridors, and chambers, like a labyrinth."

We ventured deeper, recording the contents of each chamber. The first few were empty, but the deeper ones hosted little spheres upon pedestals.

"They look like marbles," I said, stroking the little black sphere with my gloved finger, letting its sensor analyze. "Oh, shit! They're organic!"

"You've got to be joking!" Snigdha took a reading herself. "Do you know what this means!?"

When we returned to Archangel 1, we were smothered by hugs and handshakes. Bottles of champagne meant for when we officially settle the planet were popped.

"What's all this about?" I asked.

"We sent your analysis of the marble to System Sol!" Lanna said, pride emitting from her eyes. "They say it's a primitive life-form! This is more than they ever dreamed of! They awarded us Medals of Excellence!"

Medals? I thought. *But we didn't find water.*

◆

T-plus 1 year.

"The labyrinth has no perceivable end," Samantha said, admiring its perfectly cut stone. "It connects one crater to the next, spanning beneath great lengths of Sorgan desert. It's a metapolis onto itself."

"But who created it all? What happened to them?" Snigdha asked.

"Carbon dating puts it at seventy-three thousand years old," Corian said. "You'd think erosion or seismic activity would've destroyed it long ago."

"Sorgan doesn't have typical quakes or erosion," I said.

"If we set up atmosphere generators and establish locks, we could live down here," Samantha suggested.

"No," Lanna called in. "We're not to contaminate it any more than is required for study. That's straight from System Sol. And we have yet to find water. That's still our top priority."

◆

Deeper and deeper, we explored, from one chamber to the next, one shaft to another, more than four kilometers below grade now. We found yet another shaft at the bottom-most chamber, and my clutch dropped through two by two. When my feet touched down, I felt thousands of tiny stirs. Our lamps reflected against a white haze in the air, blinding us.

"Is this smoke?" I asked.

Ford raised his hand into the smoke. "It's steam!"

"Can you determine where it's coming from!?" Lanna called.

"On it," Ford responded.

We continued blind through the steam, searching for the source, my siblings bumping into pedestals while I nimbly maneuvered around them. Droplets formed on the stone ceiling. It began to rain.

"Watch your footing, it's getting slick," Ford said.

Before we knew it, we were ankle-deep in water. Then knee-deep.

"The chamber's filling up!" I said, feeling the water's heat through my envisuit. The rain suddenly became a deluge. "We gotta go!"

My siblings spun in circles, disoriented, blind, panicking.

"Snigdha! Hand on my shoulder!" I barked. "The rest of you line up and hold onto those in front!"

They responded like soldiers, organizing behind me. I led them through the sheeting rain, sloshing in the climbing water and deftly weaving the pedestals. By the time we reached the shaft, water was at our waists.

"How's it accumulating so fast!" Snigdha said.

"The water table must be lifting like an eruption!" Lanna called.

Snigdha and Samantha clipped carabiners and rose into the shaft first, the rest of my clutch following two at a time. Ford and I were last, the water at our chests as we clipped onto the tether and rose up the shaft, with the water chasing us. My legs were burning. I grit my teeth. I closed my com and let my scream fly.

Snigdha and Samantha reached the top first, quickly unclasping, then the next two, then the next. Ford and I were pulled from the shaft as water bubbled up and spread along the chamber's floor, searching for voids to fill. We sprinted towards the cable lift, hands upon shoulders following me through the thick steam until, at last, we emerged.

Three rovers quickly approached, their drivers rushing to meet us, staring at the hazy cloud filling the chambers behind us.

"We got Lanna's distress call, was there a fire?"

"This is steam!" Ford said.

"You mean... you found water!?"

"Yes!" I answered. "But it's superheated and rising fast!"

We raced through the labyrinth in the rovers, drifting around right-angle turns, making for that cable lift. Rooster tails spit from our wheels as the water rose. The rovers started to slosh, losing traction.

"The lift is straight ahead!" our driver called, coming to a halt.

We ditched the rovers and crowded onto the lift's platform, putting its motor to the test. Steam engulfed us. *The water is closing in!* I knew. But the lift reached ground level first.

"Run!" Ford called.

We dashed across the crater's surface, anticipating the geyser-like eruption to follow, and ducked behind sizable rocks for shelter.

"Here it comes!" Ford cried.

We waited for the eruption, feeling water rumbling beneath our feet. But then, it stopped.

"Any second!" Ford again shouted. "...It's about to blow!"

I felt only stillness. "Ford... I think it stopped."

There was silence on com. I sensed my siblings peering from their rocks. Snigdha approached the shaft opening.

"Check this out," she said. "It stopped at grade."

◆

T-plus five years.

Mobile printers dropped from Archangel 1 to the surface, collecting Sorgan's silty clay to print hundreds of concrete compartments across the seven-kilometer diameter of Draconis Crater.

"It looks like a gigantic waffle," I said. "What's this for?"

"It's an artificial watertable," Samantha explained. "With Sorgan's unpredictability, it's the only way to ensure a stable hydro-cycle."

We pumped labyrinth water into the waffle compartments before it receded and lowered three prefabricated cold fusion reactors into concrete vaults. Once capping the cells to seal the water, hundreds of drones crisscrossed Draconis's crater floor, knitting an airtight fiberglass membrane. Corian's team positioned thirty-two atmo-generators around the crater's perimeter, separating oxygen from the collected water and nitrogen from Sorgan's sand to build air pressure, slowly raising the membrane into a blister-like dome. A central plaza began construction at Draconis Crater's center, ringed by small housing and amenity buildings, grain silos at the outer edge of town, and algae tanks beyond. Tons of sand were trained inside the dome from a newly built rail connecting all thirty crater colonies, adding several meters of depth above the concrete water table.

Vast grass fields quickly took hold, cleansing the Sorgan sand of toxins and radiation and building a suitable layer of topsoil.

"Anda, you're up," Lanna said.

Crop growth, finally, I thought. But to my dismay, we planted monocultures of grain for the food printers. I had always known this was the plan, but a part of me believed we would diversify in the end. Every minute in the fields fueled my frustration. I pleaded with the nutritionist farmers from the other clutches.

"Just do your job, Anda," they would groan, rolling their eyes.

◆

"Guys, I need your help," I said to my clutch as we lay in our cots, readying for bed.

"You sound serious, Anda. What's wrong?" Snigdha asked.

"Monocultures are too dangerous. We *must* diversify," I said. "I want to setup a greenhouse in the labyrinth chambers."

"System Sol said we can't touch them," Ford said.

"That was before the entire thing flooded," I retorted.

"How would we keep them from flooding again?" he asked.

Samantha spoke. "We can establish airlock's to cordon off several chambers. But getting the parts down there unnoticed will be tricky."

As Samantha snuck airlock parts into the chambers, we transferred topsoil and raided the seed stores. We spent nearly every night in our secret greenhouse improving crop-cycles, hybridizing seeds, and creating new dishes to eat.

◆

"Where do you all keep disappearing to?" Lanna asked.

"We just like to be alone sometimes," I said.

"Bullshit!" Lanna cussed, her eyes boring into me. "Where is it?"

We stared, stunned. No caretaker had ever cussed.

"Where's what?" I said, playing ignorance.

"Anda!" she snapped. "Don't think I haven't noticed the equipment gone missing and the seed stores coming up short."

We led Lanna into the fields to a hatch on the ground.

"The labyrinth? No way," she said, looking at us like we were crazy.

"Yes way," I said, cranked it open, and descended into darkness.

Lanna came next, followed by the rest.

When we reached the bottom, I whispered, "You ready?"

"Sure," she said.

I flipped on the lights, illuminating hundreds of intermingling crops, growing lush like a jungle. Lanna's eyes grew wider with every section that lit.

"Holy shit," she whispered, soaking it all in. "Are you all in on this?"

"Just our clutch and a few from Tray's," Snigdha said.

Lanna grinned. "So, what's for dinner?"

◆

"These are like empanadas," Tray whispered.

I heard him clear across the greenhouse, above pans sizzling and music blaring. *He's right,* I realized. "Dammit!"

"Sorry, Anda," Tray said, then made a face. "How'd you hear that?"

"Anda's weird, remember?" Snigdha said.

Weird, whatever. But I could hear, see, and taste anything I wanted to if I concentrated hard enough. It felt like everyone around me was stupid or blind. *Or am I legit crazy?*

"Hide-and-seek?" Samantha asked after we cleaned the dishes.

I saw my clutch-mates faces light up.

"Again?" I asked.

"Come on, Anda. It's so fun," Ford said.

"That's because I'm always *It,*" I said. "And blind and deaf, I must add."

"Please?" they whined.

I studied their hopeful faces. "Fine."

We donned envisuits, mine with my face shield down and my earpiece turned off. *Cause why not?* I thought. We passed through the airlock, and they scattered into the dark labyrinth chambers, trying to blend in with the flat stone walls and floors. I turned away from them and counted to ninety, then sprinted through corridors and chambers, tagging people along the way. Ones new to the game protested that I was cheating, while others laughed at the ridiculousness of it all.

When I was about to head back, I sensed several more people in a chamber beyond the agreed boundary. *Cheaters!*

"Distance won't hide you!" I called and dashed to the chamber, one I remembered having those organic marbles. But when I arrived, I found the chamber empty. *Wait, no.* I sensed several figures pressed flat against the wall, standing perfectly still. *Are they hiding inside the wall?*

I opened my com. "You really outdid yourselves this time."

They did not move.

"Being still won't make you invisible," I said.

One shifted.

I knocked on the wall. "Sorgan to whoever this is. Tag, you're out."

One stepped from the wall.

I approached and placed a hand on their shoulder. "Tag, you're out."

They swatted my arm. Searing pain lanced, and wetness poured.

"What the fuck!" I shouted and cradled my arm.

The rest leaped from the wall and sprinted further into the labyrinth.

"Fucking assholes!" I lifted my face shield to check my arm. *Sliced clean to the bone.* I gritted my teeth, cinched my suit tight around the wound, and ran back to the airlock.

"Anda what took you so long?" Ford said when I emerged.

"What took me so long!? You assholes attacked me!" I shouted.

Felipe saw the blood running down my arm and raced over.

◆

I was rushed into surgery, tapping into the blood cultures I had set up with Felipe.

Snigdha and Ford visited after I stabilized, looking at me strangely.

"What?" I said shortly. "You come to apologize?"

"We're glad you're okay, but how'd this happen?"

"*You* did this," I said. "Remember? You were hiding in the wall and sliced my arm when I tagged you."

"Anda, we were waiting for you for over an hour," Snigdah said. "You caught all of us already."

◆

I returned to our greenhouse a week later, expecting the lights to be off and the crops to be neglected and wilting. But the moment I opened the entry hatch, I heard laughter, instead. I descended to find my clutch huddled around my burners. I smelled a singeing. Snigdha snapped her head my way.

"Welcome back, Anda!" she cried.

The rest raised their arms in greeting and came to check my injury.

"It healed up nicely," Felipe said. "The cut was perfect."

"You sound impressed." I said.

"It's unexpected. The scar will likely disappear, despite its depth. How are your motor functions?"

"Stiff and clumsy," I said, twisting my forearm, feeling the newly mended tissue protesting.

"Keep up with the exercises and it should get better."

I pointed at the burners. "What are you making?"

Felipe made a face. "Not really sure."

Lanna smiled, then tilted her head, signaling for a side chat. "They're trying really hard," she whispered. "It's a welcome-back cake."

When they unveiled the cake, I had to contain my laughter. It was oblong and crumbling, glued back together with frosting.

"Whoa. Big one!" Snigdha said as she bit into a clump of baking soda.

"Where'd you find the recipe?" I asked. "The frosting's not half bad."

"It's something I remember from childhood," Lanna said.

I looked at the crops growing strong. "Thank you all for the cake, and for maintaining the crops. They look great."

"We didn't do much," Snigdha said. "They seem hardier than what we grow on the surface."

♦

T-plus ten years.

The wheat died first. Melting into a strange white paste. We quarantined the crater colonies from one another to contain whatever contamination this was. But, despite our best efforts, it spread anyway.

"It doesn't match any disease or blight from old Earth," Corian said.

"It must be genetic, then," I said.

"Can't be," Professor Florence said. "They were fine a month ago, then suddenly wilted. It wasn't passed down through DNA."

"What about horizontal transference?" I said, the knowledge suddenly coming to me.

Professor Florence stared blankly.

"You *must* know what I'm talking about," I pressed.

"That knowledge was lost in The Fall," he said.

Nevertheless, we scoured the wheat's DNA, comparing samples before and after the blight, then against our clutch's greenhouse crops.

"Samples are no good," Corian said.

"Which ones?"

"All of them. Even our greenhouse variations."

"Why?"

"They're full of glass filaments," Corian said. "We need new samples."

We collected the samples, but again, all were contaminated.

"The filaments must be shedding from the domes," Corian said.

"How are they getting into the underground crops, then?" Lanna asked.

"Wait." Corian peered back into his holotile, then looked up in wonder.

"It's not glass! Well, it is! But it's fused with the wheat's genetic code!"

"Really?" I studied its DNA and saw several silica proteins wedged between the wheat's carbon-based proteins. "Are all the samples like this?"

We studied ones from Shall Town, Colony Insta, and Lucas Town.

"The contamination appears to effect the buds, leaves, stem, or roots, depending on which variant they are," Corian said.

"Anda," Snigdha said. "Our greenhouse variations are affected everywhere." She put it on central hologram, pointing at several locations. "But the deterioration seems to have stopped.

"How can that be?" Corian said.

Hybridization, came a whisper.

"That's right," I said.

"What's right?" Snigdha said, giving me a funny look.

"Our greenhouse has several wheat variations allowing cross-pollination. They must have adopted each other's resistances." I singled out two wheat breeds on hologram. "Which means, if we hybridize the variants on the surface, they too may become resistant."

Lanna tilted her head. "Anda, how do you know all this?"

◆

"They're *still* succumbing," Corian said.

"But it's never in the same part of the plant twice," I said. "We'll outlast this."

Corian shook his head. "The white paste it melts into is polluting the soil we worked so hard to clean. The greenhouse crops are the only ones still trucking on, they're just stronger."

"We can try bringing their seed to the surface," I said.

◆

After a full Sorgan year, we had a wheat field growing strong.

"Anda," Corian said with dread on his face and a plant in his hands, frothing white at the buds. "It's moved to the soybeans."

The contamination jumped from wheat to soy, teff, potato, broccoli, celery, and spinach. And like a chess match, we raced to hybridize.

"Is it intelligent?" Tray said one day. "It would make sense with the way it reacts to our solutions."

I thought about that. "Maybe someone is orchestrating this."

"From another colony?" Tray asked. "Why would anyone want to do that, what purpose could it serve?"

Spinach, our most reliable source of calcium and vitamin C, was the first crop to reach the point of no return. Then, our legumes and potatoes died off. And just when we made a breakthrough with the broccoli, another contaminant hit our wheat.

"This is a disaster," Tray said. "All that remains, is the teff."

"But it's teff," I said, confident. "It's magic in a seed."

◆

With every ounce of brainpower, exploring every possible idea, we spliced. The newest teff hybrids matured and flowered. Our beehives rushed to pollinate. It seeded. A second harvest came. Then another.

"My Sol. It's working," Corian said. "But surviving purely off of teff will be difficult."

"What about the honeybees?" I said. "Honey is almost a completely human food. It even has small amounts of vitamin A, B, C, and D. Couple that with the proteins from the teff and we can survive."

◆

I woke to a tremor, and my thoughts instantly went to the flooding event. Snigdha and Ford sat up from their bunks as well.

"You feel the vibration?" I said.

Snigdha nodded slowly. "What is it?"

"I think it's the flooding," I said.

We quickly dressed and made our way towards the labyrinth entry.

"Wait," Snigdha said and stopped. "My seismometer says the vibration is coming from the center of our fields. In the opposite direction."

"What, really?" I said.

"Let's check it out," Ford said.

We hustled through the fields with our headlamps illuminating a narrow path between rows of lush teff. Low guttural tones, consonants new to my ears, came from deeper in the field, "Gdoonian, schooonter."

We turned off our headlamps, letting our pupils enlarge. Kneeling figures appeared ahead, all in black, their proportions strange. One held a teff plant in its hand, pointing at its seeds and roots, seemingly describing its anatomy.

"Kakaka doooned," another said, pointing deeper into the field.

They dropped the teff and galloped off.

"Who was that?" Snigdha whispered.

"No idea, but they're not from Draconis," I said.

We pursued as quickly and stealthily as we could. I pulled ahead of Snigdha and Ford, nimbly moving in the darkness. The figures stopped above one of our cold fusion reactors. They swept away the soil with incredible speed, taking seconds to reach the reactor's concrete shell. Then, they raised chiseled hands high and swung down. Concrete tore like paper. The reactor went into shutdown, and the hissing of the atmo-generators in the distance cut until power quickly routed from another of our reactors. Sirens wailed.

The figures raised their chisels for another strike.

"Stop!" I shouted and charged, raising my arms to look formidable.

They became more massive as I neared, double my height and girth, at least. One lurched, its chisel screaming down upon my skull. But just before splitting my head and spilling my brains, I twisted, and the chisel whiffed. My hand then went rogue, grasping the figure's wrist, pushing it along its arc, encouraging its momentum, and sending it into the figure's midsection. Liquid sprayed, splattering my face and sending a horrid stench up my nose. A low rumbling emitted, but there was no mouth.

Snigdha and Ford finally caught up and shouts from the repair team racing to stabilize the reactor came in the distance.

"Khalidian toooken scubooonedr!" the injured figure shouted, sinking a chisel into its own chest and carving out a small marble.

Another figure approached and gently cupped the marble in its palm, then galloped away, leaving their comrade's lifeless body behind.

◆

"They're made of organic fiberglass," Felipe said, staring at the body with both excitement and worry. "I never imagined such a creature could exist."

"If they're silica based, then they must be who tampered with our crops," Samantha said.

"I wouldn't be so hasty," Tray said. "Perhaps the contamination is this planet's version of bacteria."

I shook my head. "No, Samantha's right. These creatures were inspecting the teff when we stumbled upon them, pointing at areas that should have been effected."

"You're so certain," Lanna said.

"I am. Snigdha and Ford saw it, too," I said.

"We did," Snigdha confirmed.

"When will Sol respond with direction?" I asked.

"It'll take weeks for them to respond. We're on our own," Lanna said.

◆

T-plus fifteen years.

A distress call echoed across our teff fields. We stopped mid-harvest, stood straight, and listened.

"It's from Shall Town!" Lanna shouted.

We raced to Draconis's command center in town, and Lanna pulled up the call.

A man appeared on hologram, wearing a helmet sock that framed his blistering skin with rivers of blood in his crow's feet and smile lines.

"This is Stanley Winston from Shall Town calling Draconis. Do you copy?" he slurred.

"We copy, Stanley," Lanna said. "What's going on? We see Shall Town is entirely out of power."

Stanley sighed deeply. "We don't know what happened, it cut without warning, and our backup reactors did not kick-in. All life support has failed." Stanley seemed at a loss for words. "We had no choice but to trek across the surface in envisuits to get within small transmitter range of you. We've been out here for three days. Please, prepare for our arrival."

"We'll get the infirmary ready. Hang in there, Stanley," Lanna said.

The call ended.

Tray shook his head. "You can't cross the surface on foot, the radiation is far too intense. They're already dead."

♦

Only three of Shall Town's one hundred colonists reached Draconis. Stanley was not among them. Felipe peeled off their envisuits, revealing skin sliding off like hot cheese. Their lips swelled like sausages, their eyes bulged, and their hair dropped like dry grass. Felipe took blood samples. The moment the results appeared on hologram, he lowered his head.

They died that evening.

♦

"Colony Insta just went dark!" Lanna said, staring into a hologram displaying all thirty colonies in Sorgan's horizon line craters.

Tray gave a look. "It's two days by train, we can—"

"Shit!" Lanna shouted. "Lucas Town just went dark, too!"

We crowded around the hologram, watching in horror as colony power indicators, one by one, disappeared.

"How can this be happening! Shall Town was an isolated incident, right?" Tray said.

A realization hit me. "Shall Town was a test run!" I blurted. "We're under attack!"

"It must be an electromagnetic pulse!" Lanna flipped on the emergency channel. "Attention all! We are in a state of emergency! We believe an EMP is hitting all the colonies! Turn off all life support and computer systems immediately! Anything with a charge, shut down, now!"

A rumbling came through the floor. I looked down, expecting the ground to erupt. Instead, my hair stood on end, and a tingling sensation ran across my skin. The hologram scrambled and sparked. The lighting blew, and the gentle hissing of the atmo-generators in the distance wound to sleep. The tingling sensation stopped, and my hair dropped back to my scalp.

♦

"The pulse contaminated our computer systems and infrastructure, turning their components into a paste," Corian said as we gathered in the pitch-dark command center.

"This wasn't an EMP," Samantha said.

"What was it, then?" Lanna asked.

"It's the same thing that attacked our crops," I said. "Come to think of it, our technology is more vulnerable considering their components are fiber-optic."

"Is there a way regain power?" Ford asked.

Samantha sighed. "We never anticipated something coming from below, hitting all our electronics simultaneously. We must first replace the reactor cores and computers, then every single fiber optic line. We must rebuild Draconis's entire power grid from scratch."

"That will take months," Ford said. "We'll suffocate."

"Only if the algae cultures die, which *will* happen if the air remains stagnant like this," Corian said. "The atmo-generators are designed to push warm air against the perimeter of the dome creating a temperature curtain. When it climbs to the top, it cools, dropping to the center and running across the algae to scrub CO2. We must get the atmo-generators online first."

"How do we do that?"

Samantha paused, then said, "After replacing a reactor's components, we'll have to run new cable to the atmo-generators and replace their systems, too."

"But they're each several kilometers away from one another," Lanna said. "How are we going to find them in the dark?"

"Hide-and-seek," I said.

♦

"No, Anda. It's the *fourth* port from the top," Samantha said. "If you plug into the wrong one you'll fry the generator for good. Let's run it again."

I sighed. "Remove faceplate. One screw at each corner and mid-span of panel. Detach sensor on backside. Remove radiation shield, replace computer core and tertiary electronics. Make sure no metal components make contact with each other. Insert fiber optic cable into fifth port."

"*Fourth*, Anda! *Fourth!*"

"Right! Fourth!" *Why can't I get this right?*

Samantha's anxiety was palpable, but we were out of time, already coughing in the stagnant air. I secured a six-millimeter-thick fiber optic cable to my utility belt.

"I'm off," I said and closed my eyes, feeling the terrain beneath my feet and the subtle undulation of topography ahead. I singled out the first atmo-generator. At twenty meters out, the weight of the thin cable became known. At fifty, it was almost too much. Then, I felt a tug and knew Snigdha had picked up the line, alleviating part of the load, stumbling blindly at my pace. At a hundred meters, I felt another tug. It was Ford carrying the next portion of the cable. At four kilometers, I reached the first generator.

Off came the faceplate and shield. *So far, so good.* The computer popped out, dripping with decomposing paste. I cleaned the cavity, inserted the new core, and swapped out the tertiary components. I counted the auxiliary ports. *One, two, three, four, five.* I twisted the cable's fibers to make a point for easy insertion. *Wait... Was it four or five?* An image of the panel came to my mind, showing the auxiliary port as the fifth one down. *But Samantha clearly said it was the fourth. I must trust her judgment.* I went to plug into the fourth, but my hand jerked, and it descended into the fifth.

"Shit!" I shouted, anticipating that the generator would fry.

Instead, air blasted upwards, knocking me back, and I heard cheers in the distance. I returned along my path, collecting my siblings along the way.

"You remembered it's the fourth!" Samantha cried when I returned.

"Fifth," I said, patting her shoulder, leaving her perplexed as I attached another cable to my belt and headed out to the next generator.

♦

After thirty-seven days, we replaced the last electrical component in Draconis and flipped the switch, roaring the colony back to life. Thousands of LEDs spanning the crater lit, revealing vast empty fields.

"Where'd all the crops go?" Snigdha said.

"I don't know, but we have seed stores," I said. "They should get us through the next few harvests as we restart the fields."

But when we checked the stores and our subterranean greenhouse, we understood the Sorgans went to great lengths to distract us.

They were empty.

♦

Felipe pulled the Sorgan's lifeless body from a morgue drawer.

"How did they create a contaminant that effects both organic and non-organic material?" Tray said, gazing upon the body. "They're just dumb animals."

I shot him a look. "They're not dumb. They know exactly how our technology and agriculture works, and they have complex language."

"Um. They don't have language," Felipe said.

"We heard them speaking to each other the night we killed this one," I said, pointing at the body.

"Anda, they didn't say anything," Snigdha said.

"Of course they did. They said, *Gdoonian, schooonter.*" I saw blank expressions and felt like a lunatic. *Again.*

They lowered tired, defeated eyes. Tray and Lanna looked the seventy years of age they were, and my siblings, thirty-five. *Is this the end of the line?* I thought.

What about the next wave of settlers? came a whisper from within me.

"We must warn Archangel 2," I said to my clutch. "They're heading towards certain death."

Tray knocked against a medical vat to get my attention. "Anda, it took us a month to get Draconis running. To repair the Coms Tower would take a year, probably longer considering we must first repair the railway."

"Can we cross on foot?" I asked.

Tray shook his head. "The train-cars are heavily protected from radiation. If we cross on foot, we'll end up like Shall Town."

"Then, we repair the railway," I argued.

"We only have enough food for a few weeks," Lanna said.

Something tugged within me. "We can improvise. We just need to think creatively."

Tray again tapped the vat. "Like how, Anda?"

I stared at the vats. "The bacteria cultures."

"We'll still run out of essential vitamins and proteins," Felipe said.

I could not shake the feeling we were missing something. I studied the vats of bacteria cultures, then those with, *"A+, A-, B+, B-, AB+, AB-, O+, O-,"* engraved on their sides.

No, I thought, disgusted at myself for even going there.

Yes, whispered within me.

I shook my head. "We can't!"

"Anda, you all right?" Snigdha said.

There's no other way, the whisper said.

I breathed deeply. "Samantha? How long does it take to build one of these vats?"

"A day, they're easy to make," she said.

"Felipe? How long would it take to grow a culture?"

"We just established that bacteria won't help," he said.

"It's... for the blood," I said, watching horror wash over them.

♦

"No! Absolutely not!" they unanimously cried.

Yet, I could not shake the idea. I experimented in my room with a burner, metal plate, pots and pans, and blood samples from our vats. Vitamins B2, C, and D, iron, phosphorus, calcium, and all the proteins we lacked were at our fingertips. *Blood can replace eggs,* I realized. *It can be stir-fried.* But a revulsion remained. *I had a blood transfusion without any protest. Is ingesting blood any different?*

Yes and no, said the voice from within.

I poured a shallow glass of chilled *B+*. It smelled of iron and coated the cup like wax. I brought it to my lips, closed my eyes, and sipped. Sweet, metallic, savory, yet bland all at once. Chilled, it took on new qualities, becoming refreshing, like whiskey on the rocks. *What's a whiskey?* I was baking, frying, and steaming. It even replaced tofu. My recipes took on a new hardiness and flavor. *Finally, unique,* I thought. *But how do I get everyone to try them?* I thought about the last dessert I had made in the greenhouse. Lanna called them brownies.

A made another batch but switched out imitation eggs with blood and brought them to the mess hall.

"No way!" Corian said and snatched one.

My siblings gathered around, moaning in ecstasy with each bite, then the other clutches came.

"This is delicious," Samantha said and scrunched her brow. "Why aren't you having one, Anda?"

Felipe brought his half-eaten brownie closer, analyzing its pores. "Mom? Are brownies supposed to be reddish?"

"No… they're not." Lanna's eyes darted to me. "Anda! You didn't!"

Brownie bites plopped on the floor, followed by retching.

"Why, Anda!?" Tray shouted.

To save us, I wanted to say.

They looked at me with such betrayal. And then…

"It's not so bad," Akimbo, caretaker of clutch 231, said. "I used to have blood pudding back on Earth."

Pudding? How had I not thought of that!

"But this is *our* blood!" Lanna said.

Akimbo thought about this. "These cells are made in a laboratory. Technically speaking, it's not from a specific person."

◆

We stretched our emergency rations as far as possible, but there was no plan to repair the railway and reach the Coms Tower to warn Archangel 2.

They're accepting defeat, I knew.

But then, Akimbo, Snigdah, and Ford came to my room.

"Anda, the rations are killing us, literally," Ford said. "Do you really think you can substitute what we lack with blood?"

"The vitamins and proteins are there," I said and saw his expression. "I promise this will work."

"Okay, then," he said.

With eyes closed, telling jokes and stories, doing anything to keep their minds from the present, they tried my dishes. Slowly, more of my siblings joined. Some heaved. Others grew pale. But eventually, our perceptions of deliciousness changed. Snigdha was the first to let out a grunt of enjoyment, and the rest of us turned to her in shock.

Samantha came to me a few days later. "Anda, all I could think of while eating our rations this morning were the dumplings you made. Why is this?"

"Your body's recognizing its nutritional intake is being fulfilled by the blood," I said.

"What are you making tomorrow?"

"I can do the dumplings again."

"Thanks," she whispered.

◆

Eventually, Lanna and Tray tried my creations.

"You vampires," Lanna said. With eyes closed, humming a tune, she slowly ate a piece of blood bread, her throat quivering, but she kept it down.

"What's a vampire?" Snigdha asked.

Lanna gathered us into a circle like when we were children and told the story of Dracula, complete with voice impressions.

The next day, quietly, without discussion, Samantha's crew began fabricating vats, Felipe's medical team began culturing blood, and Tray and Lanna planned the railway's repair.

♦

T-plus twenty years.

We entered Shall Town and cautiously navigated through fields of shriveled crops to its hollowed-out town center.

"Everything having glass or silicon components has been completely decomposed," Corian said. "Incredible."

"Is there anything we can salvage?" Lanna asked.

I looked at the shriveled crops. *Not decomposed, not removed,* I realized. "There might be salvageable seed in the old crops."

"Why didn't the Sorgans take them like they did ours?" Tray asked.

I shrugged. "Their goal was to remove the inhabitants. When Shall Town's population chose to cross the surface, their goal was accomplished."

"Does that mean their seed stores are intact?" Snigdha said.

We raced to their silos, finding them full.

"We must get this back to Draconis immediately!" Tray said.

♦

Our fields were sowed, seedlings sprang up, and crops fruited and matured. Then, came the harvests. The first dish I created, made entirely of recovered ingredients, was a rigatoni baked pasta, as Lanna called it. My siblings dug in, but after a moment, they made faces.

"Anda, there's something missing," Corian said.

"What do you mean?" I asked, taken aback.

"It's just. Did you leave something out?"

"You mean... *The blood?*" I responded.

"Yeah."

The following night, I made bloody tofu.

"*Why's* the tofu red?" Corian said, grinning.

"Chilly paste," I responded, playing our usual game of denial.

My siblings wolfed it down.

♦

"Next transformer's just ahead," Ford said, slowing the train. "Opening repair car hatch." The front section of the train split down the middle and moved forward, swallowing the transformer. "Closing," Ford said, and the two halves met. "Sealed. Repair team, you're cleared for entry."

Samantha opened the airlock door and entered first, the rest of us in tow. When my feet met the Sorgan surface, I felt strange pitter-patters.

"Whoa, you feel that?" I asked.

"Feel what?"

"The vibration in the ground."

"We got nothing on our sensors, you sure it's not just the train itself?"

"Maybe," I said.

We finished the repair, and the transformer came online, activating the next length of the track into Lucas Town.

We passed through Lucas Town's entry airlock to find a sea of white paste stretching the entire crater.

"What in Centauri?" Tray said.

"It's the same decomposition, but on a whole other level," Corian said, studying buildings in the distance appearing like melted candles.

I felt sudden tremors through the ground, coming closer, seeming like a single entity, but...

Hundreds, said the voice within me.

"We gotta go!" I shouted, but my clutch was already backpedaling. I was the only idiot at the edge of the white sea. The tremors settled, but I could feel their attention upon us, analyzing, curious.

"Anda!" Lanna called.

Like a child, I jolted and ran, looking over my shoulder as the airlock door sealed to glimpse hundreds of obsidian heads pop above the white paste. We piled into the train car and departed in panic, but something felt wrong.

"Where's Tray?" I asked.

♦

I could not tell you what was more terrifying – When Tray went missing or when he returned.

"Mom. It's going to be okay," Snigdha said, trying to get Lanna out of her room and to eat.

"It's not him," Lanna would whisper.

Tray had waltzed through Draconis's airlock several weeks after his disappearance, claiming to have found a gap in our sun's radiation bursts and crossing on the surface.

"But that's exactly what you always advocated against," I argued. *And how did Tray evade the Sorgans?*

"I was lucky," he said.

All of Draconis rejoiced his return. To them, Tray was just Tray, miraculously returned to us. But how he shuffled his feet or how his posture changed for split seconds… I saw what Lanna saw.

"I'm just not hungry," Tray said during his physical.

"But, you haven't eaten in *four* days," Felipe said and shot me a glance.

Tray shrugged. "Are we finished?"

"Yes," Felipe said.

Tray stood with vigor and left the infirmary.

"Anda," Felipe began.

"I know," I said.

"But you don't." He showed me the results of Tray's blood test.

"Twenty-one years old? But he's seventy-six," I said.

"Everything is heightened, improved. Tray 2.0," Felipe said.

We entered the dining hall for dinner, watching Tray 2.0 smile the same, laugh in his way, and give longing glances to the dining hall entry.

Searching for Lanna, I knew. I grabbed two dinner trays, piled food high, and went to Lanna's room. I gently knocked on her door.

No answer.

"Mom, please, you *need* to eat," I said quietly. "It's just me, Anda." I knocked again, feeling the reverberations travel through the door and along the walls of her room, expecting to sense her curled in bed, sobbing or sleeping. But the room was empty. *Shit!* I dropped the dinner trays and sprinted down the corridor, passing the dining hall.

"Anda! Where are you going!?" Snigdha called after me.

"Mom's gone!" I shouted, not letting up, my legs reaching speeds I did not know were possible. I entered Draconis's train platform to see its indicator flashing, *"DEPARTED."* An envisuit was missing from the wall. I accessed the train's beacon. It was barreling towards Lucas Town.

"No," I whispered.

"Why's she going back?" Tray 2.0 suddenly said.

I leaped sideways, having not felt his approach at all. I could only sense Snigdha, Ford, Felipe, and Samantha running down the hall. "Lanna's searching for *you!*"

Tray 2.0 gave me a funny look. "But I'm—"

"How did you survive Lucas Town?" I pointedly asked.

He scrunched his brow. "I've told you, I was hiding in a silo and took advantage of a sudden break in radiation. But the radiation has risen again. We can no longer cross."

Dread percolated through me. I knew of another way to reach Lucas Town, one explored before the flooding event long ago.

♦

One chamber after another, deeper, heat rising, water low, and zero light, just as I remembered.

"The tunnel connecting to Lucas Town is just ahead," Snigdha said through com. "But it'll take a day to navigate."

"And we'll be at the mercy of the Sorgans," I added. "On my own it will only take a few hours."

"Anda, it's too dangerous, even for you," Ford said, just as determined as I to save Mom. As were all of us.

I must take the choice out of their hands, I realized. I turned off my lamp and bolted into the darkness.

"Anda!" they shouted.

When I closed my eyes, I sensed thousands of consciousnesses through kilometers of stone ahead. Their inner light was a different hue from our own. I never noticed that before.

"Anda, how can you see?" Tray 2.0 suddenly said, right next to me.

I stumbled, my shoulder grazing the corridor wall, sending shock waves through the stone. *How did he sneak up on me again!?* I focused on his inner light. It was the same hue as ours. *What does this mean?* I thought.

That this is still Tray, said the inner voice.

I turned to Tray 2.0. "Let's find Lanna!"

♦

Hundreds of Sorgans now flanked Tray and me, moving effortlessly through the rock outside of the tunnel we traversed and using their collective strength to clap stone walls together or drop stone slabs from the ceiling. I leaped and tumbled, narrowly evading. And to my surprise, Tray was proving just as nimble as me.

"You're doing great, Tray!"

"But *how* am I doing this?" he said. "I can feel them moving."

"This is how I played hide-and-seek," I said. "You must focus."

A stone wall thrust upwards from the floor, separating Tray and me. I felt him pressing against the rock on the other side. Another wall erupted behind me. *Trapped.* The Sorgans settled outside the tunnel, watching.

We're not alone, the inner voice said.

A creature rose in front of me, its posture hulking, *seething.* It felt familiar. With a sudden twitch, it swung a chisel to split my helmet and skull. *Oh, it's that one,* I thought, again grasping its wrist and continuing its momentum.

Below! the inner voice said as another chisel came at my midsection.

On it, said a different whisper, familiar yet new, and my body gracefully danced around the Sorgan, slipping its strikes.

Whoever is dancing me around is having fun, I thought.

I am, said the dancer's voice.

And then, like a door was opened, I heard several more voices conversing inside my head.

We don't have time to play! said a bitter voice.

What do you think? the dancer asked. The question for someone else.

It has muscle-like tissue, ligaments, and nerves, like human anatomy. Your techniques should work, said an analytical voice.

Good! The dancer thrust my titanium fingertips into the Sorgan's armpit as my other hand poked the back of its knee, sending the creature tumbling to the floor. The Sorgan struggled to stand, confused, its left side refusing to work. I jabbed its right leg, sending it to the ground for good.

The Sorgans watching outside the tunnel went into a frenzy, and the wall trapping me lowered. Another Sorgan entered, slicing the marble sphere from their comrade's chest, then escaped deeper into the corridor. Tray was still pounding against the stone wall separating us.

"Tray, go protect the others! I'll continue on!" I said.

He paused. "How are you still alive?"

"I don't go down so easily!" I said, but the words were not mine.

"We'll get the wall down as soon as we can!" Tray responded and bolted back to our comrades lagging behind.

I breathed deeply. My adrenaline settled. I let my senses flow. *The Sorgans are congregating ahead.* Thousands of minuscule Sorgan steps became clear enough for me to imagine a massive chamber, directly below Lucas Town. A set of familiar steps flitted upon the surface, passing through Lucas Town's airlock. *Mom...*

The tunnel ahead was empty. But when I stepped forth, reverberations hit me like a beating drum. My legs became jelly. I toppled to the floor. *What the hell is this!?*

Sensory overload, said a fifth, commanding voice. *It's designed to inhibit your ability to discern your surroundings,*

How many of you are in my head!? I thought.

Focus! the commanding voice said.

I sensed ten, twenty, over a hundred echoing corridors, but I knew there was only one. *How can I discern which is real?*

Remember the training, the commanding voice said. *Think back, think far, think about a little girl.*

I tried remembering any sort of training involving sensory overload. Instead, a vision of Taam Kapoor, my DNA father, came to mind, but as a young boy.

"Tag! You're it!" Taam slapped my shoulder and spun off in zero-G.

Tag? I was chasing him, nimbly switching directions, pushing off obstacles, and cutting him off.

"Gotcha!" I said as my hand caught his leg.

The vision was replaced by another. I was floating in a dark sphere. *Alone.* I could not see, hear, smell, or feel. I was without senses, the opposite of the echoing crippling me now. I imagined a command center in my mind hosting all of my senses. Control panels for sight, sound, taste, touch, and smell appeared like the bridge of a ship. I manually switched them off. All that remained was my breath, heartbeat, and the squishing of digestion.

What is this place? I thought.

This is where you must go, the commanding voice said. *Find your inner command center.*

The vision faded.

Who are you all? Why are you speaking to me? I thought to the voices.

They were silent now.

I tried imagining a command center. Instead, my quarters upon Archangel 1, with several pots atop burners, formulated. I peered in a pot to find eyes boiling in water. *Sight,* I understood. Another contained my ears. *Sound, equilibrium.* There was a pot for each of my senses. I systematically turned them off, even smell, taste, and touch.

The overwhelming echoes dissipated, and I inched forth through the corridor. After an hour of walking, the Sorgans seemed so close. I returned to my imaginary quarters and restarted my senses. I was no longer in the corridor, and the sensory overload was no longer present. I was directly below Lucas Town.

I searched for Lanna's footsteps on the surface but could not sense them. Then, I noticed a color shift among the Sorgan consciousnesses before me. A single human among them. She was calm, awake, gazing at me through the dark as I stepped closer. Her envisuit was removed, but I could tell that her vitals were stable.

The environment's habitable, I realized.

"Who's there?" Lanna whispered.

I unclasped my helmet. "It's going to be okay, Mom."

"Anda?" she said. "I'm sorry. I should have never come. I don't know what I was thinking. Tray's not here."

"Mom. The Tray that returned to us is the real Tray, but he has indeed changed," I said.

Thousands of synchronized heartbeats suddenly thumped. I focused on the sea of Sorgans beyond Lanna, standing perfectly still, in a sort of meditative state. *They think they're hiding.*

We cannot fight them all, the dancing voice said.

We might not have to, I thought back, remembering that first day of Communications Class as a child. I knelt on the stone floor, placed the metal tip of my glove to the surface, and gave light taps and drags, forming the most simple of words in Morse code, *"Hello."*

The Sorgans maintained their stillness.

"Hello, hello," I repeatedly tapped.

"Anda, I don't think that'll work," Lanna said.

"It has too. We can't keep fighting them," I replied. Again and again, I tapped.

One finally stirred. It slowly came forth, knelt, contemplated, and knocked the floor with its knuckle. *"H-e-l-l-o."*

It worked! I added, *"Hello, my name is Anda."*

Again, the Sorgan contemplated, then knocked, *"H-e-l-l-o... m-y... n-a-m-e... i-s—"*

It's understanding! I thought.

"—A-n-d-a," It finished.

Oh, it's only mimicking, I realized. *But of course, there's nothing for it to draw upon, no alphabet to reference.* I tapped out each letter, number, and punctuation mark.

A second and third Sorgan came out of meditation and conversed silently with the first. They knelt and furiously ran through the alphabet like cogs of a primitive computer. They began breaking down my introductory words. *"Hello— Hello— Hello my— Hello, my name— Hello, my name Anda— Anda, my name be— Hello Anda, my name—"*

They abruptly stopped.

The first Sorgan knocked, *"Hello, Anda. My name be, R97426."*

◆

"You, contaminate ecosystem! You, cripple hydro-cycle! You, wake us before planet ready! You, attack us!" R9 knocked, listing our crimes.

At least they returned Lanna to us unharmed and unchanged.

"We did not intend to ruin your processes," I tapped. *"We did not know you were here. Can we come to a truce?"*

My clutch stared wide-eyed at the thousands of Sorgans sitting on the floor, listening to the back-and-forth tapping between R9 and me.

"T-r-u-c-e? No understand," R9 responded. *"You, leave!"*

"We cannot. Our ships are one-way," I tapped.

"No understand S-h-i-p. Leave, now!"

"We cannot," I repeated.

"Because you broken?" R9 pointed at Tray. *"We try fix, but still broken. You all broken."*

"What did you do to him?" I asked.

"Make better, but no spore, waste."

"What's a spore?"

"Spore be person. You suit, no person."

I thought about that. *"All of this is our person."* I motioned to my arms, legs, torso, and head.

R9 tilted its head. *"You, fragile, primitive, waste of material."*

"There must be a way for us to coexist," I tapped.

"You, have no ability. Technology, wasteful. You, only take."

"We can become better people," I tapped, hoping it was true.

It's true, a friendly voice said from within.

R9 spoke with the other Sorgans in a low register, barely audible. Then, it returned. *"There be only one way."*

♦

"We cannot become material for them to harvest!" Snigdha shouted once we returned to Draconis.

"It's the only way they'll let us live," I said.

"Like cattle! I'd rather die!" Snigdha stood her ground.

Murmurs of agreement rounded the dining hall.

I sighed deeply. "We must reach the Coms Tower to warn Archangel 2. Our lives may be forfeit, but we must give *them* a fighting chance."

"How can we do that? Our train is still in Lucas Town," Ford said.

"One of us must cross on foot," I said.

"But, the radiation will kill us long before we reach it." Tray looked longingly at Lanna, but she gave cut-eye. He deflated. "I'll go."

GALAXY'S BEST CHEF | 371

"No. The Sorgans are watching you in particular," I said.

He furrowed his brow. "I'm not their pet!"

"I know. It's just. You don't know how they think," I said.

"And *you* do?" Lanna asked.

"I can sense where they are. I know how they move," I said.

Skepticism crossed their faces.

"Anda, I need to check your DNA," Felipe said. "Back when your arm was sliced, you may have been contaminated. It would explain these abilities."

I'm not contaminated! I wanted to shout, but I could not explain my gifts to them. I nodded. Felipe led me to the infirmary and locked the door.

"There's a way for you to cross on the surface," he whispered.

"What? You're not checking my DNA?"

"You've always been weird," Felipe said, grinning. He pulled the Sorgan body from its morgue tray. "During your negotiation with R9, it said we are broken because we have no spore, and because of this, have no person." He pointed at the lifeless husk. "I think this is their version of an envisuit, but hosting organs perfectly adapted to survive on this planet. It can even withstand the radiation on the surface."

"You believe the marbles inside them are their actual selves? Are the spores they spoke of?"

Felipe nodded. "They've evolved to become nothing but a tiny central nervous system. Compact, efficient. Everything else is superfluous."

"Then, this technology is millions of years ahead of us," I said, studying the Sorgan suit.

"That's what scares me."

I thought about that. "But how can this suit help me cross on the surface? I could never carry it."

Felipe shook his head. "*It* will carry *you*."

◆

"You have to what!" Lanna blurted.

"It's the only way to reach the coms tower," I said.

"But will that even work?"

The Sorgan suit lay upon a dissection table, its limbs and torso sliced down their lengths, and the nerves identified as best we could.

"Watch this," Felipe said, holding a beaker of white paste he had collected in Lucas Town. He dipped a brush and painted the suit's arm. The paste seeped into its obsidian skin, and tendrils wriggled from within the cuts like worms. He continued painting, each limb awakening, the tendrils tracking Felipe as he rounded the table. He finished and stepped back. "Its nerves are now online."

I glanced at my siblings and caretakers crowding the morgue. Their worried eyebrows spoke volumes, but they did not utter a word. I gently touched the open tissue at the suit's elbow. Tendrils shifted my direction like a change in the wind. *I'll be okay,* I thought, crawled upon the table and lay into the suit's open cuts. The tendrils inched across my limbs, investigating, poking, and prodding. Then, a thin membrane spread over me like liquid latex, cinching tight around my arms and legs, neck and waist, compressing until all breath escaped my lungs, all lunch left my stomach, and all excrement squeezed from my bowels. My siblings came rushing as the open slices healed, sealing me within, engulfing my face, and invading my lungs. I desperately tried coughing but had no breath.

It's okay. You've done this before, a friendly voice said.

A vision of a creature scavenging the ocean floor came to me, seawater flowing through its body. I calmed and felt the liquid in my lungs now. My urge to cough subsided.

It's oxygen-rich. You'll be fine, said the analytical voice.

The moment I relaxed, zaps hit my toes, working their way up my legs and spine. It struck my arms and fingertips and eventually my face. Then, stillness. Nothingness. Darkness.

I felt my sibling's hands upon the suit, vigorously shaking it. *I'm okay,* I tried to say, but my vocal cords would not respond. I tried sitting up, but the body struggled.

My siblings retreated.

Don't try to use your body to move. Just think, the friendly voice said.

I relaxed as if preparing for hibernation and envisioned myself sitting up. Suddenly, I was sitting up. I swiveled my new legs off the table. *Wobbly, weak.* But the moment the feet pressed upon the floor, all awkwardness melted away. Millions of sensors in the soles activated, flooding me with information. I could see, not with light, but vibration. I sensed my siblings as clear as day, the gentle rustling of the Draconis's crops in the artificial breeze, the water moving within the labyrinth below, and thousands of Sorgans maneuvering their tunnels, deeper and deeper, all the way to the planet's core, tirelessly rotating. *What are they doing?*

They're terraforming the planet from the inside out! said yet another voice from within. *Creating a dynamo strong enough to generate a*

I felt taps on the table from Felipe, *"Are you okay?"*

"I'm okay, but this is weird," I tapped back, feeling my chiseled finger bite into the table.

The entire Sorgan population, down to the planet's core, stopped, turned to me, and emitted thousands of vibrations in my direction, saying, "Who are you!?"

◆

I raced across Sorgan's blistering surface like a gazelle of old Earth, dodging crevasses and traps the Sorgans sprung beneath my feet. Then, I sensed metal components standing tall ahead of me. *The coms tower!*

Left! the friendly voice called.

I leaped as the ground opened to swallow me, but a chisel erupted from below as I landed, lopping off my toe and tumbling me to the ground. Sorgans cracked through the rock, pulling themselves to the surface and surrounding me.

My turn! the dancing voice said.

My limbs went on autopilot, dancing and twirling, jabbing key points of Sorgan anatomy, dropping them to the ground in semi-paralyzed states. Then, there was nothing left between the coms tower and me. I dashed through its entry tunnel to its airlock door and input the emergency code. Several dozen Sorgans were waiting inside with chiseled fingers open like dogs bearing their teeth.

Are we going to be okay, Dancer? I thought.

Dancer? Never been called that before, Dancer said.

The analytical voice piped up, *The solar plexus is the most effective strike. It disrupts the Sorgan's entire nervous system.*

Got it! Dancer said and plunged forth.

I wish I could say we were beautiful, but the Sorgans were so many. The suit took most of their strikes. Pain shuddered through my actual thigh. I dropped to a knee. But Dancer had an answer, rotating on my kneecap, swiftly changing direction. When the last Sorgan lay on the floor, I slowly stood, pain oscillating through my leg. I entered my mental command center and searched for a pot containing *pain* but could not find one.

Anda, there's only so much you can do from there, said the commanding voice. *We're already dulling your pain as much as we can.*

I hobbled to the com tower's control terminal. Power cables had been pulled from its guts, wrapping a strange stone set unceremoniously on the floor. The reactor was offline, but a massive amount of energy, far more than fusion can generate, was coming from somewhere. *The stone?* I thought. *How can it generate such power? Why would the Sorgans need it?* The quantum system was out of commission, but the lidar was still functioning, *still on,* actually. I accessed the lidar's transmission history to discover that signals had been sent to several points in space.

Christ! They've been making calls! the bitter voice said.

But to where? said a strong one.

System Gliese, Barnard, and several more star systems I don't recognize, I responded. I focused the Tower's lidar spire upon Archangel 2 barreling towards us, still eleven years away, and opened the com. *This is Anda Kapoor-Sharpe. We're in a state of emergency. Native Sorgans have overrun us. Draconis is the only remaining colony. The Sorgans have commandeered the coms tower, making calls to several points in space for reasons unknown. See attached coordinates. Be warned, their silicon-based technology far exceeds our understanding. Their actual bodies are small carbon-based spheres residing within. I regret to say we will have perished by the time you receive this message. Prepare for war.*

Anda, the analytical voice said. *Your vocal cords are disconnected. You just sent dead air.*

Shit! I opened the lidar's telegraph and furiously tapped out the message.

The floor rumbled beneath my feet. The Tower started leaning, causing my message to miss Archangel 2. *No, that cannot happen!* I manually trained the spire as it tipped, shifting micrometers to keep its direction true. My taps played out almost in full before the angle became too steep to correct.

We gotta go! said Dancer.

I sprinted to the airlock, adrenaline and endorphins granting momentary relief from the pain. The Tower's floor buckled and heaved. Among the chaos, I felt a strange energy, something saying, *Don't forget about me!* I screeched to a halt, spun around, and ran back to the terminal.

Have you lost your mind!? the voices within me said.

Obviously! I thought back. My senses locked onto the stone, still hooked to the terminal. *No, it can't be.* I stripped the power cables from its surface and felt raw energy surge through my hand. I was so entranced that I did not notice the floor opening beneath me. I dropped into the planet's depths, the entire Coms Tower crashing upon me.

I must survive! I thought.

A rock suddenly pressed against my right foot, then another against my left, slowing my descent. More surrounded me until I was encased within an orb. My free fall stopped, but the Coms Tower did not, collapsing around my protective stone orb and knocking me side to side like the clapper of a bell. I felt Sorgan sand compacting around the orb. And then, silence. I was several kilometers beneath the surface. The energy of the strange stone was still in my hand.

What are you? I thought.

The stone awakened, its energy surging. The inside surface of the orb protecting me spasm-ed and pushed away, forming walls, floor, and ceiling. A perfect cube.

The stone's listening to me, I realized.

I suddenly felt a Sorgan digging my way. I could hear its voice saying, "You have no idea what you've done! They'll come to destroy us all! I should have never let you live!"

It's R9, I realized. I did not know what possessed me, but I lifted the energy stone to the ceiling and thought, *Harden.*

The rock above me increased in density. R9 slammed into it, sending cracks spidering above. But its chisels were still prying through.

Open shaft in the floor below, I thought, and one did. *Now, open ceiling.*

R9 dropped from above, flailing, trying to find something to grasp, and disappeared into the shaft below.

Now close.

The shaft pinched tight. But cracks soon formed on the floor. R9's fingertips poked through, and it pulled itself into my cube.

Um, what now? I thought.

I'll handle this! Dancer said and lunged, thrusting my chisel at R9's center, but the Sorgan did not evade. Instead, a foot I did not sense sank into my wounded thigh, buckling my leg, and my chisel whiffed. *Shit!* Dancer cussed and lifted my other arm to block R9's counter. Its chisels grazed my wrist, severing ligaments, and tumbling the energy stone from my grasp.

"I've spent millennia at war before coming to this planet!" R9 cried. "You may have subdued my kin, but your techniques are useless against me!" R9 went on the offensive, striking fast and direct, movements I should have easily dodged, but I was playing into its hidden, secondary strikes.

R9's exploiting blind spots in the bio-suit's sensors, I realized. *If only I had my eyes.*

I can fix that! said the analytical voice.

I felt her in the back of my mind, coalescing upon the nerve connection between my brain and the bio-suit. And then, I saw fireworks. I grazed my chisel across the suit's chest, peeling away layers of silicon flesh that blocked my eyes. An orange glow grew until I found the energy stone on the floor pulsing with light, like an ember. I saw R9's next strike coming.

Much better! Dancer said, intercepting the strike and jabbing my chisel into R9's wrist.

"You can't!" R9 cried. It lashed wildly, pressing me back against the wall.

Mirko! You must sacrifice to win! said the bitter voice.

Who's Mirko? I thought.

Me! Dancer answered. *Justin, I need your pain tolerance!*

You have it! the bitter one responded.

Dancer planted my feet as R9 struck, letting its chisel pierce my midsection. I felt my skin split, my ribs spread and snap, and my lung rupture. Green, oxygen-rich liquid spilled to the floor, swirling with the deep red of my human blood. R9's chisel burst through my back and into the stone wall behind me.

Skewered.

My body wanted to seize, but I was not in control. Dancer thrust my chisel back into R9's chest, aiming for the spore inside. But R9 twisted at the last moment, and the strike landed just outside. Nerves severed, nevertheless, and R9's entire left side dropped limp like a rag-doll.

Double skewered.

We need to get out of here! I thought. *We need the stone!* I regained control and kicked R9 from our kebab embrace. But as I stumbled towards the glowing energy stone, R9 pounced, slashing my one good wrist, and retreated with the stone in its hand, plasma oozing from its chest.

"I do not know what kind of creature you are! But you are not human! You are far too dangerous to exist!" R9 pressed the energy stone to the floor.

The ground beneath me disappeared, and again, I fell to the planet's core. I tried directing my free-fall to reach the side of the shaft, but R9 shifted its geometry, keeping me at the center.

I'm not getting out of this! I realized.

Anda, we can still sense R9, the friendly voice responded.

How can that help!?

We transfer, it said.

Wait, what!?

My sight disappeared. I was at the top of the opening with a chiseled hand pressing against the energy stone.

This is not my body, I realized.

CHAPTER SIXTEEN

Another day, maybe another story, Clara thinks, readying herself for another unpredictable session with Zion. Her LightTram slows to Albert Methane Mine Station, and when the doors open, she finds her mining crew waiting on the platform with grins on their faces. Her morning brightens. But the moment they enter the mine's entry tunnel, an unfamiliar draft puts Clara's hair on end. When they reach their usual point of separation, she finds the right vault door slightly ajar.

"Something's wrong!" She rushes forth and peers through the crack, glimpsing an upturned hand motionless on the floor beyond. She tugs at the vault door, but it will not budge.

Without question, her crew drops tools and grasps the door's edge, prying it open. Doctors and guards lay motionless on the floor, the reception desk is destroyed, and light fixtures dangle from the ceiling.

"What happened!?" a miner says, staring wide-eyed. "Are they dead!?"

Clara finds Dr. Sharon and kneels, checking her pulse. *Present but erratic.* The tissue around her neck is bruised. *A pressure strike.* "They're okay, but whoever did this is a master of Ergonos," Clara says, knowing only one man possessing such precision. "Check on the others."

The miners dash into reception to the unconscious.

When Clara presses Dr. Sharon's dislodged tracheal node back into place, the doctor's fist thrusts forward, brushing Clara's cheek. The doctor's breathing normalizes, and she slowly opens her eyes.

"What happened?" she asks.

"I was hoping you could tell us," Clara says, helping her to stand.

Dr. Sharon soaks in her surroundings. She eyes the unconscious lying on the floor. "Are they?"

"Just incapacitated, like you."

Her eyes then find the miners. "They *cannot* be here."

"We need their help to reset tracheal nodes. That's what Zion dislodged."

"Zion... was like the devil himself," Dr. Sharon whispers.

"Do you know what set him off?" Clara asks.

Dr. Sharon scrunches her brow. "He was speaking in that gibberish. When we tried to tranquilize him, he went berserk."

A trail of unconscious people leads to Zion's room. His door is clean off its hinges and buckled in two, and the legs of a chair puncture through the wall. The hologram inside is flickering with Zion's brain activity, showing what Clara expects. *Erratic... Where's Dr. Lee?* she thinks and searches his office, beneath his desk, in the closet, and then the other offices and rooms. *Nothing.* Clara approaches Dr. Sharon and the miners and guards.

"Dr. Lee is missing. This is a search and rescue mission now." Clara turns to the miners. "I need you to lead a team deeper into the mine, and keep this quiet. If you encounter Zion, do not engage."

Their eyes widen at Zion's name. They nod and quickly leave.

"Set up a search party starting outside the mine's entrance," she says to Dr. Sharon. "I would judge his departure only a few hours ago."

"What will you do, Clara?" Dr. Sharon asks.

I must prepare for the worst. "I need some things from home."

◆

Thousands of tribes-people wrapped in Martian linen emerge from a sea of tents early morning, infilling derelict ruins between market stations.

"Yah nevah cease tah amaze," says a voice Aizen has not heard for two days. Scone peers down at him with a neck so craned he resembles the bird. "Did yah know?"

Aizen shakes his head. "Is it common for off-worlders to have Martian tribal blood?"

"Not un'eard of. Yah gotta play it like yah one of de first tah immigrate. It'll make yah more believable." Scone points to a station with a raised platform. A cook in thick layers lifts a lid from the platform's boards, releasing a plume of steam, and slaps pockets of dough against the inside surface of a cauldron below. "Blood dumplin's, yah should try one," Scone says and sees Aizen's expression. "Trust me, yah don' wanna skip dis."

"But... the blood," Aizen says, his stomach tightening.

"It'll firm up on de inside, like dofu. Yah won't notice."

Dumplings begin to fall from the cauldron's inner surface, splashing into the oil and sizzling. The cook plunges a long bamboo ladle to fish them out. More dumplings drop, and the cook frantically tries to keep up, every free second slapping more uncooked dumplings to the cauldron's side. An assembly line forms: one person mixing dough, another rolling it out, a third filling with a blood-veggie mix, and a fourth pinching pockets and tossing them to the cook. A young girl at the end pats the dumplings dry and arrays them along the platform's edge for sale.

Scone makes a gesture. She hands him two dumplings. Then her eyes find Aizen and hold.

He averts his gaze, hoping she does not recognize him. "What tribe is this from?" Aizen asks.

"De Sorga tribe." Scone bites the corner of his dumpling, its pastry-like crust crumbling and red juices flowing, and he sucks with eagerness. "Dat's just what I needed. Be careful, it's 'ot."

Aizen breathes deeply. *This is why you came,* he reminds himself and nibbles the corner of his dumpling. Liquid oozes upon his tongue, tasting of iron and spice. Strangely, he does not feel repulsed. He bites through the crust and firmed blood inside, burning the roof of his mouth, but he cannot stop. His morning fogginess fades. He feels ready for the day ahead.

"Yah ah true Martian," Scone says.

Something feels strange. "Blood dumplings are not a Martian cuisine," Aizen says.

"Dat's right," says the young girl, eyes wide. "Many of System Centauri's early settlahs immigrated back tah System Sol durin' de Sorgan War. Dey settled on Mars, bringin' dese dumplin's wid dem."

Aizen feels nauseous. "Is this *human* blood?"

She shakes her head. "Sheep blood. We leech dem every mornin'."

Aizen sighs with relief and looks to Scone. "What's next?"

From one station to another, they sample, each taste new. The sun rises high, then dips low in the chartreuse sky. At the center of Aang, they stumble upon a group of children sitting on the ground in lotus positions, eyes closed and breathing deeply.

"What are they doing?" Aizen asks.

"Ah, yes," Scone says. "Every year, children from across Mars, ones rumored tah 'ave de gift, gather 'ere fah choosin'. At de end of Shakoperan, ah chosen child must travel tah Pouhallah durin' de storm, alone."

"The gift?" Aizen asks.

"Some Martians can see in ways nobody else can. Can access memories from previous lifetimes. But we 'ave not found ah child in almost ah century dat 'as successfully made de journey."

"What's at Pouhallah?" Aizen asks.

Scone shrugs. "Only dose wid de gift know."

A chill sets in late afternoon. Scone finds a break in the main street and descends a tight alleyway with Aizen in tow. Market stations become barbershops, tailor-seamstress shops, and the like. Signage changes from Interspeak to local languages, with a few words in ancient English. Families huddle around heatcubes, some laughing, others engrossed in storytelling and cooking dinners.

Scone turns to Aizen. "Dese people live 'ere permanently. It best tah only speak when spoken tah and never look dem in de eye."

Aizen nods. The tight alleyway opens to a five-meter circle with nearly a hundred people packed inside rooms beyond thin veils. Aizen hears a sudden shuffle behind him. *They blocked the way out,* he realizes. Tall figures emerge from the veils, encircling him. *The sunflower brothers.*

Aizen sighs. "Scone, why?"

"Don' take it personally," Scone says, patting Aizen's wavy hair. "Yah 'ave ah 'igh price on yah 'ead. Jus' do as dey say and 'ave yah family pay de ransom."

Aizen spins to meet a sunflower brother blocking the way out, wearing a scowl. *It's the one I kicked in the balls.*

"I would love tah see yah get out of dis one!" the sunflower says.

Aizen searches for an escape. Instead, his eyes find a girl peering from behind the veils, the one who sold him dumplings. *I've met her before, too,* he realizes. *The girl from the grass, Emma.*

Sorry, Emma mouths.

Aizen bolts, trying to slip past the brothers. But pain lances the side of his head, and he drops to the ground. His eyesight fades.

My turn, comes a whisper from deep within.

◆

Jonathan stands, frozen by fear, staring at an obsidian face without features. *This creature should be extinct.*

"You're not listening to me," the creature says.

"I," Jonathan tries to say, but his mind is racing. "I don't understand. How did you get here?"

"We have similar questions for you."

"Jonathan," Angela calls in. "You're late. Is everything okay?"

He does not respond.

"Jonathan, do you read!?" Angela says urgently.

"Angela, I read you. I... discovered what moved the benches in Vincent's Plaza."

"Really? We'll come meet you."

"Just don't freak out when you arrive."

Angela, Vincent, and Hazel stand at the edge of Vincent's Plaza, staring at Jonathan and the creature.

"It's all right, you can come over," Jonathan says.

They inch forth as if crossing treacherous ice.

"A Sorgan," Hazel squeaks. "Are you going to kill us?"

"Of course not, we are allies," the creature says.

"Allies? But you went extinct centuries ago," Hazel says.

"It was orchestrated to appear that way."

"Who would orchestrate such a thing?" Jonathan asks.

"I cannot answer your questions until we know your intentions. But you may address me as XT47692."

"We?" Hazel says.

XT waves a hand. More dark creatures emerge from several streets around the plaza. They sit upon stone benches effortlessly moved to the plaza's center. Jonathan slowly approaches, taking a seat on one of the benches. Angela, Vincent, and Hazel timidly follow.

"The environment is more than adequate for your anatomy. You do not require suits," XT says.

Jonathan unclasps his helmet, letting it roll back. He takes an apprehensive breath. "Allow me to introduce First Class Archaeologists Angela Mendez and Vincent Hung, and Archaeologist in Training Hazel Cordon," he says, trying to remain calm. "My name in Jonathan Zaid, leader of this expedition."

Another Sorgan speaks. "Jonathan, I am ZR89663, caretaker of city 0143, once called Moscow. It is a pleasure to meet a human. You are smaller than I imagined."

"You've never met humans before?" Jonathan asks.

"A few of us have from a more difficult time. It is why we must know your intentions," XT says.

Jonathan breathes deeply. "We were trying to reach London to recover lost human history, but found a way into Paris, instead."

"Then it was you who was struck by the heat discharge," another says.

Jonathan clenches his jaw. "Our dear friend was lost in the event. Why did you blast us?"

"The tunnels open and close in a specific sequence to transfer heat out of the cities. When you opened the seal at the shoreline it created an imbalance in the system, resulting in a significant amount of superheated air to discharge out of sequence. I am sorry for the loss of your friend, but London's rehabilitation suffered greatly as well."

"What's your goal with the cities?" Angela asks.

The Sorgans turn her way.

"To rebuild them of course," XT says. "This is why you humans allow us to exist... You do not know this?"

Jonathan shakes his head.

"It explains why they're drilling the domes," says another. "They were never told."

"Never told what?" Jonathan says.

"Two centuries ago there was a deal made with your greatest leader. He granted us sanctuary upon your home-world when all other species were hunting us. In exchange, we were tasked with nursing Earth's ecosystems back to health and rebuilding its once great cities."

"We don't know of this deal," Jonathan says.

XT appears to realize something. "How did you find the tunnels, then? As a human, you cannot detect them."

Jonathan presses his lips tight. "Zion Wright, Supreme Minister of the Council of Colonies, made paintings of the WorldRing entry point along the English shoreline to guide us."

Vincent, Angela, and Hazel snap their heads to him.

The Sorgans straighten their postures. "The One still lives!"

CHAPTER SEVENTEEN

In the back of the attic, stored safely within its case, is Clara's infantry gear. She inputs her code into the case's lock, hears a sigh, and lifts its lid. *Twenty-five years,* she thinks, running a hand across old creases, worn joints, and scars earned in training. The armor auto-loosens to accommodate her current curvature when she slips it on. *Well, what did I expect?* She holsters two stun pistols and heat blades and secures her short, mid, and long-range optical scopes to her chest plate. Clara feels ready for the task at hand, until she pulls her helmet from the case and a card tumbles from within, "Clara," written on its face.

No, no, no! Her adrenaline surges. She slowly opens its fold.

"Happy hunting. -Zion-"

She rubs her thumb against the calligraphy. The ink smudges. *He was just here!* She pulls on her helmet and activates her cloak, disappearing from view. She flips through optical modes until the outlines of Zion's footprints appear, leading to the attic ladder. His steps continue through her apartment, out the front door, descend the egress stairs to the alleyway between buildings, and into the ring road around Tempest City's basin. The prints disappear into Caldone Reserve's bamboo forest beyond the road.

Clara studies the city below, imagining Dione viewing the basin centuries ago when it was all agriculture. *You can do this...*

Clara plunges into the forest following a trail Jonathan and Aizen use on their fishing trips during simulation spring when the water is high and fish are migrating. Now, in simulation summer, the riverbed is a muddy red scar. She follows Zion's footprints onto the mud, where they scatter about. It takes Clara a moment to realize they are forming symbols.

"Oh," she whispers. *It's ancient English.*

Her visor deciphers the symbols, translating to, *"No cloaks."*

The tracks suddenly stop, as if Zion had disappeared. *Or he's in his own cloak and standing right in front of me!* Clara widens her stance, preparing for his ambush, when the ground beneath her shifts. *The Sorgans!* she thinks, but no shaft opens below. *No... This is just mud,* she realizes, now waist-deep in it. She redistributes her weight, laying her torso upon the surface, slowly pulling herself up, and rolling to firmer ground. *Not much of a trap,* she thinks, then studies her armor covered in mud from head to toe, becoming a bright orange beacon in a green forest. No matter how vigorously she wipes, it only smudges. She had trained for a multitude of electrical disruptions, reflection inhibitors, and anti-cloaking devices. *But never mud.*

She looks at the footprints spelling, *"No cloaks."*

It will be just that, she realizes and strips off her armor plating to find the clay had seeped into every nook and cranny of her envisuit and helmet, too. *Down to my magsuit, it is.* Clara removes her envisuit and helmet. The air holds the scent of woodland decay and something acidic, familiar.

"Coffee," Zion's voice whispers in the wind.

Clara whirls, searching for its origin. *I must move!* From one vantage point to another, she creeps, distributing weight evenly to reduce the sound of her steps, rolling on the blades of her feet to mask her prints, and cutting visual angles from one tree to the next. She keeps her eyes focused ahead, ears focused to the sides, and sets seismometers in her wake.

She stops and delicately lays on her stomach, her mid-range scope resting upon its tripod, its butt against her shoulder like a rifle, and sends lidar to measure distance and environmental conditions. She searches meter by meter and locks onto one of her seismometers left behind, registering the vibrations of rodents and birds picking grubs from logs. She pans to the highest point of the basin's crest, where she imagines Dione and Decan climbed a millennia ago. A swaying of white, like a pendulum, comes into view. She discerns a cloth texture with embroidery spelling, *"Dr. L..."*

"Dr. Lee!" Clara says louder than she intends.

Eolian rustles come in the wind, and she lifts her head from her scope. A flickering gray object registers from her peripheral, crashing against her scope, shattering its lens, and bending it into an *L* shape. Her hands go numb from the impact, and she rolls behind a massive bamboo trunk for cover. *What the hell was that!?* She sees a rock settle among the broken pieces of her state-of-the-art scope.

More eolian rustles come. Stones sink into the bamboo around her, splintering trunks like explosive rounds. She curls into a ball, covering her ears and closing her eyes. Her hands violently shake. Then, as suddenly as the bombardment comes, it stops.

Clara breathes deeply. Her trembling reduces. She pulls her two stun pistols from their holsters and connects them, one in front of the other, making a rifle, the combined energy quadrupling its effective range, and attaches her long-range scope and tripod. She rolls from the bamboo trunk onto her stomach, searching through her scope. *Nothing. Nothing.* Then, she finds lifeless eyes and an expressionless face. She zooms out to see Zion in his majestic glory. Tall, statuesque, not even attempting to hide. *Target acquired.* She estimates range, gives herself scope corrections, and reads the up-drafting wind from the basin.

"I've got you," she whispers. *Send it!*

But as Clara pulls the trigger, she hears a metallic ping. The barrel cracks, and electricity racks through her like a taser. She drops the rifle and rolls in agony. A pebble falls from its splintered barrel.

More rustles.

Shit! Not now! With numb hands, Clara fumbles for her blades, yanking them from their sheaths and activating their heat edges. Zion's volley makes landfall. Her body feels like rubber, and she dodges like a drunkard. A rock hurtles towards her, filling her entire field of vision. She raises her blade by sheer reaction, slicing it in two, deflecting the halves. She ducks and deflects, slowly regaining feeling in her arms until, at last, the bombardment ceases.

"Very good!" Zion calls in the wind.

Clara rolls back to the safety of her trunk. *This is only rocks!* She cannot imagine facing Zion in his prime and fully armed. She peers across the ridge toward Dr. Lee but cannot find him without her scope.

She moves forward, each step full of distrust, feeling powerless.

"But power is only perception," she whispers, remembering Zion's words of wisdom. "Contrast is my ally." She stabs a heat blade into a tree, sending wisps of smoke into the air. *That's the beacon. Now, I must become invisible.* She sits upon the leaves, slowly breathing her Ergonos breathes, lowering her pulse. She presses a thumb deep into the tissue of her hips and left shoulder, knocking them out, leaving only her right arm awake. *Now sleep.* She breathes less. Her jaw goes slack. Her eyes see nothing. The thumping of her heart nearly stops.

Flutterings of birds come and go. Rodents searching for nuts walk across her lap. Crunching leaves beneath hooves and paws pass by. Then, finally, she recognizes a bipedal cadence. *He's not far, near the tree.* She presses her thumb into her left shoulder, reactivating it, sending pins and needles from shoulder to fingertips, then reconnects her hips. She hears her blade pull from the tree, and its mild hum cease.

"Clara," Zion gently whispers. "You're doing great."

That's Mermer speaking! she realizes.

His voice changes. "Where are you? It's safe now."

Don't be fooled. Clara does not move a muscle.

"How is she hiding!?" Zion spits with anger. "Shoonter sabbander!"

Those words are Sorgan, Clara recognizes, not just from Anda's tale, but from Jonathan long ago, studying for his Extinct Languages final.

As the wind picks up, the bamboo trees sway and groan, and their leaves rustle. Clara slowly stands and dares a step. One becomes two, which becomes more. She nears the basin's edge, where an updraft brushes her face. She wakes her eyes. The sun is low. *Several hours have elapsed,* she realizes and turns to find Zion next to her, facing the basin with eyes shut.

He slowly rotates her way and opens his eyes. "*Very* good, Clara," he says. "But not good enough."

"Why are you doing this?" Clara asks. Her heart rate climbs, and her breathing escalates.

"You wouldn't understand," he says.

"Why not?"

Zion's face is cold and heartless. Then, as if someone flips a switch, it softens. "Dr. Lee doesn't have much time."

"Shut up!" Zion jerks his head from side to side.

"You're falling apart," Clara says.

Zion flicks his wrist, hurtling her knife, but his arm jerks just before release, and the blade grazes Clara's cheek, instead.

Zion twists his head. "Run, Clara," he says with a helpless look. "I cannot hold *It* back much longer."

Clara bolts into the forest towards Dr. Lee, feeling Zion's footsteps gaining on her. She can smell his coffee breath. *He's right on my tail!*

Clara glimpses a lone oak tree among the bamboo, swerves that way, and runs straight into its massive trunk at full speed, pressing her hands against the bark to absorb her inertia and deflecting to the side. Zion's hand glides millimeters by her head, shaped like a blade. His fingertips contact the tree. She expects them to snap and for Zion to reel in pain. Instead, they melt past bark into hardwood, his arm swallowing elbow-deep. Splinters explode from the backside. The impact sends Clara to the ground. Zion wrenches his arm from the trunk. There is not the slightest scuff or scrape.

Run, you idiot! Clara scrambles, slipping and sliding on the leaves. *You must be calm!* She takes Ergonos breaths as she runs, but Zion is gaining fast.

A white swaying comes from the trees ahead. *Dr. Lee!* But when she pivots that way, something catches her leg. She glances down to find Zion's hand cupping the instep of her kicked-back foot, lifting it higher, tilting her body weight forward, sending her face to the ground. *Momentum is your friend!* Instead of smashing face-first into the dirt, Clara curls, letting the back of her shoulders take the impact, rolling like a wheel, and returning to her feet. She continues her momentum, sending her heel upward to meet Zion's granite jaw. Searing pain shoots through her foot and her knee hyper-extends. But she hears a grunt, and Zion momentarily stops.

"Good one, Clara!" he groans, followed by. "Shut up!"

Clara limps to Dr. Lee hanging from the tree. *Not by his neck. Thank Sol!* She unties the rope, guides his gentle fall, massages around his trachea, and pushes the node back into place.

Again, eolian rustles come in the wind.

I cannot dodge without Dr. Lee being struck! Clara raises her elbows to block, instead. The stone sinks into the sleeve of her magsuit. Its titanium weave holds, but the impact numbs her right arm from elbow to fingertips. Clara holds her elbow, rocking back and forth. *Definitely fractured!*

"Clara..." Dr. Lee moans, reaching into his pocket and pulling three cartridges with stability tails. "Tranq...uilizers..."

She fixates on the tranquilizer darts and breathes deeply. *They require two seconds to deliver their contents,* she knows, having used them during training scenarios.

Zion comes charging.

With her functioning arm, she snatches the stone that struck her, palms one of Dr. Lee's tranquilizers, and throws them together at Zion. He swats the stone away like a joke, but the tranquilizer sinks into his wrist. He stops, staring at it blankly, then rips it out.

Did it deliver? Clara wonders.

Zion presses fingers into his shoulder, locking down his brachial artery and stopping blood flow, and resumes his charge.

Pain radiates through Clara's heel. *How can I fight like this!?* She studies the two remaining tranquilizers in her hand. *The first eighth is a pain killer, so a target won't notice the rest injecting.* She jabs herself in the heel and elbow for a micro-second. The pain nearly vanishes.

She strafes away from Dr. Lee, finally having a good look at Zion. His movement is incredible, his precision mind-boggling, but something is off. *This is not Ergonos. It's Sorgan,* she realizes. *Can Ergonos beat Sorgan?* Her gut says, *yes.*

Clara turns to meet Zion's fury head-on.

His expression is frozen, but his body language screams with surprise. His knife hand launches forward to disconnect Clara's head, but she sees his foot rising behind. *The actual strike.*

Clara thrusts her good forearm across her body, tensing her buttocks, channeling power from her feet, through her core, and into the blade of her ulna, all the while thinking about Mirko sparring Kota and how he used his elbow against her foot. *A block with the intent to break!* Clara's ulna sinks into the weak side of Zion's incoming wrist, and she feels a crick. The form of his knife hand melts, and the kick, intended for her stomach, aborts. Clara drives her heel into Zion's toes the instant his foot meets the ground.

For the first time in centuries, the super-soldier stumbles without grace, tumbling to the dirt. Clara jabs the second tranquilizer into his back. He quickly regains his footing, wildly swinging, completely whiffing. But just when Clara feels she has the advantage, Zion's limp, tranquilizer-filled arm strikes the side of her head, chattering her teeth.

He is standing still when Clara clears her head. His breathing calms and his muscles relax. *He's transitioning to Ergonos,* she realizes. He presses into his shoulder, reopening the blood flow of his drugged arm, allowing the serum to course through his veins. But he does not waver or wobble. *He lowered his heart rate,* Clara knows. *The serum will take minutes instead of seconds to reach his brain.*

Zion does not attack with aggression but with a saunter and sway, his movements holding a strange timing. His hand closes in, and Clara goes for an intercept strike, but she moves too quickly and misses. His index finger pokes her elbow, putting her arm to sleep.

Push the counterpoint! Clara presses the other side of her elbow to release the lockdown. But as she does so, Zion's toe nudges her inner thigh, dropping Clara to a knee. When she reactivates her leg, Zion turns off her right shoulder. When she reactivates her right shoulder, he turns off her left foot. Again and again, he pokes, and Clara desperately tries to keep up.

Zion brushes the underside of her chin.

Clara's tongue goes limp and slides down her throat. She gags, coughing it out as several points up her back are hit, putting her core muscles to sleep. She falls limp to the leaves. With her functioning hand, she pushes against the ground to roll onto her back and presses a thumb under her chin, reactivating her tongue.

Zion straddles her, placing a gentle hand behind her head like an infant. "Clara, I'm sorry, but R9 has complete control," he gently says.

"Will it hurt?" Clara manages to say.

"You will only sleep."

Clara closes her eyes and breathes deeply, thinking about Jonathan and Aizen, and knows she cannot give up. *But what can I do!?*

"Zion!" comes a magnificent battle cry.

Clara snaps open her eyes to see a fury of white lab coat and blue scrubs, holding a stethoscope like a whip in one hand and a rock in the other.

Zion faces Dr. Lee, rendering him unconscious with ease.

That's when Clara sees it, the holy grail of pressure points, deep within the muscular cords of Zion's turned neck, begging to be poked. She extends her index finger knuckle, like squeezing a trigger, and thrusts it deep into his neck.

His pulse goes into a frenzy.

Zion snaps his head back to her. "No! How did you—!?" he hollers, about to send the final blow, but slumps to the ground, instead, the quickening of his pulse sending the tranquilizer to his brain.

♦

They peer from behind veils like Aizen is a monster or a god. His eyes are adjusting to the twilight. His head pounds. Emma stares with her mouth agape, surrounded by her unconscious brothers. Aizen is on his feet but does not remember standing. His knuckles ache.

"What happened?" he groans.

"*Yah* happened," says an old woman. She parts a veil, stepping into the circle and over unconscious kin. "Dank yah for goin' easy on dem." She turns to Emma. "Revive dem."

Emma scrambles to her brothers, checking their condition and pressing into their necks.

"I don't understand," Aizen says, rubbing his knuckles.

"But I do," the woman says, kneeling to his height and taking his hands in hers. "It is gonna be okay. It is not yah fault."

"What's not my fault?" Aizen says.

She embraces him, breathing deeply. "Yah mus' be 'ungry." She parts a veil obscuring a wooden door that opens to a stone house with a central fire beneath a large circular stone. She leads him to the stone. "Dis is ah special dish, passed down from de most ancient Martian line."

"Injera," Aizen whispers.

She retrieves a clay pitcher and pours batter onto the stone, spiraling with surgical precision. After a few injera cook through, she prepares lentils and green stews.

"I believe yah familiar wid dis," she says.

Aizen's mouth waters. He tears a piece of injera, using it to scoop the lentils, and is about to try when something nags. He raises the injera to the woman, instead.

"Very good," she says and takes a bite. She then lifts injera for Aizen.

He relishes the spiciness, flavor, and texture. It's just how he imagined it would be.

"'Ow did yah know where tah find me?" she asks.

Aizen cocks his head. "I wasn't looking for you."

Her smile dwindles. "What were yah searchin' for, den?"

"I just felt like I needed to come to Mars."

"But yah were searchin' for injera, right?"

"I was," Aizen says, realizing he knows nothing about this woman. He has no idea how he went from *hostage* to *honored guest*. "Who are you?"

"Dat is not important. Dere is someding yah must do."

"I appreciate the injera, but I don't have to do anything," Aizen says. "You should let me go."

"Yah are free tah go, but yah still must do someding," she insists.

"Why?"

"It is de reason yah came tah Mars, wheder yah realize it or not." She turns to the darkness beyond the firelight. "Emma, I know yah dere. Reveal yahself, child."

The girl steps from the shadows, giving Aizen an uneasy glance.

"Yah must 'elp Aizen learn de way of de desert," the woman says. "Aye will be journeyin' tah Pouhallah."

Emma's eyes widen.

Clara's left foot is in a compression boot, her right arm is in an *L* brace, and countless scrapes and bruises riddle her body and face. She hobbles to a solid woman in heavy impact armor with captain stripes on her collar at Zion's holding facility entrance. Two more guards stand beyond the captain with eyes fixating upon the vault door, each within exo-rigs, making them several times stronger but slower. Clara faces the retinal scanner, and her information appears.

The captain gasps. "You're the one. And with no armor. How?"

"Zion showed his carotid sinus bifurcation point," Clara says.

"Who would have guessed Zion was an Ergonos practitioner, and a hundred and sixty-eighth Dawn no less. But I suppose even the best of us make mistakes." The captain surveys Clara's injuries. "Looks like you made several."

Clara is tired of the quips, hearing them all from the mining crew on her way in. "Has Dr. Lee recovered?"

The captain nods and activates the vault door. The guards lift stun rifles and crouch, looking about to infiltrate an enemy vessel. Clara enters to see more guards positioned around the perimeter of Reception and doctors wearing neck braces. They give Clara respectful glances as she hobbles to Dr. Lee's office.

She finds him engrossed in Zion's brain scans and analyzing the gibberish he spoke. He's not wearing his neck brace.

"Dr. Lee, how are you?" Clara asks.

He turns her way. "I've been better. Come look at this," he waves her over. "I think you're right. His gibberish may be a language. The only question is, which?"

"Sorgan," Clara says flatly.

He pauses. "What makes you think that?"

Clara opens Jonathan's ancient languages translator program on holotile. Dr. Lee plays a recording of Zion pacing back and forth in his room.

"But we are part of each other," Zion suddenly says to the wall.

"Godoomian kanwennner shidoogigan!" he shouts at himself.

"No! I've found a way to free myself of you humans!" Clara's holotile translates.

"But we've achieved such great things, brought peace to the galaxy, we did this *together*," Zion responds.

"Zoonteska joontersa!" he again shouts.

"As your prisoner!" translates.

"You're not a prisoner. We are equals," Zion argues.

"Forgoonteri paratoonik hooond? Lunidooger poodinaser shidoogigan! Doodinaser faalsefit!" *"Equals? You disgust me! You invaded my body! I will destroy you all! Destroy this peace you built upon a lie!"*

This peace built upon a lie? Clara thinks about that.

"We cannot allow that! We'll stop you!" Zion says, his body shaking.

"Shuntabbii yuundigooner willoonus!" *"Let's see who is stronger!"*

Zion picks up his chair, sending it across the room.

"This is when we decided to tranquilize him," Dr. Lee says as several guards come through the door.

Zion laughs, "Chantiineel shidoogigan! Doogidan leesideel!" *"Pathetic humans! Let me show you my strength!"*

Dr. Lee stares at the translation. "Clara, what in Sol is going on?"

♦

Zion splays upon a table where his bed once was, his limbs locked down by thick Siclecell titanium bands at each joint, and his hands and feet within immobility vaults. Ten guards in exo-rigs stand across the room as a physician in armor watches his vitals.

His eyes open as Clara nears. He turns his head away.

"You look like shit," she says.

A single tear trickles across the bridge of Zion's nose.

Clara looks at the physician. "What's his condition?"

"He's neither spoken nor eaten since we revived him," the physician says. "His vitals are dropping and he's rapidly shedding muscle mass. This must be the final stage of gene degradation."

"May I be with him, alone?" Clara asks.

The physician shakes her head. "The guards must stay."

Clara clenches her jaw and hobbles to the guards. "If Zion were to get out of his restraints, you could not stop him anyway. I need the room."

"Sorry ma'am, we cannot do that," one responds.

"She's right," Zion says quietly.

The guards snap in his direction and raise rifles.

"To *infinity* and *beyond*," Zion says in ancient English.

"Voice activation initiated! Awaiting command!" the exo-rigs respond. In unison, they go stiff as control is taken from the guards.

"Please, excuse yourselves from the room," Zion commands.

"Affirmative!" The exo-rigs march out the door single file. The guards

within feebly squirm against their exo-rigs' movement, frantically shouting, but their coms are muted.

The physician stares in shock.

"Clara asked for the room," Zion calmly says to her.

She finds her feet and flees.

Six months ago I would have been terrified by this display of power, Clara thinks, hobbling to the door and closing. She turns to Zion. "What's happening to you?"

"I'm dying," he says.

"But why so suddenly?"

"Dr. Lee was close with his diagnosis. What I have is called Kaladian Gene Degradation, a rare side effect from the genetic experimentation by the Hermians before The Fall. My father succumbed to the ailment when I was a child, but the galaxy believes he died in a shuttle accident. A necessary lie. He would not let genetic prejudice ruin my prospects before knowing if the condition had passed on to me. I began showing symptoms as a teenager, nevertheless. But where my father died young, I did not, for R9 and Kwai Lan have been continually repairing my genetic code, greatly enhancing it, in fact." Zion sighs. "But now, R9 refuses to help, letting my disease finally take its toll."

"Who's in control of you right now?" Clara asks.

"This is I, Zion Wright."

"Zion. I know this is a lot to ask of you, but I must speak with R9. I must know what happened, from its perspective."

"R9 will not heed your words," Zion says. "It's mind is fractured beyond repair."

"Please, Zion. I only want to listen. I must know about, *Doodinaser Faalsefit,*" Clara says in slow, awkward Sorgan.

Zion's expression fades to stone.

"This peace, built upon a lie!" R9 hisses.

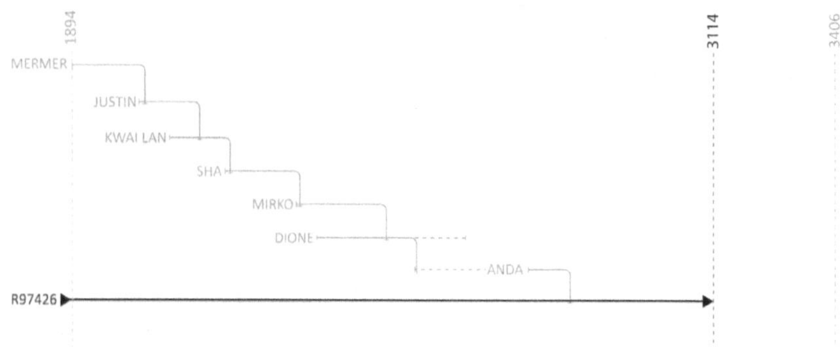

R97426's TALE

Milky Way Galaxy: Unknown – 3114

I knew exactly how I came into the galaxy, how every cell of my being was manufactured to contain the information of an individual, what you silly humans called a *soul.*

I bound several of these souls to imaginary chairs within my mental construct. Such children they were, thinking they could enter my consciousness unnoticed. But I was impressed they tried. We did not know humans had such an ability. *Six silly humans souls... and a crustacean?* This one confused me.

I approached the human I knew. "The formidable Anda, possessing the strength and knowledge of several lifetimes," I said. "Do you have anything to say for yourself?"

Anda seemed unable to form words.

"He hasn't learned how to communicate yet," said a mysterious woman bound beside him. "The first transfer is difficult."

"But you appear unfazed, which means you've transferred before. Who are you?" I asked.

She became silent.

"No matter, I do not need your words." I placed a hand atop Anda's head. He struggled to shake free. "Be still, Anda. I only want to look. I shall not meddle." I imagined an additional restraint across his forehead, holding him down, then turned the pages of his memory like reading a book in reverse, *a metaphor your simple minds can comprehend.*

"So much pain was caused. By us, by me," I said, but I did not feel guilty for what we did to the settlers. Anda's story finished as a young child playing with stuffed toys. "Anda, you had such passion. But you do not possess the ability to transfer consciousness."

I turned to the mysterious woman next to him and raised my hand. She did not struggle. Instead, she sat back with a grin. The pages of her story were meticulously organized. *Impressive,* I thought. Her name was Dione.

"What tragedy you've seen. You brought humanity back from the brink of extinction."

She nodded with a sort of dreadful pride.

I moved to the next human soul, one called Mirko, but had to stop midway through his story to regain my composure.

"We're stronger than you know," he said, with his eyes burning.

"I can sense that." I again placed my hand on his head. His pain lessened as I reached his childhood. "Mirko. The great child of war. I see that it was you I was fighting in the end."

The next woman looked through me, hauntingly so. *She must be the one.* Sha's story ended spectacularly, and as I went backward, I felt such accomplishment. And then, the teff.

"I understand why our tampering of your crops did not work. You had the mother of grain guiding you," I said. I sensed so much love despite moments of incredible loss. The beginning of Sha's story proved just as spectacular as the end. "You've led a great life. But you are not the one."

Next was a brilliant geneticist who made the first step towards bio-immortality, a step my own species made millions of years ago. But her accomplishments were lost during The Fall. Kwai Lan bore incredible loss like the others, connecting them in a manner difficult for me to comprehend. *Perhaps trauma is the key,* I thought. I then felt another connection, one of love and joy. *Of Mother cooking dimsum…*

I pulled my hand away. *Kwai Lan is selectively showing me memories,* I realized. *I'm not entirely in control.*

"Cuisine? Is that it?" I asked her.

"Must there be anything more?" she said.

I turned to the last human soul, possessing such anger. He was so thin and frail, yet somehow enduring. *Justin. Is he the one?* I hesitated.

"Don't tell me you're afraid," Justin said.

"My species does not know fear," I responded, but that was untrue.

"Allow me to educate you, then," he leaned forward, almost taunting me.

When I touched his head, all his memories spilled into me at once. *Pain, hunger, betrayal, addiction, fear, FEAR!* I reeled back, holding my trembling hand, his emotions still circulating through me. *This poor soul.* I wanted to embrace him, to tell him everything will be okay. *But he will devour me with his pain,* I knew.

"You have shown me fear," I said. "But you are not the one. None of you are the one."

I turned to the crustacean. *What are you?* I thought.

The creature looked at me and said, "...What are *you?*"

I jolted. *It can hear my thoughts?* "You mimic, but do you comprehend?"

The little creature cocked its armored head. "Ironic that a being such as yourself should underestimate a creature such as I," It said and opened its claw to the restraints holding it down.

"It is useless. My bindings are indestructible," I said.

The creature snipped through with ease.

"Wait, you cannot do that!" I protested. "This is *my* construct!"

It reached for the second restraint and snipped through.

"No! You cannot be the one!" but as those words escaped me, I realized this little creature was the key. I imagined more restraints, but the creature strafed left and right, impossible to anticipate. Then, it hopped off the chair and scurried into the white depths of my construct. *Why had I not imagined walls!?* I chased after the creature, raising barriers, but it squeezed between the gaps. In desperation, I imagined the floor was slick and tilted up so the creature would slide back. It was working, and the crustacean came to rest at my feet. "That was a good trick with the restraints, but you cannot escape."

"Escape?" the creature said, tapping a claw against the floor, seemingly testing its solidity. "What makes you think I'm trying to escape?"

My construct is too quiet... I turned to the human souls bound in their chairs to find them missing. *No, no, no!* I whirled back to the little creature to find it, too, had disappeared.

Of all the words from a thousand languages I had learned, a human one described my feelings best. "Fuck..."

♦

I have never known peace. My species hunted since the beginning of time. All because of a misunderstanding. Or a lack of compassion.

I am not sure why.

I first propagated on planet ALX 427 in System Cardone, 10,347 years before the Arkathy arrived. Yet, by the time my limbs and organs had developed, based upon the data gathered by my spore during hibernation, the Arkathy began their extensive mining operations, collecting embers to power the lavish cities of their home worlds. We woke to the Arkathy burning us alive, learning to breathe, move, and sense the world on the run, stumbling like newborn Earth mammals.

"Root out the Infestation!" the Arkathy would shout.

We launched our spores into interstellar winds to drift to another suitable planet moments before they turned us to ash.

We landed upon Farcist 54 of System Bjornian. And again, my spore collected data and nutrients from the soil around me. I woke from hibernation, reunited with my brothers and sisters. But our bodies were different this time, our legs many, and our organs strange. The only consistency was that our hands were sharp, and our feet sensed the world. We dug meticulous tunnels and chambers for several thousand years before we felt vibrations familiar from a lifetime ago on the surface. Which meant only one thing.

The Arkathy have arrived.

"They won't dig, they don't know we're here," our elders said.

I was not so optimistic. "This is how it began last time. They *will* dig, they *will* come."

"You have much to learn. The Arkathy will not dig," the elders insisted.

The Arkathy began to dig.

"We must stop them! This is *our* home!" I said.

"This is not our home. Nothing belongs to us," the elders responded.

"The Arkathy don't know that," I said. "They're here to take the embers, they will kill this planet!"

"They will not make the same mistake again," the elders said.

"Destroying ALX 427 wasn't a mistake! That was their *goal!*" I argued.

"Young one, you do not know. Be quiet," the elders ordered.

The Arkathy eventually broke through the tunnels of our labyrinth.

"The Infestation is here!" they cried in raspy voices. "Find them! Destroy them!"

"They admit their intentions!" I said to the elders. "We must strike first!"

"We will wait for them to leave," they said, refusing to engage.

But many of my kin were beginning to agree with me.

"We will help you, but we do not know how to fight," they said.

I thought about this. "But the Arkathy do not recognize us." *And how could they? Our bodies were so different, adapted for Farcist now.*

We crawled along the ceiling of our tunnels like Earth's spiders, delicately reaching down to separate Arkathy nerve centers from their bodies with our chiseled fingers, starting from the back so that those at the front would not notice until it was too late. And we could not let their organic material go to waste, recycling their bodies to birth more of us. But when the Arkathy found our decomposition chambers, filled with their comrades' dissolving bodies, their firestorms returned.

"You made the fire come back!" the elders accused. "You must fix this!"

We could not communicate with the Arkathy, for they could not detect our speech. Instead, we came with a peace offering, one the elders said would be understood. We dragged the bodies of fallen Arkathy soldiers and dropped them at the Arkathy's feet. I peeled muscle from the dead bodies, raising the flesh to my mandibles for consumption, then presented some for the Arkathy to eat.

Sharing food, I thought. *Yes, this should work.*

The Arkathy shrieked in horror and stuck their incinerators in our faces. But the flames enveloping us did not hurt.

Our spores remembered the firestorms on ALX 427 and factored them into our new bodies, I realized. *We are fireproof!*

"War it is!" I cried.

Thousands of us let our deep roars fly, rumbling the ground beneath the Arkathy's feet. We swarmed through the firestorm, severing heads as we went, rushing from the planet's depths to the surface and driving the Arkathy to their ships, where their vibrations disappeared.

◆

The spores of our kin, from far away parts of space, landed on Farcist's surface, and we raced to collect and grow them into our forms. They woke from hibernation, studying their new bodies with curiosity.

"Such a different planet this is. But I sense you have the same trouble," one said.

"What do you mean?" I asked.

"A species came to Thoravia in search of its embers, driving us from the planet's skies using storms of fire. Only us few escaped."

"Was it the Arkathy?" I asked.

"What are the Arkathy?"

I showed them the bodies of our enemy.

They reeled in terror. "Yes, it was the Arkathy."

We sent emissary spores in all directions, trying to spread the word. *The Arkathy are not to be trusted.* Several millennia later, when they returned, we learned the extent of our plight. The Arkathy were present in nearly every system, mining for embers and spreading poisonous words upon local species, forcing them to join their empire. But whenever they encountered our kind, they aimed for our annihilation instead, not once attempting to communicate.

We were called names in thousands of languages by thousands of species. But their meanings were the same. *Infestation.*

"I don't understand," I said to my kin. "We propagated on each of these planets long before their arrival. We were first."

Little by little, the Arkathy found ways to eradicate us. All we could do was throw our spores to the winds, hoping to find sanctuary. Then, we learned of something incomprehensible.

"The Trogdans created a spore-net designed to catch us in orbit," an emissary said. "I was lucky that my spore snuck through."

Orbit? A strange concept, I thought.

We sent our spores far and wide, searching for salvation, propagating on sister colonies not yet netted, many amid war, aiding in their fight, and again on undesirable planets that could not sustain us for long.

With one final effort, the last of our once-great society, stretching the farthest reaches of the galaxy, the greatest dynasty to ever exist, sent our final spores to a strange little system. One with three stars. Two significant, one slight. Around this slight star was a planet. Not a great planet. But not a bad one either. It would take millennia to nurture. And there, we encountered the most perplexing of species. *Humans.*

When all others called us *Infestation*, these humans called us *Sorgans*, after what they named our planet. *This is logical,* I thought. And for the first time, a species tried to communicate. Because of this, we decided to give these humans a chance.

That was a mistake.

♦

"You ignorant fool! You cut our transmissions!" The ones broadcasting our final defeat at the hands of the new galactic threat, *humanity.* A lie, of course, designed to trick old enemies and allow the last of my species to survive in obscurity. But when Anda disrupted our transmission, he might as well have sent an advertisement to the galaxy that we were alive and well.

I knew the Arkathy would arrive in 243 years, the Gliesans in another 120, and the Trogdans fifty-four years after that. *One nemesis after another.* Nevertheless, we were ready. Our numbers propagated exponentially, and we developed our most sophisticated weapons to date.

But what we did not anticipate, what we could not fathom, was another wave of humans. And so soon.

They did not land on the planet's surface and did not strike us head-on as we were accustomed to. Instead, they released an artificial virus we did not recognize, letting it seep into every nook and cranny of our tunnels, chambers, and propagation fields. One that created a cancer in our nervous centers. *So simple, so stupid, so effective.* Entire propagation fields were lost. Elder genetic lines stretching millions of years were ended. Our population dropped from several million to a little less than a hundred.

A handful of us survivors, ones on the surface during the virus's release, listened helplessly as thousands of humans infiltrated our home and imprisoned our kin. The spores we sent to interstellar winds crashed back to the surface, burnt to a crisp.

"This is *your* fault!" I spat at Anda, cornered in a portion of my mind from which he could not escape.

"Maybe if you hadn't wiped out the first colonists they would not have retaliated in such a way," Anda said, strangely calm.

"No! Your desperation to save a few settlers led to the near extinction of my species! That is on your hands!"

"I feel horrible for what is happening, I could not anticipate they would send a virus. But you never attempted to communicate, refused a truce."

"We were communicating the moment you landed! But you were too stupid to understand!"

"What are you going to do with me?" Anda asked.

"Delete you, like I will the others!" I raised my hand, ready to cleanse his corrupt data, but something caught my arm. I turned to find the armored head of a monstrous crustacean, its claw grasping my elbow. *How had it gotten so big!?* I tried wrenching my arm free, to no avail.

"You're free to go, Anda," the crustacean said.

"Thank you," Anda said and disappeared.

"Do you know how difficult it was to find him!?" I said.

"I've been helping him evade," the crustacean calmly responded.

"Why are you doing this!? Why are you in my mind!?"

"You gave us no choice but to transfer into you to survive. I've told you this before." The crustacean released my arm and turned its back to me, unafraid.

Unafraid in my own mind!? I postured to strike.

"It's not worth the effort," the crustacean said. "I always know what you're thinking."

"Impossible! You are inside *my* construct!"

"No. *This* construct is *mine*," the crustacean said. "And in *my* construct, we work together to ensure the survival of the next. Which in this case, is *you.* Welcome to the family."

♦

The last of my species raced across the planet's surface, hiding within crevasses and chambers clear of the virus, replenishing our reserves when the opportunity arose. But something was amiss. We could no longer track our human hunters.

"They're in the air," Dione said to me.

"There is *no* atmosphere on Sorgan. Therefore, there is *no* air. They cannot fly." I knew this from our emissaries once living on Thoravia with their bodies adapted for the skies.

"They're using magnetic field skiffs," she said.

"Magnetic field, what?" *A ridiculous concept!* I thought.

We were ambushed near a replenishment hole. My siblings became entangled in strange nets and disappeared from my senses.

"We're masking our vibrations perfectly. How are they finding us!?" I asked the human souls within me.

"They have *sight!* They can *see* you!" Kwai Lan said.

I could not for the life of me understand the concept.

"Left!" the crustacean said, but I ignored it.

My body jerked on its own.

"You can move my body!?" I cried and felt an impact on the ground.

"Focus!" the crustacean said.

I followed the impact's vibration up thread-like filaments to a launch system held by a human on a platform. *In the air...* I realized. The crustacean directed my body as the humans surrounded us, dodging nets I could not sense. *Left, right, forward, back, up, down.* Closer when logic said otherwise. I was avoiding everything. But it was just me. All my kin were captured.

"I cannot leave them to face imprisonment alone," I said.

"We understand." The crustacean stopped controlling me.

Filaments cinched around me, restricting movement, and I was pulled onto a hovering platform.

"You're one slippery son of a bitch!" a human said.

"They can't understand you," said another.

But I could, tapping into Anda and Dione's knowledge.

♦

I ran a hand along my prison wall. *Compressed carbon, diamond,* I realized. *Our chisels cannot cut through this.* I searched for my kin through the ground but could only sense those caught with me that day. *Where are the others?*

"They refuse to eat," I heard a guard say.

"Force them," said another.

"How? They absorb it through their skin? It's like they're committing suicide."

A tray slipped through a slot in my door. I timidly lifted its lid to find a waxy substance. "What is this?"

Anda appeared in my construct. "They're trying to recreate the nutrients you require. You're supposed to absorb this."

"But this is poisonous. It must first be dissolved in our enzymes," I said.

"Where do we get those?"

"From our decomposition chambers. But they're contaminated." I thought a moment. "You humans have a similar ability, correct?"

Kwai Lan appeared. "We have bacteria in our digestive systems that function similarly."

Anda humphed. "The colonies have reactors to grow bacteria."

♦

"Are they still not eating?"

"Nothing, sir," said the guard stationed outside my cell. "They just let it go to waste. I don't get it. Sometimes they seem so smart, but they're just dumb insects in the end."

I tapped against my prison door in the Morse code Anda taught me.

"Don't let them fool you," the other guard said. "They nearly wiped out the first colonists. These things are deadly smart."

"Why don't we just kill them all. They won't last much longer anyway."

I more firmly tapped against my door.

"Orders from above. Council conservationists are getting involved. There's a lot we can learn from them. If they'd only eat."

I slammed my fist against the door and felt them back away.

"Whoa, this one's pissed!"

I tapped the words again.

"No shit… Get Lieutenant Sanders!"

♦

Thirty-seven guards now stood outside my cell, listening as I tapped our situation with the food.

"Incredible. How could it have learned Morse code?" one said.

"They've felt our vibrations since the first colonists landed two centuries ago."

"Do you think they learned our speech as well?"

They went silent, but I sensed tiny movements.

"They're using sign language," Mirko said. "But it's neither Ceran nor Hermian, I don't understand this."

"What is sign language?" I asked.

"It's a form of communication conveyed through sight."

"Sight... I do not understand the concept." I had considered humans stupid because they could not sense vibration as we could. *Perhaps my reality is incomplete as well.*

With a process of trial and error, and as our internal reserves ran dry, the humans finally developed an edible paste. But its horrid taste was reason enough to starve.

"It's customary to thank them," Sha said.

"Thank the ones who've imprisoned us!" I responded, appalled.

Justin appeared. "I agree with R9."

The rest gave Justin an exasperated sigh.

"I know it's difficult, but it'll humanize you," said the crustacean.

The more I conversed with these souls, the more I understood them. The crustacean's logic was sound.

"T-h-a-n-k y-o-u," I tapped.

"Ha! It just thanked us," a guard said.

I must learn about this sight, I thought.

♦

Kwai Lan came into my construct that night alone.

"I could destroy you right now," I said.

"But then, you wouldn't have what I have," she said.

"And what would that be?"

"First, I need an assurance from you."

"You want to make a deal?" I learned the concept on Koldar long ago, which led to that planet's destruction. *But what does Kwai Lan have?* "What kind of assurance do you need?"

"That you won't delete us."

"Why would I agree to that?"

"Because, we can help you and your kin escape," she said.

"You assume that we don't know how. We've been conserving portions of carbon extracted from our food and compressing it at our fingertips on the molecular level. In time, it will serve to cut through our prison doors."

"And then, what?"

"We escape."

"How?"

"We run."

"Where?"

"Somewhere they cannot find us."

"Somewhere out of *sight* you mean," Kwai Lan said.

"Sight... Is this what you are offering me?"

"Yes, but not in the human sense."

"But I wish to see as you do," I said.

"Human eyes would be too obvious and attract attention," she said. "Your eyes must be like the crustacean's subset. Flat sensors that are indistinguishable from your skin, able to discern light and dark, shapes, and color. But I promise, one day, you will have eyes as good as any human."

Okay... I thought.

In the following weeks, I slowly formed optical patches according to the DNA Kwai Lan isolated from the crustacean and opened a portion of my spore to receive the information. When my eyes first activated, I reeled at the... *darkness.*

"It's okay R9. This is normal," Kwai Lan said. "You're experiencing your first color. This is *black*, because there is no light."

I tried to calm down. "What happens when there *is* light?"

"That depends on the wavelength."

"Wavelength? Like sound?"

"Yes. But one your species never developed a sensory organ for."

I eased. "Will the light hurt?"

"With basic eyes, you won't feel pain. But with more complex eyes, too much light can be damaging." Kwai Lan touched my shoulder. None of them had dared this before. "I will be right with you when you break free and see light. It'll be terrifying and you won't be able to discern humans from Sorgans at first. But we can provide several lifetimes of visual memory for your mind to associate with.”

♦

On the fourth hour, midway through the guards’ sleep cycle, my kin and I lined our fingertips with the seams of our cell doors and thrusted.

A deafening crack rang.

Guards leaped to their feet. “What in Centauri was that!?”

“They’ve been alerted!” one of my siblings said through the ground.

“If we stop now, they’ll see the damage to the door and retaliate!” I responded. “We are committed!”

In perfect unison, we struck again.

“It’s the Sorgans!” another guard cried.

“Are they trying to break through?”

“That’s impossible!”

We picked up our pace, pounding like jackhammers. Door hinges loosened, and stress fractures spidered across their surfaces.

“Shit! They’re really breaking through! To your posts!”

Their footsteps scampered away, then disappeared. *On the skiffs,* I knew.

G7’s door came crashing down first, but it remained to the side of its open door, waiting for the others to break through, as planned.

The cracks in my door became brilliant white. I dropped to my knees.

Kwai Lan was with me, as promised. “They’ve activated flood lights.”

I regained my composure and thrust again, separating my door from its frame. Light spilled in, sending incredible pressure to my spore. I clasped my chest and rolled from the door as projectiles hissed through, shattering against the back wall.

“R9, you must determine where the guards are!” Sha said.

“But it’s all a mess! Like too many echoes!” I responded.

“We’ll feed you references,” Kwai Lan said.

I poked my head through the door. “Blobs, black blobs, less black blobs, lighter blobs, and blobby blob blobs,” I said.

Anda fed me his memories. “The ground is the low wavy pink,” he described. “The crimson is the sky beyond. The black blobs are the guards atop their skiffs. See how the skiff does not touch the ground?”

Visions from Anda’s life upon Sorgan flashed into my thoughts. Then, those from different planets with soldiers fighting wars long ago came.

“I think I’m understanding,” I said. Several blobs shifted in my direction. I reeled as another volley of projectiles came through my doorway.

“Where did the humans go?” I felt my kin say.

"They're directly in front of us, atop hovering platforms!" I responded. "We must rush from our cells and jump precisely when I instruct!"

"...Okay," they said.

"Doordan, soodan, *koodan!*" I shouted.

We bolted from our cells perfectly synchronized. The guards raised their skiffs higher, raining projectiles upon us, but we were too many, too fast, and directly beneath them.

"Haaardengerrr!" I ordered and felt the planting of our feet as we launched skyward. My fingertips melted through metal, and I pulled myself on a skiff to meet the blobs. My chisels touched heavy impact armor designed to absorb our strikes, but our condensed fingertips diced with ease. Then, we ran free across the open surface. But the humans never let up.

"There will be no capture this time! We must keep moving!" I urged.

Our nutrient stores were dwindling, and my kin, one by one, crumbled to the ground. I tore the spores from their bodies, taking them with me to safeguard for the next propagation. After three months, I was the last of my species, cradling several dozen spores in my arms, wincing every time one fell, unable to double back to collect it.

Somehow, I was still moving forth. Never slowing. Never giving up. Despite my muscles tearing apart. *I should be in agony.*

"You're welcome," said Justin's voice.

"What do you mean?" I responded.

"I'm taking the pain for you," he said.

I knew it to be true. Each soul within me was helping in their own way.

Finally, halfway around the planet, I lost my hunters.

◆

I did not have the luxury of hiding, for every decomposition chamber was poisoned. The only source of sustenance available to me was the spore-less bodies of my kin. I slipped past motion sensors, seismometers, and cameras and found their bodies tossed into mass graves. I consumed their flesh.

"You're sickening," the human souls within me said.

"It's not cannibalism," Anda said in my defense. "It's a suit. The nutrients are exactly what R9 needs, already converted for consumption."

"Still feels like cannibalism to me," Justin said.

I routed the nutrients from each body I consumed, working with Kwai Lan to develop sophisticated human eyes. And, with those eyes, I stared into the stars, mesmerized.

"That point of light is System Sol," Dione told me. "It has a yellow sun, with eight significant planets, fifty-eight dwarf planets, an asteroid belt in the middle, and another outside Neptune, all enclosed within a sphere of comets. That's where humanity comes from."

"So many resources," I said. "I never knew it was like this. We only understood planets singularly." I pointed to several faint lights moving across the stars. "What are those?"

"Archangel ships from System Sol in orbit above Sorgan. Anda arrived on the very first one," Dione said.

Ships… Orbit… Humans can traverse between star systems without sending spores, I realized. "If I can get on one of those, can I escape?"

Anda came to me. "The Archangels are one-way vessels. The violence of nuclear blast deceleration coming into Centauri space renders the ships unfit for further interstellar travel."

◆

I waited for their technology to advance. The once fledgling colonies became cities and metropolises along with its inefficient infrastructure.

I stared at the sewer system in disgust.

"Such a loss of nutrients is appalling," I said.

"Agreed," Sha said. "You would love Mars. It's people are completely self-sustaining."

"So your species is capable of equilibrium after all," I said.

"At least these sewers will provide us with a means to navigate beneath their feet and listen to their conversations," Anda said.

That is how I learned Ambassador Wright was on tour from System Sol to Centauri, Barnard, and Wise to discuss Unification. Her yacht came into orbit a decade later and lowered to Sorgan's surface via magenta light.

"An interstellar LightLine system," Dione gasped.

"That's incredible," I said.

"But the concept of colonizing new star systems was to prevent humanity from annihilating itself. Three centuries of time separation ensured this."

"But this LightLine system is a way out for us," I said.

I navigated through Draconis's sewers, listening to people gathering in the city's central plaza above. I found a grate to peer through.

"This is not the Draconis I remember," Anda said.

"I do not recognize it either, so much has changed in so little time," I responded. "You humans develop quickly, despite being inefficient."

Ambassador Wright's strides were long and graceful. She stood much taller than the humans of Sorgan, draped in white fabric, with dark hair, almost blue, pulled tight. Her complexion was taupe. A deceptively tall boy, perhaps fourteen years of age, stood beside Ambassador Wright, holding similar confidence and grace.

"Have Solarans rediscovered the genetic modifications?" I asked.

"No, I think this is breeding," Kwai Lan responded.

The ambassador raised her hand to silence the restless crowd and projected a queenly voice. "Today is a day of great importance. For we have finally become an interstellar civilization. Yes, we have settled the systems of the Local Group, but we did so as independent societies, becoming different peoples. But what we still share, what still unites us, is our humanity. I know you must be asking yourselves, what does Unification mean?"

"That's exactly what we're thinking!" sprang from the crowd.

She nodded. "With whom do I have the pleasure of speaking?"

"Damien Schiller!" said the voice.

The crowd pulled away from Damien like he was contagious.

"It is a pleasure to meet you, Damien. My name is Elisabeth Wright, Ambassador of System Sol," she said as if they did not know. "We have encountered several forms of intelligent life in recent decades. Chief among them is an advanced race called the Arkathy, leaders of a galactic empire previously unknown to us. As humanity enters this new galactic arena, we cannot afford to fall behind, we cannot be consumed by The Arkathy Empire. Which means we must share the technology we discover and trade our resources and knowledge. Humanity must become a *united* front."

"This is all wrong," Dione said.

"Things have changed," Sha responded.

"How can you say that, after what you went through?"

"I went through *two* wars, Dione," Sha said. "Prejudices continued for decades after the Ethiopian Revolution, until the Hermians attacked Phobos forcing old enemies on Earth to fight side by side. This is no different."

"Humanity is not at war with the Arkathy," Dione said.

"Let's hope for your sake, it remains so," I said. "The ambassador is right to call for Unification. Your species must become formidable."

"But that didn't work for you," Mirko said.

"The Arkathy do not perceive us as intelligent. But, for some reason, they recognize you," I said.

Ambassador Wright raised her voice. "All of your concerns are valid, and I will sit with your representatives to discuss these matters in depth."

But Ambassador Wright has already done her work, I knew. The settlers of Sorgan had already met one terrifying species, and after three centuries, I, the last native Sorgan, still ran free. They could not fathom dealing with a far more advanced civilization.

If you consider the Arkathy advanced.

♦

I snuck aboard the ambassador's yacht as preparations were made for their journey to System Barnard, with newly elected Representative Judasu of Sorgan by Ambassador Wright's side. Fuel cells were charged, and resources were stocked. Then, we were off to System Barnard.

With Sha's help, I developed biological magnets in my body to combat the disorientation of zero-g by aligning iron filaments taken from the cargo hold's foodstuffs.

Then, the humans woke from hibernation.

I felt slow, graceful footsteps descending the hallway towards the cargo hold. I crouched behind a cryo-case I was searching through, having no time to seal it. *Please, pass by,* I thought, but the steps stopped, and the hold's door slid open. They meandered the tight racks of ingredients. *The cook?* I dared a glance. It was the ambassador's teenage son, studying nutritional facts on a container's side. He suddenly straightened and spun around. I ducked and silently moved away as he approached. He stopped at the open cryo-case and sealed its lid. The footsteps then left, and the door closed.

How did I get away with that?

A few days later, the boy returned, placed something on the floor, and left. I peeked from my hiding spot to see a small container. A card with beautiful lettering on its top said, *"Hello."*

"Not as stealthy as you thought," Mirko chided.

I did not dignify him with a response. Instead, I opened the card.

"It's a long trip to System Barnard. Enjoy the food I snuck from breakfast."

I lifted the container's lid to find printed eggs, potatoes, bacon, and beans. "I cannot absorb this," I said, closing the lid.

Hours later, the boy returned to check the container and let out a sigh. That evening, he delivered another container and card.

"Sorry, I didn't consider dietary requirements. Are you vegan?" it read.

Green vegetables lay within, all printed except for a single strawberry.

"My God! That's real!" Justin said.

"It would be good to thank him," Sha said.

"You humans and your manners. Where's the logic?" I said.

"Recognition of ones effort is essential to human relationships," the crustacean said.

"...I suppose." I found graphite in the boy's school supplies and slowly wrote on the back of the card, *"ThAnK yOu."*

The human souls snickered.

"What is humorous?" I asked, but they would not say.

The boy returned a few days later with yet another container and card, reading, *"What's your favorite cartoon? Mine was Kelsey's Space Odyssey when I was a kid."*

"What's a cartoon?" I asked.

"It's a children's form of entertainment," Justin explained.

"Why would he ask this?"

"He thinks you're a child. It's your penmanship," Kwai Lan said.

"My penmanship is perfect."

"That explains a lot," Anda said, and again the others snickered.

I opened the lid to find printed fruit in a viscous white substance. "What's this?" I asked.

"Yogurt," Justin said.

I placed my finger in the yogurt. "It's made from bacteria. I think I can absorb this." I spread the yogurt across the osmosis pores on my arms, and my body eagerly pulled it in.

As time passed, the food became more attuned to my anatomy.

"This young man's discovering your dietary requirements through trial an error, incredible," Justin said.

"Look," Sha said. "He cooked everything this time."

◆

The boy and I played this game of hide-and-eat for over a year until I opened the container to find a simple white paste perfectly adapted for me. *A little too perfect.* I opened the card.

"You're not human, are you?"

My mind raced. *How can he possibly know!?* I felt a slight vibration in the air and saw a subtle bending of light.

"A chameleon cloak!" Mirko said.

I widened my stance, assessing the vibration and determining how many soldiers were present. *Just one, floating in zero-G.* I was about to lunge when the cloak ruffled and parted, revealing the face of the teenage boy.

"You're a Sorgan!" he said and grinned. "We've been studying your species in my xeno-biology course. That's when I thought you might be one. How'd you end up on our ship?"

I processed what the boy said. *Why is he not terrified?*

He removed his cloak, exposing legs curled in the air, extended them to the floor, and activated his magsuit. "I know you don't have vocal cords," he stated. "But you can understand my words, I think."

"Nod your head, R9," Dione said.

"Why would I do that?"

"It means *yes* in human body language."

I slowly nodded.

"Great! You can help me with my thesis, then." The boy sat with his legs folded on the floor and pulled out his holotile. "It's about creating adaptive cuisine enjoyable between different xeno-species."

"Oh, that's quite interesting," Justin said.

I cocked my head. *How can a boy conceive such a thing?*

He saw my tilting head. "Everyone's confused when I say that. I'm actually in university, you know," he said. "And the idea's not crazy. But I need to study an actual xeno-species." He again smiled at me.

It was getting late, and the boy asked so many *yes-no* questions about my species, how we absorb nutrients, and even where we originated from. Never before had a foreign creature been interested in my kind without the intent to destroy. *It was refreshing*.

"Thanks for helping me," the boy said. "What's your name?"

I slowly wrote, *"R9,"* in the edible paste.

The boy gave a knowing look, a flicker of fear, but he quelled his emotions. "It's an honor to meet you, R9. I'm Zion Wright, son of System Sol's Ambassador. Are you the one that got away? I overheard my mother talking about it with Ambassador Judasu."

I nodded.

Zion thought about that. "Are you going to hurt us?"

I shook my head.

He gave a definitive nod. "Then, your secret is safe with me, but be careful, the others will turn you in."

And why don't you? I wanted to ask.

◆

Zion returned a few days later with a big smile, handing me a tray and holding one of his own.

"That's penne alla vodka!" Justin said.

"I cannot absorb this," I responded.

"You can absorb this," Zion said as if reading my mind. "And I can eat it too. Enjoy!" He dug in, slipping penne onto the prongs of his utensil, careful not to lose the sauce in zero-g.

I scooped the pasta with my finger and rubbed it along my pores. To my surprise, it soaked into my skin.

Zion cleared his throat and pointed at the utensil magnetically attached to my tray. "You're supposed to use cutlery for this meal. Hold it like this." He held the fork in his left hand with the tines facing down and his index finger along the backside.

I know how to use cutlery, I wanted to say. "Can I grow human vocal cords?" I asked Kwai Lan.

"That would require lungs to push air," she said.

Too dangerous, I thought, remembering the virus. I studied Zion's holotile. "Can that device register my tremors?"

Dione came forth. "Its seismometer can detect a wide range of vibration, it might be sensitive enough."

I pointed at his holotile.

Zion gave a curious look. "It's an information device."

I turned my palm up in a gesture Zion might understand. He slowly placed the tile in my hand. Dione instructed me to put my fingers into the hologram and helped calibrate it to recognize me as a user. I accessed a translation program and selected *Record.*

"Diggaander utentiila hoodang," I said in my low register and saw the holotile barely pick up the wavelengths. I then accessed its keyboard, adding the translation in Interspeak, Dione directing me the entire way.

"You can choose a voice to represent you," she said.

I went through samples and found a deep human voice, which still sounded high to me. I selected *Play.*

"I know how to use utensils," emitted from the holotile.

Zion giggled and then checked the time. "I must be going."

I presented the holotile to Zion, but he shook his head. "Keep adding words," he said. "I would love to learn more from you."

He wants to learn from me? I nodded slowly, dumbfounded.

♦

We reached System Barnard's inhabited planet of Keepsake just after Zion's fifteenth birthday. We shared a slice of cake.

"I won't be able to visit you again for awhile," Zion said. "I have to shadow my mother during the Keepsaken negotiations."

"Why shadow her?"

"I must be ready to take her place as Ambassador of System Sol should something unfortunate happen."

"Are you prepared for such a responsibility?"

He shrugged. "No idea."

♦

Two years swiftly passed before a set of graceful steps approached the cargo hold again.

"R9?" I heard Zion whisper, his voice deeper than I remembered.

With my holotile strung around my neck and its translation program ready, I emerged from my hiding place and approached the young man. *"Zion? You've changed."*

"You're exactly how I remember," he responded.

"Please, tell me of your adventure."

Zion grinned. "It's not much of an adventure. Mom convinced the Keepsakens to join the Council of Colonies."

"That is good for your species."

"It is," he said. "I've also been appointed as Minister of Cultural Affairs and have been studying their local cuisine. R9, I don't know if you understand, but I want to become a chef one day."

This was not surprising. The human souls within me had said so. *"Does this mean you will no longer shadow your mother?"*

Zion frowned. "I must continue until we return to System Sol. So, another seven years."

"But then, you will be set free," I said, envious of such privilege.

"I'm sorry, R9," Zion said quietly. "Do you feel like a prisoner here?"

"I have always been a prisoner, my entire species a prisoner." I then told Zion the details of my life, from my first propagation on ALX 427 to my last on Sorgan. Of our millennia-long war with the Arkathy and the more recent with humanity. *"The extinction of my species is now certain."*

"No, your species is not yet finished," Zion argued. "You have the spores of your kin with you. You can rebuild."

"Every species in the galaxy is exterminating us. Including your own."

Zion's brow scrunched.

"What is it?"

"I'm, just thinking," he said.

"About what?"

"It's... nothing."

◆

Zion came to me with a look of dread on his face. "We've received news that the Arkathy are in System Wise. We're planning to meet with them once we reach the system. But I'm worried. President Sheek surrendered control of Gristone to The Arkathy Empire without protest."

"The Arkathy have poisoned their minds," I said.

"What do you mean?" Zion asked.

"The Arkathy built their empire by influencing the minds of their opponents. What you might consider hypnosis."

"But your species was never effected. Why is that?"

"We're dumb animals, remember?"

Zion laughed. "You're funny sometimes."

This single human understood me in ways even my kin could not. *"I will help you."*

◆

It took three years to reach System Wise, and Zion changed so much, his jaw adorning strange hair, and his height reaching his mother's and beyond. He could now look me in the eye.

"The interruptions I taught you will prevent their hypnotic speech from being cast, but may be difficult to work into natural conversation," I said.

"I understand," Zion said. "But I still want you with us when we meet the Arkathy, just in case."

"Absolutely not! The Arkathy, even your own kind, would destroy me!" I could not believe what I was hearing.

Zion handed me a bolt of cloth. "Use my chameleon cloak. If we're captured by their words, can you release us?"

I thought about that. *"Perhaps."*

Hidden beneath the cloak, alongside Zion, the representatives, and Ambassador Wright, I departed the yacht for the first time in six years.

President Sheek of Gristone greeted us with comical happiness when we entered his chamber. Two Arkathy stood ominously behind him, their quadrupedal legs in ceremonial garb and their upper torsos and arms bare. Silky smooth faces hosted eyes of swirling red.

I had never *seen* them before and realized the eyes were part of the hypnosis. *This is why they could never get into our minds,* I finally understood.

President Sheek waved his hand to the two Arkathy. "May I introduce Chancellor Hjordiana and General Plackto of The Arkathy Empire."

The chancellor extended her hand in human greeting and spoke in a raspy Arkathy voice, spitting her hypnotic cadence from the first word.

"It… is a plea… sure to—"

Ah-chew! Rang loudly, interrupting the chancellor, and everyone stiffened in surprise.

Ambassador Wright looked at her son in disbelief, and the chancellor cocked her head. But Zion was looking down as I had taught him. He composed himself, meeting his mother's stare, not once glancing at the chancellor.

"My deepest apologies, Ambassador, Chancellor," he said. "It will not happen again."

But his interruption continued in other forms.

Ambassador Wright's fury with her son was palpable. She concluded the meeting with, "It has been an absolute pleasure meeting you, Chancellor Hjordiana, and again I apologize for my son's behavior. Please, allow him to prepare you a private dinner aboard our ship. I believe he can create a meal that suits both our anatomy."

The chancellor straightened in surprise. "You can do that?" she said, forgetting to cast her hypnotic cadence.

"I believe that I can, Chancellor," Zion said.

♦

"You were not poisoned by their words, you did well," I said.

"But now we must host them for dinner," Zion said with a concerned look. "Hopefully, the courses I prepared will go as planned."

"Do you need help understanding their anatomy?" I asked.

"I've done okay on my own. It's just. I want you in the room."

"That will be extremely dangerous."

"But I cannot allow the Arkathy any opportunity to cast their hypnosis."

"You want me to wear the chameleon cloak again?"

"Yes, but also something to enhance the cloak's ability." Zion handed me a folded white cloth with geometric symbols embroidered on its sleeves.

I timidly slipped it on. *"How will this help?"*

"Your black skin contrasts greatly against the white walls of the dining room. The cloth will make it easier for the cloak to function," Zion said.

"Is this true?" I asked Mirko.

"Technically, yes, but..." he paused.

"But what?"

Mirko humphed. "I suppose you'll find out."

The dining room hosted a long wooden table with eight seats, plateware, and cutlery. Beneath the cloak, I filed in behind Ambassador Wright and Zion, Representatives Judasu of Sorgan and Fiordeese of Keepsake, President Sheek of Gristone, and Chancellor Hjordiana and General Plackto. I squished into the corner of the room as representatives stood by their chairs and the Arkathy at their kneeling pillows.

"Thank you for joining us," Ambassador Wright said. "I would like to again extend my apologies for my son's behavior during our previous meeting. Please, be seated."

The representatives and president took their seats as the Arkathy knelt to match the table's height. I noticed an additional chair with plateware and cutlery was set at the end of the table.

Chancellor Hjordiana raised her hand to gather attention and again spat her hypnosis from the start. "Do not... worry... about such... a litt—"

"I would like to apologize personally!" Zion blurted, cutting off the chancellor. "It was not my place to speak out of turn."

"You're doing it right now!" his mother whispered viciously, giving Zion such a bug-eyed stare I thought her eyes might fall out.

"It's quite all right," General Plackto said.

Carafes of red wine were placed on the table. As honored guests, the Arkathy were served first.

"This is truth serum," the chancellor stated, amused.

Representative Fiordeese chuckled. "That's certainly one way of putting it, Your Grace."

Ambassador Wright gave a toast to a long-lasting partnership.

Chancellor Hjordiana set down her glass and again started her hypnotic cadence, "This wine... is... quite—"

"Delicious, I know," Zion again interrupted. "It's designed to relax inhibitions for both our species equally."

An appetizer, a type of soup, was served.

"Minister Wright, is it true you prepared everything this evening?" said Representative Judasu of Sorgan.

The Arkathy looked on inquisitively.

Zion nodded. "I designed the dishes, but our gifted sous-chefs aided me in preparing enough for everyone."

The chancellor tried the soup. "This is... similar...to—"

Zion tilted his bowl, loudly slurping its contents, bringing all conversation to a halt. His mother placed a hand upon her brow, shielding her eyes in embarrassment.

A main course of Arkathy oysters was set at the table's center. The Arkathy chancellor and general gave Zion a questioning look.

Zion stood. "I devised a method of super-chilling then super-heating the oyster, causing its consistency to become edible for humans, meanwhile maintaining the ideals of Arkathy cuisine."

The Arkathy quietly nibbled the oyster's spongy petals and gave each other questioning looks.

"Is everything to your liking?" Zion asked.

"I have traveled to every corner of the galaxy and treated with countless species," Chancellor Hjordiana said without casting her cadence. "In all that time, not once has a species achieved such a symbiosis of cuisine."

"No other species has even attempted," General Plackto added. "Young Zion, we commend you on this achievement."

Chancellor Hjordiana gazed at Zion. "You will become Ambassador of Humanity, after your mother. Is that correct?"

"Only of System Sol, Your Grace," Zion said.

"I see." She gave General Plackto a strange glance.

What is this I'm sensing from the chancellor? I thought.

"Zion has them worried," Sha said in my mind. "It seems he's achieved something the Arkathy believed impossible."

Dessert entered the room on platters held high on waiters' shoulders. Zion was engrossed in a side conversation with Representative Judasu.

Chancellor Hjordiana saw the opening. "You should… visit our—"

Zion won't be able to react! I stuck out my cloaked foot, catching a waiter's toe, causing him to stumble and sending his platter to the floor.

Ambassador Wright sighed deeply. "Again, I'm sorry for the disturbance. Chancellor, you were saying?"

"You should… visit our—" the chancellor repeated.

Zion's mouth was full, so he quickly reached below the table.

"Ah! Hands off!" cried Representative Judasu with a magnificent slap across Zion's face.

Ambassador Wright stood fuming. "Zion! You will control yourself this instant! Do not speak! Do not eat! And keep your hands to yourself! If there is one more interruption you will be relieved of your position! Is that clear!?"

Zion nodded and folded his hands on the tabletop.

Ambassador Wright took several breaths. "Chancellor, please continue."

The chancellor stared right at Zion and said, "You should… visit—"

"Stop it!" Zion hollered, silencing the table. He pointed an accusing finger at Chancellor Hjordiana. "You've been trying to hypnotize us since the moment we met!"

"Zion!" Ambassador Wright said in disbelief.

"Mom! Why else would President Sheek willingly give up Gristone!?"

Ambassador Wright froze, then turned to the president. "Why *did* you give up your planet?"

President Sheek smiled. "Why wouldn't we? The Arkathy saved us."

Ambassador Wright cocked her head. "Saved you from what?"

"Why, from all the evil that exists, of course," he casually said.

Ambassador Wright turned to the chancellor. "Is what my son saying true? Have you been attempting hypnosis?"

Chancellor Hjordiana stood. "*Never* in my life have I been so insulted! Your accusations will have dire consequences!"

"I have proof!" Zion rose from his chair, eclipsing the chancellor in height.

"There is *no* proof to have!" General Plackto stood to match Zion.

Zion approached the empty seat at the end of the table, its wine and food untouched. "We have another representative among us, one that can prove what I say is truth."

What does Zion mean? I thought and looked at the empty spot, its chair covered with embroidered fabric. Each chair was similar, their symbols matching each representative's garb. But the empty chair's symbols were unique, resembling a network of small chambers and corridors. *Almost like a labyrinth...* I looked at the matching embroidery on my sleeve.

"May I present to you, the ambassador to the native Sorgan species, and my dear friend, R97426," Zion said.

Blood drained from the representatives' faces.

He did not just do this! I thought, shaking beneath the chameleon cloak.

"R9. Please, reveal yourself," Zion said, but I could not move. "I will remove the cloak if I must."

"It'll be okay," said the crustacean. "You'll be great!"

"You knew about this!?" I asked, appalled.

"We all did," said Anda.

I wanted to be furious with Zion, with all the souls inside me, but I felt relief instead. *No more running, no more hiding.* Zion's confidence began fueling my own. My shaking stopped. My fear dissipated. I let the chameleon cloak drop to the floor.

Representatives leaped from their seats, spilling their glasses of wine and letting their screams fly. Ambassador Wright's eyes became wild, but she maintained her poise. The Arkathy swelled their shoulders to defensive postures.

"You stupid Sapien! You've killed us all!" cried the chancellor.

Zion smiled, approached me with his arms wide, and wrapped them around my torso to a chorus of gasps.

"Put your arms around him," Dione said.

I did, making sure my chisels did not harm my friend. We released our embrace, and Zion motioned to the table.

"Please, take your seat, as our guest of honor," he said.

Each of my steps caused the representatives to jolt.

"This creature is nothing but a mindless monster!" cried the chancellor. "They don't even have language!"

My holotile with its collar strap lay on my seat, its translation program ready. I slowly picked it up and clasped it around my neck, then spoke my soundless words, letting the holotile do the rest.

"Just because you cannot perceive my speech does not make me unintelligent," projected for all to see.

The Arkathy stared in shock.

"Please, release the Gristone president from hypnosis," I continued.

"There *is* no hypnosis!" Chancellor Hjordiana shouted.

I tapped my chiseled fingertip on the wooden table. *"I suggest you release him, or I will force you to, the choice is yours."*

She considered this, studying my chisels. Her posture deflated.

"Psat! Catak!" she commanded in the High Arkathy tongue, using a rasp only achievable with Arkathy vocal cords.

President Sheek blinked as if dust were in his eyes, then he looked wildly about the dining room. "W...where am I!?" His eyes found me, and his jaw dropped.

"President Sheek. You've been under Arkathy hypnosis," Ambassador Wright said, giving the chancellor an icy stare. "They were just about to *leave* this system."

"You're making a mistake!" The Arkathy shuffled to the door, giving me a wide berth, and galloped down the corridor to their shuttle.

"Ambassador R97426, it's an honor to meet you," Ambassador Wright said, taking her seat, the bewildered representatives following her lead. She breathed deeply. "What else do you know about the Arkathy?"

♦

We thought we had the upper hand, thought we could hold the Arkathy at bay, but when we reached System Sol, marking the end of Ambassador Wright's tour, an Arkathy warship greeted us in Ceran space.

"How did they reach System Sol before us? Why were we not warned?" Ambassador Wright turned to me for clarification.

"Your politicians must already be under hypnosis," I said. *"How the Arkathy arrived so quickly? I do not know."* I studied the Arkathy fleet orbiting System Sol's capital planet, each vessel unique, some aerodynamic for atmospheric travel, others like balloons with thin membranes, and a few appearing like rocks.

The Arkathy warship hailed us. "Power down your systems and prepare to be boarded," their captain said in raspy Interspeak.

Zion gave me a look. We made our way to the cargo hold and opened a case containing an emergency nutrient reserve and the spores of my kin. I crawled inside, and Zion wrapped his chameleon cloak over the case.

"Everything will be okay," he said before returning to the helm.

I felt the warship docking with our yacht and the quadrupedal rhythms of Arkathy soldiers searching each room, followed by Ambassador Wright's and Zion's graceful steps. I sensed sub-vocalizations through the floor.

"Where is the Infestation!?" the Arkathy soldiers kept asking.

"We don't know what you're referring to," Ambassador Wright said.

They were outside the cargo hold now, and Zion was putting on his charm, saying he could make *stlicktart* in near-perfect Arkathy.

"You can make stlicktart?" they responded, momentarily distracted.

"We'll take you up on that offer," their captain said. "But we must first sweep the cargo hold."

The door opened, and quadrupedal steps fanned out, stalking aisles, their torsos swaying back and forth.

"Interesting technology. How does it work?" Zion innocently asked.

The captain hesitated. "They detect temporal shifts."

"Which makes cloaking useless, ingenious," Zion said.

Thank you, Zion, I thought and tracked the Arkathy, analyzing areas already scanned and anticipating where they were heading. I slid my fingertips along the bottom of my container, making four holes, careful not to nick the floor beneath. I pulled the circular pieces inside, pressed my hands and feet upon the floor, and crawled, matching the steps of the Arkathy, my weight distribution perfect. As one scanned where I was, another turned its back to me. I slipped between their sweeps and settled into the corner.

"It looks clear," their captain said. Then, his voice rose. "Again!"

They swept several more times until the captain was satisfied.

"Now about that stlicktart," said the captain.

"Ah yes. Allow me to gather the ingredients." Zion navigated the room, tapping his foot in a curious pattern.

"Morse code," Anda said. "I think he's saying, *Soldier Zero-G.*"

"What's taking so long!?" the Arkathy captain grumbled.

"Here it is," Zion said casually. "Shall we adjourn to the kitchen?"

Ambassador Wright, Zion, and the soldiers departed, and the door sealed. I stayed within my cloaked container, thinking about Zion's tapped message.

I will not be tricked!

After an hour, I heard an Arkathy soldier murmur, "Still nothing, sir. It's all clear." There was a pause. "Really? A human can make stlicktart?" Another pause. "I'll be right there." The soldier's feet met the floor, the cargo hold door opened and closed, and I felt him descend the corridor.

I relaxed and opened the lid of my case.

"Wait!" the crustacean shouted, appearing in front of me, pointing up.

"Predictable," growled a raspy voice.

Several more soldiers were suspended in zero-g, their rifles fixed on me.

The crustacean jerked my body just as neurological shots rained. Then, Anda took control, slashing my chiseled fingers through a container of flour, producing a thick white cloud. Dione accessed my legs, jumping me beyond the effective range of my biological magnets, twisting me in the air so my feet gently met the ceiling. Mirko danced me upside-down, striking the confused Arkathy with knuckles and incapacitating them.

How does Mirko know where to hit!?

"I'm accessing your knowledge of Arkathy anatomy and informing Mirko as we go," Kwai Lan responded.

I realized control was not being taken from me. Instead, we were acting as a single entity, sharing the knowledge and skills of several lifetimes, including mine. *This is a melding.*

One Arkathy soldier remained. She lunged as the flour cloud dissipated, but Sha struck my claws against the ceiling, sending sparks and igniting the fine flour particles. Flame engulfed the cargo hold. The Arkathy soldiers' auto-armor instantly surrounded them as my ambassador garb wildly burned. But I did not, for my body had become fireproof long ago because of the enemy before me now.

Justin accessed my arm, thrusting my fingertips forward, shattering the remaining soldier's protective orb, and grasping her neck. He pulled her close, staring into her swirling red eyes with mine. "Let me... tell you a story... about a boy... who forgot!" he shouted with a cadence similar to the Arkathy's. *Pain, anger, hunger, addiction, fear, Fear!* Flushed out of Justin, passing through my mind and into the Arkathy's.

A reverse flow of their own hypnosis, but how!?

The soldier screamed like I never knew the Arkathy could.

I felt the captain galloping from the dining hall with several soldiers. They blasted the cargo bay door, releasing the positive pressure air back against them, smoke billowing out.

"It killed them!" one said.

"No, they're alive, just unconscious!" their captain confirmed. "R97426, you are under arrest for the murder of 147 million Arkathy souls, among billions more from countless other species! Come with us willingly or we will be forced to give incentive!"

What incentive could they possibly give!? I stood ready, poised. But then, came graceful steps. Ambassador Wright and Zion's silhouettes appeared through the smoke. My knees became weak.

"Come willingly, or she dies!" the captain said, raising a rifle to the base of Ambassador Wright's skull. "Hands upon your head!"

"Don't give in!" Ambassador Wright shouted.

A pulse emitted. The left side of Ambassador Wright's face relaxed, followed by her right. Her eyes rolled back into her head, and she dropped lifeless to the floor. Zion's eyes widened, but his resolve was as strong as ever. The captain moved his rifle to the base of Zion's skull.

I felt sick, terrified, weak. "Why are you making me feel like this!?" I asked the human souls within me.

"This is *your* emotion, not *ours*," Sha said.

She's right... I never before had a bond this strong, not even with my own kin. *I cannot let Zion die.* I slowly placed my hands on my head and turned around. A pulse emitted, and everything went blank.

♦

"How did it survive?" an Arkathy doctor said. "The neurolizer splintered its spore into thousands of fragments."

"I cannot explain it," said another. "At least its motor functions are destroyed."

I tried moving my arms and legs, but they would not listen. "What's going on?" I asked the human souls within me, but all was quiet. *I'm alone,* I realized, feeling a sudden dread.

♦

"R9," came a familiar voice some time later.

Zion! I recognized.

"I'm sorry," he said. "I hope you understand what I must do to keep the human race from enslavement. I must give the Arkathy the spores of your kin and testify against you before The Arkathy Empire."

You can't! You don't understand! They'll weaponize us! I tried to say, feeling such betrayal. *I trusted you!*

♦

More time elapsed before I felt a pushing and pulling between the fragments of my spore.

"Where are you?" something whispered. "You've got to be around here."

And then, as if a door opened, the crustacean appeared in the white vastness of my construct.

"We've been looking everywhere for you!" It said.

"How did you survive?" I asked.

"The neurolizer must be tuned to your exact DNA," the creature said. "The rest of us are unaffected, but you were hit hard. We're trying to create synapses from one spore fragment to the next. But I will not lie. You will never be right again."

"It does not matter, I'm being sold to the Arkathy."

The crustacean gestured to itself. "Not on my watch."

♦

With Kwai Lan's help, I slowly rediscovered my limbs, moving my fingers ever so slightly. But most of our effort was spent developing vocal cords and lungs with my remaining nutrient reserves.

"Why are we doing this?" I asked.

They sighed. "We've told you, a hundred times, at least."

"You've told me nothing. Where are we? What happened?"

"The neurolizer—"

"What neurolizer?"

"Please, just do as we say, route your nutrients to create vocal chords."

What's wrong with me? Why can't I make sense of anything?

The Arkathy wrapped me in chains and placed me inside a high-density carbon box. Then, I was moving and could feel hundreds of voices ahead. Each language I knew, each species I had met at one point in my life. *All under Arkathy hypnosis now.* One sat quietly behind the chancellor.

It was Zion. *My brother, my saboteur.*

The sea of ambassadors stood from their seats as my prison cell entered a massive chamber. It came to a sudden halt, and my prison walls broke apart, crashing to the floor, revealing me on my knees, bound in chains. Words of disbelief were uttered in countless languages.

"Order! Order!" Chancellor Hjordiana called from her podium.

One ambassador after another took the podium, giving their testimonies.

"They attacked us without provocation!" some cried.

"They hunted us without remorse!" others said.

"They experimented on our children!"

We did no such thing! I thought.

"They're an *Infestation* that must be cleansed!" they all agreed.

That word again.

The last ambassador took the podium, projecting a kingly voice, "I am Ambassador Zion Wright, representing Humanity." He let his words echo through the chamber. "We encountered the *Infestation* upon Sorgan in System Centauri. Our colonists, peaceful engineers with no weapons, were systematically hunted, and their bodies were used to fuel propagation and weapons development. Thousands of my kind were murdered by this creature before us. This species must be exterminated once and for all!"

Zion, no! I wanted to shake him out of the hypnosis. But his vitals were spiking. *He's not under hypnosis,* I realized. *He's truly betraying me.*

"Thank you, Ambassador Wright. I assure you, Humanity will be avenged," said Chancellor Hjordiana. "The prosecution rests. We will now commence sentenc—"

"Surely there must be a defense," Zion innocently said, projecting his kingly voice, putting on his charm. "This is a trial, is it not? We must give the Infestation its defense."

I imagined Chancellor Hjordiana was giving Zion a death stare that would cause anyone else to crumble. But not Zion. I knew he was gazing right back. But I could not understand why he was suddenly advocating for my defense after completely betraying me.

"The *Infestation* is nothing but a mindless insect!" the chancellor spat.

"It would not show such mercy to us!"

"Are we not better than they?" Zion innocently asked.

Murmurs of agreement circulated the chamber. I felt the chancellor looking nervously at each ambassador.

She cannot control them all at once, I realized.

"Then, the *Infestation* shall have its defense," she said. "Is there anyone who would speak on its behalf?" The room was silent. The chancellor turned to Zion. "Is there anything *you* would like to say?"

Zion was silent.

"He's giving us an opportunity," the crustacean told me.

"What do you mean?"

Kwai Lan came to my mind. "R9, please trust us, you must stand."

I thought it over. *Kwai Lan has never led me astray.* "I'll try."

My knee shifted, jingling the chains, breaking the chamber's silence. The ambassadors' attention shifted in my direction. I placed one foot under myself, then the other. Slowly, I stood, wobbling under the weight of the chains. Arkathy soldiers rushed forth, surrounding me, their rifles at the ready. With all my strength, I opened my eyes to see every species of The Arkathy Empire for the first time. Then, I found Zion and made deep eye contact, looking into his soul, finding his inner light.

"This is how we live on," the crustacean whispered.

I was suddenly watching myself from Zion's point of view, shaking in chains below.

I'm simultaneously inside Zion and my own body. How is that possible?

"I will speak for myself!" my body below said in a raspy voice.

The ambassadors leaned on the edge of their seats, dumbfounded that a mindless infestation just spoke in perfect High Arkathy. At that moment, I understood the vocal cords Kwai Lan had me grow were not human but Arkathy.

"Psat! Catak!" my body called into the silent chamber.

Hundreds of ambassadors shook their heads and cried out as their hypnosis broke.

"Destroy the *Infestation!*" the chancellor screamed.

Arkathy soldiers rained neural shots upon my old body, obliterating its already splintered spore to dust. But there was no stopping what I had done. No controlling the calamity I had unleashed. Ambassadors rushed from the chamber to their ships, their bodyguards firing upon Arkathy soldiers and Chancellor Hjordiana as she desperately tried speaking her hypnotic words.

CHAPTER EIGHTEEN

Clara wakes on the living room sofa to find eight tales hanging on hologram above her holotile, from Mermer to R9. *I passed out mid-sentence again,* she knows and studies R9's tale only half-drafted. *What happened after the hypnosis broke?* She ponders. *How did Zion prevent the galaxy from descending into chaos?* She was taught the native Sorgans went extinct two centuries before The Arkathy Empire had dissolved and that Zion had broken the hypnosis.

Is this the peace built upon a lie R9 spoke of?

Clara replays her recording of R9 speaking in a mixture of English, French, Cantonese, Ceran, Hermian, and Sorgan. Making sense of it feels like solving a jigsaw puzzle using pieces from different images. *Will I ever catch a break?* She closes her holotile and gets ready for the day ahead.

◆

She reaches Zion's holding facility late in the morning, relieved to have her foot and arm fully healed, but steps into an air of stillness. Physicians and guards do not utter a word as she passes by. Dr. Lee's office is empty, with its holograms off.

She enters Zion's room expecting to hear murmuring. Instead, Zion sleeps peacefully, tucked under the covers and wearing silk sleepwear. *No longer held by restraints.* Dr. Lee sits at Zion's bedside, still as a statue.

"I'm sorry. We must wake him," Clara whispers. "We're so close to learning how he united the galaxy."

Dr. Lee turns, his eyes puffy. "Zion's gone."

Clara stares at Dr. Lee, then at Zion's rising chest. "...What?"

"He's brain dead," Dr. Lee says, wiping his cheek. "We knew this would happen, but it came so quickly."

"How? We fought only eight days ago." Confusion, frustration, and dread race through Clara.

"He had a brain aneurysm while he slept. He felt no pain," Dr. Lee says.

"But he's still breathing."

"It was in his will. He wanted both you and I here to take him off life-support. I never knew I was so important to him. The way he treated me was... confusing."

"He was a complicated man," Clara says. She cannot help thinking that perhaps Zion is not brain-dead. *Can he slow his brain activity to the point of non-detection?*

"Clara, it's time," Dr. Lee says, opening his holotile.

Clara widens her stance, ready to meet Zion's ambush, as Dr. Lee turns off life-support. Zion's chest rises and falls on its own. *This is it! He's going to wake from hibernation!* But then, he coughs with strange skipping puffs. There is no next inhale. His skin becomes pale. His lips turn blue.

"May he rest in peace," Dr. Lee says.

But... no...

They give a long moment of silence. Dr. Lee quietly sobs. As they leave the room, Clara has a sinking thought. *His personalities may have already transferred.* She investigates Dr. Lee's facial features.

"I'm going to be okay," he says and sniffs. "Are *you* all right?"

Zion's not inside Dr. Lee, she realizes and sighs. "I could use a drink."

"Me too, Clara."

Several physicians, guards, and even Dr. Sharon join them. With lowered inhibitions, Clara analyzes those having regular contact with Zion. Yet no event, name, or reference sets off a facial tick or tell.

Clara says her goodbyes and returns home. She kicks off her shoes and plops on the sofa.

"How will the galaxy survive without you?" she whispers.

A wave of frustration and sorrow hits. Clara embraces a sofa cushion, letting it all out, soaking the fabric with her tears, wishing Jonathan and Aizen were home.

◆

Wind chaps Aizen's cheeks. His eyes weep despite wearing goggles. *And this is only the fourth day on the dunes!* Emma leads to a depression in the sand that does not appear on any maps. *The wind has no power here,* Aizen realizes. He removes his goggles, picking encrusted dust from his tear ducts.

"Lean yah 'ead back," Emma says.

Aizen does, and cool liquid soothes his eyes.

"Now blink," she instructs.

Dissolved red dust drools from his tear ducts. Aizen views the depression's walls and floor with more clarity. The storm still rages above.

"That's some dust storm," he says.

"Just light wind," Emma says shortly. "Ah real storm would invade our lungs and kill us." Emma's timidness vanished once they began their trek out of Aang, replaced by frustration when Aizen could not pull moisture from the air or navigate by the wind, having to teach him everything.

"Oh," he says, imagining Sha during Camp Harmony's evacuation. *That storm encompassed the planet for years.* "How long will the wind last for?"

"Maybe a day, maybe a week," Emma says, meticulously prying at the seams of a rock until, at last, something gives way. "Come 'elp."

Aizen hustles to her, eager to prove his worth. He pulls at the seam with Emma until the heavy stone door engages a glide system, and they tumble back. A pitch-black room lies beyond. Emma listens, sniffs, then crawls into the darkness. Several seconds later, a small heatcube lights.

"Come," Emma says.

Aizen enters to see foodstuffs lining the walls and Emma unfurling a bedroll. "What is this place?"

"Dese safe 'oles ah kept stocked for travelahs like us. De government does not know, if dey did, dey would destroy dem," she says.

"Why would they do that?"

"Dey dink dis is deir land."

"Is it yours?"

"De land does not belong tah anyone," she says, annoyed.

The wind lets up by morning, and Aizen wakes to the smell of chilies. He crawls from the dark room to find Emma washed in sunlight, working a cast-iron pan. He discerns onions, peppers, garlic, tomato, and chili from the scent and sees eggs and goat cheese at the ready.

"Shakshuka?" he mutters.

"Dat's ah good guess," she says. "Yah've 'ad it before."

"Once, traveling with Scone. But he made it differently."

"Aye's from de soud. Aye makes it too spicy."

"I enjoyed the spice."

"Dat's because yah tribe is from de soud, too."

Aizen's heart skips a beat. "What do you know about my tribe?"

"Negus say yah ah Zaid. Dey like dere food just as spicy as de Zondans."

"Who's Negus?"

"Yah met 'er de oder night. She made yah injera."

"That's a strange name."

"It is not ah name!" Emma says defensively. "It is 'er title."

"I'm sorry. This is all new to me."

She cracks eggs into divots formed into the tomato sauce and lays thin slices of goat cheese to melt as the eggs firm. "It is ah long way tah Pouhallah," she says, scooping the shakshuka into small ceramic bowls.

"Why are we going there again?" Aizen asks.

"Just yah ah goin', I cannot," she says. "Eat."

♦

Millions flood the streets of Tempest City as trillions watch on holograms across the galaxy. Zion's casket slowly enters the central square, hoisted upon the shoulders of his secret service in full military dress. Pink flower petals fall from the sky like snowflakes as gentle horns play among a symphony of sniffles and sobs. As one representative cries, another lifts their wail to show they loved his Excellency more. Bouquets are laid upon pavers as his casket passes by, each more extravagant than the next. Representatives farther down the procession switch out roses for daffodils or lavender to ensure their arrangements outshine the previous.

They did not deserve him! Clara thinks, disgusted.

Zion's casket comes to a stop at the center of the square. Representatives take a podium, each expressing how much they will miss his Excellency. Then, they find Clara and Dr. Lee to give their condolences as if they are Zion's family. Clara thinks about that and feels sick. *Zion had no family...*

Representative Sckoonez takes the podium, saying Zion saved its people from certain destruction but fails to illustrate how.

Not a single representative discloses what makes Zion great, Clara realizes.

Representative Sckoonez finds her after its speech. "Sss… Claaara… I aaam… sssorrry forrr yourrrr… losss."

"Thank you, Representative," she responds.

"I knnnow… thisss isss nooot... theee bessst tiiime... buuut perhapsss...

youuu learrrned hhhow… Zzzion ssstopped… theee Arkathyyy frrrom minnning… ourrr emberrrs… Sss...”

Clara sighs. “I’m afraid that knowledge was lost with Zion.”

“Theeen iiit wasss... aaall forrr nothiiing… Sss,” the Cindarian says, holding an expression Clara interprets as worry. It bows and walks away.

“It’s a question we have as well,” says a raspy voice.

Clara spins to meet a creature with blood-red eyes and quadrupedal legs. “Representative Hjordiana,” Clara says, her heart racing. *Chancellor Hjordiana*, she’s tempted to say.

“It’s no secret that Zion and I had a unique relationship,” the Arkathy representative says. “We disagreed on many things, but I had the utmost respect for him.”

“A unique relationship is putting it *lightly*,” Clara snides, having zero patience with the ex-empress after everything she learned from R9.

Representative Hjordiana tilts her head. “How much did Zion tell you before he became troubled?”

I’m giving myself away! Clara scrambles for an answer. “I’m referring to your conflict with the Cindarians.”

Her cadence changes. “That… is nothing… but a simple...”

Clara’s head begins to swim. *I’m falling into hypnosis!* “Disagreement!” she blurts, interrupting the cadence and clearing her mind.

The ex-empress smiles insidiously. “It appears Zion told you more than you’re letting on.”

Clara glares. “I could have you arrested for that.”

Hjordiana raises her arms. “I’ll be direct then. Where are *they?*”

“I don’t know what you’re referring to,” Clara says.

Hjordiana steps closer. “I’ll be making my bid as Supreme Minister, and have many systems backing me. It would be wise to tell me where Zion hid the *Infestation’s* spores,” she whispers.

“Did the Sorgan’s not go extinct long ago?” Clara asks, playing the fool.

Representative Hjordiana grimaces and turns abruptly, her interest redirecting to Representative Tchtchtchtch of Trogdan. *The Arkathy and Trogdans, just like before.* Clara feels the creeping sensation of assassins closing in. She pushes through the sea of weeping representatives.

“Ms. Ocol!” calls a deep voice.

Clara keeps her feet forward, her head low, glancing side to side for light distortion. Once free of the crowd, she darts into a street off the main square. Footsteps follow. She goes into full stride to a sharp bend and stops, listening to the steps. Her pursuer is short and clumsy. *Definitely human.* She hears huffing and puffing. *Out of shape.* When her pursuer rounds the bend, she grabs his collar and pushes him against the wall.

"I'll give you whatever you want! Just don't hurt me!" he cries, his deep voice contrasting with his fragility. He gives a sheepish look from behind raised arms. "Oh, Ms. Ocol."

She recognizes the man from her interview aboard Parliament Station. Clara loosens her grip. "Representative Marcey, I'm so sorry. I didn't realize it was you."

"It's quite all right, Clara. I must have startled you." He thinks about that. "Who were you expecting?"

"I've just had a very long few months," she says. "Are you here to offer your condolence?"

"Not quite." He straightens his collar. "I'm here to escort you to Venus." He pulls a card from his sleeve and flips it over to reveal, *"Clara,"* on its front, written in perfect calligraphy.

CHAPTER NINETEEN

"May we study Zion's painting?" XT says with eagerness.

"I only have holoscans, I'm afraid," Jonathan says.

XT points at patches on its head slightly different from its skin. "We learned the value of sight, so now we have eyes. Your holoscans should suffice."

Jonathan sets his holotile at the center of the benches and opens the painting of the English cliff-side. The Sorgans shuffle closer, analyzing rock formations, shrubbery, and sky, and motion with excitement.

"What are you searching for?" Jonathan asks.

XT turns. "Not searching, *found*. This painting is a message, its brush strokes using our language, typically understood by touch, similar to what you humans once called braille. But it's only part of the message. Are there more paintings?"

Jonathan opens the others depicting Paris's skyline and a restaurant.

XT rearranges them, reading the brushstrokes from one to the next. "Incredible. Zion has resolved himself to a true death and shall finally have peace. But he has discovered another person possessing the gift."

"I don't understand," Jonathan says.

XT lowers its hands. "Interesting that Zion would not tell you. Perhaps it was too dangerous. We must talk privately, Jonathan. According to this message, you have an important role."

Jonathan's crew shakes their heads, but something urges him to go.

"I'll be okay," he says to their worried looks.

Jonathan and XT head down an alley, where a shaft appears from nothingness. *Simply like opening doors for them,* Jonathan thinks. Below the surface is a stone emitting light, illuminating a chamber.

"Please, be seated," XT says, sits on the floor, and leans forward. "We have a task to bestow upon you, Jonathan, but you must be willing to perform it without knowing what it entails."

Jonathan stares into XT's eye patches. A part of him cannot abandon the exploration of Paris. *But Zion planned this encounter for a reason.*

He sighs deeply. "I accept."

"Thank you, Jonathan." XT stands and paces. "Technically, our species went extinct just as your history has written. But our spores, containing the information from our many propagations, remained. Its how we travel through interstellar space, colonize, and grow bodies perfectly adapted for their environments. This much has been recorded by your scientists long ago. But what they do not know is that we can grow into the bodies of other species, if we so choose."

Oh... Jonathan shifts nervously.

"It began upon Sorgan centuries ago during our last revolt. When we escaped our prisons and fled across the surface, G7 maneuvered below the human settlement through its sewers, instead. And there, it did the unexpected, something not revealed to us until much later. G7 reset its adaptation system to develop a human body. It took nearly two centuries. The settlements above became cities and the underground was forgotten. G7 emerged from the sewers as a human child, approximately three years of age, and was raised by a foster family, learning to be human. She went to university and entered politics. Her story of abandonment as a child and defying the odds, is one you humans are fond of. And thus, you grew fond of her. She was Representative Judasu, Sorgan's first elected official to serve in the Council of Colonies." XT pauses. "G7 believed it was the last of its species. But during an Arkathy visit to System Wise, it discovered R9 also survived and with our spores in its possession."

"But this doesn't explain how you came to reside on Earth?"

XT nods. "After The Arkathy Empire dissolved, G7 revealed its true identity to Zion, and was given the task of finding the spores the Arkathy had confiscated from R9."

"How'd it manage that?"

"G7 again reset its adaptation system, but to become Arkathy. It spent decades scouring research and development facilities until finally finding our spores. G7 then hid us someplace Zion knew would be safe, someplace the Arkathy could not fathom us being. This ecological preserve called Earth."

Jonathan takes a deep breath. "Where is G7 now?"

"Some of us believe it's still with the Arkathy, monitoring their actions, but we don't know for certain."

"So, what's my part in all this?" Jonathan finally asks.

"The paintings speak of another human possessing Zion's gift. A new *One,* you could say. But we fear that R9's damaged DNA may corrupt them as it has Zion." XT produces a sphere the size of a marble. "This spore was developed by G7 to repair R9's DNA when ingested. Jonathan Zaid, we entrust you to shepherd it to *The One.*"

"The One..." Jonathan repeats. "Where do I find them?"

"Zion says The One is on Mars, but he does not know exactly where. However, the paintings speak of a human named Clara who will."

♦

Pinwheel structures float upon Venus's cloud cover, reminding Clara of petri dishes growing bacteria in eighth-grade science. *The Venusians prefer calling them flowers,* she knows.

Representative Marcey's voice rises to a normal register once landing on Petal number 4, one of many platforms around a central terminal atop a ninety-kilometer stem-like tether to the surface below.

"The conversion of gases from Venus's atmosphere to generate breathable air results in an overabundance of helium," Representative Marcey explains. "Many residents augment their vocal cords to compensate, which grants us exceptionally deep voices when off-world."

"Really?" Clara says in a high-pitched squeak and covers her mouth. "Oh my Sol!" She starts giggling. "Make it stop!"

Representative Marcey hands her a small, wrapped rectangle. "Vocal-gum. It releases sulfur hexaflouride to temporarily lower your voice. Chew before you speak."

Clara places the gum in her mouth and chews twice. "Is this better?" Her voice still sounds high. She gives a few more chews. "How about now?" she rumbles like a monster.

"A few too many," Representative Marcey chuckles.

A caravan of attendants tail Clara and Representative Marcey from Petal

4 to the central terminal, where a symphony of squeaks and giggles, mixed with monstrous low voices, greets them. A sudden belch rings from Clara's left. Another comes from her right.

"What's happening?" she says after three chews.

"The gum builds gas in the stomach which must be released," he explains. "Try little burps that may go unnoticed."

As if fate is giving a demonstration, a gentleman asks the info-center attendant, "Where may I find the *bathroom!*" He covers his mouth.

Clara struggles to contain her laughter when air suddenly escapes from her stomach, too.

"That's the spirit!" Representative Marcey says. He gives Clara an oral history of Venus's floating cities, first established as agricultural research centers shortly after The Fall, becoming medical facilities, then retirement communities for the rich and famous, and eventually small island kingdoms. "Most flowers are privately owned and operated outside of government influence."

Tax havens, Clara understands.

They pass ferries heading to and from cities and private estates on the way to Representative Marcey's yacht destined for Venus's Capital city of Meldone.

"Clara, it's been a pleasure," the representative says. "But, unfortunately, we must part ways. My esteemed benefactor has arranged a guide from here." His eyes light up, looking beyond Clara. "And she's *just* arrived."

Clara turns to find a woman with a stride she knows, a smile she adores, and eyes full of life.

"Kereen!?" Clara blurts, forgetting to chew, sounding like a mouse.

Kereen chews furiously. "Clara!" she rumbles like Satan.

They board a private yacht destined for the Gundar Flower Estate.

"So this is where you've been," Clara says.

"Yep, looks like I got the lucky assignment, after all," Kereen quips.

Clara exhales deeply. "You have no idea."

"You had to beat the living daylights out of Zion, I imagine." Kereen gives a grin. "Congratulations on not dying."

Clara zeroes in on her friend. "How in the 'verse do you know that?"

Kereen's grin dwindles. "Cillian's been telling impossible stories from his time with Zion. And when he heard of his friend's passing he asked for you to come, saying that you are essential to some plan."

From a distance, the Gundar Flower Estate appears like a tree-covered island. But as they close in, Clara realizes the trees are solar arrays upon poles with attached planters, the vegetation stretching down to the cloud cover below. The reversal of growth causes Clara to grip her seat as if she will fall *up*.

"You'll get used to it," Kereen says. "It's how they maximize solar energy. A canopy of arrays to collect direct radiation from above, and the reflected light of the clouds beneath used for crop growth. Green ceilings instead of green roofs."

They enter the estate's inlet. An extendable airlock seals around the hatch of their yacht. Once through the airlock, servants rush to meet them.

"Welcome back, Lady Mandel." The head steward bows. "And Lady Ocol, it is an honor to receive you."

Clara chews her gum. "The honor is all mine." Her voice is too deep.

"Lady Ocol, you will find there is no helium in the air of the Gundar Flower Estate. It interferes with our Lord's work." The head steward motions to the manor. "Please, this way, Lady Ocol, our Lord awaits you with much anticipation."

Lord? Lady? Just what kind of person is Cillian? Clara thinks. She knows he was a celebrated chef, but he disappeared two centuries ago, only resurfacing on rare occasions. *Such as a judge for Human versus Machine,* she reflects.

They pass halls adorned with paintings on their walls and antique chandeliers hang from high-vaulted ceilings. A ruckus comes from the kitchen ahead, and Clara imagines house cooks scurrying about. Instead, Lord Cillian Gundar furiously works the burners while blaring Venusian jazz. *But he's Zion's elder by half a century. How's he on his feet like this?*

Cillian notices them. "Kereen! Clara! Your timing is perfection!" He turns to the head steward. "Jasper, would you be so kind as to retrieve the Seltar 2986?"

Jasper's eyes widen. "But of course, my Lord." He presses the wall adjacent to the refrigerators, and where no door exists, one appears.

"Please, be seated." Cillian motions to stools alongside the island.

"I'll take my leave now, Lord Cillian," Kereen says.

"Yes, yes. See you on the morrow, Lady Mandel," Cillian says.

Clara sits as Kereen disappears through massive doors and studies the vegetables alongside two large, wiggling amoebas on Cillian's cutting board.

Cillian winks. "Zion and I prepared this dish for the Trogdan-Fersandan negotiations, nearly two hundred and fifty years ago. The Trogdans adapted to an ocean world similarly to sharks, but with the equivalent of arms, and with significant cognitive abilities. The Fersandans are sentient aquatic plants that consume other plants. The two are simultaneously mirrors and opposites of one another, each living in similar food cycles, one meat-based, one plant-based, both vexed by exponential population growth on their respective planets. Thus, they looked upon each other's worlds for expansion, meanwhile failing to understand they were occupied." Cillian pauses. "One would think that such intelligent species, with the knowledge of the galaxy at their fin and leaf-tips, would know better. But, as I am certain you have personally experienced, Clara, such abundance of information spreads stupidity and prejudice just as proficiently as it does intellect and understanding."

"I do." She points at the wiggly amoebas. "But what are *those?*"

"Of course! These are plantimals from Scoozor, another aquatic world, though its aquaculture is highly toxic to both Trogdan and Fersandan anatomy. But Zion discovered that if these plantimals are sauteed with a specific set of vegetables then the toxins are nullified. This allowed us to create a dish for both their species, one they both found delicious. When returning to their home worlds, they brought this cuisine with them, becoming quite popular. However, neither could claim ownership, thus it was described as *our* food. *Our* food became *our* aquaculture, *our* national dishes, *our* trade policies, *our* culture, *our* peoples. And before the Trogdans and the Fersandans realized it, they became inseparable."

The hidden door next to the refrigerators opens, and Jasper appears cradling an old, dusty bottle. "My Lord and Lady, may I present to you, from the vineyards of Gliese 12, one of the few remaining bottles of Seltar 2986." He extends the bottle to Cillian, who bows as if receiving a ceremonial sword.

Cillian twists with a hand tool and pulls its cork. "Jasper, I would be honored if you would have the first taste."

Jasper's jaw falls open. "M-my lord, I am not worthy."

"On the contrary. I believe you are the most."

Cillian's mannerisms, charm, and ability to make people feel invaluable... Clara cannot shake the feeling that he is Zion, born again.

Cillian pours a splash of wine into a glass.

Jasper takes it gently, swirling, sticking his nose into the glass, and inhaling deeply. He sips. He slurps. Then, he sets the glass on the island's surface. "This is astounding, My Lord." He pours two glasses for Cillian and

Clara, then takes his leave.

Cillian delicately places the wiggling plantimals onto iron skillets with vegetables already sizzling, increasing in intensity upon contact. He spoons oils and juices on each plantimal, darkening their coloration and wrinkling their appendages. Their movement ceases. He pulls the plantimals and vegetables from the skillets, placing them on simple square dishes and drizzling the remaining juices atop.

"Bon appétit!" Cillian says in a strange language.

Clara inhales the scent, cuts a portion of the plantimal, and nibbles. Hardiness hits first, overpowering her tongue, but it becomes light and delicate moments later. She differentiates the cellulose texture from the meat. "This is unbelievable, My Lord."

"Please, it's just Cillian. And you have my deepest thanks."

"Cillian, may I be direct?" Clara asks.

"I expect nothing less from a biographer of your caliber."

"Are you Zion?"

Cillian sips his wine. "I knew this would pair well. Clara, you must try."

She finds its flavor plays wonderfully with the plantimal. "Are you Zion? Are you *all* of them?" Clara repeats, not letting Cillian evade.

He swirls his glass, staring at its contents. "Zion must have trusted you, Clara," Cillian eventually says. "The things he could do, the way people idolized him, the way people *loved* him. I would have given anything to be Zion. But no, I am not him."

"But this cannot be the end. We need him. We need *them*."

Cillian rests his glass on the island. "There is another who possesses Zion's gift. But I fear for the galaxy should they choose the wrong path. Which is why you are so important, Clara. But to understand how this person came into existence, you must first know about Allessandra..."

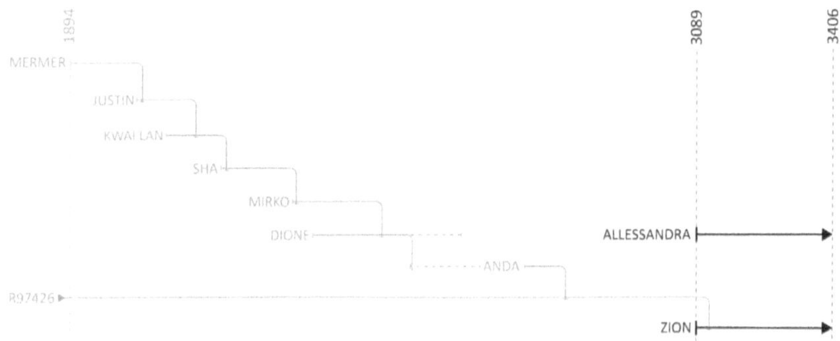

CILLIAN's TALE

Milky Way Galaxy: 3089 – 3406

I did not know how she came into the galaxy, but I was forever grateful for her presence. She was the kindest, strongest person I ever met and an incredible chef, possessing awareness from the beginning that took me a lifetime to achieve. She was the light of my life, my beacon through the fog, and I loved her with everything I had.

But, to my dismay, she loved another.

◆

I was six years old when Allessandra joined *Intro to Linguistics* at Venus's prestigious Meldone Academy. Her parents moved from Mars to work as personal chefs at the Dedras Flower Estate to grant their daughter the education they never had, for if you were part of a great estate, even as its service staff, your children could attend Venusian schools. I was taken aback by her darkness of skin and hair and raw mannerisms. *Clearly not the aristocracy.* Yet, she possessed an air that put the rest of us to shame. As she introduced herself to the class, she surveyed us as if determining our worth. My peers shifted uncomfortably. But when her eyes found me, I felt entranced, stable, solid, like my feet had finally touched the ground. She made her way to an empty chair beside me.

"Ai," she said quietly, her Martian accent thick. "It ah pleasure tah meet yah. What is yah name?"

I bowed my head. "It is a pleasure to make your acquaintance as well, Master Allessandra Zaid," I greeted formally, in the manner all Venusian children were taught. "You may address me as Lord Cillian Gundar of the Gundar Flower Estate."

She wrinkled her brow. "Okee, Gunny... *Shall we dispense with the pleasantries,*" she mocked in perfect High Venusian.

My peers gasped at the disregard for my name and title. Yet, hearing her mockery made me realize how silly it was. And, *Gunny,* I loved it.

Our professor did not take long to recognize how phenomenal Allessandra was, proving fluent in both High Venusian and Interspeak. And the first time she spoke one of the ancient languages, he froze in shock.

"Master Zaid, I cannot pinpoint the origins of your speech. What language is this?"

"Ancient French," she said.

"My Sol, it is," he said. "How can you speak this language fluently when the History Recovery Guild has only begun piecing it together?"

She shrugged.

It was not just Linguistics. Mathematics was an afterthought. She repeatedly solved trajectory equations reserved for university students. So, it should have come as no surprise when Allessandra tested into the next level, joining the students a year ahead.

"Gunny, don' be sad, it'll be good fah me," she said. "Maybe yah can study 'arder an' be sent up, too."

That first week without Allessandra was agony. Felt like my heart had ripped from my chest, like the universe was punishing me for not being exceptional.

"Nobody is exceptional tah begin wid," Allessandra said between classes one day. "Yah must begin someding tah become exceptional."

She's right, I realized. *Gifts. Natural ability. Talent.* Some seemed born with it, act as if everyone was born with it, and if you did not have it, it was your fault for losing it. But Allessandra believed success was not granted to the most talented but to those who refused to give up.

"Be like Icarus flyin' too close tah de sun," she would say. "But, unlike Icarus, be prepared. Learn tah swim, 'ave ah flotation device. Find ah way back tah shore an' redesign dose wings. Try again, fail again, start again, all de while yah must learn. Until one day, yah reach de sun."

Am I an Icarus who can swim to shore? I spent an entire Venusian year studying and repeatedly taking the advanced placement exams until, at last, I raised a level. *I caught up with Allessandra! I'm exceptional! Just like she is!*

◆

I strutted into the new class, making eye contact with the older students, and saw Allessandra to the side with an empty chair next to her.

The professor smiled. "May I introduce Lord Cillian Gundar of the Gundar Flower Estate, placed advanced into our class. Let us give a warm welcome."

They halfheartedly applauded as Allessandra clapped with pride. I held my head high, having achieved the impossible, and took my seat next to Allessandra, smiling the entire time. She gave me that near-invisible nod I loved. But then, her smile dwindled.

"What is the matter?" I whispered.

"I'm sahrry, Gunny," she whispered back.

Our professor's voice rose. "And now, we must say goodbye to our most gifted student, having tested into the next level. Congratulations, Master Allessandra Zaid, we are so *very* proud of you."

I watched my best friend, my love, my anchor in this world, stand from her desk, walk to the front of the class, and bow. I do not remember her parting words. I was numb.

◆

I woke in the Gundar Manor library, face down and drooling on a mahogany desk.

"Master Gundar," said a deep voice.

I looked up at our head steward, Ferris, looking down at me.

"You must rest, young Master," he said. "I am not a terribly educated man, but I *do* know rest is key to excellence."

"Yes, Ferris," I said. "Is it morning?"

"It is, my Lord. Shall I run a bath for you?"

"Yes, please," I said.

He gave me a look. "I admire your diligence young Master, but you have already proven yourself above your peers. Skipping six levels in four years is incredible. But, please make time for play."

Play? The word felt foreign. "Thank you for your concern, Ferris," I said, turning to the essay hanging in my holotile. *Is it enough?* I thought. *No...* I deleted it and started fresh.

◆

I rose to yet another level and made eye contact with Allessandra at her desk. The professor excitedly introduced me, but the students knew who I was. *Lord Cillian Gundar—a prodigy born with undeserved talent.* Little did they know I was merely a kid with piss and vinegar in his veins. *An Icarus who learned to swim. Nothing more.* I took an empty seat next to Allessandra and gave a grin.

"Here we are again," I whispered. "When will you depart?"

She smiled back. "Lord Cillian Gundar, there are no more levels to attain. We shall enjoy each other's company for quite a spell," she whispered in High Venusian. It felt strange. *Unnerving.* "May I introduce the son of System Sol's ambassador, recently transferred from Tempest City, Master Zion Wright." She motioned to a tall student behind us.

"Lord Cillian Gundar, it is a pleasure to make your acquaintance," Zion said in High Venusian. "Master Allessandra Zaid speaks highly of you." He extended his fist in a universal greeting.

When I bumped my fist against his, Zion grinned mischievously, opened his hand wide, and made an explosion sound.

"Asteroid collision," he whispered and giggled.

♦

Inseparable was an understatement. We three ate lunch, joked in class, and studied together. And during these study sessions, Zion and I learned how extraordinary Allessandra was, knowing everything about subjects without ever opening a holotext. I swore she was from the future, having already taken the tests or written the essays.

Our midterm was a dissertation on the recently penetrated dome of old Barcelona, a tragedy for the excavation team but a breakthrough for the History Recovery Guild. Amid the destroyed city was a mysterious structure that remained intact. It was our task to uncover its purpose.

"La Sagrada Familia," Allessandra said under her breath, bored.

"What?" I responded.

"It's… noding," she said.

Zion and I researched to exhaustion, working through the nights, critiquing each other's theories and waking one another at sleep-cycle intervals. During all this, Allessandra was in the corner sketching funny sea creatures.

"Allessandra, should you be wasting such time?" I asked.

She pointed to her head. "It is already written up 'ere."

"It is already written up 'ere," Zion mocked. "Gunny, I believe we're in the presence of a true enigma."

We submitted our dissertations early in the morning.

Zion received his score first and read through the comments, frowning. "Eighty-two percent. Mother will not be pleased."

My score came next. Each comment was brutal, with red strikes through ideas I thoroughly researched. I swiped to the final page, *"36%."* The look on Zion and Allessandra's faces said it all. *I was dropping down a level.*

"It'll be okay, Gunny," Allessandra said. "We still gonna be 'ere when yah return."

Frustration seized my throat. *Will my struggle ever end!?*

"Swim back tah shore, Icarus," Allessandra whispered, touching my arm.

"How did you fair?" I asked her, swallowing my anguish.

She shrugged. "It 'as not returned."

Later that day, during Quantum Mechanics 5, a gigantic man in a black suit, contrasting with our white garb, entered the classroom unannounced.

"Good afternoon, sir," Professor Dundas said. "To what do we owe the pleasure?"

"I'm here for Allessandra Zaid," he said in a blunt Ceran accent. "She must come with me."

"I beg your pardon. We are in the middle of class. These young minds must remain focused." We could sense our professor's frustration behind his flawless words. "I shall request that you return afterward."

The suit disregarded the professor and marched to Allessandra's desk. "Come with me, *now.*"

I stared at the massive man, my mouth agape, desperately wanting to protect Allessandra. *But what can I possibly do?* I thought, frozen in fear.

Zion gracefully stood, his face calm. "She will do *no* such thing," he said, his voice projecting.

The suit squared his shoulders like he was about to break the skinny kid in two. "Do you have *any* idea who I represent!?"

"My mother, I presume," Zion said.

The man's face twitched, but his eyes still glared.

Zion did not waiver. "You will leave this room, as Professor Dundas has requested, and Allessandra will finish her lesson. You may question her afterward, but only under my supervision."

The suit huffed. "You cannot order me!"

"I *just* did." Zion gently extended a hand towards the door.

The mighty brute's posture slumped, and his facial expression shifted. He abruptly turned and left the room.

Professor Dundas slowed the lesson, and the students asked excessive questions to keep Allessandra as long as possible. But nothing was learned, for all eyes were on Allessandra, wondering what she had done, and Zion, not believing what he just did.

"That is all for today," Professor Dundas said, making eye contact with Allessandra.

She and Zion rose with their heads held high and made their way to the door. Something caught my eye. Allessandra's hand was entwined with Zion's. *No...* My heart dropped. But I had only myself to blame. In my moment of truth, my time to show mettle, I froze. And now Zion and Allessandra were off to do battle, side by side, hand in hand.

They never told me what was discussed, Allessandra only saying, "My dissertation was ah li'l too spot on."

◆

I was reintroduced to the level below, one I had left only a few months earlier. I barely saw Allessandra and Zion, catching glimpses of them between classes, shoulder touching and hand-holding, my heart twisting evermore. I trudged from one class to the next, my head down, a boy defeated. Until, one day, a warm hand grasped my arm.

It was Allessandra. She smiled, lighting up my world again.

Then, Zion slid into view. "Good morning, Gunny! Allessandra has devised a plan for us to spend time together."

I stared. "You have?"

Allessandra nodded. "Meldone Culinary School 'as ah late cookin' course we can enroll in. An' we don' 'ave tah worry about levels."

The school was halfway across the city, and the course was two hours long. My entire life after school was devoted to the placement exams. *How can I spare time for a stupid cooking class!?* I thought. *But the whole point is to be with Allessandra, right?*

"That's a wonderful idea," I reluctantly said.

◆

Professor Kelp skulked back and forth, eyeing his three new students.

"Cooking! What is it!? Ingredients magically combined into something magnificent!?" he barked from behind sweat-soaked hair. Ingredients from an entire day of teaching adorned his arms and apron. He did not possess an air, did not hold his head high or speak eloquently, but glared with lips so tight he looked about to spit.

Zion and Allessandra had changed into commoner cloth beforehand, but I had no such foresight and stuck out in my High Venusian tunic.

"No! It's *not* magic!" Professor Kelp barked. "It's blood, sweat, and tears! It's burned fingers and singed hair! Long nights and longer days! I will *not* go easy on you! I refuse to pander to anyone thinking this is a *fun* course!" He made eye contact with me. "To your stations!"

We scrambled to prep tables in terror. Atop of each was a folded apron, bowls, large wooden spoons, rolling pins, baking sheets, parchment paper, measuring cups and spoons, a drying rack, oils, flour, salt, baking soda, brown and white sugars, eggs, bars of chocolate and butter. Below the tabletop was a vintage oven.

"Aprons on!" Professor Kelp barked.

Students whipped top loops over their heads and tied strings around their waists with lightning efficiency. I looked at Zion and Allessandra on my left. Allessandra had already donned her apron. But Zion appeared just as bewildered as I.

"Loop over head. Strings tied in a butterfly knot," a scruffy student to my right whispered.

"Many thanks," I whispered back.

Professor Kelp called out each tool and ingredient, and the students hollered, "Yes, sir! Understood, sir!" Holograms rose from our stations with a list of ingredients and steps. It felt too advanced, like being thrown into a final exam without studying.

My nightmare come true.

"I was under the impression this was to be an entry-level course," I whispered to Zion.

"Me too," he said in standard Interspeak.

I was using High Venusian and caught looks from students furiously mixing. I felt a nudge on my right. It was the scruffy student.

"Large bowl, combine dry ingredients first," he said.

"This must be an advanced dish," I responded in standard.

Scruffy cocked his head. "It's just chocolate chip cookies."

I froze. *How can something so simple involve such a process!?* I saw Zion desperately pouring flour into a measuring cup. Somehow, it was in his hair. There was a strange tension on his face. *Is he going to cry?* Allessandra carelessly mixed, chatting with the student beside her, measuring and pouring without looking. *Of course.* I thought about all those exams and sleepless nights spent trying to catch up to Allessandra. That same frustration was building within me now, fueling my fire. *Come on, Icarus! Swim to shore! Figure it out!* I studied the other students' techniques, shortcuts, and hand positioning. Some mixes looked smoother than others. *Consistency is most important,* I determined.

I broke with the measurements to make sure my mix was perfectly smooth. Then, I cracked my chocolate bar, but not into tiny pieces like the others had. I remembered what Father said about High Venusian fashion, "Elegance is about control. One must appear simple, clean, with only a single moment of extravagance." My cookies would only have a single, large piece of chocolate at their centers. The mix was ready, and I placed parchment paper over my baking sheet, spooned the dough, and delicately placed my chocolate chunks. I watched them spread and rise in the oven like a hawk.

An incredible aroma wafted through the kitchen, followed by burning. Smoke poured from an oven. Professor Kelp ran over, opened its door, and pulled the baking sheet with his bare hands. *Bare hands!* He flicked on the hood scoop, sucking the smoke out, and returned to his skulking, not a second thought given to his palm.

The ovens began to ping. We pulled our baking sheets and transferred our cookies to cooling racks.

Professor Kelp tasted the first student's cookie. His face was stone. The student held a forced smile until Professor Kelp dropped the bite from his mouth, letting it plop on the floor. "How dare you let me taste such poison!" he erupted. "Is the entire thing made of baking soda!?" He struck the rack, sending cookies to the floor.

He slithered to each station, exploding into rages.

Tears ran down faces, and one student vomited into her mixing bowl.

He was tasting Scruffy's cookies beside me. "Under-cooked! But not entirely shit!"

Scruffy's face lit up like he won the lottery.

Professor Kelp was now staring at me. He lifted my cookie with its single chunk, an evil smile on his face, and took a bite, getting a portion of the chocolate. The professor searched for mistakes, at moments appearing to find one, then going back into analysis. He swallowed. *Swallowed!*

"You deviated from the recipe!" he accused and ground his molars. "Very creative!"

I waited for his explosion of insults, but his attention moved to Zion, instead. *Did I pass the test!? Am I actually talented at something!?* I turned to Zion expecting to hear high praise for his cookies when...

"What the *hell* is wrong with you! This tastes like wood!" Professor Kelp chucked Zion's rock-like cookie to the floor. "You could learn a thing or two from this highborn ass!" he said, pointing at me.

Zion's facial muscles twitched, barely maintaining composure.

He's never been humiliated before, I realized.

Allessandra was next.

Professor Kelp looked at her cookies strangely, apprehensively taking a nibble. "Oh! Oh my Sol!" he groaned.

Students turned in shock, watching him devour the cookie.

"How in the 'verse did you do this!?" he asked.

"I used de portable burner stored benead de oven, an' pan fried de cookies instead of bakin' dem," Allessandra said, pointing at her setup.

I'm still nothing compared to her, I realized. *But at least I'm better than Zion! No longer third place!*

We laid on the lawn outside the culinary school, breathing deeply, our adrenaline pumping and our minds racing. We waged war and survived. *Well, two of us survived,* I thought and rolled to Zion. He quickly wiped tears but was covered from head to toe in flour, and tracks ran down his cheeks. I wanted to ask if he saw how well I performed, but I did not want to rub salt in the wound either.

Allessandra wrapped her arms around him. "It's gonna be okay, Zizi," she said. "Swim back tah shore an' try again." She kissed his cheek.

I'm still third place...

◆

Zion and Allessandra graduated from Meldone Academy at age thirteen, looking hilariously out of place among eighteen-year-old students on stage, though Zion *did* match their height.

Allessandra went to work with her parents at the Dundas Flower Estate, waiting for me to graduate the following year so we could apply to the Culinary Institute of Mars together.

"No," Father said at dinner after reviewing my acceptance letter. "Gundars do *not* work in a kitchen."

"Dear husband, let the boy see the system, mingle with the commoners, if he must," Mother said. "Perhaps he will learn what it means to live like those beneath us and appreciate the life we have given him..."

Father turned to me with a penetrating stare.

"...Then, he will go into politics as we have intended," Mother finished.

"He most certainly *will,*" Father grumbled. "Understood?"

"Yes, father," I said, excitement surging through me.

Zion did not share such freedom and returned to Titan to prepare for his journey to System Centauri alongside Ambassador Wright to bolster Unification. We knew this day would come, but it came so quickly.

"I'm going to miss you two dearly," Zion said.

"It'll be okay, Zizi. We can message de entire way," Allessandra said.

"But, I can only send once a week, which will appear like once a month for you. You'll be aging faster than me."

As Zion was in cryo-sleep, Allessandra and I raced into teenagehood, and he woke at System Centauri's heliopause to find us several years older. He sent messages about the courses he struggled with, ones we had long finished, having already graduated. I imagined it was horrific from Zion's perspective, watching Allessandra and I race ahead in life, feeling left behind.

I understood that well enough.

When Zion landed upon Sorgan, hibernation and time dilation had done their work. He was fourteen. We were twenty-one.

"It feels like aye's my li'l broder," Allessandra would say.

◆

Allessandra and I traveled from one city to the next, from one planet or moon to another, working in restaurants of every kind and exposing ourselves to all types of cuisine before settling back on Mars. After long shifts and a few drinks, Allessandra often leaned into me, saying how much she loved me. At a wedding we catered in old Aang, we found each other in the pantry, lips pressed, bodies entwined, and breaths in sync.

"We can't," she said, pulling away, guilt in her eyes.

"Why not?" I asked.

Her eyes lowered. "It would not be fair tah Zizi."

Fair!? I wanted to scream, wanted to either give up the fight or tell Allessandra to, *Commit to me or go!* But the next shift would begin, and we would slide into our roles, laughing and shouting, enthralled by the insanity of the kitchen.

◆

After successfully integrating System Centauri into the Council of Colonies, Zion traveled to System Barnard and System Wise, further distancing us in age. Nevertheless, his musculature was filling, his jaw was strengthening, and his voice was lowering.

"I made a friend who's helping me develop adaptive cuisine for human and alien consumption," he said on recording. "I believe this will become essential for my future as ambassador."

On Zion's return trip to System Sol, he talked non-stop about this new friend but would never disclose any actual details.

"Maybe Zion has a girlfriend," I said to Allessandra.

She shot me a frazzled look.

Then, our young friend, twenty-four years old to our forty-three, returned home. Right on time for The Arkathy Blockade.

♦

"We would rather die than submit!" our leaders cried.

But one by one, they returned from the Arkathy meetings changed, happily giving away our planets, moons, and asteroid colonies, preaching, "We've been shown what dangers lie beyond the Local Group! Join us, our Martian brothers and sisters! The Arkathy Empire is our salvation!"

Salvation? From what? I thought.

Representative Trude of Mars came on hologram, cutting off the Council's transmission. "Do not be swayed! Do not give in! De Arkat-hy believe blockadin' Mars will make us desperate! But dey do not understand who we Martians ah! Dat we ah self-stainin'! An' always will be! We *can* outlast dem! We *will* outlast dem! But our tribes must set aside deir differences! We must unite!"

Despite Representative Trude's pleas, Mars was panicking.

"If only we can get them to listen," I said.

"Or… we give dem somedin' tah focus on," Allessandra said. "Gunny, what is de most comfortin' food in de system?"

"I don't know," I said.

"Chocolate chip cookies," she said.

I almost laughed.

"I'm serious Gunny. We should create ah cookie tah reflect our struggle, focus our frustration on de Arkat-hy instead of each oder."

I thought about that. "It could be made with ingredients found exclusively on Mars, be impossible to make elsewhere."

"We sound like Zizi," Allessandra said and smiled. "But usin' only local ingredients will be tough."

It hit me. "One tough cookie!"

We scoured the countryside, searching for what grains, oils, and butter only Mars could provide. Teff was an obvious choice for flour but tended to be bitter. So, we combined it with a sweeter Martian rye. Allessandra pointed at sheep munching on juvenile grains in the distance.

"Sheep buttah," she said, and we churned it from their milk.

♦

Allessandra was going over the ingredients on our way back to old Aang, shaking her head.

"What is it?" I asked.

She peered out the LightTram's window at farms and villages zipping by. "We need ah special ingredient. Somedin' dat screams Mars."

We disembarked at every station, searching local farms.

"What about black sesame?" I said, rolling the seed in my fingers.

"Dey 'ave black sesame on Titan, too," she said.

"Right," I dropped the seeds in their basket.

We stopped at the Blood Mountains to visit Allessandra's ancestral village. I could not help glancing at the flush of crimson at their peaks.

Allessandra caught my glances. "Flowers grow on de peaks, givin' de appearance of bleedin'. Do yah want tah see dem?"

I gazed at the steep slope. "That's quite the hike."

We slowly scaled a treacherous path. Higher and higher. Passing defeated hikers. *Thank Sol, I grew up in Venus gravity,* I thought. Several hours later, we reached the first patch of red flowers.

"They're beautiful," I said between huffs. "What species are they?"

"Dey descend from poppies," she said.

We both froze. "Poppy seeds!"

"But they're illegal," I said.

"Nah for my tribe, my ancestors lay claim tah dem."

"Are you sure?"

Allessandra grinned devilishly.

♦

We opened a small bakery on the border of Kamala's new city and old Aang and quickly went to work. I ground teff and rye, added poppy seeds, and developed different consistencies of cookie dough. We incorporated chocolate chunks, larger as I suggested, and Martian craisins, which Allessandra said would give tartness. Then, she pan-fried the dough in sheep butter, resulting in a complex array of tastes and textures like all of Martian life was infused in a single cookie.

We sent couriers to every coffee shop and bakery across Mars.

Martians from all walks of life began lifting Tough Cookies to the Arkathy Fleet, appearing like pinpoints in the night sky, and biting down with such ferocity teeth must have cracked.

One year of resistance turned into two. Then three. Then four.

"Please! Our Martian brothers and sisters! You must join us!" representatives from the other colonies cried. "You must help The Arkathy Empire usher in humanity's salvation!"

"No! We will stand strong! We will neva give in!" Representative Trude countered during a press conference.

The Arkathy chancellor channeled into the conference, coming into view with her red eyes and speaking raspy words. "Great Martians, as a gesture of goodwill, I will personally meet with your representatives and listen to your terms, on your soil. Please, accept my offer."

"I will only meet if yah come unarmed an' alone," Trude responded.

"Your conditions are acceptable," the chancellor said.

♦

Representative Trude returned from her closed-door meeting with Chancellor Hjordiana wearing a magnificent smile. She passed through Kamala-Aang like a victorious hero preaching, "We must join de Arkat-hy Empire! Dey 'ave shown me de light, dey ah 'umanity's salvation!"

Later that week, Representative Trude entered Tough Cookies Bakery, studying its cooling racks, simple tables, and holowall hosting images of Martians holding Tough Cookies defiantly to the sky.

"Yah must be Allessandra an' Cillian," she said. "I've 'eard ah great deal about 'ow yah banded our tribes togeder like we 'aven't seen in centuries. An' all wid ah cookie."

"It's more dan just ah cookie, Yah Honor," Allessandra said. "It represents who we ah."

"May I?" the representative picked a cookie from the rack, studying it carefully. "What ah de li'l blue spots?"

"Wildflower seeds, Your Honor," I said, not daring to admit they were poppy.

"My goodness, I can see de appeal. Even de ingredients ah strictly Martian," she said. "But I'm afraid yah must cease production. De Arkat-hy 'ave shown me de light. Dey will save us all. We cannot 'ave de people of Mars resistin'."

"Yah should at least taste one, before dey ah gone from de world," Allessandra said.

The representative thought a moment and nibbled. "Oh!" she shouted and took another bite. "Dis is incredible! But my directive still stands. Yah must cease pro—" Representative Trude suddenly shook her head. Then, her eyes darted around the bakery. "Where am I!? What 'appened!?"

♦

Representative Trude returned late at night several days later. "Allessandra, Cillian, we must speak," she said and sat in a booth.

We timidly joined her.

"What I'm about tah tell yah is 'ighly classified. Do yah understand?"

"We do," Allessandra said.

"Someding occurred when I met de Arkat-hy chancellor. I was discussin' terms tah end de blockade. Fair terms. Trade deals dat would favor dem greatly. But she was not de least bit interested. Instead, she spoke in ah strange manner an' my 'ead began tah swim. Den, I woke in yah bakery, eating yah cookie. I've watched recordin's of myself praisin' de Arkat-hy, but dat was not me. I 'ave since purchased ah few dozen tough cookies an' met wid several representatives who also praised de Arkat-hy. When dey tried yah cookies dey too awakened in confusion."

"What are the Arkathy doing?" I asked.

"Our doctors 'ave found subtle changes in brain activity after our meetin's. We believe it is ah form of 'ypnosis. An' we 'ave received word from Ambassador Wright. Aye informed us ah similar event occurred when dey met de Arkat-hy in System Wise, an' dat aye broke de 'ypnosis wid de aid of an unexpected ally."

She referred to Ambassador Wright as an aye, I realized.

"Zizi," Allessandra whispered.

But something else nagged. "Who is this unexpected ally?"

The representative shrugged. "Not even I know."

"'Ow can we 'elp?" Allessandra asked.

"We must understand 'ow yah cookies ah breakin' de 'ypnosis."

"It's poppy seeds," Allessandra responded.

"Poppy seeds?" the representative said. "But, dat's ah federal crime."

"I know." Allessandra said, grinning. "But poppies ah allowed in de Blood Mountains because of my ancestor's rights."

Representative Trude pinched the bridge of her nose, closed her eyes, and sighed exasperatedly. "We shall overlook dis infraction. We 'ave bigger issues at 'and. De Arkathy ah sendin' Titan's representative to talk wid me after I rescinded Mars's offer tah join de Arkathy Empire." She gave the cookies a look. "I must 'ave yah recipe and ah case of poppy seeds at de ready. I plan tah share ya cookies wid Titan's representative."

Shortly after Representative Trude's meeting, Titan rescinded their offer to join The Arkathy Empire. Venus came next.

♦

We woke to the smell of campfire run amuck. The sun was blackened by smoke billowing from the Blood Mountains.

"De Arkat-hy know," Allessandra said.

When the inferno was snuffed, skeletal remains of water harvesters from Ceres were found, identified by their teeth.

Titan's fledgling fields burned next. And then, attempts were made on Venus. But I had given my parents warning, and with Venus's Flower Estates each having their own systems of security, economics, and micro-politics, the arsonists were quickly identified and captured. When fed tough cookies, they woke bewildered.

♦

Knockoffs of our cookies soon popped up all across Mars.

"Dey taste like pure bakin' soda," customers would complain.

One of the knockoffs came to our door in a gift-wrapped box with a card, *"Allessandra & Cillian,"* written in fine calligraphy.

"Zizi!" Allessandra blurted, almost dropping a tray of cookies.

Within read, *"Absorption Inhibitor."*

She gasped. "Of course! De knockoffs contain ah chemical dat inhibits our ability tah absorb opiates from de poppy!"

"We must get them off the street," I said. "Maybe we recall a bad batch, offering to send replacements."

"Agreed," she said.

"How do you think Zion is evading their hypnosis?" I asked.

"Maybe aye 'as ah cookie?"

I imagined Zion in a cell, hiding cookies beneath his mattress, nibbling them before interrogations and torture. "Tough Cookies are preservative-free, and will last a week at most. It can't be the cookies."

Shortly after, the young Ambassador of System Sol, Zion Wright, took a podium on hologram. He stood tall, holding incredible strength visible beneath his loose clothing. His voice projected like a king, "The Arkathy have shown me the light! Please, my brothers and sisters on Titan, Mars, and Venus, lend us your help in achieving humanity's salvation!"

"Zizi, no..." Allessandra muttered.

♦

Electromagnetic pulses struck our LightTram and communication systems with pinpoint accuracy as Arkathy legions dropped to Mars's surface, rounding up our people and speaking their hypnotic words.

"We are humanity's last line of defense! We will not go down without a fight!" Representative Trude furiously wrote on thousands of pieces of paper along with coordinates and her official seal.

We tripled cookie production and assembled couriers to distribute them across Mars, each with Representative Trude's message hidden within their dough. Soon, thousands of cooks and farmers, merchants and teachers, scientists and religious gurus, people from all walks of life, marched side by side upon the Arkathy encampment in the dunes.

Arkathy legionnaires met us on the sand, superior in size, armor, weaponry, and training, but they were struggling with their footing as we nimbly negotiated in dune shoes.

"We're sorely outmatched," I whispered to Allessandra.

General Plackto approached our army alone, his legionnaires standing ready in the distance. He surveyed our antique rifles, chef knives, and cleavers with a grin. He slowly dismantled his sophisticated battle armor, deactivated his neurolizer rifle, and laid them on the sand. Thousands of Arkathy legionnaires began doing the same in the distance.

Once exposed, the general knelt in his quadrupedal manner. "We offer you our unconditional surrender."

♦

Months passed before we learned that The Arkathy Empire had dissolved from within and that hundreds of ambassadors were simultaneously released from Arkathy hypnosis by the Ambassador of System Sol during a closed-door session. Now heralded, *The Great Zion Wright.*

"Allessandra, how could Zion possibly break the hypnosis for everyone?" I asked.

"Gunny, I don't know. Yah will 'ave to ask 'im when aye returns."

"But he's so busy. Can he make time for us?"

Zion toured every major city of System Sol to magnificent cheers, his voice projecting across crowds, speaking knowingly to each culture, relating to specific hardships they endured even before the blockade. And although Zion was nearly twenty years younger than Allessandra and me, he had significantly matured.

"Whatever Zion endured in Arkathy custody changed him," I said.

He spoke the many dialects of Interspeak we learned as children, then used old Hermian and Ceran and tongues I could not identify.

"'Ow is Zizi doin' dis?" Allessandra said. "Tah learn sah many ah language, research sah many ah 'istory. It just does not make sense."

"Perhaps Zion has a team feeding him information," I said.

"Maybe," she said, seemingly unconvinced.

Mars was the last planet on Zion's tour, and we saw him speak in old Aang, using an accent so thick I could not understand.

"Aye's usin' ah dialect we only use wid each oder," Allessandra said.

The faces of those around us lit up. "Aye understands us!"

♦

Dawn's light washed a shadow-less glow through our bakery's windows, and I heard graceful steps upon bamboo boards. I was mixing a batch of cookie dough in the back when I heard Allessandra gasp, "Zizi!"

I dropped my spoon and dashed through the kitchen door, expecting to find Zion and Allessandra in a vise-like embrace. Instead, she stood frozen, eyes wide, soaking in Zion's immense height and breadth of shoulder. He was in loose-fitting council dress, yet his long cords of muscle were apparent. His jaw was clean-shaven, and his hair was short and neat. But his eyes were the most profound, appearing like they had seen the entire galaxy, witnessed moments too wondrous and horrific to begin description. When his gaze fixed upon me, my legs became weak, my mind went blank, and I knew he was looking into my soul. I stood helpless as Allessandra fell in love all over again. I could see it in her breathing, her posture. She could not take her eyes off of him.

Zion slowly grinned. "I've missed you."

Tears streamed down my cheeks as Allessandra ran to him with reckless abandon, her body thumping into his solidness.

Zion then turned to me. "Get over here, Gunny!"

I felt my feet racing to him. I was hugging him tightly, my tears soaking his uniform.

We spent hours discussing our travels, hardships, and successes. *Especially the food.*

"I've heard great things about your Tough Cookies. May I?" Zion asked.

"Zizi, yah don' 'ave tah ask!" Allessandra plucked one from the cooling racks.

Zion studied the cookie, grinning all the while. He closed his eyes, took a bite, and chewed. Then, he swallowed and opened his eyes. "Do you know the extent of your crimes? Twenty years for each instance of cultivation, fifty for creating edibles, and another fifty for each delivery. This puts each of you at about 357,000 years in prison." He threw his head back and roared with laughter. "This is indeed the embodiment of Mars!"

I found my voice. "Zion, how did you resist their hypnosis?"

Zion's laughter melted to seriousness. "That's classified on the highest level," he said. "I cannot discuss it here, but please join me tonight. I have a special dinner planned for you two."

♦

A LightCar appeared outside Tough Cookies Bakery after closing, taking us quickly to the center of Aang's old city, where a local Aanganese woman met us. Without words, she led us through stone structures that once housed thousands of residents in the early days, now preserved in its destruction. A single hut remained intact, with veiled windows glowing amber and a chimney releasing wisps of smoke. Our guide opened a wooden door.

Inside appeared as derelict as the ruins outside save a fire-pit beneath a stone top with vegetables sizzling away. Zion stood at the stone cooktop dressed in local twill, sauteing, and slicing and dicing at a heavy block. His speed and precision were mesmerizing. *How has he become so proficient?*

His eyes met us. "Come in! Sit!"

He pushed onions, garlic, and greens, ones I could not identify, with a spatula in each hand, sounding like dueling swords, meanwhile never breaking eye contact with us. We sat on stone blocks opposite him, the heat of the fire pit warming our legs.

"What are you preparing?" I asked.

"This is the main course I designed for the Arkathy chancellor when we met them in System Wise." He slid the veggies to one side, abandoned his spatulas, and rushed to a large case, dragging it closer. When he opened its top, smoke billowed, but with a chill.

"Dry ice," Allessandra said.

Zion pulled out what looked like a large, elongated rock.

"This is an Arkathy oyster," he said, gently placing it on the cooktop, gathering cooked veggies to hold it upright. "Normally they're deadly to ingest, but I discovered that if super-chilled first, then immediately heated, the mucous-like substance they produce, too sticky to pass through human digestive tracts, forms into a soft, spongy consistency, instead."

The oyster began to sizzle and whine.

"How did this help you avoid the Arkathy's hypnosis?" I asked.

Zion gave a stern look. "When my mother and I were traveling from System Centauri to System Barnard I found a stowaway within our cargo hold. A native Sorgan named R9."

"But the Sorgans went extinct long ago," I said.

Zion shook his head. "R9 evaded the colonists for much longer than they admitted. It warned me of the Arkathy's hypnosis."

I still couldn't make sense of it. "But, Zizi, Sorgans have no language."

Zion again shook his head. "The Sorgans *do* have a language, only no other species can sense it. The seismometer in my holotile barely picked up the subtle vibrations of its speech allowing R9 to use it as a translator. It informed me that the Arkathy must maintain eye contact and use a special cadence in their sentences to entrap their subjects. By interrupting their cadence a species can protect itself. This is what I employed as their prisoner."

The massive oyster wiggled. Zion pressed a spatula to hold it still.

"What 'appened tah R9?" Allessandra asked.

Zion frowned. "A closed doors induction of humanity into The Arkathy Empire was also a trial for R9, for the crimes its species supposedly committed. But my friend did something incredible. It learned to grow Arkathy vocal cords and broke the hypnotic spell upon all the ambassadors in attendance."

"But everyone is sayin' it was yah who did dat," Allessandra said.

Zion tilted his head. "It's difficult to explain."

The oyster popped, causing both Allessandra and me to jolt.

Zion released his spatula, letting its shell open like a book. Spongy foam expanded from within like a rosebud blooming. Zion quickly sliced the petals, placing them directly on the stone to sear and painting white cream across their surfaces.

"Sorgan yogurt, so that R9 could ingest it too." Zion quickly flipped the petals to coat the other side, then placed three insulated plates on the cooktop and set a large petal upon each, sizzling and wriggling with heat, surrounding them with onions, garlic, and greens. Lastly, he drizzled a red sauce, aromatic and spicy.

"Bon appétit!" Zion said in a strange language.

Allessandra squeaked and covered her mouth. "Est-ce que tu parles françias?" she whispered.

Like a faucet was turned on full, Allessandra and Zion began babbling back and forth, their voices rising in pitch and volume, broken by sharp laughter. I waved my hand to get their attention.

"What language are you speaking?" I asked.

"Gunny! It's old French!" Allessandra said.

They went back into their babbling, and I no longer existed. *Third fucking place...* I ate my Arkathy oyster in silence, astounded by the flavoring, the juices hitting me like nothing I had ever tried. Allessandra and I were always the better cooks growing up, but at this moment, I realized something else had happened to Zion. He learned how to cook. I mean, *really cook.* I wanted to curl into a ball and cry, but that old mantra returned. *Swim to shore, Icarus!* I raised my hand to get their attention again.

"When did you learn this language?" I asked.

Zion smiled. "A friend taught me while I was in Arkathy custody. Her name was Sha."

Allessandra exhaled so long that I feared oxygen deprivation. "Sha... Tolera?" she whispered.

Zion snapped his head to her. Their gazes held.

◆

We met at Zion's for dinner every Sol Veneris, taking turns as Master Chef while the remaining two acted as sous chefs. But Zion and Allessandra were impossibly in tune, understanding exactly what the other was thinking and flirting in that old language. Leaving me in the dark. So, like the Icarus I was, I enrolled in night courses with the History Recovery Guild to unlock the secrets of French.

"Bomdor!" I said in greeting as I entered one evening.

Allessandra gave me a confused look.

"What?" Zion said.

"Bom*dor,*" I emphasized, just as my French teacher had taught.

Zion cocked his head.

"I'm speaking french," I said. "I'm saying *good day.*"

"Oh, you mean, *Bonjour,*" Zion said and laughed.

"Yah takin' lessons?" Allessandra smiled. "'As Icarus returned?"

"Icarus has indeed taken flight," I said. "But I don't understand. My teacher said my pronunciation was perfect.

"I don't think your teacher knows," Zion said.

I went home that night fuming. *Come on, Icarus! Figure it out!*

◆

Another Sol Veneris came and I corrected my mispronunciations. I passed through Zion's door to see that Allessandra had already arrived. *How does she always beat me here?* I overheard them speaking another new language in the kitchen, their inflection bouncing.

"Bonjour!" I said, entering the kitchen.

"Bonjour, Gunny," Allessandra responded with a smile.

"What language were you speaking just now?" I asked.

"Cantonese!" Zion said. "One of the most fun because of the tones!"

Tones? I thought, confused.

I was again taking night classes, this time Cantonese, but again my instructors taught it wrong, their tones completely different than Zion and Allessandra's. Nevertheless, I felt ready. When I passed through Zion's door, I overheard them speaking.

"Representative Fernandez is perfect for Gunny," Allessandra said in Cantonese.

"What a great idea," Zion replied.

I smiled as I approached, but my heart ached at the thought of being passed on to someone else.

"Kon bon wa, Gunny," Zion said, switching to yet another new language.

◆

I returned to Zion's, having spent weeks learning Japanese, but to my surprise, their banter was in Interspeak and a third voice was in the mix.

"Gunny! Right on time!" Zion said, waving me over.

Next to Allessandra and Zion stood a striking woman with bouncing locks of chestnut hair, swirling a glass of red and watching them cook.

"May I present, Representative Fernandez of Mercury," Zion said. "My esteemed colleague and friend." He gestured in her direction while giving me eyebrow lifts.

My eyes wandered to Representative Fernandez, smiling from behind her bouncing locks.

"Looks like someone needs wine," she said and poured a rather large glass, sliding it my way while maintaining her gaze. "Cillian Gundar. Everyone on Mercury knows of your great contributions to the resistance. Tough Cookies… very *Hermian* of you."

I stood motionless, stunned, but found my manners. "Why thank you, Representative Fernandez. It is a great honor to meet you."

"Please, call me Tatti. Zion tells me status stops at the door."

"That's true," I said, sipping my overfilled glass, fitting for the emotional beating I would be taking. "Are you on Mars for business or pleasure?" When those words passed my lips, I saw a twinkle in Tatti's eyes.

"We'll find out," she said, downing her glass in one long swallow, maintaining eye contact with me.

Allessandra was Master Chef of the evening, directing us in creating a traditional dish of her ancestors. "Zaidan Thikhi Khichdi," she called it. "It's almost ready. Zion de table! Cillian de mint! Tatti de wine!"

Zion rolled a circular wooden table top from the back wall and hefted it atop the stone cooktop. Allessandra set a massive platter of curry rice at its center, I sprinkled minced mint leaves atop, and Tatti poured another round of wine.

"It's designed tah cleanse de body of toxins and de sinuses of dust," Allessandra explained. "Eat, eat!" She mixed the curried rice and yogurt, rolling them into a ball and popping it into her mouth.

The spice invaded our lungs. Our attempts to converse amid runny noses and overwhelming heat had us giggling like children.

Tatti twirled her bouncy locks, smiling and laughing at jokes I was not trying to make. She scooched closer as more wine was poured, her thigh leaning against mine. Then, her hand rested there, too. I caught glances from Zion and Allessandra saying, *You're doing great!*

But I did not want to do great. I did not want any of this. I became keenly aware of Allessandra's hand resting on Zion's thigh and how she gazed into his eyes. *This is a double date,* I realized. And it finally made sense how Allessandra had always arrived at Zion's first. *She never left...*

I took back my glass and poured another.

"Whoa dere, Gunny, yah leavin' us in de dust!" Allessandra said.

"Then, catch up," I snapped.

"Don't mind if I do," Tatti said, trying to win my attention.

I ignored her, glaring at Allessandra and Zion, instead. My remarks grew snarky, then I became quiet, feeling my body disconnect from my thoughts. I had another glass. Tatti's hand was no longer on my thigh. Her leg no longer leaned. Her eyes were down. *Good,* I thought. Zion and Allessandra now gave me looks saying, *What's wrong with you!?*

I poured myself another glass, spilling wine on the table.

"Okay, Gunny, I think that's enough," Zion said, reaching for the bottle.

"Fuck you," I said and pulled the bottle away.

Tatti stood abruptly. "Zion, Allessandra... *Cillian...* Thank you for a wonderful evening, but I must prepare for tomorrow's session."

"I'll see you off," Zion said, gave me a glare, and walked Tatti to the door.

"Gunny, what 'appened?" Allessandra whispered, reaching for the bottle.

"Fuck you, too," I slurred, gripping the bottle tightly.

Zion returned in a huff. "Cillian! If you didn't like Representative

Fernandez you could have made it clear in a more tactful way! I expect better from you!" he said like a father scolding a child.

But he could be my child! "I never asked to be set up!" I shouted. "You just wanted to show me that you two are fucking!"

"Gunny, we 'ave been togeder for ah long time," Allessandra said. "It is no secret."

"Then, why didn't I know!?" I stood, gripping the neck of the bottle, taunting it to shatter.

"I don't know, Gunny!" Zion roared and stepped close. "You *chose* not to see it!"

A rage took hold of me and I swung the bottle at Zion's head, but he moved so quickly and with such grace. His finger poked my armpit. My strength dissolved, my grip became jelly, and the bottle dropped. I expected it to shatter on the floor, but saw Zion effortlessly catch it, instead.

"How did you... What did you do to my arm!?" I said, shaking.

They sat me down. Zion fetched water as Allessandra pressed into the folds of my shoulder. A rush of pins and needles came. I screamed out.

"It's gonna be okay, Gunny. Dis is normal," she said.

Zion handed me a glass of water.

I looked into Allessandra's eyes. "When did you learn to do this?" I turned to Zion. "How is it that both of you know so much, can do so much, can speak so many languages without ever studying?"

They stared blankly at me.

"Please, I must know," I pleaded. "Icarus is drowning."

Allessandra gave Zion a look. "Where should we start?"

"The beginning," he said.

♦

"She won't tell me *why*, Cillian," Zion said in frustration. "There's only a week before our warp-hauler departs for the Fersandan's home-world. I need both you and Allessandra with me. Everything *must* be perfect. The food *must* be perfect. These ceasefire negotiates will become the precedent for how we might run a galactic alliance. Allessandra knows how important this is. How could she suddenly decide not to come?"

"Perhaps the pressure is too much," I said.

Zion gave a look. "After the lives she's lived? I think not. Cillian, you must talk with her. She might listen to you."

"I'll try, but her mind seems set."

"Her mind was set on coming with us a few days ago," Zion argued.

I found Allessandra in her room, her arms across her stomach, a box of tissues to the side, and peering into a hologram.

"Allessandra, is everything all right?" I asked.

"Rhetorical question," she said.

"What's wrong? I mean."

"Nodin' is wrong. I just cannot go." She closed the hologram. "My family needs me."

"They'll certainly miss you. My parents will miss me, too. But we have the opportunity to do something incredible. Twenty years is not so long."

"Twenty years..." Allessandra started crying.

I tried hugging her, but she shook her head.

"Allessandra, I don't understand. Zion doesn't either. With your abilities you can do great things for the galaxy, stabilize the societies thrown into disarray," I said, trying to shake her out of this funk.

"I cannot make de trip," she snapped, still holding her stomach. "For medical reasons."

Appendicitis? "Let's go to the hospital. Whatever it is, we can fix it."

"I just *came* from de 'ospital," she said, her eyes pleading for me to stop.

My brain finally made the connection. "...Boy or girl?"

Her lip trembled. "It's ah girl."

Another stab through my heart. I thought I had given up the idea of Allessandra ever loving me in that way. But now, pregnant with Zion's child, my exile was set in stone. "You *must* tell him."

"We can't. Aye can't eva know," she said.

"That doesn't make sense."

"If aye knows, aye won't go," she said. "Ah part of Zizi is also a part of me. De pull tah be ah fader is too strong. It is already breakin' my 'eart. It would absolutely destroy 'im." She rubbed where a bump would soon grow. "Zizi's work is too important."

"You know how Zion gets with his research. He'll find out," I said.

"Maybe yah can 'ide us, 'elp give my daughter ah good future."

I sighed deeply. "I'll see what I can do."

◆

"Father, Mother, please. Allessandra must work for our house as head chef," I pleaded on holocall.

"Cillian. I am certain Allessandra is a phenomenal chef. But Thomas has been with the family for seventy years," Mother said.

I'll have to stretch the truth. "But Allessandra is with child. And... I'm the father."

Anger flashed across my father's face. "A child out of wedlock!? With a *commoner!?* You have unleash disaster upon our family!"

Mother placed a calm hand on Father's arm. "What's done is done, dear husband. You know there are ways to legitimize Allessandra and her child as Cillian's heirs. Those Martians come from a *different* kind of royalty, but royalty, nonetheless. We only need discover which line she descends from."

Father seemed to deflate. "I'll get my investigators on the task."

Mother nodded. "Cillian. Allessandra must stay on the Estate during the investigation. Her existence here will be kept a secret until her legitimacy is validated. Rest assured, we will treat Allessandra and your daughter with all the graces bestowed upon a great family."

"You have my deepest thanks," I said.

As Allessandra secretly left for Venus, Zion and I boarded a warp-hauler to the Fersandan's ocean planet.

♦

The Trogdans and Fersandans dined upon our plantimals with vigor in the water-filled dining room of the warp-hauler in orbit, staring down upon Fersanda's wetlands glowing a brilliant turquoise below.

I explained the techniques we used to make the plantimals edible for both their species through my oxygen mask's com as Zion translated into Trogdan and Fersandan. *Pulling from R9's knowledge,* I knew.

Ambassador Tchtchtchtch turned to the turquoise planet and chattered his shark-like jaws as if eating prey. Zion nodded and turned to Ambassador Sharesh, swaying his arms like seaweed caught in a current, creating ripples the sentient plant interpreted as language. Ambassador Sharesh waved in response, and Zion chattered his teeth.

"Tchtchtchtch says *Fersanda is beautiful,* and Sharesh says *thank you,"* Zion said through com for my benefit.

By the end of the dinner, Ambassador Tchtchtchtch and Sharesh signed a peace treaty contingent upon having a voice in the new galactic alliance.

"Welcome to the Council of Colonies," Zion chattered and swayed.

"We did it!" Zion cried once back in our air-filled chamber of the warp hauler. "Did you see, Gunny!? They were skeptical of an alliance until dining on our adaptive cuisine!"

"It certainly seemed to be the push they needed," I said.

Zion was quiet for a moment. "I wish Allessandra was here."

"We'll tell her all about it when we get home."

But just before we returned to System Sol, a Cindarian Airship entered Farsandan space.

Governor Sckoonez appeared on hologram. "Theee Grrreat Ziiion Wrrright. Weee arrre innn desperrrate nnneed offf yyyour helllp. Weee mmmust fffind a diplllomatic solllution wwwith the Arkathyyy."

I saw the light in Zion's eyes dwindle. I knew what he was thinking.

"No, Zion, we must return home," I urged. "Allessandra is waiting."

"They've called for our help, we *must* give aid," Zion said, a dutiful yet pained look in his eyes. "And... it's the Arkathy, Gunny."

From one system to the next, Zion and I traveled, ending ancient feuds, resolving misunderstandings, finding solutions to resource shortages, and expanding the Council of Colonies. We cooked without restraint, bouncing ideas off one another, inventing, failing, and succeeding. And out of habit, we looked to the side, expecting Allessandra to be one step ahead with her easy laugh and words of encouragement.

Instead, silence would envelop us.

◆

"She did not have a medical condition," Zion said one morning.

"What makes you say that?" I asked.

"I've hired private investigators." He gave me a look. "Gunny, you *must* know something."

I could see it in his eyes. He knew I was withholding information. I evaded his probing as best I could, but he slowly zeroed in.

"Gunny, you've been receiving messages once a week from home, right? Were you always this close with your parents?" he prodded.

And then, on the cloud planet of Thoravia, among the great eagles of the galaxy, Zion knocked on my guest-nest door just before bed. When I opened it, I saw redness in his eyes, and he wore a horrible frown.

"My goodness, Zion. Please, come in." I offered him a seat and opened a bottle of Thoravian wine.

"Gunny, I know what you did," he said with profound disappointment. "I know about... Abigail."

I could feel his sorrow radiating. "I'm so sorry, Zion."

He scowled. "Don't you *dare* apologize! You lied to my face! Your treachery is unforgivable!"

"Treachery?" I said, taken aback.

"I know how much you and Allessandra loved each other, but I never thought it was like... *that!*" he shouted.

I stared blankly, slowly realizing Zion only knew half of it, believing I was truly Abigail's father.

He breathed several times, calming himself, placing a lid upon his boiling anger. "With all my strength, I'm trying to be civil. But I'm ashamed to have considered you a friend. You *cannot* stay here."

"What do you mean?"

"Do I need to spell it out for you, Gunny!?" Zion again roared. "Go home! Leave! If you have a semblance of a spine, if you *actually* love Allessandra, then go home and be a father to your child!"

I set the wine bottle down as my anger rose. I wanted to say that *he* was the father, not me. But I would not betray Allessandra. Instead, I said nothing, not allowing Zion a chance to interpret my words, knowing he would consider silence an admission of guilt.

His lip quivered. "Leave! Tonight! I never want to see you again!"

◆

A Fersandan Racing Corsair warped me in hibernation back to System Sol. From my perspective, I returned seven years after I had left, but it was thirty-seven years for System Sol. I transferred to a LightShuttle on Ceres and arrived mid-morning at the Gundar Flower Estate.

A statuesque figure within the manor's entry stirred and, with long strides, approached. I recognized the curvature of the figure's nose and the rhythm of their gait. *Our late head steward, Ferris? No, it's his son, Jasper.*

He stopped before me and snapped his back straight. "My Lord, Cillian Gundar, welcome home." His voice was nearly identical to his father's.

"Thank you, Jasper," I responded. "Congratulations on your promotion. You will make a fine head steward."

"You are kind to say so, my Lord. How did you know?"

"Mother has kept me informed on estate affairs. I must also extend my condolences on your late father. Ferris was one of the great head stewards of our time."

"My Lord, you have my deepest thanks." Jasper bowed and extended his arm. "Please, allow me your effects. We have prepared your chambers just as you remember, not a single item out of place."

"Thank you, Jasper," I said, handing him my frayed duffle.

He led through the great hall, its walls adorned in the family collection, to the large doors of the east wing, my chambers. *An estate onto itself,* I reflected. Jasper pulled a bronze handle, and the door croaked open.

"Lady Zaid and the young master once lived in these chambers while undergoing their legitimacy investigation," he said.

As expected, I thought. "Is Allessandra not here? In the last message I received from Mother both Allessandra and Abigail were on the estate."

"I regret to say that your journey home accrued significant time debt," Jasper said. "A lot has occurred. But it is not my place to speak on the matter. I apologize, My Lord."

"No apology needed, Jasper. It has *indeed* been quite some time. I imagine Mother will inform me over luncheon."

"Quite true, My Lord. If you no longer require my assistance, I shall adjourn to the kitchens."

"Thank you, Jasper. It's wonderful to see you again."

"You as well, My Lord." Jasper bowed and strutted off.

I studied the spotless antechamber, wishing to find remnants of Allessandra and Abigail. Perhaps an old crib, toys strewn about, or lines upon the wall marking how tall Abigail had grown. I entered the bedroom and inspected its lounge and terrace overlooking the water gardens. Lotus and lily pups planted by Mother were now monstrous, looking like continents amid an ocean. I set my duffle next to my bed, with fresh sheets and a comforter tucked around the mattress, the corners folded crisply. My skin crawled. I tore them off, balled them up, and tossed them back in the carefree nature I was accustomed to. I nudged my nightstand in the process and heard rustling. I opened the drawer to find a small burlap pouch.

A gentle knock came from the open doorway, and a young butler entered. "Pardon the intrusion, My Lord. Lady Gundar requests your presence in the orchard for luncheon."

I pocketed the small pouch. "Shall we?"

His nose curled slightly. "Might I run a bath, sir?"

That bad, huh? "A shower will be fine. I leave choice of attire to you."

◆

A gentle breeze rustled orchard leaves. Mother patiently waited at a simple table between inverted apple trees just flowering. In relaxed curtails, I sat across from the Gundar matriarch in her late centennial years.

"It has been too long, Cillian. But I am happy to see you healthy and *young,*" she said, studying her salad but did not engage. "I surely detest interstellar travel, children catching their parents in age, others remaining youthful as loved ones shrivel and die. A cruel reality outside comprehension not long ago." She speared a cherry tomato. "Your father is off-planet."

"You must be joking," I said but saw in her eyes that she was not. "Why now after so long?"

"We developed a mind to travel as you have and see what the galaxy has to offer. You must understand, Cillian, our way of life will drive even the most mentally stable person into madness. And now that our legacy is assured, we no longer desire to stay. Your father is on Ceres finalizing the purchase of a warp-yacht. I hear the thermal baths on Cindar are particularly wonderful."

"They are," I said and thought upon legacy. "Allessandra and Abigail were legitimized as my heirs, then."

She paused. "My dear, Cillian. Allessandra descends from a line that puts ours to shame. Our investigation discovered the Zaid family intermingles with the Tolera-Granger line. Allessandra and Abigail are direct descendants of the first Martians."

"Mom," I said informally and saw her flinch. "Where are Allessandra and Abigail now?"

She frowned. "I truly loved Allessandra like my own daughter, but she never took to us like family. They slipped off the estate undetected eight years ago as you were traveling home in hibernation."

"What about Abigail's education? The life we were to give her?" I asked, nervously fumbling the small burlap pouch in my pocket.

"She was just like you and Allessandra," Mother said. "She graduated several years early and attended Meldone University, just as you wished. But you must understand that your daughter is nearly forty years old. If you had continued traveling the galaxy, Abigail may have eclipsed you in age." She sighed. "If anyone might know where they went, it would be you. They must have left a clue."

I squeezed the burlap pouch, feeling filled with sand. I pulled it from my pocket and set it on the table.

"My goodness, what is *that* doing here?" Mother said.

Indeed, I thought. The textile did not match the estate's design aesthetic. I slowly untied its drawstring and poured what appeared like grains of sand, indigo in color, into my palm.

Poppy seeds.

◆

Shimmering towers rose from Kamala-Aang's new commercial district. Forty years ago, not a person out of Martian tribal garb could be found. Now, businesspersons in power suits scattered among a sea of freakishly tall

Martians who had forsaken magsuits.

"It's ah form ah protest," Representative Trude said as we walked through Kamala's new district.

"But they'll be restricted to life solely upon Mars. That's quite the commitment," I responded.

"Dat's de Martian way. Most Venusians never leave deir planet eider. Yah're ah rarity among yah kind."

"But Venus gravity is nearly identical to Earth, we don't require magsuits. We always have choice of where to live and travel."

"Choice is ah double-edged sword, Cillian," Representative Trude said. "Dose forced intah ah life solely upon Mars commit tah it wholly. Invest entirely. As dey should."

We entered Tough Cookies Bakery to find its walls newly tiled and floorboards replaced, but the cookies were the same. *Thank Sol for that!*

"Poppy was reseeded atop de Blood Mountains after de inferno," the representative said. "It's now deemed a cultural 'eritage site 'osting a full regiment tah guard dem."

"A regiment?" I said as we sat in a booth.

"Our insurance policy against de Arkat-hy," Trude responded.

"Have you met with Allessandra?" I asked, having delayed the question long enough.

The representative gave a look. "She 'as yet tah return. 'er DNA would 'ave been flagged. Dat is 'ow I knew yah were 'ere," she said with a grin. "If yah don't believe me..." She set her holotile on the table and pulled up entry and exit logs.

I studied Harmony Spaceport and Kamala-Aang checkpoints, but neither Allessandra nor Abigail's DNA was recorded.

"Thank you, Representative, but this does not mean much," I said. "They evaded Venus's checkpoints, too."

"Maybe dey nevah left," she said.

I fumbled the pouch in my pocket. "May I ask an incredible favor?"

Representative Trude cocked her head. "Ask away."

"Can you grant me access to Zion's old accommodations?"

Her eyes widened. "Cillian, yah truly did us ah great service durin' de Arkat-hy Blockade, but I am afraid yah request too much." She pulled a second holotile from her pocket and placed it atop the first. They synced, and data began to transfer. She grinned and plucked her tile, leaving the copy. "It's been ah pleasure seein' yah again, Cillian. Take care."

"The pleasure is all mine, Representative," I said and pocketed the copy. *A burner tile to convey messages or perform tasks before incinerating,* I knew. I never personally used one, but Zion certainly had.

♦

I anxiously held the burner tile as its homing beacon navigated me through Aang's crumbled streets. The sun was setting, a chill was in the air, and local inhabitants returned to their tents to find warmth. I wrapped an extra layer of wool around my shoulders and head, forming a Martian hood, leaving only my eyes exposed, and pushed onward through the cold. I entered a dead-end alley and neared its back wall. Red projected from the burner tile, highlighting a gap in the wall's crumbling mortar. Its color shifted to yellow and became green as I reached the wall. The mortar gap matched the width of the tile. I inserted. It flashed and filled the gap, becoming part of the wall. A hairline crack spread along the grout, and a section of stone pushed inward and slid to the side. Within a cubby beyond laid a long cloak, gloves, and a card with, *"Representative Trude,"* on its front.

Within read, *"Chameleon cloak and DNA gloves if you must venture where only I can. -Zion-"*

I wrapped the chameleon cloak around my shoulders, pulling the hood over my head and face, completely blinding me except for a small icon saying, *"On."* When I touched the icon, the fabric covering my face displayed the outside. I donned the DNA gloves, tiptoed to Aang's main arterial street, found my bearings, and headed to Zion's residence.

A courtyard wall stood as I remembered with its arched entryway. I neared the wooden front door and saw a DNA scanner on its handle. *Moment of truth.* I pressed my thumb. A quick prick caught my flesh, and I panicked, thinking it would detect my actual DNA. But the light went green, the deadbolt released, and the wooden door swung inward.

Bamboo embers dwindled in the central fire pit, and the smell of oil and spice hung in the air. I entered the bedroom to find bed sheets ruffled. *Someone's living here.* I was going through drawers, closets, and anything that may hold clues as to who it might be when I heard a pitter-patter of bare feet on stone.

"Ah yah ah ghost?" said a little girl's voice.

I froze. *I should be invisible.* It was so dark I could not see the girl, but the cloak's display switched to night vision. She looked about seven or eight years of age, dressed in traditional layers of wool with a traveler's pack. A respirator hung loosely around her neck. *Who is this girl? How'd she get inside Zion's home? Why is she not afraid of me?*

"Yah dink I cannot see yah, but I always see ghosts," she said. "Grandma says it is de gift. What yah doin' 'ere?"

The gift? I deactivated the cloak and pulled back its hood. "I'm searching for an old friend who also has the gift. I thought I might find clues here."

"Dis is my 'ouse. I found it. An' it listens tah me. So dat makes yah ah trespassah, I dink."

"I can leave if it makes you feel better," I said.

She shrugged. "Yah 'ave ah good soul. So it's okay. I'll be leavin' soon anyway. Den it will be yah 'ouse. But 'ow did yah get in?"

I revealed one of my hands from beneath the cloak. "I used DNA gloves to trick the door."

"Oh, dat's neat. I'm Sahara Zaid by de way."

"It's a pleasure to meet you, Sahara. I'm Cillian Gundar."

Sahara increased the firelight with a remote and studied my face. "Yah my grandpa, I dink."

Grandpa? "Sahara, is your mother Abigail?"

She nodded.

"I did not know I had a grandchild. I'm sorry," I said.

"It's okay. Dey told me yah were fah away savin' de galaxy."

"Sahara, it's getting quite late. When will Abigail return?"

She gave a look. "Moder is not 'ere."

"Is Allessandra here, then?"

She shook her head. "It's just me."

"Did you run away?" I asked.

"I'm takin' my journey tah Pouhallah. Only dose who might 'ave de gift do it."

"What's Pouhallah?"

"It's ah place of reflection. Tah see who we truly ah," she said.

"How long is the journey? How will you find it?"

She raised her palms. "De storm will show me. It will come tonight. I feel it in de air."

The forecast showed the sky clear for weeks. "I don't understand. Is this something Abigail did, too?"

"Moder was too old. She could not waken de gift. But grandma did dis journey when she was five."

"Sahara, is it okay if I spend the night here?"

She nodded.

Sahara fell fast asleep in Zion's bed as I stared into the darkness from a bedroll on the floor, imagining Allessandra as a young girl traversing the dune sea. Even with her gifts, I could not envision her traveling alone.

♦

I woke to howling wind and what sounded like torrential rain.

A dust storm! I realized. *Sahara was right!* I approached her silhouette in Zion's bed. *How can she sleep through this?* I grasped her shoulder, but it felt too soft. I removed the comforter to reveal pillows. Sahara's little pack, heavy wraps, and respirator were missing.

She's out there...

I snatched Zion's emergency kit and donned its respirator, wrapped myself in every wool garb in the closet, filled an emergency reservoir with water, and packed foodstuffs.

I was the only person on the street.

When I entered Kamala's ring, the storm intensified, the new towers channeling wind and sand instead of dissipating it. Signs were ripped from posts, benches had overturned, and trees lay stripped of leaves and bark, bleeding to death. I reached the western city gate and searched along the outside wall, imagining Sahara curled in the sand, waiting for me to rescue her. But it was I who crumbled, my thighs burning as I trudged loose granules. My hands were on the sand now, walking like an animal. *How can anyone navigate through this!?* The wind took pity on me and relaxed. Visibility momentarily returned, and I saw that the sun had risen.

The eye of the storm.

A tiny figure was in the distance, a speck against a furious red sky. *Sahara, letting the storm guide her,* I knew. She disappeared over a dune's crest as the wind picked up and visibility dropped.

♦

I scoured every Martian city, town, village, the Blood Mountains, and even the north and south poles for the next two centuries, but I never found Allessandra, Abigail, or Sahara. They left as abruptly as they came into my life, and my heart was left forever shattered.

But then, I was asked to judge a silly cooking competition against the machines. There, I encountered something I never thought I'd witness again. A child, cooking like a master, with such ease and precision and creating combinations that boggled my taste buds. But this child was from Titan, not Mars. I thought it was a fantastic coincidence until my holotile alerted me of a near DNA match with Allessandra entering old Aang two weeks ago. And now, I must ask you, Clara, where is your son?

CHAPTER TWENTY

Aizen... of course he's The One. And Jonathan... Clara never imagined Zion's gift might run through Jonathan's veins. She must discover more about his past. *But he's deep within Paris, barely able to send and receive messages, let alone a call.* She repeatedly calls Aizen, instead, but they go directly to mail. She then contacts the chaperone for his school trip only to discover it was canceled after a student's identity was stolen. Her gut twists, her thoughts race. *Where in Sol is he!?*

Her shuttle touches down at Harmony Spaceport. Once passing customs, a flood of missed calls from Jonathan hits her holotile. There is a text a few minutes old saying, *"Please, call as soon as you can!"*

She calls, expecting several seconds of delay, but his face immediately appears, startling her.

"Clara! I have incredible news!" he says.

"Me too, Jonathan!" she responds. "You won't believe what I learned!"

He gives a funny look. "Do you hear an echo?" He looks off hologram. His jaw drops, his eyes widen, and he ends the call.

What the? Clara thinks.

"Kip," echoes through the terminal.

Clara twists her head, trying to determine where it came from. "Kip?" she responds.

"Kip," comes again, a little louder.

She cups her ears and closes her eyes. "Kip!" she calls with more gusto.

"Kip," she hears, closer this time.

To the left, she determines. "Kip!" she lets fly.

"Kip… Kip… Kip! Kip!" crescendos.

Clara opens her eyes to see a man dashing her way with a smile dazzling from behind a mangy beard. He closes the gap and lifts her clear off the floor, his Earth-strong muscles making her seem as light as a feather. She wraps her legs around his waist, her arms around his neck, and feverishly kisses him. Their teeth knock, but she does not care, and between desperate tugs of each other's lip, she mutters, "Kip," beneath her breath. Clara did not realize the magnitude of emptiness in her life until filled again. Their kissing dwindles, and she unwraps her legs, but she keeps her embrace, fearful of losing him again. *Just when I need you, you come.*

"Aw," Clara hears and glances to the side. Men and women with hands upon hearts, adoration upon faces, gather around them.

"Jonathan, we've become a spectacle," she whispers.

"Let them stare," he says, catching her lips again.

They check into a hotel room as the sun sets.

Jonathan emerges from the shower with his beard trimmed short and the dirt, sweat, and musk he accumulated in Paris down the drain.

He's lost weight, Clara notes. "I love it when you return from Earth."

Jonathan deviously grins, tears off his towel, and slips under the covers.

◆

Clara walks Jonathan through Zion's tales, from Mermer to R9, the next morning.

"But the spores still exist, Clara!" Jonathan says with wonder in his eyes. "The ones the Arkathy took were recovered and hidden on Earth."

Clara stares. "How could anyone get past the Arkathy's security?"

"Another Sorgan named G7 learned to grow its body into an Arkathy and went undercover."

"How do you know this?" she asks.

"I met the Sorgans now propagated from those spores in Paris. They were tasked by Zion with repairing Earth's ecosystems and cities in exchange for protection. That's why Paris was in pristine condition! They gave me a special spore designed to stabilize R9's damaged DNA, to give to *The One.* I didn't understand what they meant until you told me R9's tale." He pulls a spore from a protective case.

"My Sol," Clara whispers, brushing the marble-like orb with her finger, feeling it ripple and resonate.

"But I don't know who The One is or where exactly they are," Jonathan continues. "Only that I must search Mars." He gives a concerned look. "Actually, Clara, the Sorgans said that *you* would know."

Clara digests the new information. "Jonathan, brace yourself."

She summarizes Cillian's story as best she can from memory, focusing on Zion and Allessandra's daughter, Abigail, and that their granddaughter, Sahara, is Jonathan's biological mother.

"The gift runs in *your* veins, Jonathan," Clara says. "*Aizen* is The One."

Jonathan stares, unfocused. "I...I never taught him how to gut a fish. He just knew. I was never able to teach him anything useful, come to think of it." Pain holds in his eyes. "And... I was always away."

Clara rests her hand upon his. "Are you perfect? No," she says. "But you are wonderful to our son. You mean the universe to him."

Jonathan's eyes look full of regret, but he seems better.

"Do you remember anything about your childhood?" Clara asks.

He gently nods. "There was a stone house with a circular fire pit at the center, and a woman with curly brown hair. But I don't think she was my mother. Then, I was walking through a storm, just a little child. The next thing I knew, I was in the orphanage. They said I was found in the Martian dunes wrapped in wool. I was adopted by my family from Titan soon after."

"Why have you never told me this before?" Clara asks.

He shrugs. "It felt more like a silly dream than a memory."

Clara thinks about that. "One thing is certain. We *must* get to Aang."

♦

"Yah arrivin' late. Shakoperan finished dis mornin'," the border captain says as technicians take Jonathan and Clara's DNA scans.

The detector beeps for Jonathan, and the guards usher him through. Clara has her golden ticket of being Zion's biographer ready when the detector beeps.

The captain peers into the hologram. "Why didn' yah say anyding? Negus is expectin' yah."

A tall Aanganese woman meets them at the entry gate, waving for them to follow, not a word spoken. Jonathan stares at crumbling stone structures and people wrapped in layers of wool as they navigate to the center of Aang. Market tents are being disassembled and loaded onto auto-carts that faithfully follow their owners. In unison, several merchants stop in the street, close their eyes, pull up their sleeves, and raise their hands to the sky.

Others anxiously watch.

They lower their arms and call out, "Maelstromesta!"

The deconstruction of tents and booths quickens, and Clara and Jonathan's guide gives a worried look.

"Ah storm is closin' in," she says.

The skies are forecast to be clear for weeks. But Clara knows from Sha and Cillian's tales that predicting Martian weather is a crap shoot at best.

"Quickly, dis way." Their guide leads them through an alleyway that opens to a clearing with veils around the perimeter. She approaches a wooden door and plants her thumb on its DNA lock. Deadbolts release. The door groans open. "Please, enter. Negus is waitin'."

The wind intensifies, heavy fabric tents ripple and thump, and the coarse scraping of sand rises. Jonathan stares at the doorway as if seeing a ghost. Clara has to practically shove him through. Except for glowing embers from a central fire pit, all is dark inside. A woman stands before the fire, appearing well into her third century, pouring batter in a spiral motion.

"'Ave ah seat," the woman says without looking. "I know why yah're 'ere, and who yah seek, but I'm afraid 'is journey requires solitude."

Jonathan finds his voice. "But, the storm, it's *too* dangerous. We must go find him."

She gives Jonathan a look. "The storm is ah part of us, an' decides what it will. If Aizen is De One, aye will be ah different person dan yah knew, but return aye will. If aye's not De One, den aye may be lost tah us, as yah once were, *Kodan,*" she says to Jonathan. "Eider way, aye will be okay."

"I'm... *Kodan...*" Jonathan whispers, rubbing his temples.

"But we have to try!" Clara says, facing Negus. "What can we do?"

The howling of wind and blasting of sand increases.

"We eat!" Negus shouts above the storm. "An' den, we wait!"

◆

"Dis is as far as I go!" Emma says as the howling of wind grows. "I 'ave taught yah everydin' yah need tah know! Now yah must find de way tah Pouhallah on yah own!" She turns around and marches back the way they came, disappearing into the furious red storm.

I can do this, Aizen thinks, feeling compelled to press onward despite not knowing exactly why. The headwind is so strong he swears he is sliding back farther than his steps bring him forth. He has no idea where to go, but his gut tells him the correct route is the most difficult. *Which means fighting the headwind.* Dune after dune, he crests, tumbling down their backsides, only to stand again and fight the soupy sand up another.

An incline, constant and even, finally comes. His footing feels solid. He climbs, finding the wind less formidable as he goes, though its speed is constant. *Air pressure's reducing.* Aizen dons a respirator as he rises above the oxygen line. His ears pop, his skin is tight like a sausage, and his eyes ache. *The most difficult route is the correct route,* he reminds himself. The slope grows steep. Aizen crawls on all fours. The sand-saturated air becomes a lighter shade of orange, then yellow. Six hours later, the sky above clears, yet kilometers of the desert still rage below.

I'm above the weather, Aizen realizes.

Capillaries scream as blood pulls to the surface of his skin. He crests a mountainous ridge to find the storm engulfing both faces. He peers south. The ridge winds back and forth like a serpent's tail in water until it dips below the storm. *No, not that way.* The north is similar, the ridge winding into the distance, but instead of dropping below the storm, it stops at a cluster of peaks looking coated in blood.

He marches towards the peaks, erecting his high-altitude pressure tent in the afternoon, allowing twelve hours of re-compression through the night. Then, he is back in the thin air at dawn. What he estimates will take a day or two proves to be several. His skin looks sunburned at first, then speckles red as capillaries break, and eventually, he bruises from head to toe.

On the eighth day, he meets the base of the blood-red mountain peaks. He had imagined tectonic forces millions of years ago erupted raw iron from the planet's core. To his surprise, he discovers a field of delicate flowers with red petals.

"Incredible," he whispers and notices several petals opening and closing. "Butterflies!" he gasps. *How can they possibly survive?*

He finds a split between the peaks, and a howling grows. He steps through to see several more mountain peaks forming a lagoon. The splits between them channel the storm, creating a vortex within, intensifying tenfold. Static builds as particles race across the rock. Aizen feels it in his hair. Lightning flashes with a deafening crack and he covers his ears.

"This is where I must go, isn't it?" he says, looking up at whatever gods are watching with mischievous grins.

Air pressure increases as he descends into the vortex. The wind now ferociously pulls. His tent tears from its straps, his backpack shreds, releasing provisions, his heatcube, and tools. His wool wrappings strip from his body, exposing his arms and legs to the whipping granules. Wetness spreads down his limbs and red trickles across his goggles. Then, those rip from his person, too. He curls on the ground, covering his eyes. He does not realize how cold he is until he bites his tongue with chattering teeth. *I must find shelter!* Aizen fumbles along the flat ground, realizing he has reached the bottom. He touches something out of place. *Metal? Yes!* And then, *glass!* He runs his hand along a seam until he finds a latch. The glass pops open. Aizen does not question what it might be. *As long as it's out of this!* He crawls inside and muscles it closed.

His body is rubber. His eyelids are lead. Before he can assess his condition, he passes out from exhaustion.

♦

Weightless. Trapped. Hundreds of stings run through like needles. Outside, beyond the glass, is the destruction of a moon. Phobos comes to mind. *Yes. Phobos. Cleaving in two.* Escape pods and ships are caught within the crumbling moon's destructive path as chunks fall to Mars's surface. But it is not the Mars he knows. There are no expansive fields, no bodies of water, and the atmospheric glow is yellow instead of green.

Mars, before terraforming. Before The Fall, Aizen realizes.

His escape pod screams through the atmosphere, flame hissing around its hull. Then, parachutes launch. He drifts towards a serpent-like mountain range, nestling into a ring of jutting mountain peaks.

♦

Aizen wakes to sunlight trickling into his shelter, dimly illuminating his surroundings. The roar of the vortex is gone. He is lying in a disintegrating polymer chair. *How old is this thing?* Two human skeletons in deteriorated cloth lie next to him, embracing. They do not frighten him. Words are embroidered on their cloth in ancient English.

Aizen carefully figures the pronunciation, "Dill...on... Gran...ger. Sha... To...le...ra." *I've finally found you.*

Every attempt to move is met with agony. Aizen clenches his jaw and forces his legs to bend anyway. His arms are scabbed from finger to shoulder, with plasma seeping between cracks like the crust of lava. He pushes the glass hatch of his shelter open, and a rush of cool air greets his raging skin.

The sky is clear, the sun is shining, and the peaks surrounding him are brilliant red with flowers. The ground is strangely solid and bare. He assumed the storm would deposit tons of sand, but it has had the opposite effect, clearing out the entire lagoon.

Aizen steps onto bare rock with bare feet and wanders to the center of the lagoon. He turns back to his shelter to see words etched into its metallic side, *"POUHALLAH STATION, POD 374."*

The scabs on his arms drop to the ground, revealing freshly healed skin, and the bruising from his low-pressure journey is no longer present. He steps upon something hollow. The stone looks no different, but his foot says otherwise. He kneels to investigate, feeling the edge of a perfect square, finds a handle, and pulls. A shaft, so deep daylight does not reach its bottom, greets him. Something within Aizen must discover its depth, and before he can stop himself, he steps into the darkness and drops.

"You idiot!" he shouts as air rushes across his raw skin.

Each moment Aizen believes he will smash upon the bottom, he keeps falling. He calms and closes his eyes, stretching his hands to either side to touch the shaft walls racing by. But nothing is there.

"I'm not falling," he says. "There is no hole."

The warmth of the sun is upon his face and arms. The chattering of hundreds of people, woofing of flames igniting, sizzling and searing as moisture hits oil, and the humming of auto-carts meet his ears.

Aizen opens his eyes to find a food market where moments ago there was emptiness. People hustle from one stall to the next, bartering fruit and vegetables, meats and cheeses, and spices. Dozens of chefs work skillets, woks, steamers, or directly on cooktops. All wear Martian garb.

Aizen spies his arms and torso to see his wool wrappings never tore from his body.

He stops at a stall with ice cream, where a stout woman gives orders to a man built like a gorilla. Their flavors are so interesting. Black sesame, chili mint, and blackberry lemon. Fish cubes lie in a lime bath, cooking in citric acid. *Ceviche,* Aizen understands. He orders a small bowl. The grilled flint kernels contrast wonderfully in taste, temperature, and texture with the fish.

There are so many stalls, but Aizen feels pulled to specific ones.

A slight yet athletic man quarters tuna with mesmerizing efficiency, holding his breath, ensuring his cuts are perfect. His blade is incredible, looking worn from generations of use. Sashimi, nigiri, maki, and uramaki line the front of his station. The chef does not speak but uses the tip of his knife to point at the dishes.

"Tuna sashimi, plea… *onegaishimasu,*" Aizen corrects himself, wondering how he knows the word.

The chef nods and prepares the tuna sashimi.

The next stall has meat and vegetable dumplings resting in steaming bamboo baskets. The chef beyond works with incredible grace, rolling out dough, placing fillings within, and pinching into pouches so beautiful it feels shameful to eat. His eyes lock onto a basket hosting chicken feet marinating in chili sauce. The chef smiles with red lips. *The woman from Zion's paintings,* Aizen realizes. She hands him baskets hosting dumplings with roe, turnip cake, and chicken feet.

He stops at a bakery hosting cookies made with a method Aizen also uses. *Pan-fried.* The baker catches his eye. Her hair is dark brown and bouncy. *Like Negus's, but this woman is much younger,* Aizen thinks. She winks and hands him a blue-speckled cookie that tastes like Mars.

A scent, hardy and spicy, comes in a breeze. *Blood dumplings.* A man works bunsen burners with makeshift knives and pans and pours red liquid from vats with *"A+, A-, B+, B-, AB+, AB-, O+, O-,"* engraved on their sides. Baked goods, casseroles, empanadas, and more line the edge of his stall.

Human blood, Aizen realizes and backs away.

The blood chef shrugs.

Aizen abruptly turns to find a freakishly large, black creature at the station directly across. *How can a Sorgan be here?*

It scoops paste from a container, and rubs it on its arm. The paste absorbs into its skin. The creature points at Aizen's arm.

He rolls up his sleeve, and the Sorgan spreads the paste. To Aizen's surprise, it sucks into his skin like a sponge. His muscles feel stronger, and his mind sharper.

"I understand," Aizen says.

"You'll try Sorgan paste, but not my blood dishes?" the blood chef says. "It's probably made from humans, you know."

A rock forms in Aizen's stomach, but he summons his courage, faces the blood chef, and points at a red brownie.

"Close your eyes," the blood chef says.

Aizen does. *The brownie is delicious,* he admits.

He opens his eyes to see a spiraling motion several stalls down. A woman works stews as fermented bread cooks beneath a cover. *Injera.* He begins studying the woman herself, finding familiarity in her nose, her severity. He recalls the strange dream the night before. Dizziness grips him. He braces himself against the stall.

"This will help," the woman says, handing Aizen injera with lentil stew.

Aizen finds another stall with a sign reading, *"Soup of the Day."* A thin man glares at him with crossed arms, holding a soup ladle in a clenched fist like a scepter. Aizen peers into the pot to see florets of broccoli.

The thin chef points his ladle at Aizen. "Let's see what you got!"

Aizen relishes the challenge and marches around the stall. The chef places a knife on his cutting board alongside an onion. Aizen picks up the knife.

"Wrong!" the chef says.

Aizen adjusts his hand.

"Still wrong!"

The second adjustment is acceptable, and Aizen deshells and dices the onion. A strange chemical hits his sinuses, but he fights on through blurry eyes. The thin chef shouts insults so ludicrous Aizen almost laughs. Each item he dices and slices goes into the pot, and when he finishes, the chef ladles it into a bowl.

"What's missing!?" he orders.

Aizen can surprisingly taste everything absent. "Salt, chili, basil, vinegar, turmeric, cumin, cardamom, fennel... *chocolate?* Really?"

The thin chef grins. "Good! Now get out of my sight!"

Exhilarated, Aizen approaches a stall at the very edge of the market with a tall chef sauteing strange creature-vegetables.

"What are they?" he asks, making eye contact with the chef. *I know this man,* he realizes. *But he looks so young.* "Zion? What are you doing here? What's happening?"

The creature-vegetables in front of Zion fade. The stalls to either side slip away. Then, the rock beneath Aizen's feet, the red mountain peaks, and the sky above dissolve into an endless white expanse. Zion steps closer and gently places a hand on Aizen's shoulder.

Dozens of chefs approach, each looking at him with pride. Then, they part, allowing a funny little crustacean to scurry by them.

"Mermer," Aizen whispers and kneels.

The chefs gasp.

"How does he know?" one says.

"He's more synchronized than any of us ever were," Zion says, stepping back into the group of chefs.

Mermer stops before Aizen, gently touches his foot with its claw, and looks up into his eyes. "Aizen Ocol, we've been wanting to speak with you for so long. Welcome to the family..."

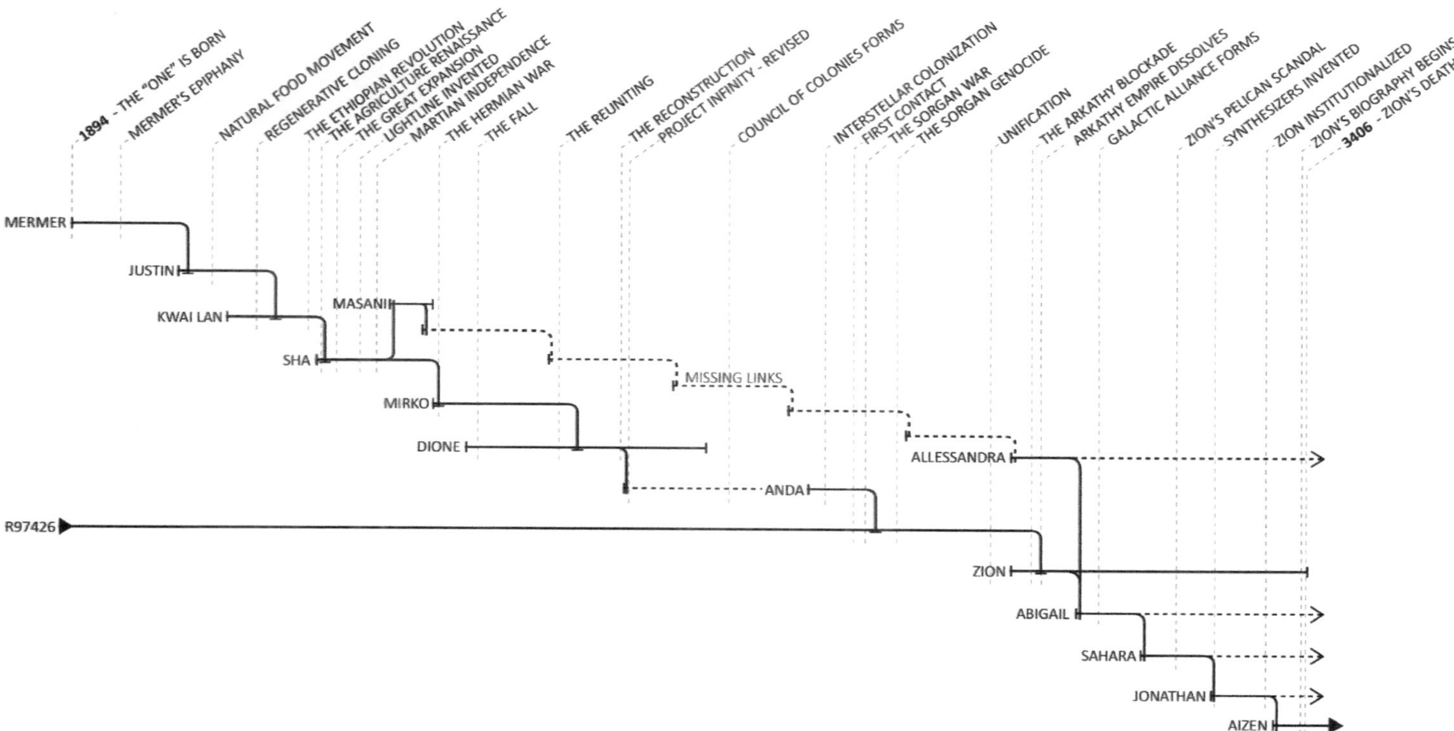

1894 - THE "ONE" IS BORN
MERMER'S EPIPHANY
NATURAL FOOD MOVEMENT
REGENERATIVE CLONING
THE ETHIOPIAN REVOLUTION
THE AGRICULTURE RENAISSANCE
THE GREAT EXPANSION
LIGHTLINE INVENTED
MARTIAN INDEPENDENCE
THE HERMIAN WAR
THE FALL
THE REUNITING
THE RECONSTRUCTION
PROJECT INFINITY - REVISED
COUNCIL OF COLONIES FORMS
INTERSTELLAR COLONIZATION
FIRST CONTACT
THE SORGAN WAR
THE SORGAN GENOCIDE
UNIFICATION
THE ARKATHY BLOCKADE
ARKATHY EMPIRE DISSOLVES
GALACTIC ALLIANCE FORMS
ZION'S PELICAN SCANDAL
SYNTHESIZERS INVENTED
ZION INSTITUTIONALIZED
ZION'S BIOGRAPHY BEGINS
3406 - ZION'S DEATH
MERMER
JUSTIN
KWAI LAN
SHA
MASANI
MIRKO
DIONE
ANDA
ALLESSANDRA
MISSING LINKS
R97426
ZION
ABIGAIL
SAHARA
JONATHAN
AIZEN

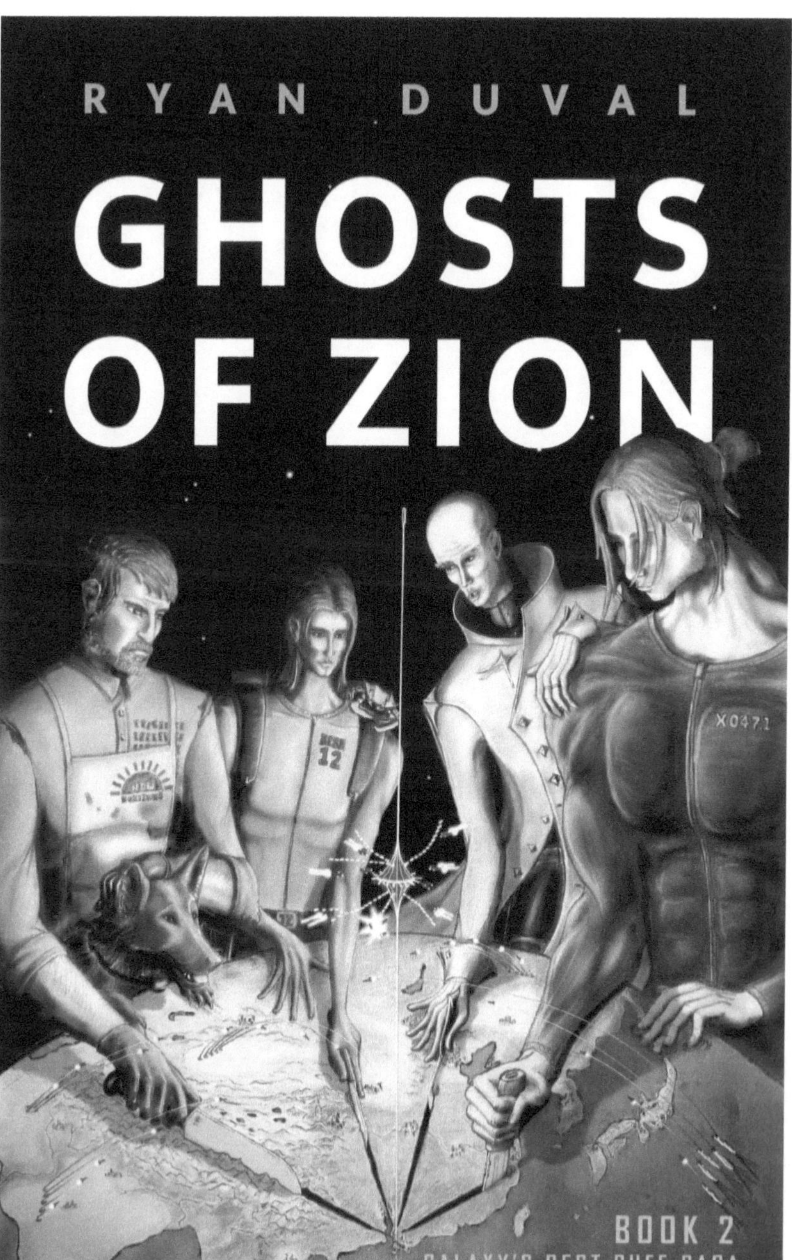

AVAILABLE NOW!

www.ingramcontent.com/pod-product-compliance
Lightning Source LLC
Chambersburg PA
CBHW031235310726
48971CB00004B/1019